What If They Lied (just a little)?

CLARK THOMAS RILEY

ISBN-13: 9781983111723

DEDICATION

My mother, Margaret Crim Riley, made sure I did my homework, and she regularly met with teachers at school in parent teacher conferences. My father, Thomas Leslie Riley, pushed me to the best education possible. My wife, Debbie, put up with so much while this work underwent its multi-decade incubation. My children, David and Sean, inspired me with their unending enthusiasm and bright curiosity. My Novel Workshop Group made sure that this work was worth reading.

CONTENTS

ACKNOWLEDGMENTS

The value of a novel workshop group cannot be exaggerated. Our regular meetings foster a commitment to writing that the rest of the world cannot. The camaraderie of the group cultivates a desire to please our fellow readers. Lucy Hoopes has contributed her critical grammarian mind. If you do not find yourself lost in the reading, it is likely her commas and attention to antecedents that are to be thanked. Lauren Goodsmith is one of the finest writers I have had the pleasure of knowing. Her insistence on honest relationships and proper cause and effect has relieved you, dear reader, of arduous suspensions of disbelief. She also speaks wonderful French. Alex Duvan has urged passionate relationships between the characters and is ever properly impatient with storyline *cul-de-sacs* or tangents. Margaret Rooney and Gail Mitchell were crucial finders of inconsistencies and ambiguities, most of which I hope to have squashed. Other members of our group have joined since this work was first completed and their valuable contributions to my future publications will be acknowledged when the ink and electrons of those works meet paper and screens.

1 DEAR GRANDFATHER

February 24, 2015

Dear Grandfather,

We are safe now, but I was really not sure we would make it. When we were leaving the city this morning, the Admiral told Dad that the roads were safe, but the bad soldiers had captured some of the streets during the night.

We were only about ten miles from here when we were ambushed. The soldiers shot out our tires, and they made us stay in the van. There were about fifteen of them, and they all had rifles and pistols. One man — I don't think he was the leader, but everyone seemed scared of him — told us to keep still and shut up, or he would kill us. I think he would have — maybe even though we did keep quiet. He was huge. They took Tiffany into a building near where they caught us, and were away from us for a long time.

The government sent out Marines to rescue us. Fortunately, our soldiers were very good. They shot the big guy after rushing the rebels at full speed. The government troops killed about half the rebels, and the others ran off into the neighborhoods. We were crouched down inside the van, so we were not hurt. The government troops use bigger bullets here than at home. We could hear the shots hitting the car, and they made a second snap like they went through the outside of the car.

The rebel troops didn't last long after they were shot. They must have been in awful pain, but they didn't yell out or anything — except the big guy kept cursing the government soldiers.

When they got to us, the troops set up positions around us, and they guarded us and gave us blankets until an armored personnel carrier arrived. They all seemed to know Dad, and all of them seemed really worried. Tiffany was gone when they searched the building, and they were still looking for her this morning. We drove in a convoy until we were back at base. Several Department staff people met us, and they took Dad off to meetings. I'm here in the old cafeteria with some of families of the Department officers.

The woman in charge, Sarah, says she doesn't know when we'll be able to leave, but that they can get all the supplies they need for a long stay. She says the new President is a good man, and she thinks this will be over soon.

I hope so. This has been awful. I don't think I ever want to visit Washington again.

Your grandson,
Jeremy

2 BULL MARKET

Monday, February 24, 2014

Few predicted the surging economic recovery following the disastrous opening of the third millennium. Those who grew up during that boom time remember a period of low unemployment, good wages, and falling food prices. Families with substantial investments saw their portfolios triple or quadruple over the course of a decade even as inflation remained at bay.

In no small part, societal fears following the string of attacks beginning in 2001 drove a rapid expansion of security industries. For skilled professionals, an array of robots and scanners awaited design and assembly. In the lower tiers of the working class, jobs as watch keeps and guards were plentiful and well compensated. Crime reached new lows as citizens swapped substantial personal liberties for safety.

James Garrette III lived at the top of the fiscal food chain. Over the course of three decades, he paid his dues among the biotechnology *intelligencia* in an institute posing as a non-profit, amassing a nine-figure fortune along the way through inside connections and timely exits from doomed ventures. His academic credentials were thin, but he provided the token image that the organization needed, and was a ready hatchet man for those of the company who stepped out of line.

Retirement lay a year or so in the future for Garrette, and he spent much of his time giving speeches and collecting honorary degrees from one college or another in exchange for a dollop of the Institute's largesse.

On the morning of February 24, 2014, James Garrette III stayed home to review his portfolio. The national markets had been flat for nearly two months, and he felt an impatience shared by those who had not experienced five consecutive down days on the market in many years.

Particularly troubling were several of his major industrial genetics holdings. They had begun to fail despite having viable products and what seemed sound business plans. His financial advisor of many years joined him for coffee.

"Have the insurance companies put out a hit on any of the products? I know they hate having to pay for the Gen-Cor heart stuff."

"No, Max, that's not it. Look, all across the line, sales are actually up. Somewhere between sales and production costs, our growth is losing steam," Garrette replied.

Max Carlton took the sheaves of paper and laid them out in a neat row, carefully aligning the edges. He squinted, his face drawn into a sour pucker. Garrette watched him closely, like watching a ferret on the trail of a rodent. Garrette knew Carlton's face would begin to redden as he homed in on an offending cash leak. Carlton's wispy white hair did little to hide his pink skin.

Presently a crimson glow spread over Carlton's face. "Why has the support staff line increased so much?" His attention shifted between two sheets. "It's easily risen forty percent. That's the item to look at."

Garrette scowled. "That's a problem, then. Gen-Cor had to beef up that part of the budget last year to lower security staff turnover. You know how hard it is to keep competent people."

Carlton looked as if he was in possession of some choice tidbit of news. "Actually, Dick Johnson over in Treasury was showing me some preliminary figures last week. The market for security people is finally beginning to tank. What Dick's people are seeing is that companies are trimming security as the hysteria gradually wears off. Face it — those are non-producing resources, and they'll devour the bottom line just as you're seeing there. What's the price-earnings on Gen-Cor, anyway?"

"Eighteen last quarter."

"Oh, you can do better than that. They've got to cut some fat. You have any leverage with them?" Carlton asked.

Garrette nodded. "They need the Institute's test results. Their head of HR will throw a fit. She's a bleeding heart, but she can't overrule the board." He paused a moment. "I just hope Laura doesn't find out, either."

Both men let out a roaring laugh.

"How the hell did you manage to raise a liberal daughter? I know she doesn't get it from her mother," Carlton queried.

"Beats me… Beats me. She's a smart kid, but when she gets locked onto a cause, she's tenacious."

"Well, you've got until spring break. What's that? March? April?"

Garrette responded, "Actually, I've got a longer reprieve. She's going down to Mexico for spring break. Something about the *maquiladoras*."

"And who's paying for that trip?" Max Carlton returned to his sour face.

Garrette nodded and looked down.

"You're not helping matters encouraging her, you know. Case in point

— I seem to recall that Gen-Cor will eventually set up production along the border."

"Hmmmm… I didn't think of that. I don't imagine my little hotheaded crusader is going to stir up too much. She's smart enough to know what makes her world move."

"Whatever. You'd better start leaning on Gen-Cor now. Earnings reports are due in a month. There's fat to burn," Carlton said, looking up.

Garrette was built for a corporate suit. Slightly overweight, slightly bald, slightly graying on top, his dark mustache closely matched his dark skin.

On the other hand, Max Carlton looked old. His pale skin wrinkled and cracked in places, revealing an unhealthy pink beneath. He had preserved a trace of Commonwealth accent that he could revive as needed for purposes of intimidation or fund-raising.

Garrette paused for the briefest of moments to reflect on the fat he would cause to burn — people with families and responsibilities. But these sentimentalities no longer lasted more than an instant. These decisions can be numbing if repeated often enough.

3 S.U.V.

Monday, February 24, 2014

Eight cylinders, more space in the back than he'd ever need, a frame that could tow a battleship, and mounting brackets already in place for more gear than he would ever own. This was the truck Jack had dreamed of since … forever.

"So, ya any closer to getting it?" Ed asked.

Jack turned to Ed and sighed, "Naw. Not really. I mean, if I were a jerk, I've got the savings to cover it, but — you know — things are kinda up in the air."

Ed pursed his lips and looked back at the truck. "Jenny?"

"Yeah."

"Anything new?" Ed asked.

"No. She had the full battery of tests Tuesday, and we'll hear day after tomorrow."

Ed turned to Jack again. "Scared?"

"She doesn't show it. She's pretty much thrown herself into her work — putting it out of her mind."

"No. I mean you," Ed pursued.

Jack murmured, "Yeah."

For a while silence enveloped the two men, preoccupied while admiring the multi-ton toy in its show-window home.

"You got that coverage thing straightened out?" Ed continued.

Jack frowned. "Not completely. Jenn's diagnostics are mostly covered under my insurance. Two years ago coverage would have been complete. For that matter, the Alliance would have covered Jenn's expenses two years ago, but they all agreed to drop their coverage. Man, that was a tough call. It was either five with insurance or all seven without. I'm not complaining. They did the right thing. But we lost the gamble."

Ed shook his head. "Yeah, I remember when our Institute coverage was the envy of the University. It was better than even commercial places."

"Tell me about it. I raised the dependent coverage last year. It's still so anemic, I'm going to have to pony up this year. I knew I could pay for one more, but we weren't so sure. We wanted to put more money into savings. When she started telling me about those stomach pains, something in the back of my head made me sign up. I didn't even ask her."

Ed looked at his friend amazed. "Aw, man, you never do that. I don't remember you ever doing anything without her OK. So what's the problem with the coverage anyway?"

"Don't know. It's just taking a lot longer to be approved than I expected. We need to get on with the other tests, but these things cost thousands and tens of thousands. It just bothers me. I don't know why. You think I'm getting paranoid?"

Ed raised an eyebrow. "Naw. I think you're an excellent judge of character and you know you can't trust these admin characters anymore."

"Yeah," Jack agreed.

They watched the truck going nowhere for another ten minutes, and then each headed home.

4 ECON 101 AND TEARS

Friday, February 28, 2014

"That's why you're here, mister. I have no sympathy or patience for your regrets," Vice President Bailey snarled. "We need someone who can punch holes in their arguments and sink 'em."

David Kincaid rued the day he left the Senate to become Chief of Staff. He once loved the roar of the crowds. He thrived on debate. He was one of the few politicians to whom the serious media would turn when they needed an analytical mind on Capitol Hill and David was proud of that. He had, after all, graduated top of his class at Carolina and had been at the top of his game politically then.

"Well," Kincaid replied, "in this case, Senator Kreis is absolutely correct. And we're asses to suggest this stupid, shortsighted position. The French are much better situated to secure the delivery corridor. They know the people; have the history and political currency. We would go in there green. You know very well that the Shia still don't trust us, and the Sunnis hate us outright. It'll cost half a billion more than if we just paid the French."

Bailey was unmoved. "Remember who you're working for, David. We're not yielding this real estate to the Frogs. Half a billion is chump change when you're looking at this acreage. Proven reserves. Proven reserves that could flow through U.S. hands — our hands." Bailey tapped his finger on the mahogany desktop to emphasize each point.

Kincaid particularly enjoyed debating this subject in public. He always won, and had been the Senate's most eloquent advocate for a radical crash program to end U.S. and even world dependency on petroleum. His arguments were strong, backed by science and statistics. By his efforts alone he reckoned that new-energies research funding had quadrupled. Seven years from beginning his crusade, he had been cutting ribbons on power plants that lighted whole cities without burning a lump of coal, without swallowing a barrel of oil, without producing a pound of nuclear waste. He was proud of that — as proud as he was of anything he had ever accomplished in his life.

And now here he was, being asked — no, 'ordered' — to defend and promote the very fossil fuel dependency he despised. The ugliness of his predicament had devoured him for months.

"No, Jim, sending our troops into the middle of this mess is wrong, and no amount of territorial gain can justify it. I'm out of here. You're on your own." Kincaid rose to leave.

"Sit down!" Bailey barked. "We're here to work out our strategy. I don't have time for your damned temper tantrums."

Kincaid turned back to look at the Vice President. "Just a bit ago you said, 'Remember who you're working for.' Thank you. I had forgotten. By law and by paycheck, I'm working for the people of the United States of America. And, as God is my witness, it is my duty to work for the people of the world. This land grab plan of yours — and I know it isn't coming from the President — is doomed to fail. It'll cost thousands of lives and poison the diplomatic well for decades. I don't support it, I can't support it, and I won't support it."

Bailey's face was aflame, but he remained seated. Kincaid could see his jaw flexing, his eyes narrowed and icy.

Kincaid smiled. "You didn't run this by the President, did you? He has no idea what's going on with this scheme, does he?"

Bailey closed the folder of papers before him. His lips were thin and tight.

"Who is in on this anyway? Defense? Treasury? Carlton? If the President needs my support on this so badly, maybe I should talk to him about it in private."

Bailey swept his hand across the table, hitting the folder, sending its contents flying through the office air. "Get out! Get out!" He shouted. The veins in his neck stood out in stark relief.

"I was just leaving." David Kincaid walked out, pulling the door closed with a soft click.

Bailey's secretary, Janet, watched him intently. Even after all this time, he couldn't tell exactly what she was thinking. He addressed her, "A man who is right has no need to be angry. A man who is wrong has no right to be angry."

She smiled. "Well said."

He shrugged. "Can't claim credit for it. Mahatma Gandhi."

"I should have known." She looked at the closed door and lowered her voice. "If you ever have a staff vacancy, please let me know."

Kincaid chuckled softly, and then whispered back, "I get that a lot."

He walked out of the office, down the stairs, and into the cold late winter sunshine. His security agent was waiting at the door. Another trapping of this office he didn't originally care for. Still, Frank was faithful and a willing ear to David's frustrations. Probably kept him sane.

"How'd it go, Mr. Kincaid?" Frank asked, smiling.

David shrugged, but flashed a mischievous grin. "We won."

Frank returned the grin. "Again."

They both laughed.

"Tell me, Frank, would you put up with this situation? Everything I've ever worked for seems like it's going down the tubes. I'm ordered to develop and implement policies that will be disastrous, while perfectly good solutions die from neglect. In two years the North Carolina Senate seat will be open. I'm thinking of running for it."

Frank walked along, quietly alert.

"I don't get to talk to the public anymore. There's no clash of ideas. It's a monoculture in there."

"You're still sittin' right next to the source of power, and you know that," Frank offered.

Kincaid looked down. "I don't know. I used to think so — right next to the source of power. A wall is, too, but that doesn't change anything. Bailey has his agenda, and nothing seems to deter him. Not logic. Not results. Not anything."

"Then you should definitely quit and run for the Senate," Frank agreed.

David turned to Frank. Frank was making a special effort to look around, ignoring the bluntness of his agreement. "Mr. Kincaid, where are we going?"

Kincaid stopped, a puzzled look on his face. He thought for a moment, and then turned around, pointing down the street. "Treasury. I almost forgot. A briefing on monetary policy. As if enough hasn't gone wrong today."

"You're losing it, sir," Frank offered.

"I know; I know. Thank you. I think I'll quit and run for the Senate."

* * *

"How certain are you about this?"

"Almost a hundred percent, Mr. Kincaid. We've been monitoring the E.U. accounts. They've set up all the transfer links. The word of only a couple of heads and it's done. No approvals or votes needed. In less than ten minutes time, their dollar holdings would drop by twenty percent."

"That would put us at what? Thirty, thirty-five percent?"

"No, sir, I'm afraid it's worse. The drop last week hit us hard. We'd be down to about twenty-five percent. The dollar would drop from the second world currency to third place. Like I said, it could be accomplished in less than ten minutes."

"Is there anyone I can talk to?" Kincaid asked.

Harry Jackson, Deputy Secretary for Currency, leaned forward, arms folded, resting on his elbows. "The French, for starters. They seem to think we're about to do an end run around them in Iran. They could use some reassurance."

Kincaid's heart sank. Apparently it showed in his face.

"We're not doing an end run around the French, are we, David?" Jackson looked desperate, panicked. "Please, God, tell me we're not."

"Bailey was trying to convince me we needed to do that very thing not half an hour ago," Kincaid muttered.

"You've got to stop them, David. You have got to stop them."

Kincaid looked over at Frank. "Let's get our butts over to Sixteen Hundred."

Frank nodded.

* * *

"Sorry about the hassle, David. The gatekeepers have their orders. But you're here now. What can I do for you?" President Miller was dressed in a tuxedo and was in the process of tying his tie when Kincaid arrived.

"The Vice President was telling me about a proposal to invade a portion of Iran to secure the pipeline route. To even suggest that is the height of irresponsibility. We should be talking to the French and the other E.U. partners. We need to have them involved. They know the people; have the history and the political currency. If we go around them, Mr. President, the consequences will be very grave. The Iranians are expecting this move. They'll defend their territory with a zeal we haven't seen since Viet Nam. And that's not all: I've just spent the last three hours at Treasury; the Europeans are about ready to drop over half their dollars."

"Jim briefed me on your conversation, David. Frankly, I'm not sensing much of a team effort from you. That pipeline carries over ten percent of our oil. Jim thinks it's a matter of national security."

Kincaid exploded, "Bullshit! That pipeline carries the lowest cost oil to his damned donors' ships. He's prepared to gamble the fate of this country to make twenty or thirty people twice as wealthy as they are now."

The President wore a mischievous smirk. He was dressed in splendid array and appeared ready to leave. "I'm depending on you to get our staffs together and lay the groundwork for assuring our access to that oil. Now you and Mr. Bailey try to find a way to play nice. Want to join me?"

With the crush of his recent schedule, David had lost track of the evening calendar. Try as he might, he couldn't remember tonight's event. "What is it? Oil Barons' Ball East?"

Miller frowned. "Eagle Coalition."

"Pass."

The President smiled. "Eh, it was worth a try. We'll talk about this on Monday. Right now, it's show time."

"No, I'll see you tomorrow — Saturday morning, eight o'clock. It's on the schedule. I definitely remember that. We're going over your Face the Nation interview. We need to use that appearance to calm the Europeans. It's important. I know you're not ready."

Miller looked back. Kincaid drew no comfort from his expression. The Chief of Staff had a bad feeling the President wasn't planning to rehearse on Saturday morning.

Kincaid made his way to the east entrance and the parking lot, passing dozens of couples from the Eagle Coalition. He recognized most of them — overweight white men with their wealthy wives or their trophy wives. None of them appeared to recognize him. Perhaps they thought him a servant. He wasn't dressed the part of a dinner guest. He smiled a moment. He was a servant. He hoped he was a faithful servant. Difficult, though.

Frank was waiting, talking with the guards. He rose as David approached. "How'd it go, Mr. Kincaid?"

"Call it a draw."

"Sorry. Where to now?" Frank asked.

"Let's call it a day. I'll be back tomorrow about six. We have a rehearsal for Sunday's broadcast. I get the distinct impression he's going to be a no-show."

"The President?"

"Yeah," Kincaid replied.

"If I may say so, that's not a good idea on his part. The last time he was on, I could have done better."

Kincaid stopped, and turning to his aide and friend, smiled. "Frank, never sell yourself short. You could do as well or better than President Miller almost any day. You have a better grasp of the facts and a practical attitude that's lacking here. You definitely could have done better."

"So, you going to resign and run for the Senate?"

David grinned. "I'm going to regret saying that, aren't I? Not this weekend. We have to save the world as we know it. We have to keep the French from being so pissed off at this administration that they set off a dollar sale that sinks our economy. I might be able to influence that if I can get the President to say the right words Sunday. At least put it off for a little while longer."

"You know, you sure aren't the optimist you were when you came here."

"Sorry. I guess, like you said, it's getting to me. You know, I used to unload all this on Mary. It would be our anniversary next Wednesday — the fourth of March."

"I know you miss her, sir. She was a fine lady."

"That she was. Funny how I always remember our anniversary now. I usually forgot it when she was alive." They had arrived at their cars.

Someone had decided that David did not need an agent after hours, though the logic of that was never clear. "Look, you go home to Cathy and give her enough love for the both of us. Treasure her. I'll see you Monday."

"Yes, sir. Have as good a weekend as you can."

* * *

"We'll find a way." Jack's voice cracked as he tried to comfort. "I'm not sure how right now but we will."

Jenn was still sobbing.

"Dr. Johnson has a lot of contacts. He suggested Dr. Morgan at Vanderbilt. Their program has had the best success rate."

Jenn's tests confirmed the presence of a particularly aggressive non-Hodgkin's lymphoma. Today's session in Dr. Nielson's office had been brutal. Nielson was as sensitive and gentle as she could be, but laid out Jenn's prospects unambiguously. The cancer was fast growing and had already spread. Jack felt pinned to his seat in the office; he could only imagine what Jenn was feeling. The bombshell was Dr. Nielson's prognosis — three to four months.

Jenn was still sobbing. "I love you, Jack."

"I love you, too." He felt her body quaking with each sob. He held her all the more tightly, and she would not relax her embrace.

It must have been well after eleven before they fell into fitful sleep.

* * *

"But there must be some treatments — experimental treatments — somewhere."

Dr. Randy Johnson shook his head slowly. "That's still one of the tough ones. The survival rate hasn't budged in a decade. The best treatments might give a month or so, some time, but the treatments are rough — really debilitating."

Jack hung his head. This wasn't what he had expected. "What about Dr. Morgan at Vanderbilt?"

"He's the one with the extra months."

"But I think I remember he reported remissions."

"Not with this class of cancer." Johnson had Nielson's papers in front of him. "Different chromosome locations give the same outward presentation, but have very different roots. Jenn's is a rare one — exact pathways aren't even known. They'll be throwing everything at her, hoping that something sticks. That being said, Jack, I need to be completely honest. The prospects just aren't good. Even if your treatment team uncovers something new, Jenn's going to need your full support. Now — before the storm — would be a good time to do things you've put off — fun things, trips. In a month or so, it may be out of the question."

* * *

"I'm going to be here only for two days. I e-mailed you my schedule more than a month ago." Laura Garrette sliced a deep red tomato into thick slices for two of the sandwiches she called "Powerhouse" — whole grain bread, romaine lettuce, alfalfa sprouts, an organic Muenster cheese, and some kind of sauce with just a little kick. Very healthy, very low fat. No wonder she cut such a slim and energetic figure.

Her father leaned back at the table. "I just thought you might stay around for dinner Wednesday night. The Prestons will be coming. His company is about to have a lot of openings for biochemists. I'd think you'd be interested," he suggested.

"Another publicly-funded miracle about to be patented and make still more fortunes for your evil corporate friends?" Given the deep, even brown of Laura's eyes, her father continued to be amazed how she could make them flash with indignation and reproach. He wouldn't have tolerated such talk from anyone else. Carlton was right. He did indulge her.

He folded his arms. "We always get back to this spot, don't we? If some company doesn't produce these 'miracles,' no one gets them. If there's no profit, no company produces them."

"Yes. Back to this spot, the one where you gloss over the billions spent from the public treasury to make the discoveries only to have them turned over to your friends to make obscene — obscene — profits to the point that the people who need the treatment — the people who paid for the discoveries in the first place — can't afford them. 'This spot,' as you call it, is the spot where rhetoric and reality diverge."

Garrette admired his daughter more than he could ever tell her, more than he could admit to himself at times. "Perhaps you're right. You have a fix?" He faced her with hands open in honest appeal.

She set down her knife and rinsed and dried her hands, came over to him and hugged him. "Oh, Daddy, I love you. Even if you are an evil capitalist baron," she whispered.

He laughed, knowing that she was smiling. He knew she loved him.

"And I am, in fact, working on a fix," she said. "You know those nasty *maquiladoras* down along the border — the ones that monster Carlton sends his work to?"

Garrette was careful not to nod as that would be a winning agreement for her arguments against Max Carlton and he did not want to fall into that trap again. He sat down at the table and folded his hands beneath his chin, waiting for her story. She finished making her sandwiches. She delivered one to him. She brought two glasses and poured a light Chablis into each.

"Thank you," he said.

She continued, "Anyway, Ritner Corp was in the process of closing one of their plants — nutritional supplements or something. The plant was up to code but they were consolidating operations to Nuevo Laredo and didn't need the Matamoras setup. Now it just happens that I knew two non-profits that had just gotten substantial grants and were looking to do something big. There are four biggies coming off patent next year, two for AIDS, and one each for arthritis and uterine cancer. With that Matamoras plant we can close the loop. We control production and distribution." She took a bite of her sandwich and chewed for a while. "How's that for a fix?"

"How old are you? How do you find all this out?" He asked.

"All I have to do is play the dumb little black girl at your dinner parties and listen to the conversation," she said. "Half the time, they're complaining about losing control of something. I just have to be sure we're the ones who get control when they lose it."

Garrette was enjoying his sandwich, but now he paused, frowning. "You need to be careful. Some of those things may be privileged communications."

"At our house? At our dinner parties?" She laughed. "I don't think so. And if that's the case, I'll remind you that some of the solutions discussed are quite illegal. And furthermore, what are they going to do? Complain and not get invited to dinner and lose the Institute's connections? Once again, Father dearest, I don't think so. How's the powerhouse?"

"Good. Delicious. So tell me. How is it that my sweet little bleeding heart is such a ruthless business woman on the side?"

Laura smiled and shook her head. "Pragmatist, Daddy, pragmatist. Just doing what we have to do to make life better for a few more people by all available means."

"Hmmm. You know you wouldn't have those means without the money it takes for your kind of access, without the resources it takes for the education that allows you to — admittedly brilliantly — put these schemes together."

"You're not trying to make me feel guilty, are you? I could just as easily overhear all these conspiracies as a servant," she retorted.

"But you would never be a servant."

There. He saw again the hot flash of those deep brown eyes.

"We have a responsibility to help others. Remember, you always drilled that into my head when I was little. Personal responsibility. Corporate responsibility. I'm totally overwhelmed now doing responsibility. The economy is crumbling and the weight is falling on the shoulders of the bottom half of our society."

"Whoa. Just a minute, young lady. Let's talk — pragmatically — about reality. Numbers. Look at the numbers. Wages are good and rising apace with living costs. Unemployment is basically frictional, and inflation is completely under control. I'm not sure in which universe that constitutes 'crumbling,' but in this universe that's called a sound economy."

Laura pondered as she carried her dishes back to the sink. She turned to her father. "You're right. You're right. But we're seeing more people at the

Center every week, and they're in ever more desperate shape. Something's not right. I can feel it."

"Don't judge an entire economy by a local reading. A single big layoff can do that locally," he cautioned.

She frowned. "Maybe. But I hear the same thing from other centers all across the States."

"Could well be that pantries are just closing down, consolidating, shifting their populations to the remaining ones. Point is, the national numbers say the economy is doing great, and everybody wins in the end when that's the case."

"You're right — I hope. Just wish it'd get great for the folks I serve. Look, I gotta go. Be sure that plate gets into the dishwasher. I did the dishes last time."

"Right. And where are you going? I forget," he asked.

"Flight lessons. I'm half way through. More takeoffs today and maybe start doing some landings."

Garrette shook his head again. "Crazy girl. Be safe."

"You know I will. Love you, Daddy." She kissed him on the forehead and bounded from the kitchen.

* * *

Saturday, March 1, 2014

At five minutes before eight on Saturday morning, David Kincaid strode into the briefing room two floors below ground level in the White House Executive Office Building.

"Good morning, ladies and gentlemen. I hate Saturday meetings as much as you. Let's keep things efficient and get home quickly. The President was supposed to be here, but … he had a 'schedule conflict.'"

A groan rose from the veteran members of the staff.

"You all should have your briefing folders, but first … I believe we have some bright new faces."

Kincaid turned to his secretary, Tracey Atwood, who was awaiting her cue.

"Yes, sir, we have three new members. Jon Mason is joining us from the University of Chicago. He is an expert on Islam and Near-Eastern studies. His credentials include four years' liaison between the Oriental Institute and the religious communities in Baghdad and Tehran."

David shook Jon's hand. "Welcome, Jon. I'm looking forward to some very specific discussions. Did Ms. Atwood set up a time?"

"Yes, sir." Jon seemed a little nervous.

"First time in the White House?"

"Yes, sir. Does it show?" Jon grinned.

"Nah. Don't worry. In a day or so, you're going to be so busy you won't know where you are."

Jon smiled broadly.

Tracey continued her introductions. "We have two new White House Fellows. Dr. Sarah Tyler is joining us for six months. She's just received her doctorate in agricultural economics at Rutgers."

David extended his hand. "Sarah. Banks of the Old Raritan, if I recall correctly. Are you up on tobacco?"

Sarah nodded. "I hope so, Mr. Kincaid."

David looked around and whispered. "You can do 'Mr. Kincaid' for about a week. Then if you're staying, among the team it's 'David' or 'sir' and 'ma'am'. In the southern tradition." He gave a little nod.

She giggled. "Yes, sir."

"And this is Ms. Anna Colbert. She will be with us for one year. She has a bachelor's in French literature from Dickenson and a master's in foreign policy from Georgetown."

"Oh, good. Ms. Colbert, you're going to be very, very busy today. Did Ms. Atwood brief you on our not-so-little problem?"

"Yes, sir." Anna had an uncommon air of sophistication about her and was quite pretty as well. David couldn't pin that sense on one single thing. She offered her hand with confidence, and she didn't have the awestruck look of many new fellows.

"Have you been here before?"

"No, sir. First time, aside from helping liaison with the French Embassy," she replied.

Again that confidence. Maybe it was her lips. Upturned, again, pretty.

David gestured for everyone to be seated. An agenda appeared on the briefing screen behind him. The dozen people around the table opened their briefing folders in unison, like a choir ready for the introit. "Item one, as you can see, is tomorrow's Face the Nation. State… Summary of the briefing sheet, please."

Each member took her or his top page. Peter Benson rose. "Our primary concern is to reassure the E.U., the French in particular, that we have no intention of invading Iran to 'secure' the Al Wadi oil pipeline. In particular, we need to have the President note that we have no ship movements in the area and that our ground forces are not at any heightened state of readiness."

Peter looked concerned. "Sir, I really wish the President were here. The wording is important. We've honed this list as best we can, but he has to read it and understand that each word is important. The last time, if you'll recall, he only glanced at it and ad-libbed his way through the answers. It took us a month — a month we didn't have to waste — to put out the fires."

David looked grim. "I will personally see to it that he reads the paper in my presence, and I will let him know the importance of the diplomatic-speak. Are we briefing the allies in advance?"

"Yes, sir. May I ask you personally to contact your counterpart with the French? I spent two hours this morning talking with Ambassador James in Paris. The French understandably feel shut out. A personal call would be helpful."

Kincaid looked at his watch. "You've been on the phone with them two hours already today?"

"Well, sir, it's five hours later there," Peter replied.

"I'm thinking of you. Thank you. I appreciate the diligence."

Peter acknowledged the compliment. "Thank you, sir."

He had an uncomfortable look, and David leaned back, waiting to see how much Peter wanted to say more.

"Sir, this is just an exercise in futility, and could actually be damaging unless we actually don't have plans to do anything about the pipeline."

Peter sat down.

The ball was in Kincaid's court. The Chief of Staff responded slowly. "No, I don't know that."

Peter registered his disappointment.

"Truth is, I'm not sure what they're up to. And I'm pretty sure that the President doesn't know any details, either. I do know that the Vice President believes that the Al Wadi pipeline is vulnerable to cutoff, either at the political level in Iran or by sabotage in Iraq. If he had his way, we'd post troops all along the pipeline tomorrow."

Sarah had been scanning the group. "Mr. Kincaid, what's so specifically critical about the Al Wadi?"

"Sorry. A little background. Peter, please make corrections as we go."

Peter nodded. "Yes, sir."

Kincaid began calling names and handing off the conversation as in a college class. "Kathy — Treasury — oil."

Kathy was the White House Chief of Staff liaison with the Department of Treasury. "Our petroleum margins are so thin, the loss of even a few percent of our supply would send prices through the roof with a ripple effect throughout the economy. The situation is substantially more precarious than even the media have portrayed it." She saw Sarah's raised eyebrows. "Yeah. Scary. I know. If you look at all the chokepoints in the bulk flow of oil, we've pretty well covered ninety-five percent of the flow. If ever the Iraq supply actually resumes, that would be another ten percent and frankly everyone would breathe a lot easier. But it's been over twenty years since Iraq exported any significant amount."

Kincaid nodded. "James — State — what about that Iraqi oil?" Attention shifted to the rear of the room.

"Basra is almost repaired from the 2008 catastrophe and will begin shipping within six months to supplement the Al Wadi pipeline. Oil from interior Iraq is a minimum twelve to eighteen months away even if everyone behaves. Said pipeline can give the world millions of barrels a day from Iran but that makes it the number one target in the world when we are seen as the beneficiaries. Fortunately, it's an Iranian-Iraqi-French project and both the Iranians and the Iraqis enjoy working with the French."

Sarah was waiting for a punch line.

Kincaid picked up the tag team presentation. "Our administration — which is to say, the Vice President — has gone out of its way to offend the French on a number of occasions and they in turn have been understandably comfortable making maximum points — and profits — from their positions in that little corner of this troubled world."

"And we can't just mend fences with the French because …?" Sarah threw open her hands.

A murmur of a chuckle made its way around the room among the veteran members. Sarah bit her lip.

"All right, everybody. Polite. Every one of you has asked the same logical question. Seems when we've been here long enough, we forget it's logical." He turned back to Sarah. "Mending fences is exactly what we need to do. That's what Peter's list is for. Or at least his list should keep us from breaking more fences.

"Unfortunately, Dr. Tyler, Mr. Bailey's most loyal base constituency has a mean streak in regards all things French. The origins may be lost in the mists of time or fog of war or some such metaphor, but the Vice President can count the votes by the tens of thousands for each French joke or slur. He and his political strategists have the numbers and they've honed the insults to weapons-grade. President Miller is a man of sound intellect and I'm personally embarrassed by all of this, but that's where we are. It's a hole so deep; I'm not sure how to get out. In part, that's where Ms. Colbert comes in."

Anna jerked her head up from her briefing papers and quickly looked around.

"I'm hoping to elevate our relationship with Paris. I'm hoping we can link up below the radar and get the old dialog back. The Vice President was pretty dismissive of the whole idea but didn't say no. And, though he would love for us to go back to Iraq, we can't because — Matt — defense…"

Matt took the handoff, "We're pinned down in Saudi Arabia, we've essentially emptied the bases stateside, and our back is to the wall with troop strength as it is. We desperately need more troops overseas but retention is in the toilet and recruitment is a joke. Even the mention of a draft will get you fired at the Pentagon. The mere suggestion is enough to ignite a firestorm. And now with the China problem, there's no place left to draw troops from. We need the whole EU, especially the French, to keep the upper Gulf quiet, even if it means shutting out U.S. companies in the area. Needless to say, that is not a popular stand with the Vice President."

Kincaid took the lead again. "As Wednesdays numbers show, our economy is just zipping along and is going to need all the fuel and lubricant it can get."

Sarah nodded as she looked over Wednesday's briefing papers on GDP and unemployment. "Oh."

"Everyone had a chance to look over Peter's bullet list for the President? Any additions or corrections?"

The room was quiet for a moment. Then Anna raised her hand.

"Ms. Colbert, what are we missing?"

"I don't know much about the specifics yet and the bullet list is of necessity brief, but we may want to pay some more attention to the language if the goal is to draw the French back to us. I see all down the list 'France … France … France ….' The French would like to be seen as a people, same as us. I sense that the President won't go out of his way to embrace them in his interview, but is his language suggestible? Moldable? If those are words."

Peter and David looked at each other. Kincaid spoke. "It's happened before. This is likely all he'll see before he goes into the studio. How can we improve it?"

"If he'll have this before him, put in the name of the people — the French. Sounds like 'our friends' won't fly, but how about 'our allies'? Evokes long ties, better times, and military honor. President looks strong, French look good."

"But, hopefully not too good." It was James, the State Department liaison. "We can't bring the French image down in the eyes of the pipeline people. Ironically, we may be better off with the French not liking us — at least publicly — than having them buddy-buddy."

"Publicly?" Kincaid asked.

"Yes, sir. If we can engineer some two-tiered thing out of this. Keep Sunday morning's show for domestic consumption and put a different face on for the folks in the EU. The media here are going to focus their laser-like vision on whatever comes out of the President's mouth. They're not going to give much coverage to what appears in the overseas press."

Kincaid put his hand to his chin. "And is there something that we have left that will do that?"

"Yes, sir. Glad you asked. They've wanted more slots at JFK and Dulles for their transatlantic flights. We've resisted that for years. With Air Atlantic going belly up this week — for this last time I think we'll all agree — seven slots open up. Three at Dulles, four in New York. Let 'em have them. They get the victory, the U.S. press says 'so what' and buries the story on page one million while it's page one over there. They look good on the home front and in the Gulf. Everybody wins."

Kincaid was searching for holes in the plan but couldn't come up with any. He turned to Peter. "Any chance we can get through to the French Chief of Staff? Today?"

Peter smiled. "Ambassador James is spending the afternoon on the tennis court with him." He looked up at the clock showing the time in Europe. "I'm guessing they'll be finishing up in about two hours."

The Chief of Staff looked energized. "Great! OK, who's covering Transportation?"

A hand rose off to Kincaid's right.

"Brenda. Any complications with this? Can I give him a definite?"

"Not that simple, sir. The gate allocation has to go through public comment period and the Hill can jump in on this one. If anyone objects, it could be a couple of years."

"Ah, that's not what I wanted to hear. Is anyone likely to object?"

"I know Southwest has its eye on those Washington slots. New York is probably safe."

"Will we win if we push hard on the Washington gates?" Kincaid asked.

"Toss up, sir," Brenda replied.

"OK. I can live with that. At least we have something to talk about. Ms. Colbert, are you ready to help me with my French. I haven't had any serious French since high school. Ms. Branson." He put on a wistful smile that brought a relaxing laughter to the room.

Anna paused for a moment. "I'll do my best, sir."

"Lovely. Transportation — please get Ms. Colbert the details so she'll have the words ready. Peter — work with State to get a good connection at just the right time. Find us something nice and friendly to say to start off the conversation. Whatever the Vice President and his crowd feel, I've got no bone to pick with Monsieur Cartier, and Mr. Bailey isn't going to object if it gets us closer to that oil.

"Are we good to go on this topic?" Kincaid paused. "OK, moving on to money closer to home. Treasury — why is California complaining about wanting more unemployment assistance? Didn't they get a copy of Wednesday's numbers?"

Kathy was passing around a limited number of copies of her special report. She slid the final one to Sarah who perked up at being included. Kathy began, "California is dealing with an almost eight percent unemployment rate. The state personal income numbers have not been good, and they're down to the bottom of their reserves. In another forty-five to fifty days, they stop writing checks."

Kathy looked at David Kincaid. He was concentrating on the sheets before him, his brow knit into a tight frown.

"That would be bad, sir. Really bad," Kathy continued.

"How did they get in this mess? California, of all states, should be sailing on the crest," he asked.

Kathy looked frustrated. "I don't know, sir. We're going to be putting them up against the other states, but we're just getting the numbers in. New York's not looking all that hot either — tentatively. A lot of California's legislators are blaming immigration."

Before Kincaid could call out 'Homeland,' Luke was ready. "Not immigration. Not legal or illegal. Homeland's numbers are good on this. I believe them. Net migration is almost zero. It's completely consistent with the trend we've been watching for the past year. The illegals are finding it harder to get jobs and conditions are actually better in Mexico, Costa Rico, and Panama than they are for them in California."

Kincaid pursed his lips. "OK, Kathy. Let's assume that California's numbers are good. Please hazard a guess as to what's going on."

"Well, sir, the only thing I can see is that the jobs are migrating to the heartland, where the cost of manufacture is supposedly lower. It's not going overseas, or we'd be seeing a B.O.P. spike to account for this big a problem."

Jon and Sarah both look baffled.

"Balance of Payments," Kincaid offered in translation. "The Treasury Department tracks money flows across each state's border, whether internally or overseas."

"Sorry, sir," Kathy continued. "Balance of Payments. We don't have good data for the past couple of months yet. I should have that next week. California, New York, and a couple of other big states track the numbers independently as well. The heartland states don't have the budgets to do that. I'll let you know as soon as Treasury sends them over."

"Fair enough. What do we do in the interim?" he asked.

"We find some money to tide them over, sir. There really isn't another option."

"Thank heavens the governor is a party man. I can hear the Vice President's lecture already. Should this be high profile or low key?"

"The President is addressing the ABA … American Bankers Association … Tuesday. That would be the time and the group. Keep it off radar except for the Wall Street Journal types."

"You'll get me a briefing, and work with Cameron and Janet on the speech?"

"Yes, sir," Kathy replied.

The Saturday briefing continued for another fifty-five minutes.

"Thanks to all of you for sacrificing this chunk of your Saturday. Peter, if you'd staff the revisions to the Presidents point page I'll go over it with him this afternoon. James, if you'd kindly let the Ambassador know that I'd like a moment of Monsieur Cartier's time." Both raised their hands in acknowledgment on their way out. Kincaid turned to those remaining.

"Well, what do you newbies think of our operation here?"

Sarah spoke up. "Wow, it's so informal. I'm not sure what I was expecting."

David smiled. "We're humans. Really. Don't let the back and forth fool you though. Your colleagues are professionals to the core and deadly serious when they get down to business. You won't find a more dedicated bunch who love their country more than the folks who were just in this room. You're going to be part of it, too — some of you real soon." He nodded in Anna's direction. "Make sure to keep me in the loop. I'm at least as human as the rest and I miss things. When it gets chaotic here, which is most of the time, channel your need to see me through Tracey. She's my gatekeeper and she's got a really good idea of what needs my attention and what you can do on your own. For now, I need to get ready to butter up my French compatriot and go see President Miller. I will see most of you on Monday. Thanks."

He stood up and stretched as the others made their way to the door.

Sarah lingered at the doorway, then turned. "Mr. Kincaid, there's something bothering me about Kathy's California numbers."

"Oh?"

"I'll talk to her later. It's that plant in Riverside. Seven thousand people laid off."

"Yeah. That's gotta be tough," he agreed.

"But that plant was unique. It assembled the last parts of the stealth bombers. My brother is a mechanic in the Air Force. There isn't another plant producing those things. Anywhere."

Kincaid was waiting and getting a little nervous about his time to rehearse French. "And…?"

"Those jobs didn't move to the heartland and we can't outsource something that sensitive. Those jobs just vanished — poof."

Kincaid tilted his head, holding out his left hand. "Meaning…?"

Sarah had her pointer finger out on her right hand, beating the air, searching for her answer. Finally, she looked up. "I don't know. I'll have to talk to Kathy." She turned and left the room.

Anna covered her mouth to avoid laughing. The Chief of Staff opened his hands helplessly.

Brenda returned with a folder of information about the gates opening up in Washington and New York, and handed them to Anna.

"Well, sir, let's see what you want to say. Airport French isn't all that different from Airport American."

* * *

In the front seat of the Piper 1066, Laura Garrette continued her checklist. The 1066, a favored tandem-seat single-engine plane, was designed originally as an inexpensive entry-level craft. The Piper design team had wisely concentrated on producing a plane that was not only thrifty but also easy to keep in the air. As a result, it had rapidly become the preferred vehicle for getting beginners into the sky and back alive.

"Chocks and chains — off. Flaps … check. Fuel — seventy-two — good." She called off each item she verified. Her instructor wouldn't say anything unless there was a mistake. "Aircraft registration …" She laughed.

"What's so funny?" the instructor asked.

"I still say having aircraft registration part of the checklist is stupid. Like we'll crash is it's not registered."

"Homeland Security, honey. They don't like strange aircraft flying around. Remember, the terrorists used airplanes a dozen years ago for the New York attacks."

"And those weren't registered?"

"Back to the checklist, hon." Linda Hill was a patient instructor.

"Rudder …" Laura continued the list to its completion without further input from Linda.

Laura was a nearly ideal student. In addition to being a quick study, she enjoyed the experience and spent far more than the minimum time in the school's simulator. Now, she went through the motions instinctively and guided the plane gracefully onto the tarmac, observing each check and lookout exactly when she should. In her fashionable prescription sunglasses, she exuded an air of elegant competence that would have been perfect in a spy movie or romantic adventure.

With clearance from the tower, she eased the throttle forward and began her run down the long concrete strip. Her eyes darted about in a circle checking her margins, checking the way ahead, checking temperatures, pressures, and airspeed. At precisely one hundred eighty knots, she eased back on the wheel and was airborne. Today's flight plan called for a short trip toward the beaches of Delaware and Maryland's Eastern Shore with a variety of navigation exercises, practice in stall recovery, and a series of simulated emergencies. She was always calm and focused through the class, but she usually relaxed at about five thousand feet, a little under a mile. From that altitude, she could take in the breadth of the land — farms, crossroads, rivers and streams. Yet she was still low enough that she could make out some details of homes, cars, and people going about their business.

It would have been fun flying over her home, but their Bethesda acreage was well within restricted airspace. Several pilots a year had lost their licenses by carelessly straying within what the aeronautical charts clearly proclaimed the "North Washington ADIZ" – Air Defense Intercept Zone. In 2008, a student pilot had demonstrated tragically how serious the "Intercept" term was taken. In addition to the pilot and instructor, twelve people in an office building had died as the flaming wreckage crashed onto their roof.

Today, there would be no adventures aside from the pleasant exhilaration of sailing the clean air above the DelMarVa Peninsula.

"Ready to take her down, Laura?" Linda signaled the last phase of the lesson. Two hours had passed in what seemed the blink of an eye.

"Ready if you are." Laura switched her radio to the landing frequency and cleared their approach with the tower. The strip was visible twenty miles away in the bright Saturday morning air. Though she loved the nautical feel of using her manual flight slide rules, she would stick with the digital flight computer this morning. It took its input feed straight from the instrumentation along the airfield and was by far the safest procedure to follow. Her plane could react immediately to any changes as they happened. She had plotted the landing with the hand calculators in the past and had been impressed how a small change in the wind could nudge one off course. She adjusted her trim, slowing their approach to exactly what was expected. If anyone were plotting their progress along the glide path, her descent would have overlaid the centerline precisely.

Though an orchestra of technologies was assisting her at every point, she still found her heart pounding as the ground began to rise to meet her craft. She wondered what it must feel like landing without the aid of all these machines out in the bush of Alaska or Australia or The Wild Places. Today, she touched down in the middle of the accumulated tire marks at the end of the landing strip. The touchdown was a bit heavier than she had hoped, but drew no comment from the rear seat so it must have been all right. She coasted down the centerline slowing for her left turn onto taxiway 014.

"Well done, Laura. As close to a perfect landing as you'll get."

5 JAMAICA

Saturday, March 1, 2014

"What'cha doing?" Jennifer Pullman walked into their study.

Jack was busy at the computer. "Just a little research on something fun I thought we might do. What do you think?" He slid his chair away from the table so that she could move in to look.

"Jamaica?" She showed only mild curiosity.

"Yeah. We'd talked about going there some day. Warm beaches, tropical breezes, island paradise."

She was still looking at the screen picture of a couple frolicking in the bright blue Jamaican water. "We did, didn't we?" Still the same distant interest.

"I thought maybe I'd take some vacation time. Maybe next month?"

Jenn smiled. "They're telling you 'Have fun while you can,' aren't they? Sweet. But I think I'll decide what's fun from here on. If some miracle happens, we'll talk Jamaica. Right now, let's talk San Diego."

"I was thinking I'd skip the meeting this year. Spend more time with you."

Jenn scowled. "No! I've been looking forward to San Diego. I enjoy our trips. Remember, the first time I noticed you was in that debate back in '96."

Jack smiled his first smile in several days. "Yeah. As I recall you were quite abusive."

"I didn't understand debating rules then. Dad dragged me with him because he was coaching one of his stars. Whom you trashed if I remember correctly," she laughed.

"That's why you got abusive. In the morning, I was just barely ahead of her — Rachel?"

"Uh huh, Rachel. You were so on-target in the morning. And so cute.

You had me completely captured. And I was agreeing with everything you stood for. Wow!"

"You sat with me at lunch. Then … came the afternoon," he reminded.

Jenn shook her head, still smiling. "You switched sides and totally destroyed every point that you'd made in the morning. I felt so betrayed. And poor Rachel."

"She wasn't ready. She hadn't researched the opposing arguments. Most of all, she actually supported the morning side and opposed the afternoon side in her heart. It was obvious. She stumbled and I took advantage of that. I wasn't mean about it, was I?"

Jenn sat down in the recliner. She looked tired but contented. "In hindsight, no. But between you being so good knocking down the morning-you and running circles around Rachel, I thought you were cocky and mean. Good thing you were still so cute. Otherwise I'd never have spoken to you again."

"Uh huh. I came over after the match to ask for your number or email address. You called me a jerk and a pig and stomped off."

Jenn giggled. "Yeah, I said that, didn't I?"

"But you still got hold of me a month later."

"Sure did. Couldn't get you out'a my mind. Tracked you down through my dad."

"I love you," he whispered.

"Yes, I know. Let's make love."

Jack grinned. "Now?"

"Now, tomorrow, every day. Let's make love on that beach above San Diego. Let's be wild, memorable, scandalous. Will my ever-analytical lover do that for me?"

He grinned more broadly and nodded. Abandoning Jamaica, he crept toward the recliner. She pushed back in the seat in mock terror. Climbing onto the chair, he carefully planted his knees to either side of her legs. She giggled. He braced his arms on the recliner, bent down and kissed her softly on her lips. She closed her eyes, savoring the moment. After quite some time, he raised his upper body part way and began undoing her blouse buttons starting at the top and working his way down. She smiled watching his progress. Often at this point, she would playfully ask, "Do you need any help?" She knew he found that mildly irritating so she just watched peacefully.

Having unbuttoned the last blouse button, he carefully parted her fabric. She was not wearing a bra. Perhaps he knew that, perhaps not; but he was mildly surprised and pleased. She had decided what she wanted and planned accordingly. He looked for a while into her soft brown eyes. They were so beautiful.

He bent down again and kissed each of her breasts. They still had the firm substance of youth — "perky" he described them. Her nipples were rigid in anticipation and she was beginning to breathe more deeply. He rose up and pulled his shirt off, flinging it somewhere to the side with a bit of drama. She giggled, reminded of an old *Pink Panther* movie scene. He returned to kissing her breasts, kissing her mouth, and kissing around her neck. She wrapped her arms around him, gently scratching his back.

"Ah, that feels so good." He moved off the chair, kneeling on the floor unbuttoning and unzipping her pants. No panties. She was serious. She lifted her butt a little so that he could slide the pants away. She now reclined open and naked save the blouse still shrouding her arms. He kissed her thighs and traveled upward. Her face was flushed by the time he reached her lips again.

She pushed him back carefully and rose from the chair until both were standing. She pulled off her blouse the rest of the way, flinging it in the general direction of his shirt. She kneeled and undid his belt, his button and zipper, and slid his pants to the floor, returning his pleasantries with kisses and strokes from the bottom until she reached his lips, standing again. They kept a large, soft comforter beside the recliner in the study for these occasions and they quickly spread it on the floor. He lay down on his back and invited her atop. They worked together in practiced silence but for the sound of breathing and rhythmic friction. Jenn closed her eyes tightly, lost in rising tension, more and more intense until she released. They paused while she sobbed silently as she always did. This reaction had puzzled Jack long ago, but he was pleased now at her peculiar expression of happiness. She relaxed and lay on top of him, her long brown hair flowing over his chest with her ear to his heart. From time to time, she would turn her head and kiss him.

As her heart rate returned to normal, she rolled off him and onto her back. He caressed her face, her breasts, her bottom, her legs, kissing as he went. When he was quite certain they were both ready, he took her hand and she sat up, smiling. This was her preferred way. He stretched out on the fabric while she positioned herself above and guided his insertion. They worked together until he released with great intensity. He could feel his muscles relax throughout his body in response to his climax. He wiggled his feet, listening to his ankles crackle. She smiled sweetly. This was one of the phenomena that signaled a most satisfying time.

She waited quietly as the last of the tingles worked through his body, and then she lay down again on his chest for a very long time — perhaps twenty minutes or so. Jack thought she had fallen asleep.

But she wasn't. "When I'm gone, you're going to have to find a woman who really likes sex a lot."

"What? I hope I didn't hear what I think I just heard. If I did, I think we're not giving the future the chance it deserves."

She ignored his protest. "You know, you're really, really good at pleasing me and your next mate should be appreciative too."

"This is creepy. Don't you have any hope? It's 2014 after all. We're going to beat this monster."

"Maybe. I don't know. If I don't, then I've got maybe thirty chances to make love with you — tops. After that, you're on your own. I just figure if we talk about it now, I can actually have some say in the future. Is that creepy?"

"I don't know," he murmured.

"Whatever. You should find someone who's more flexible, interesting. I'm a one-position lover. You don't seem to mind. In fact, you seem to be fine with that. But you should have more variety. And don't settle for the first woman you make love to."

Jack lay flat on his back looking at the ceiling. "I can't believe we're having this conversation."

She continued, "I'm actually finding it quite liberating. I was afraid talking about her would be difficult. But you're the best thing that ever happened to me, and I just want to protect my investments. How's that for practical?"

Jennifer turned to face Jack. Her nipples were firm again and there was urgency in her voice. "I'm trying to think of some candidates. Patricia?"

"Yuk! No one from the lab gets near me. I'm really fed up with them on a lot of counts these days."

"Oh? You used to hold them out as model workers."

"Before I worked with them every day all day. They're selfish spoiled brats. All they think of is what more they can get. I prefer my women generous and thoughtful — obviously."

"I see. Well, she should definitely push you harder into politics than I have. You've given enough to the Institute and they clearly don't respect you. You'd make a great and honorable public servant."

"Hah! I'd go nuts," he laughed.

"No, no, no. You're patient, you're persuasive, you're honest …"

"And I can see too many sides of every issue, I don't or won't take stands, and I hate political games."

"So Jennifer II gives you the stand and you run with it. Promise me you'll find a hardheaded woman. Someone who'll use you for greatness."

"We're going to see this through," he said, clenching his jaw.

"This isn't a discussion. It's a request. Promise me."

Jack looked distressed.

"Promise me!" she insisted.

"I promise."

"Promise what?"

Jack closed his eyes. "I promise if you don't get over this that I will search for a hard-headed woman who'll use me for greatness."

"Close enough."

Now she was staring at the ceiling. He opened his eyes and turned his head toward her. She was smiling serenely.

Suddenly she giggled. "Or maybe even if I do get better, you should have a mistress who'll drive you to greatness. Think about it — two women working together on you." She was gleeful.

"Oy. One woman is more than I can handle already."

Jennifer laughed, and then turned to attack him, tickling and kissing. They tumbled in naked play until they were both exhausted, and then lay in one another's arms until overtaken by a long Saturday afternoon nap.

The screen saver had long obliterated Jamaica and the computer screen was dark.

* * *

Anna made her way through the labyrinthine second basement corridors until she came to the designated room. David Kincaid was waiting, studying his notes beside a machine with an array of lights and buttons, a telephone handset in the middle.

"Ah. Right on time. Thank you. I just talked to our ambassador and Monsieur Cartier should phone back in about fifteen minutes. Have you ever used one of these contraptions?"

Anna shook her head.

"Have a seat. Let me give you a really quick orientation. Don't worry; the beast is very user friendly. It's a machine designed to prevent diplomatic nightmares. Watch. The main handset here is the only two-way voice part. Here on either side, the handsets just listen. That way, there won't be any strange breathing for the other end to hear. Then you have our lights on top here. Every thing to the left is local, as marked. To the right is the remote location."

"And the other country has the same setup?" she asked.

"Yes indeed. It's one of those delightful things that we often work out behind the scenes — technical background. It never makes the news, but helps keep the world running smoothly. Each feature evolved out of some embarrassment or dispute. The plans for this beast were validated by a whole bunch of engineering committees and working groups with really long boring names, and it was implemented smoothly. Kinda encouraging, really."

Anna agreed.

"Now, the lights on top are important. You have two for local, two for remote. The first one is recording. Green — recording is on; red — recording is off. The second is for open mike. Green — everyone in the room is listening; red — only the center handset is live. The toggle switch under each light gives control. They're very clearly marked and are probably some of the best human-engineered controls in the world." Kincaid looked at the clock. "I see you have the list of phrases for me. After our initial pleasantries, you'll be the one on the two-way phone."

"Isn't this a little on the high-powered side?" she asked. "I've only been here two days.".

"Welcome to the human side of the inter-nations. We're not negotiating any treaties or threatening to launch missiles. We're just a few public servants doing our jobs keeping in touch. We're letting each other know what's bothering us, or how we can help. You remember the earthquake in Syria last year?"

"Yes sir. It was a major disaster. I also recall we lent a lot of assistance despite rather high tensions between the two countries at the time."

"Exactly," he confirmed. "Everything was arranged through this very phone. Everything was planned person-to-person. Every move that might be misconstrued was explored here first. This phone is executive office to executive office. It doesn't replace anything that State does. That's why we have the record button. When the green light is on, someone over in Foggy Bottom will be reviewing what I say in a matter of minutes. No loose cannons, no independent operations."

"I'm impressed," she said.

Kincaid smiled. "Me too. It's one of the more satisfying elements of this job — keeping people in the loop instead of shutting them out."

Anna returned his smile. He resolved he would find ways to elicit that smile as often as possible.

"As for your being here only two days, you're a White House Fellow. You've been selected from the best of the best. We have complete confidence you'll do fine. I've never been disappointed."

"What's to prevent someone from tampering with the machine so that it doesn't show the recording or open microphone?"

"Nothing but honor, I suppose. If you watch from outside the workings of government, you might get a pretty jaded view of what goes on. But I'd say we have a pretty good operation, really. It's not so different from any of the other commerce of life. Most of us, most of the people we deal with are honest, hard-working people. On a typical day, a billion transactions will be executed fairly and efficiently. A few tens of thousands will be fraudulent or botched. That's not a bad record. But what you hear about are those that go badly. Same here. In a few minutes, we're going to assure the French chief of staff that we are not doing anything sneaky, and we're going to give him something that will make his job easier on Monday morning. In return, he'll help us stay out of more trouble than we're already in over in the Gulf. Win-win for the cost of a phone call. And you and I and whoever is on the machine over there and maybe a few low-level diplomatic types are the only ones who will ever know about it. Person to person. That's where the good power resides."

The machine gave a gentle chirp and he took the sheet that Anna had prepared. "How do you say 'I hear you beat our ambassador again'?" He quickly added, "…in tennis?"

"*J'entends que vous battez notre ambassadeur dans le tennis encore.*"

Kincaid picked up the green two-way handset and nodded for Anna to pick up the set on the right of the machine. "*Bonjour, Monsieur Cartier. Ça va?*"

"*Bonjour, Monsieur Kincaid. La vie est bonne aujourd'hui. Et tu?*"

"*Trés bien. J'entends que vous battez notre ambassadeur dans le tennis encore.*"

"*Je pense qu'il me laissait gagner.*"

Kincaid turned to Anna, who whispered back. < "*I think he was letting me win.*" >

Kincaid agreed. "*Il est un bon homme.*" He studied Anna's notes and continued. "*Je suis heureux d'avoir Mlle Anna Colbert en tant que mon interprète. Elle parle français bien meux que moi.*" < *I'm pleased to have Miss Anna Colbert as my interpreter. Her French is much better than mine.* > He handed the green phone to Anna and picked up the black listener to his left.

Cartier addressed Anna. "*Bonjour Mlle Colbert. Je suis enchanté pour vous rencontrer.*" < *Good day, Miss Colbert. I am delighted to meet you.* >

"*Merci, Monsieur Cartier.*"

So began the session with David Kincaid speaking with his colleague through Anna.

"Monsieur Cartier. I wanted to let you know that President Miller will be interviewed tomorrow on Sunday morning television and will likely be asked the usual questions about our operations in the Persian Gulf. I wanted to be sure to give you a chance to ask any questions in advance and to allow our country to avoid any confusion about what he might say."

< "*Like last time?*" >

Kincaid smiled. "Yes. Like last time. I presume that you share our concerns about the Al Wadi pipeline."

< "*Yes. Of course. We are quite proud of our French engineers, and of our smooth cooperation with both countries in the region. We would really prefer not to have any feathers ruffled.*" >

"Yes, sir. I can appreciate your position. That is part of why I wanted to call you. I wanted to assure you that we are as content as possible to stay out of the way of your enterprise. Would I be wrong to assume that a little bit of complaining about your operations would not be a problem?"

Cartier laughed. < "*I think our President would be pleased to complain in return. Of course that assumes that you do not have any mischief afoot.*" >

"President Miller is supposed to stress tomorrow that we are absolutely not interfering. He is supposed to point out that we have no ship movements or aircraft redeployments. He's supposed to point out that our troops are at stable strength levels with normal rotation." Kincaid emphasized each "supposed" and Anna interpreted the emphasis.

Cartier laughed again. < *"I'll let my boss know what your boss is 'supposed' to say. Is there something that you would like my boss to say in public in return?"* >

Kincaid was visibly relieved. "Actually, Monsieur Cartier, I think we have some good news for your President. With the loss of our Air Atlantic Company, there will be several gates vacant at several airports. We anticipate considerable competition for the Washington gates but we would be very supportive if our dear ally made known their need for the New York gates."

< *"Ah. That is good news indeed. The President will be pleased. Shall I have him watch President Miller's television show?"* >

"Um… Perhaps the ambassador could provide him a video of the highlights."

Another laugh. < *"Well, Monsieur Kincaid, I appreciate your call. Right now, Ambassador James I believe owes me one of your quintessential culinary delights — hamburgers on the grill, though he tells me there is no ham involved. Peculiar language English."* >

Kincaid grinned.

Cartier continued, though Anna stopped interpreting. The conversation went on for several minutes before there seemed a final point. "*Mlle Colbert, vous devez vider ce vieil homme et venir travail pour moi.*"

"*Oh, non, non monsieur.*" She was speaking more rapidly, more heavily accented, very natural. She looked up at David Kincaid. "*Ah, il n'est pas tellement vieux.*" She sounded almost flirtatious.

"*Est-ce que je peux satisfaire lui parle une fois de plus?*" < *"May I speak to him once more?"* >

"*Oui. Au revoir.*" She handed the phone to Kincaid. "He wants to talk to you directly." She did not pick up the listening phone.

"Charming young lady. It's good to see your interpreters have improved."

"Ah. As has your English. Quite good."

"Not as good as her French. I wanted to thank you again for the advance notice. I'll see to it that we behave predictably."

"Thank you. Enjoy your meal. *Au revoir.*"

He hung up the phone and turned to Anna. "Well, that seemed to go well. You did great. He was quite impressed. Thank you."

She rose to leave. "My pleasure, sir. Did the French language come back to you?"

"A little, maybe. You two speeded up there at the end. I think I caught something about 'he's too old'."

"Oh, no. We do need to work on your French if we're going to be talking to Monsieur Cartier very often. I said, '*il n'est pas tellement vieux*'."

"Ah." Kincaid showed relief, hoping she couldn't be certain he didn't know the words.

"If you don't have anything else, I'll be on my way," she demurred.

"Thank you so very much. I'm going up to visit the President now, and see if we can put on a good show tomorrow. I'll see you Monday."

"Yes, sir." She turned and headed down the corridor.

David waited as patiently as he could. He needed to find a French-English dictionary or a computer with translation software on it. He wasn't sure how to spell *tellement.*

6 FRIENDLY TURF

Saturday, March 1, 2014

David Kincaid rode elevator seven to the third floor, got off, and turned right. Even as one of the President's closest confidants, he kept his identification card close at hand, ready for the perpetual phalanx of identity checks. His ready compliance kept him in the good graces of the Marine contingent. He made a point of knowing each of their names and backgrounds.

"Corporal Tull, good afternoon."

"Good afternoon, Mr. Kincaid. Thank you." Corporal Jeff Tull took the proffered badge, swiped it through his card reader, and then dutifully compared the string of random numbers and letters on the back to his access list.

"So how's the girl friend? Mary?" Kincaid asked.

"Not good, sir. I think she dumped me."

Kincaid's face clouded. "Oh, not good, not good. I'm sorry."

"She said going out with a Marine's too unpredictable. She wants someone with reliable hours."

"Hmm. I can see that would be a problem. You taking it OK?"

Tull returned the identification card. "Yes, sir, I think so. I kinda felt it coming."

"Well, for what comfort it may offer, you're enviably young, and will be a prize catch for the young lady who truly deserves you."

Tull grinned. "Thank you, sir. The President's expecting you."

David pushed open the door and entered into hallowed space. Looking forward at the President's desk, little had changed in the twelve years since he first walked in as a junior congressman. Behind him though, to his left and right, the banks of technological gadgetry had grown in number, complexity, and sophistication. The Oval Office production facilities now put to shame the big television studios of 2002. Still, he took comfort seeing the President of the United States of America at his ancient wooden desk with a simple pen busy writing on a yellow legal pad.

"David! Come on in. How the Hell are ya?"

Kincaid grinned. "Mr. President. Quite well, thank you. Yourself?"

"Good, good. I got your talking points. Please thank your staff. Cameron and Jean sent up an opening, too. There're several things I know you want to go over with me here …" The President eyed the thick folder in Kincaid's hand. "… and probably some more."

Kincaid looked down. "Oh, no, this is mostly for Monday. But I was hoping we could go over some tone issues this afternoon."

"So I don't make an ass of myself like last time?"

"I wouldn't put it that way, sir."

Miller nodded. "No, you probably wouldn't. Too polite. But look. I know I didn't handle that well. Caused a ruckus, created three international incidents, and sent the stock market down five percent."

Kincaid grinned again. He enjoyed talking with President Miller one on one without the Vice President's influence. Miller was generally honest, open, and friendly. His clear, often elegant, conversational style had helped him win easy re-election last year, and helped maintain his high approval ratings.

"Well, Mr. President, we handled it. Hopefully, tomorrow will be a more positive experience for all of us. In particular, we're hoping you'll spread a little good will with the E.U., including the French."

"Yeah. I notice a big chunk of your paper devoted to that. Here. Sit down. Make yourself comfortable."

"Thank you. The staff feels that the right words could get us back toward their friendly side. We really need calm in the Gulf, both with the arms and with the oil. You know we're spending a lot more there than we need to — you've seen the numbers. If we could throttle back those costs, your excellent economy should be able to put us almost in the black by term's end."

"You guys already talking legacy down there? I'm not dead yet."

Kincaid chuckled. "I'm never *not* thinking legacy, sir. It's mine too."

"Uh huh. And what are you thinking for '16? Run for the Senate seat in North Carolina?"

"Not seriously. Senator Kreis is doing a great job. I think we're all better off with him there than me."

"He's a good man, I grant you," the President agreed. "After the transition, you take some time off to reflect. I know you've got a long public service career ahead."

"Thank you, sir. Now about tomorrow …"

"Yeah. Do I really have to deal with Jacobs again?"

"Yes, you do," Kincaid replied.

"He doesn't like me." The President was clearly in a playful mood, donning his 'put upon' look.

"It's his job. He's new enough that he has to make an impact and you know that. Especially now. You got confrontational last time and he used that quite skillfully. That's why we put humility as item one on the list. I'm sure Jacobs can handle the difference but he probably won't be expecting it. Gives you an edge."

President Miller nodded.

"Also, note the little bio sheet on him. Lot's of nice tidbits. Work some of those in gracefully."

"Where do you people find this stuff? You've even got how many puppies his dog had when Jacobs was five."

"He's a celebrity. People collect this stuff. Tracey just punched in the right agency. They have things about you that you probably didn't know."

"OK. I'll commit this to memory tonight."

"Will you have time?"

"Tiffany has a dance. I actually blocked out the whole time to get ready. Thought you'd be impressed."

Kincaid smiled. "Indeed I am. This bodes well for tomorrow. Any questions about our suggestions on the language?"

"No. It's good. I like the 'allies' and 'resistance' references. Very clever. Nostalgic." The President looked up at a very pensive Chief of Staff. "What's going on up there?"

Kincaid paused a few seconds. "We really need to rework our attitudes. The Europeans own half our companies; we own half of theirs. For two-thirds of our populations, we're literally cousins. This belligerence or condescension, or whatever it is, isn't healthy or productive. You mentioned legacy. Mutual respect wouldn't be a bad thing to have on the books."

Kincaid watched the President rock back and forth in his chair. Miller had his inscrutable face on. Kincaid continued. "It might be a hard point to sell to the Vice President, but it's your entry in the history books, not his."

Miller's inscrutable look gave way to a mischievous smile. "I think you're right. Both about it being a good idea and Bailey hating it."

Kincaid lowered his head. "Why is it we keep this up? Seems as long as I remember, we've had this public squabble with the French. I don't remember how it started or what fuels it."

The President continued to rock back and forth. He pursed his lips in thought. "Don't fully know myself. I'm not a history major — poli sci. But this 'squabble' goes way back. Probably started as jealousy. You know, the French way of life — or at least our stereotype — loose, carefree, unhurried. Clashes really badly with our image of the driven American —

struggling to get ahead. Next you had arrogant troublemakers like de Gaulle. Then for dessert they best us pretty consistently in diplomacy and they cash in when we lose. Pushes our little boy buttons. And I think they know that."

"Hmm. Points well taken. Still I wish we could alter that." David replied.

"Could happen. Probably take something pretty dramatic. But Polish jokes essentially died with Lec Walesa and Solidarity. Germans became heroes resisting in Berlin. Could happen. After all, they did give us Lafayette and Lady Liberty."

Kincaid nodded. "So are you good to go with our language here?"

The President agreed. "Of course. 'Allies, resistance.' Got it. Now I'm also going to do some bragging about our numbers. I didn't see nearly the volume of crowing compared to our tone exercises."

"Again, point well taken, sir."

"You look tired, David. You need a break."

Kincaid managed a trace of a smile. "Yes, sir. Don't see it coming any time soon, though. The fact that I didn't focus more on our accomplishments is telling, I guess. I didn't used to be the worrier, you'll remember. Used to focus on a bright future. Now that it's here, all I can think about is how fragile it is; how quickly this bubble could burst."

"Tell you what. I'm going to be seeing you at, what, seven tomorrow? I don't see anything on your list where we have a disagreement, and Bailey's not here to change that. You get some rest, I'll memorize my lines and we'll look forward to the Miller and Jacobs show tomorrow."

"Hard to argue with that, sir. I appreciate your time, and I'm really looking forward to it. Hope you are too." As Kincaid rose from his chair, the top folder in his bundle fell to the floor disgorging its contents on the carpet. "Yes, I guess I do need a rest."

The President helped gather the papers, and began looking over them. "So what's going on in California here?"

"Haven't gone over that with the Vice President."

The mischievous grin reappeared. "The Veep's not here. Promise I won't tell. C'mon."

When Kincaid seemed neither willing to talk or even smile, the President continued soberly. "Maybe we have some fences to mend in our own house. There are times when the tension between the two of you approaches unhealthy and unproductive. Seems to have gotten worse lately."

Kincaid sighed. "There's an awfully wide gulf between us."

"Gulf? You hate each other's guts."

"I don't hate him," Kincaid protested.

"No, that's probably true. You wouldn't allow yourself that. But he hates you. That is true. I can think of about a hundred reasons he might, but what do you think are the top reasons for this — as you call it — gulf?"

Kincaid reflected a moment. "We've got completely different core values. I'm a farmer, he's a hunter-gatherer; I like the deal, he likes the conquest; I enjoy the nuanced, he likes it black and white."

Miller laughed. "Well said. That's part of why I like having you around."

"Do we have any uncertainty in that?" Kincaid asked.

"Oh no. Of course, if Bailey had his way, you'd be gone in a flash. But I need you both. When the two of you agree — which is more often than either of you realize — then I know I've got a sure policy. When you don't, I play you off each other until I'm satisfied. Very Machiavellian, eh?"

Kincaid finally smiled again. "Well, I guess it works for you."

"It does. And for the country I might add."

Kincaid continued, "That actually touches on another thing that keeps bothering me. I still don't like the private security he maintains on the side. It doesn't feel right to me. Too feudal. We've talked about this before."

"Yes. And nothing's changed. His circumstances are still different. His family connections put him at risks way beyond those of the office. We would need an act of congress — literally; you know that — to provide that much more security for him. But he foots the bill himself. He's doing us a favor."

Kincaid rubbed his face. "Yeah, I suppose."

"But you still don't agree."

Kincaid shrugged.

"OK. Now I've promised not to tell. What's with California?"

Kincaid looked around out of habit before beginning. "Unemployment numbers have come in way higher than we expected. Revenues just the opposite. They're on track for a payroll meltdown in another month and a half. I want to put together something to tide Governor Barnes over."

The President was skimming the papers as he replaced them in the folder. "Yeah. I see. Gotta help Bob out. Good man." He continued to scan columns of figures. "Are you sure about these numbers? California should be our crown jewel."

"No, sir, I'm not sure. We're going over them. That's part of why I'm not ready. These are based on state figures, which should be a little behind ours. Kathy and Sarah are trying to close the gap."

"Sarah?"

"One of the new fellows. Pretty sharp."

The President nodded. "You pick good people. Another reason to keep you. Isn't Jacobs going to ask about this?"

Kincaid paused. "He shouldn't know about these numbers. They're deep confidential and pretty obscure. Still that is a hole. Sorry. What would we say?"

"I think you basically covered it there. We're studying the numbers. Of course, we stand with the people of the great state of California, and expect the Golden State to be more golden than ever. We'll work with their fine governor to make sure that prosperity reigns from top to bottom and everywhere in between."

"Not bad." Kincaid nodded. "Maybe approaching schmaltzy, but not bad."

"I'll work on it. Jacobs would love to ambush us on something like that. You got any other folders there I should be aware of?"

"No, sir," Kincaid grinned. "Everything else is internal staff papers. And stop thinking he's trying to ambush you. Be your charming, relaxed self. Be sensitive to when he's asking something you haven't studied. We have the best staff in the world to cover the nitty-gritty details. You'll get back to him on that. I think we're good. Anything else I can get for you, sir?"

"Go home. Get some rest. I've got my marching orders. I'll be ready."

"I'm looking forward to tomorrow, sir," Kincaid said as he rose and headed toward the door.

"Two puppies. Biscuit and Romper."

Kincaid turned around slowly.

"I really do read what you send me," Miller said.

"Thank you, sir. How did you know their names though?"

The President grinned broadly and slapped his hand on the desk. "I called his mother. Swore her to secrecy."

"Good night, Mr. President. I'll see you in the morning."

"Good night, David. Thank you, and thank your staff."

Kincaid went through the doorway and closed the door gently. "Good night, Corporal Tull."

"Good night, Mr. Kincaid."

Kincaid looked at the time. "Watch about over?"

"Yes, sir. About half an hour."

"Quiet afternoon. Must get a little boring."

"I've got my coffee, sir."

"Excellent. Now let's keep an eye out for the right young lady for you — your soul mate."

Tull smiled. "And for you too, sir." He immediately became sober. "I'm sorry, sir. I didn't mean that the way it sounded."

"Why not?" Kincaid looked pensive. "Somewhere, some gentle soul is my match again. I like your thinking."

Tull appeared relieved.

"We'll watch out for each other, eh?"

"Yes, sir."

"Good night." Kincaid made his way out through the maze to the parking lot. The setting sun bathed the white granite and marble of the capitol's towering buildings and monuments in a golden orange glow. Amidst the cleanly trimmed shrubs, he could spy the first precocious crocuses closing up for the night. His breath still materialized like wisps of orange sherbet in the chill. Today had been good. Tomorrow had possibilities. And life was as under control as it ever got.

7 AMBUSH

Sunday, March 2, 2014

"Morning, beautiful." Jack had the kitchen table set and coffee brewing when Jennifer stepped in. Her hair was wrapped in a large blue towel, still damp from her shower. She wore her large terry housecoat. Jack poured two large orange juices, leaned over, and planted a kiss on her lips when she walked over to him, then handed her one of the juices.

She took the juice and sat down at her place at table. The morning light streaming in the kitchen window caught on a bouquet of fresh carnations. "How pretty," she said.

Jack turned from the stove and smiled. "Saw them last night at the Super Fresh. Thought you'd like them. I've never seen that orange-flecked variety before. Eggs?"

She checked out the orange-flecked carnation, taking a deep whiff of its fragrance. "Nice. One egg. Mind if I turn on the TV? Ben Jacobs Hour's on in about 15."

"Yeah, yeah. I definitely want to see it today. The President's on."

"Right. That didn't go so well last time," she said.

"Well, Miller was off his game. He wasn't ready and when he got caught unprepared, he tried to fake it. You can't do that with Jacobs, who's as serious as they get."

Jennifer smiled. "I know."

"Sorry. This is my game. I love it. What the President should have done was go as far as he knew, and then stopped. He would have gotten points for that. He could have just left the subject hanging. Jacobs wouldn't get anything by pushing past a polite stop."

"You should volunteer to coach him."

Jack smiled. "I'm sure he's got the best coaches in the world, but it only works if he follows their advice. They have access to the best information sources on the planet. They're wired and networked. They don't need an amateur."

"So how come he blew it last time?"

Jack frowned. "Wish I knew."

"Well, if he blows it again, you apply," she insisted.

"We'll see. I think my lab job's a lot safer bet."

Toast popped up a perfect fragrant brown. He gave the skillet a shake and sprinkled a dash of Italian seasoning on the egg. He looked over at Jennifer, serene and beautiful in the warm morning light.

* * *

Laura sipped an organic tea while flipping through the front sections of the *Post.* Despite a well-stocked refrigerator, nothing appealed to her. She settled for a bowl of some fancy cheese cubes, likely left over from one of last week's dinners.

Her father was off for tennis at the club with someone. It was too early to call anyone on the west coast and the clinic wouldn't open for another forty-five minutes, but it would be swamped until about noon if it were a typical Sunday.

She pulled up the television schedule to see if anything worthwhile was on. "Oh great." She spied the listing for the Ben Jacobs Hour. "It's time to play 'let's pretend.'" She hesitated for a while before finally turning on the T.V. She continued to flip through the Sunday business section while enduring the last four minutes of commercials.

"Let's see. Layoffs in airlines, auto, computer, manufacturing. Do we see any openings? Nooooo. Oh wait. Yes, we do. Another monster military contract and the Army misses its recruiting goals again. No wonder things are going so well. Somewhere." She looked around their luxurious empty kitchen. "Here."

* * *

Kincaid had been in the studio for nearly an hour. He had chatted with the camera crew and the lighting crew. He had sat in the chair and traded practice banter with Ben Jacobs's director while the crews finalized camera angles and sequence.

"So Mr. President, when do you have something negative to say about the job picture?"

Kincaid smiled his most Presidential. "When Hell freezes over."

Laughter from the crew.

"And when do we expect that?" John Brightman continued the mock interview.

"Well, Ben, it's almost spring here in our nation's capitol and we're expecting a long, hot summer."

"OK. Got it." A technical voice in the dim nether world beyond the lights called out. "Any idea what color he's wearing today?"

"Predicting charcoal." Kincaid then pointed to his left shoulder. "Little flag pin here. Red, white, and blue." He grinned.

More laughter.

"I think we're ready, Mr. Kincaid. Thanks for your assistance."

"Always a pleasure, John. I think I see our host arriving now."

Ben Jacobs breezed in, trailing a small retinue of prompters, researchers, stylists, and assorted deputy assistants. He was young, but possessed an air of uncommon maturity.

"Ah, Mr. Kincaid."

"Mr. Jacobs," Kincaid replied.

They shook hands.

"Ben and David?" Jacobs suggested.

"Works for me."

"Everything comfortable on the set?"

"Like home away from home." Kincaid turned and swept his hand around toward the crew beyond the lights. "I hope you appreciate the backup you have here. Best of the best."

Kincaid and Jacobs applauded the crew.

Kincaid continued, "Congratulations on your ratings, Ben. Number one again I see. Way number one."

"Thanks. We try. Same for you. I don't think our last encounter did any lasting damage."

"Naw. He sulked for a few days, and then blamed you for being a bully and enemy of all free people everywhere, then got over it. But no sneaky questions today, OK?" Kincaid grinned.

Jacobs drew back, appalled. "Never!"

They both turned toward a commotion on the right. "Looks like it's show time," Jacobs said.

President Miller strode on to the set smiling broadly. He and Jacobs shook hands and exchanged pleasantries. Kincaid stepped back to his usual spot between cameras three and four. Makeup swarmed in to do their final touches. The President wore his charcoal suit with flag pin. He turned to find Kincaid at the edge of the light and flashed a quick smile, nodding when he located his Chief of Staff.

The clock displayed nine fifty-nine and forty seconds. The director called for quiet on the set and began the count down. "On five, four, …" He became silent and with his fingers indicated three, two, one.

* * *

Jack sat down across from Jennifer, two eggs and some sausage on his plate.

The familiar logo appeared on the television. "Live from Washington, this is the Ben Jacobs Hour, with today's special guest, the President of the United States."

Jack watched their demeanor intensely. "They both look relaxed. Both have notes on the side, but they won't have time to refer to them."

Jennifer giggled. Jack turned to her and stuck out his tongue.

"I think he looks stodgy in dark gray," she observed.

"Projects an image of power. He wants that, needs that."

Ben Jacobs appeared on screen. "Good morning and welcome. It has been a long time since a President of the United States has entered a second term with an approval rating over fifty percent, and has been apparently untouched by scandals. Our guest this morning, President Bill Miller, appears to have pulled this off." Jacobs flashed a Cheshire smile. "Or has he? We'll find out when we return after this break."

"Cheap stunt." Jack seemed genuinely disappointed.

"You don't think he has anything?" she asked.

"Not a chance. If he did, the network would have pulled out all the stops to boost viewership. This is going to be mostly questions and answers or at least questions and evasions."

* * *

After the break, Jacobs continued, "We're back with the President of the United States. Mr. President, the history of presidential second terms for the last century has been one of turmoil and conflict. To what do you credit this extraordinary run of high ratings?"

"Well, Mr. Jacobs, things have been going rather well. That's seldom been the case for second terms. I have to give credit first to the American people for their hard work and good attitudes. There's nothing we can't do when we're all pulling together, and that has been the case.

"Second credit goes to our country's amazing support team. Our Vice President, our chiefs of staff, the hundreds of support members of the executive branch have toiled tirelessly to keep our country on track. As you have often pointed out, I'm a pragmatist. I want the job done and done right. And I'm not too picky about calling on folks from what we traditionally call left or right, red or blue. What the people of this great land expect is performance and caring. You'd love to hear — though I'm glad in a way that you don't — the arguments that we sometimes go through while putting together the programs and policies that have worked so well. All these different ideas, diverse philosophies, and really smart people — it's amazing. But in the end, the bottom line is we will craft something that serves the public good. Perfect policy? Not in this lifetime. But optimized to work.

"And third, but by no means least is the working relationship we've forged with the legislative and judicial branches of our government. Recall if you will the animosity and acrimony of a decade ago. Here we are today, a divided government, but I can say without fear of contradiction that there has seldom been a climate of greater trust and respect than exists between my office and those of Senator Kreis and Representative Carter. When we pull together, there's nothing we can't accomplish.

* * *

Jack nodded. "Nice opening. Set's expectations well. Don't expect perfection. Give lots of credit. Jacobs can't shoot at him without hitting the whole crowd. The President seems relaxed, too. Obviously did his homework this time."

Jennifer had moved from her chair to sit in Jack's lap. He directed most of his attention to the interview. She had wrapped her arms around him, kissing his neck, occasionally glancing at the TV.

"Good," She finally commented. "He could use a break. Sounds like he's trying to do the right thing."

Jack turned and kissed her on the cheek. "Yeah. I don't think he has that grab-everything mentality of the last couple of administrations. But he's a pragmatist, and he's been pretty lucky with the economy. Jacobs isn't going to get much on him there. Foreign relations may be another matter. Let's see."

* * *

Laura popped a couple of cheese cubes in her mouth. She scolded the television. "Jeez Jacobs. Pull the plug on this. He's running on like syrup. I should have had pancakes for breakfast. Ask him about the shelters."

* * *

Jacobs turned to his next page of notes. "In all this near-perfect world at home though, there are some dark clouds that draw our attention. As I'm sure you're aware, the financial picture in California has darkened dramatically in the past month. What's going on there in our most populous state, and what does it portend for the nation as a whole?" Jacobs's carefully rehearsed inflection around "As I'm sure you're aware..." bordered on triumphant.

Kincaid shifted from foot to foot. Having almost missed this point in the briefing, he wasn't sure the President would deliver either a confident reply or a safely non-committal response. This was precisely the situation in which he lost control last time. And where did Jacobs get those numbers, and how much more did he know?

The President shook his head slowly and grew serious. "You know Mr. Jacobs, our team got that state report, and we've been studying it in detail. Frankly, it's a bit of an enigma. Of all states, California should be a prime beneficiary of the good times. At this point, we're not sure what to make of the numbers."

The President continued, "But what we are sure of is that we stand with the people of the great state of California and with their extraordinary governor, Bob Barnes. I talked with him yesterday to let him know that the federal government stands shoulder to shoulder with the state. We do take any rough spot seriously. Personally, I think and hope that we're seeing some kind of fluke or statistical bubble, and expect the Golden State to be more golden than ever."

Kincaid was delighted with the response. Almost identical to their office meeting, but spiked with just the right blend of caution. But Kincaid did not recall the President mentioning any contact with Governor Barnes. He watched the President closely.

When the camera shifted to Jacobs and his attention was directed there, the President turned immediately in Kincaid's direction.

Kincaid tilted his head quizzically.

The President held his hand open as if pleading.

Kincaid carefully pulled out his silenced phone, and held it to his ear as he raised his eyebrows.

The President gave a tiny slow nod.

Kincaid crept back from his station, turned, and headed out beyond the muffle doors. He made his way to an empty room and called the White House switchboard operator who patched him through to Sacramento.

"Good morning Rachel. This is David Kincaid. Yes. Fine. Yourself? Excellent. May I please speak to Bob?"

Governor Barnes came on the line. "David. Good Morning. Been watching the Ben Jacobs hour here."

Kincaid winced. "Yes sir. I thought I ought to talk to you about that."

"Yeah. Good. I must be getting really old. I don't remember talking to the President yesterday. Imagine that."

"Yes sir. The fault is ours. What the President surely meant to say was that we will be consulting thoroughly with you to get to the bottom of this. You know we don't take you or your state for granted."

"Well, it would have helped plenty if you hadn't closed those two plants."

"We're going to do something about that. I'm not sure what, but something."

"I'd appreciate that. Look, I had some more bad news come across my desk Friday. Doubt you've seen this yet. Our personal bankruptcies and late payment rates have been shooting up here. What the Hell are the other states doing that we're not? I look at the national numbers and figure we've missed the boat on something."

"Again Bob, I don't know. We've got our people on it but just don't have an answer for you yet."

"Well, let's meet on this A.S.A.P. And I'm guessing if anyone asks, I was talking with the President yesterday."

"He would consider that a very kind gesture."

"OK, I'm getting a vague recollection of a conversation. Looks like Jacobs is moving on. You'd better get back in the studio David."

"Thank you Bob."

Kincaid let out a sigh of relief and walked back to his spot.

With camera on Jacobs again, the President looked over to Kincaid.

Kincaid held a hand close to his chest and gave a thumbs-up.

The President smiled before turning his full attention to Jacobs who had been reading a list of various charities that had been reporting substantial increases in calls for help.

"I've seen those lists and I'll be honest Mr. Jacobs, I'm not sure what to make of them. On the one hand, we have our financial data carefully gathered on a continuous basis by professional researchers all across the country — and around the world for that matter — showing a steady, robust economy with some of the lowest unemployment on record. The stock market, which is one of the most sensitive indicators of our national health, has been pretty steady, even if not showing the enthusiasm one might expect.

"On the other hand, you have reports like the list you just read of communities under stress. I want to say this as carefully as I can because I don't want it misconstrued. There is a disconnect between the two worlds that begs explanation. Part of the problem with your list is that it is largely anecdotal, largely devoid of data, and sporadic on top of everything. When faced with two contradictory lists, one well researched and verifiable, and the other almost completely undocumented, which am I going to give greater weight? It can be agonizing. We really strive to do the right thing."

* * *

"Well done. Transferred the argument right back. Presents a clear case for his position, leaves himself open to the other but requires Jacobs to substantiate the list, which he can't. Displays a desire for compassion without having to do anything."

Jennifer rested her head on Jack's shoulder as she watched the show. "Who do you believe?"

Jack started at her question. "I hadn't even considered the charity list. Now I know that sounds cold …"

"Yes it does," she confirmed.

"… but the President is right. The facts simply don't bear out an increase in any of the hallmarks of poverty — homelessness, hunger, and other signs of decay. The one thing he really avoided was the point that those charities need a sense of urgency for fund raising. Admittedly they probably don't have the resources to provide documentation like the Department of Labor has but I don't see them trying … which inevitably leads to the question of whether the charities are really seeing a change or it's mostly marketing. I believe the President when he says he doesn't know. But he sure is skeptical. As am I."

* * *

"You asshole! You're calling us all liars, aren't you?" Laura shook her fist. "You come down to our clinics and our soup kitchens, you pig-headed, arrogant, elitist jerk! We'll show you some numbers. We'll show you real people." She picked up a cheese cube and hurled it at the screen. It hit the President in the right cheek leaving a greasy smudge. "Take that, pig!" She sent another flying for good measure. This cube impacted between camera changes causing minimal damage aside from another smudge.

* * *

The President and reporter swapped lists, quotes, challenges, and explanations for another five minutes without effect.

Jacobs continued smiling. "Yes, it's easy to see why you seem to have broken the second term curse. Let's move on to foreign affairs. Tensions in the Gulf have recently taken a turn for the worse. In particular, the Iranians and Iraqis continue to issue warnings about the Al Wadi pipeline. Why is that?"

The President laughed. "I think you're asking the wrong president. This is interesting. We're on our third question and again it's facts versus rumor, innuendo, and speculation. Here are the facts." The President leaned forward toward the camera. He counted on his fingers. "First, we are and we have continually honored the desires of the Iraqi people and have never violated the integrity of Iran. Second, our troop and fleet deployments are obvious to the whole world. You don't need to take my word for it. You can literally go check for yourself. We could not support any mischief even if we wanted to — which we don't. And third, we are quite prepared to work with our good friends and long-standing allies, the French, who have invested so heavily their skills and resources in this pipeline. We have no issue here. The rhetoric, I sincerely believe, is for home consumption. I hope that some day we can move beyond it. Abroad, as at home, there is nothing we can't accomplish if we pull together."

"My, that is quite a change in atmosphere, Mr. President," Jacobs said.

The President leaned back and relaxed in his chair and resumed his smile. "Just yesterday, I was talking about atmosphere with my fine chief of staff, David Kincaid. We were talking about old friends, how they can sometimes argue, how they have spats. But the mark of true friendship is that in the end, they're still friends. The French were the guarantors of our nascent democracy, our early example of Parliament, our continuing inspirations with their resistance in World War Two. While we wish that we had been the ones to co-sponsor the Al Wadi pipeline, it is they with whom we will be doing business and that is a comfortable outcome as I see it."

* * *

"Whoa. That's quite a change." Jack had his arms wrapped around Jennifer. "I'm guessing our forces are so stretched that they're basically doing a strategic retreat."

"Ooooh, you're so sexy when you talk that way. Makes me turn to jelly inside." She tried to remain serious but began to giggle before she finished her delivery.

Jack tightened his hug and nuzzled her chest.

* * *

Laura had expended a dozen or so cheese rounds by this time. The spent casein ammunition lay scattered on the table and floor in the vicinity of the television. The tube itself had grown blurry from her hits.

* * *

"Finally, Mr. President, the matter of atmospherics leads us once again to Vice President Bailey. His speech to the Petroleum Import Council last month basically set off the latest row in diplomacy. Questions continue to be raised by the press and members of both parties in congress about the Vice President's appropriate role in many of these areas given his family's deep ties to the oil industry and with some of the strident anti-Islamic voices of the religious right."

Kincaid watched nervously as the President paused, scowling. At this moment, control meant everything. Nothing would be gained by an argument.

The President shook his head only a bit. "You know, if this were baseball, I think this would be ball four and I'd take my base." He looked into the camera, almost pleading. "Where are the facts? Upon what do we base these concerns? I'm listening. I'm waiting. OK. Let's review what we've got. The truth is that Vice President Bailey is a wealthy man. For decades, his family has worked hard and invested wisely. In many ways, they were and are the quintessential American Dream personified, pulling themselves out of poverty and up through our unacknowledged class strata. But in our system, once you have achieved success, it seems you transition from example to target.

"Where are the facts? The Vice President long ago transferred management of his financial affairs to an approved blind trust. That trust is overseen at the federal level by agencies beholden to all three branches of government.

"As for his association with a wide range of religious groups; that is a normal part of our policy of outreach. Presumably, you're referring to Dr. Richards's Crusade for Moral Clarity. I don't mind saying that I have problems with some of his group's positions. I'm no theologian, but I sense that sometimes he thinks outside the Book. So it makes headlines if we have a dialog with them. But our meetings with the World Council of Churches or Catholic Youth the same month get buried on page one hundred and you can forget any air coverage at all. Is that fair?"

"With all due respect Mr. President, the World Council of Churches and Catholic Youth are considered safe and constructive by most people.

Associating with them is deemed normal and hardly newsworthy outside the circles of those most directly affected. Paul Richards has been described variously as a loaded gun and a ticking bomb. I'm no theologian either but I've never met any theologian who would endorse his or his group's stands."

"So what shall we do, Mr. Jacobs? Ignore him? Disregard his input? Shun his fourteen million followers?" The President spread his hands outward, inviting.

"A lot of us are skeptical of those claims, Mr. President. We hear fourteen million. But it's hard to swallow that one in twenty Americans belong to the Reverend Richard's movement. It simply flies in the face of our personal experiences."

"The facts again Mr. Jacobs. The facts." The President punched his finger on the arm of the chair for emphasis. "When my administration initiates a program whose purpose is unpopular with the Crusade for Moral Clarity, we can count on an outpouring of responses from them. While we may not read each note in depth, we do run our email through sophisticated programs to check for duplicate addresses, fake addresses, or other indicators of fraud. We get tens or hundreds of thousands of emails, tens of thousands of letters. When we began our push for the Gender Rights Protection Bill, we received over five million communications."

"All negative, I'm sure."

"Huh. You have no idea."

"I'm sorry Mr. President, but this is exactly my point. The public is of rights concerned when a small — though we might argue that — group holds such sway at the very center of power in this country, especially with a group whose very name is offensive to many millions of people around the world."

The President looked tired for the first time in the interview. "Mr. Jacobs, I do not necessarily disagree with much that you are saying, but this is a democracy. The people decide the direction we will go, every four years in my case, every two or six for some of our representatives. We listen to the concerns of the citizenry and we take those concerns into account, or we look for other employment. Frankly, I'd like to hear from some moral and ethical perspectives other than the Crusade from time to time, but it seems they rarely write. Why is that? Seriously. Why?"

"I don't have an answer for you, sir." Jacobs turned to the camera. "You, the people out there listening, have you let your thoughts be known? The decisions that shape our lives depend on the input our leaders and representatives receive. You are not powerless. Your input matters. Send an email to thePresident@theWhiteHouse.gov or send a postal letter to The President of the United States, 1600 Pennsylvania Avenue, Washington, DC. We'll put that information on our web site, BenJacobsShow.com."

* * *

Jack tilted his head back. "That was interesting. I wonder if Jacobs knew he was going to do that? It seemed pretty spontaneous. The President was actually falling behind. You could see the frustration, and he invoked the 'it's not my fault' defense, which is pathetically weak. It's almost like Jacobs's on his side."

Jennifer raised her head and turned to Jack. "Well, I hope he is."

"Hmmm. Point well taken."

* * *

Laura bounced in her chair. "Yeah, yeah, yeah. Right, Jacobs. Let's all write to our benevolent leaders and drown out the Nazis and send them packing. Why didn't we think of that? Gee. But you forgot to remind your viewers to enclose their ten thousand dollar campaign contributions so they'll actually read the letter." She ran low on cheese but threw another two cubes. "My aims pretty good this morning. Better than yours, Jacobs."

* * *

Jacobs turned back to the President. "Mr. President, building on your baseball analogy, I'd have to call your last answer a strike. Much has been made — by us, by the Congress, by advisors in your own party — of the Vice President's wealth or, more precisely, the handling and display of his wealth. You have defended the Vice President on his use of personal security, his use of family-owned planes. Your arguments have been persuasive, and your loyalty to the Vice President admirable. But Vice President Bailey continues to be a source of concern for the public."

The President folded his arms, preparing for another round on this old subject. His gaze fixed on Jacobs, and the camera caught a tick or two as his jaw clenched.

Jacobs continued. "Well, we've done our own investigation and have recently uncovered striking evidence that the Vice President's blind trusts may be peeking. The correlation between the stocks held by his trusts and the legislative programs he supports have been remarkable and, according to our analysis, no mere chance or coincidence. As you can imagine, this raises many disturbing questions. Again."

The President showed no surprise, only irritation. "What is it about this great country that we have come not just to distrust, but actually to despise wealth? Those who are diligent, who do their homework, who gather the information and resources, and who take the risks have earned their compensation. I don't normally argue with the umpire, but on this I have to take a stand. We have been over and over and over the matters of Vice President Bailey's wealth, and his connections, and his lifestyle. It's an almost tabloid obsession; perhaps because it is so very rare that a person with Jim Bailey's gifts would devote himself to the public good. I depend on his skills and his commitment to help keep this country on the path to greater prosperity. Perhaps a few, perhaps a lot of people find his style abrasive, aloof, whatever. Truth be told, Mr. Jacobs, the Vice President and I have had some pretty heated disagreements from time to time. But the Vice President's life has been under a microscope for at least twenty years, and no one has provided a shred of convincing evidence that he has behaved other than honorably and within the law. Shrewdly, to be sure, but honorably."

"Mr. President, your question has two parts. The first why have we the people come to — as you put it — despise wealth? All of us lived through the excesses of the first decade of this century and have seen up close the corrosive effect of greed in the service of the rich and powerful. There is little reserve of sympathy for the well off.

"The second question — if I may rephrase — is along the lines of 'why do you keep flogging a dead horse about the link between the Vice President's public service and his wealth?'"

The President grinned broadly. "Not my words, but I suppose that is the general drift."

"Well, sir, the study we have undertaken has looked at that connection in a fundamentally different way. As you have correctly pointed out before, if the policies that you endorse and execute are truly the best for the country, then any wise and competent investment organization will follow the lead of the administration as those organizations evaluate their investment."

The President nodded, appearing satisfied.

"But, as our investigations have revealed, the trusts that hold the Vice President's wealth made their investment decisions well before the policies were announced. Their ability to target specific industries, even down to specific companies and subcontractors, is remarkable, even uncanny. We studied forty major investment organizations and were struck by the ability of the Windham Trust — unique among them all — to anticipate the detailed direction our government would be taking. Can you explain why that would be, Mr. President?"

* * *

"Oh, dear! Not good." Jack scowled as he watched. "The President better have a strong answer for that. Whether or not Jacobs has something, an innuendo alone can be devastating in this climate. It'll play for weeks and drown out everything else around it. Jacobs is going to have to produce those studies, and both sides will pick them apart, but the administration hardly needs a distraction like this."

Jennifer, soft, warm, and comfortable, wriggled in his lap. "You just remember I always thought Bailey was a crook. If my lover will recall, I asked why I couldn't vote for Miller for President and that other guy for Vice President."

"Hmmm. Whether or not he's a crook, just looking like one can be enough. Let's see how Miller handles this. It's the first new thing that's come out of the show today."

* * *

Laura had called a cease-fire in the cheese siege. "Aha! The worms are coming out of the corpse! Doesn't matter that your snake has hurt so many people with policies of neglect. Never mind the denial of justice. Never mind that he builds a legal fortress around his rich buddies. Oh! He took some more money. Now we get worked up. You wait until this rotting mess gets opened up. Then you'll smell how really bad things are."

She popped a few more cubes into her mouth as she mumbled her attack. As her descriptions grew more graphic, she began to lose her appetite.

Laura waited for the camera to return to the President. "OK, Miller, Jacobs's gotcha. How're you going to escape this time?" When the President reappeared, he seemed calm, but displayed nothing resembling confidence. "Ooooh, he's really gotcha." She fired the final three rounds, one hitting the President in the teeth, two in the forehead. "Damn. I'm good."

* * *

The President began slowly, deliberately. "You have couched this conversation in academic clothes, but you are, in effect, making some very serious charges about ..."

Jacobs interrupted. "Mr. President, we in the press have danced around this for far too long. Our investigation has been thorough as no other has been. Let's not beat around the bush any more. We do believe and have overwhelming evidence to support our belief that the Vice President of the United States has used his office and his influence to add substantially to his fortune.

"Mr. President, I am providing you with an unabridged copy of our investigative report and we are making available highlights of our investigation on our web site at the close of this program. I look forward to a response." Jacobs reached to the table at his side and handed the President a tome the size of a large city phone book.

The President looked stern. "I see by the clock that we are nearly out of time. Very dramatic. Obviously springing charges like you have and presenting this ... monster ..." the President held up the red-covered report with both hands, hefting it and turning it for the camera "... in a way that is impossible to respond to creates an impression that you have found something. Well, Mr. Jacobs, that's not the way justice works; that's not the way our government works. I will take this report seriously, of course. It will be read line by line, I assure you. You've put your reputation and the reputation of your network on the line here. I have confidence in Vice

President Bailey and our team and look forward to presenting our reasoned and responsible reply." He placed the copy quietly down on his table so as not to further emphasize its size. The camera caught his jaw clenching.

Jacobs stared back at the President, then turned to face the camera. "We look forward to your response and will cover it completely. As the President has pointed out, our time together is drawing to a close. You have been watching the Ben Jacobs Hour with our most special guest, the President of the United States of America, Bill Miller. Please join us next week when our guest will be the Secretary of the Treasury, William Deatherage. And stay with us twenty-four-seven on our interactive website, BenJacobs.com. For all of us in the Washington studio, this is Ben Jacobs wishing you peace and prosperity until we meet again."

On screen the customary credits rolled, and the screen faded to black followed by commercials. The director called out the end of live coverage.

Kincaid left the shadows between the cameras and headed toward the fuming President.

He was addressing Jacobs with an unmistakably sharp edge. "That was a damned cheap trick, a stupid theatrical trick."

Jacobs made no reply.

"What the Hell did you want to accomplish? Have we withheld anything from you? Hasn't this been the most open administration in two decades?"

"No, sir. Respectfully. You are blinded by your loyalty to Vice President Bailey, sir. Maybe you and maybe David Kincaid are being straight with us, but Bailey is not. Read the report, Mr. President. Read the report. You don't need to point out that my reputation is on the line. I look back at the history of investigations that turned out to be graveyards of over-eager reporters. I have no intention of joining them. Read the report, sir. Read the report."

The President rose. "You don't ambush me like this." He turned to Kincaid. "Ambush." The President walked quickly from the studio without another word.

Though no one else had left the set, it remained very quiet in the wake of the President's anger. Several of the technicians began to prepare in silence for the next show.

Kincaid walked over to the table and retrieved the report the President had left behind.

Jacobs spoke. "It's true, David. And I think you know it or feel it. Please, I beg you, read the report. We had to do it this way to get his attention."

Kincaid raised his hand. "No, don't go there. We're both professionals." He did not show any anger, only fatigue. "The President is right. It was cheap theatrics. Whether there is anything in here or not, it was a stunt, and a disrespectful stunt. And don't get all pious on me. It won't work. Your timing was a business decision quite unrelated to the content of your investigation. It was distasteful, and you should be above that. With your talent, you don't need to play games. If this is quality work, it will stand the test of time, and your position will be secure. If it's trash, no amount of surprise will save it." He paused, carefully crafting his continuation. "I'm going to begin going over this report the moment I leave the building. My staff and people at Justice will be going over it with a fine-toothed comb within twenty-four hours. If what you say is true, there will be consequences for the Vice President. If not, there will be consequences for you. Don't take this road, Ben. There are better ways."

Jacobs stood quietly as half the crew continued their work and the other half watched the two men. Jacobs seemed wanting to come up with a forceful response, but remained silent.

"You're too good for this, Ben." Kincaid put the report under his arm and walked slowly to the exit as the lights dimmed on the set.

* * *

Laura sat fuming as credits gave way to commercials. She took the remote and switched off the set. Only then did she saw the reflection of a man standing behind her. Frightened, she jerked around to face the intruder.

Her father leaned on the doorframe, grinning.

She scowled. "How long have you been there?"

He paused, enjoying the element of surprise. "Since the break before last."

"Very sneaky. Jacobs was talking about Windham Trust. I've seen envelopes from Windham Trust come here for you … are we in trouble?"

Jim Garrette relaxed his smile. He straightened up and walked over to the counter near the television, carefully avoiding stepping on cheese cubes. He took a plate and gathered some of the cubes from the countertop, putting a few in his mouth. "We're not in any trouble, and I doubt that anyone else is, either. Windham is one of the most selective investment houses in the country — maybe the world. They don't take customers off the street. You have to be invited to invest with them. Dr. Carlton recommended us. The minimum was half a million when we joined."

"We? I don't think *we* should be involved in anything that the pink monster recommends. We?" she demanded.

"You are the heir apparent, little girl. As I said, the minimum investment was half a million a decade ago. It's something like three-quarters of a million now. And there are plenty of restrictions on the time period that it has to be held. Plus, there's additional up front money. In return, we get one of the highest staff-to-customer ratios in the industry, and returns that are," he gestured toward the blank television screen, "as you see, the envy of the country."

"Jacobs talked about insider trading with the likes of Bailey."

"Noooooooo, my child. He insinuated it, hoping that people would jump to that conclusion, which apparently they have."

Laura bristled.

Her father continued. "Their investment officers travel in the most informed circles of society. They research their investments more exhaustively than just about anyone else. They don't leave holes open for doubt. Other firms have neither the resources nor the mandate to do that. That is why we get a return that's about four percent better than the other guys when you take out that which we pay ahead and that which Mr. Jacobs neglects to include."

Laura sat intransigent, arms crossed.

"Look," said Garrette, "let's put this in perspective. You told me yesterday that you got that pharmaceutical company up and running on the border."

"It's not up and running yet, but we've secured everything we need. That's not the …"

He raised a hand and continued, "And how on earth did Laura Garrette, a graduate student in Political Science from Georgetown, manage to leverage the millions of dollars and considerable human capital to do this?"

"I told you, I heard …" She stopped.

Garrette's smile turned cat-like. He had his daughter trapped. Didn't happen very often these days. "You listened to conversations at your parent's dinner parties and were able to connect the dots brilliantly, and you have the brains, the intuition, and the will to carry out an ambitious and worthy project. Congratulations. You've displayed all the kinds of skills that Windham uses so that we can keep the lights on and the refrigerator stocked."

Laura's eyes narrowed. She got up, fists clenched, and stalked out of the kitchen, growling.

Jim Garrette gathered a few more cheese cubes and took her vacated seat. He chuckled to himself. "My beautiful daughter, the graduate student, growled at her father." He smiled broadly and then popped the cheese into his mouth.

8 UNINTENDED CONSEQUENCES

Monday, March 3, 2014

David Kincaid was not looking forward to Monday morning.

Frank waited at the head of the parking space as Kincaid pulled into the garage. "My cousin Scott can get you a good deal on a house down in Raleigh," he smiled.

"That bad?" Kincaid appreciated the humor, but knew it was meant to brace him for the morning.

"Let's just say they'll want to keep the tours away from the Oval Office. The Vice President was doing his stiff-walk really fast and didn't look happy. I haven't seen anyone who's left the office smiling."

"Maybe I should go back to bed. What'd you say your cousin's name was?"

Frank chuckled. "Oh, don't let 'em grind you down, sir. You'll get through this. Just another bump in the road. A big one, I'll grant you, but still a bump."

Kincaid put the Jacobs report under his arm. The two walked from his car to the security check near the office. Kincaid had brought the staff donuts and offered one to Frank.

"No, thanks. Gotta watch those things." He patted his stomach. He was not noticeably overweight, but a little heavier than he wanted.

Kincaid nodded a greeting to each staff member as he passed through the hum of activity. He arrived at his outer office just as Tracey was finishing a phone call.

"Good morning, Mr. Kincaid." She stopped, wrinkled her brow in thought, and then crossed her arms. "No, that's a lie. Let me start over. It's good to see you, Mr. Kincaid. Unfortunately, the President and the Vice President would like to see you upstairs."

Kincaid closed his eyes. "Now?"

"Yes, sir."

"Lovely. OK, let Abigail know I'm on my way up. Please arrange to have several copies made of this, or, better yet, get hold of Ben Jacobs and see if you can get the complete file. I don't want to deforest the country printing it. Tell Peter to get a team together to take it apart. We've to get some kind of response out today."

"Is it true?"

"Hard to say what's true and what's not. That thing's over eight hundred pages. I was able to say awake through about two hundred and fifty. There's a lot I don't understand about their methodology, but it raises some disturbing scenarios. That's why we have to get on it right away." He turned back toward the door. "But now, I actually do think we've got trouble."

"Why is that, sir?" she inquired.

"Of all the questions you could have asked, you asked, 'Is it true?'"

Tracey shrugged. "I'll get this to Peter."

He left the donuts on the table in his outer office. On the way to the elevator, Kincaid tried to envision the different scenarios he would be facing in the Oval Office with both Miller and Bailey there. As he rode the elevator, he realized there were just too many possibilities and decided to clear his mind and relax. He approached the President's office security check. "Good morning, Corporal Tull."

Tull looked quietly over to Abigail Jackson, the President's secretary, then back to Kincaid, and shook his head before quietly resuming his check.

"Come on, someone has to have something encouraging this morning."

"Whole lot of shouting going on, sir."

"Hmmm. Can't imagine the Vice President was too pleased with the report from yesterday's show."

"I don't know about that, sir. I don't think that's what it's about. It's been more the preacher — Reverend Richards."

"Richards?"

"Yes, sir." Tull handed back the Chief of Staff's identification. "I'm finished. Good luck."

Kincaid walked slowly toward the door. He paused there to look back at Tull, who had returned to his papers, then to greet Abigail.

She offered her hand toward the door, apologetically. "Sorry."

Kincaid took a deep breath and strode into the Oval Office. The President was seated in his chair, arms crossed. The Vice President was standing off at a distance, arms also crossed. He turned to Kincaid as the Chief of Staff entered.

"What are we going to do about yesterday's disaster?" The Vice President was nearly shouting already.

"Are we talking about the report? I'm staffing it now."

The Vice President shook his head. "No, no, no, that will fall on its own. What are we going to do about our gaff insulting the Crusade?"

"What?" Kincaid asked in surprise.

"We essentially called them fanatics and crackpots," the Vice President shouted.

Kincaid recalled the references to the Crusade for Moral Clarity only vaguely. The other matters seemed to outweigh anything to do with Paul Richards.

"The switchboard has been jammed since about noon yesterday, and we're still getting e-mails at the rate of over a hundred thousand an hour — hopping mad."

"Just what was it we said?" Kincaid looked back and forth between the President and the Vice President.

The President spoke. "Apparently when I mentioned the Gender Rights Protection and asked for other views, The Crusade took it as an attack."

"Damned right," The Vice President joined in. "This is our most loyal base, and their convictions are strong. You dismissed them as if they were a cult. Of course they're up in arms."

Bailey was directing his irritation at Kincaid. The Chief of Staff was tempted to remind the Vice President that it was the President who had been interviewed, but knew that observation would not be well received. "OK, leaving aside whether they're a cult or not, what did the President say that was wrong? And what are we supposed to do about anything he said?"

"We issue a statement immediately to show our respect for their viewpoint and apologize for impugning their integrity."

"Impugning their integrity?"

"When you go on and on about checking their e-mail for possible fakes, that sends a pretty clear message that we think they're liars."

Kincaid grew aggravated. "Bullshit! We run everyone's e-mail through those programs."

"Well, they're not everyone, and this is the first they're hearing about it. The Crusade includes the moral pillars of this society. They deserve our respect."

"Fine. We'll issue a clarification. This is a distraction from the real issue that was raised yesterday — the report," Kincaid reminded.

"I'm dealing with that hatchet job. Jacobs didn't check his facts, and he's jumping to conclusions like a kangaroo. We'll have a rebuttal out by the afternoon."

"You have a copy of the report?" Kincaid asked.

"He put it on his damned website. We'll tear him a new asshole over this. He's dealing with fallout from the Crusade, too," Bailey sneered.

"The web stuff is just an excerpt. I'd like your people to sit down with the group we're putting together and have the full report in front of them.

We need a really airtight response on this to make it go away. Atmospherics aren't going to suffice," Kincaid cautioned.

"Atmospherics? I suggest you get your damned head out of the clouds, David. That report is nothing more than re-warmed allegations and innuendos, as you will soon see. Go ahead and check it out. But don't lose sight of the real bomb he planted, stirring up trouble with our religious constituency."

The President intervened. "OK, that's enough. Jim, Ben Jacobs has leveled extremely serious charges at you. I'm sure he's wrong, but this is going to take more than a rebuttal unless you've got one as thick and detailed as that damnable encyclopedia he tossed at me yesterday."

The Vice President stood stiffly. President Miller seldom interfered with his operations.

Miller continued, "I want the response to come from outside your office. David has the staff and the respect of the Press Corps. I'd like him to head the investigation ..."

"Investigation?" Vice President Bailey stared at the President.

"Unless you have a better word for it." The President turned to Kincaid. "Can you spare Peter for a bit? I know how clean and thorough his work is."

Kincaid's hands were folded in front of him, and he was relaxed. "He's already on it, Mr. President."

The President nodded. "Good." He turned to the Vice President. "I expect absolute — cheerful — cooperation between your people and the Chief of Staff — my Chief of Staff. Look, Jim, I'm not out to hang you. God knows I've stood beside you all these years. This matter has to be put to rest right now. We've got too much we want to do to let this distraction fester."

The Vice President stared sullenly at the President. The room was strangely silent. Finally, Bailey walked over to Kincaid and stood far closer than necessary. Eyeing the Chief of Staff, he spoke to the President. "Yes, sir, I think that would be a very good idea. There's probably nothing that David Kincaid would rather do than find some dirt on me. And when his witch-hunt turns up nothing — and nothing it will — then you can rest comfortably knowing your faith in me was warranted. Then we will deal with Jacobs and his people."

The President had been watching Kincaid for his reactions, but returned swiftly to the Vice President. "We will not be 'dealing' with anyone! As distasteful as that interview was, the story will rise or fall on its merits. Show that you've been defamed, that Jacobs was an arrogant ass; show that the press has gone hysterical. Whatever. But for God's sake, don't throw fuel on the fire."

The Vice President displayed no emotion.

"Was there anything unclear about what I just said?" Miller asked.

"No, Mr. President."

"OK. Fine. Now, what do you have on your schedule today and tomorrow?"

Bailey looked at his watch. "I'm running down to the wire on a meeting with the Foreign Relations Council now, and I'm basically booked back to back for the next week."

The President sighed. "We need to discuss what we're going to do for Bob Barnes."

The Vice President's scowl returned. "You said yesterday that we'd stand by him. Frankly, we've coddled those bastards long enough. The longer we keep propping them up, the longer it'll be before they get their houses in order. California still has a lot of fat to trim."

Kincaid was through holding his fire. "That's bullshit and you know it! California is one of the best-run states. Barnes got the 'Clean and Lean' award from that watchdog group just last month. Look, your own report said he was getting more service per dollar than any industry. Besides, California doesn't have anything to cut without damaging infrastructure. The bulk of what I see is that any cut is going to wind up costing a lot more than it saves."

Bailey ignored Kincaid and addressed the President. "If you're handing out financial gifts, where do you propose finding the money?"

The President's elbow rested on his desk, and he put his chin in his hand. "Wasn't this precisely why we developed the States Assistance Fund? With revenues from the past year, we should be flush with reserves in that account."

The Vice President shook his head. "You're putting yourself on a slippery slope, sir. That fund was meant for catastrophes on the scale of Katrina or Donald. If you set a precedent with California, the other forty-nine governors will whine their way through that fund in no time."

"But the other states aren't having problems like California, Jim. DOD closed two huge plants there. That alone added a point to their unemployment."

Kincaid, who had fallen into deep reflection, spoke now. "Sir, unaccustomed as I am to agreeing with Vice President Bailey, he has a point. What Ben Jacobs said yesterday was correct. We're picking up a lot of indirect signs of softness across the country. We've got to do something for Bob — we owe him that and more — and then we need to find out what's going on at the base of this. We're missing something in our analysis."

The three men stood at the vertices of their triangle of frustration for several seconds.

The President brought the stalemate to a close. "All right, we've got work to do. Mr. Vice President, on your way out, please tell your staff to give David's people everything they need without a fuss."

"Yes, sir," Bailey replied.

"David, help me get something together to satisfy Governor Barnes."

"Yes, sir," Kincaid replied.

The Vice President eyed the Chief of Staff. Then he turned and left the office.

Once the quick footsteps that characterized the Vice President's agitated moods faded, Kincaid turned to face the President. The President stared back with his best poker face.

"OK, David, what are you thinking?"

"It was a big report."

"I know. I had to lift it on television. That was embarrassing."

"Actually, you handled it quite well, sir. I watched the replay several times. You were cool, factual, with just a hint of controlled outrage. I haven't been to the office to see the snap polls but I think you may have actually won that round."

"Doesn't matter, though, if the Vice President's done something."

"Actually, sir, it does matter. Again, I watched the replay. You made your sincerity very clear. You said you'd take it seriously, and that's precisely what you're doing. No, I think you handled it fine. And if Jacobs is wrong, you're really going to come out well."

The President got up from his chair and paced a bit. Finally, he went to a window overlooking the South Lawn. "'...if Jacobs is wrong...' Do you think Jacobs is wrong?"

Kincaid wished that he had not phrased his reply that way. "Sorry. That's not what I meant."

"Oh, yes, it is. It is, and that's why I'm talking to you right now. Hey, it's just you, me, and..." — he gestured to one of the priceless antiques — "...the Remington statue. We got rid of the recorders decades ago. You're my Chief of Staff and my closest confidant. And even though you don't like Vice President Bailey, you are, nonetheless, unbelievably fair-minded and surprisingly objective. Do you think — *think* — that Jacobs has something on the Vice President? I need to know your gut feelings."

The President was nearly pleading.

Kincaid thought hard. The President seemed to appreciate the Chief of Staff's discomfort. Kincaid began slowly. "Like I said, it is a big report. It's also dense. Lots of really obscure — at least to me — economic terms. I'm not stupid, but I can't say that I followed much of it. Every conclusion was couched in terms of probabilities and improbabilities. The report's over eight hundred pages. I read maybe two hundred fifty pages, and I didn't find anything in those pages that anyone I know would call a smoking gun. It's ambiguous to me. Don't worry, though; when whoever Peter gets together finishes it, I should be able to give you a yes or no."

The President stood gazing quietly out the window.

"It's a bump in the road, Mr. President. You're doing fine. In regard to this, you're handling the situation by the book. It's going to be OK."

Still staring, the President mused. "Ever have a feeling that something bad is about to happen? Like those animals that sense earthquakes and storms?"

Kincaid smiled. "If it's any comfort, sir, those legends have been mostly debunked."

"Yeah? I didn't know that. That's good, I guess. I wish my own history of hunches wasn't so good."

A knock on the door interrupted their ponderings. The door opened, and Tiffany Miller peeked in. "Am I disturbing anything?"

At the sight of the First Daughter, both men lit up with broad smiles. Tiffany had entered the White House a shy fourteen-year-old and had blossomed into a beautiful, self-confident young woman. Having honed her skills in public speaking and public relations, she was widely admired and respected for lending her support to several causes, including the battles against AIDS and land mines. She occasionally found herself at odds with her father's administration, and the disagreements boosted her credibility with the public.

"Come in, come in! Please!" the President said.

She entered the room. She gave a hug to Kincaid, who was closer to the door. "Were you guys beating up Mr. Bailey?"

Kincaid looked at the President with a grin. "No, I don't think so. Why?"

She smiled. "I passed him in the hall downstairs. He definitely did not look happy, and he was doing that walk of his." She did a credible imitation of the Vice President's angry stride as she went over to her father. Both men were laughing hard as she embraced him.

"So," he said, "how was the dance? I didn't get a chance to ask you yesterday."

"Oh, great, just great. Nothing more romantic than a date with a frightened fella and three Secret Service agents."

"Sorry," the President demurred.

"Yeah, well, at least it was fun, unlike your Sunday. That was ugly."

"Was I that bad?"

"Not you. Jacobs. He was being a jerk. Like you said, he just threw it at you and said 'bye.' That's not fair. We were watching the show at the dorm. Even Shannon said it was a cheap trick."

The President turned to Kincaid, who gave a quick thumbs-up. The President explained, "Shannon is my chief critic at Georgetown. She had a lot of 'improvements' to suggest when Tiffany had her here for dinner."

Tiffany grinned and shrugged.

Kincaid could see the President's spirits lifting as he turned back to his daughter. "Were we too rough on the religious folks?"

"Huh?"

"We've been bombarded with angry calls and e-mails about slighting the Crusade."

"That's weird. I don't even recall much about that. Shannon certainly would have picked up on it. I mean, you mentioned Richards, but he's a nut case. Anybody with sense knows that."

Kincaid chucked. "Your daughter is wise beyond her years. Listen, you guys, I have a report to take apart along with everything else I had planned for today." He bowed to the young woman. "Tiffany, it is always a joy to see you. Thank you for cheering up your dad. Mr. President, I'll send up good news as I get it."

Tiffany gave a small wave. "Goodbye, Mr. Kincaid."

He walked out of the room smiling.

Abigail looked up. "Well, good to see almost everyone's in a better mood."

Kincaid nodded. "It helps when you send in an angel." As he left, he glanced over to Corporal Tull. The young Marine was nodding in agreement.

* * *

"Pretty long face, even for a Monday morning." Jennifer watched Jack as he got ready to leave for work.

"Evaluations. I hate evaluations."

"That's because you want to be nice, and evaluations aren't always nice."

"Yeah."

"And?" she persisted.

"And I'm tired of those three always grouching about money. They're paid more than any other techs in the department. I've got a limited pool of money to draw on for raises. I've given up a big chunk of my own share three years running. But it's never enough. And I don't get any appreciation for it."

"Then why do you keep it up?"

Jack sighed and sat down in the chair by the door. "It's probably like you said: I want to be nice."

"Have they earned the raises?"

"Maybe. But no more than me. Leslie got her master's, but we've already incremented for that. I get so tired of Elsa and Patricia going on and on about hair and dresses and such. Then they wonder why women don't get promotions."

"It's worth wondering about," she said.

"Yes, you're right. But in your case, you focus on the tasks at hand and the advancement path. That's why you move up. If you focused on hair and dresses, you'd still be in an entry-level job."

"I am concerned about my looks."

"Yes, but you don't dwell on it." Jack looked at Jennifer. He did not have the time or desire for an argument. "You make a decision, you act on it, you get dressed, and you are fabulously beautiful without diverting your brain into the wilderness."

"Cop out," she retorted.

"You're fabulous." Jack wrapped his arms around her, smothering her with kisses.

She giggled. "Remember, I've got women's group tonight. You're on your own for dinner."

"I'm meeting Ed." Jack tried to get to the door before it was too late.

"Are you going to that stupid shooting gallery again?" Jennifer scowled.

Jack paused. "Firing range. It's relaxing. It costs almost nothing."

"I still don't like it. I don't like the guns, and I don't care much for Ed, either."

"I've known Ed for fifteen years. He's not such a bad guy," Jack replied.

"I've seen enough. I don't care for his guns, he drinks too much, and his attitude toward women is disgusting." Jennifer crossed her arms.

"I'm working on that."

"Well, you'd better. I want you to change him, not the other way around. He's a bad influence; or, at least, he's not a good influence."

"I'll work on him." He kissed Jennifer again. "I promise."

Jack went out the door for the twenty-minute drive to work. He focused on the unpleasant task ahead. His patience had grown thin with the passing years. If his exposure had only been to Leslie, Elsa, and Patricia, he would probably have had the same feeling toward women as Ed did. Fortunately, Jennifer had found him; that had made all the difference in the world. "Jenn's probably right."

Jack tried to break off his thoughts of Jennifer as he felt again a rising panic and unease. He arrived at work at eight thirty-seven, about half an hour before his technicians. By the time he had finished discussing individually their evaluations, it was eleven-thirty.

At one-thirty, the Institute's secretary asked Jack to come to the office.

"Jack, I just got this back from insurance. Your claim's been denied."

He stared at her. "What? Why?"

"Says here 'Code 508: Pre-existing condition.'"

"How can that be? We didn't find out about her cancer until last month. She went on my policy in January."

"I don't know, Jack. Look, I've got a call in to the benefits manager. I hope it's just a clerical error and we can get it straightened out today. Otherwise, I'll definitely file the appeal. You've been with the Institute for fifteen years. I'm sure they'll stand up for you."

"Thanks, Doris. In the meantime, what do I do about the bills?"

Doris grimaced. "Yeah, billing. Did she have all her medical work done here?"

"Yeah. Other than the office visits. But Neilson's affiliated with the hospital."

"That helps. Let me talk to Alicia over in billing. I'm sure they'll want you to pay at least a little earnest money, but let me check. OK?"

"Thanks again. This really hasn't been a very good month for us and today everything seems to be going down the tubes."

"Oh, yes, evaluations." She suddenly brightened. "Ah, I do have at least one positive note." She reached into a pile of papers to her right, thumbed down about half an inch, and retrieved a signed slip. "Your leave was approved for April." She handed him the slip.

He smiled. "Good. I think I told you we're going to San Diego."

"Yeah, the big debates. Should be a good time."

"Uh huh. I wasn't going at first because of Jenn, but she insisted. Really wants to go." He grinned.

"Well, have a good time. I'm glad they approved it."

Jack looked surprised. "Was there any question? I've got the hours. That should've been routine."

"Should've been. But headquarters has been going over every application with a magnifying glass lately. Like they're trying to squeeze out every dime. Last I heard, they're rolling in dough, but squeezing every nickel and dime out of you guys. Pisses me off."

Jack shook his head. "Doesn't make sense. Not like it was fifteen years ago."

"No, it's not. Have we really been doing this for fifteen years?"

"Yep," he said.

"Amazing."

"You're my hero again, Doris. Don't let 'em grind you down either. Please let me know if you need anything from me on the billing. I keep pretty good records, you know."

Doris nodded. Jack left the office heading back to the laboratory without a trace of a smile.

By six in the evening, he would be quite ready for the firing range.

* * *

Jack squeezed off a final round and examined his target. He shook his head, took the paper and left the room to join Ed at their usual table. Jack removed his ear protection and sat down. A drink was waiting. Appeared to be a cola.

Ed was drinking a beer. "You don't have the look of a champion there, Jack, old boy."

Jack laid his target on the table for Ed to see.

"Ouch. You're gettin' worse. Not supposed to work that way."

"Tell me about it, Ed. One-fifty. I did one-seventy-five last week."

"Aaah, you've got a lot on your mind. Sick woman, asshole bitches workin' for you, and a rich master who doesn't give a shit whether we live or die." Ed picked up Jack's pistol and examined it. "Plus this cheap-ass popgun of yours. It's an embarrassment."

"Thanks, Ed. You really know how to cheer a guy up."

Ed chuckled. He finished inspecting the pistol, instinctively checking that the chamber and magazine were empty.

"And you've got to stop calling them bitches," Jack said. "It's a reflex for you, and it's going to get you in trouble. The Institute's cracking down. It may seem harmless here — a point I'm not conceding — but it'll get you fired downtown."

"Yeah, yeah, I know. Hard to change how you feel, though. And those… what would you call them?"

"Employees?" Jack offered.

Ed frowned. "… yeah, those tight-assed employees are driving you nuts as fast as all the other shit you're takin'."

Jack laughed as he shook his head. "You're hopeless."

Ed leaned back, his large frame filling the chair and then some. He gazed at the ceiling. "Yeah, that's what they tell me, that's what they tell me."

Jack returned home about an hour before Jennifer. By the time she was due to arrive, he had tea ready and a video cued in the player in case she was in the mood. He had the bed ready with fluffed pillow and extra comforter in case she was tired.

They fell asleep watching a romantic comedy.

9 COMPETENCE

Wednesday, March 5, 2014

Kincaid arrived in the conference room to find Kathy sitting in her usual spot two seats to the right of the head chair. She raced through a stack of papers, placing into one stack those that seemed of no interest. Other papers she marked with a check or circle and placed in a second, closer pile.

"How goes the war, Ms. Kathy?"

She looked up a moment, flicked a smile, and returned to her sorting as she talked. "Good morning, sir. It's going well enough. Jacobs's story dumped another ton and a half of paperwork on us."

"That much?"

"Maybe an exaggeration. Just a ton."

Kincaid poured a cup of coffee. It smelled good — a hint of hazelnut. "Have you had time to look at any of the report?"

"A little. Peter said you've started the first two hundred or so pages. He's divided the rest up into sections. Each of us has a block. I'm six hundred to eight hundred."

"Have you found anything interesting?"

She waggled her hand. "Hard to say. Some pretty obscure analysis and awfully cautious conclusions."

"That's my impression, too," Kincaid concurred. "The stuff's been up on Jacobs's website for over a day now. Any feedback from our adoring public?"

"Not a peep. Odd, if there was any substance, don't you think?"

Kincaid nodded. "So, who've we got coming and where are they?"

She looked up. "Meeting was pushed back half an hour. Peter sent out the notice."

"Wow, I'm actually early then. Mark your calendar."

She smiled. "Anyway, Peter has a rep from Treasury and one from

Justice. And he's asked Sarah to sit in."

"Sarah Tyler?"

"I still can't get over your memory for names. Yes, Sarah Tyler. A lot of the analysis utilizes pipeline theory. Neither Peter nor I are up on that. Apparently that's one of Sarah's favorite areas of study."

"Pipeline. I should remember pipeline theory. My old roommate in college was into that. Can't say I recollect it though. That was a while ago."

"It's the study of how to detect and measure the effect of special, sometimes secret, information flow in a network. It's mostly used in economics, but it's now being applied more broadly — biology, military, politics."

"Ugh. I don't get into politics," he shuddered.

Kathy laughed.

"Oh, did Sarah say anything to you about the California plant closings?"

Now Kathy grinned.

"What?"

"That girl is a stitch. Yeah, she talked about the plant closings and maybe twenty other things."

Kincaid frowned. "Hmmm. Our conversation on Saturday was pretty fragmented. Does she have a problem with focus? Is she taking the fellowship seriously?"

"Oh, don't get me wrong, sir," Kathy protested. "She's spot-on in her analysis and as quick a study as I've ever met. It's just that her brain gets way out ahead of her mouth and she winds up with some hilarious phrasing. No, she's really fine and she'll be a big asset to us in this mess. She's got the energy we've been short on."

"Good. We had a full plate before *Encyclopedia Jacobsii.* Speaking of which, how's the conference coming?"

Kathy groaned. "I hate planning those things. I know it's important, but I just don't have an aptitude for banquets and all."

Sarah appeared in the doorway. She balanced two large books and a stack of file folders under one arm, a paper plate with bagel sandwich in her hand, and a large Styrofoam cup in her mouth.

"Do you need some help?" Kincaid started to move in her direction.

"Dwo fank vue." She looked around the table. Kathy patted the seat to her right to suggest a landing place. Sarah glided over to the spot and slid the papers onto the desk, set the plate down, and then removed the cup from her mouth. "But I appreciate the offer."

Kincaid looked at Kathy, and they both shook their heads. He turned to Sarah. "We have coffee here in the room. Quite good, actually."

"Excellent. I'll remember that."

Kincaid resumed his conversation with Kathy. "The dinner?"

"Like I said, I'm not good at party planning. I'll get with the dining room staff this afternoon."

Sarah perked up. "Party?"

Kincaid explained, "Kathy's in charge of the dinner honoring the AIDS fighters May twelfth after the main conference. Big to-do. Tiffany Miller will be the unofficial host. Several celebrities. But Kathy's not having fun planning the party."

"You're kidding. I love parties. I was on our prom committee in high school. I was just in charge of decorating the gym until Joyce Johnson came down with mono. By the time I was finished, we had the prom at the Hilton." She placed a victorious finger in the air. "And we got it sponsored by the Passaic Mall, so it cost only half what they'd spent the year before. Very cool. At Rutgers I put together the economists' summit in 2013. Amazing what banks will give you in return for getting their names on the napkins. I even got Greenspan to give the banquet speech. What's not to love about that?"

Kathy stared at Sarah for a moment, and then turned to Kincaid. "She followed me home. Can I keep her?"

He chuckled. "Maybe. We'll see. Only on a not-to-interfere basis."

Peter entered the room with two others in tow.

Kincaid recognized Bob Matthews from Treasury. "'Morning, Bob. Thanks for joining us."

Peter introduced Michael Bershak from the Department of Justice.

Another three staffers joined the meeting. Once pleasantries had been exchanged, Kincaid motioned for everyone to be seated. "Again, thanks for coming. Is there anyone who did not see yesterday's interview between the President and Ben Jacobs?"

Two of the newcomers raised their hands.

"Peter, can we get them a video of the program?"

Peter nodded.

"As you know, mixed in with the usual chit-chat of the interview, Mr. Jacobs made a charge that the Vice President has been benefiting from his position in government, specifically insider trading through Windham Trust. By way of evidence, Mr. Jacobs presented us with a study he ..." Kincaid turned to Peter. "Did his team do the study or someone else?"

"The study was produced under contract by Frankel and Associates of Bristol, Connecticut. They're a widely respected economics consultant firm."

Kincaid saw Sarah nodding in agreement. "He presented us with this study he had commissioned. On air he made it sound like an indictment of the Vice President. I've read part of it, and Kathy's read part of it, and Peter has divvied up the rest." He offered his hand in Sarah's direction. "Our newest White House Fellow, Dr. Sarah Tyler, has a portion." He looked at Matthews and Bershak. "And we will be providing you gentleman with the full set of data. The President has given us the task of investigating the report and preparing a public response — the sooner the better. We are to work independently of the Vice President's office, but the President has ordered the Vice President's staff's full cooperation."

Bob Matthews tilted his head. "Ordered?"

Kincaid rubbed the back of his neck. "Maybe not the best choice of words, but I think it's common knowledge around here that the Vice President and I are not on good terms. This episode has the potential for a lot of friction. I'd like us to do our best to be professional in our thoroughness and our respect for his office."

Matthews seemed satisfied.

"Neither Kathy nor I have picked up on anything obviously bad in the report. Peter? Sarah?"

Peter shook his head.

Sarah took her copy and leafed through it. Kincaid could see numerous red markings on the pages already. "The people from Frankel are using pipeline analysis to try to pinpoint an unusual appearance of capital." She looked up at the blank expressions around the room. "OK, you're out in the desert and come across a big patch of greenery, an oasis. All around there's bits and pieces of vegetation so you know that generally some water is available. But in the oasis there's lots of water. No obvious stream, but there it is. Usually the water has traveled through some hidden aquifer — a natural pipeline — and bubbled up in this one spot. The plants aren't any better adapted than the surrounding vegetation; they just have special access to the water. In this case Windham Trust is the oasis. Frankel says Windham's people are good, but aren't that much better than the other firms, yet they're way more successful, so there must be a pipeline of economic news feeding them. Windham's investor list is very closely held, but at least a few are known. The only investors of the known list with access to information consistent with Windham's investment decisions are the Vice President's family and, specifically, Vice President Bailey."

Bershak responded, "Did Jacobs get the rest of the list?"

"I don't think so. That's a huge hole in the report."

"Couldn't Windham just be very good observers of the flow of capital from Washington?"

"Yes, absolutely. But the Frankel position is that many firms — they list about thirteen — invest very heavily in federal fund research, yet none of them comes even close to the success rate that Windham has achieved. You'd think such success would draw a lot of attention, but Windham is super secretive."

Matthews looked uncomfortable. "This all sounds plausible, but pretty mushy at its core."

"Yep." Sarah was unfazed. "Pipeline analysis usually starts out that way.

Most of the smaller cases I studied didn't turn up anything. The theory relies on the difference — the oasis — really being substantially different from background. When you see that many trees, you know without a doubt that something is going on, but it takes geologists with lots of soundings to actually trace the aquifer back to its source."

Peter put his hands over his face in mock exasperation. "So, Sarah, what is our geological equivalent?"

"You're not going to like it. You'd have to get Windham's and the Vice President's records. You'd have to see the actual facts that they used in their investment decisions. The analysis in my section of the report demonstrates pretty convincingly that there is a pipeline of some sort, but only suggests that Vice President Bailey is the most likely source from the known list."

Bershak's face clouded. "You're right; I can't say that I like it. It basically calls for a fishing expedition based on the Trust doing unusually well."

"Funny you mention fish. One of the ways that some oasis sources have been traced is by the fish in the water of the oasis. If you find a certain species in the water and there are, say, five possible sources of the water and only one of them has that species of fish, then you've pretty well traced the source without a lot of explosives."

Bershak smiled. "Do we have any fish in the report?"

"No, sorry."

"Well, that helps me, at least, to know where we stand." Kincaid refocused the group. "So what we need today is a schedule for gathering enough facts to lay this to rest or ask for more horsepower in the investigation. The President has given us a mandate to use anything legal. Bob and Michael, if you would please help my people get together a basic and sufficient probe, we'll execute the plan and meet again to determine what to do. In the meantime, if you could come up with a safe and secure statement for the weekly press briefing tomorrow morning, that would be greatly appreciated. Peter — tasteful but serious."

Peter smiled. "Yes, sir."

"If no one needs anything from me, I have several overlapping previous engagements. If you guys are still here around noon, please join the President for lunch. I think we're having either Australia or National Forestry for lunch."

"Austria, sir." Peter smiled.

Everyone laughed, including Kincaid.

* * *

In the late afternoon Sarah continued her work on the Vice President's report. She shared a small cubicle with Anna, currently at the State Department until Friday. Sarah had taken advantage of Anna's absence, and both desks were covered with sections of the report and stacks of supporting documents.

"Looks like you're well on your way to making our one-ton quota." Kathy had quietly appeared at the entrance to the cubicle.

Sarah giggled. "Yeah, it's like our research papers, only a lot more immediate."

"Find anything useful?"

"Bits and pieces. The folks at Frankel did a great job. Didn't miss much, as best as I can tell," Sarah mused.

Kathy looked at a sampling of documents beside the report itself. "Where did you get these?"

"Several online databases. Mostly for academic studies, but it's amazing what you can piece together from stray tidbits."

"Can we talk about the banquet? I can come back later if you're hot on the trail."

"Ooh, no, I can use a break." She looked at two folders in Kathy's hands.

"These are the overviews for the two dinners I'm supposed to be in charge of, but Mr. Kincaid said to make sure we keep our focus on the investigation and the tobacco project."

"And the unemployment mystery…" Sarah added.

"And the unemployment mystery. Right. Doesn't sound very focused does it?"

Sarah shook her head. "But I like it that way. If I don't have chaos, I make it," she grinned.

"Speaking of unemployment mystery, I got some of the states' figures in today. You're right; those jobs aren't being picked up anywhere else so far. Maryland turned in a respectable employment number, but it was just even. No big gains other than an expansion of the solar plant in Frederick that compensated for the port closure."

Sarah frowned. "Very strange. We've got to find where those jobs are popping up, otherwise you can't account for the national employment numbers. They have to add up in the end, or there has to be a much, much bigger underground economy blooming in about the last three years."

"I'll have New York, Tennessee, and Florida this week. Now, about the banquets…"

"Yeah, you said something about the AIDS conference this morning. What's the second one?"

"Presidential Medal of Freedom two weeks later. More glitter. Lots of press. I have no ideas."

Sarah picked up the first folder and began to browse. "OK, AIDS first, right?"

Kathy nodded.

"When?"

"April 25."

Sarah looked up quickly. "Oh dear. That's much time."

"Well, it's mostly staffed. This place is non-stop dinners."

Sarah returned to browsing. "What's the menu?"

"I'm not sure. Why?" Kathy asked.

"I know several of these people keep kosher. Also, do they all have parking instructions?"

"Parking?"

"That was a big problem when I did the economics summit. We don't want to invite these kinds of people and expect them to find parking and just walk up to the door," Sarah murmured.

"You don't mess around, do you? I think someone on the Marine Corps staff is responsible for that — security and all."

"Right." Sarah looked skeptical. "Press?"

"Ron handles that."

"Does he have all the bios?" She shuffled through the folder. "Where are the bios, anyway?"

"Actually they've decided to keep it kinda low key," Kathy replied.

"What? You've got some of the biggest star power in the world doing generous, heroic stuff, and you want to keep it quiet?"

"We're getting a lot of flack from the religious folk." Kathy frowned and then rubbed her face.

Sarah sat back in her chair crossing her arms, her black sweater and long black hair contrasted with the rising red in her cheeks. "Religious folk? You've got to be kidding. This work is a mitzvah if ever there was a mitzvah." She picked up the seating chart. "And who are these people I see? Methodist, Catholic, Presbyterian, Jewish, …"

"OK, sure, the mainline groups are on board. It's organizations like the Crusade we're trying to avoid. They've opposed nearly every successful program. Seems anything that works involves some moral compromise or some group they target."

"So what? They're miniscule. What's this big obsession with the Crusade anyway? Why are we even paying attention to them?" Sarah tapped her pen rapidly on the table.

"Votes. They're a very tightly disciplined voting block. Have you been to their web site?" Kathy raised her eyebrows and pulled at her sweater. "They have a section called 'The Devil's Gallery.' It's pages of programs they oppose and pictures of legislators from national all the way down to the county level who they think are opposing God. Every time a program is defeated, they draw a line through it. Every time one of those candidates loses, they put an 'X' through the picture. Take a look. It's scary."

Sarah shook her head. "OK if I talk to Ron?"

"Sure, but you're not going to get very far. Bailey keeps him on a pretty short leash."

"Huh? The Vice President has his own press spokesman. I thought Ron worked for the President."

"If only it were that simple," Kathy sighed, apparently resigned to the situation.

"Never mind. I get the picture. Tell me how I can help with this. For all the hassle, it could be fun. Other than the AIDS part, of course. I've wanted to meet some of these people for a long time, especially Dolores."

"Uh, she's the 'hooker' Dolores."

"I know. I did a short study on her group a couple of years ago. Wound up with a lot more questions than answers, in part because I could never actually get through to her." Sarah leaned into her hand, brows knit in concentration, eyelids narrowed.

Kathy reassembled the AIDS folder, removing six sheets into a separate pile. Kathy's manners were all business. "Well, my young apprentice, here is how you can help." She handed Sarah the six sheets. "Dietary needs, parking, and background checks for our biographies. You seem to really know how to dig, and we don't want anyone listed with the wrong spouse or occupation."

Sarah reached for her coffee and raised it to her lips as she scanned the seating chart again.

Kathy continued, "Guests have to be outta here by eleven. They tend to want to linger and soak up the ambience."

"Duh."

Kathy smiled and pulled out the second folder. She carried herself elegantly, in modest attire.

Sarah watched her closely. "Are you going to be there?"

"Where?" Kathy looked up from her folder.

"The AIDS dinner."

"I don't know. Hadn't thought much about it. Crowds aren't my thing. I wind up at a few of them for want of anything else to do."

"What about your boyfriend? Girlfriend? Significant other?"

Kathy put her chin in her hand as she leaned on the table.

Sarah put a finger to her chin. "Sorry. That was rude and presumptuous of me. Not my business."

"Don't worry. My life's pretty much an open book. Not a lot to tell, actually. Don't have a boyfriend. Haven't for a while. The adventure here keeps me pretty tied up."

Sarah pouted. "Too bad."

Kathy flashed a trace of a smile. "Now, part two."

Sarah scooted her chair closer to the second folder.

"Presidential Medal of Freedom. May ninth. Much higher profile than the other. Lots of press. Chauffeured limos, personal escorts, the works."

"Uh huh, I see."

Kathy picked up a two-page list. "Here's the roster. Usually the honorees have at least one guest. These are the names with their guides. Can I get you to do diet and bios on them, too? Any errors, get them to Ron ASAP and see to it that his people have them fixed. Don't rely on their word for it. Check."

"Right."

"Thanks, Sarah. This helps me a lot. As I said, I don't enjoy dinner planning in general. This is the first time I've felt comfortable about it."

"Hey, we'll have fun. Just think like you were being invited to the dinner itself. What would you like to see? Visualize. This gives me a chance to see the kitchen too. Whom do I see in catering?"

"That would be Mrs. Gillenwater. She's great if she's on your side. Just don't get on her wrong side," Kathy warned.

* * *

Tuesday, March 25, 2014

About as far away from an AIDS benefit as could be found, the annual gathering of the Windham Trust was convened in darkness at the secluded Pembroke Estate in Herndon, Virginia. Heavily armed uniformed security verified the identity of the invited guests as they arrived, escorted them to a peripheral parking zone, and then assisted them into waiting limousines for the two hundred yard excursion to the conference center. Uninvited guests would be grounds for expulsion from the Trust. Chauffeurs were escorted separately to an outbuilding where they could enjoy a supervised rest while their employers attended to business.

All around the room — white faces. Suits worth more than an average monthly salary. Watches on old arms. Watches costing more than the suits. Plates of perfectly prepared food. Bland, but perfectly prepared. The plate or, more properly, the privilege to consume the perfectly prepared food on the plate, cost more than the watches.

Given the "contribution" he was asked for, Jim Garrette calculated each bite cost a bit over five hundred dollars. He looked around the room at all the white faces. If history was predictive, then each bite would return three thousand dollars. The hands beyond the watches on the old arms in those suits controlled three quarters of the largest economy on the planet. All those white faces. Except for the servers and, of course, him.

The faces on those suits were waiting to hear from Max Carlton.

And yet …

And yet Jim Garrette could not stop thinking of his daughter, of her disdain for these people and this atmosphere. In particular he could not remove her words "pink monster" from his mind. He watched Carlton at the head table conversing with his hosts. Pink. Too much time indoors. Too little air and too little sunshine. Why did she have to be so right so often?

By the looks of the dishes being removed and coffee being served, the time was at hand for Max Carlton's keynote address. He was not going to "predict" the future. Predict means to speak of events beforehand — pre-dict. Carlton was going to dictate the future. Speak the words, and they would be fulfilled.

As the tables were gradually cleared of plates, the brown faces, the black faces, and the plain working faces vanished. Only the faces of black-shirted security, with expressions from harsh to mean, remained aside from the faces atop the suits. Somewhere someone who could be trusted would be turning on a broadband transmitter to jam any signals being sent out. When one pays the poverty line for a plate of bland food, one does not get frisked. But neither does one get trusted.

Carlton approached the podium. The assembled worshippers maintained their silence as he took a small, folded set of sheets from his breast pocket. The incandescent lamp on the podium was early twentieth century. The paneling behind the speaker was a rich, dark mahogany. The drapes were dark red velvet with golden cords. The congregants continued to sip quietly of fine brandies or wines that had been until this evening cataloged and tracked like museum pieces.

Carlton straightened the papers and adjusted his glasses a little lower on the bridge of his pink nose. "For twelve and a half years, we have lived in the security economy. Those of you who followed the Trust's guidance have done quite well, as the public and corporate coffers have poured their considerable resources into all manner of being safe." He spoke with a smooth, distinct accent, perhaps South African, perhaps a Commonwealth accent, or a combination of them. It added a note of authenticity to his words and kept the assembly enthralled. "Those days are over. The others don't know it yet and won't for another six months to a year, but the days at the trough of personal surveillance and countermeasures are over.

"Twelve and a half years ago, a small band of lunatics, with less funding than any of you here, simply walked through our airport gates, and the rent-a-cops merely sleep-walked through their duties. After the disaster, the resulting hysteria led to one of the largest shifts of capital in the history of the world. And I'm compelled to remind you that much of it shifted your way."

A murmur of uncomfortable laughter washed over the room.

"But the people have tired of watching for the wolf to return and will no longer bankroll huge staffs sitting at entrances or walking halls. They have grown weary of badges and special locks and access codes. Our studies show conclusively that a year from now the security segment of the economy will contract seventy to eighty percent — employment, services, products, everything. Get out while you can. You have been warned."

No one in the seats showed any reaction to his statements. Carlton had visited many of them pointing out the large chunks of their bottom lines allocated to non-productive assets. "So what happens to this infrastructure? Though the hysteria spawned by the agents of 9/11 may be subsiding, the commonplace parasitism that is an integral part of the human condition persists as pernicious as ever. Theft, shrinkage, and embezzlement still account for an unacceptable share of the waste in your organizations, exceeded only by the incompetence and vanity you tolerate. And I hope I need not remind you that, often as not, the perpetrators of these thefts are the very employees responsible for your security. It is time for that to change.

"As you well know — as you must certainly know — I have little patience for computers. For the most part I regard them as distractions. I do not have one in my office. I do not own one. Those who serve me are responsible for operating those machines and presenting me with the distilled information that I require. If they cannot do that, then they serve no function and are gone. I know that some of you are quite proud of your prowess with your terminals. You shouldn't be. Many of you spend entirely too much time staring at screens. Your time would be better spent thinking, better spent figuring out how people in this world operate, better spent staying on top. Your responsibility to yourself is to do what others are not capable of. Let the machines replace them, not you.

"However, some things have changed dramatically with the computing machines. In the past months I have had the opportunity to tour in depth the laboratories producing the machines that will replace most of your security staffs and the security staffs throughout business and government, both civilian and military. I have personally tested some of the new developments and can tell you that the achievements are remarkable. I have taken part in security tests at an airport in the Midwest. Undetected by the passersby in the terminal, the video surveillance identified everyone by name if they had been through the ticketing process. The system displayed their destination, their occupation, and their annual income. And the system accomplished this in real time with one hundred percent accuracy for over an hour while I was there. The airport was crowded, and the traffic moved fast. During that hour three sex offenders, eighteen parole violators, and three hundred fifteen individuals without identification in the system were flagged and arrested or detained. Of the three hundred fifteen without identification, two hundred seventy three were in this country illegally and were taken immediately for deportation.

"I cite this system as a first example. It is mature, it is working, and it is ready to deploy. And it is secret for the moment. The Transportation Security Administration will announce system-wide implementation in two months. This system will enhance security at our airports, rail centers, and public buildings an order of magnitude and will eliminate nearly a hundred thousand federal employees for a savings after installation of over five billion dollars in the first year alone. The thoroughness, economy, and reliability of these recognition systems are such that none of the agents of 9/11 would have passed even the first gates of any of the airports. None.

"As massive as the conversion will be on the federal level, it pales in magnitude to the private savings. These systems are scalable from factory to office to home. Advances in miniaturization coming out of our defense laboratories and patented by our companies will make this technology ubiquitous. Concurrent advances in software, again fully patented and protected, will replace in short order much of the staff you now pay to support and manage your enterprises."

A murmur spread through the assembly. Carlton's conversion had been abrupt indeed.

"I sense that many of you are skeptical, as well you should be. You should never take the word of anyone for anything. That philosophy has certainly served me well for a very long time. Many of you are skeptical. So let me ask you this. How many of you called me at the office last week?"

About forty hands went up including Garrette's.

"And with how many of you was I impatient?"

All the hands went down.

"And that didn't seem odd?"

Laughter for a moment.

"How many of you received the information you desired?"

The hands went up again.

"How many of you did not receive the information you sought?"

Hands went down. Garrette couldn't decide whether this exercise was annoying or amusing.

Carlton paused. He pushed his glasses higher on his nose. He turned to the side, picked up his wine glass and took a slow sip. He returned to the podium, letting his gaze sweep across the room.

"I was not in the office last week. I have not answered my phone for the past two weeks. Nor has my staff. You were talking to only one machine — a single machine. As many as seven of you at once were conversing with chips and circuits. Your questions were analyzed, processed, and answered correctly. The only residue of your conversation was a concise synopsis I received. One of you 'talked' with 'me' for over an hour. The distillation of your call occupied less than a minute of my time.

"Yet not one of you realized, despite the uncharacteristic courtesy and patience extended to you, that you were not talking with me. These chips and circuits are ready to replace, at a fraction of the salaries you are currently paying, the call center people, watch staffs, and machine crews at your enterprises. The chips and circuits do a better job at a tiny fraction of your payroll costs. And they don't argue."

As Carlton continued to rail against the wasted time and resources that he saw in each enterprise, Garrette reached out and picked up his place card. This place card was the only physical item he or anyone else would take home. It was very plain — four inches by six inches, creamy Bristol Vellum in landscape format. The Windham Trust device was engraved at the top, a slate blue circle inside a thick-thin double border of slate blue with the ever-present "WT" in fancy script. Nowhere did the words "Windham Trust" appear. Below the device he read "Dr. James Edward Garrette, PhD." At first he couldn't believe that it was engraved, but turning the card over, he spied the telltale impression of the gravure process. Back on the front, he saw his account, 147, in tiny Copperplate Gothic in the lower left corner. Since he had been inducted into the Trust, it had not even doubled in membership. He took a moment to look around the room. Easily three-fourths of the membership was present.

Garrette returned to the heart of the card. "The membership would like to thank the sponsors of our dinner, who have graciously invited the membership to their open houses and receptions." On Jim Garrette's card, there were seven receptions listed; five hardware firms he did not recognize and two biotechnology firms he did. He was the one who had recommended the two familiar names. He smiled to see the invitation to QuantaLab's wine and cheese show-and-tell at their Florida facility. The event was scheduled for one-thirty in the afternoon on Thursday, April 10, in room 1205 of the headquarters building in Sarasota. Garrette smiled because room 1205 would be eight stories above the roof of the building. Unless he called the phone number, no wine and no cheese would be expended, and no tours would be given. On April 10 at one-thirty in the afternoon, Jim Garrette would purchase $6,025,000 in QuantaLab shares through his personal broker, five thousand times the room number.

Each card in the room was unique. Each member had made known the amount he wished to invest for the coming year. The pool of stocks targeted by the Trust and recommended by the membership had been divided up and randomized. True, the Trust would make purchases of some of these stocks, but would also purchase known losers and ploddingly reliable issues to dilute the reported gains. Each member would purchase the designated stocks on the staggered schedules on their cards through their own brokers. None of the sophisticated monitoring programs of the SEC would notice even a ripple of activity. The purchases on the cards would be completed within a month, the cards would be destroyed with class three shredders, and about two weeks later various government departments would let bids for new security technologies that could only be supplied by firms on the place cards around the table. That the SEC would not notice a pattern was a given. John Brisbane, who owned the firm that produced their software, was sipping sherry three tables away from

Garrette. Non-trust friends in the inner circles of the assembled titans would congratulate their acquaintances on their bold investments, and the titans would be held up as examples of the risk-takers who made this country great. In actuality, no risks were involved. A small number of low-level GSA analysts were compiling new equipment specifications guaranteed to be filled from the listed companies. The poorly-paid low-level analysts would resign sporadically over the next six months and would be hired by companies on the list at five to six times their previous salary, but never, never by any company that would have fallen under their analytical gaze. As always, it is difficult to retain good government employees at the lower levels.

10 CHANGES

Saturday, March 29, 2014

San Diego proved all that Jack had hoped for and more. Since arriving Friday night, he had spared little thought for the lab's backbiting or the bills mounting because of the Institute's stalling. He had divided his time between preparing for his Sunday sessions and enjoying Jennifer's tourist delights. Saturday morning was spent at San Diego's zoo with pandas, koalas, and peacocks. She ate more junk food than he had seen her eat since first they met.

They walked the rocky beach north of La Jolla in late afternoon, picking up stones and examining omnipresent kelp washing ashore. Her skirt fluttered in a light breeze. Jack wore cut off jeans. It was the first time he had been barefoot outdoors in … he had a hard time remembering when last he had walked barefoot outdoors. Saturday had been cloudless and bright, warmer than a typical late March day. The sun was setting on the horizon, about one disk width above the ocean. Only now did high cirrus clouds catch fading rays, coloring with warm colors.

Jennifer faced Jack. "I want to make love to you."

Jack looked back and grinned. She was flushed with more than sunset's glow. "Sounds fine with me. Let's head back."

"I want to make love to you here. Now," she insisted.

"With all loving respect, I don't think that's a good idea on several levels. Let's go back and enjoy a warm, passionate evening inside."

"Now!" She began unbuttoning her blouse. "It's always memorable in movies. I want to make love to remember."

"For one thing, we could be arrested," he reminded her, glancing in both directions and upward from his limited field of view of rocks in the cove. He didn't see anyone. "For another thing, the temperature is going to drop fast in …" He observed the sun hovering half a disk above the horizon. "… about ten minutes."

"Then better get a move on, lover boy." She was not to be deterred. Nor was this a whim. Her blouse was off, rolled up as a pillow. No bra. She released her last skirt button and unwrapped it. No panties. She spread it over pebble-strewn sand, a soft cushion below her blouse pillow.

Jack bit his lower lip. She was so very beautiful. Treatments were already taking a toll on her weight, and he might have noticed her ribs highlighted in the orange suffusion. But he saw only her graceful hips, her elegant arms, her perfect nose, her nipples. She was so very beautiful.

Having donned her chosen attire, Jennifer set to work on Jack, who surrendered to her determination. He placed his jeans, his shirt, and his undergarments in spots where her back and buttocks would rest.

They embraced to breakers' deep thunder on granite. He caressed her, stroked her, and excited her in every way that had ever worked. When she reached climax, he knew he had pleased her beyond her fantasy. She rolled over, smiling and serene.

"You're on top today," she said.

Jack savored their lovemaking, releasing well after the red hues on the rocks had dimmed. They giggled, they laughed, and gathered what covering they could from clothing strewn about where they lay together.

Their reverie was short-lived. Above the waves' thud, they heard a dog barking. Jack scurried to find underwear in the dim light as Jennifer struggled to shake sand from her blouse, giggling as she did.

The dog, a German shepherd, appeared around a huge boulder to the south. Silhouetted on the other end of its leash was a uniformed figure. The dog barked, but did not seem particularly aggressive.

"What's going on here?" the man asked.

Jack struggled to pull on his underpants. He sensed a keen vulnerability in front from the approaching canine. "Officer, we were …" He hoped he would fare a whole lot better with his words tomorrow, but this evening verbs, nouns, adjectives, and even adverbs failed him completely.

"Never mind." The officer seemed at once both stern and kindly.

Jennifer had gotten her blouse on and wrapped her skirt around her, but that was all. She leaned on Jack and smiled meekly. "He's my husband."

The officer shook his head. Jack could see 'Beach Patrol' embroidered above his left pocket, adorned with a badge. "Well, that's nice. But you know very well you can't do that here." He pointed at the sand.

"We're sorry, officer. We're not from around here," she offered.

"I see. And sex on beaches is allowed in … ?"

"Maryland, sir."

He raised his eyebrows, still shaking his head. "I have my doubts. On the other hand, I haven't seen you here before and doubt you will be doing this here again."

Jack shook his head no.

"Why don't you get dressed before you freeze?" He looked up and down the beach. "I gotta cite you for something in case someone's watching. There's a lot of serious things I could write up, but you seem like a couple of nice kids, and we can sure use your tourist dollars, so I'm going to give you the minimum — nudity outside of official zone."

Jennifer could not stifle a small puff of a giggle. The officer smiled in return as he wrote their ticket with information Jack provided. The dog wagged his tail, and Jennifer reached out to pat its head and receive a friendly lick. "Thank you, officer."

He handed Jack the citation. "Enjoy your time here. Indoors preferably."

Jack bowed out of instinct.

The officer resumed his trek north, giving the leash a gentle tug. "Come on, Rusty." He glanced over his shoulder as Jennifer wrapped her arms around Jack. "Be glad I came along when I did, folks. In about half an hour, tide comes in here with fifteen-foot waves; this beach is under water and cut off from north and south. People drown here every year."

Jennifer and Jack joined hands and walked south past the boulders bordering the cove. Jennifer started laughing. Jack tried to grab her to tickle, but she broke free, and they raced, howling, in moonless darkness all the way to their rental car.

* * *

"So how was your flight?" Anna tried to draw Laura Garrette from her funk.

"It was OK. I've got enough hours for my license. I just wanted to be up there alone." Laura leaned back in her chair, arms crossed. "You know, I'm just not in a mood to practice tonight. It just seems so irrelevant."

Anna set Laura's sheet music in front of her. "It will be if we don't practice."

"I spent the rest of my day working with the coordinating committee trying to come up with money to fund our soup lines. You know, money's just drying up. What's going on with you people up there in the Big House?" Laura scowled at her music, arms crossed more tightly.

"You agreed — no probing. You know I couldn't say anything even if I knew anything. And I've told you — let's see … I think seventy-one times — I'm on the diplomatic team, not in any domestic role." Anna Colbert was patient with her friend, but growing weary.

"I'm sorry. Look, I've had a rough day, all my centers are having rough times, and every other coordinating committee is having a rough year. When is your boss's boss's boss going to do something?"

Anna set her music aside. "It's only boss's boss. If I give you a little background, just between you and me, can we get on to music?"

"Yeah, I guess."

Anna was not satisfied. She folded her arms, waiting.

"OK, OK! Just you and me. Tell me something to help me understand what the hell is going on."

Anna began, "A couple of my best friends in the staff office *are* on our economic team. They don't know what's going on, either. They're seeing the same numbers as you are. Indicators at the national level are all steady and strong. But state numbers are all heading down. They'd love to have some way of accessing data from your centers, but it's not available. Surveys of investors, which we do have access to, paint an oh-so-rosy picture."

Laura felt uncomfortable with Anna's last sentence. She looked at her. Her friend was not one to exploit family differences, and Laura sensed no trace of a dig. Laura's discomfort was entirely from within. For all she knew, Anna meant the information as good news. "So what are your friends doing?" Laura asked.

Anna sighed. "They're gathering information. They're looking under every stone for a reason. They're serious about it. Mr. Kincaid is as dedicated a public servant as I've ever even heard of. He wants the best for everyone. As soon as he knows what's going on, we'll be finding a fix."

"I suppose. But you could start by fixing that slimeball Bailey."

Anna frowned and shuddered. "I don't want to talk about him except to say he makes my job as difficult as he does the economics team's."

Laura had calmed down.

Anna tapped again on Laura's music. "I kept my promise. Can we get to work now?"

"Hmmm. Thanks. I'll keep it between us two. At least you give a different perspective on it. Hey, if your money people need some data, give them my number. One of our volunteers is a biostatistician from College Park. I'll bet she could get you some useful stuff."

"Thanks. I've got your number in my phone." Anna moved tonight's music closer to Laura.

Laura smiled and then cleared her throat.

* * *

Sunday, March 30, 2014

Jack was in full command of verbs, nouns, adjectives, and particularly adverbs by Sunday afternoon's debate, defeating competitors from across the country with ease. His stiffest challenge was a final contestant from the University of Chicago, but his Chicago opponent lost ground by following an argument into a logical *cul-de-sac*. It helped that among those topics Jack chose to prepare for, he had anticipated the final one — "Resolved: the federal government should fund job transition centers to accommodate job training needs wrought by changes in technology." Historically the organization chose topics inflamed by White House actions and usually topics of a social nature rather than military.

Jennifer was waiting at the stage door as he finished. "Way to go, big boy. Crushed 'em pretty good. Course, I hope you don't believe what you said up there."

He finished on the negative side, arguing ineffectiveness of large programs applied to passing phenomena. "You sure you want to talk about this?"

They walked out of the hall, through the building, and onto their host campus. The college provided an idyllic backdrop with its broad promenade perched over the Pacific, majestic eucalyptus trees providing fragrant broken shade from bright afternoon sun. They walked hand in hand, looking down on the same coastline they had so enjoyed the previous evening. It was high tide, and impressive breakers submerged the friendly sand beneath. Dull thuds of powerful water on rock carried on the wind.

She answered, "Talk, yes; argue, no. After all, you're the grand champion. You were almost as good when you argued the affirmative." Jennifer drew close to him as they strolled the sea cliff walk. She was enjoying herself, though she looked very tired.

"To be honest, I don't know any more. To win a debate you have to ditch emotions and focus on facts to the exclusion of everything else. I've been doing it so long, sometimes I don't get any feelings back after it's over."

"I'm not sure that's healthy," she murmured.

"You're right. A lot of monstrosities are built on top of impeccable logic," he agreed.

"Do you believe what you said when you were in the negative today?" Jennifer looked up into his eyes.

He looked back into hers, noting as always their deep brown beauty, their utter sincerity. Jack wondered what message, if any, his eyes sent. "Oh, definitely I believed it. Every statement was rigorously true. And you know every point was philosophically strong and defensible."

Jennifer looked away to ground.

"And I know that's not what you were asking. Do I support consequences of the affirmative or negative?"

Jennifer lifted her head, closed her eyes, inhaling the salt air. Small tears formed in her eyes and journeyed down her cheeks. "We haven't got much time, Jack. I can feel it going. I won't get to see the ocean again. I won't get to hear you kick butt again. We haven't much time. I so want to plant some passion before I go, some special mission that'll take root and bear fruit. That may be all I can do."

She turned back to him. She saw his dull panic masked by expressionless face. After wiping her tears, she continued, "Kind of a downer, huh, right after our big triumph? I'm sorry. I didn't mean to do that." She reached her arms up around his neck. "I love you. I'm so proud of you."

He embraced her. "I love you, too."

After a bit she released him and stepped back. She shook her hair and took another deep breath. "Now answer my question."

"Which question?"

"Do you believe — *feelings*, not facts — what you said when you were in the negative today?"

Jack motioned to a bench. He sat down, and she nestled on his lap, leaning her head on his shoulder and closing her eyes. She was not heavy, not nearly so heavy as she should be. "I'm resigned to the correctness of both positions and to the idea that what is right and best is somewhere in between. I know by power of money and influence negative will prevail, in the short run, at least. Still, when money and power prevail too long, everything falls apart. So eventually positive will prevail."

"You're hopeless." She did not open her eyes. "There has got to be some feeling in there somewhere. I know you have feelings. I know it when we make love. I know it when you come home from work frustrated."

"OK, so what's different about those times? Making love to you is personal. Making love to you doesn't have a down side, a negative."

"Other than almost getting arrested?" she asked.

Jack smiled. "Other than almost getting arrested. But that's a very small down side." He stroked her arm. "As for coming home frustrated, my frustration is with the stupidity of my overlords and the greed of my workers. Neither one is looking at the long-term picture, and I know I will eventually pay a price. Which means that we will pay the price — you and I."

"I see," she whispered.

"Seriously. Maybe that's what you're picking up on. For the most part, what's the point of passion? Making love? Yes, there's a reward for passion. But with government job programs, what does passion get you? Nothing a rational discussion won't. Other than heartburn. All the feeling in the world won't change outcomes."

"You're wrong," she said.

"I hope so."

Jennifer shifted her body and twisted her head up to look at him. "And what about work? You don't like going to work any more. You get angry. What are you going to do about it?"

Jack gazed out over deep blue water. From time to time a sailboat would slip into view out at sea, parallel to the shore. "I don't know. I don't see much changing."

"Then you change it. Quit," she said, following his gaze.

"But I love my work. And you've always been so proud of what I do!"

"Times change, lover. Life is too precious to squander it in despair. If you're not going to leave irritations behind, get rid of them."

Jack looked down at Jennifer. "Fire Leslie and the crew?"

"Sure," she replied.

"Now who's cold and calculating?"

"No, you're not following me. You run this lab because you love it. You're passionate about your work. They're not. Elsa, Patricia, Leslie — they're smart; they're talented; but they're in it for money, not passion. And they're stuck right where they are. Those women aren't going to make more than cost-of-living raises going forward because they've risen as far as they can go. You asked if I meant fire them. Actually, no. But tell them to get ready to move on. Guide them out. You can be humane to them and to yourself. Get someone in there who has room to grow. Everybody wins."

"Hmm. Hadn't thought about it that way."

"Yeah, you've been in the same spot too long. Like those fossils at headquarters."

Jack sighed, "Not much I can do about them, though."

"You're still not listening. Quit. Move on. Start looking for something that excites you. Not to be morbid, but you're not going to need so much salary in a while. Do something worthwhile others can't afford to do because they can't afford someone like you. Are you hearing me?"

Jack was silent. Jennifer waited.

"I think so," he said finally, "You're right. I know it. But I'm afraid of the leap."

"Good! Then you heard me right. Be afraid. You have to be afraid. Then do it. Don't do anything if it doesn't make you afraid at first." She moved onto the bench, laying her head on his lap. He stroked her hair gently, silently.

* * *

Monday, March 31, 2014

Sarah threaded the White House's subterranean labyrinth. In only a month since she'd arrived, the maze had become familiar. The White House workings seemed not so much machinations of a great world power, but rather a large hotel or corporate headquarters. Her missions before her official day began were to get menus to the kitchen, arrange for parking, and provide biographies to the press office. At her current pace, Sarah figured it would take precisely half an hour.

The kitchen was huge, with staff in constant motion when she arrived at 7:45. Main breakfast dishes arrived for washing, and a myriad of pastry carts for individual breakfast meetings were leaving on their appointed routes. Massive trays of meats were in final stages of preparation for far fancier noon meals, each serving prepared with the exquisite attention to detail that marked lunch in the most powerful dining rooms on earth.

One junior chef pointed Sarah to the corner office where Ms.

Gillenwater oversaw operations. She was on the phone imploring some staffer to get her list in as quickly as possible. Sarah looked around Ms. Gillenwater's office. It resembled pictures she had seen of World War II military war rooms where invasions were planned. A large board across the back featured a tight list of events with dates and colored magnets signifying stages of preparation. From accompanying notes scribbled in erasable marker, Sarah gathered she did not want her events to have any red magnets. She looked down Ms. Gillenwater's list. Despite the AIDS dinner being only four weeks away, it was not on the board. She saw the Medal of Freedom dinner in May. It already had a yellow magnet on its guest list block.

Ms. Gillenwater finished her phone call and looked up. "May I help you, miss?"

"I have guest lists for the AIDS banquet and the Medal of Freedom dinner," Sarah replied.

"Oh, good. I was hoping we wouldn't be waiting until the last minute again." She took the two lists from Sarah and examined them, then paused. "I'm sorry. Toni Gillenwater. It's been too busy here today. Forgot my manners."

"Sarah Tyler, Ms. Gillenwater."

Ms. Gillenwater smiled. Perhaps in her seventies, with well-managed white hair, she reminded Sarah of her grandmother. Her smile propagated into a series of happy wrinkles. "My friends call me 'Miss Toni,' and anyone who brings in guest lists this far in advance is my friend."

Sarah smiled and bit her lower lip as Miss Toni changed the Medal of Freedom magnet to green. She looked for AIDS Banquet without success. She opened a smaller calendar on her desk, going over entries until she found it.

"I hadn't heard anything about this for several months. I was afraid they'd cancelled it." Miss Toni added the dinner to her operations board and placed a green magnet for guest lists. She looked at the long list. "But this many people are going to be crowded there. It would be better in the Grand Ballroom. Seems appropriate to be there, anyway, don't you think?" Miss Toni had obviously dealt with controversies surrounding this particular dinner before.

"Yes, I do. Can you change rooms?" Sarah asked.

Ms. Toni walked to her office doorway and looked out to left and right, then returned to the board. "Technically, yes," she whispered. "I am, after all, manager. But people upstairs can override my choices. Ron — Ron Kowalski, the press secretary — would be most likely to notice and say something. I doubt it matters much to him, but he can be cowed pretty badly by the Vice President."

"…who doesn't want the dinner publicized? I see," Sarah finished.

"I doubt he really cares himself, but politics…" She tossed her hands out in resignation. "Only the President and Mr. Kincaid can say yes if he says no."

"I work for Mr. Kincaid," Sarah offered.

"Ah. Working for and being are two very different things in this world."

They looked at the board together. Very impressive. Important names noted in margins of the board comprised a list of the world's most powerful people. Ms. Toni had already written 'Grand Ballroom' for location. She looked at Sarah and winked. "It was available. Let's keep it there until we're told otherwise."

Sarah nodded. "Thank you." She prepared to move on to her next visit but paused for a final comment. "I noted special diet and kosher needs on those lists."

Toni peered at one list through the lower half of her glasses. "You can't imagine how much you've helped me. Are you taking this over permanently?"

"I don't think so. I'm an economist. I volunteered to help out Kathy Whiting."

"Well good for you. I like Ms. Whiting. They work her too hard, and she doesn't complain enough. She's a good-hearted woman."

Sarah nodded. "She warned me there would be flak over the AIDS banquet. Just out of curiosity, you seem pretty interested in the event. How come?"

"Our church sponsors a local free clinic. The national head of free clinics is being honored. I just think it's the right thing to do."

Ms. Toni's phone rang and she raised her hand to wave goodbye. Sarah returned Miss Toni's wave and headed to her next station.

* * *

Parking was a matter of security and security was the Marine Corps detachment responsibility. Sarah arrived at the parking desk still on schedule to complete her tasks by 8:15.

"Yes, Ma'am. May I help you?" Corporal Tull was the embodiment of readiness in his crisp uniform.

Sarah had vague memories of ROTC units at college, which never possessed this crispness, even on drill days. But, then, they weren't Marines. "I have parking lists for the AIDS banquet and Medal of Freedom dinner," she said.

Tull took her second set of lists. "Yes, Ma'am."

"You don't have to call me 'ma'am'."

Tull grinned as he looked over her lists. "Actually, I do. It's a show of respect. My little sister would be 'Ma'am' here."

"OK. I haven't done this before. Do I get passes? Tickets? Does someone else take it from here?"

He looked up at her from the lists. She was looking around and felt a little underdressed against the snappy uniforms of men and women passing on their urgent business. She wore a simple gray skirt with white blouse and her perennial black sweater. Her simple pin seemed pallid compared to so many rows of ribbons.

She turned back to Tull. He was staring at her, almost transfixed. She cocked her head. "Yes?"

Tull blinked and returned to his task. "Sorry, Ma'am. I don't think I've seen you around before."

"I've been here only a month. A month today, in fact. I'm in the Chief of Staff's office."

Tull marked out a block of numbers on a log sheet he had retrieved from his desk. He smiled a big smile. "Mr. Kincaid's a fine man. A true gentleman."

Sarah expressed surprise. "Does he come here often?"

"Ah, no, Ma'am. I pull duty outside the 'big office' fairly often. He comes by there almost every watch. He always has his ID ready and everything in order. Funny how you notice little things. But it makes a lot of difference when you have hundreds of people to put through every day. Plus he knows everyone by name."

Sarah nodded.

Tull made an entry in one of his myriad logs. "OK, I've got you taken care of here. Normally, everyone waits until last minute to get these lists to us, but you've got it all squared away well ahead of time. I've got spots for all your guests. Please, please emphasize to them they need to bring some form of government ID, like a driver's license. Passes will be at the North-East gate an hour before your first guests are allowed in." He pulled out a sheet identifying gates and handed it to her.

Sarah smiled. Her father always said "squared away," and she hadn't heard it for a long time.

"And you can really help us if someone with clearance could be at the gate to vouch for any guests who forget their IDs," Tull continued, "Dr. Tyler, this takes care of AIDS banquet. MoF is a bigger operation with limos and escorts and all. Someone will be with you about a week before to verify the lists and give you more details."

"How did you know my name? You said you've never seen me before," she asked.

Tull pointed down to her left side where her badge was clipped on.

"Right." She grinned. "Well, thank you … Captain?" She realized she was going to have to learn what the stripes and stars and bars meant, and quickly.

Tull grinned in return. "Corporal, Ma'am. Enlisted. Just below sergeant."

She raised her index finger for emphasis. "Well, thank you, Corporal Tull. Thank you very much."

"Yes, Ma'am," he replied, smiling.

She headed for the door. On a whim, she spun her head around. Tull was watching her, a pleasant smile still on his face. As soon as she eyed him, he dropped his gaze to some papers before him. She turned her head back to the hall, narrowly missing a uniformed man with what appeared to be a silver leaf on his lapel. Up until now a young man watching her so closely might have been irritating, but she felt instead a little flush in her cheeks. She grinned, putting her tongue to her teeth for a moment, and went on.

* * *

Still on schedule, Sarah arrived at the press secretary's office with a single envelope of biographies. The area seemed empty compared to the kitchen and Marine outpost. She approached the door whose number she had been given. Inside, a man, his back to her, removed pictures from the wall, one after another, and placed them in several sturdy packing boxes. She looked around. Shelves on one side were empty, desktop cleared.

"Mr. Kowalski?"

The man turned around. She recognized press secretary Ron Kowalski. Her eyes darted around the room. Several boxes were already stacked, a large roll of movers tape on top.

"Yes?" He returned to dismantling.

Sarah looked back at Kowalski. "I've got bios for the AIDS banquet and Medal of Freedom dinner."

"No disrespect, but you'll have to take that up with the Secretary of I-Don't-Give-a-Shit."

"I beg your pardon?" Sarah put her free hand on her hip as a scowl darkened her face.

Ron Kowalski continued his packing, placing bundles of papers in boxes with angry thuds. He was a rough cut compared to most White House staffers, his sandy red hair close cropped and his suit, if you could call it such, much less formal than the local norm. After packing about ten more bundles, he raised his head and looked at her. "I'm not going to be able to help you, miss. I'm outta here. An hour ago, I got offered a senior analyst spot with NBC, and I'm taking it. I'm kissing this sorry asylum goodbye."

"Well, good for you!" Sarah put both hands on her hips. "I'm glad for you, or sorry for you, or whatever. But I've got a job to do myself. Just tell me to whom give these."

He looked down at her stack of biographies. "In the past, I'd have said give them to Mila, my assistant, but she's going with me. She's not even coming in today. Or tomorrow. Or ever. Actually, you know, for the first time since nineteen forty, this office will be completely vacant."

"This is ridiculous! I expected the President of the United States of

America's press office to be crawling with staff," Sarah exploded.

Kowalski straightened up and, facing Sarah, folded his arms. "Yeah. You would, wouldn't you? It was like that five years ago. Until Bailey began to meddle. He's gutted my office. He's run off my staff with his approval protocols — love that word 'protocols' — , and he's made living almost impossible, all while building up his own media kingdom outside the White House."

Sarah waved her hand back and forth, shaking her head and sending her hair dancing. "Whoa, whoa, whoa, whoa! Am I in the right office? I thought this was the President's press office, not the Vice President's."

"My point exactly, young lady." Kowalski raised his left hand and began ticking off points on his thick fingers as his anger increased. "Bailey controls my budget and can sit on a personnel request forever. Bailey controls clearances, and no one gets cleared if he so elects. Bailey controls security reviews." He shifted his hands to produce air quotes for 'security reviews.' "If he wants to bury a release, it won't get reviewed until weeks or months after the event. And, if you dare to go around him, you find yourself talking to the FBI for a couple of days." He had run out of fingers. "It's sad to see how we've been torn down to this sorry state, but after today I'm his worst nightmare. All the news organizations smell blood in the water and are buying the best sharks they can afford." Kowalski opened his hands in a wide shrug, turning away.

Sarah's face reddened. "I'm sorry about how bad things have gotten for you. I really am. But I'm still just trying to do my job. You have no right to be rude to me, no right to treat me this way."

Kowalski lowered his folders and leaned on his hands quietly, speaking once he calmed down. "You're right. You're absolutely right. My mother didn't raise me to be this way."

Sarah tilted her head to one side. She sensed his sincerity.

He shook his head slowly. "I'd love to blame my rudeness on Bailey, but I'm responsible for what comes out of my mouth, no matter what." Ron Kowalski faced her again, his face kinder. "With your forgiveness, I'd like to start over, please." He extended his hand. "Hello. I'm Ron Kowalski, former press secretary."

Sarah smiled and put out her hand. "Hi. I'm Sarah Tyler."

Kowalski perked up at once. "Ah, Doctor Sarah Tyler. Well, this *is* an honor. I'm glad I got to meet you face to face before leaving."

His high profile recognition caught Sarah off guard. She glanced at her security badge. Corporal Tull had gotten her name from her tag and, though it did contain the title 'Dr.', Ron Kowalski could not have seen it from where he stood. "You know me?"

"Oh, yes indeed. You're part of the group investigating our beloved Vice President." He resumed his packing, but more calmly, addressing

Sarah often. "You've become a person of great interest all of a sudden, along with Peter and Kathy."

"Really?" she asked, obviously stunned.

"Uh huh. Peter asked me to gather some material for you." He paused and crossed to a seven-inch pile remaining on a bookcase. He picked it up and handed it to Sarah with an exaggerated bow. "Bailey's office asked — no, 'asked' is way too mild a term — ordered me to report what questions you were asking and what I gave you."

Sarah examined the stack in her hand and frowned. "And have you?"

"Hell, no!" He looked at her as if her question were absurd. "If I think I can help bring him down, I'm certainly not going to tip him off. And if there's anything you need from me from now on, don't hesitate to call. I don't have any new cards yet, but I'll get you all my contact information as soon as I have something definite."

Sarah continued to stare at the stack. "This isn't turning out like I thought. I came here to do agricultural economics. Instead, I'm playing detective on the Vice President for the President. I'm way out of my league and area."

Kowalski chuckled, grinning. His rumpled shirt lent him the air of a comfortable old friend. "You were chosen because you have a brilliant analytical mind. Peter said so, and frankly, I've never known him to be wrong …" he paused, seeming to search his memory "… about anything."

"We haven't found anything, you know. Everything is innuendo and speculation."

He nodded. "Oh, you will. You will. I may not be a brilliant analyst, but I've survived a long time in this town by knowing people. You're this close." He gestured with his fingers. "I don't know anything specific, but I can feel it. Otherwise his people wouldn't be going to battle stations over these checks of yours. Go through that pile I just gave you. He rubs elbows with big money brokers, most of them operating on the edge of legality." Kowalski walked over to her, took the stack, set it on the table, and flipped about halfway down, pulling out a sheet of yellow legal paper with a list of names. "See this?"

Sarah nodded.

"This is my guess of who's in Windham Trust based on who's with whom in pictures and articles. I can't prove any of it, but I'd stake my honor on it. Now, don't you go taking it as gospel."

"You've been looking into Windham, too?" Sarah asked Kowalski, her eyes wide.

He grinned. "Actually, I started this list about two years ago, before the reelection. On my way in to work one day I heard a story about someone — Hebert, I think — going to jail for defrauding the government of a lot of money. The story mentioned Windham. I didn't think anything about it at the time — sorta subliminal, I suppose. Later that morning Bailey came into my office — we had seven people then — and ordered me to destroy any material with Hebert in it."

"No shit!" Sarah exclaimed.

"You'll find it all at the bottom of the pile. Since then, anytime he's ordered something removed, it's gone onto the heap." He picked up the pile again and placed it in her hands atop her biographies. "Enjoy, but watch your back. He can be a very dangerous man." He gave a smug smile. After a pause he asked, "Anything else I can get you this morning?"

Sarah shook her head. "Guess not. I'll ask Mr. Kincaid what to do with the biographies."

Kowalski winced.

"What?" she asked.

"I feel really bad. I haven't talked to him, and I know he deserves better. Mr. Kincaid's stood up for us more than a few times and helped me through some of my low points — my many low points. I feel like a coward bolting this way."

"So go tell him. Now."

He sighed. "I'm afraid he'd talk me out of it." He looked into her eyes. "Don't worry. No matter what happens to Bailey, Mr. Kincaid will come out OK. So will President Miller, I think, though he should have reined in that shitball Bailey a long time ago."

"Well, we gotta do what we gotta do," she sighed, hefting her new paperwork. "Thanks, I guess. Hope your new job turns out well. See you on the tube?"

"Don't know. Maybe. Don't much care as long as I'm honestly employed."

Sarah left the press office, and Ron Kowalski continued his packing.

* * *

"What do you mean 'laid them off'? How can you cut those services?" Laura had listened to her food pantry's newest client with a scowl.

"It's simple. My supervisor came back from the meetin' cryin'. She said the county was runnin' so far behind budget they was havin' to lay off more people. They already closed three rec centers last month, and they've got a hirin' freeze — even on police." Anita was a pretty, petite woman, a graceful blend of Filipino and Caucasian. Her face showed the strain of her predicament. "I've never been here before and thought I never would be."

Laura began to pack a bag with standard staples — three boxes of macaroni and cheese, four cans of various vegetables, a large bag of rice. A special treat this week courtesy of a local grocery chain was a two-pound jar of instant iced tea mix. Laura noticed the wedding ring on Anita's finger. "Does your husband work for the county, too?"

"No, mum, Benny's in the Navy over in the Gulf — on *USS Carl*

Vinson. They're supposed to be gettin' a raise in July, but it won't make up for losing my call center job. It's sad. One reason I got my job in the first place was our county's preference policy for military spouses." Anita's lip began to quiver. "What am I goin' to do? I don't want to live on charity."

"This isn't charity," Laura replied, her lips firm as she packed in an extra bag of rice. "This is payback. I know what 911 centers do, and I've got a pretty good idea what they pay. You were just paying it forward. When things get back on track, you're going to be sitting here doing this or doing a food drive at church."

Anita smiled at last. "Thank you, mum. Bless you." She walked out of the pantry carrying her bag.

Laura watched her leave and then leaned forward, her hands planted on the table, her jaw set. "She's the fourth new one today, Charlie. What's going on?"

Quietly, in the background, Charlie pre-bagged rations according to their standard list. He sported a black tee shirt with a cerebral message 'In the Kingdom of the Blind …' on the front and '… the One-Eyed Man is King' on the back. His long hair was a throwback to the nineteen sixties or seventies; he was in his late fifties. "Like our lady said, she got laid off. Got laid off from a job everyone figured was absolutely secure. It's the same story with almost every new client. At least I've got total job security."

Laura was deep in thought as she continued to lean on her hands. Charlie had nearly finished his bagging when she jerked alert. "I can't believe I just let that go. You're unemployed, you turkey!"

Charlie laughed. "A growth industry, m'lady, but it's still more sinister. What gives everyone the creeps is learning there will be fewer 911 operators. What the county hasn't said much about is our operators are being replaced by robots."

Laura crossed her arms. "All right. Fool me once —"

"No, no. I'm serious. The county contracted for five of those new machines from Brisbane Technologies. Even if the economy turns around, those jobs are history. Each twenty-thousand-dollar machine replaces at least three shifts each with a thirty-thousand-dollar-a-year-with-benefits worker. Robots work 24/7 without breaks or car problems or school meetings."

"You are one depressing son-of-a-bitch, Charlie."

"Hmmm, thanks, I guess. Hey! I've got a shirt saying 'Reality Sucks.' Think I should wear it tomorrow?"

"No," she replied.

Charlie dragged a chair to Laura's desk and placed it with the back toward her. He straddled the seat backwards, folded his arms on the back and rested his head on his arms. "OK, Massa Lady, don't tell me you don't have a plan."

"If I had a plan, you'd have heard it already."

"True." Charlie nodded as best he could. His chair rocked beneath him. "So, instead, I will review your situation and some of your options."

"Could I stop you?" she asked.

"No."

She raised her hands off her desk and sat in her chair.

"One. Our center is barely maintaining an even keel. We have enough funds to survive, even though visits are up fifty percent over last year because you've busted your butt for new contributions. Two. You cannot sustain your effort because you have too much else going on, and it's making you very bitchy."

"I am not bitchy," she interrupted.

"Hey, this is my lecture. Wait your turn. Where was I? Oh, yes, it's making you very bitchy. Three. You know in your gut our situation is getting — and will continue getting — worse. These changes are systemic — embedded in the very fabric of our society — *ergo*, you are going to have to come up with a fundamentally different approach to getting people jobs because we can't keep this up; we are just one little center out of thousands and thousands who are seeing exactly the same armies of highly skilled unemployed."

"You are one depressing son-of-a-bitch, Charlie."

"You already said that. Of course, I'm depressing you because you know it's true, but you haven't shifted your thinking to a new path yet, and are afraid of the enormous task ahead of you. Once your thinking reaches a higher plane — which it will — then you'll transform into Joan of Arc Woman, and great powers will tremble before you."

Laura giggled as Charlie put his hands together and bowed in her direction, bumping his head on the chair back. "OK, you've got all this insight as usual. Why don't you fight the system yourself?"

"Because I'm lazy and disorganized," he replied, shrugging.

"You're not lazy."

"Laziness has different forms. I like pretty new ideas dancing in my head, but it doesn't do anything for my self-esteem to catch them and put them to work. I'd rather see them dancing."

"Did you ingest anything back in the seventies you shouldn't have?"

"Oh, yeah! But that's another story for another day. Presently, I am your muse. I attach myself to you and your people because you will use me and abuse me for the good of all mankind. Plus, of course, you feed me. But time's wasting. You need to mass your armies."

Laura looked at Charlie, sitting smug and inscrutable. "And do any of your dancing ideas know how to mass my armies?"

"Absolutely. Our county is running out of money. We may be 'governed' by sleazy politicians at the top, but those people who're saying we're running out of money are mostly long-term bureaucrats with nothing to gain by lying. In fact, honesty makes their jobs easier because they don't have to appear in hearings later. So I believe we'll soon be out of money and I take that as a given, despite what I read in the *Post* about ultra-rich people like you seeming to be doing well. More on that later."

Laura had once been annoyed by Charlie's candid references to her wealth, but had come to appreciate it was to him a mere statement of fact without agenda. Though it could be embarrassing in a crowd, one-on-one it was OK. She was curious as to what he was envisioning for her as a consequence of her family's situation.

Charlie moved through his analysis. "Given that money is drying up, something has to be done — now — to save the system before all money is gone. You know — use your last gas to get to a gas station, or it gets really tedious. Anyway, we need jobs that pay decent wages. What do we have that's not being replaced? Intellectual jobs like teaching? No. We certainly need more teachers, but they take public money — money that's running out. Artists? Need 'em, but art doesn't pay. Or doesn't in the present. You have to be dead for awhile." Charlie grinned just a little. "Gardeners? Doesn't pay enough. Grocery clerks? Oops, they're almost gone. But stocking people are harder to replace by machines because they use judgment. Programmers? Aha, now we have a need and the pay. Oh, but no one wants to program because it takes years of being a geek with mostly one-time dates and a mentality that takes years to breed. Banking? No, already almost completely automated. So basically the jobs still available in any abundance are all very low wage, even if they are intellectually satisfying or require big training. You can't count on governments at any level to require your people to pay more, since your people will dismiss them indirectly through our ad-rigged elections," Charlie finished, and sat still.

Laura waited. "Hold on! That's it? Those are your dancing ideas?"

Charlie's grin widened. "Ha! You missed the logical flaw in there. And you weren't taking my description of you seriously."

Laura buried her face in her hands. "You're giving me a headache," she mumbled.

"OK, gardeners, artisans, teachers, clerks — all low pay. Most — most — of society low pay. Why? Takes the same body. Takes the same thought power. Why? *Because we allow it.* We accept low wages. The wealthy …" he stretched out his palm in her direction. "… assume correctly that society will go along with the assumption these jobs will pay low. Any one individual who bucks the system will just be replaced by another who doesn't. As long as most accept this, then it will remain true. The entire world economic system is founded on this core acceptance. As it has been, so it will be. Not!"

Laura listened intently. Charlie might have a few neurons out of place, but no one doubted his basic understanding of the universe. Perhaps no one ever realized his basic understanding of the universe might be useful.

He continued, "Your army is ready, Joan. They are poorly trained and have wanted a leader for two thousand years. But now their backs are to the wall. They possess the most powerful motivator of all life — fear. Fear of starving. They will follow a leader who will convince them they will survive. They can be misled by a huckster, or truly led by a saint. Either way, it's going to happen. And there's a lot more choice involved in this than most people realize."

Laura was thinking. "So rich people …"

"You rich people. Make it personal, think from within so you can correctly grasp the concepts."

Laura frowned. "So, we rich people are going to pay more money to people we don't now because…?"

"Because you will realize it's the right thing to do. And because you won't have a choice against a well-trained army. First principle of attack is early application of massive, overwhelming force. Do not lose your first battle or you may not have a second battle."

* * *

Wearing an uncharacteristic frown, Sarah stood before Tracey's desk at 8:21.

Tracey looked up as Sarah entered the office. "Bad weekend?"

"No, actually it was quite productive." Sarah shook her head. "But Monday's not starting off so well. Is Mr. Kincaid available?"

"Not really. He's in there." Tracey nodded in the direction of the staff meeting room. The door was closed. "He's got Treasury, Justice, and other sorts you don't want to talk to on a Monday. What's on your mind?"

Sarah held out guest lists, somewhat wrinkled from their morning journey. "I was going to drop these off with Ron Kowalski, but Ron's resigned, and I'm not sure who should get them."

Tracey grinned. "Ron resigns about every three months. Kinda like one of those regular geysers. He'll calm down after he talks to Mr. Kincaid."

"Uh, I don't think so. He seemed pretty serious. He said he and Mila are both gone, he's been hired by NBC, and Mila is going with him. As fast as he was packing, he'll be gone in twenty-five minutes or so."

Tracey's grin vanished. She pointed to the meeting room door. "Knock and go on in. Tell him what you just told me."

Sarah proceeded to the door, knocked, and opened it. Tracey had said "Treasury" and "Justice," but Sarah was still surprised to see the actual Secretary of the Treasury and Attorney General in person. Glancing around quickly, she noted Peter and Kathy from the home team and several others who must have come with the Secretaries.

Kincaid looked up from his notes. "Yes?"

"Sir, —" Sarah paused, a bit hesitant in the presence of the assembled officials. "— Tracey thought I should let you know that Mr. Kowalski has resigned."

The room erupted in laughter. Kincaid waved his hand for silence, but was still smiling. "Sorry. Ron quits fairly regularly."

"Yes, sir, that's what Tracey said. But this time he's clearing out his office. He's taken a senior analyst position with NBC, and Mila's going with him. He'll probably be finished packing in less than half an hour."

Kincaid's face paled. He leaned back in his chair and put his hands to his temples. After a moment he leaned forward again and pulled his notes together, putting them in a folder. He looked over to Peter without a word.

Peter nodded. "I've got it here, boss. Good luck."

Kincaid handed his folder to Peter, rose from the table, and headed to the outer office, holding the door for Sarah. Once outside the meeting room, he asked her, "How did you happen to be down there?"

She held out her lists again. "I was trying to get the AIDS banquet list to him. Apparently there's no one left down there."

Kincaid rubbed his chin. "I have an awful feeling that's right."

He looked to Tracey, who without a word, held out her hand to Sarah, who handed Tracey the lists.

Tracey scanned them, flipping through pages. Then she looked up at Kincaid. "I'll have something for you just in case."

"Me?" Kincaid's eyebrows went up.

"Regular Monday press briefing at 10:30. Two hours." She paused. "Unless you'd like Mr. Bailey's people to take it."

Kincaid scowled. "Yeah. Thanks. Just in case." He headed down the hall.

After he was gone, Tracey swiveled back to Sarah. "Glad you caught this. It could have been much worse."

"Will he talk Mr. Kowalski out of leaving?"

"You said Mila's going, too?" Tracey asked.

Sarah nodded.

"Probably not, then. Ron and Mila have been kind of an item for a while." Tracey was shaking her head. "And if he's been offered such a senior position, I can't imagine why he would stay around here for more abuse." She sighed. "But Mr. Kincaid's going to try. Maybe he'll get Ron to delay a few days, or a few hours at least." Tracey glanced over toward the meeting room. "Who's got the meeting?"

"Peter," Sarah replied.

"Good."

* * *

At 10:30, the White House press room was ready. Every chair was occupied, and more reporters stood in the side. Altogether there were probably fifty percent more people than city fire code permitted.

David Kincaid entered exactly on time. A murmur rose from reporters. Several of them still watched the hallway expectantly. Kincaid strode to the podium after placing a stack of handouts on the table by the door. "Good morning. I have two announcements and three clarifications. After that, I will be glad to take your questions."

Murmuring grew louder. Looking about sternly, Kincaid paused until the room grew quiet.

"First, on behalf of our entire staff office, I want to offer our heartfelt congratulations to Ron Kowalski, who has this morning accepted a position of senior news analyst for National Broadcasting Company. Ron will be sorely missed by all of us." Kincaid paused, then grinned as he fumbled through his pile of notes. "Trust me, I'm missing him already."

Nervous laughter swept the room.

"Most of you have complained from time to time about Ron's ability to answer your questions obscurely and ambiguously. We relied on him for that, and he was a master. I will note for the record that all of you seemed to get the answers you needed by decoding his complex responses. He has been and will continue to be a dedicated public servant, committed to truth. Some might think he is on the 'other side' now. I do not. I believe he will be telling the same story, just from a different perspective.

"We have not chosen a successor to Ron at this time." He looked up from his notes and pointed to the table beside the door he had entered. "If you're interested, or know someone who is, please leave your résumé over there. If Ron allows it, we will be hosting an appreciation reception for him. Tracey will post particulars in the ready room.

"Second announcement, and I'm sorry this was delayed: as you know, the International AIDS and HIV Symposium will gather in Washington next month. It will showcase the — unfortunately — few triumphs in the war on this scourge and highlight many challenges remaining. The White House will host a dinner and reception for some notable warriors in that struggle. I have summaries of the invited luminaries with brief references to what they have done in service to mankind.

"Next some clarifications. First, the Snake River flows through more states than Idaho, as a number of you pointed out, and we have no intention of removing that river from Wyoming, Oregon, or Washington. The reference was specifically to restoration of fisheries in Nez Perce National Forest Hell's Canyon stretch of the Snake.

"Second, our contribution to Somali reconstruction effort is one point five 'B,' billion, dollars, not 'M,' million, which would have been totally inadequate, wouldn't it?

"Third, President Miller will be visiting the Kentucky State Fair in August, not July."

Kincaid closed his folder of notes. "That's all I have on my list. Now, what's on your minds?"

Kincaid had observed long ago the intensity of a press briefing could be reliably predicted from the number and vigor of hands rising at the beginning of the briefing. Today all hands shot up as one. He took a deep breath and pointed to the senior correspondent.

The reporter from *The Times* rose. "Mr. Kincaid, is it true Ron Kowalski was pushed out of his office by Vice President Bailey?"

"No. Ron Kowalski has been attached to the President, not the Vice President, and anyone who knows Ron knows that no one pushes him anywhere. He left because he had an offer to do work at the top of his field with better technology, more appropriate compensation, and a much, much nicer office. I hope to visit him when he settles in. I understand the coffee's pretty good over there."

Kincaid pointed to a second reporter in the middle of the room. Several in the vicinity pointed to themselves, uncertain of whom he meant to select. "Sorry. I'm not so familiar with your names as Ron was. The woman with beige sweater."

"Yes, sir. To follow up, it's been obvious for some time Vice President Bailey has been systematically dismantling President Miller's press apparatus. Isn't this, in reality, a final blow?"

Kincaid tried to conceal his annoyance. "That's a question for Ron Kowalski, but you're here, I'm here, and we're having a press briefing. Whether an apparatus is in place or not, we are communicating quite freely."

"But the President has no spokesman now."

Kincaid crossed his arms. "I am the President's spokesman for the moment. Other tasks for which I have responsibility won't permit me to do this forever, but if you have a question, comment, or complaint, I assure you I have the President's ear."

She nodded and shrugged.

He pointed to his left. "Young man with red tie." Three reporters glanced down; two of them were wearing blue ties.

"Sir, can you give us an update on the Vice Presidential scandal?"

Kincaid chuckled. "No, and I'm not beating my dog any more — in fact, I've never had a dog. Nice try, though. In regard to our investigation of Ben Jacobs's report, it has consumed considerable time and resources." Jacobs, sitting in row seven, looked up at once from his notes at mention of his name. "Three members of my staff have been evaluating his report. So far, I've learned more than I ever thought I'd know about pipeline theory, and I've come to appreciate anew how industrious and well-connected the Vice President's family is, but we have found no wrongdoing by Vice President Bailey … in complete agreement with the actual contents of Mr.

Jacobs's massive report." Kincaid looked at Jacobs. "Our study should wrap up soon, perhaps within a week. If anyone has information of which we are unaware, you've got our phone numbers."

He pointed to his left. As a practiced politician, he had the ability to stand outside his body and watch himself, making sure his choreography fitted the audience's needs. "Next."

"Mr. Kincaid, could you give us your impression of the Vice President's mood at this time? And are you in a good working relationship with him?"

Kincaid paused, studying the reporter. Then he looked around the room briefly. "How many of you have been covering me since my House days?"

Five hands rose.

"One tradition I've developed over — gee, I guess — decades is to partition my press time into two segments, one for matters of substance and fact, and another for what I'll call 'personality stuff.' It's not so much either is more important or profound, but personality stuff can't be documented, voted on, or funded. After cameras and microphones are off, we can gather up here off this podium and talk about personality stuff. When video and sound are on, I only intend to talk about official matters." He looked for the five who had raised their hands. "Hasn't it worked out pretty well over the years?"

All five nodded in agreement.

"My relationship with Vice President Bailey falls into the 'personality stuff' category. If you're interested, I'll be here afterward."

The reporter smiled. "But who decides what category a question falls in?"

"In this room, I do. This is my show. When I'm in your studio, you make the rules, and I follow them." He watched the reporter for a bit. "Since I didn't answer your first question, you still have a turn."

"Sir, can you enlighten us on the White House's turnabout on the AIDS banquet?"

"Turnabout?" Kincaid asked.

"We were led to believe the White House had cancelled it for fear of offending various religious groups," the reporter continued.

"I don't know who led you to believe that, but this White House has done more than any other — ever — in taking a leadership role in the fight against this and many other global pandemics. Reality check — look at our budget, our truest proof of all. We have increased real dollars contributions to research and outreach every year since taking office. If anyone questions the President's commitment, I would remind them that his own brilliant daughter is the gathering's official host. As far as various religious groups are concerned, I'm not aware of a single major religious group being left out of our programs. Many of America's churches, synagogues, mosques, and other houses of worship are central to this most compassionate mission."

The reporter responded. "Dr. Paul Richards of the Crusade for Moral Clarity has described any involvement with the Conference as 'making a deal with the devil.'"

"Did he? I was not aware of that. I would invite Dr. Richards to be a part of our efforts to heal the sick. If he has a better way, I hope he will present it — with clarity."

Kincaid's response set off a buzz. He waited for chatter to die down and selected the next reporter. He tried his best to select a diverse mix of media, genders, ethnicities, countries of origin. "Ron always made this look easy. I've got to ask him how he chose whom to call on."

"Mr. Kincaid, the governor of California has expressed alarm at deteriorating economic conditions in his state. Other governors are echoing his concerns. The President had given assurances that our government was taking those concerns seriously. What is the White House doing to act on Governor Barnes' predicament?"

Kincaid looked again at Jacobs. "Ben, your program really rearranged most of my days."

Ben Jacobs put out his hands, as if to surrender, but said nothing.

"The same people who were tasked with checking on our Vice President have also been tasked with responding to the stresses reported by the states. To date, the President has released some money from the States' Assistance Fund. This move was in part a demonstration of the seriousness with which we view any potential downturn, but also an attempt to buy us time as we study this situation. If that sounds like a bureaucratic delay, it is. The last thing we want to do is act hastily, maybe imprudently, in ways that could make matters worse. There is a lot of money involved — your money — and we want a solution, not a patch. I can assure the good people of California and other states we are paying attention and we have some very bright and dedicated people working to make sure every American can reach her or his potential.

"Additionally, I was meeting with the Secretary of the Treasury this morning to see what we can do about better numbers to support our efforts at getting the economy running smoothly at all levels. Part of our challenge is that the data upon which we base our programs is often slow in reaching us and incomplete. We're working on that, too."

The press briefing continued for another twenty-seven questions until Kincaid called time at eleven-thirty. Six questions were deferred to the personality session, which continued until just before noon.

Kincaid ambled back to his office, glancing at his watch to verify it was lunchtime. Trying to be objective, he judged his performance had been adequate, but not memorable. Probably for the best. Priority one, he needed to get a new press secretary. He enjoyed the back and forth with reporters but the exchange had consumed half a day he could not spare.

On his return trip, Kincaid stopped by the east dining room and picked up a healthy sandwich — tiny salad greens and some cheese on whole grain bread. As he approached the staff dining room, he could hear a raucous discussion in progress.

Actually, calling it the staff dining room was a stretch. This room was where they did almost everything not requiring an elegant polished table. The staff dining room hosted their regular meals, internal meetings, parties, presentations, and anything else of an informal bent. Here the table was smaller, and there were more chairs of a cheaper grade. The chairs didn't match.

Kincaid entered with his sandwich and fruit drink to stumbling applause and some bravos voiced through stuffed mouths. He shook his head as he smiled. Peter, James, and Matt each had variations on a burger theme. Tracey and Kathy ate garden salads, Tracey with her usual blue cheese dressing and Kathy with her usual French. Anna dined on a salad with perhaps a vinaigrette. Sarah demolished a cheeseburger along with a large stack of French fries and a bowl of ice cream.

"Was I as bad as I think?" Kincaid asked.

Everyone hooted away the question. Peter spoke for the group. "It was pretty awesome, sir. We watched it down here and some commentary afterward."

"You got tape that quickly?"

"It was on live," Matt replied.

"Really? Why?"

Matt continued, "Let me back up just a little. It was on Wolfe Network live at first. It seems someone told them Ron's office was empty and his briefings would be cancelled. When you showed up, the other networks added coverage."

Kincaid had not yet touched his sandwich. "That doesn't make sense. Ron wouldn't do that. Anything in the analysis worth mentioning?"

"Except for Wolfe, it was pretty straight reporting of Ron leaving and investigations continuing. Wolfe went on for a while about turmoil at the White House and a growing conflict with evangelical Christianity."

Kincaid took a quick bite of his sandwich and continued after a drink. "Great. I'm glad they have their usual laser-like grasp on reality."

James coughed and spoke up. "I don't think lasers have grasps."

"Even light sabers?"

Matt corrected him. "Light sabers aren't lasers. They're energy weapons, but not lasers."

Kincaid was grinning. "Darn. I wanted some adjective with 'laser' in it."

"Laser-like focus?" Anna offered.

"Do lasers have focus?"

Everyone looked at Matt, who put down his burger. "Hmm. Collimated beam, very sharp. It's actually a core characteristic of lasers. Yeah, I guess you could say 'laser-like focus.'"

"Good. I'm glad Wolfe has its usual laser-like focus on reality." Kincaid continued with his sandwich.

"However, I don't expect the laser lobby will be pleased with your analogy," Matt suggested to a chorus of 'boo's.

"Well, thank-yous all around to Kathy and Sarah for the banquet material. Without them I wouldn't have had much to say."

Kathy spoke up. "They were all Sarah's."

"Really? Very impressive. Careful we don't make our reporters lazy. It was rather well annotated, I notice. When did you have time to do all this?"

Sarah smiled. "Thanks. I finished it up this weekend."

Kincaid frowned. "Very diligent, but don't overdo it. We all need rest, too."

"Rest will be this coming weekend. I'll be off Friday for a family gathering," Sarah responded.

"Oh, now I'm going to look bad. I need tobacco research by Monday. Can you hand off any to someone else?"

Smiling, she pulled out a thick report from her briefcase and handed it to him.

Kincaid flipped through her report quickly, rotating material sideways from time to time to scan a chart or table. "Well, have a great weekend. Where are you going?"

Anna grinned. "She won't tell us. Big secret."

"No, it's not. It's just a private family gathering down at a beach in Georgia. When I get away, I like to be away," Sarah said to Kincaid.

Kincaid chuckled. "Was that what I was hearing down the hall?"

Matt spoke this time. "No, that was earlier. Sarah was making disparaging remarks about the Medal of Freedom winners."

Kincaid confronted Sarah in mock indignation. "But it's our nation's highest civilian honor." His cryptic smile indicated he had his own doubts.

"I wasn't exactly disparaging the winners. Not all of them. Some of them, yes. There are plenty of good people on the list, but a lot of losers — losers who were losers when they were winners … of the medal."

Kathy rested her face in her hands. "That's why I love working with her."

Sarah had a French fry in her hand, waving it like a stick. "I mean, really, look at the list — if you can find a copy. None of the usual people around here even had an up to date copy. I had to go to the web to find it. Look back at the honorees. Some of them are even in jail … or should be." She pulled her list out and read some names. "For instance, 2004 … Tenet, Franks, Bremer. Good grief. We're still digging out from messes they made. Half of these people wouldn't pass the rest stop test."

Sarah continued to study the list while the room fell silent. As they looked at one another, everyone seemed afraid to ask the obvious question.

"OK, I think I'm the senior person here," said Kincaid. "What exactly is the 'rest stop test'?"

Sarah raised her head from her list. "Ah, when we were little, my family would drive down to the National Seashore and we drove the New Jersey Turnpike. I was a handful back then."

"Back then…?" Anna asked.

"Hey, this is my story. Anyway, my dad was always looking for ways to keep us occupied on the trip. One year he had a prize of ten bucks to the first one of us who could memorize all the names of rest stops on the New Jersey turnpike and tell something about the person each was named for. I beat my big brother, and I still remember them to this day: Lombardi, Hamilton, Edison, Cleveland, Kilmer, Molly Pitcher (just one of only two women to be honored), Stockton, Wilson, Cooper, Whitman, Clara Barton (the other woman), and Fenwick."

Peter had been listening carefully. "I counted three women. What about Joyce Kilmer?"

"Ah!" Sarah shook her fry violently until it broke. "Almost everyone thinks that, especially since they only know the 'Trees' poem. But he was a guy. So there."

"And this has to do with Presidential Medal of Freedom … exactly how?" Kincaid insisted.

"Oh, yeah, right. My point was when a politician names a rest stop on the Turnpike, they're going to be really careful whom they pick. Their choice will be in front of the whole public, every class, every hour of every day. Millions of people are going to stop in to get a bite to eat or take a leak, and they're going to see names. Any politician who names a rest stop after some jerk is going to have it in their face forever. There are consequences. With the Medal of Freedom, except for some alumni magazines maybe, their story is mostly buried on page one thousand seventeen. No real consequences. So I'm just saying the Medal would be more meaningful if we applied the rest stop test."

Kincaid agreed, "Good point. Just how did this come up?"

Peter answered, "Richards."

"Ah. I hope someone informed Dr. Tyler I was not happy about it either."

Sarah put the fry into her mouth. "Yes, sir, and I still say it's a black mark on the Medal. Richards is a homophobic, anti-Semitic, misogynistic demon and has no business being held up as a positive role model."

"Succinctly put. While that may or may not all be true, he's being honored for schools his organization set up. They've achieved some amazing things as far as test scores go. Academy Christiani are the ones often held up whenever we get back into voucher and testing debates."

"Hmm." Sarah dipped another fry in ketchup.

"Skeptical?" Kincaid inquired.

"I've tutored some Academy graduates. I wasn't impressed."

"You're the numbers person. They take the same tests as public school kids do."

"I know. I don't understand it."

"Anyway, that's why he's receiving the Presidential Medal of Freedom. Vice President Bailey nominated him and the President approved it. The Medal doesn't need anything more." Kincaid returned to his sandwich.

Sarah frowned as she pulled out another fry and used it to stir her catsup. "Still, it's a black mark — in my opinion. Sooner or later, someone's going to have to step up to him."

Kincaid sighed. "Again, I can't disagree. But I know I wouldn't want to be the one taking him on. He can be ruthless."

Sarah continued, "Yeah, I know. Kathy told me about The Devil's Gallery. I went there, and it's creepy. How does he get away with it, anyway? He's a non-profit, and his site is so extreme partisan."

Kincaid raised a cautionary finger. "That's an example of how smart he is, boys and girls. Everyone keeps calling it 'his site' or 'the Crusade's site.' It's not. It looks like it's his. The motif is the same, and links are identical. But it belongs to one of his parishioners. It's completely private and completely legal without affecting the Crusade's tax status. Believe me; we've checked. There are three of our important congressional allies in the fights of their lives, and all three are on that Gallery. Even if there were something I could do, I don't know if I'd have the stomach for a fight with him."

A Marine appeared in the doorway. Sarah looked up to see it was Corporal Tull carrying a message board. She watched as Kincaid put down his sandwich and took the board. He flipped through messages, initialing each and making an occasional notation. Mid-way through the stack, he stopped and read one message twice. "Did Mr. Johnson see this?"

"No, sir, Mr. Johnson's out and won't be back until fifteen hundred."

"Ah." Kincaid added more notes. "Please be sure he does."

"Yes, sir."

As Kincaid continued to scan the message traffic, Tull caught sight of Sarah.

His eyes were clear ice blue. She broke into a grin and then tried to stifle it. Her effort was only partially successful, leaving her mouth with a friendly but mangled expression. Tull's own grin propagated a set of dimples on his cheeks. Kincaid handed back the board.

"Thank you, sir." Tull straightened smartly, and left the room.

Sarah watched him until he was gone, then glanced around the room.

No one had been paying attention. "Is Corporal Tull really a corporal?" she asked.

"No," Matt responded, "he's really Generalissimo Frito but we call him Corporal Tull to protect his cover."

Kincaid addressed Matt first, "I'm sure there's a good reason for her question." Then he returned to Sarah. "Jeff Tull is indeed a corporal in the United States Marine Corps. Dare I ask why the question?"

Sarah had French fries in each hand, waving them in unison as she continued. "Well, I was reviewing rank symbols, and sergeants outrank corporals, right?"

"Last time I checked, yes," Kincaid agreed.

"It just seemed to me he was a bit older than some sergeants down in the security office. That's all. Just curious."

"Yes, good point, and a good story. Jeff Tull graduated from the University of Illinois Business School and was working in Human Resources at a big Chicago firm — Jackson and Gallagher, I think — when he began to feel a need for more purpose in his life. In the end he left and enlisted in the Marines. So, yes, he is a bit older than some of his sergeants. And even some officers. I'd say he's about your age."

She raised her eyebrows. "He left Jackson and Gallagher for the Marines?"

Kincaid set down what remained of his sandwich, rested his elbows on the table, and placed his fingertips together. "OK, this is for everyone. Don't ever — ever — assume a career in the military, even starting at the most junior enlisted level, is a step down. There are many motivations for their choice — lots of them noble in the extreme. Our lives are in their hands every day, especially around here. They serve with dedication and distinction. And in the case of the Marines, they serve with single-minded devotion."

Sarah nodded.

Everyone finished lunch and proceeded to afternoon tasks.

* * *

Thursday, April 3, 2014

The group meeting in the lab office had already twice come close to shouting.

Their eighth-floor office was a simple affair, a rectangular room with four desks, each with a set of bookshelves. The technicians occupied three desks to the left as one entered and Jack occupied the corner desk on the right. All desks were the same size and made of the same material. Along the wall, between Jack's desk and the door, was a large bank of filing cabinets containing fourteen years of test results, acquired for the researchers their facility supported. At the far end room was a small refrigerator.

The office space was functional throughout. The only concessions to human occupants were myriad family pictures and meager bric-a-brac on desks or hung on corkboards at the back of their desks. The room boasted no windows save one in the single door. Harsh fluorescent lights typical of offices of this vintage illuminated the room.

Jack was firm. "I don't care how closely you think you can monitor heated stir plates, they're not to be used for stirring acetonitrile. It's too volatile a solvent and much too flammable."

"Those stir plates are rated for organic solvents." Leslie stood by her desk, closest to the door. "That's why we bought that particular model. By warming the solution, we cut two hours off prep every day."

"They're rated for *polar* organics — ethanol, propanol, pyridine. Not ether or acetonitrile."

Leslie's cheeks were flushed, her demeanor sharp. "You don't trust us to do our jobs. You never do. We've told you — we stay with our work. We don't neglect anything. We save two hours a day using authorized equipment doing it exactly the way other labs do. We've got a lot of work to do, you know. You don't have to face everyone coming in here wanting to know if their samples are ready."

"Why not? Why aren't you sending them to me? That's part of my job. If you're getting grief from other labs, send them to me! Do it. If they can't understand, I'll talk to the investigators themselves. My job is to run this lab safely and properly. It's your job, too. You don't have to jump every time another tech comes in and says they want something right now. If you're not comfortable telling them, … send … them … to … me."

Leslie folded her arms.

Patricia spoke up. "When you micromanage our work like this, it's really discouraging. Every time we come up with an innovation, it's either shot down or tied up in so much paperwork or research it's not worth it."

"This is hardly micromanaging. I'm responsible for this lab — for its efficiency and its safety. If your workload is too heavy, we'll get another tech. Or we'll set up another station. We can do that. We have resources."

Elsa jumped in. "But not enough for a decent raise."

It was Jack's turn to fold his arms. "Is that what this is about?"

"In part, yes." Leslie said. "We're expected to comply with all this and we do. But what do we get in return? The same pay as last year after you take into account cost of living."

"I was hoping we were past salaries. I really was. We've been over the pay thing for hours and hours. You've always been recognized for your good work by being paid at the top end of the salary scale for your positions. Like I laid out last week, we've been given a certain amount for salary next year. It included raises, which you all received. I recommended the same percentage for myself as I did for you, and this was the first time in three years I've put in any increase for myself. The Institute's endowment has not done well this past year. There isn't any more money for salary increases."

Elsa spoke. "You just said we could hire another person. If we've got money for that, why not more for us?"

Jack hung his head as he spoke, his voice trembling just a little. "We don't have money for another technician in the budget we were given. I meant if we honestly need more help for our workload, I would work to get our budget increased to accommodate another worker. … if we really need another."

"But you won't go to bat for those of us already here." Leslie's lips pressed together in a thin line.

"This conversation is over. If there are no other items, this meeting is finished." Jack had difficulty getting his words out.

Leslie wasn't finished. "You know, this is not the only place needing our skills."

Jack pointed toward the door.

"Fuck you!" Leslie unfolded her arms and marched from the room.

Elsa and Patricia looked at each other.

"Any other items?" Jack folded his arms again.

Elsa shook her head and got up, heading for the lab.

Jack sat back down at his desk. He raised his hand and watched it for a moment. It was shaking. He laid his hand on his desk. A pile of papers and unopened envelopes stared back at him. One envelope was from the Institute's health benefits administrator. Jack shut his eyes. "That's not going to be good news. Someone would have called if I had any good news." He set the health benefits envelope to the side and continued through the stack, pulling out new orders or charges into one pile, dropping advertisements into his recycle bin.

Jack was almost finished with his sorting when he picked up an envelope from Division of Fines and Collections of San Diego County, addressed to him by name. He paused a moment then opened it. For the first time in quite a while, he smiled. It was a copy of citation 08934872 for forty-five dollars for violation of County Code V-1748, Nudity Outside of Official Zone. He chuckled, almost laughed out loud. "Well, that was forty-five dollars well spent. Jenn's going to love it."

He looked up at the clock — five after eleven. The University Lecture started at eleven. The research was an area of particular interest since it involved overriding exon control in specific disease states. He set the citation down on top of urgent mail in the center of his desk, got up, and dashed for the elevator.

11 THE CALM

Friday, April 4, 2014

Laura met the Montgomery County sheriff in his office. In a jurisdiction of this size and complexity, such a meeting would have normally been impossible to set up, but Laura had announced herself as Dr. James Garrette's daughter. The officer managed to adjust his schedule to fit her in between other meetings. She had considered bringing Charlie, since he was the source of her information, but had decided against it. Charlie, despite his critical observations, was prone to introduce a certain element of chaos into meetings.

"How may I help you today, Ms. Garrette?" The sheriff was all business, but well mannered. His people skills had kept him in office through five tumultuous election cycles.

"I'd like to find out more about the replacement of the 911 call center workers with robots."

"Excuse me?" The sheriff looked at Laura in disbelief.

Laura had trusted Charlie's information. Every time he came up with these conspiratorial stories, the stories panned out. Some day, though, he would be wrong. "I'm told that the County has contracted for five Adminatron 541 units to replace twenty 911 dispatchers."

The sheriff shook his head. "I don't think so. That's my department and I certainly would know about it. With all due respect, I think you've been misinformed."

Laura sat for a moment, frowning. "So there was no meeting in the County Executive's office last Thursday afternoon approving a contract with Brisbane Technologies for five Adminatron 541s?"

His expression changed quickly. The Sheriff's ongoing feud with the County Executive was the stuff of legend. "I hope to hell you're wrong. Excuse my language. Give me a moment, please." He leaned over to his phone. "Linda, get me Bob over in procurement." He turned back to Laura. "I'm being totally honest here, Ms. Garrette. I don't know anything about this. Where did you hear about it?"

Laura hesitated, and then offered a truthful non-answer. "I work with several food banks in the area, and we're getting a lot of new people, including some from the call centers."

"We did have to reduce staff because of the budget crunch, but not because they're being replaced by —"

The phone rang and he picked it up, saving Laura the task of explaining Charlie. "Yeah, Bob. Sheriff here. Do you know anything about some answering machines being purchased for the call center?" The sheriff's frown turned angry. "When the hell was someone going to let me know about this? … I don't give a shit. That's my department. No one consulted me on this, and I don't know anything about it. He's messing with my people, and he's talking about changing the security operations of this county with some goddamn machines I've never heard of. … Yeah, I know you're not the one. Sorry. It just pisses me off to be hearing this first from a social worker who's already catching the consequences. … OK. Listen, Bob, sorry to fly off the handle. I appreciate your being honest with me. I'll keep your name out of it. … Yeah. Sure. Hey, let's catch a beer tonight. … Yeah. Meet ya there about five-thirty. Thanks again."

He gently set down the receiver, glared at the phone, and then looked up at Laura. "Ma'am, I owe you one. That kinda blindsided me. I'm sure you've got plenty of reasons to be upset about it, but I've got a reason to be upset too — a special one. One of my Guard buddies was killed over in Kuwait last year. His widow got a job at the call center in part because of the veterans' preference. I'll march into Hell to be sure she doesn't lose her job over this. And that goes for the others, too. You have my word on it."

"Yes, sir. Thank you." Laura replied.

"Are you with the County?"

"No, just a volunteer coordinator." She handed him her card.

"Just a volunteer, huh? Says here 'National Coordinator'." He grinned. "Hey, when I called you a social worker on the line with Bob, that was a compliment. After all, my wife's a social worker. But 'volunteer coordinator' is good, too. We need all the help we can get these days." He handed Laura his card in return. "If you need anything in my department, this is my direct line." He pointed to the second number on the card. "It goes straight to Linda's desk and bypasses the switchboard. Are you good at yelling and screaming?"

Laura grinned. "I've been known to raise a little rabble. Why?"

"When this goes public — which I guarantee will be in just a few hours — there're going to be plenty of public meetings, and a lot of noise might be helpful. I've been the good cop all my life, but this is getting out of control."

She reached out and shook his hand. "Thank you for your time, Sheriff. We've got each other's contact info now. As they say, I think this is the start of a beautiful friendship."

* * *

Jack returned from the lecture a little after two-thirty. The presentation had been weaker than the title implied, but he had stayed around to talk with the researchers to see what progress was being made in the area of exon-regulated control. He didn't learn anything new, but had gotten a good lunch out of the exchange.

Back at the office, he looked around. The three techs were in the lab. "I could go next door and get into another argument and start the weekend upset, or I could leave early and spend a longer than usual evening with my wife. Let me think about that. Gee, hard choice. And now I'm talking to myself." He turned to leave, then turned abruptly back to his desk. There were no new messages. He went through the pile of urgent mail, frowned, and scratched his head. Then he caught sight of an envelope near the edge of his desk, smiled, and reached back for the citation. It had a stain from a coffee cup. Jack thought he had taken the cup with him to the lecture. He picked up the citation and then looked again at the top of the urgent mail. He shook his head. "I'm losing it."

Jack walked to the parking garage without saying goodbye to anyone.

* * *

David Kincaid looked up from his desk. Four-forty. If he could get that last bit of information, he'd be completely ready for Monday. He got up and walked down the hall to the office where Sarah worked. He looked over to Sarah's side of the office, her desk covered with stacks of papers and bound reports. Amidst the paper tide were a couple of coffee cups and an opened bag of ginger snaps. The wall was festooned with flip chart sheets inscribed with cryptic flow charts; circles and boxes connected with lines and arrows bearing numbers. The scene had a certain psychotic aura about it.

He turned to Kathy. "Have you seen Sarah? I wanted to take the tobacco research home this weekend, but I don't want to rummage through her wonderland."

"Remember, she's gone south for the weekend, sir? I can call her on her cell, though."

"No, no, I'll get it Monday. I'll just leave a note. I remember now. She deserves some peace and quiet. Both of you do."

Kathy smiled. "Thank you, Mr. Kincaid. I'm good. I've got a quiet weekend. Picasso exhibit at the National Gallery. Ron got me a VIP pass before he left."

"Good deal," Kincaid smiled. "Enjoy. See you Monday."

From Kathy's office, the garage exit was one hallway away. Kincaid headed in the opposite direction, traveling half-way across the White House basement. He turned and headed back to the parking lot along the south corridor two doors beyond Peter's office. He stopped at the doorway and looked in. Anna was busy writing on a legal pad. Her desk was mostly cleared. A vase of gerbera daisies sat to one side. The wall behind her was decorated with the kinds of prints one buys in Paris near Notre Dame. The books at the bottom of her bookcase appeared to be State Department manuals, but the top shelf contained smaller volumes including several very slender ones. Poetry? She wore a plum colored sweater, very elegant over her black blouse.

"Have a pleasant weekend, Ms. Colbert."

She looked up and smiled. She seemed to Kincaid to smile with her eyes as well as her mouth. Her lipstick, a subtle shade of rose, had obviously been selected to complement her sweater. "And you as well, sir. Do you have plans?"

"The usual. Getting ready for Monday's press briefing. Church on Sunday and maybe the farmers' market. You?"

"Quiet. Church on Sunday. Maybe take in the trail along the canal."

"Enjoy. See you Monday."

"Good bye, sir."

When Kincaid arrived at the garage, he stood for a moment, alone before the heavy door. "Are you out of your mind? You're fifty-five years old. Get a grip." All through the Friday capital traffic, he could not purge the images of gerberas and rose lips.

12 RECKONING

Monday, April 7, 2014

David Kincaid drove south on 13th Street from his apartment in northwest Washington. He enjoyed this drive down the broad boulevard past old brownstones and new, overpriced condos. He especially enjoyed the view at the intersection with Massachusetts Avenue, where the street rose and he could glimpse the Washington Monument and the rooftops of some of the Smithsonian museums bordering the Mall, a classic view of his beloved city.

Today, however, his thoughts were not on the view, but on his press briefing at ten. Peter had gathered about twenty-five résumés of potential press secretaries, but it would be weeks before they would complete the selection process. In the meantime Kincaid was determined to keep the weekly briefing on track with the same informal rigor that had characterized Ron's stewardship.

His eyes on the road ahead, Kincaid practiced his answers to expected questions.

"'No. The Government' is not telling people what to grow. We are merely' … no … 'but we are certainly exercising our responsibility to inform the shepherds …' … too quaint; need something else … 'America's hard-working farmers that the future of tobacco farming is extinction …' too fancy? I like extinction ... … 'and we are offering the services that taxpaying farmer expect … Yes, maybe even demand ... to help them achieve an orderly transition to profitable, sustainable, and healthful agricultural products.' Yeah. That's good. We expect a …'"

Kincaid broke off and shook his head. "Jeez, I need Sarah's numbers '… percent drop in demand each year. That's *x* number of farmers who will lose their land if they have not made the transition. We will not stand idly by and watch that happen …' That's good."

He rounded the final bend, and the White House loomed into view.

"Uh oh."

The sidewalk was lined with reporters filing urgent "live from the White House" pieces. Antenna trucks were parked across the street. Whatever was going on had developed since five this morning. National Public Radio had delivered a fairly bland report back then. He switched on his car radio, but it offered no help. The story on at the moment covered the ailing British monarch.

As Kincaid approached the entrance to the parking lot, a number of unaffiliated reporters recognized his car and dashed in his direction. He kept the windows up and slowed his approach. They were shouting questions he couldn't make out and trying to get him to roll down the window. He eased through the throng and waited as two Marines gently but firmly persuaded the crowd to step back. Once inside the gate, he made his way quickly to his parking spot, where Frank was waiting.

Kincaid got out and grabbed his brief case. "I missed something. What's going on?"

"Not completely sure, sir. I only caught a fragment of it on the radio on the way in. Apparently one of the staff, Sarah Tyler, was on the news."

"Is she OK?"

"I don't think anything happened to her. Something about her activities over the weekend. Something about being nude."

Kincaid turned to Frank as he fumbled for his identification. "Really?"

"That's all I know, sir." Frank turned to look at the line of reporters. "They're sure making a big deal of it, though. Must be something more."

The two men finished the security check and walked quickly toward the staff area.

Kincaid pointed ahead. "Go see Peter. See what he's got and what we need. I'll check in with Tracey and meet you there as soon as I can."

They split up. Kincaid entered his outer office, where Tracey was waiting for him. She had on her 'serene' face. Her hands were together in front of her. Kincaid took a deep breath and willed himself to relax.

She spoke, "Sarah was featured on Ben Jacobs' report this morning. Apparently the annual family retreat is at a naturist resort. Someone took home videos and gave them to Jacobs, who then put them on about seven o'clock this morning. Sounds like it was a snotty little report."

"Does that have anything to do with the reporters out there?" Kincaid waved his arm in the general direction of outside.

"Oh, yeah. Seems several groups are very upset about our decadence. The Crusade was especially harsh on her, as I understand."

Kincaid frowned. "Did she do anything wrong? I mean, she wasn't stripping on national TV or anything like that, was she?"

"No, sir, I'm certain of that. I think the press has had a slow news week or something. They're all over it."

"This is ridiculous. In the first place, it's an egregious invasion of privacy."

Tracey looked back at him in silence.

"Right. Where's Sarah now?"

Tracey pointed to Kincaid's office. He had not noticed that the door was closed. "She's crying. Very upset. I don't think 'devastated' would be overstating it. I talked with her a bit. She was just having fun on a family outing."

Kincaid turned toward his office. "Have Peter get me some briefing points on naturist resorts please. See if anyone has seen the video and can give me a short summary."

Kincaid knocked gently on his door and went in, closing it behind him.

Sarah was sitting in one of the large chairs in front of his desk. Her eyes were red, and she clutched a tissue that should have been replaced some time ago. He saw no trace of the confident, outspoken Fellow of Friday.

She looked up at him. Her lips quivered. "I'm so sorry, sir."

Kincaid avoided his desk. Instead, he pulled up another chair beside her, took the box of tissues from his desk, and handed them to her. "I'm not aware of anything you've done to be sorry for. What happened?"

She spoke with difficulty, halting to catch her breath from time to time. "We were just at the park, the same as we've done every year I can remember. We were just playing volleyball. That's all. The same as we do every year. Somebody must have had a camera. I don't know who or why. Cameras are against the rules there. No one should have been taking pictures. But they were. And now they're on TV. All over the TV."

He felt torn between his urge to offer advice or to simply listen. "I'm sorry. You're being exposed to the ugly underside of this city. He had no right to put you on. I can't imagine what he was thinking. Your vacation games are none of his business. I ... I just don't understand."

"He was laughing at me."

Kincaid felt a flush of anger.

Sarah began sobbing, her voice a hoarse squeak. "And he called me a whore!"

Kincaid blanched. "Ben Jacobs called you a whore?"

Sarah wiped her eyes while shaking her head. "No, Richards. On national television. He called me a whore. I heard it. My family's heard it by now."

He felt his arms heavy and a rising stomach-churning anger. He closed his eyes. Had she been in the room, Tracey would have advised him to breathe slowly and wait before saying anything. He followed her unspoken advice. When Kincaid felt control returning, he opened his eyes.

A tear rolled off Sarah's cheek.

"You are not a whore. You are a good and loyal servant of the people who has been terribly wronged today."

"Am I being fired?" She pressed her trembling lips together.

Kincaid dropped back in his chair. "No, absolutely not! You've done nothing wrong. You are the one who's been violated by this mess. Did you think we would fire you?"

She held out a small stack of folders that had been in her lap. "Your note said to bring all the stuff I was working on to your office. I thought you were letting me go."

Kincaid looked at the folders, then to Sarah. "No." He took one of the tissues and reached out to dab her eyes. "Oh, no. I see how that must have looked this morning. I put the note on your desk Friday after you were gone. I just needed — actually still need — the report for this morning's briefing. We're putting your plan into action. This morning was going to be the launch. We're not letting you go. We need you more than ever."

Sarah smiled weakly.

"You've got a lot of people here who'll stick up for you. You going to be OK?"

Sarah nodded.

"I still remember some of my first bruisings. I hope this will be of some help. This town has a short memory. The news part will blow over in a day or so. Some of what happened this morning is more serious. I'm not sure what's getting Richards all lathered up. Probably has something to do with the last Jacobs interview. We'll have to do something about what he said. That was totally wrong. I can only imagine that Peter's got something in the works."

Sarah's tears had stopped, and her speech was returning to normal. "I'm just sorry this mess is taking so much time. I know we've got so much to do."

Kincaid scratched his head. "Sometimes things don't go the way we've planned. I'm not going to minimize what's happened to you. We're going to talk about it as much as we need. We may take it up a little later today. The nation's business is going to come sweeping in without much pity on our own situation. You sure you're OK for now?"

She nodded again. "Yes, sir. Thank you. I'm feeling a lot better."

"Talk to Tracey." Kincaid smiled. "That's what I do when I'm bruised. I know people have no idea how important she is in keeping this little patch of the country at peace. The things she's talked me out of …" He shook his head.

Sarah grinned.

"OK. You're going to get a lot of unsolicited advice. I'll start first. You may wish to keep a low profile for a day or so. Sounds like the press knows what you look like, so you may want to have someone take your car to another parking place, and then you can take one of the tunnels that'll get you away from the hubbub here."

"I don't have a car."

"Oh. Do you live close by?"

"No, sir, I have an apartment in Laurel. I take the Metro in."

"Wow. That's seems like quite a commute."

"No, sir, not really. I use the time to get the reports done. It's not so bad. I'm saving for a car, but it'll take a while."

Kincaid could see her relaxing. "What kind of car is our economist looking at?"

She grinned. "I've had my eye on one of those hybrid VWs. Bright yellow. With the flower holder."

Kincaid almost laughed. "That makes sense. Are you close to getting it?"

Sarah shrugged. "It's about twenty-five K. I'll have to wait awhile, but I don't mind. The commute's not that bad. I guess I'll be wondering who's watching now, though."

"Good point. I'll see if we can arrange something until this is old news."

The phone console on his desk buzzed. It was Tracey. "Mr. Kincaid, the President wants to see you right away."

"We're finishing here. I'll be right up."

"Abigail says Mr. Bailey's in with him behaving badly."

Kincaid hung his head. "Right. Thanks."

"I've gotten you in trouble, too, haven't I?" Sarah frowned.

"Not really. If it weren't this, it'd be something else. The Vice President gets upset whenever the Crusade's involved. He's looking to the '16 election, and he considers them a big part of his base. Kinda ironic if you ask me. He's never struck me as a particularly religious man."

Sarah listened quietly.

"But that's another story. I'm talking too much. I've got to go see what's going on upstairs. Tell you what. You know the back way to the briefing room?"

She nodded.

"Go back to the booth before the briefing starts. I'm sure there will be questions about your game. You'll see how we handle these things."

"OK," she said.

Kincaid got up and walked to the door, turning the knob. He paused and looked back at her. "Who won?"

"Sir?"

"The game. Who won?"

"We did. Our team won. Seven-five," she replied.

He nodded. "Good. Congratulations." He turned and left the room, wishing for all the world he had some idea of how he was going to handle the situation.

Tracey was looking through printouts on the table in the outer office.

"How is she?"

"I think she'll be OK. Can you keep an eye on her?"

Tracey nodded.

"Did Peter … ?"

"He was in here an hour early, sir. I've never, ever seen him that furious. Only the second time I've ever heard him use profanity. Something about Dr. Richards. What's going on with him?"

"I have so little information, I'm at a loss. But I think I'm about to find out. Did Peter get anything on the naturist resorts?"

"He's busy with security right now. That's what I'm doing." She opened her arms to the papers on the table. "Want a sun-filled, fun-filled vacation? The resort they went to typically hosts up to two hundred families in summer."

He grinned. "I look paunchy enough in a normal swimsuit. Anything less would be a disgrace to the species. Besides, Myrtle Beach is a little more demure. Wish me luck. I've got to go give the Vice President his sedatives. Do me a favor, please. Get Peter and have the briefing room detachment 'lose' Ben Jacobs's credentials. Put them on my desk."

"Yes, sir. With pleasure," she smiled a wicked smile.

Kincaid walked down the hall, boarded the elevator, and rode alone to the office level. His ID was still in his hand from entering the White House.

Corporal Tull had morning duty and was looking grim as he filled out the inevitable log entries.

The Chief of Staff could already hear muffled arguments from the Oval Office. He finished his check-in and looked over to Abigail.

"Welcome to Monday, Mr. Kincaid," she offered.

He opened the door and stepped into the Oval Office. The President was seated at his desk looking weary. Vice President Bailey paced off to the left, but wheeled around as Kincaid entered.

"You! Can't you keep your little hippie commune down there under control?"

Kincaid ignored the Vice President, and addressed the President. "You sent for me, sir?"

"Yes, David. The Vice President tells me that one of your staff was involved in some sort of sex scandal down in Georgia over the weekend. In my other tasks this morning, I missed the news, and Mr. Bailey has been a bit scant on the details. Can you please enlighten me?"

"I'm not sure, sir." Kincaid alternated his attention between the President and the Vice President. "I'm not aware of any of my staff being involved in a scandal. Dr. Tyler was vacationing with her family at a naturist resort, and some peeping Tom took pictures like it was the girls' locker room in high school and gave it to Ben Jacobs, who showed it on TV this morning."

"What was she doing?" the President asked.

Kincaid replied, "Playing volleyball."

"That's it? Is that illegal?"

"That's it. And no, volleyball's not illegal, at least not in Georgia." Kincaid sensed that the President was unimpressed with the situation.

The Vice President crossed his arms and started walking toward Kincaid. "You have no appreciation for the seriousness of this, do you? We have tried for six years to cultivate the image of the cleanest, purist White House in history. It takes only one sick episode like this to derail everything."

Kincaid turn to the Vice President. "What 'sick episode'? Do you know something I don't?"

"She was prancing around naked on national television, god dammit!"

"She was playing volleyball. Someone filmed them without permission. She's a private citizen, not an elected official, sir. Ben Jacobs had no right to barge into a family outing and post it like that."

The Vice President's face was red, and he made a series of poking motions with his finger. "You're talking about the image of the office of President. What are your plans for damage control here, David?"

"I plan to ignore it to the extent possible except for a long talk with Ben Jacobs."

"Oh, no." The Vice President was shaking his head furiously. "You are going to take this seriously. At a minimum, you are going to fire the little bitch and make it clear we do not condone such lascivious behavior."

"The hell I will! Dr. Tyler has done nothing wrong. The only discipline is going to be exercised on one Ben Jacobs."

The Vice President put his hands on his hips. "Then you will be fired, mister."

The President spoke up. "Jim, you're in my territory. I haven't seen a clear account of what's happened here."

The Vice President turned, pleading. "Mr. President, something has to be done to fix this immediately. I've got a fund-raiser in New Hampshire in ..." — he looked at his watch — "... three hours. I'll be back in the morning. For your sake, this has to be fixed by then. By your leave, sir."

President Miller waved, and the Vice President left the office. They waited until the sounds of the Vice President's quick steps were gone. "David, make this go away. We have too much to do to have a distraction like this. Find out what happened. Don't leave any loose ends. If you have to let her go, do it. The national interests come first. Don't lose sight of that."

"Yes, sir."

Kincaid turned to leave the Oval Office. Only then did he realize that the door had been left open. He walked slowly toward the elevator.

Corporal Tull rose from his seat, standing at attention. His grim look was gone. Kincaid looked around to Abigail. She gave him a quick, determined nod and raised fist, the first time he'd ever seen her do that.

Kincaid had an hour to prepare for his Monday briefing, and he had not yet read Sarah's notes.

By the time Kincaid rode the elevator down and returned to his office, Sarah was gone and Peter was waiting with Kincaid's briefing clipboard.

"What have you got?"

Peter handed him the clipboard. "About Sarah?"

"Of course."

"Plenty of background. None of it reflects badly on her at all. For now, sir, put it out of your mind and concentrate on the briefing. I see you've pulled Jacobs' credentials. What did you have in mind?"

"I don't know. I'll have to wait until I get details. But we can't roll over on this, can we?"

"No, sir. I suggest we don't go much beyond showing our great offense taken, though."

"Right." Kincaid looked over to where Sarah had been sitting. "She brought the tobacco work, but I don't see it."

"I put it on your desk." Peter pointed to the stack of folders. "Executive summary is on top." He looked at his watch. "That's really all you have time for. Want me to get a mike? You can use the earpiece."

Kincaid shook his head. "I've tried that. It really comes over as contrived. How much have you read?" He picked up the stack and glanced over the labels.

"I skimmed the top four. If you get moving, you might take a look at 'Legislative Implementation.'"

"Come in with me. I'll introduce you and may hand off some of the questions."

Peter cocked his head. "I haven't been up before the national press before, sir."

Kincaid shrugged as he turned to Peter. "They're not so bad overall. They're just doing their jobs like we are. If you tell them a good story, they'll print it or air it. If you tell them the truth while you're at it, it won't come back to bite you later, no matter how ugly it is. And right now, you've got more facts already in your head than I have time to absorb in a day. Just answer any questions I hand off to you with what you actually know. That already tells them the answer's not obvious. I've always found a simple 'I don't know; I'll get back to you' will take care of the stumpers — as long as you actually do get back to them. I learned that from Ron."

"I'll give it a shot, sir," Peter agreed.

"Thanks. You'll do fine. Now let's see that summary."

Kincaid sat reading the papers until Peter called time. They got up and headed to the press room, stopping in the outer office long enough for Peter to pick up a stack of handouts. Kincaid thanked Tracey on his way out.

Peter looked over to his boss. "I can see in your face that you're still worried about Sarah's video. Don't be. I've learned a lot this morning that we can go over later. The main point is that Sarah's more than innocent. It's not going to be a problem — for us."

Kincaid noted Peter's odd phrasing and sighed. "Good. Thanks. That does make me feel better."

As they approached the presenters' entrance to the White House press room, Kincaid heard a lot of chatter. "Natives are restless today. This could get rough."

"Great. I picked a fine day for you to talk me into this." Peter was shaking his head.

"Take a deep breath." Kincaid put his hand on the door handle. "It's show time."

Kincaid's detached political self was in charge. A casual glance at the crowd; confident strides toward the podium; calm offer of a seat to Peter. Remember the press; resolute approach to the podium— be careful not to trip; check of microphone and light while ignoring the reporters; no sniffling or touching the face; setting the notes on the podium; spreading them a little so he could access each page individually without fiddling.

Kincaid reflected on his first real speech, in sixth grade. He wondered if it was as good as he was remembering now. Jane Swanson in the second row of Mrs. Hamor's class told him later she thought it was a good speech, so it must have been. That was a long time ago.

He looked up, unsmiling, from the podium and surveyed the group. Once the talk died down, he began. "I have one announcement and two clarifications. First, the President has called a White House conference August fourth through the sixth to focus on this country's plans to assist the transition away from tobacco cultivation. The American farmer expects and deserves every service possible to compete and prosper in today's global economy. Our American farmers are the best and most progressive in the world with many crops. Tobacco should not be one of them. The curse of this weed with all its health, environmental, and economic downsides is now recognized on a global scale. In this country, we have drastically curbed the use of tobacco, and we are working in concert with nations around the globe to eventually eliminate its trade. Cultivation of tobacco as a cash crop is a recipe for extinction. We cannot responsibly stand by and see our farmers lose their land when we have the capability to warn them."

Kincaid looked up from his papers. The reporters were quiet. They were taking few notes.

"I have two clarifications. First, the rotation troops for the Kuwait forward base rotation will come from the eighty-second, not the hundred-first division. The members of the hundred-first will be returning for a well-deserved homecoming. Finally, our new ambassador to South Africa will be James P. Kerson, not John Kerson. My apologies for getting John's hopes up.

"Those are the announcements and clarifications I have at this time." Kincaid braced himself. "What questions do you have this morning?"

Nearly every hand shot up. Kincaid pointed to the senior correspondent.

"Mr. Kincaid, would you please comment on this weekend's incident with one of the President's staff members?"

Kincaid looked down. He adjusted the alignment of his pages of the tobacco report. The reporter's question, he noted, was carefully crafted to mask any agenda behind it. He looked up again.

"In the past few hours, I have become aware of a gross invasion of the privacy of one of my staff while on a family vacation. The matter is under investigation and will be handled appropriately." His answer didn't seem to have much impact. Kincaid moved on to the next hand. Their order was impossible to track, so he chose more or less randomly from different locations in the room.

"Mr. Kincaid, the events of the weekend have raised quite an outcry around the country. Could you be more specific in the actions the White House is considering?"

Kincaid crossed his arms. He frowned as he leaned into the microphone and lowered his voice. "I don't think there was anything unclear in the answer I just gave. I don't have all the facts concerning the matter. Quite frankly, from everything I do know, there is no issue beyond an assault on the dignity of one of my staff. I believe this matter rightly belongs in our post-briefing get-together off the record. We have substantive issues of national importance to deal with, and I'd like to move forward with those."

Sarah watched from behind the mirrored glass at the back of the auditorium. She murmured, "Oh, sir, they're not going to let you off that easy." She bit her lip. "They want our blood."

Kincaid pointed to a third questioner, a reporter from the Wolfe Group.

"With all due respect, sir, this story is of considerable interest to the public. It raises more ethical concerns at a time when the White House is already under increasing scrutiny over the Vice President's conduct. A member of this press corps has been barred from here after uncovering the story. And prominent members of the American faith community are calling for her dismissal and your firing if you do not dismiss her."

Kincaid's detached political self abandoned him. "People, we have lost focus here. This country is wrestling with immense problems that affect everyone from the kitchen to the boardroom. There are economic and military challenges before us that require our serious attention. This weekend, one of my staff played volleyball on her vacation, and we are discussing her attire. They must be scratching their heads in Europe right now. There is no story here. This is about fashion and personal choices for leisure time, not morality. Is it the novelty of these resorts in this country that's got everyone all abuzz? Grow up, people. What you wear or don't in the privacy of a resort is a personal decision. Ten years from now you're going to be wondering what the fuss is about.

"As for your colleague, Ben Jacobs, I have pulled his credentials for review. I am personally responsible for that. I pulled them because I want to talk to him about why he found it necessary to ridicule a dedicated public servant. If he wants to take me on — fine. I've entered that area of politics where combat is the normal and accepted practice. Satirizing and lampooning me I can accept. I signed on with that understanding. But you do not subject the innocent to publicity that can bring out the dangerous elements of our society. How would you react if I posted a photo of your daughter or your son or your niece or your nephew on the news, even in their prom regalia?"

The press corps was busy writing and recording now.

Kincaid's face felt warm. He had leaned forward to the edge of the podium light, which cast bold shadows over his face. "How would you react if some scavenging jackal called them 'whore' on national television as a result of that coverage? I pulled Mr. Jacobs' credentials because he has exposed a private, non-political citizen to attack by those who recognize no boundaries in their quest for position and power. That reporting was irresponsible in the extreme and cannot go unchallenged. I will be talking to Ben Jacobs personally … and very soon."

Kincaid's hands were animated now, and he punctuated his delivery with an occasional fist on the podium. "Now, as to the 'prominent members of the American faith community calling for her dismissal' and my firing, I know that can refer only to Dr. Paul Richards. Focus, people. Focus. Dr. Richards heads a group with many adherents, but he does not speak for the entire American faith community. Regardless of what he says, he speaks for himself. As an American, he is entitled to his opinions and beliefs. But when he treads upon the dignity of others and holds the innocent up to callous humiliation, then I am compelled to defend those who are attacked. Dr. Richards is welcome to call for my firing, but let's get one thing straight: I am responsible for the office of Chief of Staff to the President of the United States. Richards does not run this office. Not now. Not never!"

Kincaid's detached political self suddenly returned, rather puzzled at what had just transpired. Under normal circumstances, he would have corrected this last ingrammaticism. The phrase should have been "not now, not ever" or simply "never." He had known better than to use double negatives since Mrs. Abbott's fourth grade class. He hoped she wasn't watching. Under normal circumstances, he would have merely restated the answer or noted it with a [*sic*] in the official transcript. But the detached political David Kincaid recognized a good stopping place. Nearly the entire press corps was on its feet, cheering wildly. He would want later to replay the audio and video of this moment to hear the rain of pencils, pens, and at least one laptop hitting the floor.

It was time now to appear calm. Smiling or gloating was out of the question. He needed to appear dignified while he figured out what he had done and where to go from here. The applause continued. He needed something distracting. He eyed the pitcher and glass of water beside it. He'd never used them before, always wondering how long they'd been there and what might be growing in them. He was relieved to see ice in both; they had to be fresh. It helped to have competent people in charge of such details. He wasn't sure if he was thirsty or not, but picked up the glass and took a sip. His hands were trembling. Probably not enough to show on television, but he didn't want to spill anything. He set the glass down and grasped the sides of the podium. The clapping was dying down, and he figured that he looked reasonably dignified.

The reporters took their seats, gathering their notes and writing instruments. Back around the fifteenth row, a reporter was listening to his laptop hard drive. He didn't look happy.

Kincaid glanced to his side. Peter was trying to appear serious, but Kincaid caught a bit of a grin around Peter's eyes.

He turned back to the press corps. "If there are no more questions about the national emergencies swirling around what we did on our spring breaks, I'd like to move onto something light. Pestilence? War? Famine? Death?"

A wave of nervous laughter swept over the room. Only about half the hands went up, a more measured pace than previously. He pointed to the middle of the room to a face he recognized.

"Susan. NPR."

The questions from that point on were about the tobacco conference, half of which he handed off to Peter, the continuing problems with the state budgets, and the growing protests in Iraq and Iran. In the personal session afterward, he fielded questions about Dr. Richards and about Vice President Bailey. His answers were mostly playful and the banter civilized.

As the clock approached noon, Kincaid concluded the briefing and left with Peter. Outside the room, he took a deep breath. "Well, my young apprentice, you had immediate answers for four of the five questions you got. That's better than I usually do. What was that one you need to follow up?"

Peter smiled. "John Haley had some question about links with A.T.F., but I'm still not sure what his question was. I've got his cell number, and I'll be calling him at two this afternoon."

Kincaid spied a scowling Ben Jacobs standing by the Marine check-in desk, arms crossed. Kincaid turned to Peter. "Go on to lunch. I have some business to attend to here."

Peter smirked. "Enjoy." He walked down the corridor toward the offices.

Kincaid walked straight to Jacobs. "You! With me! Now! We've got to have a serious talk."

Jacobs was defiant. "You have no right to bar me from this. I am a credentialed member of the press corps. You do not order me around."

Out of the corner of his eye, Kincaid noticed that the reporters leaving the briefing had stopped and turned their attention to the two of them. He saw Jacobs glance in the same direction, and detected a flicker of hesitation. Kincaid pursued. "OK. Fine. You want to talk about this right here, right now? I can live with that. I want you to convince me why it was necessary this morning to subject one of my staff to all the prurient interests lurking about in society." Kincaid was pointing his finger at Jacobs' heart.

A small mob of reporters began to take notes. Jacobs hesitated, shifting his eyes between Kincaid and the mob.

Kincaid flicked his head in the direction of his office. "Let's go, Ben, unless you prefer this forum."

He could feel the warmth of his anger. As they strode down the passage, those ahead stepped aside. The military types snapped to attention as Kincaid approached, then glowered at Jacobs as he passed. This was not proper protocol, but Kincaid knew the theatrics would be helpful.

He entered his outer office, Jacobs in tow. Tracey had not left for lunch. She looked at Jacobs with icy calm.

"Would you please get Mr. Jacobs' boss …?" Kincaid could not remember Jacobs' editor's name. He wrinkled his brow, snapping his fingers in the air.

"Saul Bedlow?" Tracey offered.

"Yes, thank you. In about seventeen minutes."

Tracey nodded ominously. Kincaid watched Jacobs carefully. Again, the reporter's emotions were barely discernable, but he wasn't happy. Kincaid suspected that the story had not been cleared before airing, and Jacobs' minute, almost imperceptible, wince more or less confirmed that. Kincaid opened the door to his office, ushered Jacobs in with a wave of his hand, and closed the door.

"Ben Jacobs, what the hell were you thinking when you ran that piece?"

Jacobs was still defiant, but far less emphatically so than during their first encounter. "That was a legitimate news story. It concerns the situation at the White House."

"How?" Kincaid demanded.

"The climate of disorder."

"What?"

"The office is losing control of its people," Jacobs stammered.

"Ben, she was playing volleyball. Volleyball, Ben. She was on vacation. We don't control people on vacation. Did she do something wrong? And since when are you tracking everyone's vacation habits?"

Jacobs looked down at the floor. He was quiet for a moment, and then looked to the side. "Dammit."

Kincaid waited.

"I made a mistake. Look, we're not tracking anybody's vacation. We received that tape just a little while before air this morning. It seemed relevant at the time. It was a mistake."

Kincaid relaxed a little. "Received the tape? From whom?"

Jacobs looked up. "First, I don't know. Our people verified it wasn't doctored and that it was Dr. Tyler. Second, if I did know, it would be protected material."

"I won't go there. You know I support confidentiality. But you also know I'm holding you accountable for what you do with the information you get. And you were way out of line to broadcast this. Dr. Tyler's volleyball game is of no political consequence, and your airing put her at risk. What you did has personal consequences. We're not talking about press freedom, Ben. We're talking about civility."

Jacobs brought the palm of his hand up to his head. "Look. I made a mistake. I can't call it back. I will fix it. I don't know how at the moment, but I will fix it."

Kincaid was pondering Jacob's answer when Tracey's voice came over the phone console. "Mr. Bedlow on line one, sir."

Kincaid could see Jacobs wilt. He punched a button to put the conversation on speakerphone. "Hello, Saul."

"David. I'm not sure what's going on, but pulling my reporter's credentials is serious business. I'm…"

Kincaid interrupted. "Are we free to talk, Saul?"

There was a pause. "I'm in my office with Jane Steele, chief counsel for the network."

Kincaid smiled. "Hello, Jane. I believe we met at the tort reform conference last summer."

"Your memory is good, David."

Kincaid sat down in his chair and continued. "Saul, Jane wouldn't be there with you if you didn't realize how serious Ben's piece was this morning. It was absolutely actionable."

Jane began, "David, I think we —"

"But I think we can avoid a lot of nastiness. Your cub reporter is sitting in time-out here in my office. We're working on a plan to get out of the hole we find ourselves in."

Kincaid listened. Silence.

Jane replied, "And what were we considering?"

"Do we agree that this morning's piece was way over the line?"

"You know I'm not going to say that, but I would stipulate that some might interpret it that way," she replied.

Kincaid continued, "Nicely phrased. Ben apparently acquired a piece of video, doesn't know where it came from, but had the good sense to authenticate it, and then proceeded to broadcast a private holiday game to the nation to the great embarrassment of Dr. Tyler. Obviously there's a lot of repair work to be done. If this were the Vice President's office, he'd be plying her with the most vicious sharks in the legal pool. He'd likely be going for Mr. Jacobs's scalp, don't you think?"

Silence, again.

After a few seconds, Kincaid resumed, "Anyway, I think Ben is getting ready to write a really, really good apology, and I'm guessing that the network would be more than happy to air it this evening — same amount of time as the piece in question." Kincaid waited for their reply. He could hear a muffled conversation on the other end of the line.

Jacobs shifted nervously from foot to foot, looking around the office at pictures on the wall.

After a little over a minute, Bedlow returned. "David, does Ben agree to that?"

Kincaid looked up at Jacobs, who gave a quick nod in the affirmative.

"Yes, Saul, I'm even giving him a pad of White House paper and a real White House pen so he can get right on it."

"Ben, when you get back to the office, give me a call. We'll be waiting."

Jacobs closed his eyes. "Yes, sir."

Kincaid's brow wrinkled. "Now don't be too hard on him, Saul."

Jacobs opened his eyes immediately.

"He's young and impetuous, but he's got more talent than any other five of your front line staff."

"That's high praise coming from you. We'll take that into consideration." Bedlow sounded sincere.

"This investigation of his has caused me a lot of paperwork, Saul, and I want him to finish it so our work's not wasted. He's either going to win a prize for investigative journalism uncovering corruption or for investigative journalism on how suspicions can be dead wrong. Either way, you win."

"I see. And is Ben on the right track?"

"I truthfully have no idea. But you'd best pair him with someone older and wiser to keep him from self-destructing." Kincaid looked into Jacobs's face. "Hold on a minute if you would, Saul. And Jane too. I'm sending Ben on his way."

Kincaid flipped the phone back to handset. He picked up Jacobs's credentials, note pad, and pen, and handed them to him. "Go see Tracey. Let her know I returned your papers, and she'll ask the Marines not to beat you up on the way out."

"Yes, sir. Thank you."

Kincaid waited until Jacobs had left the office and closed the door. "All right, Saul, he's on his way. I meant what I said. He's a good kid and will do you proud if you give him some guidance. He's onto something even though it probably won't turn out how we expect. He can dig in places we here can't go. I'll look forward to his reports."

"We'll keep you informed, David. I'm sorry about hurting your staff."

"Ah, yes. About that. I'm sure Ben's public apology will go a long way toward making things right with Dr. Tyler."

* * *

Shortly after seven that evening, Laura and Charlie met in the sheriff's office with supervisors of the Montgomery County emergency call center.

"No, ma'am, nobody told us anything about this." The senior supervisor was in his sixties, though years of night shifts had aged him considerably further. "And I, for one, believe the Sheriff. But how can they do this to us? I can't imagine there's any machine that can handle what these operators do. But it's just like this county exec to stab us in the back. The people on the switchboards do heroic work, as do their families. That's why we have the Veteran Family Preference. Some of their spouses are on their fourth or fifth rotation overseas. It's just not right."

Laura removed a handful of papers from her briefcase. "Charlie and I were able to get hold of some of the contracts for the work."

The Sheriff looked up at Laura as she handed him a portion of the stack. He flipped through some of the pages, his face turning red. "God damn them all! They've had this in the works for over a year." He looked over more papers. "They used a budget they knew I wouldn't see. I don't suppose you know when they're supposed to do this, do you?"

Charlie browsed through his stack. "Matter of fact, we do. Looks like they're going to start Monday, May fifth. According to this, the installation workers are being told it's for a brokerage firm. They'll be working in the spaces adjacent to the current call center. All the cables for the call center pass through the new space's overhead already. The plan is to have the Brisbane machines begin taking the calls line by line and to let the operators go as the machines become operational. They expect the transition to take about a week. The crew has already done installations in Oxford, Mississippi, and Salt Lake City."

The Sheriff and the supervisors looked at each other. After a while, the Sheriff spoke. "OK, guys, I don't know if what I'm about to suggest is even legal. I'm fairly sure I'll lose my job over it sooner or later, but there comes a time when ya gotta take a stand, and I think now's the time. We're not going to let them turn the call center over to robots. I'm in good with the people in inspection and licensing, and I'm sure we can ball up the project with them for months. But to stop it permanently will take action by the County Council. At the moment, I doubt more than a couple of Council members are even aware of this project. We're going to need a lot of community support, and that means this rotten mess has to be made public. Did you get these documents legally?"

Charlie looked up at the ceiling. "Possibly not."

The Sheriff frowned. "Then try to keep my name out of it as long as you can. I'll run interference for you as I'm able."

Laura nodded. "Good. The permit papers were filed last week, but they were given routine provisional approval by licensing. The application says *Brokerage Office* on it. What do you need to get going?"

"Just some story in the paper or on the radio. Something with names and mention of the fraudulent application." The Sheriff rubbed his chin.

"Done. Charlie can get the radio coverage. I have contacts at the *Post* and *The Times.*"

"Doubt *The Times* will help much here. The owner's in pretty thick with the county exec."

Laura flashed a smile. "Normally you'd be right, but his granddaughter is one of the workers who'll lose her job."

The Sheriff grinned in return. "You don't miss much, do you? I'm glad you're on our side."

She grew serious. "We're up against some serious money. I hope you feel that way when this erupts in flames."

* * *

Kincaid rubbed his face and looked up at the clock. Five forty-seven. He'd been holed up for almost four and a half hours straight. He'd done only about half of what he wanted, but that was a remarkable achievement. He heard a knock at the door. "Enter."

Corporal Tull appeared with a large mug of coffee. "Thought you could use this, sir."

"Oh, wonderful. You didn't have to do that, but blessings on you and all your future children."

Tull grinned. "I asked Ms. Tracey if there was anything you needed, and she said you were falling asleep and needed coffee."

Kincaid took a sip. It was a rich, aromatic blend. "I've had my door closed. What made her think I was falling asleep?"

Tull smiled.

"Right. She always knows. Anyway, I really appreciate it. Good coffee, by the way. I like the hazelnut. A little frou-frou for a Marine to be carrying isn't it? Hope I don't get you in trouble."

"Naw, I won't tell if you won't."

Kincaid sensed that Tull had more on his mind than bringing coffee. "And how are you doing today?"

"Permission to speak freely, sir?"

"Of course," Kincaid replied, smiling.

"That was a heroic thing you did this morning."

"The briefing? Not really. Jacobs was out of line, he hurt one our people, and I called him on it. You stick up for your men, right? Or in this case, one of our women."

"That was magnificent, too, sir. I was referring to Vice President Bailey."

"How do you know about that?"

"I was on duty outside the office. You left the door open when you walked in."

"Ah, yes." Kincaid looked at his watch. "Are you still on duty?"

"No, sir, I just wanted to hang around and let you know what I thought."

"Thank you. But let's keep it between us. That's not the sort of thing that should get around."

Tull grinned again. "Yes, sir, just you and me. Though maybe a few in the detachment may have gotten wind of it. We'll keep it quiet."

"You know, it's really amazing how much hubbub could come out of a stupid home video."

"Sir?" Tull seemed surprised.

"The video. I've spent half my day squabbling on the national stage because some jerk took a movie and gave it to a reporter." Kincaid took a long sip of the warm liquid.

Tull's surprised look remained. "Then you haven't talked with Mr. Benson yet?"

Kincaid set down the cup slowly, feeling suddenly uneasy. "No. Peter's been working on it, too. Talking with Major Reed, if I recall correctly. I haven't seen him since the briefing."

"That was no home video, sir. Whoever took it might have wanted it to look like a home video, but it certainly was not."

"Really?" Kincaid expression tightened.

"Major Reed went over it in our Time Out for Instruction this afternoon. We were learning how to fill out the security breach forms. He's escalated it to a possible security threat."

"Security threat? A volleyball game? Admittedly, a naked volleyball game. But how is that a security threat? And why does he think it wasn't amateur?"

"Did you notice the swing set behind the volleyball net?"

"I haven't seen the video. I hadn't planned to."

Tull paused. "You went up on stage and defended her without even seeing the film? Gutsy move, sir."

"Or stupid."

"It can be a fine line. Anyway, the swing set. The Major was showing us the angles of the frame. He did some math calculations — I followed them a little then, but probably couldn't explain it now — and was able to establish a zone from which the movie was taken. The camera was set up between six hundred and eight hundred meters from the game."

"Whoa, that's almost a football field … good Lord, that's nearly eight football fields away."

"Exactly, sir. The camera gear to take shots like that cost hundreds of thousands of dollars. And cameras aren't enough. You need computer programs to stabilize the image and track your target. In the video, you can see the frame jump from time to time while the software makes corrections. The Major has some buddies at CIA who owe him some favors. With the way the frames behave, he thinks he can probably get a make on the gear, even down to firmware revision. It's a limited audience for this kind of spyware. He'll track down who did the filming."

"But why would anyone go to those lengths to film a volleyball game?"

"He doesn't think it was the game they were after, but Ms. … Dr. Tyler. There were thirty-seven people in the game and on the sidelines. For over eighty percent of the clip, she's the target. The software allows that. He doesn't know why. Maybe trying to embarrass the President or set up a kidnapping. That's why he's escalated it."

"She could be in danger, then."

"Probably not. That was part of our discussion. Whoever's behind it has had plenty of opportunity to grab her if that was the point. He's concerned enough that he's providing her with a locator and some training, but he's pretty sure they were trying to embarrass the President through her."

"I'll talk to Peter before he leaves. Thanks for bringing me up to date."

Tull nodded but didn't leave.

"Something else on your mind?"

"I had been wondering — just thinking about it, about asking Dr. Tyler out."

Kincaid leaned back in his chair. "Ah, I see. It wouldn't have anything to do with the video, would it?"

Tull recoiled in horror. "No, sir. I mean, she is cute in the pictures, but she caught my eye a while ago. She's got … spirit."

"Spirit," Kincaid mused. "I think we need a stronger word than spirit. She's a human tornado some days."

"Yes, sir," Tull grinned.

"Still, I doubt there's any rule against asking her out if your intentions are honorable, which I have no doubt they are. Just be prepared for her to be cautious. She's been through a lot in the last twenty-four hours."

"Understood, sir."

"Then go for it. She's a fine person, and you two should have a fun time."

"Thank you, sir." Tull smiled and left.

* * *

Jennifer sat on Jack's lap, wrapped in a blanket and Jack's arms, watching television. The evening news was mid-way through coverage of the morning's press briefing. The clip finished with Kincaid nearly shouting, "Not now. Not never."

She smiled, almost giddy. "Wow! There's something you don't see very often. Someone actually standing up for the people who work for them."

"He's probably sleeping with her."

Jennifer jabbed her elbow into Jack's ribs. "You are an insufferable cynic, Jack Pullman. Look, I'm the one with the nearly-perfect track record here, and I say he's just being noble."

He hugged her and gave her a peck of a kiss. "Really? May I remind my seer that he works in the same office with the Vice President you loathe."

She shook her head. "You are wrong, my love. He works in the President's office, and he does not get along with that jerk Bailey. If you have to be jaded, then the Chief of Staff's probably getting back at Bailey."

"But he's been defending the Vice President, if you'll recall."

She kissed him on the forehead. "You haven't been watching. Next time they cover him answering questions, watch his face. There's something about his eyes and mouth that tells you he doesn't believe Bailey. And their feuding is common knowledge anyway."

Jack raised his eyebrows. "Oh, really? I hadn't heard that."

"It's been on *Entertainment Tonight* for months."

"Oh, gee, wow. I didn't know that. It must be true, then."

"You, sir, are a snob as well as a grumpy old cynic. You want a rational argument? OK, Mister Ace Debater, how about this? They called the President's and First Lady's split when no one even knew about their troubles. And that thing with the governor of Missouri."

Jack tried to recall the details. "OK, they get it right from time to time. Everyone gets lucky occasionally."

"No, no. They almost always call it right and they call it first. Those people may be running the country, but they're still people. And in the end they behave like people, for better and for worse. They're not machines."

Jack smiled, "OK, I'll give you the point."

"Ooh, goodie! That makes me ahead, doesn't it?"

"Not a chance." Jack got up, lifting Jennifer into the warm corner of the couch he'd just left. "I'm going to start dinner. Stir fry OK?"

She smiled. "Sounds great." She looked back to the news. "Oh, lookie there. It's Ben Jacobs. And he's about to say he's really sorry for what he did."

"What? What makes you think that?" Jack asked.

"Look at the eyes, lover boy. Look at the eyes. Bet you a chick flick he's about to apologize."

"You're on. If I win, we see the new James Bond piece."

Jennifer smirked. "You just want to gawk at Katie Baker."

"Watch the TV."

* * *

Kincaid checked his watch after finishing his coffee. Six forty-seven. He could hear Tracey getting ready to leave. He followed her routine by sound and was waiting for the rattle of car keys when he heard other voices.

"Is he in?"

Kincaid recognized Anna's voice and strained to hear more, but indiscernible mumbling ensued for over a minute.

Tracey finally spoke. "Oh, yes, he'll definitely want to see that. Go wake him up."

He heard her car keys at the same time there was a knock on the door. "I'm not asleep, thank you. I've gotten quite a lot accomplished."

Anna and Peter entered smiling.

Kincaid rested his arm on his desk and his chin in his hand. "Doesn't anyone ever go home around here anymore?"

Peter spoke first. "Not when we're having this much fun. The afternoon snap polls just arrived. You'll want to look them over."

"But not until after you watch the news." Anna clutched the poll results.

Kincaid held out his hand for the report. "I'll probably listen to the news on my way home or replay it from the download."

"Then you don't get to see the polls," Anna insisted.

"Why do I need to see the news live?"

"Ben Jacobs called and asked … no. How did he put it?" Anna turned to Peter.

"Humbly requested your attention to the seven o'clock national news."

Kincaid looked to Anna. She held the papers tightly. He smiled. "Are you at least going to tell me why I want to see the numbers? I'm guessing I'll be pretty well roasted."

"Nice try, sir. We think you'll want to digest the numbers before you meet with the President in the morning."

"I didn't know I was meeting him in the morning."

Anna and Peter looked at each other.

She turned back to Kincaid. "The Vice President will be back from New

Hampshire around eight-thirty. You've assaulted his favorite prime base. The whole volleyball story from start to finish is number one on every news outlet from print to broadcast to web in the U.S. and half of Europe. And, as you'll see from the numbers after you watch the news, it's altered the political landscape. So you'll be meeting the President in the morning. Besides, Abigail called and said she was setting aside half an hour at seven thirty tomorrow morning."

Kincaid sighed and reached into his desk for the remote. "Have a seat. But I'm out of popcorn."

Anna chuckled and took the seat next to his desk. She set the papers face down in her lap. Her skirt featured a pattern of warm browns, and she wore a dark red sash for a belt. She had replaced the White House standard issue string lanyard of her identification badge with a demure gold chain that complimented the rough texture of her dark brown knitted sweater. A strand of hair fell forward, curving toward the screen, following the curve of her cheek when she looked down at the papers.

Kincaid turned quickly to watch the screen as she raised her head in his direction. Peter had taken a seat on Kincaid's other side close to the television. The broadcast opened with another story of the monarch's illness. Security was extremely tight at Royal Hospital in London and spokesmen were tight-lipped. But workmen had begun telltale preparations in Westminster Abbey and the country was obviously being prepared for a somber announcement. The second story reported more arrests in Riyadh after anti-American riots had killed over forty a week ago. The Saudis were dealing harshly with the disturbance, but the crackdown seemed only to escalate the violence.

Nearly fifteen minutes into the broadcast, after a long series of commercials, the network's chief executive appeared on camera. "Good evening. My name is Saul Bedlow, and I am the one ultimately responsible for what you see and hear covered by our network. We at CDBS strive at all times to provide accurate and informative coverage of the events that affect your lives. Sometimes, though, we ourselves are the news. This morning, we aired a story that, on reflection, did not meet our standards of newsworthiness. Here to explain is one of our brightest young reporters, Ben Jacobs."

"Good. They're going to give him a chance." Kincaid watched Jacobs's body language as the reporter appeared. Kincaid had wondered how they would handle the background and the messages conveyed by the props of the setting. The network had gone with a seamless background of slightly off-white. Jacobs was seated on a simple stool with armrests. He wore dark tan slacks with a tan sweater, white shirt, and black tie. His eyes were cast down, his hands folded in front of him, his straight black hair hanging loosely. He raised his head and faced the camera.

"My parents taught me that I am responsible for what I say and do. They taught me that when I make a mistake, I am to take ownership of that mistake and correct it to the best of my ability. This morning I aired a story about the private vacation of a dedicated member of the White House staff, Dr. Sarah Tyler. Though I checked the authenticity of the story, I did not properly consider whether the story was appropriate for the news or whether it would embarrass Dr. Tyler or her family."

Jacobs opened his hands. "When I report on individuals involved in wrongdoing, it is inevitable that some will be shamed or ridiculed. That is part of our protective reaction as a society, part of our aversion to harmful behavior. On the other hand, when we trivialize or ridicule others solely for the purposes of amusement or gain, then we damage core pillars of civility and common decency. And that does not promote the common good. This morning I aired the private moments of people enjoying life and the company of family.

"Why I did that is not entirely clear to me. Perhaps the novelty; perhaps I thought it would bring high ratings. Certainly the piece attracted the level of interest I anticipated. I and I alone was responsible for the decision to show some of the footage. I did not follow our established procedures, which would certainly have raised the serious issues of privacy that now confront me."

Jacobs got up slowly from the stool, folded his arms, bowed his head for a moment, and then faced the camera again.

Kincaid watched Jacobs. "That was a risky move on live television. He could have slipped or bumped the stool. He's good."

Anna turned to Kincaid. "Surely this isn't live. That required a lot of rehearsal."

"I think it's live." Peter pointed to the bottom of the screen. "There's no network logo or banner across the bottom. They'll record the first take clean, then add those as needed for rebroadcast."

"Oh. Wow." Anna nodded.

Jacobs continued. "The bottom line is that I took a moment of joy and family fellowship and exploited it as sensational and odd. My exploitation was wrong. I cannot undo my action, but I will do what I can to redress the injury I have caused. To begin I offer my deepest apology to Dr. Tyler and to her family and friends, and I hope that my apology will be received in the spirit it is offered. To those whom I try to serve, I beg your forgiveness for this lapse of judgment. If you found my offering this morning titillating or scandalous, I implore you to reflect on your feelings as I have on mine. We should be about a more noble level of discourse. We should be concentrating on the serious issues that confront our country and our world.

"For my part, I pledge to do just that. I thank you for your understanding."

Jacobs turned slowly and walked off camera. The set was silent for a moment and then a voice-over delivered the usual disclaimer that the views expressed did not necessarily reflect the views of the network.

Kincaid watched closely, noting the respectful silence at the end with nothing but the empty stool on screen. "That was well done. I think he's probably closed the public phase of the episode." He turned to Peter. "But I understand we have a lot more questions coming out of this."

Peter turned around as Kincaid muted the volume. "How do you know about that?"

"I have spies everywhere. I see you when you're sleeping, I know when you're awake, I … well, you know the rest."

"OK. Major Reed ran the video by the guys in remote sensing down at Langley. The video had to have been captured by a computer-controlled camera developed originally for DOD by a defense contractor in Florida. The Major contacted them. They made seven of those cameras. Six are in use overseas and one was stolen about eight months ago. That's all he had as of four this afternoon."

"Well done, young man. Keep me apprised of developments. Does the Major have any concerns for Sarah's safety?"

"No sir. At least not from any politically motivated corners. Obviously there could be some interest in her person as a result of the story. He got several volunteers to escort her home for the next week or so just to make sure there's no harassment."

"Good." Kincaid turned to Anna. "Do I get to see my death sentence now?"

She smiled and placed the polls on his desk, spreading them out before him. Peter came over to point out details on the three sheets.

"These results are about two hours old but have been consistent through the day. I'm guessing Jacobs's *mea culpa* will only improve the numbers. I was particularly struck by the response from those who considered themselves evangelical conservatives."

Kincaid leaned forward, pondering the spread. "Hm. That's good. Not sure what it means, but perhaps Dr. Richards's grip isn't so strong as we usually assume."

Anna drew his attention to the last page. "And take a look as some of the comments. The polling organization records those after the base interview is over. 'At last stands up to the Crusade' 'About time' 'Finally showing some backbone.' Interesting reactions, don't you think?"

"Are they saying that about me or the President?"

"Both. It's the first time the White House has broken eighty percent approval in three years. Even on the economy."

Kincaid leaned back in his chair. "Huh. It's a strange world sometimes.

Maybe I should use poor sentence structure more often."

Anna giggled. "I think everyone recognized that little slip as passionate loyalty. It was a sign of authenticity that's hard to fake."

She was looking straight into his eyes. Her eyes were beautiful, medium brown with flecks of green and gold. She was that close.

"So if I'm sincere, I should use bad grammar."

She nodded and smiled sweetly. "Apparently so."

* * *

"Thus within a week all twenty workers will be replaced." Laura went over details of the 911 center replacements with the reporter from *The Times* just as she had with the *Post* an hour earlier.

This reporter did not seem so interested as the one from the *Post.* "As you said, these replacements are happening all over the country. How is this one newsworthy?"

"The people who are being replaced are spouses and children of the men and women who are serving in the Gulf. These are important, meaningful jobs with good pay and benefits. The county will be cutting the support from twenty people at a time when it's almost impossible to get a similar job."

The reporter jotted down the information half-heartedly. "Unemployment is only four percent. Wouldn't seem to pose much of a challenge."

Laura finally flashed anger. "Bullshit! Look around here, lady. This is a food pantry. When I started volunteering here five years ago, we were seeing a hundred fifty a week. We're seeing five, six hundred a week now. And it's not just the always-poor like five years ago. We're seeing middle-class families, well-educated middle-class families who haven't found alternative jobs in a year or more. I don't care what the unemployment numbers say, I'm telling you what I see. Something's disconnected and there's no clear explanation."

By this point, the reporter was writing quickly. She looked up as Laura paused. "You know, now that you mention it, I've been doing a lot of these stories lately. Not that they get in the paper or on air. But I've had the same odd feeling like something's wrong that I can't put my finger on.

"I'm going to write this up. I still don't think they'll use it as is, but you said you had a human-interest angle that would clench it?"

Laura smiled. "Yeah. I thought you should interview one of the workers who'll lose her job. Anita Howard will be terminated around May seventh if this plan goes through."

"Anita Howard? Isn't she…?"

"Walter Howard's granddaughter-in-law. Yes. Your publisher's granddaughter-in-law's job will be replaced by a machine on or about May seventh. Her husband is serving his country aboard the *Carl Vinson* out in the Gulf. They're expecting a child in July. She'll be terminated with no insurance, pregnant and alone while a cold megacompany makes millions using fake permits — all with the secret knowledge and consent of a handful of elected officials. Sounds like human interest to me."

The reporter was alert and eager now. "Can you get me in contact with Ms. Howard?"

Laura smiled again. "She's upstairs."

* * *

Jack and Jennifer had fallen asleep two-thirds of the way through *Patchwork*. The video was stuck on the end credits when Jennifer woke up. She nudged Jack. "Hey lover, the movie's over. Bed time."

Jack sat up, twisting to loosen muscles. "We'll have to watch it again a little earlier next time. When did we drift off?"

"Right after Goldberg made his escape."

"I don't remember that. Definitely need to watch it again."

"Go turn off the lights and let's get to bed. Tomorrow's going to be a bad day."

"She may have some good news for us." Jack hung his head.

"Jack, tomorrow's going to be bad. We have to prepare for that. I can feel what's coming, and there's no turning back. I don't have much time, and I want to make the most of every day. We don't have time for alternate endings."

Jack trudged to the kitchen to set up coffee for the morning. Jennifer had been cleaning out cabinets and the refrigerator. She had given away the two plants that had lived on the kitchen windowsill since they had arrived in the apartment. She knew Jack couldn't take proper care of them, so they would die and he would feel guilty for that, as well.

Jack was finding lots of these unannounced preparations. She wouldn't let him help with them, preferring that he concentrate on the insurance and medical paperwork she loathed. He would be dealing with the lawyer to file an appeal for the coverage denial, and he would continue to plead with Plantagenet Pharmaceuticals to get Jennifer enrolled in their drug study. He still heard rumors that their new MetaStop was remarkably effective against her specific cancer. Friday he would go down to Richmond to talk directly to one of their investigators under the guise of seeking a lab management position. If it would give him access to the drug, he'd take the position at any cost.

He doused the kitchen lights and returned to the living room. Jennifer was barely awake. He scooped her up and carried her to the bedroom. It was far too easy a task now. He wanted desperately to cry out, to shriek and to rage. Instead, he held her tightly, laid her down on the bed, and added an extra comforter. When he came to bed, he wrapped his arm around her.

She smiled. "That's a good movie. You seemed to like it even if it was a chick flick."

He struggled to keep an even voice. "Hey, you found a chick flick with Katie Baker in it. Even the geezer was well acted."

She snuggled tightly against his chest. "Sam Neill's not a geezer."

"No, but he played one. Do you think a young thing like her could really be happy with an old guy?"

"Sure. She might have been young, but she was wise. And he wasn't that old. Happens all the time."

"And you don't find that sexist?"

"No." Her answers grew shorter and quieter as she drifted back to sleep.

Jack pulled himself up and kissed her.

"Hmmmmm." She sighed.

He laid his head on his pillow as tears streamed down his face.

13 A WOMAN SCORNED

Tuesday, April 8, 2014

David Kincaid drove warily toward the corner opening onto the White House. This morning, he had carefully watched the morning news on two channels and listened to Public Radio as he drove.

The radio made no mention of the previous day's tempest, but both television stations had shown footage of protests outside the White House gate. Wolfe Network interviewed one outraged septuagenarian on the picket line, likely meaning that there were some good camera angles, but little substance.

As he rounded the corner, his suspicions were confirmed. About twenty placard-bearing citizens were marching with posters or holding up signs at Camera Point, the spot where people can stand to assist cameramen positioned across the street. That broad plaza is a safe and easy place to set up even the larger video units, the angle providing a beautiful classic White House backdrop.

Kincaid glanced quickly at the lofted signs, catching the text on a couple of them. They appeared handmade and included "Pray for our President" and "Why do you Hate God?". There were no camera crews at the moment, the two pieces on the morning news having been produced Monday night. He entered the gate without fanfare, and the Marine on duty made no mention of the protests a hundred or so feet away.

At seven in the morning, the corridors were relatively calm, resembling more a major hotel than one of the centers of world power. Carts of food and briefing papers wheeled by dedicated staffers were the traffic of the hour. Kincaid exchanged pleasant greetings with each worker, stopping just a moment to receive a happy update on Consuela's new granddaughter.

Arriving at his office, Kincaid unlocked the door, stowed his sweater, and donned his suit coat. He checked his desk. Peter had still been working in the office when Kincaid departed for an evening dinner in Alexandria. He found a copy of the final snap poll of the day along with a note "See Maj. Reed after TOfI around 10 — P." TOfI must be *time out for instruction* as best Kincaid could figure. The poll was essentially the same as the one they had shared with him during the evening news. Anna mentioned that the President would have the numbers on his desk, but that the Vice President's copy would be delayed a few hours. Devious staff. Ordinarily a Vice President should be able to count on his assistant to keep the reports up to date, but Janet was probably in league with Peter and Anna. Kincaid smiled.

He folded the final poll, placing it in his breast pocket, and left the office, locking the door behind him. The elevator was fast this time of day, and he finished with security checks and stood outside the Oval Office in near-record time.

"Good morning, Mr. Kincaid." Abigail was working on something resembling a picture frame.

"Good morning. Am I dead on arrival, or will I live to fight another day?"

She looked up smiling, then turned toward the door for a moment and lowered her voice. "He'll try to seem upset for a while, but he won't be very good at it. He's already seen the numbers. Go on in."

Kincaid knocked gently, opened the door, and walked in. The President had a spread of photos across his desk and a small pile of newspapers to the side. He had a magnifying glass out looking at the pictures. He seemed intent on comparing some details in the pictures and didn't look up immediately.

"David, I think we need to review what I mean by 'make this go away.' Tell me something: how much detail did you have about your staffer's holiday before you went into the press briefing yesterday?"

"Not much more than what I said when I was in here, Mr. President. Peter had already begun an investigation and assured me that there was no wrong-doing on our part."

The President finally looked up. "So, basically, intuition."

"I have faith in my staff, sir. We're very rigorous about our background checks, and I have full confidence in Peter's analysis."

"Some day, David, your intuition is going to fail us, and we're going to be sitting in the middle of deep shit." He was staring at Kincaid, watching for a reaction.

Kincaid knew the President wanted to provoke him. He was using "intuition," a word he seldom used. Kincaid waited, keeping his expression as unrevealing as possible.

"But today is not that day. I presume you've seen the snaps."

"I glanced at the ones from last night."

"Not bad. First time we've broken seventy in a long time. Weird town, Washington. You know what was on the news this morning?"

"The protests outside the gate?"

The President appeared surprised, looking in the direction of the windows. "They're still out there? No. Not that. They're doing follow-ups on clothing-optional resorts. You're not getting a cut of the action are you?"

Kincaid grinned, throwing his hands into the air to disclaim any relation to this news.

"Weird town. But on the serious side, I want to know what was behind this story. Did you notice how many cameras were out there yesterday? Didn't that strike you as odd, even for this section of the zoo?"

"Truthfully, sir, I had a lot on my plate and didn't have much time to think about it, but now that you mention …"

"I had dinner with Saul and with Mel Berndt last night," Miller interrupted.

"That must have been fun. Both major media heads at one table."

"Yeah. Very revealing. Jacobs wasn't the only one who got that video. Consolidated received it. Wolfe, too. But their videos had notes attached claiming it was a sex club. The note raised so much suspicion that they knew better than to air it on their networks. For whatever reason, Jacobs didn't have the note, didn't check with Saul, and decided to run the story at deadline. Everyone saw him going with the story, figured they were going to miss out on something, and piled on."

Kincaid folded his arms. "Really?"

"So, David, I want to know what the hell's going on. Who's behind this and why."

"Yes, sir."

Both men stopped at the sound of quick, hard footsteps outside the door. The President turned to Kincaid. "He's early."

Vice President Bailey entered, face flushed. A sheaf of printouts dangled from his hand. Immediately, he directed his anger to Kincaid. "Are you trying to goddamn destroy me?"

"No," Kincaid replied in a matter-of-fact tone.

"You attacked one of the nation's leading religious leaders from the very office of the President of the United States."

"Richards?"

"Don't be a smart ass. You've assaulted our most reliable base of support."

"He called one of my staff a whore."

"And I notice you haven't fixed that problem, either."

The President had been watching the back and forth, bemused. "Excuse me, gentlemen. I don't want to delay your pleasantries, but I'm having more company over later this morning."

"My apologies, Mr. President." Bailey turned to Miller, who had put his hands together to rest his chin. "I came back as quickly as I could to deal with this catastrophe. With all due respect, sir, how long are we going to put up with this cowboy?" The Vice President extended his free hand, pointing stiffly at Kincaid.

The President unfolded his hands and leaned back in his chair, swiveling in Kincaid's direction. He tilted his head back and forth several times. "I'm sorry, David, I just can't see you herding cattle." He swiveled back to Bailey. "Mr. Vice President, do you know something I don't? We're looking into yesterday's event, and we're not finding any problems on our end. The snap polls show enormous support for my Chief of Staff's defense. Am I missing something?"

Kincaid noted Bailey's brief surprise.

"I haven't seen the numbers, sir, and I'm not aware of any investigation results."

The President moved some of the photos on his desk, picked up the poll sheet, and handed it to the Vice President.

Bailey scanned the tables of numbers. His cheek twitched once. He flipped the paper over, finding the reverse blank. "This is meaningless."

"It's seventy-three percent approval, Jim. That's not meaningless."

"Mr. President, it's seventy-three percent of a random sample. If I ask the general population if they'd like free beer, I'll get seventy-three percent or maybe more, but that doesn't get anyone free beer. What counts is motivation, Mr. President." He lifted up the stack of papers. "We're getting slammed by those who actually take the time to make their voices known. You can ask anyone what they think, but it only matters what they do. The people who take time to write are the ones who take time to vote. You know that as well as I do. And we're getting e-mails down in the comm center running five to two outraged at yesterday's affront."

The President took the stack of e-mails from the Vice President and began to thumb through them. He looked over, frowning, to Kincaid.

The Vice President continued. "You must realize, sir — surely you must — that what we get done in the time remaining depends on the support of people who actually take action. Dr. Richards's followers are as organized and reliable a demographic group as there is. And now you, through David's recklessness, have slapped them in the face. We cannot afford to lose this group. Our margins for a lot of the work we need to accomplish are just too thin."

The President opened the stack at various places, reading the comments aloud. "... outrageous insult ... never been so insulted or humiliated ... ashamed of the leaders of our country ... how could you abandon us? ... why do you hate God so ..." He looked up at the Vice President. "Five to two?"

"Yes, Mr. President, since late yesterday afternoon. And they're still pouring in by the hundreds of thousands. I can only imagine what the real mail will be like, since the liberals don't use real mail very much anymore — too much work for them." He cast a baleful look in Kincaid's direction.

The President set the papers down, looking at them, perplexed. "Any thoughts, Mr. Kincaid?"

"No, sir. I defended a staff member against a specific attack. I certainly did not include anyone else."

"Pretty angry stuff here." The President lifted the e-mails again.

Kincaid reached out and took them. With a sinking feeling, he flipped through several. He looked at the e-mail addresses, which indicated all kinds of services. The writings ranged from short, hot notes, to rambling discussions. There were a few notes of support but they were short and polite by comparison.

"Any ideas, David?" the President implored.

Kincaid shook his head. He read a few more from almost a ream of paper. He took the stack and flipped through hundreds of missives. It was difficult to respond in light of the e-mails, e-mails from a very powerful and focused group. His mind turned to The Devil's Gallery.

The Vice President folded his arms and turned to the President. "Something has to be done to repair this, Mr. President."

Kincaid stalled for time. He flipped the pages again with his thumb. Something didn't seem right as the pages flew by. He checked again, this time flipping the pages from the top side of the paper.

He looked up calmly, addressing Vice President Bailey, "Save your paper. These are fake."

Bailey's face reddened. "Are you out of you mind? These came right off the printer in my office, right out of the e-mail system. They've passed through our spam-detection software already. Are you going to impugn these good people, too, in the face of all evidence, you arrogant ass?"

The President leaned back wearily. "David?"

"I'm not sure of every detail, sir, but Matt explained to me about e-mails awhile back, how they go station to station. That information is captured in the header here at the top of the message. We normally ignore it like it's gibberish. When I flip through these, every letter is different except these four lines at the top." Kincaid was looking at a sheet halfway through the stack. "After the sender's address, they all go through something called 'smxch.eastva.com'. All of them — no matter who's sending. No matter their e-mail address. And the times are all within a few minutes of each other. I just don't understand why Mrs. Ronald Parsons would be e-mailing us from Norman, Oklahoma, at three-seventeen in the morning her time."

The Vice President narrowed his eyes. "If you don't understand and you're not sure, perhaps you'd best check it out before dismissing it."

The President shook his head. "All right. That's enough. I don't know what's going on, but I want answers. Mr. Vice President, please check out our filtering software. David, get me some answers that will stick. And I want hard answers. No intuition. Is that completely clear?"

Both answered at once, "Yes, sir."

"Now get out of here. I have a country to run."

They left the Oval Office together. Kincaid did not want to ride down on the elevator with Bailey. He approached Abigail's desk, hoping the Vice President didn't have any business with her. Bailey continued toward the elevator, but turned back a moment as he left. "Nice try, David, but it won't work. You're going down."

Abigail looked up at Kincaid. She lowered her voice again. "Are we trying to avoid talking with our playmates?"

Kincaid looked hurt. "How can you think that? I just wanted you to know that Consuela's granddaughter is home now and doing fine."

She grinned. "Ah, thank you. I'm glad to hear that. Who's Consuela?"

* * *

Laura was in the midst of restocking when Charlie entered the center holding two newspapers aloft triumphantly.

"Way to go, Joan. They're below the fold, but both stories are front page. *Post* and *The Times*."

"Look, Charlie," — she took the papers — "I've been thinking about the whole Joan of Arc metaphor, and I'd like to try something else, OK? She died in the effort, as you'll recall."

"Sure did. But, wow, what a way to go. Burned at the stake. Spectacular."

Laura shook her head and began reading the stories.

Charlie was grinning. "Sheriff called. They're going to be making their move about ten-thirty if you want to be around."

She drew a deep breath. "This is moving awfully fast. We need more people there for backup — someone to take pictures, gather information. If it's not coordinated, it'll die on the vine."

"Then get on your phone, boss lady. The wheels are rolling. Lead, follow, or get outta the way."

Laura looked at the shelves, still partially stocked, then at her watch. "We've got to open in three hours. How're we going to do that?"

"Go with what you've got. The food line will wait. The enforcement won't."

She got up, brushed herself off, and picked up her jacket, checking for keys and cell phone before heading to her car. Charlie followed and buckled himself in the passenger seat as she reached the head of the legal justice center by phone. "Dan, I'm heading over to the call center. Yeah, it's about the story this morning. The county is about to confront that tech company …" She turned to Charlie, making a circular motion with her hand.

"Brisbane Technologies," he confirmed.

"… Brisbane Technologies. There's going to be a lot of fallout with the county exec, and we need to be ready to pick up whatever we can. Have you got anyone? Good. I'm on my way."

Laura made seven calls on her way to the call center in a nondescript office complex near College Park. Dan was as efficient as ever. Three law students from Georgetown were already waiting, notepads in hand. She had barely introduced herself when she spotted two sheriff's cars arriving. Her group approached cautiously. One emerging officer was familiar to her from the meeting at the sheriff's office.

He looked at Laura. "Who are these people?"

"Legal Justice Center. They're observers."

"OK, but don't get in the way. This should be a simple violations service. We don't want any kind of confrontation."

The students nodded. The deputy showed them a copy of his citation charging the company with securing a construction permit by fraud. They handed back the paperwork.

The other deputy joined the group, and the two officers took the lead, entering the building and taking stairs to the second floor. Laura, Charlie, and the students stopped halfway down the hall as the officers went to room two thirty-one and knocked.

At first there was no answer. They knocked again more loudly. Presently, the door opened, blocked by a very large man.

"What do you want?" he demanded.

The deputies looked at each other, then at the hulk looming in the doorway. "We have a report of unauthorized construction and are here to order an immediate halt."

"Fuck you! This is none of your concern. Get outta here," the hulk demanded again.

Laura looked at Charlie, who seemed uncharacteristically perplexed. One of the students began to take notes.

The deputies persisted. "Sir, that's really not an option. We're here to enforce a county action. May we please come in?"

"No, mother fuckers! Maybe you didn't hear me. I said get outta here. This is none of your business."

One of the deputies looked down the hallway to Laura. The hulk followed his gaze. When he caught sight of them, he smashed the closest deputy against the far wall, sending a crashing sound reverberating down the hallway. He slammed the door shut and proceeded swiftly in Laura's direction. The students stepped back.

"Who are you?" he growled.

Laura stepped forward in challenge. "Doesn't matter. Who are you? What are you hiding in there?"

"Get out. This doesn't concern you." He caught a glimpse of the student taking notes.

Wheeling in her direction, he reached out and grabbed the notepad. Grasping the fresh pad in his hands, he tore it in half. "Get out!"

Laura heard a number of footsteps behind her, but didn't turn her back to the hulk.

"Let me handle this, Hercules. Get back to your work."

The hulk gave Laura a sneer, but turned back toward the office. He stopped only to spit on the deputies midway down the hall. The one he had slammed into the wall was holding his shoulder. As the hulk opened the door and went in, the first deputy assisted his injured companion to his feet, and they made their way toward Laura.

Laura turned to the voice. Two black-shirted officers with insignia similar to Homeland Security accompanied a short, balding man. He presented his badge for only a second. She was able to read only "Henderson."

"I'm going to have to ask you folks to leave. Mr. Hermann was not very tactful in his communication, but he was correct that you should not be here. This is not your concern."

The injured officer spoke up. "The hell it isn't! We're here enforcing a county ordinance. Who are you to block us?"

Henderson was icy. "You're on federal property, son. This is an emergency call center in a federal district. We have jurisdiction, and I am going to ask you once again to leave."

Laura felt heat rising in her face. "Federal district? Since when do you have say over a county call center? And how the hell did you find out about this?"

"Read the statutes, ma'am. I don't have to tell you that. I'm asking you nicely for the last time. Please leave the premises now."

Laura turned and headed to room two thirty-one.

"Stop her."

Laura accelerated to a run. She arrived at the door and threw herself against it without effect. The two black-shirted officers grabbed her by the waist and neck. She heard Charlie call out to release her. She turned to see him running in her direction followed by the able-bodied deputy.

The black-shirts released her, pushing her in Charlie's direction. Then she heard the sound of rounds being chambered in two guns. She looked at Henderson, who was just getting off a radio-like device.

"All right. Please come with us. You're all under arrest."

* * *

Wednesday, April 9, 2014

Jack sat quietly as the Plantagenet interviewer finished her notes. The trip from Frederick to Richmond in the wee hours of the morning was catching up with him.

The interviewer finished writing, gathered her notes together, and tapped them on the table for alignment. "You know, Jack, we've had an awful lot of really highly qualified lab managers applying for this position."

Jack nodded.

"You'd be giving up a lot of salary and benefits for this job." She raised her eyes to meet his.

"Your research is top of the line here. You're taking the basic research I've been working with for the past decade and making it practical."

"Uh huh. One common thread that runs through all our overqualified candidates is that each has a friend or relative with a condition that might be addressed by MetaStop. You know about MetaStop?"

Jack paused a moment, and nodded again.

"I can't get you close to those studies, Jack. Every milligram in existence is in the clinical trials. It's all spoken for by people who are in the same condition as Jennifer. People with families too. There's a finite supply, Jack, and it can't be stretched. I'm sorry."

Jack buried his face in his hands. "How did you know her name is Jennifer?"

"You applied for the clinical trials … three times. When we started getting so many stellar applicants, we began crosschecking the applicants against the trials list. Our labs would love to have your talent, or any of the other ones, but a job here won't get you the MetaStop you're looking for. For that matter, it's still a clinical trial and there's no guarantee MetaStop will ever be approved. The work's just that — a trial. It wouldn't be fair to you or our lab to bring you in with groundless expectations." She closed the file folder.

Jack took a deep breath. "Well, thanks anyway. You're right, of course. Still, if you know anyone I could contact, any alternatives, anything at all, would you let me know?" He held out his Institute business card.

She looked over the card, and then put it in her pocket. "I will. I promise. It probably won't help, but one of our board members is a scientific officer of your Institute. He doesn't have anything to do with the detailed workings of the company, but he might know something or someone."

"Who?" Jack leaned forward.

"Dr. James Garrette."

Jack sat back in his chair, dejected.

* * *

"Thank you, Matt." Kincaid raised his hand as Matt left the office with the stack of e-mails.

"Nice going, sir. I'm amazed the Vice President let you hold them; much less take them with you. Matt's like a kid in a candy store. He'll get to the bottom of it. Count on it." Peter smiled from the comfortable chair by the door.

"The V-P was caught off guard, and wasn't thinking clearly. Peter, am I spending too much time on this? Why am I devoting these hours when there's so much serious stuff going on?"

"Because you smell a rat and your intuition is telling you it's a whole lot more than someone's embarrassing Sarah."

"And you seem so sure, too. Why?" Kincaid drummed his fingers on his desk.

"Track record, sir. You and I have been having these talks since '05, and the answer is always the same. Somewhere in your circuits where you can't even identify, the dots are connecting; and your circuits are just very good at picking the right dots. Matt could probably give you some nice neurological explanation that neither of us would understand, but doesn't use the word 'intuition,' and we'd all nod. I just know what I've seen. You're not wasting your time."

"Thanks. I feel better." Kincaid replied.

Frank appeared in the doorway. "Eleven o'clock over in Treasury, sir. We've got to get going."

Kincaid looked back to Peter. "Can you and Anna get the airport gate papers together for the afternoon? I'd like to go over those with the President before he leaves."

"Yes, sir." Peter got up, grasping Frank's shoulder on the way out. "Watch out that the boss gets there. He's thinking deep thoughts again."

Frank smiled. "Will do, Pete."

After Peter departed, Kincaid folded his arms. "What's with the 'we'? I don't need an escort to cross the street."

"The sidewalk is loaded with protesters sir."

"And you think they're going to attack me?"

"No." Frank shook his head. "You'll get into your usual 'talk' with them and you'll never make the meeting."

Kincaid sighed. "Did Tracey put you up to this?"

"No. I put me up to this. I know how you love to wade in. You'd convince half of them if it took you all day. You'd rather be doing that than meeting over in the basement of Treasury."

Kincaid shrugged. Frank was probably right. David got his coat and they walked out under the portico, past the main entrance guardhouse, and west toward the Treasury building.

As they made their way through the pickets, Kincaid nodded and smiled at each sign bearer. Most smiled and nodded back.

Kincaid turned to Frank. "Don't you find this a bit eerie?"

"Just keep walking, sir," Frank admonished.

They traveled another thirty feet. "It's like we're in another dimension or something." He looked back at the twenty or so people they had just encountered. Turning back ahead, he saw the elderly man with the sign reading 'Why do you hate God?' "Excuse me, young man."

"Sir, your meeting."

"Only one minute, I promise."

Frank sighed expressively.

Kincaid extended his hand, and the man placed his leaflets under the arm carrying his sign. The man shook hands firmly.

Kincaid smiled. "I'm from North Carolina. What's up here?"

"The President's been attacking our church, and we're here to let him know we don't appreciate that."

"Really? The President?"

"Or at least some of his people."

"Ah." Kincaid nodded his concern. He looked at the sign again. Though it appeared handmade from the street, there were telltale characteristics of a printed sign up close. "When did this happen? I must have missed it. Been kinda busy lately."

"I think it was Monday — after that girl from his office did her strip-tease on television."

Frank tugged on Kincaid's sleeve. "Sir, your meeting."

"Right. Well, my good man, I've got to go. What are your flyers there?"

The old man looked down. "Oh. We're supposed to be handing these out. They gave them to us along with the signs." He handed Kincaid a sheet of green paper.

"Thanks. I'll be sure to read it. Where do I get these?"

"Crusade headquarters."

Kincaid tilted his head back. "I thought that was in California."

"Oh, no, the regional headquarters is over on K Street." He pointed generally north and west. "That's where we're stayin' and gettin' our *per diem*."

"Good to know. Thank you, sir." Kincaid looked down at the paper. "Ah, I see it wasn't the President. It was that Kincaid fellow attacking Dr. Richards. I didn't think the President would do that. Well, you keep up the good fight, sir."

"God bless you," the old man acknowledged.

They crossed the street, Frank watching for traffic as Kincaid read the broadsheet. "You just couldn't resist, could you?"

"Hey, I took only a minute, like I said."

"Seven minutes. And we will be barely on time. Why couldn't you let it ride?"

"We walked right through fifteen, twenty-five people protesting what I said, and not one even recognized me. If I'm going to be demonized, I'd like the demonizers to at least know who I am."

"They're not demonizing you, sir."

"Ah, my faithful companion, for once you are wrong. Read it."

Kincaid handed Frank the paper and watched for the two of them as they continued their journey.

Frank read aloud. "…but he has fallen under the demonic spell of David Kendall, his apostate chief of staff, and is in danger of losing touch with the faith that our country was founded on." Frank turned to Kincaid. "So you are a demon. Well, that explains a lot."

"Hey!"

Frank was laughing.

"Plus they misspelled my name and have a dangling participle. But they got right the part at the bottom asking for donations, complete with name, address, and everything else."

"Maybe you should join up. Might save you yet. Maybe they have some kind of exorcism."

They began walking up the steps of the Treasury building. "Good idea. We Presbyterians don't have that. I'll fill it in this afternoon. Remind me why we're here again."

* * *

Sarah sat immersed in tobacco data, her desk strewn with stacks of Department of Agriculture and Commerce reports. Kathy combed state budgets from 2012 and 2013.

Sarah raised her head. "Did you ever notice how people have a sound shadow when they pass by the door?"

"What?"

"Listen. Hear the vent noises? Kind of a low level hiss. Now. Someone's coming. Listen while they pass." Sarah suggested.

Matt walked past their office.

"See?" Sarah asked.

"OK. Yeah. Are you having a hard time concentrating?"

"No. I was just noticing that."

Kathy sighed and looked up at her clock. "It's lunch time. I think you're ready for a break."

"Go on ahead. I have just a little to transfer here. I'll catch up with you in a bit."

Kathy placed her computer on secure screen saver and walked out into the hall.

Sarah continued copying and pasting rows of tobacco production figures into her spreadsheet. She was just finishing with the 2008 export numbers from Mozambique when the hall noise dropped and stayed down.

"That was quick. Forget something?"

She looked up. Instead of Kathy, she was looking into the face of Ben Jacobs, though she took a moment to recognize him without his television lighting and makeup.

"You!" Her voiced dripped cold indignity. "Who let you in?"

Jacobs's head drooped. His hands were behind his back. "I checked with Mr. Kincaid and Ms. Atwood. They thought it was OK."

"You hurt me. You may have put me in danger."

He lowered his head farther. "I know. I'm sorry. If I could undo it, I would. In a heartbeat."

Sarah crossed her arms and scowled. "What are you doing here?"

He raised his head and brought his hands from behind his back. "I've come to apologize."

Her scowl softened. She looked down from his face to his hands. In one was a large bouquet of pastel flowers; in the other a box covered with maroon velvet, tied with a golden ribbon. "I thought you apologized last night. At the end of the news," she said.

"That was a public apology. It was you I offended, so I thought I should apologize to you personally."

She kept her eyes on the flowers and the box. "Are those for me?"

He held them out to her. "If you'll accept them."

She reached out and took the flowers. Burying her nose into the bouquet she breathed deeply the spicy clove scent. "Freesias. My favorite."

"I know."

She looked up at him with what scowling she had left. "How can you know that?"

"I asked your mother."

"You talked to my mother?" she exclaimed.

"Hey, your boss asked my mother about my dogs." Jacobs opened his arms.

"Good point. Guess we started that. How did it go with my mom?"

"She said I was a *mashugana*, but that there was hope for me."

Sarah shook her head. "That's my mom. Her first encounter with the most powerful man in news, and she calls him crazy."

"But she said there's hope for me."

She looked at the velvet box. It had fine gold lettering on it reading 'Sean Riley, Chocolatier.' "Whoa, I've heard of these. If you got me freesias, then this must be…"

"Chocolate dipped apricots," he finished her sentence.

She tore open the wrapper. "I thought you had to reserve stuff from him weeks in advance."

"You do. Normally."

She looked up grinning. "I see. Someone had to call in a lot of favors, I'm guessing."

He shrugged.

She lifted the lid. Half the pieces were apricots, the other half an assortment of elegant designs and flavors. There was a note inside — 'For a most gracious lady. May these treats bring you contentment. Sean Riley.' She lifted one of the fruits and bit into it, half on the chocolate, half on the uncovered apricot. She closed her eyes and a smile spread across her lips. "This is considerably better quality than I'm used to."

"You're probably not used to being paraded around the world unexpectedly."

"Around the world?"

"Sorry. For a few hours, it was the most downloaded video clip."

Sarah leaned her head back and stared at the ceiling. "I don't know whether to be mortified or smug." She brought her head back to see Jacobs's pained look. She gazed down at the box and then lifted it in his direction. "Want one?"

He began to raise his hand to decline, but changed his mind and reached for one of the assortment. "I've never had any, actually." He bit into the piece, a chocolate covered cherry. "Wow. He said he only used fresh fruit. It's a real black cherry inside. Mr. Riley said to refrigerate the box when you get home."

"Thanks."

"So is there any chance we can put my blunder behind us?"

She looked at the freesias and the fine chocolates. "Probably. I'm not very good at staying mad at people unless they're persistent jerks. One thing I learned out of this was that there are a lot of people around here who actually care about me."

"Mr. Kincaid?" Jacobs asked.

"A lot of people, but he's probably at the top of my list. You're lucky he was the one who handled it. Reminds me a lot of my brother."

"Oh?"

"When I was growing up in West Orange, New Jersey, there was a bully in our neighborhood. We always had to watch out for him on the way home from school. He liked to rough up the little kids." She frowned. "Anyway, we were on our way home from second grade one day and hadn't been paying attention. The bully sorta ambushed us. He pushed me down and took my stuffed rabbit and threw it into the yard with the mean dog. About that time my brother came around the corner and saw what was going on. My brother is two years older than I am, but younger than the bully and a head shorter.

"My brother came running at the bully at full speed, arms swinging everywhere. I still don't know how, but he landed some pretty effective punches on him and wrestled him to the ground. I remember the bully rolling over, and my brother practically screaming, 'You leave my sister alone!' From that day to this, he's been my biggest hero in the world. He even got a big stick and went into the mean dog's yard and got my rabbit back. On Monday, I kinda got a second big brother."

Jacobs was nodding. "Am I really the bully?"

Sarah looked up quickly from a second apricot. "No. You were insensitive, maybe a little thoughtless, but I don't think that was intentional." She looked again at the flowers and chocolates. "And you're doing a pretty good job of trying to fix it. No, Richards is the bully. He was cruel and calculating. He meant to hurt me. But don't you ever do that again to an innocent person. Save your fire for the bad guys. There are plenty of them."

Jacobs raised his right hand. "I promise."

"Actually, you're more like Bobby Jenkins. He sat behind me in third grade and put glue in my hair."

Jacobs burst into laughter.

"It's true. Come to think of it, he had to read his apology in front of the whole class, too. Yours was better, even allowing for the age difference."

"I really meant it." Jacobs replied.

"You'll probably want to keep your writer under lock and key, though. Mr. Kincaid's looking for a new presidential press secretary, you know."

"I wrote it," Jacobs said.

Sarah raised her eyebrows. "Yeah? Like I said, it was good. Besides, you sorta got me a new car."

"Really? How so?"

"My Uncle Aaron, my dad's super rich brother, gives his nieces and nephews cars for their twenty-fifth birthdays if they've completed college."

Jacobs folded his arms. "Aaron Tyler? Big Apple Auto?"

Sarah frowned. "Yeah. I know you don't have anything on him."

Jacobs shook his head. "Oh, no, on the contrary. He's a major patron of the arts and education in the New York metro area."

"Well, I've always known him as Uncle Aaron. He comes to all our family gatherings — birthdays, Bat Mitzvahs … volleyball. Anyway, he was going to give me the car on my birthday in December, but he and Mom figured I needed it more now."

Jacobs put his hands together. "I think I should probably go before I do something to spoil the moment. I'll let you get back to your work." He started to turn.

"Thanks for the apology. It really means something to me." She took another bite of apricot. "And for the fruit."

Jacobs smiled, turned, and left.

* * *

James Garrette paced back and forth. His face was flushed, his tone harsh. Laura sat in the living room chair. Her arms were folded, her face sullen.

"You had no business being there. You're lucky you're not in jail, young lady. You were trespassing, pure and simple."

"The hell I was. That building is public. The call center is public. I was never anywhere that it wasn't my right to be. I was totally correct to be finding out why my customers are losing their jobs to some corrupt politician's scheme."

He wheeled and leaned on the arm of her chair. "You were breaking the law."

She faced him, teeth clenched. "Bullshit! I was on public property with —I'll remind you — deputy sheriffs. I was the one with the law. That Henderson guy was not law enforcement. I don't know what company he's working for, but it's not the government at any level. The only person he seems to report to is Pinkie."

Garrette hung his head. "You really should show respect and gratitude. Dr. Carlton's intervention saved you and your friends a boatload of grief and probably a lot of criminal charges."

"Oh yeah? What is his involvement in all of this, anyway? And how did he find out about it so quickly? And you. How are you mixed up in all this? I think I have a right to know what my own father is involved in."

"You don't have any right, but I'll tell you. Max Carlton is my boss. And he is my friend who has been very good to me and to my family over the decades. He is also a good friend of John Brisbane, whose company is upgrading the security equipment for the county. You're just lucky he was in a position to know who you are."

"If I was breaking the law, why wasn't I taken in? Huh?"

"What?" Garrette started.

"If I was breaking the law, despite my being with real law officers, seems like they would be conspirators, now doesn't it?"

"Don't muddy the issue."

"I'm not the one being muddy. Henderson and his two evil elves took five people at gunpoint from public property and then let us go because that old man waved his magic wand and said make it go away. Excuse me if I'm not all giddy grateful."

He sat down in the chair facing Laura, the look of anger changing to fatigue.

Laura waited awhile, her arms still crossed. "You OK, Daddy? If I'm in this deeper than I could have imagined this morning, you must be in even deeper."

He leaned back in the chair and sighed. "Where did you get your smarts? Between your mom and me, there isn't enough to explain it."

Laura uncrossed her arms and drew up her legs onto the chair. "You're not trying to change the subject, are you?" Her voice was quiet.

"No … yes … I don't know. When I got the call this morning, I was in a committee meeting. I was irritated at the interruption. Dr. Carlton ordered me to come and 'take charge' of you, and I was worried about my job. I remember being furious with you when you wouldn't leave the Brisbane office without your friends and associates. I remember that all I could feel was irritation, worry, and anger." He hung his head and sighed again. "Despite the fact that you were in the right."

She studied him, limp and old looking. "How involved are you in this?"

"I think you said it — deep," he sighed.

"What's involved? Can you get out?"

"I don't know. Maybe not. You remember asking me about the Windham Trust investments?"

She rested her chin on her knees and raised her eyes in his direction. "Uh huh. You get big envelopes from them every few weeks. Windham's linked to Vice President Bailey. Where is this going?"

"Brisbane Technologies is one of our biggest holdings with Windham. We have about seven million dollars of Brisbane stock."

She rocked back and forth. "Seven million, huh? I thought you told me half a million in Windham."

He shook his head. "That was a decade ago. Between additional contributions and performance, just that one part of the portfolio is about seven million now. The other things have done almost as well."

"Other things? Are the 'other things' as shadowy as Brisbane?"

"Some," he murmured.

She closed her eyes. "Can you get out?"

"I don't know. It all happened so gradually. Fifteen years ago, I was just a science administrator at an obscure research institute. When Dr. Carlton arrived, he took me under his wing and gave me opportunities I could have only dreamed about. The chance to benefit from it all came bit by bit. An investment opportunity here, a private conference there. And it's all paid off so well. So well…" He slowly moved he arm, sweeping around their expansive living room.

"What does Pin… Dr. Carlton get out of this?"

His face wrinkled as if to laugh, but he couldn't. "Information. The Institute's research has always been on the cutting edge, and with government budgets tight as they are, we're even further out ahead of everyone. He gets to know every discovery and research direction months — even years — ahead of anyone else. Everything we do these days gets locked down in patents and agreements. Our institute has a whole wing of lawyers who go after the people who used to be my friends and colleagues. It bothered me at first … until I got used to it. It bothers me a lot now, yet I can't do anything about it."

"Why not?"

"Men with guns and black suited elves. You've just now been introduced to them. Brisbane's not the only one who does that."

"Daddy, you've got to get out of this now," she implored.

"It's not that simple. We're in this and valuable to them. They're not going to let us just walk away."

"Who is 'us'?" she asked, startled.

"Windham doesn't have any qualms about using families as leverage. And they watch us more closely than you can imagine. Your group's pharmaceutical company on the border?"

"I don't like the feel of this," she said.

"Dr. Carlton warned me that he sits on the boards of two of your donor organizations, the Newport Trust and the Birmingham Foundation. He told me that if you don't back off, then those donors will — his words — be unable to continue supporting the border projects."

Laura continued to rock back and forth.

Garrette turned his back to her. "I'm so sorry."

* * *

Friday, April 18, 2014

"And Peter, is Senator Kreis on board with the change?"

"Yes, sir. The gate at Kennedy will be repurposed on Monday. The Senator said thanks for getting the N. C. State folks onto the Tobacco Commission."

Kincaid turned to Anna. "And will Jean Cartier be on hand in New York?"

"No, sir, he sends his regrets. They're tied down with the G-9 conference coming up and the first Al Wadi oil arriving at Basra. Ambassador Bonet will represent the Republic."

"Good. Who are we sending?" Kincaid asked.

"You," she smiled.

"Me? I don't remember."

"It's been on your calendar for weeks. I'm going up Sunday afternoon and you and Frank will fly up Monday morning."

Kincaid had just turned to Peter as Tracey entered the room. "Mr. Kincaid, the President needs to see you immediately. There's been a development."

"Anything more specific?"

"No, sir."

He got up from his chair. "OK, you two get things together for Monday. Maybe you can get home before dark. Have a safe trip up, and I'll see you Monday morning."

Kincaid checked his pocket for his badge and headed to the Oval Office. After check-in, he turned to Abigail. "Can you tell me what's going on?"

"Wish I could, Mr. Kincaid. The Vice President is in there, Defense is three minutes out, and they're on the line with the war room and the Joint Chiefs."

"Great," he cringed.

He walked into the Oval Office, closing the door behind him. The Vice President was engaged in an animated discussion. Two Navy officers manned a set of charts. Ahmed, the President's favored Arabic interpreter, sat quietly on the couch by the Remington statue. Kincaid caught his attention and spread his hands in question.

Ahmed shrugged and shook his head. Kincaid took that as a good sign. He walked over to the President's desk. Sensing his arrival, Miller looked up.

"Oh, good, David, you're here. Some of our people appear to have been captured north of Basra."

"Captured?" Kincaid tilted his head.

"Yeah, but everything is befuddled. All we're going on is a couple of radio transmissions — not very clear at that — and a hell of a lot of confusion as to where they were when they were captured."

Kincaid approached the desk, quickly scanning the maps. They were marked with several Xs in pencil, question marks, times, arrows, and markings in the gulf indicating ship positions. "Who's involved?"

The President was looking back and forth between the Vice President and the officers. "That's just part of the problem. We don't know. Depending on where they actually were, it could be anyone. And..." — he looked sternly at the Vice President — "...depending on where they were captured, we could be in a world of shit."

Kincaid examined the main map more closely. The Al Wadi pipeline had been heavily penciled in. Two of the Xs were in the desert in Iraq between the pipeline and the Gulf. But one mark was to the west of the line about twenty miles inside Iran. Kincaid felt goose bumps on his arms. "How long ago did they go missing?"

The President turned to one of the officers.

"About 1700 Zulu, sir. About three hours ago."

"And no idea who got them?" Kincaid asked.

The officer shook his head.

Kincaid looked at the positions again. "What were they doing there?"

The Secretary of Defense walked into the office.

The officer continued. "They were on routine reconnaissance patrol. The security of the pipeline is Worry Number One for us."

Secretary Banks was alongside Kincaid, who continued his questions. "I can believe that for these two points. The Iraqis don't like us wandering around their country, but will tolerate it. Not this one, and they shouldn't." He pointed to the X deep in Iran and looked around the room.

Both Bailey and Banks looked very uncomfortable. The President drummed his fingers on the desk.

Secretary Banks spoke. "There may have been a failure of their Global Positioning System unit. These patrols will operate for a week or so at a time. If their unit wasn't working properly, they could have strayed that far."

Kincaid noted the deliberate silence of the two officers. "How many of our people are we talking about? It was my understanding that every soldier has a GPS."

The Vice President provided details. "Four members of the patrol are missing. We don't know the details. Frankly, the details aren't important at the moment. We need to get our people back. Whoever is holding them is going to extract a heavy price."

Kincaid looked at Bailey, then at Banks and then turned to the President. "Mr. President, there can be no good reason for this point in Iran. I don't care whether their GPSs were working. The pipeline is massive. No one could have crossed it without knowing what they were doing."

Miller turned to Bailey. "Mr. Vice President?"

Bailey crossed his arms, looking down dispassionately at the map. "We've had some intelligence to suggest that Tehran was using some of the pipeline structure to mask the installation of missile launchers pointed at the Gulf. We've been sending in patrols to get an accurate assessment."

Kincaid turned to the President. "Sir?"

"I was not aware of the patrols, David. I'm learning about it same as you."

Kincaid turned to the Secretary of Defense. "Bob?"

"The directive came from the White House, David. I was not comfortable with it, but agreed that the possible threat had to be verified. I assumed the order came from the President. I hadn't had the opportunity to confer with him since we started last week."

"Where are they, Bob?" The President's face was beginning to redden.

"Those points are our best guesses, sir."

The President stood up abruptly. "Stop bullshitting me, you two. Where are they?"

The Vice President pointed to the location inside Iran. "Most likely here, sir."

"Who has them?"

The Vice President shook his head. "We don't know."

"Who has them?" The President repeated the question more forcefully.

Secretary Banks spoke quietly. "It's true, Mr. President. We don't know. The main satellite has just passed over. We should have some more information in the next couple of hours."

"And I'm guessing we have no way of knowing how to get them back, since we don't know who has them."

Banks shook his head. Kincaid broke in. "Where is State in all this? If our people have been captured in Iran … I don't even want to think about it."

The President walked behind his desk, hands on hips. "I thought it was a military problem up until now. I'll call State. David, could you contact the French? They're the ones who could get caught in the middle here. I don't want them in the dark, too."

"Yes, sir," Kincaid agreed.

Miller turned to Banks. "Mr. Secretary, what are we doing about a rescue attempt?"

"We've put the airborne assault and rescue on alert, sir. There are Seals and Rangers ready if we can locate the patrol."

"All right, let's get some solid information here." He turned to the two officers. "Thank you, gentlemen. Please brief Secretary Banks on what you've shown me." The President turned to his right. "Ahmed, looks like I don't need you yet. It's Friday afternoon. Do you have responsibilities?"

Ahmed stood up. "No, Mr. President, I'm good for the day. Thank you for asking."

The President nodded. "If I may impose upon you please stay around for a few more hours."

"As you wish, sir. I will be down in Mr. Kincaid's area. I have some questions for Matthew." With a nod, he was off.

The others gathered their papers and made their way to the outer office.

"Mr. Vice President, Mr. Kincaid, please remain." The President waited until the doors closed, then stood, his arms folded, looking at Vice President Bailey.

"Sir?" The Vice President's cheek twitched.

"Don't you ever — ever — do anything like this again!" Miller shouted. "If our troops have been captured by the Iranians, we are looking at a diplomatic and military catastrophe. What else is going on that I don't know about?"

Bailey had been averting his eyes, but immediately faced the President after this question. "Nothing, sir. This was a small reconnaissance operation. They were not armed, except for standard side arms."

"They were operating inside another sovereign country, Jim. They were on patrol inside godamn Iran. We have men in uniform inside a powerful, hostile sovereign country uninvited."

"Sir, we don't…," Bailey began.

"Shut up! Whether or not that's where they've been captured, and regardless of where they're being held, it's obvious that they were sent there under my name, even though I had no idea they were there. Why did you send them?"

"I was completely honest, sir. We needed the reconnaissance."

"The French are there on scene, Jim. Don't they let us know if something is developing?"

"If you can believe them, sir."

"Have they ever been less than forthcoming, Jim? Have they ever lied to us?" Miller demanded.

"I don't know…"

"No, Jim. No. The answer is no. We have always enjoyed full cooperation with our French counterparts. What's more, we are now completely dependent on them to manage this pipeline and provide a reliable source of oil."

The Vice President remained stony-faced.

"Now, I'm asking you again. Is there anything else going on I don't know about? Military, industrial, anything?"

"No, sir," Bailey replied, stoic.

The President raised his hands and ran his fingers through his graying hair. "We have to deal with this now. But it won't be over. This is an unbelievable breach of responsibility putting those men in there. Go find Bob and let me know as soon as you've located our troops. Have a plan ready."

The Vice President turned to leave, and caught sight of the Chief of Staff.

Kincaid could tell that Bailey wanted to give him some unpleasant gesture, but couldn't.

Only the President and David Kincaid remained. A warm April setting sun illumined the Washington Monument visible through the office window. The President had turned to watch the peaceful vista. "We're in for a hell of a ride this time, David. I know you'd like to say, 'I told you so.'"

Kincaid managed a trace of a smile. "I'd never do that, sir."

"I know. That's why I said it for you. You've earned it. You know that more than a few commentators have said I've been too detached." He turned to watch for Kincaid's reaction. "They're probably right. And if those boys are in Iranian hands, I'm going to go down like Jimmy Carter."

"I'm not sure that's such a bad outcome, sir. He's become one of the most respected politicians of that era."

"Yeah, but it's taken forty years." He shook his head. "Look, this thing is going to be moving fast when it breaks. I'm going to need all your people. Get them up to speed. Talk to your French counterpart first. We need to contain the damage as much as we can. So far, nothing's blown up and nothing is on fire."

"Yes, sir. Anything else?" Kincaid asked.

The President paused, frowning. “How is your fellow coming on the investigation of Bailey’s dealings?”

“Sarah Tyler? She’s gathered lots of data. We lost sight of her desk weeks ago. No smoking gun, but she says it could be weeks before she has anything worthwhile … if, indeed, there is anything to be had.”

“Let me know if you find anything. Even if you’re uncertain, let me know. I’ve had enough surprises, and something feels very wrong. We could be in for a perfect storm of bad news.”

“I think we’ll be fine, sir,” Kincaid assured.

“You don’t believe that, and you’re a lousy liar. I think I’ve got another five appointments, and then I’ll come down. Tell me before you leave.”

“Yes, sir. I don’t have anything planned this evening.”

Kincaid left the Oval Office and turned to Abigail. “Could you please call my office and have Ms. Colbert meet me in the Comm Room?”

“Yes, Mr. Kincaid.”

By the time he arrived at the communication room, Anna was waiting outside the door.

“Some of our troops were captured on patrol near the Al Wadi pipeline. We need to get them back, and that may well involve military action in the vicinity of the pipeline. We’re going to let Mr. Cartier know where things stand.”

“That doesn’t sound good. Who captured them?” she asked.

“That’s part of the problem. We don’t know.”

Kincaid typed in the number to call.

Anna put on her headset and looked to Kincaid. “It’s a bit after ten in the evening. I doubt he’d be in his office.”

“True, but they should be able to patch us to him.”

He was surprised to hear Jean Cartier answer personally.

“Oui?”

Anna began interpreting.

< “Ah, David, I was expecting your call.” >

“Expecting?”

< “Yes. It seems we found some things you lost out in the desert.” >

“That is precisely why I’m calling. The President and I have just found out about a problem in the last hours.”

< “Then would you mind telling me what your troops were doing almost forty kilometers inside Iran?” >

Anna looked at Kincaid with alarm. She pushed the privacy button. “He’s not happy.”

“He shouldn’t be.” Kincaid nodded to Anna and she went on line again. “Monsieur Cartier, the President and I had not been informed of this mission. Had we known, we certainly would not have authorized it.”

< “Ah, I see. Perhaps your President should keep a closer eye on

Monsieur Bailey, then.” >

Kincaid frowned. “An interesting comment, my friend.”

< “Our Ambassador Bonet is a keen observer of personalities. We are fortunate indeed to have him in your fair city. But I digress. You are the fortunate ones that your soldiers were kidnapped rather than captured by the Iranian army. I suspect we can get them back for you but it will be expensive, especially for your dear friend Mr. Bailey.” >

Kincaid relaxed. He watched Anna grinning at some inflection buried in the nuances of the French. “I'm listening.”

< Your people were captured by a band of tribesmen. Your people may have been equipped with the latest night vision equipment and sensors, but they're no match for these nomads who ply the desert. >

“My information is much more limited than yours, Jean. Were there any casualties? On either side?”

< Fortunately, no. They wisely did not put up a struggle. My Legionnaires tell me your men were armed only with pistols and were quickly surrounded by fifty or so men with rifles and very sharp knives. Now, David, if we may, shall we return to the question about why your people were out in the desert? I can only assume there must be a most important reason to undertake a mission of such risk. >

Kincaid paused, shaking his head. “The reasons are not altogether clear at this time. Vice President Bailey tells us that they were on a reconnaissance mission, that they were investigating reports of missile launchers hidden beneath the pipeline. His explanation is unconvincing. The truth is that neither the President nor I have good information at this time.”

< I appreciate your candor. Perhaps the charts they were carrying will clarify the matter. They were not prepared by your military, but rather by Universal Oil. >

“Universal? The Vice President's former company?”

< Former? David, David, David, we really must sit down on Monday and have a long talk. I will be bringing their papers with me. I think your Dr. Tyler will find them most interesting. >

“I look forward to meeting with you in New York, though I'd been under the impression that you weren't able to attend.” Kincaid looked to Anna. She shrugged.

< Well, yes, that was the case. But this development has much more important implications than the G-9 meeting. Besides, I'm tired of reviewing menus and seating arrangements. > He added a couple of phrases in a brusque undertone.

Anna grinned. She did not interpret the last two phrases.

Kincaid continued. “You said that this incident will be expensive for Vice President Bailey.

< Ah, yes. Assuming that we will be receiving rights to the gate, President Gastagne will personally accompany your brave soldiers back. The tribesmen will, of course, be expecting a gratuity for their desert hospitality … and their silence. >

Kincaid rubbed a hand over his face.

< Your pause betrays you, David. Let me guess that the gratuity is a problem. I'll spare you the lecture on mature diplomacy. I'm sure that our diplomats with a simple transportation fee can make arrangements. >

"Thank you, Jean. I'm sure that can be arranged, but it doesn't come out of the Vice President's budget."

< That wasn't what I was referring to. Monsieur Bailey is trying to scuttle the transfer of the terminal to Air France as we speak. >

Kincaid leaned forward. "The transfer is already essentially accomplished. We got the last senator to agree this afternoon."

< Yes, with a certain board position that Monsieur Bailey's security apparatus must approve. But he had hoped the terminal would be given to an airline operated by one of his close associates. >

"I'll see that the President is aware of this. We will make a big show of the Legion's rescue. I presume it was a heroic operation."

< How heroic do you require? >

"Something dashing, thrilling. You've seen the movies."

Cartier laughed. < I'll see what we can do. By the way, do you need your geo-positioning devices back? The tribesmen rather fancy them and would find them quite useful. It would make negotiations proceed more smoothly. >

"Interesting, Jean. I was told that there was only one GPS and that it must have broken."

< You really need a better source of information. No, each soldier had a hand held device. Our desert friends broke one when it was dropped, but the other three are working quite well. They play a game trying to match each other's position looking only at the device. Quite amusing. So then we are agreed — our brave Legionnaires rescued your people from a band of lawless kidnappers ten kilometers inside Iraq, and your people had one damaged geo-positioning device. >

"Can the tribesmen be trusted to back that story?"

< As long as we are — as you say — the high bidder. >

"Thank you, Jean."

< A pleasure as always, David. *Au revoir* until Monday. >

Cartier hung up the phone. Kincaid and Anna looked at each other.

Kincaid spoke. "Well, that went relatively well. Hard to imagine, but we and our French friends probably just saved several thousand lives and hundreds of millions of dollars."

Anna shook her head. "Amazing. And that's all it took?"

"We were lucky this time. Had it been the Iranian Guard instead of the cross-border 'businessmen,' the outcome would have been much different. Let's get upstairs before they do something stupid."

On the elevator, Kincaid turned to Anna. "When I explain the situation to the President, watch the Vice President carefully for his reactions. I'll watch Secretary Banks. I'm curious about how closely they interact."

"Yes, sir."

The elevator door opened.

After signing in, Kincaid turned to Abigail and gave her a thumbs up sign.

"Oh, good. You're the first person who hasn't looked like the grim reaper. Somehow the media have gotten hold of the story."

Walking into the crowded office, he found the President seated by a table covered in charts. Secretary Banks and an admiral were explaining different options. The Vice President conferred in a corner with one of the two generals present.

The President looked up for only a moment. "We're finalizing a strike plan now, David. The carriers have been given the three locations. Helicopters are ready to head into the air under close air support."

Kincaid fixed his eyes on Banks as Anna watched Bailey. "That would be a tragic mistake, sir."

President Miller raised his head quickly. "Oh?"

"Yes, sir. The local French Foreign Legion rescued our people about an hour ago in a raid right here." Kincaid pointed to the spot ten kilometers inside Iraq. As Secretary Banks surmised, the group's GPS was malfunctioning. The men had been captured by a large group of desert tribesmen traders who operate along the border."

Banks heaved a loud sigh, but he smiled. "Thank God! Do the French actually have them?"

"Yes, Mr. Secretary. They'll be back here Monday morning as the first passengers to arrive at the new French concourse at Kennedy. I believe you'll want to be there to greet them, Mr. President. President Gastagne will be escorting them."

"But of course!" The President beamed. "About time we've had something to celebrate."

"Um, Mr. President, the concourse transfer hasn't been approved yet." Kincaid turned to the Vice President, whose expression had changed from perplexed to sour.

"Oh, yes, it has. Senator Kreis was on board as of this morning."

Bailey continued. "That agreement is contingent on his nominee's getting on the tobacco board, and his nominee isn't cleared yet."

"God damn it, Jim!" the President slammed his hands on the table and rose halfway from his seat, cheeks flushed. "They just helped us avoid a war. A war, Jim. Your people have the job of clearing these guys. It's the fucking tobacco board. I don't care if they've nominated Osama bin Laden, Jim. Clear him now! If you can't do it, I'll do it myself. Personally. Understood?"

"Yes, sir."

The President plopped back in his chair. "All right, everybody, while this is still fresh, I want to get procedures in place so this doesn't happen again. Secretary Banks, we will be keeping David and me in every loop going forward. Is that clear?"

"Yes, sir," Banks replied.

"I want a detailed report on the timeline of this operation by the end of the day." The President turned to his clock. "Shit. It's past the end of the day. I want a report in three hours. Everybody is dismissed except for those who are planning Monday's event — David, Ms. …"

"Colbert, sir." Anna nodded.

The President turned to the Vice President. "Would you like to welcome our French heroes, Jim?"

"No, sir. Thank you."

"Fine. Bring me the paperwork with that clearance before you leave. I want to sign it myself." Miller pointed to door. "Go!"

The President remained seated, serene amidst the aides scurrying to remove charts and papers.

Kincaid moved toward a set of French doors to the side of the Oval Office and motioned for Anna to join him. He kept his voice low. "You've seen a number of classic photographs of Presidents looking out these windows. This is what they see."

A faint trace of dusk tinged the otherwise dark sky. Bright floodlights illumined the Washington Monument and the World War Two Memorial while a constant stream of night traffic moved oblivious to the events that had just transpired.

Anna murmured, "Very beautiful. I would think this view helps keep focus during chaos." She turned a moment back to the room to see a petty officer gathering the last papers into a portfolio. She whispered, "What reaction from the Secretary?"

Kincaid gazed at the brilliant obelisk. "He seemed genuinely relieved. I didn't sense he was trying to hide anything. You?"

"The Vice President is probably taking his antacids now. I haven't seen him too many times in person, but he seemed as upset as I've ever seen him in any press picture. I don't sense that he was expecting anything you told the President. He even flinched when you said there was only one GPS."

Kincaid nodded. "You nearly laughed when Cartier was talking about my friend Monsieur Bailey. What was that about?"

"A little hard to interpret on the fly, sir. There's a French sitcom about a nice man named Jacques who's forever getting in trouble because of his friend Marcel, a shady character. Marcel's kind of a petty criminal. Monsieur Cartier was saying that 'your Marcel, Monsieur Bailey' was not going to be happy."

Kincaid chuckled and turned toward the President. Miller was still in his seat though the table had been pulled away and returned to the side. His eyes were closed and his head tilted back a little. Kincaid and Anna approached quietly.

"So, how far inside Iran were they?" The President kept his eyes closed.

"About forty kilometers — twenty-five miles give or take."

The President opened his eyes and turned to Kincaid. "What the hell were they doing there?"

Kincaid opened his hand and nodded to Anna, who picked up the story. "According to Jean Cartier, they were carrying maps from Universal Oil, cameras, and geopositioning devices. They were lightly armed and didn't put up any resistance. That probably saved their lives. The Iranians have invited the Foreign Legion to help with current security of the Al Wadi, and to train their security forces for deployment along the pipeline."

The President looked back and forth between the two. "I thought there was only one malfunctioning unit."

"No, sir, one was dropped after their capture, but the other three are perfectly functional. They knew exactly where they were."

"How soon before the Iranians know about this? Or do they already?"

"The tribesmen are pragmatic businessmen and are being well compensated for their hospitality. Jean thinks they're likely to keep quiet."

The President read from a small scrap of paper. "I have a note from Abigail that the press already has word 'the Iranians have attacked and captured a platoon of Americans serving in the Gulf.' Any idea how that got out?"

"No idea, sir." Kincaid was shaking his head. "However, it would be well to nip any speculation as quickly as possible before the story takes on a life of its own. Let me make a few more checks and clear up some details and I'll give a quick briefing to the press pool."

"Right. And I want a thorough debriefing of those soldiers. I want to know for certain what their mission was and who instigated it."

"I agree, sir. In fact, I was going to suggest Admiral Brown come up with us to meet them and take command."

"Bill Brown? Good man. Any particular reason?"

"Forgive me, sir, but I'd feel more comfortable with him than with someone the Vice President would choose. He would also have good cover, since he has exceptionally good relations with President Gastagne."

"Don't I remember something about an affair?" the President asked.

Anna joined in. "Close, sir. When Admiral Brown was attached to

NATO and serving in Paris, he had a rather well publicized, very proper dating relationship with the President's daughter, Michelle. All indications were that it was honorable, and President Gastagne seemed delighted. In fact, when Michelle decided later to take up with one of their rock stars, he was quite vocal in his disappointment. The rock star affair was all over the European tabloids. President Gastagne and Admiral Brown are still very good, very close friends."

The President smiled. "It's a complicated world, isn't it?"

Kincaid nodded again. "Yes, sir. If you don't have further need of us, we'll get the press taken care of and make arrangements for Monday."

"Good. Is there anything you need from me?"

"Do you speak French, Mr. President?" Anna asked.

"*Un peu.*"

She smiled. "I'll be there if you need any assistance, sir."

They turned and began walking out. Kincaid stopped briefly at the door. "Have a good weekend, Mr. President."

* * *

Once Sarah had entered her last data set into the computer, she transferred it to the modeling programs running on mainframe computers at Rutgers and Fort Meade. She watched the results return showing projected cash flows for tobacco products around the world and how those flows changed with different proposals they were considering. Though the transactions represented billions of dollars, it hardly seemed so since the displays dropped the last six digits of each number to save space on printouts. With the initial run it seemed their program would cost about twice what they had hoped. But this was still well within the projected healthcare cost savings, and she was still missing the inputs from North Carolina and Alabama. Those would probably bring the cost down a little. The ambient noise from the hallway dropped again, and she turned to see who was still around at this late hour.

"Corporal Tull. Hello."

"Good evening, ma'am."

"Are you still on duty? It's past eight," she asked.

"No, ma'am."

"Then drop the 'ma'am.' Can I order you to do that?"

"I don't think so. But I'll try."

She giggled. "I don't think there's anyone around here who can sign anything."

"No, m… no. I just came to see how you were doing; see if things are OK."

"Thank you. Actually, life calmed down quite a bit after Mr. Kincaid cleared up protocol with Mr. Jacobs. In fact, Ben Jacobs has been rather nice since that. He brought these." She held forward the box of chocolates.

Every other spot, where the apricots had been, was empty. "Try one."

Tull picked a lumpy cluster. "Mmmm. Blueberries. And they're fresh. Not dried. Very good."

"So, what do off duty Marines do on a Friday night in Washington?" she asked.

"Shine shoes, practice saluting, stand at attention…" Tull looked up to see her expression — half serious, half puzzled. They both began to laugh. "We do the same things everyone else does. In fact, that's part of why I stopped by. I was wondering — and there's absolutely no pressure — if you would be interested in going with me to our Bible group Sunday night."

She paused. "Um. I'm not sure. I'm Jewish, you know."

Tull mirrored her pause. "OK," he began slowly, "I know that's great with our group. Two of the members are rabbi students. It's a study group. We're not proselytizing. And our discussions are pretty lively. I think you'd enjoy it. But, again, there's no pressure."

"Let me think about it. I'm not saying no. OK?"

"Yes, m… yes. I wrote down my cell phone number here just in case." He handed her a slip of paper.

"Thank you," she said.

He nodded, grinning. The grin produced those dimples again. He turned and walked down the hallway.

Sarah listened until she heard the elevator doors close, and then drummed on her desk with her fists. "Yes!"

* * *

Saturday, April 19, 2014

Jennifer was more successful than Jack at holding back despair. "It just makes more sense, Jack. I like Lindale. I've been a volunteer there for five years. They're set up to take care of me better than here. Look, I'm so weak I can't even walk to the bathroom without taking a rest. You'll actually get to spend as much quality time or more with me in hospice than you do now because you won't have to be constantly making modifications to the place. Plus you can keep working hard, which would make me happier. I can spend the time concentrating on writing."

"You're right, of course."

Jennifer wrapped her arms around Jack, and kissed him on the neck. "We both have a pretty good idea of the time horizon here, and I want to make use of every minute left. Now you listen to me carefully and don't interrupt until I'm finished, OK?"

Jack nodded.

"Promise. I want to hear it. 'Cause you're going to object to the first half."

"I promise."

"OK. Lindale is putting me up at no cost for now. I argued with them, but Janille says my work there, especially the legal stuff, has been worth a fortune to them. I know we were planning to pay for my time there out of savings and a little retirement, but Janille wants to do this out of gratitude and kindness, and it would be an insult to turn her down. Got it?"

Jack nodded meekly.

"Long after I'm gone, when you and your hard-headed wife — remember, she needs to be hard-headed — are fabulously wealthy, maybe you can make an obscenely huge donation, name a wing after me or something."

Jack managed a tiny smile.

"Now help me get the rest of this packed. Whatever's left we can donate. In fact, the Lindale Center has a 'helping closet' for families in serious financial need. That would be a good start."

Under instruction, he helped pack four nightgowns, most of her underwear and socks, toiletries, seven books, three writing pads, a box of ballpoint pens, an audio recorder with extra batteries, and the three pictures she kept on her dresser. The lid closed without effort. Jack slowly carried the suitcase that had never seen Jamaica to the front hall.

14 DESCENT

Monday, April 21, 2014

Laura was reading articles in *The Times* and *Post* about their run-in at the Montgomery County call center. The pantry would not open for another ten minutes and she didn't want to look outside yet. "Charlie, we're in this deep, aren't we?"

"Oh, yeah. We're lucky to be alive. Or maybe not. Those goons are probably preparing a horrible death for us right now."

"You're not making me feel any better."

"Oh. I'm sorry. Was I supposed to be doing that? OK, how about this? No, not too deep, and we've uncovered a lot of really bad dirt and will be given glowing credit for it in our obituaries."

"You're sick." She tossed the paper onto the office table and returned to filling in her logs. "I think someone got to the *Post.* Their report's really toned down and they used *trespassing* about ten times. But I think Anita's father-in-law must still be pissed off. *The Times* is giving our incident pretty decent coverage."

Charlie had pushed the recliner back and rested with his hands on his chest. "But the papers are still only talking about economics."

Laura looked up. "…and…?"

Charlie didn't move. His jazz festival ball cap was pulled down low on his face and his hair stuck out from the back of the cap. "I've had this notion in my head that they had an awful lot of horsepower there if the only mission is to put a room full of hard-working Americans out of work and skim off a bunch of tax dollars."

She folded her hands on her desk. "The contract is worth half a million, Charlie."

"Uh huh. That applies to dozens and dozens of county projects — projects that displace the same number of potential taxpayers. But they don't have black-shirted commandos with Israeli and Chinese weaponry and shoulder-mounted encrypted communications gear. And they sure don't have Armani-suited skinheads like Henderson on call."

Laura pulled the newspapers back and re-read the stories. She looked up. "Please tell me you just forgot to take your paranoia meds this morning."

He lifted his cap and turned to face her. "Yeah, that's it." He wouldn't say any more.

Laura waited about a minute before giving in. "All right. I doubt I'm going to believe anything you concoct, but what do you think is going on?"

Charlie pulled the cap back down and rested his chin on his chest once more. He wiggled to get more comfortable. "That building is right beside the line-of-sight between the downtown DC transmitters and the central Maryland switching station. And … it's also at the intersection with the line between Andrews Air Force Base and Camp David."

"So you think they're spies?"

"Not exactly. You didn't happen to notice while you were playing footsie with the goons whom they were working for, did you?"

"Homeland Security — DHS — I definitely remember them saying that."

"Not exactly."

Laura lowered her head into her fists, mumbling through her knuckles, "You're irritating me."

"Henderson kept referring to Homeland, but he never actually said he was one of them. That badge case of his was really, really nice — definitely not government issued. And the badge was bimetallic — silver and gold. Government issued badges are just silver. Trust me. I know. Finally, while I was fighting for my ladye faire, I got painfully close to the shoulder of head goon Hercules. That patch was Brisbane Technologies, not DHS."

"So what? DHS hired them," Laura suggested.

"Why? Why bring in this much muscle to convert a call center — a civilian county call center? Is Anita that dangerous? I don't think so. We've cracked a little piece of veneer off a project these guys didn't want anyone to know about. And did I note that Carlton is involved?"

Laura nodded.

"He goes straight up to the top. Well, at least to Bailey's office. Carlton is the perfect nexus of oppressive government and the dark side of capitalism. The fact that he stepped in to protect us — you — tells me that you must be awfully important to him. And I doubt it has anything to do with this pantry or your pharmaceuticals on the border. I really think you need to have a quiet look at your daddy's portfolio."

Laura watched Charlie, unmoving but for his lips, ball cap still pulled over his eyes. She got up from her desk and headed toward the front door.

"Let's open up, it's time. Oh, shit, there's gotta be thirty or forty people in line already."

Charlie got up from the recliner and stretched. "On the other hand, Carlton's probably the reason we're not attending that funeral this morning."

Laura tilted her head. "What funeral?"

"Ours."

* * *

"Yes, sir. And they'll each need to sign these." Peter handed Kincaid a pair of documents in elegant diplomatic folders. "Normally they could be signed by deputy secretaries of state but it looks great on television to have the two presidents signing. Be sure to secure the pens and get them to Secretary Zink. She needs to certify them for gifts."

Kincaid smiled. He looked up at the clock. Seven forty-five. "I've got about an hour and a half before Marine One arrives. I'll get some coffee and go over the message traffic. Anything else before I go?"

"No, sir. I talked to Anna about half an hour ago. She says they've got the place looking really nice — flags, banners, white chairs for the dignitaries and press. Sounds like a good show."

Peter got up to leave. They both turned their heads toward the hall at the sound of a distant argument. "Sounds like Sarah," Peter offered.

"And Corporal Tull," Kincaid added.

They began to make out fragments of the exchange: "…but that's not what it says…," "…it's a continual revelation…," "…relying on tradition, not documentation…."

Kincaid rubbed his chin. "As I recall, they were going out on a 'not' date last night."

Peter grinned, shaking his head. "Doesn't sound like it went very well."

The pair in the hall had lowered their voices somewhat, but the words were distinct now. Tull seemed to give up his argument. "*Oy.*"

"You can't say that," Sarah said.

"What? Why not?"

"It's Jewish. You're not Jewish."

"It's a word, a nice expressive word. It doesn't belong to anyone."

"It carries cultural connotations. It has history."

Tull's tone changed. "I've got to stop here with the message traffic. Are you free tonight?"

Peter and Kincaid exchanged puzzled glances.

"I'm finishing up the AIDS banquet arrangements this afternoon. I should have it cleaned up by six-thirtyish. I want to try the new Five Guys."

"OK, I'll stop by then." Tull entered the outer office and greeted Tracey.

Peter shook his head again. "Have a pleasant trip, sir."

"Thanks." Kincaid watched Peter leave and waited for Corporal Tull.

The pattern was familiar. The Corporal knocked gently on the doorframe and announced his presence. "Mr. Kincaid? I have the morning traffic."

Kincaid motioned with both hands. "Come in, come in. We couldn't help overhearing your conversation. Sounded like a rough Sunday evening."

"Sir?"

"With Dr. Tyler," Kincaid replied.

"Oh, no, sir. Actually it was wonderful. I think she was kinda skeptical at first, but we have a very academic group, and she has home court advantage. Didn't take long for her to become the hero — heroine? — of the group, either. We have two rabbinical students. I had called them rabbi students — she corrected me pretty early. Moshe and Aaron have always dominated the group because of their studies, and they stifled discussion. She listened for about ten minutes and then took them on. By the time the group wrapped up, Moshe was arguing with himself."

"Hmm, I didn't realize she had that much background."

"That's the amazing thing, sir. She doesn't. We talked about it on the way back to her place. She said she was arguing from 'first principles.' She said they were drawing conclusions they couldn't support with facts or consistent arguments. Several of the Christians — she insists on 'Gentiles' — finally started participating again. It was fabulous."

Kincaid smiled as he began initialing the documents on Tull's clipboard.

"And she is funny," the corporal continue.

"I've noticed that." Kincaid finished the messages. "Looks like a quiet weekend otherwise."

"But sounds like it could have been bad, sir."

"How much do you know?"

"Only what I hear, sir. And that's as far as it goes. I watched your press briefing Friday night. I think the French probably appreciated what you said."

"Well, I hope you're right. The French saved us from a serious self-inflicted wound. I'm very grateful for their help."

"Safe journey, sir." Tull took the clipboard and left.

Kincaid tidied his desk, handed his finished paperwork to Tracey, and headed for the President's office.

* * *

As their argument grew louder, Jack closed the office door. "This is not a matter for discussion. That was a dangerous and very stupid thing to do. We've had this conversation twice before. You do not heat acetonitrile on a hot plate. Ever. Period. If it had boiled over, we would have had a disaster. Have you ever seen acetonitrile burn?"

His three technicians were seated, arms folded. Leslie was red faced, near tears. "This is ridiculous. Your rigid rules are putting us further behind. You act like this was some whim. Unlike you, we're at the job, right there. We monitor the temperature. We stir the mix. In the process, we change a three-hour dissolve into twenty minutes."

"And risk a fire that could take out this corner of the building."

"You're not listening. We're on top of things. We're paying attention."

"What's the hurry? What is so important about speed that you're willing to take risks like this?" Jack spread out his hands with the question.

Elsa joined in. "You see? You don't have to put up with everybody coming to us wanting to know when their samples will be ready. You don't know what that pressure is like."

"Bullshit. They come to me and I tell them the samples will be ready when they're ready. We can't change the chemistry or the physics. Their turnaround time is determined by the machines and the protocols."

"And then they come to us."

"And you know why? Because when they do, you bend the procedures. You alter the list. You let them bully you. You don't have to do that. Send them back to me. That's my job. That's what they pay me for. If there's a genuine need for faster turnaround, then we'll budget for more equipment, more people. But I really don't see a genuine need for more speed."

"But it doesn't even need to cost anything, Jack. We just need to heat the solvent to cut the time wasted dissolving the monomers."

"Fine. Find me a heater that's OSHA-approved for heating acetonitrile, and I'll put in for it today."

"There's no such thing." Leslie turned her head away.

"Have you looked?"

"Yes."

"Well, I wonder why that would be." Jack put his hands on his hips. "Do you think that's maybe because it's … too … dangerous?"

The three were scowling.

"I was three hours late because I visited the hospice this morning. I assumed that I could leave things in your hands, and this happens despite my earlier warnings. I have to be able to trust people when I'm not here. The next time something like this happens, I'll be putting letters in your HR jackets, or worse."

The red on Leslie's face deepened. "Don't you threaten us."

"That's not a threat. That's proper procedure."

"We don't have to take this. There are plenty of labs that will respect what we do."

Jack pointed to the door.

"Fuck you, Jack." Leslie left the room, slamming the door.

The other two rose quietly and left for the lab. Jack waited a moment and then fell into his chair. He leaned his head back against the wall and closed his eyes. Finally pulling himself forward, he turned to face his desk. His eyes traveled above the piles of paperwork to Jennifer's picture framed above his desk. It was surely the best picture he had ever taken. It really caught her joy, her smile, her chestnut brown hair blown back gently by a late May breeze beside a trail up in the Catoctins. He'd taken the picture about an hour before sunset, and the warm sun tones painted her face in its truest hues. They had later made love beside the trail.

* * *

President Miller and President Gastagne were in a jovial mood by mid-afternoon. From the time the gleaming white Air France Airbus pulled up to the terminal, both men had been swathed in *bleu, blanc, et rouge.* The Boys Choir of Harlem offered the *Marseillaise* and *Star Spangled Banner.* The French furnished a cadre of highly decorated legionnaires and two discreet security escorts for the returning American troops. After President Miller, in broken French, declared his passionate amorous love for all the French people, Anna stepped in and provided the remaining interpretation. President Gastagne accepted Miller's "advances" with dry and gracious humor.

After speeches and signatures and abundant pictures, the two presidents left the concourse for meetings and dinner at the Waldorf-Astoria. Kincaid, Cartier, Anna, the troops, and several military escorts remained in the reception lounge.

A senior officer pleaded with Kincaid, "But I have my orders to take these men for debriefing, sir."

Kincaid looked at the officer's nametag. "Colonel Jones, the men will be leaving with Admiral Brown."

"But, sir, my orders came directly from Vice President Bailey."

"No, Colonel, your orders come from the President of the United States at the personal request of the President of France. And Admiral Brown outranks you by — what? — four grades."

"Yes, sir!" Colonel Jones saluted Admiral Brown and left the concourse.

Kincaid turned to Admiral Brown. "Anything I can do for you, Bill?"

The admiral had his tongue in cheek. "No, sir, thank you. The President called me with instructions. I've got a limo down on the tarmac. We'll slip out quietly." He winked.

Kincaid nodded, smiling. "Make it so, Admiral."

The four troops followed Admiral Brown down the jetway, through a door, and down the ladder to the waiting vehicle, leaving Cartier, Kincaid, and Anna alone.

< Ah, Ms. Colbert, I finally have the pleasure of meeting you face to face. I can only say that you are even more charming in person than on the phone. You really should ditch these lost souls and come to work for us. >

< You're too kind, sir. I actually did work for you for two summers

several years ago at the embassy in Washington. It was a wonderful experience, but I think I've found my calling here. >

Kincaid looked around him at the empty room. "Anything we can share with the rest of the class?"

"Monsieur Cartier was wondering if we'd be having hamburgers again tonight. I assured him the fare would be more elevated," Anna offered.

"Ah." Kincaid watched as Cartier broke into a broad grin.

They turned at the sound of running footsteps. An aide entered the room, out of breath. "Ms. Colbert, the President needs some assistance with interpreting."

Anna followed him down the corridor.

Cartier watched them leave and then turned to Kincaid. "So, David, our little charade seems to have worked in our hemisphere. Have you successfully calmed your ever-vigilant press?"

"Alas, yes, Jean. Truth is the first casualty of war."

"Yes, I think we came up with that phrase first."

"Probably. Or maybe the Greeks."

"Ah, I've been pretty hard on you, but for the most part your people have acted pretty professionally. I sense that you are as concerned as I am about the disconnect between your President and your Vice President. If you think it is dangerous, I can only concur."

Kincaid nodded. "That's why the men are going with Admiral Brown. We're also taking a number of steps to check independently what the Vice President may have been doing."

"Good. As promised, I have a gift for your Dr. Tyler." Cartier handed Kincaid a large manila folder secured with ties. "These are the charts your soldiers were carrying. Odd, to say the least, for a missile hunt."

"Just out of curiosity, Jean, how do you know about Dr. Tyler?"

Cartier's smile turned mischievous. "Hard to keep secrets between friends. How many times have I mentioned that our Ambassador Bonet is a keen observer of personalities?"

"Yes, but Sarah works deep inside the administration."

Cartier brushed his hands in dismissal. "Bonet has been embedded in the Washington fabric for what — forty years. He's endured a dozen of your presidents and eight of ours. The social and political scene in your capital is his passion, his hobby, his very life. If he merely guesses something is so, we act on it as fact."

Kincaid nodded.

"Speaking of which, he was wondering about you and Ms. Colbert."

"Excuse me?" Kincaid eyed him warily.

"The two of you seem made for one another. Two entirely-too-dedicated souls in that rough and tumble city of yours."

"Ms. Colbert is a valued member of my staff. Our relationship is strictly professional."

"I see. Well, if you are not pursuing her, perhaps I should."

Kincaid folded his arms and adopted an exaggerated frown. "You're married, Jean."

"And you're not, David. If you don't have feelings for Ms. Colbert, then be careful with your eyes when Ambassador Bonet is present. Remember a reception last month in your West Wing? He was watching. Yes, your thoughts betray you."

"I know that we came up with that phrase first."

Cartier chuckled. "True. Nasty fellow, Darth Vader. I hope I don't resemble him too much."

Kincaid shook his head and motioned toward the exit. "Shall we go see if there are hamburgers for dinner?"

"*Oui*."

The two walked down the corridor.

"You weren't talking about hamburgers, were you?"

"You'll have to ask Mademoiselle Colbert when she has finished interpreting for your amorous President."

"You're bringing more chaos into my life, Jean."

"That is what friends are for."

* * *

"Mr. Johnson, we don't pay you the salary we do for excuses; we pay you to keep the company project on its timeline. Now you're telling me that we're looking at another two months. That is unacceptable." Max Carlton carefully transferred pages of Johnson's report from one pile to another, turning them as needed to absorb the information.

"Dr. Carlton, with all due respect, we would have been finished ahead of schedule had the specifications not been changed. Every time a new feature is added, we have to revise hundreds of pages of code to accommodate the changes. This impacts our schedule, sometimes severely. If we could just freeze the specifications, our team could produce a product of the quality you need in the time we promise."

Carlton waved his hand in dismissal. "Mr. Johnson, I have told you to add people as necessary to keep this project on track. The cost of a few more hires to get our control software to the plants pales in comparison to the millions we are wasting on salaries of workers sitting in their air-conditioned booths watching dials and turning knobs."

Johnson had buried his head in his hands. "You can't just pull someone off the street and bring them up to speed on a project of this magnitude. We're talking about thousands of pages of code, complex control code for unique power equipment. The programming has to meet very stringent DOE standards. There are only a handful of people in the world who have the skills and competence to carry that out. We're lucky to have found

Josh."

Carlton continued to flip pages. "I beg to differ with you, Mr. Johnson. I note that your report shows he has not submitted his documentation in a timely manner. In fact, I see that he has not documented his code at all. That is a severe problem."

"It's not his style, sir. I assure you that his work is of the highest quality and will perform above expectations when completed. This project is as much art as engineering. We can't change the completion time by simply bringing in more people."

"Nonsense. I'd like to talk with this young man. I think he needs to be impressed with the urgency of his task."

"Sir?" Mike asked, blanching.

"Bring him in here."

"Dr. Carlton, Josh is a brilliant programmer, but not very … diplomatic. He's concentrating on the task now. I don't think a confrontation would be productive."

Carlton's face began to redden. "Mr. Johnson, your problem, in part, is that you coddle these *prima donnas.* You're afraid to tell your people to do their jobs. Bring this Josh to me."

Mike Johnson stood, but couldn't bring himself to move to the conference room door.

"Now!" Carlton demanded.

* * *

Josh Ruark stared at his huge monitor as he moved snippets of text across the screen. He muttered to himself, "Control on seven, control off six, control on seven, control off six. Dialog close five, cancel four, loop, loop, loop, next." His cubicle wall was awash in screen prints of dialog boxes, lists, specifications, photos of naked women, and his motorcycle. His bookshelf was empty save two books on Java, a thick Brisbane procedures manual still in unopened shrink-wrap, and a struggling *Philodendron.* His desk was strewn with printouts, two coffee mugs — one full — and assorted caffeinated beverages in various states of consumption. Behind him on the floor were a body pillow and tattered blanket. "Shutdown, control on six, control off five, control on six, control off five. Dialog close four, cancel three, loop, loop, next." He did not notice when Mike Johnson appeared at his cubicle entrance.

"Josh, I need you in the conference room."

"Not now, Mike; I'm updating the shutdown routines."

"It's important Josh. Please."

"Can't be more important than this." He continued moving blocks of code from one window to another.

"Just ten minutes in the conference room. There's someone who needs to talk to you."

"If she's not naked, I'm not interested," Josh continued.

"Josh, Max Carlton has been sent by headquarters to get a progress report."

"Tell him to get bent." He stopped and turned to Johnson. "Max Carlton. That name sounds familiar."

Johnson crossed his arms. "He signed your contract."

Josh returned to his programming. "How sweet. He underpaid me."

"And he's about to sign your termination. He wants to talk to you."

Josh shook his head.

"Now."

Josh wheeled in his chair and stood up to follow Johnson.

"Aren't you going to save?"

"You said ten minutes. This is a UNIX workstation on a UPS. It's been up for —" — he turned to look at a small widget on his screen and then turned back to Johnson — "— seventeen months, three days, four hours, and seventeen minutes. You said ten minutes."

"Josh, please be restrained. Dr. Carlton is a very powerful person and not so forgiving as we are."

"Of course," Josh assured.

They walked down the corridor and entered the conference room.

Carlton was still seated, finishing the last three or four pages before him. He looked up. "Mr. Ruark?"

"Yeah."

Carlton's face clouded. "You are considerably behind your timeline finishing the project for which we pay you so well."

"Bullshit! The timeline I was given got shredded sixteen months ago. You pinheads keep changing the specs."

Carlton's face flushed again. "And when do you expect to be finished?"

"When I'm done. Are we through?"

"Young man, I do not like you attitude."

"Pity."

"That's enough. I want you to cease your programming and concentrate on the documentation. My reports show that you have done none of the documentation required by your contract."

Josh leaned forward, his fists on the table, his face only a few inches from Carlton's. "My contract says document. It doesn't say when. I don't document until I've received the next to last payment. You know for a fact I've never failed to fully explain all the coding I've done for other companies, but I'll be damned if I leave my work open for someone to take over in mid-stride. You'll get your documentation when I'm ready. Got it?"

Carlton glowed red. "We will be ending your contract early, Mr. Ruark. I want you to begin handing this project over to Ms. Mattock."

Josh grinned. "Mattock? Louise Mattock? Really? Well, did you hear the one about the priest, the monkey, and the whore? No? Well, I guess that wasn't a very funny joke either. Louise is an incompetent cunt who's good at making pretty flow charts, but couldn't program a polynomial without going back to her BASIC book."

"You're fired!" Carlton shouted.

Ruark made a fist and thrust it at Carlton, his middle finger upraised. Then he turned and left the room, slamming the door behind him.

Johnson, panic in his voice, turned to Carlton. "You can't fire him. We can't do it without him. We'd have to start from scratch."

"Put Ms. Mattock on the job. Let her finish. I see that she doesn't have problems with her assignments, including documentation."

"Sir, she was hired to do the artwork and the manuals. Josh is correct. She's not competent to do his job."

"Then you need to hire competent people, Mr. Johnson. We're finished here. Get this project back on schedule."

Mike Johnson turned and headed for Josh's cubicle.

"Josh, don't go anywhere yet. I'll talk to him. I'll get it straightened out."

"Not happening," Josh responded.

"Josh, I can't make this a go without you."

"Oh, I know."

Johnson sighed. "What are you going to do?"

Josh was pulling paper off the wall of his cubicle. The naked women and motorcycles went into a pile on his desk. The screen shots and specifications went into his shredder. "I have three game companies who've been on my case to join them. One's been after me for over a year."

"Will they pay as much?"

"Not as salary."

"Do they have benefits?"

"No."

"Will they even be able to pay you?"

"Maybe. If the game sells." He picked up the *Philodendron* and checked the dry soil and curled leaves. "Mealy bugs." He set it back on the shelf. "Didn't adapt." He turned to Mike. "Tell the emperor to document this." He reached behind his computer, grasped the power plug and pulled hard. The collection of code pages vanished, replaced by a black screen with a small rainbow rectangle containing the words 'No Signal Detected.'

Johnson turned and entered his own cubicle, bringing an empty box that had been parked by the trash. He began removing family pictures and his own books from the shelves. He was cleaning out his last drawer when Josh came by.

"Joining the rebels?"

Johnson stopped packing and sat down in his chair. "I've been with the company for fifteen years. It used to be fun. I thought it was meaningful.

But for the last few years, I've just been managing projects to put people out of work to the enrichment of the big power companies. The pay's been great, the vacation, all that. But it's like golden handcuffs. After today, there's not much left for me here."

"So wha'cha going to do?"

"I don't know. I'll have to act fast. Janice's going to kill me."

"Hey, I was on the phone right after you left. Programming Palace is taking me on for a game they're releasing in January. They need a manager. Why don't you come with me? I like working for you. You don't interfere destructively."

"I thought you said they didn't pay well."

"No, not up front. But you get a share of the game when it's released."

"And health care?"

"We're kinda on our own most of the time."

"I don't think I can stomach that much risk."

"Don't worry. I'll spot you."

Johnson smiled, shaking his head. "Need I remind you that you're unemployed already?"

Josh shook his head. "Not to worry. With residuals from the last two games I worked on, I cleared six and eleven million respectively. I can cover you 'til we release this one."

Johnson leaned back in his chair folding his hands on his stomach. He stared at Josh. "Seventeen million dollars? What the hell are you doing working here?"

Josh set his computer bag down at the cubicle entrance. "Like you, I thought I could do some good. I spent ten years writing simulations of bad guys blowing up power stations. I thought it would be cool to write something to actually run real stations. Apparently I was wrong. Anyway, I don't need much money. I don't have family like you. I basically just need cash for the bike and renting women. After working for these jerks, I'll be glad to get back to blowing 'em up again."

Johnson got up from his chair, surveyed his desk and walls. Seeing nothing else belonging to him, he picked up his box and motioned for Josh to join him.

Josh had only his computer bag and backpack. "Guess I got you fired. Sorry about that."

"Oh, no, not really. Maybe you were the catalyst, but it was bound to happen sooner or later." He stopped. "Actually, I don't think he fired me. Carlton thinks I've gone to get Louise." Johnson resumed his journey to the exit.

"Don't I need to turn in my badge or something?" Josh asked.

Johnson turned to him and smiled. "Carlton didn't tell you anything, given your abrupt departure. You would be turning your badge and key in to your supervisor. That would be me. And he didn't tell me to collect anything. So…"

They walked through the exit, Josh holding the door for Mike.

* * *

About an hour later, Louise Mattock entered the conference room. "You sent for me, Dr. Carlton?"

"Yes, Ms. Mattock. Brisbane Technologies would like to offer you the position of senior programmer on the master control software project." Carlton's glasses were low on his nose and he peered at her over them.

"That would be an honor, sir. But what about Josh?"

"Mr. Ruark is no longer with us. His work had certain deficiencies which were no longer tolerable."

She smiled.

"I'm particularly concerned with an item in the progress report regarding documentation. Apparently that was something he could not grasp. I would like you to make that your first priority."

"Yes, sir." She looked around at the otherwise empty room. "Will I be reporting to Mike Johnson?"

"He apparently is no longer with us, either. No. For the time being, I would like you to report directly to me. I'd like weekly status reports until the project is where it should be."

"Absolutely, sir."

They shook hands and she returned to her office.

As she passed Josh's cubicle, she shook her head. "What a pig." At her office, she switched into heels and prepared to leave for her lunch meeting with the Help Desk Group. Her tasks as group secretary would keep her busy until two in the afternoon.

* * *

"So Major Reed's not worried about them filming me?" Sarah added Tull's pickles to her sandwich and took several of his fries for good measure.

"Nope. He's pretty sure the object was to embarrass someone in the White House other than you — most likely the President. Those cover letters the other reporters got were wrong in almost every detail. If the filmers went to the trouble of getting all that spook gear, they would have known a lot more details about you if you were the real target. Your camp is close to the lab in Florida where they make the cameras. You're probably more of what we call a target of opportunity." Tull dipped his fry into her catsup.

"I've heard of targets of opportunity before. Not always a happy outcome. And I thought Mr. Kincaid said the camera was stolen."

"That's what they first told the Major. But since he's talked more with them, he's getting suspicious. He says their explanations sounds farfetched.

Anyway, he's still on it. The Major can be pretty stubborn. He won't let the matter rest until he has the truth. He's been poking around with some of his buddies from the old days. They all seem to sense something going on in other places, as well. That's the part that's got him concerned. He suggests you might not want to be too free with whom you discuss your investigation of the financials."

Sarah set down her sandwich and looked around the Five Guys restaurant. "You think they might be watching us here?"

Tull laughed. "I doubt it. This would be a lousy place to spy on someone. You decided on the spur of the moment to come here, and it takes time to set up good snooping gear. It's crowded, which makes it tough to watch someone. And it's really noisy."

She looked around again and returned to her meal. "Good."

"How's your banquet thing going?"

"My banquet 'thing'?" She laughed. "It's good — actually probably the most enjoyable 'thing' I've been doing lately. Tiffany Miller's great to work with. Plus, I get to sample the best of the best down in the White House kitchens. And when I call all these celebrities on their unlisted numbers and say I'm from the President's office, they're ready to do anything I ask them. Kinda heady. The real bonus is that it's a great cause. Can't believe that Kathy didn't love doing the banquets. Just not her 'thing,' I guess."

"Yeah. You never know what turn 'things' will take at the White House." Tull grinned.

She smiled back. "No, you really don't." Sarah finished the last fries and gathered her wrappers. She looked up to the menu above the counter. "Shame they don't have ice cream here."

* * *

At the Waldorf-Astoria, the dining room crew scurried to clear the dinner clutter as Anna assisted Jean Cartier in packaging the diplomatic documents for their transport to Washington and Paris. The two presidents had gone off to another section of the hotel to arrange a future visit.

< I want to thank you again, Ms. Colbert, for your gracious assistance today. >

< The pleasure is ours. Our citizens still have no idea of the heartache your actions have deterred. >

Jean shrugged.

David Kincaid entered the room looking tired, but smiling. "We're wrapping up out there. Will you be staying in New York tonight, Ms. Colbert?"

"No, sir. As soon as we're finished here, I'll head down to the subway and catch the train back to DC."

Kincaid looked alarmed. "At this hour?"

She smiled. "The southbound trains depart every hour until about one.

It's not a problem."

"You'll be exhausted by the time you get to the station, much less by the time you get home." Kincaid watched her smile broaden farther, if that were possible.

"It's OK. It really is. I'll nap on the train. It's quite comfortable."

He nodded in contemplation. "I think some members of the group heading back down might have room. We could get you right to your car."

"OK," she accepted.

Kincaid left the room at a brisk walk.

< David Kincaid is a good and honorable man, *Mademoiselle.* >

< Yes. > She turned to Cartier. < Yes, he is. The best of men. >

Kincaid returned. "I've got you a ride. It'll cut a couple of hours off your trip."

"Thank you, sir." She turned to Jean, who was smiling sweetly, hands on his diplomatic pouch. < And *adieu* to you, sir. >

"*Bonsoir, ma chère.*"

Anna and Kincaid left. Jean Cartier watched them depart, then picked up his pouch and headed for the elevator, grinning and humming the *Marseillaise*, softly at first, but rising to a crescendo as the elevator doors closed.

Kincaid held Anna's hand as she stepped up into the cabin. She took her seat and buckled in. With the other passengers in place, a Marine crewman closed the hatch and signaled the pilot. Marine One rose from the open square, and the city fell away in all directions like an incandescent blanket. She watched out the window as they passed between the Chrysler Building and the Empire State Building.

"Of all the places in this great land, maybe I'm most proud of this," the President sighed.

She nodded. "As well you should be, Mr. President."

"Thank you again for rescuing me."

"My pleasure, sir. I think today went rather well."

"Even when I told the French I lusted after them? That was a stupid thing for me to try."

"I'm sure the French lust after you, too, sir. A gaffe or two in an otherwise flawless performance seems to endear people to us."

President Miller turned to Kincaid. "Ah, yes, the ingramatticism. Isn't that what you called it?"

Kincaid nodded.

The President turned to Anna. "I asked the pilot to fly close to Lady Liberty. We're allowed to do that. Seemed appropriate for the day."

They stared as the floodlit statue filled the port window. Then the pilot increased altitude, and they raced above the docks and refineries of northern New Jersey and on to the dark, sleeping interior.

The President leaned back and addressed Kincaid. "Speaking of ingrammaticisms, whatever happened with the e-mails?"

"I put Matt's report on your desk, sir."

"The left pile or the right pile?"

Kincaid thought a moment. "The right as you're facing them."

The President shook his head. "Doesn't much matter. Seems I don't have time to look at either pile these days. Give me the short and sweet."

"Matt says we use a very sophisticated e-mail filter. It reads the mail and sorts it by subject. It does the tallies; it does all sorts of things. Most importantly, it's very good at judging what is spam or false bombardments of e-mail."

Miller frowned. "OK. You were claiming that most of that stack that the Vice President carried was a bombardment."

"Yes, sir. That's the part that really got Matt excited. Turns out that the company that makes the filter, Brisbane something or another, also makes bulk e-mail programs. And for a price, they will insert a little line in the header that tells their own filtering software to let it through."

The President folded his arms. "So let me guess. The Crusade for Moral Clarity uses that bulk mailer rendering our gatekeeper impotent."

"Bingo, sir! Matt took the backups of all the e-mails and ran them through another company's filter, and the ratio was three to one in support of us. Peter and Matt contacted several dozen of the people in whose names the e-mails were sent, and none of them were aware that their names and addresses were being used. Some of them were furious. The boys looked at some of our earlier mailings, too, and found the same pattern, including on the child nutrition bill."

"How did we miss that earlier?"

"Really not our fault, sir. One of Vice President Bailey's security directives was to turn off headers on our e-mail. That morning, though, he printed from his own computer, which still had the headers printed. If he hadn't slipped up, we might never have caught it."

"David, I want to move again on the nutrition package. Should I confront the Vice President about this?"

"No, sir, I think it best that he not know what we know here. Matt will keep the other program running, and we can compare to get a better idea what's going on."

"And I want you to get Dr. Tyler any additional help she needs. I have to know what the hell is going on here."

"I'm working on that, sir. Right now I have to figure out whom I can trust in the security maze."

Anna fell asleep somewhere near the Delaware line. She was awakened by Kincaid's gentle hand on her shoulder as they began their descent onto the White House lawn.

* * *

Laura brought a heavy armful of manila folders to her kitchen table.

Charlie was helping himself to a large plate of leftovers. "Kinda freaked me out having to pass by guard houses on the way in here."

"Dad handles a lot of money and stuff for the Institute. They were worried about our safety. They're off duty this week."

Charlie brought his plate to the table. "What was it you said he does?"

"He's science officer for the Institute."

"Like Mr. Spock?"

"No, not like Mr. Spock."

"How's he different?"

Laura frowned and then shook her head. "I have no idea. Don't get me sidetracked. These are the papers I know about. Keep them in the right order. I don't want him to know we've done this. I feel bad enough already."

"OK. You handle the papers; I'll handle the conspiracy."

She ignored him and opened the folders, starting at the end. "Here's the main account list — Windham Trust."

Charlie looked over and then let out a low whistle. "Wow! I thought you said a couple of million."

Laura's face fell. "That's what I thought. He's never really talked about it. I had no idea."

"A hundred seventy-two and change. Maybe I should have been a science officer. But then again, I probably wouldn't have been happy."

Laura was staring at the balance sheet. "How can anyone amass that much so fast?" She flipped through the pages.

Charlie scanned them. "I recognize some of those companies. There, for instance — Plantagenet Pharmaceuticals, thirty-two million."

"That's logical. They license a lot of the Institute's research. Don't know how ethical it is though."

"Humor me, boss lady. Check the top of the list — the Bs."

She flipped backward and opened the page for Charlie.

He chuckled. "Well, isn't that special? Brisbane Technologies, forty-nine million dollars. Your life just got a whole lot more interesting."

* * *

"You're right. This is really good. Lindale kitchens deserve their reputation." Jack ate his last rosemary potato.

"Told you. We figure each meal could be our last, so each one has to be great." Jennifer could see his face grow serious. "Come on. It's gallows humor. What's the choice? Morose? Sulking? Wasting time on pity? I don't think so."

"OK."

She picked up a couple of pills and swallowed them with her juice.

"Matter of fact, we've got a cookbook project here — *If It's the Last Meal, Make It the Best.* I told Jody to help them get it published once we get a hundred-fifty recipes. Each person gets to submit their one most favorite dish. I submitted your minestrone recipe."

Jack leaned back in his chair, his face drained.

"All right. Let's change the subject. Leslie actually used the words *fuck you*?" Jennifer raised her eyebrows as she finished her strip steak.

Jack finally smiled and turned to snacking on the items Jennifer didn't want — gelatin, peas, and toast. "Yup. I told them if it happened again, I'd put discipline letters in their jackets."

"Good for you. It's about time." She shifted the plates to get to her cake. "Do you think she'll really leave for another position?"

"Don't know. She didn't talk to me the rest of the day, and I didn't much want to talk to any of them, either."

"You know, language like that could be grounds for dismissal."

"Maybe. If I documented it well enough, if I had willing witnesses, and if I wanted to jump through all the legal hoops. But right now I've got too much on my plate." He paused, and they looked down as one at his empty dinner plates, and both began laughing.

After dinner Jennifer read pages from that day's writing of her family history. Jack offered suggestions about word choice. She gave him a list of source material to bring back on Tuesday. They spent the last twenty minutes kissing before he had to leave. Jack noticed a tear in her eye and a waver in her voice.

15 PAYBACK

Thursday, April 24, 2014

If Sarah had hoped for a smoothly running event, her hopes were quickly dashed. From the time the first limousines arrived at the north portico for the AIDS banquet, she shuttled constantly between arrival hall and dining room, fixing glitches. One speaker had been left off the security list. John Bessimer, the great proponent of the vegan diet, had almost been served filet mignon. One Hollywood couple who had just finished a spectacularly ugly divorce had been seated next to each other.

Sarah engaged each crisis in turn, including nearly dragging the divorced former spouse into the ladies' room. When the crowd was finally seated at eight o'clock and the dinner began, Sarah moved into the shadows at the back of the room. She spied Tull in dress uniform and moved to stand alongside him. She nodded.

Tull whispered, "Tough night, huh? Sorry you took it on?"

She closed her eyes and leaned her head back on the wall. "No. I'm exhausted, but still feel kinda tingly." She tilted her head forward and looked around the assembly. Then she spread her arms wide. "Look. It worked. It came together. Everyone's having a good time and eating basically what they were supposed to get. And the cause is moved forward big time!" She turned to Tull and smiled.

Tull nodded. "You did good. You have a table place?"

She shook her head. "You have to be a bigshot to have a spot at one of these tables. These guys and gals have Nobel Prizes, million dollar movie deals; two of them run whole countries."

Tull was called over to one of the tables to answer a question. When he returned, he found Sarah scanning the crowd. "Looking for someone in particular?"

She kept her voice low. "I'm looking for Dolores."

"The San Francisco Madame?"

"Uh huh." She continued looking.

Tull leaned in and pointed discreetly to a table to the right of center. "She's there, the one with the gray suit, next to the guy with the tan jacket. They assigned me to take her to her seat. The guys thought it was funny, I guess. What's your interest in her?"

"I did a paper on her pension fund once for a class on corporate responsibility. There've been some questions that have bugged me ever since. I was hoping to get a chance to ask them tonight."

Half an hour into the dinner, Tiffany Miller rose and took the podium. She made introductions, usually with an obscure tidbit about the dignitaries she acknowledged.

Tull turned to Sarah. "Hard to believe she's only nineteen. She carries herself like royalty."

Sarah nodded. "And commands like a general. I've been working with her for the better part of two months. She has the whole thing laid out in her mind, and when she asks someone to do something, it just happens. Amazing."

The speeches began around eight forty-five. Some were humorous, some angry. They ended a few minutes after ten, and guests began to depart. Tull stayed occupied until nearly eleven escorting guests to departing cars. As best she could, Sarah kept an eye out for Dolores while attending to special requests from some of the notables. By ten thirty, Sarah's tasks were finished. Dolores had been holding court of sorts from her seat. Sarah waited until the others had bade farewell.

Sarah approached. Dolores' tailored suit complemented her stylishly bobbed blonde hair. She had the presence of a major corporate executive. "Ms. Hoffman?"

She turned to Sarah. "Oh, my. We shouldn't to be so formal. 'Dolores' is fine. It's my brand, after all." She smiled broadly.

"Yes, ma'am." Sarah extended her hand. "My name's Sarah Tyler and …"

Dolores brightened. "Ah, Doctor Tyler. David's been telling me about all the work you've put into tonight. Job well done! You serve the people well, and I thank you."

Sarah grinned and shrugged. "Just did what the First Daughter said. But I was wondering if you had a moment for a question or two."

Dolores peered around. "Looks like it's just the two of us girls. Have a seat. What's on your mind?"

"When I was doing my doctoral, I studied your company policies for a term paper in one of my classes. The return on investment for your pension fund is spectacular, to say the least. I tried to figure out how you were making your investment decisions. I even tried to contact you."

Dolores frowned. "Sorry. I apologize. I certainly wouldn't brush you off. But I get several hundred pieces of mail a day and maybe ten times that of genuine e-mail. I'm afraid you got lost in the flood. But you've got me now."

Sarah nodded slowly.

"It's a secret, though," Delores cautioned.

Sarah slumped.

Dolores grinned. "But I like you, so I'll tell you the secret if you won't spread it around."

Sarah nodded quickly now.

"First of all, tell me what did you conclude in your paper?"

"The best I could figure in the end was that you had an innate understanding of psychology, given the … industry … you're in. But I was never happy with that. There are plenty of psychologically astute corporations that don't get near your returns, and a lot of your picks really didn't make sense other than they proved really good."

Dolores crossed her arms and lowered her head, smiling. Then she looked back up. "You're giving me too much credit for brilliance. The credit really goes to the ignorance and arrogance of others."

Sarah tilted her head.

"My girls provide pleasure to a very special class of customers."

Sarah looked troubled.

"Let me guess. You're bothered by *girls*."

"Well, you don't hear the term that often any more, I guess," Sarah agreed.

Dolores conceded the point. "True. But we're a business. We market a product, and that product is satisfaction of the sex drive — mostly for men, still. They don't know it, but three million years of evolution have given them a desire for strong young women capable of carrying their children. Never mind the disconnect with their other desires and responsibilities. If they want *girls*, we'll give them their illusion. We sell the sizzle without the steak."

"That still doesn't explain the return."

"True again. So once they've had their sizzle, they think they're done. They've paid their money, lots of money, and not always really theirs, and the girl becomes invisible, like she doesn't exist. Sometimes it does make me crazy. These men — and sometimes women — will pay a thousand dollars for the highest quality climax anywhere and … what do you think happens several times a week?"

"I'm afraid to guess."

"They get on their cell phones and do business deals. Right there in the room. They may still have their pants off or their parts hanging out, but they're wheeling and dealing like they're the kings and queens of the world.

And the girl doesn't exist."

Sarah shook her head.

"But. Now this is the secret: that girl is in truth a very smart woman. Dolores does not run a cat house. Some of those girls have advanced degrees. With our grade of customer, the working conditions aren't so bad. The better lasses are pulling down a hundred thou' a year for a few hours with their legs in the air. And when the big shot's talking on the phone, the girls are listening, and they're remembering. They enter it into our log, and we invest accordingly. When the big merger surprises everyone three days later, or the super product goes shockingly bust, we've already moved our capitalist butts."

Sarah was slouched back in her chair. "Wow."

"So it's really not so miraculous. Just some girls knowing when to keep their mouths open and when to keep them shut."

"OK, it makes sense now. Ironically, I wanted to use pipeline theory to explain it, but couldn't find an angle. Just didn't think of the women as pipelines."

"Few do. But, hey, we women have exploited our invisible status for thousands of years. Being the power behind the throne ain't so bad if you don't require the cheering crowds for yourself."

Sarah finally frowned. "Thousand dollars a night?"

Dolores laughed. "Oh, no, thousand dollars or more for a few hours. These are people who can pay. These are people who own billion dollar companies, run huge organizations."

"But doesn't their spending show up and get them in trouble? I'm sorry; I probably shouldn't talk about your business this way right here, right now, but most people don't consider it a normal business expense. No offense."

"None taken. In fact, it is precisely because of our curious position in advanced society that we can charge what we do to those we serve. Sometimes they pay from their own personal funds, but we have ways of structuring our charges innocuously. It's what you expect at our level."

"But what happens when people find out? I mean, they must sometimes."

"Oh, yeah, it happens. But many of our customers have been with us quietly for years. When the wife finds out, we see three outcomes in about equal proportions. The first is with the better marriages: the guy repents, they get counseling, and the marriage survives. Those are what we call the real wives. The other two are usually the trophy wives. The second will divorce him and take him for all she can. The third won't divorce him and still takes him for all she can. Those are the cold blooded ones. Hey, you want to hear a joke?"

"I don't know."

"Ah, c'mon, it's good. Why do trophy wives always look so fresh and young?"

Sarah pondered. "I don't know. … Why?"

Dolores smiled. "When you're that cold, there's no refrigeration required." She giggled.

"Ouch."

Dolores tried to be serious. "It's true. Those trophy wives aren't so different from us. They make a great living off the heads of companies, heads of governments, heads of churches."

"Churches?" Sarah raised her eyebrows.

"Dearie, they're men. This is not a new phenomenon. Trust me, your Hebrew scriptures have a lot more heroine prostitutes than hero priests."

"Still, it's hard to believe that they can maintain the appearance." She looked up to see Dolores holding her hand up to the side of her face with fingers extended like a telephone receiver. "What?" Sarah asked.

"Just a little device we use at work. Ours is a business of emotion. And sometimes the girls, especially the newer ones, can confuse passion for love. So we use the 'phone.' Reality calling. Think about what's happening. I seem to recall that a certain pastor who has always preached loudly about love, who didn't even know you at all, called you a whore … in a bad way."

"Richards," Sarah muttered.

"Yes. Now tell me these big religious guys are any different than any other bigshots."

Sarah grew very quiet.

"Look, Dearie, my business is a trust business. My customers keep coming back because they know that what they do in my house stays in my house. The only exception is for anyone who abuses my girls. And Richards is on my shit list big time."

Sarah straightened up.

"About five years ago, he started visiting — usually at night, usually disguised. He always asked for the youngest. Asked that they be dressed up as little girls. Kinda freaky, but business is business, and all my girls are of age — certified. He had a favorite — cute as a button and pretty flat-chested — he usually asked for. But one night he started beating her. Black eye, bruises. I was ready to call the cops, but his lawyers showed up and settled with her for fifty grand. I tried to talk her out of it, but fifty is a lot of money. Richards has been banned from my place ever since."

"Whoa!"

"Oh, it gets worse. After I kicked him out, he turned to streetwalkers. Runaways, druggies. He could get away with a lot, and they wouldn't even know who he was. One of my girls found out about a fifteen-year-old he had beaten. He almost got off Scot free, but I stepped in with some lawyers with whom we exchange services. His ministries ponied up about half a million to keep it out of the press. I've set her up with social workers, schools, and an endowment for college. I feel pretty good about that part. But we had to sign a non-disclosure. That's the only thing I regret. When I think of all the people who send in offerings to him, it makes me sick."

Sarah sat for a while with her mouth open before finally speaking. "*Oy vey.*"

"Yeah, *oy vey*," Dolores echoed.

* * *

Friday, May 2, 2014

Sarah watched through mirrored glass as Kincaid finished his formal press session and stepped down to the floor for his traditional non-substantial conversations. She watched Ben Jacobs approach from the right. Kincaid turned to him and they smiled and shook hands, apparently exchanging friendly greetings. Whatever hurt feelings there might have been a while ago seemed to have healed nicely.

She tilted her head. "Hmmm…"

Sarah left the observation room quietly and headed to her car. She drove slowly out of the underground parking and inched along in the outside lot, observing the throng of White House Press Corps exiting the building.

Spying Jacobs, she drove up just behind and to his right. She called out in a raucous voice, "Hey, Jacobs!"

He turned around and eyed the vehicle carefully — a very bright yellow Volkswagen beetle with Maryland Agricultural Education plates JRSYGRL. "Uh oh." He smiled, shook his head, and called back, "I don't want any trouble. I'm innocent."

"Yeah, I'll bet. Hey, where're you headed?"

He stopped, and then approached the driver's window cautiously. "Metro station. I'm going home for a good night's sleep. I've had a good day, and I don't want to spoil it. Why?"

"Thought I might give you a lift. Where do you live?"

"Silver Spring."

"No kiddin'. My apartment's in Laurel. You're right on my way. Hop in. I'll get you there before the Metro can."

Jacobs looked uncomfortable. "I'm not sure this is such a good idea."

"Don't be a wuss. Jesus, you practically got me the car after all."

He looked in the direction of the Metro station three blocks away. Still he hesitated.

"C'mon." She lowered her voice to a flirty huskiness. "C'mon. I'll tell you a story on the way."

Looking into the distance again, his resistance faded. He walked around the front of her car and opened the passenger door. She was busy, frantically gathering burger wrappers and drink cups, stuffing them into an emptied fried chicken box, and then tossing it into the back.

"You've had this car only a few weeks, and you've already trashed it."

She grinned. "Hey, I'm a busy girl. Don't give me a hard time."

"Still I have a bad feeling about this. And you're not going to beat the Metro this time of day."

She checked her dash and her rear view mirror. She put the car into first gear. "You've obviously never ridden with me."

As he clicked his seat belt securely, the car leapt forward, and they were off through Washington's evening rush hour.

* * *

That evening at Baltimore-Washington Thurgood Marshall International Airport, the last passengers were checking in for the nine-thirty flight. U.S. Airways ticket agent Sharon Brown did her best to offer friendly competence to this most fatigued class of passengers.

"Well, Mr. Jacobs, it's an honor having you with us tonight for the redeye. What brings you out at this hour?"

"Just researching a little story. Just seeing what might come of it."

"Well, sir, I hope it's a winner."

"I have a good feeling it will be," he replied.

"Your flight's only half-booked. I've got empty seats on both sides, so you should be able to stretch out."

"Thank you. I really appreciate that."

"Anything to check?"

"No, I've just got my carry-on bag and laptop."

"OK, then, you're all set. One for San Francisco. Enjoy your visit."

"Thank you." Jacobs took his boarding pass and headed for the D concourse. He passed quickly through security and into the nearly empty promenade. "Yeah, this is going to be well worth a few nights' sleep."

* * *

Saturday, May 3, 2014

David Kincaid parked in his usual reserved White House space. The leisurely Saturday pace suited him, and he could imagine what it must have been like if this were the norm at the beginning of the twentieth century. His gate check-in would have been no less rigorous than usual, but the rhythm would have been more relaxed, more gracious.

He made his way to his office and picked up two briefing folders he had meant to take home Friday evening. He turned out the lights as he left and detoured toward the fellows' offices. He stopped at Anna's office and peered in. He did not want to turn on her office lights lest he leave some trace of his visit. In the dim light he saw that the gerbera daisies had been replaced by lilies-of-the-valley. He thought he could smell their fragrance from the doorway. Or was that Anna's lingering perfume?

He backed away from the door and headed to his car. Passing Sarah's office, he found her at her computer with a small stack of documents.

"Don't work too hard," he said from the doorway. "We don't want you burning out."

Sarah looked up quickly and flashed a smile. "Good morning, sir. Don't worry. I'm just passing the time 'til Jeff gets off duty at noon. He took Brycynski's morning watch. We're going to the National Zoo to see the pandas this afternoon."

"Excellent. Sounds like fun. Say 'hi' to the bears … or whatever they are."

"Yeah. I heard they're not really bears. Matt would probably know."

Kincaid chuckled.

"Actually, Matt would love this." She swiveled her computer screen to show him what she was working on. The window was filled with lines that looked for all the world like a pile of pick-up-sticks with little red growths.

Kincaid shook his head. "What am I looking at?"

"This is pipeline analysis software. It lets me visualize economic relationships. Look — I can rotate it through several axes." She moved her mouse along a slide bar and the pile rotated on screen. "The dots are different people. My software assigns their size based on calculated rank of importance. The yellow lines are direct lines of responsibility, usually a known investment or verified contractual relationship. See how the dots almost all connect to that big ball in the center? That's Windham Trust."

Kincaid nodded. "And the red lines?"

"Ah. The red lines are associations. Those are the fuzzy friendships, advisors, and photo-op pipelines. That's what I've been updating this morning. I've got all of Ron Kowalski's stuff in, and I'm getting ready to check the findings your French buddy gave you to give to me."

"I see. Anything useful so far?"

Sarah smiled a wicked smile. "Oh, yeah. Watch this. I noticed I kept seeing Dr. Richards's name associated with all these characters. I just finished adding him to all the associate relations, and …" She clicked on one of the checkboxes on her screen.

Kincaid raised his eyebrows. "Huh. That looks a lot more organized." The pile of straws now looked more like a lumpy potato.

"Yes, indeed. Now here's the part that Matt would love. I can do 'what-ifs.' For instance, if I promote the good reverend from associate to responsible, I get this …"

Kincaid jerked his head back. "Whoa. I don't pretend to understand all I'm seeing, but that looks significant." The potato had transformed into a latticework sphere with two large balls in the center.

"Yup. Windham Trust and Dr. Paul Richards are nearly equal size. I began to wonder when I started seeing him on all these boards. Then I checked tax records. At first — almost nothing. Then I started finding all these different foundations set up with him at the head of each. And they invest billions of dollars — billions." She rotated the sphere, beautiful in its symmetry. "No one else has this effect. And I've tried them all."

"The Vice President?"

"Well, you're either going to be disappointed or relieved." She checked the name button. "Here's Mr. Bailey as an associate …" The pile of straws looked a bit more structured, but nothing like the Richards's association potato. "… and here he is elevated to 'responsible'." She clicked again, but the structure barely changed.

Kincaid stared at the screen for a while. "It has to be good news, I guess. I'll be the first to admit I'm a little surprised. But still, it has to be good."

Sarah shook her head. "Yeah. Sure. I can tell you're no more convinced than I am. Something stinks, but it's buried deep. When I read the stories, I can feel it. When I talk to the other dots, I can hear it in their voices. I'm still missing data. Most of his blind trusts are really tight with their information. It'll probably take a court order or his permission to get at them, and I don't sense you're ready to do that yet. But to get just a hint of what I'm sensing, watch what happens if I drop everyone out but Bailey and Richards." The richly colored sphere changed to a pastel version like a thin dandelion seed head with Richards still in the center.

"Jean Cartier made some cryptic remark about the Vice President and Universal Oil. Was that in Ron's papers?"

"Universal? I wish you'd said something." She reached for her pile of papers and removed the top third of the pile down to the point where Cartier's documents began. She entered text and connected several dots. "Did he say anything specific?"

Kincaid shook his head.

"OK, I'll put him in as an association and then add everybody else back in and update."

They watched as lines began to trace on the screen. The resulting shape was nearly spherical. Bailey's dot was much larger now.

Kincaid rubbed his chin. "And …"

"If I promote him to 'responsible'?" The object became a sharply defined sphere with the Vice President now a third, smaller ball near the center. "You have to tell me these things."

"Sorry," Kincaid said.

"No problem," she laughed. "Didn't mean to be so snippy. But it tells me that I need to get some hard numbers. This project's beginning to get too big. I'm going to have to start choosing between this and the tobacco."

Kincaid nodded. "The President asked me to get you some help."

"The President?"

"I'll be talking to a couple of people over in Treasury and Justice on Monday. I don't want you moving off tobacco now. First, it's important to us, and second, I don't want to raise any unnecessary questions."

"Ooooo. Sarah the spy."

Kincaid grinned. "Not exactly. But this is the sort of delicate situation where what we do in the investigation can affect the problem itself."

"The Observer Effect," she offered.

"What?"

"I can't explain it too clearly, but it's one of the few things I remember from my only physics class, the name of that phenomenon. The very act of observing something changes it."

He smiled and looked at his watch. "I need to be on my way. And Corporal Tull should be off watch soon. Have fun at the zoo." He headed for the hall, stopping at her door. He turned back to Sarah. "Indulge me. Back up your data to an independent server."

Her wicked smile returned. "Already did."

* * *

"Sorry about the mess." Laura frowned as she surveyed Charlie's Riverside apartment. "It's just that I don't think anyone would be expecting us to be here."

"Plus I've got jamming gear here, and it's turned on," Charlie announced, clearly pleased with himself as he called out from his kitchen.

The sheriff was seated on Charlie's couch. "Jamming gear?"

"Yeah. Blocks the cell tower position query signal so they can't track you."

Laura lowered her shaking head.

The sheriff's deputies stood near the front door, and Laura's graduate friends were pulling up chairs. Anita had joined them.

Charlie returned from the kitchen with two packs of fruit drink. "Did everyone park a block or so away?"

Laura rolled her eyes, but breathed a sigh of relief as everyone nodded.

The sheriff spoke first. "OK, folks, I'll be brief. That was close over at the call center. I don't know what we stumbled onto, but it must be really sensitive. I really don't think even the county exec knows what's going on in there. As you can imagine, he was on the warpath when he first got wind of our scuffle, but he's been nice to me for the last week. I was at the site when he came to see the office area. It's like those guys had gone over the place with a vacuum. We didn't get much. But I don't think they've gone far because we still see their trucks in the area. And I appreciate that Anita and her crew dropped by when the exec arrived." He nodded in her direction.

Anita crossed her arms over her chest. "Yeah, we all gave the exec pieces of our minds. But I notice he wasn't making us any promises about keeping the center open."

One of the students spoke. "I think we're probably entering a dangerous period. I'd expect the exec to make some big and serious moves in the next few days. He's in a super-tight bind after building so much of his reputation on not raising taxes. He really can't change course. The news media don't know this yet, but his revenues are so far below projections already that he can't make payroll. He was counting on the call center automation and some other major outsourcing to stave off the nasty budget decisions. You tipped his hand, and the spotlight's on him." He turned to face the sheriff. "The county exec can't dismiss you right now without fanning the flames more, but I'm sure that as soon as the press moves on, you're gone."

Anita raised her hand. "That's what we in the union think too. We've pledged solidarity with the sheriff and his people. If the sheriff is fired, we'll start job actions immediately."

Laura frowned. "That's noble on one level but can we really jeopardize public safety, even for this?"

Anita shook her head. "Of course not. But seventy percent or more of our calls aren't really emergencies. We get confused people, kids needing help with their homework — that sort of thing. We usually give those calls some time and then pass them on to more appropriate centers. We can just say no to them and concentrate on the real emergencies and free up others to demonstrate."

Laura rubbed her hand on her chin. "I see."

Charlie had been sitting quietly. He looked around the room and observed, "Some of the records we've found may shed some light on where the next action spots will be. I had a theory about the location of the College Park call center in relation to some communication corridors before I saw this material." He looked at Laura. "Could've just been a coincidence. But in these documents, two other projects were listed in very interesting locations. One is in Franconia, Virginia and sits in the communication path between the Treasury Department and Verizon's international transmitter in Lorton." He turned to the sheriff. "I know you have no jurisdiction there, but the third site is in Suitland, Maryland, right between Treasury and Andrews. If I give you an address, could you check for those trucks hanging around there?"

The sheriff eyed Charlie, his face wrinkling with discomfort. "What's going on here? I don't like getting deep into something that has nothing to do with my job and public safety. It's one thing to defend the relatives of our vets working in a nine-one-one center, but —"

Raising his hand, Charlie interrupted the sheriff. "The county exec is getting a hundred fifty thousand dollars, cash, under the table in exchange for turning over one of the buildings of Andrew Jackson Middle School to Brisbane Technologies for unspecified purposes. He will be making the announcement next week describing it as part of 'cost-cutting measures'."

The sheriff sank back into the couch, a stunned look on his face. After a moment, he looked up at Charlie. "We'll look into it — quietly. Who is this Brisbane Technologies, and what are they doing?"

"They're a major developer of communication and security systems, mostly for the U.S. government and very large corporations." Laura was staring preoccupied at Charlie's coffee table. "They make all kinds of electronic gear for Homeland Security."

"If these are legitimate projects, can't they just go through standard County procedures to rent the spaces?"

"They're probably not legitimate projects," Charlie said.

Laura frowned. "We don't know that, Charlie. These three locations might support some kind of project, but Brisbane has almost forty other jobs in the DC area."

"All of which were publicly bid," Charlie continued.

The sheriff raised his hands. "All right, guys. I don't have time to get in the middle of your argument. Tell you what: we'll keep an eye on their activities around Suitland and College Park. Tom Welman is sheriff down in Franconia. He and I go way back. I'll have him take a look at what's going on down there. But I keep asking myself, 'What has this got to do with the law?'."

Charlie leaned forward, grinning. "Your boss is taking big money to keep quiet about shutting down part of our public safety system, and he's giving away public property to a shadowy company, apparently without a clear idea of what they're doing with it." He turned to Laura. "The three pieces of public property all just happen to be located within the lines of sight of some of the most important data transmitters in the entire country with the potential to capture … or disrupt … their communications. Seems to me that could have a lot to do with the law, now."

* * *

Monday, May 5, 2014

David Kincaid sat in his office chair, flanked by Anna and Peter. He pointed out parts of the newspaper story in front of him.

Sarah appeared in his doorway. "You sent for me, sir?"

"Dr. Tyler. How are we doing this morning?" Kincaid grinned.

"Fine … sir. Very productive … I think." She eyed Kincaid warily. "Am I in trouble, again?"

"No, not at all. I … we … just thought you'd be feeling buoyant today."

"I'm OK, I guess. Why?"

Kincaid and Anna exchanged glances.

Anna asked, "Didn't you watch Ben Jacobs's special last night?"

Sarah thought for a moment, and then grinned. "I was at church, arguing."

Kincaid nodded. "And nothing caught your attention on the radio on your way in this morning?"

She brought her thumb to her mouth, chewing gently on her thumbnail. She grinned weakly. "One O Six Rock?"

Peter did his best to stifle a laugh.

Kincaid leaned forward, his hands placed on the newspaper on his desk. "I'm guessing it's too much to ask if you've read the *Post* this morning."

Sarah brightened and waved her finger in the air. "That was the next thing on my list."

"I don't usually give my staff much direct advice, but perhaps we want to be a bit more attuned to the news, especially since we often *are* the news. I'll save you a trip for the paper." He folded his copy closed and turned it around so that Sarah could read. The lead title proclaimed "Leading Evangelist Caught in Web of Child Prostitution and Deceit." The article was complete with a classic picture of Paul Richards, shackled hands raised to shield him from the camera, accompanied by several police officers.

"Oh, my!" Sarah began reading the lead article. She put her finger on the page where it noted Ben Jacobs as the author. "I'd heard rumors that Richards had sex with a fifteen-year-old."

Anna raised her eyebrows. "'A'? … 'fifteen-year-old'?" She leaned over, pointing to a paragraph farther down the page. "According to Jacobs's research, Dr. Richards had violent encounters with at least seven child prostitutes, one of whom was twelve at the time."

Peter added, "One fifteen-year-old he beat up came under the protection of Dolores, the San Francisco Madame. That girl was more fortunate than the others. At least she got some measure of justice. These others were paid a few hundred dollars and told to keep quiet by the vice officers who were in league with Richards."

"In league?" Sarah asked.

"Apparently some members of the San Francisco vice squad learned of Richards's habits and kept close track of his movements. In return for some rather handsome payoffs from the Crusade for Moral Clarity, they were keeping things hushed up. I'd say San Francisco's going to be pretty stirred up this morning." Kincaid watched Sarah for her reactions. "Still, I would have expected a little more excitement on your part."

Sarah, still reading, shook her head. "I was on the receiving end of bad press not so long ago. I didn't do anything wrong to deserve it but I know how it hurt my family. I'm imagining what this must be like for his wife and kids."

"Fortunately, he doesn't have any children," said Kincaid. He frowned. "That came out sounding awfully mean. But I can't think of another way to say it. He didn't have any children. And as for his wife …" He reached over and turned to page three.

"Wow. That's a big article." Sarah tilted her head.

"Yeah, Jacobs must have been working on this for a while," Anna offered.

"Or he writes really fast," Sarah mumbled.

"Anyway, here … it appears she's been aware of her husband's proclivities for years. She kept quiet about it in return for a slice of the *Clarion Hour* revenues. Apparently she could do a lot of happy smiling for twenty thousand a show."

Sarah's shoulders drooped. "No refrigeration required."

"Huh?" Anna stared at her, puzzled.

"Just something I heard from a wise person once."

"Well, you can take this copy and read it at your convenience." Kincaid gently tugged on the paper, folded it and handed it to Sarah. "And we figured you might be able to use these." He handed her an envelope.

The envelope contained two tickets to the Medal of Freedom ceremony and dinner. She looked up at Kincaid.

"Seems Dr. Richards and guest are no longer on the list. His name's been withdrawn from the honorees."

She twisted her mouth and nodded.

"You'll be disappointed, but probably won't be surprised, to know that it wasn't solely for the sexual violence that the medal's been cancelled, though that would have been enough. Apparently Ben found out that the good preacher's education numbers had been fudged, just like you suspected."

"Fudged? How could he get away with that, too? Those are publicly available numbers. Anyone can check." Sarah frowned.

Kincaid sighed, "True. But it seems no one did. Richards raised the scores they reported, just a little – only a few points. And in their press releases to the media, he lowered the public school scores just a little. No one caught it … none of the hundreds of reporters who quoted it. They just took his press releases and repeated them."

"Why didn't the public schools object?" Sarah asked.

"They have neither the staff nor the time to check them either. So the short of it is that the Crusade schools didn't perform so well as public schools, after all. Oh … and 'The Devil's Gallery'? Another item no one watched closely. Turns out that the Crusade has — or had — a team of researchers scouring the country for really tight races with people they didn't like. They featured them on the targets page. If the candidate lost, they got the 'X'. But if they won, their picture simply disappeared from the site. No one checked, no one followed up. All we paid attention to was that huge gallery of defeated candidates. Anyway, Dr. Richards is now uninvited, and we thought you might want to take someone to a nice dinner. You'll be seated next to Dr. Degrado, the cancer researcher from New Jersey. Seemed a natural fit, being from your home state. Do you have something formal to wear?"

Sarah stared at the tickets. "Of course."

"Excellent. Take a look at the articles after the staff meeting. There's lots more there. The fact that the Crusade, a non-profit organization, paid Dr. Richards's bribes is a federal crime, for instance. After Jacobs found out about the sex crimes, he just kept coming up with more decay and corruption. He told me that he's got some important 'material' — he wouldn't say what — for you he needs to hand deliver this afternoon."

Sarah nodded. "I'd better get my stuff ready for the meeting." She looked up at the clock. "I've only got about half an hour." She turned toward the door.

"One more thing." Kincaid brought his hand up and rubbed the bridge of his nose. "Have you ever confronted anyone from the Crusade before?"

"No, sir, I don't think so. Why?"

"Jacobs gained the confidence of several very dissatisfied Crusade secretaries. The recordings of your volleyball game were distributed anonymously to the national press from the San Francisco office of the Crusade. That's not in the *Post* article. He called me this morning and wanted me to pass that along to you."

"Thank you, sir," Sarah said, dazed.

* * *

Sarah barely finished setting up her computer on a conference room side table as staff members began arriving.

Kincaid was the last to take his usual seat directly across from Sarah. "Good morning everyone. We have a lot to cover so let's pile right in. Matt, I think you'll find Sarah's project of particular interest. Be prepared to offer commentary on it."

Matt nodded.

"First, though, Kathy and Sarah, what good news do you have for me about our national economic picture?"

Kathy shook her head. "No good news, sir. The state reports continue to come in consistently and substantially below revenue projections. More and more every day."

Kincaid frowned. "Good news then might include an explanation of how this can be possible in light of a booming stock market and every other indicator. This situation makes less sense every day."

"Agreed, sir. It seems the state economies and the national economy have become uncoupled, though the market volatility is at record levels. The national picture … the one Wall Street uses for its cues … is still solid. We have no idea how that is, since the national structure should be a composite of the state pictures. When we plug the national numbers into our core models, Wall Street is performing appropriately. But nearly half the states have applied for the emergency fund. I hope it's well backed up or it'll run dry pretty quickly."

Kincaid's frown turned to a scowl. "Yes, Vice President Bailey may have mentioned that might happen. Do we have an alternative?"

"No, not if the state economies don't pick up soon. We'd really like to go over the base numbers but I still can't get access to them."

"I have the security request in. I don't know why it's taking so long, but I'll try to get that expedited. What else?"

Kathy shook her head.

Kincaid turned to the other side of the table. "Speaking of volatility … James, Anna, what news from Al Wadi?"

James spoke first. "The French rescue of our people doesn't seem to have upset many nationals there, though there is talk that we might have been on some secret mission farther north than was reported. The distrust throughout the Arab world and Iran is pretty intense. The briefing board mentioned something about insurgents being tracked near Riyadh. This has State majorly worried."

Anna continued the report. "Saudi public support for the House of Saud has never been lower and their security is getting more heavy-handed than usual. Ambassador Hansen quietly evacuated all dependents from our embassy and consulates as a precaution. It wouldn't take much to plunge the whole country into chaos."

Kincaid put his elbows on the table and rested his head on his outstretched palms. "Great. What should we be doing?"

Anna and James glanced at one another. She turned back to Kincaid. "Pray that no one does anything stupid and be prepared to lose thirty percent of our energy on short notice."

Kincaid leaned back in his chair. "Does anyone have any good news this morning?" He looked around at his staff. "Anyone?" Still no response. "OK, in the absence of good news, I'll take interesting news. Sarah."

Sarah stepped over to her computer and adjusted the angle of the screen so that Matt could see clearly. "Part of what I've been doing beside the tobacco and the state numbers is following up on Ben Jacobs's report from two months ago."

"Has it been that long?" Kincaid pulled out his pocket calendar.

"Yes, sir. March second. A noted research firm, Frankel Associates, compiled Jacobs's report using pipeline theory. That's a method I used a lot in my program before I came here, and I've used some of the software we helped develop to analyze what data are available. Most of the items are from newspaper clippings and records that Ron Kowalski had kept and some documents provided by Jean Cartier, Mr. Kincaid's French connection." She looked up to see her boss grinning and shaking his head.

She turned to her monitor. "What I've done is enter those relationships into my database. All the people in all the articles and clippings have some dealings with each other, but they're all linked to a private financial organization named Windham Trust. Because it's private and advises members rather than doing any investment directly, the trust is pretty much exempt from any reporting requirements. It's really tough to even confirm any memberships in the trust. But the folks at Frankel found it at the center of most of the Vice President's public associates. When I enter those associates and their documented relations, I get this." Sarah proceeded with the same presentation she had given Kincaid on Saturday morning, with the addition of the French data.

Matt sat passively through her presentation, mostly resting his chin in the palm of his hand. When Sarah finished her part, she waited while he took a sip of his coffee. He had taken no notes. The room was quiet.

Kincaid slowly turned to Matt. "So?"

"It's really pretty. I like the lattice pattern. How easy is it to enter data?"

Sarah said nervously, "Very easy. I just type it in."

"Put my name in there."

"What?"

"Just do it. 'Matthew.'"

She typed. A tiny yellow dot appeared on her screen at the edge of the lattice sphere.

"Now link me responsible to Universal Oil."

"But …" she protested.

"Please. I have a Gas America card. They're owned by Universal."

His dot grew larger and immediately sprouted links to a number of other dots.

"Now link me responsible to Brisbane Technologies."

"No way."

"Way. I'm a deer hunter. For my birthday, I finally saved up enough for an EcoLite 400 spotter scope for my rifle. Best seven hundred fifty dollars I ever spent. It's digital, with enhanced imagery and vibration compensation. EcoLite is a wholly owned subsidiary of Brisbane Technologies. That's the same technology from the same company that gave such a clear picture of someone's butt playing volleyball. I have a direct money link to Brisbane Technologies."

Sarah frowned but typed anyway. Matt's ball was now the forth or fifth largest on her screen.

"Now an associate link to your buddy, the lately incarcerated Reverend Doctor Richards."

Sarah threw up her hands, her cheeks flushed. "This is ridiculous."

"You asked me to watch. Type in the association. I'm a Baptist and he claims to be a Baptist. I was at a Baptist Convention a couple of years back where he spoke. If you get a photo from the convention and a really good magnifying glass, you'll find both of us in the same hall."

One by one, the staff turned their attention to Kincaid. Sarah finally looked at him. Kincaid nodded.

Sarah typed in the associate relationship, and Matt's sphere moved alongside Richards's sphere. She turned to him, quite calmly. "OK, I see your point. It's like my first thesis defense, which was a disaster. But I realized later that I really wasn't ready. What did I miss here?"

All eyes turned to Matt.

"First of all, I have no doubt that you're onto something, but not just because of this pretty software. I've been dealing with Bailey and his people for almost six years now, and my gut reaction is that he has enough dirty laundry to keep Jacobs in Pulitzers for decades if Jacobs could get to the actual numbers. But he won't, because Bailey is way too crafty to let his guard down.

"Your software did not dispel any of that. But it didn't advance the case for two main reasons. First, your entries are binary — either yes or no. You can't discriminate by degree. That's how I get to be as powerful as your beloved child molester right alongside what is certainly a multi-'t'-trillion dollar operation like Windham Trust. Did you program that software?"

Sarah shook her head.

"See if whoever programmed it could give you variable input — dollars, number of handshakes, degree of shadiness, whatever. I think you'll get a much more revealing picture even with a more limited amount of information. The second, and more serious, shortcoming is that these data are cherry-picked. Someone is looking for a relation and will by definition choose those data that support the desired conclusion. It's called the Easterbrook Phenomenon. Philippa Easterbrook did a survey of medical studies back in the 1980s. She found that it was almost fifty times more likely to get published a positive study than a negative study. Most importantly, her study showed it wasn't just manipulation by the drug companies. Editors by human nature aren't interested in negative results, which are boring. How much hard data do you have regarding the Vice President?"

"Hard data? Like financial reports?"

"Right."

She shook her head. "Almost none."

"Gotta get numbers."

Sarah nodded, chewing on her thumbnail. "Right."

* * *

As Kathy and Sarah walked back to their office down the hall, Kathy said encouragingly, "That's Matt's way. He wasn't trying to be difficult. He's just … direct."

Sarah shook her head. "I know. I'm not upset. He was doing exactly what he was supposed to do, what we asked him to do. I was excited about the findings to the point that I completely lost track of the flaws. I need to plug the holes but I'm not sure how. I need to get hold of the programmer."

"Do you know him?"

"Her. She works for Professor Doctrow at Princeton. This copy was a simplified version she gave me. I guess it was never meant to take on a project of this size. I don't know how much further she took it."

As they rounded the corner, they found Ben Jacobs beside the door of their office accompanied by Corporal Tull.

Tull spoke. "Dr. Tyler."

She nodded, managing to keep a straight face. "Corporal Tull."

"Mr. Jacobs was pre-cleared by Mr. Kincaid. Will you take responsibility for escorting him?"

She nodded. "I will."

"Thank you, ma'am." Sarah caught a trace of a grin on Tull's face as he turned to leave.

"Well, Mr. Jacobs," Sarah said, "Congratulations on your article and your show. They say you must have been working on it for quite some time."

"I had lots of help," he replied.

Sarah pointed to Kathy. "Mr. Jacobs, this is Kathy Whiting, White House Senior Economic Advisor."

Kathy and Ben shook hands. "Ms. Whiting, I think we met at a reception about two years ago. Mr. Kincaid relies on you a great deal. It's an honor to meet you again."

Sarah looked at a brown envelope in Jacobs's hand. "He says you have something for me."

Jacobs glanced up and down the hallway. "Is there some place a little quieter where we could go over this?"

Jacobs followed the two inside their office.

He laid the envelope on Sarah's desk and crossed his arms over his chest.

She opened it and pulled out three sheets of paper. After a moment her jaw dropped. "Holy shit." She turned to Kathy. "It's the list."

"What list?" Kathy asked.

"The Windham Trust membership list, complete with dollars."

Kathy looked to Jacobs. "Where did you get that?"

"You know I'm not going to reveal sources."

"Fair enough, but we have a lot riding on this. How do we know it's reliable?"

"Oh, you'll have to trust me on that. You don't think I'd be bringing you something this disappointing if it wasn't real, do you?"

Sarah looked up, her eyebrows raised. "Disappointing? I wish I had had this about half an hour ago. Why would I be disappointed?"

Jacobs remained sober. "Vice President Bailey's name is nowhere on the list."

16 CHANGE OF ARRANGEMENTS

Thursday, May 8, 2014

Sarah appeared at the doorway to Anna's office. "I need help."

Anna continued writing. "Uh huh. You can only imagine how much restraint it takes to keep from running with that."

"Seriously. I need a killer dress for the Medal of Freedom dinner."

Anna dropped her pen, and looked into Sarah's desperate face. "That's tonight."

"I know."

"You told us you had something formal to wear," Anna continued.

"I know. I thought I did, but turns out it's at my parents' house in New Jersey."

"Since when am I the party-dress lady?"

"Come on. A little mercy, Colbert. Nobody knows how to put things together right like you do."

Anna shook her head.

"Please. I've got the afternoon off. Just tell me where to go. I promise I won't spill your secret."

"It's not where you go. It's what you choose."

Sarah's face twisted in anguish.

"All right. I'll help. With this short notice you're going to need someone who's got alterations on the premises." She pulled out her small note pad of monogrammed ivory paper. "A block and a half beyond DuPont Circle on Mass Ave, there's a little shop called Audrey's. Ask for Audrey Andrews and tell her I sent you."

Anna looked up. She hesitated. Sarah seemed exceptionally attentive. "May I presume you're taking Corporal Tull?"

Sarah nodded quickly.

"What's he wearing?" Anna asked.

"Wearing?"

"Yes. Uniform? Suit? What color?"

Sarah bit her lip.

Anna picked up her phone. "Detachment Office, Corporal Tull, please. … This is Ms. Colbert in Mr. Kincaid's office." She waited for Tull while addressing Sarah, "I'll spare you the lecture about how you should have checked your dress almost immediately."

"Sorry."

Anna's attention returned to the phone. "Corporal Tull. Anna Colbert here. I have some questions you probably won't want to answer too loudly in the Detachment Office. Just keep your responses as brief as possible, OK? For the dinner tonight, will you be wearing a suit rather than your uniform — 'Yes' or 'No.' OK. Black? Charcoal. Excellent. White shirt? OK. Cufflinks? No, not really. They're not expected these days. Color of tie? Maroon. Fine. Straight necktie? Bow. My, you will look dashing. That's all the questions I've got. Thank you for your assistance."

She put down the phone and dashed notes on her paper. "I'm sure Audrey has several items in dark red satin, something with just a little shimmer. Should be trimmed in black. Black shoes and stockings. Tell her you need a small burnished gold purse to go with it." She handed Sarah the notes and looked at the clock. "Actually, you'd better get going with traffic what it is. She may have to take it in. I'll call her and let her know you're on your way. She'll put it on my account, and you can pay me back. I get a pretty good discount."

"You do?"

"I helped coordinate between Audrey and the French Embassy when I interned there. Anyway, get going. You two will look great."

* * *

As dinnertime approached, Jeff Tull waited alongside the corridor leading to the dining room next to the elevator to the offices below.

"Tull!" a sharp voice called from his right.

"Major Reed, sir."

"What are you doing here? You're not crashing the dinner, are you?"

Tull instinctively stood at attention. "No, sir. I'm an invited guest, sir."

"Guest?" Major Reed asked, appearing skeptical.

The elevator opened and Sarah walked out. The two men turned in her direction. Tull broke into a wide smile.

Sarah glanced at the two, and then walked up to Tull, slipping her arm into his. She turned to Major Reed. "Doesn't our Marine look magnificent, whatever uniform he's wearing?"

The Major turned back to Tull. He seemed to be attempting, without success, a stern look. Finally he nodded, grinning. "Yes, ma'am, he does. So you'll vouch for him, Dr. Tyler?"

"Absolutely. He's my date."

The Major stepped back. "Dr. Tyler, Corporal Tull, have a wonderful evening."

She bowed, and they turned to walk with other guests toward the banquet.

"Thanks," Tull whispered.

"He wasn't giving you a hard time, was he?"

"Not really. It's just you don't often have a member of the detachment as a guest at these things."

She giggled.

"You look fabulous, by the way," he offered.

"Thanks. I had some very high-level help."

"Does this have something to do with the call from Ms. Colbert this morning?"

"Yup," she confirmed.

They arrived at the broad entrance to the room, its tables and decor breathtaking. A white-gloved usher looked at Sarah's card and directed them to table seventeen. Tull held her chair as she sat down. She introduced herself to Dr. Degrado as deputy assistant economics advisor to the President and Tull as a member of the Marine Corps security detachment for the White House. Degrado gave a brief explanation of his work on cancer drugs. While he and Tull began talking about the finances of the drug approval process, Sarah reached into her purse and pulled out a nametag, which she switched with the one at her place.

Tull watched her. "What are we doing?"

"I rescued it from the trash." She turned the card so that he could see it.

He shook his head as he grinned. The card read 'Dr. Paul Richards, Crusade for Moral Clarity.' Sarah had crossed out Richards' name and affiliation and had written in her name.

* * *

Monday, May 12, 2014

During his early morning news conference, the county executive announced that all three call centers would be fully automated within five weeks, saving the county nearly thirty million dollars in the first year.

Immediately afterwards, the emergency call center began its fifty percent work stoppage.

The sheriff's staff located the new Brisbane site less than a block from where they and Laura's team first disrupted the automation work. Anita was among the protesters gathering around the new office, carrying her sign and pleading with Brisbane electronic technicians to stop work. Laura and Charlie were on their phones starting at the end of the news conference, calling reporters with word of the new location. By three in the afternoon on Monday, the road beside the new automated center sprouted a small forest of satellite feed antennae trucks as a cadre of local reporters filed their on-the-scene reports for the six o'clock news complete with interviews from the old call center workers and 'no comments' from the new.

By six in the evening, Brisbane's Henderson ordered the building locked and walked out to one of his trucks flanked by Hercules and another large security guard. Hercules cleared their path, pushing everyone out of the way with the same brute force that Laura and the deputies had experienced earlier.

At seven the county executive ordered the sheriff to clear the entire block and secure the area. The sheriff responded at eight, releasing to the press the documents that Charlie had acquired subsequent to their meeting linking the executive to Brisbane's projects.

Live on the eleven o'clock news the county executive fired the sheriff for insubordination and dereliction of duty.

* * *

Tuesday, May 13, 2014

President Miller was about half-way through a light breakfast in the Oval Office when Vice President Bailey strode in.

"Mr. President, we have a situation. One of our new security centers has come under attack."

The President stopped eating. "Attack? Where?"

"It's local, in College Park."

"What? You're not talking about that call center on the news last night, are you?"

"Call center is only part of its task, sir. It's also designed to accommodate a lot of the secure communications for Homeland Security. That center is a key component of our crisis response network."

The President leaned back in his chair, folding his arms. "The news reports made no mention of any federal offices, and I don't remember anything about this in the last six months."

"We were in the process of federalizing it, but ..."

"I still don't remember any conversation about this," Miller persisted.

"No, sir, I didn't think it appropriate to burden you with that while you're dealing with all the economic hoopla."

The President returned to his meal. "Jim, I'm a lot better at multi-tasking than you're giving me credit. Now about this call center. Seems to me like a local labor dispute that should be handled by the two squabbling parties in Prince George's County. And as for 'attack,' I'd hardly classify a standard labor strike as an 'attack.'"

"We believe there may be infiltration of the strikers by foreign agents, possibly a branch of al-Qaeda or Abu Sayyaf Group."

"And on what are we basing that? I don't recall seeing anything in the last few days' briefings."

"Surveillance videos identify several members of the protesters as possible agents."

The President pushed his plate away and straightened up. "Whoa, whoa, whoa. Back up the bus, Jim. Surveillance? Do we have a court order for that? Last thing I want on my watch is another domestic spying mess."

"We've got the damned paperwork in progress, sir. I really don't think you're appreciating the gravity of this situation. I'm sure the really last thing you want on your watch is another nine-eleven."

"Don't try to scare me, Jim. It won't work. If we've got a legitimate surveillance operation that has identified possible foreign agents, why haven't we taken them into custody?"

"The match is not as good as we'd like, and we need to get more information before we move."

"How not good is it?"

"Our best target is a Filipino woman who yields a seventeen percent match with a known Abu Sayyaf operative. And there's some guy named Charles Jones who lights up with all sorts of radical connections going back forty years or so."

"Jeez, Jim, if I don't shave and comb my hair, I've got a seventeen percent match with half a dozen terrorists. Look — either get some real information immediately or move on. This looks like something we will be staying out of. I can't think of any reason I'd get worked up over this even if the center were federalized. This is a labor dispute, pure and simple."

"Yes, sir, I'll get the information, and if it doesn't pan out, we'll move on."

* * *

By three-thirty Tuesday afternoon, all but one of the antenna trucks had departed College Park along with most of the reporters. Work continued inside the new call center, though Charlie was convinced at a reduced pace. Only five people had entered the building since dawn. Anita and her coworkers walked in front of the building, displaying their 'Stop the Dehumanization' signs to any passing cars. They received several supportive toots from passing motorists.

During a break in their quiet vigil, Anita sat with Charlie and a young correspondent from National Public Radio. They took advantage of a Bradford pear tree that offered some shade from the warm May sunshine.

"Well, Michael, looks like you're about the only one left. The others don't seem to think our situation so important, eh?" Anita shrugged.

Michael set down his bottled water. "I doubt it's a matter of importance. There was a lot of action yesterday, and that's what gets viewer and reader attention for the commercial broadcasts. My piece will take a couple of days to research and may not air until Saturday or Sunday. It's hard to market something that's important when there's no drama attached."

"Maybe you should interview Charlie. He's led a very dramatic life." She turned to Charlie, lying on the grass with his beret pulled over his eyes. "Tell Michael about the time you were in lockup with that Bush girl."

He grinned. Two days worth of gray stubble on his face glowed in the backlighting sunshine. "I don't think the adventures of Charlie Jones will necessarily help your cause. Maybe someday some of Laura's writer friends will write 'em up, make it into a sitcom or something."

Michael laughed. "You're too modest. I've heard your name a lot. You seem to be the uncontrolled philosopher to a lot of prominent activists."

"Poor misguided souls." Charlie rocked his head back and forth.

The sound of heavy trucks drew their attention to the office park' entrance.

Charlie pushed himself up onto his elbow. "Those are army. Fort Meade, I'm guessing. I have a bad feeling about this."

The three got up and walked over to the rest of the group. Charlie began talking to those holding placards, explaining as quickly as he could the etiquette of confronting armed police and soldiers. Anita picked up her placard. Michael turned on his recorder and put it in his side pocket, picked up an extra placard and stood in the middle of the group.

Three trucks pulled up to the curb and several men got out, eight from each truck. Most were soldiers with rifles and helmets. Each truck also hosted a civilian. The civilians took the lead, walking over to Anita's group.

One of the civilians seemed to be the leader. He sported a salt-and-pepper short haircut, dark sunglasses, tailored black suit, and no trace of any friendliness. "On the authority of the Department of Homeland Security, I order you to leave these premises immediately."

Charlie stood in front of the group. He folded his arms. "Authority of the Department of Homeland Security? Give me a break. You don't have authority to order any such thing."

"You're trespassing on federal property, sir, in a secure zone. Again, I'm ordering you in no uncertain terms to leave."

Charlie did not yield. "Bullshit! This is a public sidewalk alongside a private office. We are part of a lawful assembly against a county action. You have no jurisdiction here, and you have no right to tell us to do anything."

The lead civilian's face reddened, and he walked up to Charlie, getting face-to-face as close as possible without touching. "You are in a federal no-trespass zone around a Department of Homeland Security communications facility."

Charlie tilted his head and smiled. "Since when?"

The lead civilian removed his sunglasses, revealing squinting gray eyes. "Are you Charles Jones?"

Charlie's smile faded. "I don't have to answer that unless you have a warrant, which you don't, since I haven't done anything. But the fact is that

I am Charles Jones — Charlie to my friends."

"Mr. Jones, I was told you might be involved in this. We have quite a lot on you, so I'm ready." He reached into the breast pocket of his suit and pulled out a single folded sheet of paper and handed it to Charlie. "Since twelve forty-seven today."

Charlie took the paper and read over it several times. "Very poorly written. Lots of clumsy grammar." He spoke loudly, but avoided looking at Michael. "According to this paper, our federal government, without oversight, has taken over a civilian office park that happens to contain a robotic replacement for the county workers at our emergency call center. How convenient for the county." He looked around at the parking lots surrounding the four buildings in the park. "Are you going to be moving all these people out?"

"Not if they don't cause trouble."

Charlie, still speaking loudly, leaned into the lead civilian. "And how are we causing trouble?"

"I've had enough of your attitude, mister. For the last time, clear out."

"No. Not without a court order."

"I don't need a court order." The lead civilian turned to a lieutenant. "Take him into custody."

"Sir?" The lieutenant seemed uncertain.

Charlie addressed the lieutenant. "You'll be violating the law if you lay a hand on me, soldier. I'm a civilian, and even if this paper is correct, I need to be arrested by a civilian because he claims this as DHS property, not DOD. If you seize me, you may be facing a court martial. And since Mr. Suit here is a civilian, he can't order you, anyway."

"Damn it, soldier, arrest this man."

The lieutenant shook his head. "I'm sorry, sir, but he's correct. I can't without a proper order."

The civilian's face glowed red. He gestured towards Anita. "Then arrest her. She's Maria Muñoz, a known terrorist of the Abu Sayyaf Group. You have both the authority and the responsibility to intercept an enemy agent." He pointed to Anita.

Charlie threw his arms out. "What the fuck are you talking about? She's a U.S. citizen and the wife of a member of the Armed Forces. What kind of fucking fraud is this?"

"Lieutenant, do your job."

The lieutenant's face twisted in anguish. He turned to Anita. "Ma'am, I have no way of knowing what's going on here, but if what he says is true, I have to arrest you. If it's not, I pledge to you that I will do everything in my power to fix it and make amends."

As his men moved slowly toward Anita, she cried out, "I'm not a terrorist. I've never done anything wrong in my life."

Charlie stepped between the lieutenant and Anita. The rest of the protesters gathered around her. Charlie reached out, holding the lieutenant back.

"Sir, please," said the young officer, "I don't want to be do this, but I have no choice."

Several soldiers surrounded the lieutenant and Charlie.

Anita cried out again, "I can prove who I am. Here, I have my driver's license." She reached into her purse.

As she did, a cracking sound echoed around the four buildings.

"Everyone down!" the lieutenant shouted, and then quickly ordered his men into a circle around the workers, their rifles pointed outward. The workers' tightly packed group dropped to the ground.

Charlie was the first to get up. He looked up at the lieutenant, who was scanning the surroundings frantically, ordering his men toward different buildings. Charlie turned to the others as they got up one by one. Only Anita remained on the ground, curled to one side, sobbing. He reached down to help her up.

Charlie kneeled beside her, "Don't worry, warrior lady. We'll get this straightened out." He put his hands gently beneath her shoulder. His eyes grew wide. He jerked back and raised his hands in front of him. They were covered with blood.

"Oh, my God." The lieutenant grabbed his cell phone. "I'm calling nine-one-one."

Through her pain, Anita tried smiling. She looked up at Charlie. "Tell him we're here."

"Shhh. Relax. You're going to be OK."

Charlie stepped back as two of the soldiers, presumably with casualty training, kneeled down to stop the blood flow. One looked up to his officer. "Lieutenant, tell them she has a serious wound to the upper left chest. She's bleeding, but it doesn't look like anything major was hit."

The lieutenant relayed the information. Another of his men sprinted to the second truck to grab two first aid kits. Sirens sounded in the distance.

The lieutenant called to the civilians as they all walked to the lead vehicle. "Hey! Where do you think you're going?"

"We have reports to file. This development is getting out of hand."

"Dammit, you get back here! I want some answers as soon as we get this lady taken care of!" The lieutenant still held his phone to his mouth.

All the civilians calmly climbed into the lead truck and drove away.

"Damn." The lieutenant turned to his men, ordering them in squads to the surrounding buildings with orders to stop anyone from leaving — at gunpoint if necessary.

Charlie turned to Michael, speaking softly, "You have Laura's number?"

Michael nodded.

"Very quietly call her. Tell her to contact the sheriff immediately."

Michael stepped back among the placards and began his text messages, looking up occasionally to make sure the soldiers weren't paying attention to him.

An ambulance and fire engine raced around the corner toward the group. Two soldiers stepped into the road directing the emergency vehicles to the side.

Medics ran to Anita.

The lieutenant approached Charlie. "Mr. Jones, I'd like you to come with us. She'll be taken care of, but you must understand we've gotta talk to you."

Charlie nodded. "Of course. Let me say goodbye for now."

The lieutenant opened his arm in Anita's direction.

Charlie motioned to Michael out of the lieutenant's view. Michael joined Charlie beside Anita. The medics applied some kind of compress and covered Anita's mouth with an oxygen mask. Watching her, Charlie spoke quietly to the medics, "Where are you taking her?"

"Laurel Regional Hospital, sir. That's the closest with an O.R. suitable for this kind of wound."

Charlie nodded.

"Don't worry, warrior lady. You'll be back on the line in no time." He squeezed her hand. She returned his grip firmly.

As he stood up, Charlie whispering to Michael, "Tell Laura where they're taking her. Tell her to make sure the sheriff doesn't let the bullet they recover out of his sight. Those suits are going to try to pin this on our army boys. Now you make yourself real scarce. There will be people looking to keep you quiet, too."

"The DHS people?"

Charlie glanced back and forth and then shook his head slowly. "No badges. Don't know who they were. I've encountered the lead suit before. Name's Henderson, I think. You're in the middle of something big and dangerous. Make yourself real scarce."

One of the soldiers called out, "What are you two talking about? Let's get a move on. Please step over to the truck, Mr. Jones."

Michael turned to the soldier. "He was telling me this isn't his first time going to jail. Just before you guys arrived, he told me about the evening he spent in lockup with one of the Bush girls."

The soldier laughed. "No kidding? Don't worry. He's not going to jail. We just gotta get things straightened out."

Charlie walked toward the second vehicle and began spinning his story. Michael walked slowly toward his own car as the lieutenant tried to keep track of his thinly-spread forces, all the while talking to his superior on his military phone. As Michael approached his car and silently got in, Anita's coworkers engaged the remaining soldiers with questions and protests.

Michael reclined his seat back and called Laura, briefing her about the events of the past half hour as she sped toward Laurel. Then he called his office and began filing his story as he uploaded the audio.

* * *

The sheriff arrived at Laurel Regional Hospital with a host of deputies. They formed a phalanx around Anita as medics wheeled her to the operating room and his deputies cordoned off the corridors as surgeons began their work.

Laura arrived and began sharing details with the sheriff.

Minutes later, four black-suited men arrived at the hospital and made their way toward the operating room. Laura had been unable to contact Charlie, and relied on Michael's narrative about the civilians involved in the College Park skirmish. She immediately recognized the leader of this quartet as Henderson.

As they marched down the corridor toward the operating room door, Laura stepped into their path. Henderson tried to swerve around her, but she moved, throwing out her arms to block him.

"Get out of the way, ma'am. You're blocking a federal law enforcement action."

"Cut the crap! Who are you people?"

"I'm not here to answer your questions, ma'am. I'm here to uphold the law. Now please get out of our way."

Laura moved close to Henderson. "Do you know who I am?"

"I don't make a habit of remembering troublemakers. I just have them removed." He signaled for two of his men to move around them and down the hall toward the O.R.

She argued loudly with Henderson as the two demanded access to the operating room. The deputies stood firm.

"All right, miss, that does it. We're taking you in."

Laura glanced to the side and then grinned. "OK … Smile!"

"What?" Henderson turned to their right at a new commotion far down the hallway. A dozen or so reporters with cameras and lights were approaching … fast.

Laura shouted, "Hey, Joe, these are the thugs I was telling you about! They have a statement to make!"

Henderson wheeled back to Laura. "We're not done." He led his men in an attempt to bypass the reporters, but the hallway was clogged with press and security staff. In the resulting melee, Henderson's glasses were knocked off, and one camera was sent skidding across the tiles. The dark quartet exited the building to a cacophony of unanswered questions.

One of the deputies donned latex gloves, picked up Henderson's glasses, and placed them in an evidence bag.

Laura turned to the deputy. "That was bizarre. I had a run-in with that creep not so long ago, but he didn't seem to recognize me."

The deputy glanced up from his notations. "Under the circumstances, I'm not sure that's a bad thing."

Laura spent the next hour on her phone talking to contacts again and trying to reach Charlie.

The sheriff emerged from the operating room a few minutes after five in the afternoon. He saw Laura and was walking in her direction when the duty nurse called to him, "Someone from Homeland Security for you, Sheriff."

He took the phone. "No, sir, I did not get any information from her." His face wrinkled in a deep frown. "The bullet? It appeared to have exited, judging by the wound. It's probably still at the scene. … No, sir, my men have not had time to go over the crime scene yet. … No, that will not be possible. … Because she died on the operating table. Hello?"

The sheriff turned to see Laura holding her hand to her mouth in horror, tears welling in her eyes. He grinned, shaking his head while holding up an evidence bag with a small lump inside. "She'll be fine. Sore for a week or so, but Anita will be fine."

* * *

After updating the President, Vice President Bailey entered the White House briefing room. Half a dozen members of the press pool looked up in surprise as he appeared for only the fourth time since taking office.

He began his announcement before reporters had time to open their folders. "Today, members of our nation's protective forces, both civilian and military, have thwarted a brazen attempt to disrupt the national communications systems upon which our security rests. After an investigation employing some of the most sophisticated technology ever used in the war on terrorism, we have, with record speed, thwarted terrorist suspects before they have had a chance to carry out their deadly mission.

"One suspect, believed to be a member of the Abu Sayyaf Group, was killed by members of the armed services as she reached for her weapon at a communication center within minutes of the capital. Other suspects are in custody and being questioned at this time."

The Vice President started to leave.

One of the pool reporters called out, "What kind of technology are we talking about?"

"I'm not going to respond to that. We are not about to hand over our secrets to the enemy," Bailey protested.

"Mr. Vice President, the Abu Sayyaf Group is based in the Philippines, and we were given to believe that it was poorly equipped and poorly funded. How is it that they have been able to mount operations on U.S. soil?"

He scowled, continuing, "We will discuss relevant details of our finding when it is appropriate and safe to do so."

"Sir, what elements of the civilian and military forces were involved in this operation and when will we have an opportunity to talk with them?"

Vice President Bailey looked incredulous. "We will not be discussing details of our anti-terrorism tactics or strategies. That's just plain stupid. Look, you people, we just broke up an assault on the American homeland. I think it's time we paid attention to the issues here instead of trying to tear our efforts apart."

His answer launched a frenzied return round of questions. His only response was a brusque "No comment," after which he turned and left the room.

* * *

The Channel Eight news team led their 7 p.m. broadcast with the story "terrorist plot broken up near the nation's capital." The newscast graphics included a map of the Philippines with the island of Mindoro mistakenly highlighted rather than Mindanao, the home base of the Abu Sayyaf Group.

Channels Three and Eleven opened with more cautious reports of a conflict with shooting at the College Park center. They reported the death as "unconfirmed."

At 7:10, NPR broadcast a special report. "Many reporters wait a lifetime to uncover the big stories. Our cub reporter Michael Swanson found himself on his second day on the job in the midst of battle just miles from NPR's Washington offices. And his report stands in stark contrast to the official pronouncements we heard moments ago from the White House. Michael, are you there?"

"I am. I'm hunkered down in the back seat, out of sight for now, but it seems that there is some kind of clampdown underway where everything happened a few hours ago. I can see now dozens and dozens of soldiers and civilians ringing the area where earlier the group of striking nine-one-one workers I was interviewing came under attack."

"You call it an attack. Did the soldiers attack the workers striking over the closure of the call center?"

"Oh, no, on the contrary. I was standing among the picketers. The shot or shots came from one of the buildings in this complex. The soldiers actually formed a protective ring around us. I hope you'll be able to hear that in the audio I've uploaded."

"I'm playing it now, Michael." On the audio, Charlie could be heard clearly arguing, first with the civilians, then with the lieutenant. The lieutenant's words and voice seemed more a plea than an order. Anita's crisp voice said, "Here, I have my driver's license," followed by a loud crack and three less distinct pops. The audio became muffled and filled with extraneous noises as the lieutenant ordered everyone down and the recorder shifted in Michael's pocket. As clarity returned, the lieutenant was ordering his men to various buildings and then making the emergency call.

"Michael, the Vice President claims that the woman we just heard, the one he says was killed by the soldiers, was an agent of Abu Sayyaf Group, the notorious terrorist group of the southern region of the Philippines. Did you have an opportunity to speak with her earlier?"

"Killed? Oh, no, oh, no. It didn't appear to either the soldiers initially attending her or to the civilian medics that her wound was fatal — serious, but not fatal. Her name is Anita, a veteran nine-one-one worker, and I was in the midst of a conversation with her and Charlie Jones when the Army trucks arrived. We had been talking for over an hour. She seemed to me a sweet woman with a dedication to her co-workers."

"In his brief press conference, the Vice President seemed to be implying that she was reaching for a weapon. Did you see anything?"

"Mara, I was actually beside her when she was shot and was beside her as she was lifted on a stretcher into the ambulance. She was clutching her driver's license."

Mara continued, "The events of this afternoon involved both military and civilian elements. The military members were clearly from the Army, though we have not been given any of the names of individuals or of units to which they were attached. Who were the civilians and what did they tell you?"

"That's one of the big mysteries here. The four civilians rode in the army trucks and behaved as if they were in charge. The lieutenant commanding the soldiers didn't seem at all comfortable with these men and appeared to chafe under their directions, at one point challenging the orders of the lead civilian, a man Jones thinks may be named Henderson. I really don't have any more information. They left immediately after the shooting, despite the lieutenant's telling them repeatedly to remain on the scene, and they never presented any kind of identification to us. You can hear that in the audio. The whole encounter still has a surreal feel about it with …"

"Sorry to interrupt you, Michael. Actually, I'm pleased to tell you that we've just received word from reporters inside Laurel Regional Hospital, where Anita was taken. It appears that this aspect of the Vice President's news conference was likewise in error. The doctors in Laurel say that she has come through surgery, and that while she is in serious but stable condition, she is expected to make a full recovery."

"That is good news indeed," Michael sighed.

"Michael, you hang tight where you are. We have people coming to relieve you, and we're looking forward to a full report later."

"Thank you."

"This is NPR News. We will bring you more information when we receive it as we try to untangle this most confusing series of events."

* * *

The Oval Office was surprisingly quiet, despite the presence of the President, the Vice President, and David Kincaid. Vice President Bailey stood tight-lipped facing the President from near the center of the room. The President sat at his desk, hands clasping his head.

Kincaid had positioned himself to the side of the office, as far out of the way as he could manage. While he leaned against the wall, trying to decide what to do with his hands, the phrase "blending into the woodwork" acquired new appeal. At the same time, he sensed that the President wanted him there to buffer and blunt Miller's anger.

The President continued. "I have read that I run a loose, a relaxed administration. I don't mind that. We have a really great working group. I have heard that I tolerate too much dissent and rancor in my administration. I'm OK with alternative views and passionate principles. In fact I'm proud of it and truly believe that's one of the keys to our success. But now they say that my administration is in disarray, that I've lost my way. That is a problem. That is unacceptable."

Vice President Bailey took a deep breath and closed his eyes for a moment.

"Where did you get the information that you shared at your press briefing this afternoon?" the President asked.

"Sir, I told you. It was a note from my staff," Bailey replied.

"And you made no further inquiry or move to confirm it before going public? That's not like you, Jim."

"I had no reason to doubt the report, and I was excited to be able to report it. We've long been in need of some kind of victory."

The President's face contorted. "Victory? In what? Things have been pretty quiet for a decade, haven't they? Quite frankly, I think our efforts have been rather successful. Do you disagree?"

"Mr. President, this apparent calm has lulled us into complacency. Congress is moving to cut funding for the very programs that have kept us secure all this time."

"Jim, this just doesn't add up. I know you're not being straight with me. I need to be able to trust you. This whole mess has all the makings of a constitutional crisis." He turned to Kincaid. "Any thoughts?"

Kincaid started. "Sir, we're missing a lot of facts. We need clarity before we do anything."

The President turned back to Bailey. "Your office will be completely open with the Chief of Staff's investigation! Understood? If not, I'm going to put them under David."

Bailey stared at Kincaid.

"Understood?" The President shouted.

"Understood, sir," Bailey said.

"And David will be spokesman for your office until this matter is cleared up."

Bailey frowned. "Sir, he doesn't know anything of our operations."

"Apparently, Jim, neither do you. And my Chief of Staff should be aware of what's going on in the Vice President's office. He should be fully aware. David doesn't mind saying 'I don't know, but I'll get back to you' at a press conference. The press seems OK with that. You might want to learn from Mr. Kincaid's example, Jim."

Bailey continued staring.

"Understood?"

"Understood, sir."

"Now go get us the staffer who sent you the memo."

Bailey looked at the clock. Eight-nineteen. "Sir?"

"Now!" the President shouted again.

Bailey moved toward the door. He paused, looked at Kincaid, and then back to the President.

Miller looked at Bailey and said, "Mr. Kincaid and I need to talk about this catastrophe out of your presence. Please send us the staffer who sent you the memo."

"Yes, sir." Bailey walked out of the room.

The President listened for the elevator doors to close. He leaned back in his chair and looked at Kincaid.

Several minutes passed.

"Sir?" Kincaid tried to restart the conversation.

"He's lying, isn't he?"

"Obviously, it's out of character for him to make a mistake like this. I've always known him to be extremely cautious. I'll be interested in what his messenger has to say."

"Do you believe there is a messenger?" Miller asked.

Kincaid rubbed his face. "I meant what I said. We're missing a lot of facts. We should know a little more in a bit."

The President got up and began pacing the room, pausing at the window to look out at the Washington Monument. "How is Dr. Tyler's investigation coming?"

"She's making progress, Mr. President, but it's slow. I have some people from Justice and Treasury assisting quietly. If anything, the data would indicate that he's done nothing wrong other than to associate with a lot of wealthy and powerful, if questionable, men. Last time I checked, that wasn't a crime. At least Matt's been cleared."

"Matt?" The President turned from the window with a surprised look.

Kincaid smiled. "Sarah's early version of the software was a tad underpowered. Matt gave her some information about himself; and when she plugged it in, he came out one of the most powerful men in the country."

The President shook his head. "Great. How can we trust anything?"

"But she's gotten hold of a later, more sophisticated version. Matt comes out where we'd expect now, and several other characters are in their expected spots. The Vice President isn't close to the core. Interestingly, the Reverend Dr. Richards is."

"The pervert we almost gave a medal to?"

"I was going to phrase it a little more delicately, but I think we're talking about the same fellow," Kincaid mused.

"Amazing how someone like that can elude justice for so long. At least he's locked up now."

"Actually, no. He posted a multi-million dollar bond. He's preparing a defense, assembled the best team of lawyers money can buy."

The President shook his head. His phone buzzed, and he pushed the speaker button. "Yes?"

The Vice President spoke. "Mr. President, the author of the memo was Deborah Keenan. She left about an hour ago for dinner and a show in Georgetown."

"Call her cell, Jim. I want this resolved."

"I tried, sir. The call is going straight to voice mail. She apparently has it switched off."

The President silenced the receiver. "Should we send out a detail to find her, David?"

"Hmm. It's a judgment call. Probably better to wait 'til morning. I'll have the gate send her directly here. But you might keep that between us. I'm guessing you think he's going to 'have a talk' with her. Obviously, we don't want that to happen."

The President returned to the phone. "All right, Mr. Vice President. But I want you to send her to David Kincaid as soon as you see her tomorrow."

"Understood, sir."

The President turned the phone off. "David, I'm tired, really tired. It's going to get worse before it gets better, and I'm not sure what 'it' is. Get some rest. Let's get started early tomorrow."

"Yes, Mr. President."

Kincaid headed toward the door.

"And, David, thanks," the President called out.

Kincaid turned back. "For…?"

The President chuckled. "For being such an aggravating ninny, insisting on protocol."

"Good night, Mr. President."

Kincaid passed the guard, giving him a pat on the shoulder, and wandered toward his office. Before traveling the final distance, he detoured by Anna's office and was surprised to find her still at her desk finishing a phone call.

She looked up. "Good evening, sir."

"Good evening, Anna. You're working later than is healthy."

She grinned. "As are you, sir. I was talking with a friend, Laura Garrette. We both sing in the Chorus. Anyway, she's been working with the group that came under fire up in College Park this afternoon. She's trying to locate her colleague, Charlie Jones. I told her I couldn't do anything about Charlie, but I'd come and keep her company."

"Really? Would you mind a tag-along? I'd like to hear her take on things. And I might be able to facilitate finding Mr. Jones," he said.

"I'd love to have some company, sir. I'll warn you, though, she can be a hot-head at times."

"I think I can handle that."

* * *

At eight in the evening, Lindale Hospice was quiet save for the unintelligible general murmur of families talking of old times and good. The lounges and waiting rooms exuded an air not of anguish or anger, but rather of fatigue and resignation.

Tina adjusted the oxygen flow to a small tube by the side of Jennifer's face and checked the contacts on the heart and respiration monitor as Jack replayed the latest confrontation with Leslie, Patricia, and Elsa. Jennifer listened closely. She tilted in his direction, not having the strength to raise her head.

"… and so I offered them help with their résumés. I can't do anything about replacements unless they resign, and I don't really see that happening any time soon. But at least recently I haven't found any disasters waiting to happen."

"Good for you, Jack," Jennifer whispered.

Jack looked at Jennifer. "Your lips are dry. You need to drink something."

"I don't want anything to drink. I want some ice chips. Go get me some ice chips."

Tina broke from her task replacing a drip bag attached to the pole beside her bed. "I'll get you some ice chips, Mrs. Pullman."

"No." Jennifer's voice was suddenly strong. "Thanks. He needs the exercise. We're reading more of my stuff tonight, and he needs to stay awake." She moved her eyes without moving her head. They shifted back to Jack. "I want some from that machine over in the Jacobs wing. It's like shaved ice."

Jack nodded, grabbed a cup, and was off.

With great difficulty Jennifer turned her head toward Tina. She watched as Tina avoided her eyes. "Tonight's the night, isn't it?"

"I don't know what you're talking about, Jennifer."

"You'd make a lousy liar. I hear the nurses and the assistants talking. You know when it's time."

Tina lowered her head, set firm.

"Do you believe in God?" Jennifer's voice relaxed.

"Yes, ma'am. I do," Tina replied.

"I'd never thought about it much, and I guess I wasn't what you'd call a religious person, but I'm feeling something now."

"Yes, ma'am. We see that pretty often here."

Jennifer nodded slowly. "Like my being — my soul I guess — is coming loose. Like cooked chicken off the bone."

Tina shook her head, smiling at last. "I've never heard it put that way. But I've heard people describe the feeling."

"I'm ready, Tina."

Tina nodded.

Jennifer took a deep breath. "But Jack's not."

"I'll be here with him," Tina assured her.

"No. You're off in two hours. I'm good for longer than that."

"I'll be here with him," Tina repeated.

"You have a family who needs you. Go home. Sharon comes on at midnight."

"I'll be here too, with Sharon. And you can just quit your arguing unless you're going to get up and stop me."

Jennifer smiled faintly. "I'll put in a good word for you, I promise."

"Thank you." Tina's eyes were wet with tears.

Jack appeared in the doorway with her cup heaped with ice the texture of snow cones and a plastic spoon. He glanced back and forth between Tina and Jennifer. "Did I miss something?"

Jennifer closed her eyes. "Tina was being stubborn. It's OK." She turned her head and received a bit of ice. "Mmmm."

Jack sat in the chair next to the nightstand and put his hand on her manuscript. "Shall I read Chapter Seventeen?"

"No, we're reading Twenty-one tonight."

Jack frowned. "What about …?"

"We're reading Twenty-one tonight." She spoke to Tina, "He promised me he'd make love to me in the morning if I sleep through the night."

Tina smiled. "I'll be sure to leave a 'Do Not Disturb' tag on the door." She put the sterile gauze and latex gloves on her tray and then stroked Jennifer's cheek. Tina nodded and left the room.

Jack picked up the manuscript and began searching for the beginning of Chapter Twenty-one.

"Before you start, I want candlelight."

"What?" Jack asked.

"I want candlelight. It's romantic."

Jack shook his head slowly. "I'm sure it would be; but with open oxygen, the whole place would burst into flames."

Jennifer began laughing, but it turned into a cough. After a bit she settled down and continued with a weak giggle. She spoke slowly, softly. "Jack Pullman, I've so got you pegged, and you've taught me well. I just knew you'd object on safety grounds. After all, it might kill me."

Jack looked sad.

"Hey, big boy. Look in the top of my bag."

Jack leaned over and rummaged gently in her overnight bag. He retrieved a small object and broke into a big smile.

"I found it at Pier One a while back. Thought I'd save it. It's battery powered. Two double As. The box said it's good for twenty-four hours."

Jack nodded, still smiling. "I'll get some rechargables."

Jennifer closed her eyes and whispered, "I think they'll do."

Jack cleared the plate and cup from the nightstand, set the electric candle in the center, and turned it on. It was quite bright. "Nice. Probably an LED." He got up and dimmed the room lights. "Very effective."

"And no bursting into flames," she offered.

Jack sat back down with the pages in his lap, watching Jennifer.

She finally turned from the light. "Chapters Seventeen through Twenty are about high school. You can read about all my passionate boyfriends another night."

The world around them was quiet, light dim save the faux candle. Jack began to read.

'The first time I met Jack Pullman, I hated him immediately. He was cocky and aggressive. He had just humiliated my best friend and was happy about it. My wise father prevented bloodshed and calmly explained to me again the rules of competition. I protested on the drive home and for the next week. It was a sunny Tuesday afternoon eight days later that my father handed me a slip of paper with Jack's phone number on it.

'The first time I met Jack Pullman was the luckiest day of my life. All the rest is mere decoration.'

Jack's voice was cracking. He looked up from the reading. "Wow."

"It's all true. And it sounds pretty good if I do say so myself."

Jack continued reading about that debate meet so many years ago. He visualized afresh the young girl with chestnut hair, freckles, and fierce anger in her eyes. Presently he glanced at her monitor, watching the steady cycles of heartbeat and breathing. He could tell that she was getting tired. The length of the breathing cycles was stretching into the familiar night pattern.

'Jack was and is a debater's debater. He loves the completely closed argument and its inescapable truth. Passion can be the debater's enemy, substituting the force of adrenalin for the purity of abstract logic. I am a raging fire, much preferring the exhilaration of igneous argument to methodical construction. We are as perfect a match as two mortals could hope to be, a hot fire in a safe and solid stove.'

Jack read on, checking the monitor occasionally. She fell asleep somewhere around page five, and he drifted off after page seven. He slept in the chair as the pages silently fell from his lap.

Wednesday, May 14, 2014

He awoke with a start. The sounds were not right. He looked over to Jennifer. In the dim light — too dim — he could see her chest heaving. It was too dark. He turned to the candle, which was now a barely glowing flicker. "Damned battery." He turned to the monitor. The rhythmic lines were gone, replaced by a wandering trace. His heart raced as he reached for the button above the headboard and pressed it franticly.

Within seconds, Tina was beside the bed. She looked at Jennifer and then at the monitor. She closed her eyes and made the Sign of the Cross on her chest.

Jack choked, "I think you need to get the doctor. She's in distress. She's having a hard time breathing."

Tina reached over to the monitor and flipped the alarm switch to silent.

Jack looked at Tina, his face twisted in pain. "What are we going to do?"

"Take her hand, Jack," Tina said, now with powerful calm.

"What?"

"Take her hand, Jack. She needs you." Her broad working hands rested on his shoulders.

Jack took Jennifer's hand. He could feel her grasping with all her remaining might while tears streamed down his cheeks.

"Give her a kiss."

Jack leaned over and kissed her cheek as the tears rained down. Jennifer's eyes remained closed, but she smiled. "Mmmm." Her breathing had calmed, and she seemed to relax.

Jack felt her grip ease. He squeezed harder, but she gave no response.

Tina looked at the monitor. The traces no longer wandered. She took one hand off his shoulder just long enough to press a button, freezing the clock at three fifty-seven. Jack's frame shook as he sobbed into the bed. Tina remained with them until dawn.

* * *

Once Jack was able to get up again, Sharon explained the procedures from that point. Jack was given a sheet with contact numbers and people to see. The hospice staff would handle the routine tasks of making the calls that one must after the death of a person.

Jack drove toward home through the morning gloom to get some rest. Realizing where he was, he stopped at the lab to post notice that he would be out for several days and leave instructions. He took out his key as he neared the lab office. But something was different. The familiar lock had been replaced by some security keypad. He looked down the hall supposing he might have arrived on the wrong floor in his distraught state. The room number was correct. He shook his head.

Jack turned at the sound of footsteps approaching around the corner. Dr. Garrette and a woman Jack had barely recognized from Headquarters HR rounded the bend and approached him.

Dr. Garrette spoke. "Jack, we'd like you to come with us to the conference room for a little chat."

Jack followed as Garrette strode toward the conference room. The woman's expression evinced discomfort.

"What's this about?"

"We'll discuss things in a minute, Jack."

In the conference room, Garrette's briefcase was open on the big table, papers spread out beside it.

Dr. Garrette extended his hand toward the seat to the right of the papers. "Have a seat Jack."

Jack fell wearily into the chair. The woman sat down quietly across the table from Jack.

"Jack, this is Joanna Denton, our assistant director of human resources. We're here to investigate a report of some potentially serious misconduct. Ms. Denton is here to assist in this investigation."

Jack shook his head. "Sir?"

Denton leaned forward, rubbing her eyes.

Garrette picked up a small stack of papers. "Jack, would you like to explain what happened on Saturday, the 29th of March?"

Jack squeezed his eyes closed. "I'm sorry. I'm not thinking too clearly this morning. March … end of March … I was on vacation. I was in San Diego with Jennifer. What's this about?"

Garrette pulled one of the papers from his stack, turned it around, and slid it over to Jack. It was a photocopy of a citation from San Diego. It was a photocopy of the citation that Jack had received for 'nudity outside of official zone.' Jack could see the coffee stain from his cup. He stared at the copy.

"Jack?" Garrette asked.

"Sir. With all due respect, this was not a problem. It was like a parking fine. I paid it. I don't understand."

Garrette grew stern. "Jack, this is not at all like a parking fine. This lascivious behavior reflects negatively on the Institute. It's our duty as corporate citizens to adhere to the highest standards."

Jack protested, "This doesn't have anything to do with the Institute. I was on my own time on the other side of the country. I was on vacation. This has nothing to do with the Institute. The Institute has no right to be involved."

Garrette reached over and placed his finger on the address on the citation: the address of the lab. "Jack, we expect our employees to be model citizens whenever they associate with the Institute. This makes it our business. Why did you choose to identify yourself with the Institute here?"

Jack stared at the paper and shook his head. "I don't know. I guess it was the first address that came into my head at the time. I give that address ten times a day." He slumped back in the chair.

Denton took notes during the conversation.

Garrette continued. "Jack, why were you nude in public in San Diego?" He leaned back and crossed his arms awaiting Jack's response.

After a long silence, Jack looked up at Garrette. "I really don't think that's any of your business, sir."

Garrette leaned forward again, tapping his finger angrily on the desk. "Dr. Pullman, your job is on the line. The Institute regards this as a very serious transgression. I suggest that you explain yourself right now."

Jack bowed his head, speaking softly. "I made love to my wife on the beach."

Garrette put his hands on the table. "All right. I think I've heard enough. I am officially notifying you that you are suspended from your duties pending a full investigation of this incident and any other related violations." He took another sheet of paper from his stack — a notice of suspension, already signed. He put it in front of Jack. "I'll need your access badge while we complete this investigation."

Staring at the paper, Jack showed no hint of emotion. The room was quiet for some time. He handed Garrette his badge.

Finally, Garrette began placing papers back in his brief case. He looked at Jack. "And I must say that you are not representing the Institute very well now, either. Is this how you normally come to work? You're unshaven, and your clothes look like you slept in them."

"My wife died," Jack mumbled.

Denton looked up immediately from her notes, horror stricken. "What?"

"Jennifer died," he replied.

Her face clouded. "When?"

"A few hours ago. She just couldn't fight the cancer any more."

Denton closed her notebook. "OK. We're halting these proceedings right now. Dr. Garrette, I'm officially notifying you that we need to vacate this suspension. Jack is entitled to bereavement leave. Under the circumstances, the suspension is totally inappropriate."

Garrette seemed immobilized by the new information.

She looked at Jack, who was staring numbly at the paper, and then gestured to Garrette, "May I have a word with you outside, sir?"

Garrette rose from his seat.

"We'll be right back, Jack," she said as she followed Garrette to the hall and gently closed the door. She spun around to Garrette. "Were you aware of this?"

"No."

"Was Jack covered under our insurance policies?" she continued.

"I don't know. He may have been."

Her voice took on a sharp edge. "May have been? Someone with advanced cancer usually racks up substantial medical bills. I haven't seen any. They would have been passed on through your office. Did you see any big claims?"

Garrette bit his lower lip.

"Damn it, James!" she shouted. "I'd better not find out you were denying his claims. We've had this discussion before. It's bad enough the human consequences — which are hideous. But you're putting the Institute at serious risk as well if you denied his claims!" She raised her fists shaking in the air as she paced back and forth. "We will go back in there, apologize, and work on repairing the damage. This man is hurting, and he is one of us, part of the Institute family."

"We can't leave him with access to the labs," Garrette mumbled.

She turned to face him. "What? Why not?"

Garrette looked away. "Given the situation as we understand it now, he's liable to be unstable and may put our source in harm's way if he has access to the lab."

"Our source? What do you mean *our source*?"

Garrette replied, "The person who revealed this incident could be a target of retribution."

"I thought you got this ticket from San Diego."

"We verified that it was genuine with the San Diego PD, but it was initially reported by an employee of the Institute."

She leaned against the wall, closing her eyes. "This is a nightmare. I'm really afraid of what else you haven't told me. You may be my senior, but I'm telling you, you're behaving like a real ass. Let's get back in there and start straightening this out."

"What are you proposing you'll do?" he asked.

"We — we — will start by apologizing and getting him some assistance. He shouldn't be alone at a time like this."

"I don't know if we have a protocol for that." Garrette looked away.

"Then we'll make it up as we go along." She reached for the door handle.

"I'm going to have to let you handle this. I've obviously done enough damage." He backed away.

"Oh, no, you don't!" she shouted.

"I'll provide you with whatever resources you need. I can't be directly involved in this matter from this point on."

"You coward! You damned coward!"

Garrette turned and walked away.

Denton took a deep breath, turned the handle, and entered the conference room. "Jack, there is so much that's gone wrong here, and so much I was not told. First of all, I am deeply sorry for your loss. I cannot imagine what you're going through. On top of that, we've been beasts. We would have been beasts even without this tragedy. There is so much I have not been told."

Jack finally looked up from the paper. "How can you let me go for this?"

"We can't, Jack." She reached out and took the letter. "He was going to have you sign it to acknowledge receipt." She tore the paper, stacked the pieces, tore them again, and continued until she could no longer tear the stack. "For the past year or so, things have been getting more and more ridiculous at Headquarters. I'm quite certain I'd be fired for what I'm about to tell you, but I've been on the edge of quitting for months anyway, and this morning's stupidity has put me over the top. I'm resigning as soon as I can get things in place for you to do what you need to do. Did you rack up a lot of bills from your wife's treatments?"

Jack nodded.

"Were any of your claims denied?" she asked.

Jack nodded again. "Almost all of them. The denials said it was a pre-existing condition."

Denton closed her eyes. "Dammit. I'll get you the information you need to take action against them, Jack, before I leave."

"That won't bring Jennifer back."

"You're right, of course, but I suspect that others are also being denied legitimate claims."

Jack seemed to be considering this possibility.

"Right now, I'd suggest you get some rest. How long have you been up?"

He shrugged. "I slept for a couple of hours last night before … I don't know exactly. I haven't been sleeping too well lately."

"What can I do for you now, Jack?"

He looked around. "I just came by to leave a note with some instructions. I was on my way home."

"Why don't you go ahead and leave a note. I can drive you home or get you a ride if you need it."

"I can't get into the lab. Someone's put new locks on the doors."

She put her hand to her face. "I forgot about that. It's standard procedure for what he presented. Here, I'll give you the code." She took one of the fragments of the suspension letter and wrote the combination to the door and handed it to him. She glanced at the clock. "Your technicians were told not to come in for another hour and a half."

Jack shook his head and sighed. "Sounds like it was a done deal."

"That's what I thought, too," she murmured.

Jack got up and headed to the door.

"Can I get you a ride?"

He shook his head. "No, I'll be OK." He thought for a moment. "But I'm going to have problems without my badge. Dr. Garrette still has it."

"I'll take care of that. I'll go with you to your car."

"Thanks."

Jack proceeded to the lab, wrote out a short list of instructions, and placed them on Leslie's desk. He couldn't bear to look at Jennifer's picture on his desk. He returned to the conference room, and then walked with Joanna to the parking garage.

She explained to him the time off to which he was eligible, and she recommended some resources for his grieving and for eventually dealing with the Institute. Denton made sure that Jack had her phone number, and that he promised to call her.

He drove home and went immediately to the bedroom, flopping onto the bed. He pulled the comforter loosely over him and fell into a fitful sleep.

* * *

"Yes, sir. I talked with Ms. Keenan for about forty-five minutes early this morning, right after she got in. I suggested she not mention our discussion to Mr. Bailey." David Kincaid had pulled one of the historic antique chairs onto the rug by the President's desk and was leaning back, relaxed with his legs crossed. The President and his Chief of Staff were alone.

"And …?" The President was calm, but clearly unhappy.

"I sense she's being as honest as she can under the circumstances. I can feel a subtext to what she told me, a second story."

"Does she need protection?"

"You've already signed off on it. Well, Abigail did."

The President nodded.

"Anyway, the storyline goes that the security section of the Vice President's office contacted the PG sheriff's office after the shooting yesterday. They eventually got hold of the sheriff himself, and the security office was told that the woman, Anita Howard, had died from her wounds."

"And we know, mercifully, that she had not," Miller responded.

"Correct, sir. I talked to her last night. And I talked to the sheriff, too."

"Really?"

"Ms. Colbert is a friend of one of the organizers, a Ms. Garrette. We went to visit her at the hospital. Ms. Garrette was trying to track down the location of one of her colleagues."

"How did that go?" Miller asked.

"I have a few bruises, but I'll recover."

The President cracked a smile.

Kincaid continued, "She's a … strong-willed … young woman, and I would have considered what she was saying as conspiracy theory except it all seems to have happened."

"Did you locate their colleague?"

"Yes, he was with the Army detachment in the middle of all this. They were up at Fort Meade. I saw to it that he was released with apologies and a ride back. Now we need to get some reliable information from the officer in charge of the detachment."

"Reliable?" Miller asked.

"The detachment reports indirectly to the security directorate. I don't want any fouling from that direction."

"Admiral Brown, again?"

"If you're willing, sir. He found out a lot of interesting history from those troops wandering in the desert. Don't know what to make of it, but I have a feeling these dots all connect."

The President waved his hand. "Have at it. What about the woman who was shot?"

"She checks out squeaky clean. There was a good bit on her at FBI because her husband holds a crypto clearance in the Navy. In fact, she was working at the call center under PG County's Veterans Family Preference program. She seems the kind who inspires loyalty. The sheriff put his job on the line for her."

"Oh?"

"Apparently the county exec was in the process of firing the sheriff over this, but the sheriff is plowing on."

"Where does this end, David?"

"I don't know, sir. The more I find out, the messier it gets. We've already got federal and local governments, military, private corporations. I'm just waiting for a religious angle."

"Don't even joke about that." The President cringed.

"Right. But for now I need to get ready for the press briefing this afternoon. Or re-briefing. It's going to be pretty ugly."

The President chuckled. "I'm sure you'll do fine. Are you getting the cooperation you need from Bailey's office?"

"I really haven't had time to test it, sir. The first challenge will be a new press secretary. I really don't have time to do this with everything else on my plate."

Miller smiled. "You love it; admit it."

"Yes, I love it, but you can't afford to have me sidetracked."

The President nodded. "If you have any problem from the Vice President's office over the Press Secretary clearance, let me know. I have not problem overriding him."

"Count on it, sir." Kincaid got up and put the chair back in its place and headed for his office.

* * *

"No, we do not have any leads at this time. But it's still extremely early in a complicated crime investigation." Kincaid was somewhat surprised by the calm reaction to events.

"And what of reports that one of the Vice President's staff had given him erroneous information for yesterday's afternoon briefing?"

Kincaid began to answer, but grew wary. "I'm not sure what you mean. Do you know something I don't?"

The reporter eyed Kincaid. "Perhaps not."

"Well, that was certainly ambiguous."

"We're professionals." A wave of laughter filled the press room.

Kincaid smiled. "I'm not aware of anyone's giving the Vice President incorrect information. I think perhaps there was a difference in interpretation of events. It happens. I wouldn't read too much into it."

The reporter seemed satisfied. Kincaid pointed to the other side of the room.

"Has the Vice President lost the President's support? Has he lost his confidence?"

Kincaid frowned. "Absolutely not. The President and Vice President have been working together in one capacity or another for nearly two decades. The President relies on him as much as ever, especially in the security area that has been one of the Vice President's main focuses. The Vice President enjoys the President's confidence."

"And you?"

"And me what?" Kincaid raised his eyebrows.

"Do you have confidence in the Vice President?"

Kincaid paused, placing his hands on the sides of the podium and looking over his scribbled notes. "Go ahead and have a seat, John. This might be a long answer."

The reporter sat down.

"Our government has evolved a lot in two hundred fifty or so years. Changes in technologies, changes in social expectations, changes in just about everything have spurred us to adapt and alter the mechanisms by which we serve the people. But — and this is critically important — our government remains a distinctly human enterprise. No technology, no formulaic philosophy can replace the personal judgments required of the leadership of our three branches. And the people are best served when the leaders of our three branches are provided with a full spectrum of information, opinions, and options. The President, as you have so often noted, has chosen a very diverse cadre of advisors, several of whom often hold contrasting views and perspectives. I suspect you may not believe it, but I respect the Vice President's views and will gladly yield the floor to him on many matters. He and I come from different backgrounds. We come from different regions, and we each have our own traditions and expectations. Do he and I have disagreements from time to time on policy and direction? You betcha. Does he enjoy the President's ear when the time comes to make decisions? You better believe it.

"Now, that's the answer to your question as you asked it. I know you're looking for a story. Conflict in the White House. Mud wrestling in the Oval Office. But you're not going to get your enduring story along those lines. There was a shooting at an office park containing some federal offices. There was labor strife coupled to automation of some very important jobs. There was a lot of tentative information put out in the fog of the moment. Your story is probably there."

The reporter seemed satisfied. Kincaid pointed to the center of the room. "Stephanie?"

"Mr. Kincaid, the incident in College Park has apparently uncovered a massive program of automating emergency call centers across the country. A number of experts from academia, government, and the private sectors have expressed alarm over this movement. They've conveyed their concerns over what appears to be an untested technology, particularly given that it's supplied by a very small number of companies. Is the White House monitoring this, and does the President have any comment on the situation?"

Kincaid replied, "We just learned of this last night, Stephanie. At this time, I'm aware of about twenty-five to thirty call centers affected, but this is all new to us. There may be more. So far, all the work seems to be done by a company called Brisbane Technologies. I have only recently learned about them, but it's really too early to speculate on what effect, if any, their products could have on public safety, labor relations, or anything else. I'm not even sure if there is a federal role in what seems like a state and local story, though, admittedly, Brisbane is a pretty big federal contractor."

She continued, "Sir, we're told that many call center employees are considering labor actions similar to those in College Park in an effort to slow or stop the conversions of their centers. The resulting disruptions could affect public safety on a national scale."

"Again, Stephanie, we're just learning about the company and the local call centers, the same as you. Our staff is giving as much attention to the call center revelations as time allows. You identified two separate lines of interest. In regard to the technological questions raised by this automation, our science and technologies advisor, Matthew Luskin, will get back to you in a day or so if that's OK."

Stephanie nodded.

"As for the labor situation, our experts in that area, Kathy Whiting and Sarah Tyler, are pretty much tied up with the state economics issues at the moment. But we will get more information as quickly as we can. Fair?"

She nodded again.

"And as long as I'm parading my ignorance, I'll pre-answer a question some of you must have. We're still working with our state counterparts to develop an economic assistance program to deal with the continuing rise in the unemployment rate. We've begun a complete review of our data, and we're examining in detail our models for measuring the flow of capital in our economy. You know, from time to time forces new to our understanding come into play. Remember the tech bubble and burst, the housing bubble and burst, tulips, silver, gold? All of these economic anomalies worked themselves out over the course of a few years. Within those aberrant periods, it would have been difficult to predict the direction of the economy. But the core processes inherent in our societies restored the systems every time.

"For our part, we are well aware of the justified anxiety of the families and individuals affected, and we're doing everything we can to protect the immediate integrity of local economies and to hasten the end of these challenges." Kincaid watched as most of the reporters entered their notes. "I think that's all I really have for now. I've promised the availability of several of my staff and I'll post their access times on the board. Thank you for your attention. I will be available up front for a few minutes."

Most of the press packed their laptops and papers and made their way into a muggy May afternoon. Six reporters came forward.

Kincaid donned his skeptical look. "OK, Ben, ask all you want, but I'm not answering anything of substance."

Ben Jacobs put his hands to his chest in mock indignation. "You know I wouldn't dream of it, Mr. Kincaid. I was just wondering if you've been reading Vice President Bailey's speeches lately?"

"That is an odd question." Kincaid narrowed his eyes, looking at Jacobs.

Jacobs shook his head. "Just wondered." He picked up his satchel and made his way to the door.

"You're going to leave it at that?"

Jacobs smiled. "Yup."

Kincaid would have followed him, but was barraged by a stream of questions about Tiffany Miller's appearance in a popular motorcycle enthusiasts' magazine.

17 UNRAVELING

Programming Palace, Camden, New Jersey, Friday, May 16, 2014

Mike Johnson waded into the programmers' suite through the flotsam and jetsam of paper cups, chips bags, and unidentifiable formerly edibles. Programming Palace's only rule was that no part of the building was to be permanently closed by the Health Department.

"Josh? Where are you?" Mike shouted to be heard over the den of explosions and animated screams. He put his newspaper under his arm as he lifted his foot over the debris.

"Over here." Josh's voice came from a lounging area three rows over.

Mike stepped carefully into an area ringed by couches arranged around a very large video monitor. Josh slouched on the primary sofa at the centerline of the screen. He held a game controller in his hand, his face blank with concentration. From time to time, he would twitch or turn in response to some extremely violent carnage on the display. A young woman sat on the floor, resting against his legs. She watched the action with bored detachment. Her brief pants accentuated long, athletic legs. Her blouse covered the legal minimum. Long blond hair spilled onto the couch next to Josh.

She turned to Mike and extended her hand below Josh's line of sight. "Hi. I'm Lindsey."

"Ah." Mike wrinkled his brow. "I think we met last week. You've changed your hair, I think. Lengthened it?"

"Oh. No. I guess I'm Lindsey Two. Lindsey One is still at the apartment sleeping things off from last night."

"I see." Mike bit his lip and turned to Josh, still twisting with each swing of the electronic sword. "Can you pause that, Josh?"

"Nope. Just go ahead. I can multitask like you wouldn't believe. I once made it through five levels of Halo Six during a fuckin' earthquake."

"OK. I appreciate the need for relaxation." Mike scanned the debris-strewn cove. Josh's eyes were still glued to the screen. Mike sensed only Lindsey Two's attention. "Still, we're coming up on deadline for the walk-through of phase three."

"When's that due?" Josh nearly knocked Lindsey Two over as he heaved to his left, his character narrowly missing decapitation. Lindsey Two seemed mildly annoyed.

"Wednesday. This coming Wednesday."

"No problem."

Mike raised his hand to rub the back of his neck. "I don't suppose it would be too much to ask you to show me some of it?"

Lindsey Two smiled.

"You're watching it." Josh's eyes narrowed. "Now watch this." He thrust forward pressing two buttons. "Die, sucker!"

His character's blade sank into the green haired chest of a hideous creature with long, curved fangs, and Mike could guess a particularly foul odor. Blood, or a green equivalent, ran down the blade.

"Look at the flow now as it gets to the half-way point." Josh grinned proudly. "It's a full surface matrix with gravity effect. Watch the perturbations of the flow. Completely accurate shadows and here … the stream begins to break into irregular lumps and then fall off as separate drops. I copyrighted that yesterday."

Mike seemed impressed. "Wow. So you actually have phase three functional."

"And most of phase four."

"Why didn't you tell me? I was getting worried."

The screen announced the end of level four. "It wasn't due until Wednesday. This coming Wednesday."

Lindsey Two giggled as Mike dropped his face into his hands.

"You're going to be the death of me."

"C'mon, Johnson. You have to admit this is way more fun than working for those drones at Brisbane."

"Fun, yes. However, waiting for the cash to flow here gives me the creeps. You know the Brisbane stock's up almost forty percent this week?"

Lindsey Two slid up from the floor to snuggle with Josh who turned to Mike. "I'd heard something about that. What goes up must come down unless there's something solid behind it. Works with gravity; works with products."

"The news about their call center hardware and software is spreading like wildfire. At last count, it looks like over two hundred cities, including Atlanta and L.A., have signed on. That's billions of dollars of sales, Josh."

"And trillions of dollars in lawsuits as soon as they find out that it doesn't work."

Josh and Mike stared at each other. Mike was the first to speak. "Doesn't work? What do you mean, it doesn't work?"

"I know the guys who've been coding it for the last ten years. It's tough sledding." Josh reached around Lindsey Two and pulled her close. "On a good day they'll get maybe thirty percent recognition. And that's only with the testers speaking calmly and clearly. If someone's crying, or out of breath, or — heaven help 'em — speaking with a foreign accent, forget about it."

Lindsey Two turned her blue eyes to Mike. "That's true. I tried it with my little girl voice. I told the machine we had a fire, and it thought I needed to change a tire."

"But … they were demonstrating the system on television last night. A woman talked through a whole series of emergencies. Look. Here she is in the paper this morning."

"Hah." Josh sneered, handing the paper to Lindsey Two.

"Oh, my word. It's Bev. No wonder. She's Paul's squeeze. He's the main programmer on the project, and he always tests his versions on her first. She's probably the only human who scores better than fifty-fifty — with the software anyway."

Josh smiled. "And of course she's hot."

"Very hot," Lindsey Two chimed in.

"So they bring her in whenever they need to impress someone or guarantee air time. As you can see, it works," Josh said.

Mike looked glum. "Yeah. That's sad."

"Just be glad you won't be around Brisbane when the shit hits the fan."

Josh's encouragement failed to elicit a smile from Mike.

"C'mon, boss buddy. Play a round here. Our software's ahead of schedule, and our stuff actually works."

"Yeah, right. You'd cream me before I could press a button."

"Probably true. So play Lindsey," Josh offered.

"I don't know."

Lindsey Two rose to her feet and picked up a second controller. She turned to Mike with pursed lips and pleading eyes. "Pleeeaasse."

"OK, sure." Mike extended his hand and accepted the controller from Josh. The game opened with Mike's character facing a stunningly realistic rendering of Lindsey Two from across a dungeon floor. Mike prepared his hand as a small clock on the screen counted down to zero. At zero, the female character bounded across the dungeon floor, spun in front of Mike's character, and kicked his head off.

"Oops. Sorry," Lindsey Two grimaced.

Mike smiled, handing the controller back to Josh. "I can't believe I fell for that."

"You're a good sport, boss man. This is going to sell like gangbusters.

Your cut of the copyright alone will net you more than you got the whole fifteen years you were at Brisbane. Beyond the games, that algorithm has all kinds of applications in fluid mechanics and process control. This is big. Trust me. I've been here before."

Lindsey Two put down her controller. "Hey, Joshie. We should have Mike over sometime. Lindsey One could teach him some moves. You know she goes for that touch of gray thing."

Mike cringed.

Josh laughed. "Yeah, I'll bet. But we have to protect Mike's innocence. He's married, you know."

* * *

David Kincaid wished a happy weekend to each staffer as their meeting broke up and they left one by one. After a while, he and Anna were the only ones remaining, each gathering their final papers from the table.

"Big plans for the weekend?" Kincaid asked.

"Not so big, sir. My sister's coming down from Baltimore Sunday afternoon, and I'll be giving her the full tour."

"Ah. Well, I hope they have the air conditioning back on by then. When it gets hot and stuffy, I know I have a hard time staying awake."

She smiled. "I noticed."

The table was clear at last. Kincaid turned off the lights on one side of the room.

Anna paused. "Sir, there's something I've been meaning to bring to your attention, but I'm not sure of the propriety of it."

He turned to her.

"Cameron Conklin was talking to me for quite a while last night."

"The Vice President's chief speech writer?" he asked.

"Yes, sir. She and I are friends. She's thinking of quitting."

"Whoa. That would be quite a loss. She's good — really good."

"Yes, sir. But she says the things she's being asked to write are getting to her — seriously bothering her."

Kincaid placed his briefcase on the table and pulled out a chair for Anna. He took a seat alongside. "Come to think of it, Ben Jacobs asked me the other day if I'd been reading Mr. Bailey's speeches. I'll admit I haven't, and I didn't have time to get back to Jacobs to see what he meant.

The room was silent. Anna turned toward the door and listened. She lowered her voice. "Cameron brought me copies of a couple of speeches. The Vice President is emphatic about the secrecy of these. He'd fire her and worse if he discovered she'd let them out. The speeches are given before shadow groups at unannounced meetings. She's not sure who the people are, and he never gives any hint about their identity. It's making her ill, sir."

Anna pulled out a handful of papers. "I read them, and they're shocking. I can't imagine that the President is aware of these meetings and what Mr.

Bailey's saying." She handed the papers to Kincaid.

He scanned the pages — very quickly at first, and then with more concentration. "Oh, my, this is absolutely Darwinian."

"I don't think Darwin ever suggested this kind of malevolence. Darwin was more about pragmatism, survival. The Vice President is talking class superiority and rights to rule."

"Is it all right if I look these over this weekend?"

"I brought them for you. Like I said, she's ready to quit."

Kincaid looked up from the papers into Anna's eyes. A grin began to spread across his face.

"Yes?" she asked.

"Tell her she should quit."

"Sir?"

"We need a press secretary. She'd be great for that position — bright, vivacious, well-versed. She'd go from speechwriter for the Vice President to full Press Secretary for the President of the United States. Boost in pay. And — this is a big plus — she's already cleared. I'm sure Mr. Bailey will pitch a hissy fit, but I also know that President Miller admires her skill. This will work. This will be great."

Anna smiled broadly. "Yes, sir. And I know she'd love it. She and I are driving up to Baltimore tonight. I'll let her know about the offer on the way up."

* * *

Sunday, May 18, 2014

James Garrette found himself in his own kitchen under attack from two furious women.

It was currently Laura's turn launching salvos. "And you know these people, and you know what they're doing is questionable at best, immoral for sure, and quite probably illegal. You have got to put a stop to it."

Garrette slammed his fist down on the table. "And you, young lady, are way out of line. I'd like to know how you got involved in this. Have you been rifling through my papers?"

Laura leaned forward, eyes ablaze. "*Our* papers, Father Dearest. They have my name on them, too. Brisbane, Quartermaster, BioRemedia, Plantagenet, who knows who else. They've all got my name on the certificates, too."

Joanna Denton glared at Garrette. "Plantagenet? Plantagenet Pharmaceuticals? James, we have contractual agreements with Plantagenet to develop our findings. That is a clear conflict of interest. And Brisbane is handling our security conversions. You know good and well that you can't have ownership of those two or any other companies doing significant business with the Institute."

"Enough! Both of you!" he shouted. "These are my personal dealings.

They do not concern you."

Laura and Joanna shouted back simultaneously. "Yes, they do!"

Laura continued. "And what about this guy Joanna's talking about?"

"Stay out of the Institute's business, young lady. It is totally inappropriate."

Laura spread her hands on the table and rose halfway out of her seat. "When my father's morality crumbles into a heap of rubble, then it's my business, too."

James Garrette, Laura Garrette, and Joanna Denton continued to battle until nearly midnight. Joanna finally left the Garrette home, slamming first the kitchen door and then her own car door on the way out.

* * *

Monday May 19, 2014

President Miller ordered the Cabinet meeting closed to press, cameras, and microphones.

The President reviewed a page from his briefing report. "Labor, what is the situation regarding nine-one-one call centers this morning?"

"Sir, over the weekend, job actions began in over three hundred eighty call centers ranging from little towns in Iowa all the way up to New York City and L.A."

"Do we get a sense of an organized strategy across the country?" The President looked up from his notes.

"No, sir. The actions range from informational pickets to actual shut-downs of call centers."

"That's a lot of systems, Rick. There is a common thread, isn't there?"

"Yes, Mr. President. In each case, the workers found out that their centers were being automated and that the transition time was only weeks away. We're looking at only another three or four thousand unemployed at this time, but these people are all working jobs vitally tied to public safety, jobs that require lots of judgment calls. If they can be replaced by machines, it portends a real sea-change in American employment, the likes of which I haven't seen in my lifetime."

"How come this wasn't on our radars? This is big money. And it's not just the money," the President asked.

"The main company behind the voice-recognition hardware and software is one of our larger defense and security contractors. They're accustomed to working quietly. They've negotiated highly incentivized contracts with mayors and city managers. The company, Brisbane Technologies, is fiercely anti-union and has been in this business long enough to know how to avoid negotiating with labor."

The President turned to Kincaid. "Brisbane. I'm hearing their name a lot lately. If they're so all-powerful, why haven't I heard about them before?"

Kincaid took his turn. "Sir, Brisbane Technologies was, until recently, a small engineering firm operating out of Ocala, Florida, run by Vincent Brisbane. They produced such things as night-vision goggles, surveillance cameras, and the like. I understand they made exquisite precision spotter scopes for hunting rifles. About five years ago John Brisbane inherited the company from his father and started a very ambitious expansion program. One of the ways he's expanded is by going aggressively after federal contracts. Brisbane has now acquired a number of other firms producing security software and telecommunications hardware. Our best estimate is they've gone from thirty million dollars annually to over sixty-five billion."

Those in the room who had not been paying attention to Kincaid now turned in his direction.

The President's eyes were wide. "In five years?"

"Yes, sir," Kincaid acknowledged.

"Again, why haven't we heard about them all over the media? Wall Street should be giddy over that stock."

"That's just one point, sir. There is no stock. Brisbane is completely privately owned. They don't issue press releases. They won't even answer our queries about their size or scope. Most of what I just reported has been put together from indirect evidence."

The President turned to Bailey. "Mr. Vice President, tell us about this Brisbane Technologies. Their work seems to fall into your bailiwick."

Vice President Bailey took a long sip of coffee before answering. "I can't speak much about their civilian businesses. I don't have much time for hunting scopes. But I do know that they've been a critical component of our defense and security readiness. Brisbane has definitely raised the bar, pressing new technologies into our fight against terrorism. Their research and development in pattern recognition logic is showing huge promise for removing human limitations spotting terrorists and detecting the flow of capital to enemy operatives."

The President was looking down at one of his papers. "How effective is their software at detecting Abu Sayyaf agents?"

The Vice President scowled. "I don't think that's relevant, sir…"

Defense Secretary Banks broke in. "Actually, Mr. President, according to Homeland, it was a Brisbane camera that initiated the College Park disaster."

The President turned again to Bailey. "Mr. Vice President, I'm getting rather nervous about what we don't know here in the West Wing. We've got an economy that seems on the one hand to be going down the toilet and on the other hand performing the best in the history of the country. We have a big company taking over critical infrastructure tasks across the country. On an individual basis, these job actions are local issues, but collectively they're affecting us all." He turned to Secretary Zink. "And State here is telling me that our erstwhile allies are expressing grave concerns about out ability to come through on our promises. We're tied down in Iraq and Saudi Arabia, where we're having a really tough time keeping track of what our own people are doing. Can you see why I'm getting nervous?"

"Yes, Mr. President." Bailey closed his briefing book.

The President looked around the room. "Does anyone else have anything of pressing importance?"

The other Cabinet secretaries began closing their books.

The President motioned to Abigail. "Before you all take off, I'd like to introduce the newest member of my staff."

Cameron Conklin walked into the room, smiling. The Vice President glared at Kincaid.

"Ms. Conklin will be assuming the duties of White House Press Secretary effective immediately. I talked with the Vice President a little while before we began the meeting, and he expressed in no uncertain terms how much he will miss her competent services."

The secretaries shared a chuckle and gave Cameron a round of applause. Everyone rose to leave.

Miller cheered them on, "OK. Everyone back to work. Find me some answers. Mr. Kincaid, please get Ms. Conklin ready for her first session in the lion's den. Mr. Vice President, please close the door when the others have left. I think we need a little quality time, one-on-one."

Vice President Bailey waited until the room was cleared, closed the door, and retook his seat across from the President. "Mr. President, I think you owe me the courtesy of consulting me before my staff is raided. Cameron's a damned good writer. I'm going to be hard put to replace her on such short notice."

"Relax, Jim. I'm well aware of your timeline. But I need someone in that billet more than you do. I can't afford diverting any more of David's time when things are in such a mess. She's just the person we need talking to the press. I know exactly why you're anxious, but, frankly, your campaign is going to need to take a back seat to the nation's business. Besides, if you can't start turning things around, your campaign's going to be a non-starter, anyway."

Bailey shook his head. "Mr. President, this isn't about my campaign. You were talking about communications a few minutes ago. I think I should have been brought in on this."

"Sorry, but it's a done deal. Let's move on. What do you know about Brisbane and this call center thing?" Miller pressed.

"Not much, sir. My encounters are pretty much limited to military and anti-terrorist. They make good equipment and battlefield management systems. And despite that dig about a single misidentification, their track record on automated surveillance and apprehension has been nothing short of spectacular. One of our advisors witnessed a test run at BWI a while ago. Their cameras and software caught a boatload of bad guys. You know Max Carlton?"

The President nodded, frowning.

"If you can impress Max with a computer system, you know it's got to be good. I know that they've got all sorts of civilian applications in addition to the military gear. I don't know the details, but the state and local governments are going to have to move to modern technologies and the savings they bring if they're going to get their spending under control and stop holding out their hands to us."

"We're talking about people, Jim — people who need jobs, people who are putting in a good day's work for a good day's pay. We have a responsibility."

"With all due respect, Mr. President, you're sounding like David Kincaid. We've been over this for years. We keep losing sight of the fact that it's the responsibility of the individual to be fit for today's commerce. One of the reasons the financials seem like they're out of whack is that we've coddled and mothered the workers of this generation to the point that they're more like sheep than like the individuals who built this great country. Look at the real numbers, sir. Look at the indices of prosperity. We're not in the dire straits these doom-and-gloomers would have you believe. At the core, we have a strong and robust economy. The sooner these people take responsibility for their fate, the sooner we'll see boom times return."

The President had been watching the Vice President intently. "Hmmm. Seems we're not plowing any new ground. Do you have the background report on College Park for me?"

"It's almost finished, sir. And I need to add something. I think Labor has missed some common threads in the labor actions against the call centers."

The President raised a cautionary hand. "The labor actions are in support of the call centers as I see it, not against."

"We'll see. Homeland is picking up a lot of chatter in support of these strikes. I think there is a more organized hostile force at work here than Rick understands."

"Get me the damned report, Jim."

"Yes, sir." The Vice President rose and left the room.

The President closed his eyes and sighed.

The Chief of Staff poked his head into the Cabinet room. "Twenty minutes to go, sir, if you want to watch her first session with the press."

The President smiled. "That would be good, but I've got a briefing in the situation room with NSA and CIA. I'll watch her tonight on replay. You'll be with her?"

"Yes, sir," Kincaid assured.

"Good. And, by the way, I find what you told me about Bailey's speeches spot on. The Vice President was using the same language, the same words here with me just a few minutes ago."

"I'll get more on it as soon as I can, sir. But for now, it's show time."

* * *

Tuesday, May 20, 2014

In the pre-dawn quiet, Jack sat on the edge of his bed and turned the pistol over in his hands. A medium-grade match pistol, it was adequate for local competition, but not the quality needed for state or national meets. Ed had two of those. But Jack's would still be instantly lethal at point-blank range.

Jennifer had been right. He should have listened to Jennifer. She had known him so much better than he knew himself. Only a safety and a trigger stood between life and death. If not for Ed, he would not have a pistol in the house. Jenn had hated the idea of a gun in their house. She didn't like the gun; she didn't like Ed. He was a bad influence.

Jack sported at least a six-day beard. He had taken a shower Saturday or Sunday when he could no longer stand himself. He had eaten four or five times, judging by the cans in the sink. Joanna Denton called Monday afternoon. It was clear that the Institute would not be keeping him. She held out no hope. In fact, she had just been dismissed herself. While Jack sank into deeper depression, Joanna was busy plotting her war with the Institute. She tried to enlist Jack, but he was non-committal. As he saw it, everything that he had accomplished and everything he had cared about during his whole life was gone. Even his mind seemed erased. Soon it would not matter.

Jack bore no illusion that anyone would mourn for long. Oh, they'd be irritated that they'd have to take up the duties. The Institute would have to put ads for his replacement in the journals. Leslie and Elsa and Patricia would be overwhelmed by the researchers' demands now that he would not be running interference. Someone would have to deal with the body in Apartment 20. He had paid the rent only last week. The landlady would have no cause to come and check the apartment until … Jack thought that was probably not fair. He had a good relationship with the landlady. She deserved better.

Perhaps he would call just a bit before pulling the trigger. Maybe, better, he would call nine-one-one just before, and he would leave the door unlocked. There wouldn't be time for anyone to break in, and the landlady wouldn't have to face the discovery.

Jack turned the pistol over in his hands. Calling nine-one-one would be difficult. They would try to talk him out of it. He would simply hang up and be finished.

Still, Jack could not be sure he could pull the trigger. Alone, he would eventually. But maybe not if he called. Now there was a safety, a trigger, and a phone call between life and death. If only he did not have such a good landlady, this would be easier.

Jack took a deep breath and looked around the bedroom. No pictures. That was another problem. Jenn's pictures were all at work — at former work — on his desk — his former desk. Amy had called from Jenn's office. They were planning a memorial service. Amy had called about noon yesterday. Jack could tell she had been crying and was on the verge of crying again. They were already missing Jennifer. Anyone who knew her was already missing her. One woman whom she had represented, a woman who had nothing, had donated a hundred dollars to a scholarship fund they were setting up. One of the corporate sponsors had donated a lot. Amy would not tell him how much, but said it was a lot. She needed some photos of Jenn for the service. Jack felt really bad that he had told her he'd get back to her.

Jenn's photos were on his former desk in his former office. Even that beautiful picture taken an hour before sunset with the warm sun painting her face in its true glowing hues. That was the one Amy would have wanted if she knew it existed.

Jack turned the pistol over in his hands. He released the safety. As he removed one barrier between life and death, he suddenly felt Jennifer's anger presence, as strongly as if she were sitting right there. She would not put up with his self-pity. She would be up and working — hard. If she knew that Amy would be learning that Jack had taken his life, Jennifer would be so very angry. She would be so very angry that he had kept that stupid pistol against her wishes. She would be reminding him that Ed was a bad influence.

Jennifer would be telling Jack to get off the edge of the bed, clean up the apartment, take a shower, and shave. Jennifer had told Jack in no uncertain terms she did not care for beards. They made Jack look ridiculous.

Jack stood up and thrust the pistol into his carrying bag. He made the bed. He cleaned up the kitchen. He showered and shaved. Now, Jennifer would approve.

If he got going early enough, he could catch a friendly guard who would let him into the building to get her pictures before anyone came to the office. Jack began making a mental list of what he wanted to retrieve: pictures, diploma, and trophy from San Diego. That was all he could think of. His books were specific enough to the job; he might leave them behind or get some kind of legal order to retrieve them. Joanna had offered to help. He really should not have treated her with such indifference. She was fighting for him and for others, and she needed his help. He was rude to not help her.

Jack's head was clearing rapidly. He would need something to transport his stuff. He eyed the carrying bag. It was big enough. He would have to take out the pistol, though. The thought of the pistol and what had nearly transpired disgusted him. Better than taking it out, he would hand it over to Ed, who would be on duty today. Jack would pick up the pictures, his diploma, and trophy; he would give Ed the pistol, and let Ed know he was changing. Maybe Amy had some tasks for him. Jennifer would be pleased.

Jack's parking pass still worked when he arrived a few minutes after seven. He had nearly an hour to do what he needed to do.

He walked toward the main entrance. Carl was on duty. Jack and Carl didn't think much of each other. Jack expected that Carl would give him a hard time, and might not let him in to pick up his valuables.

Jack walked around the building to the loading dock. He was relieved to see Ed on duty. He would give Ed the pistol. Ed would certainly let him in for the ten minutes Jack needed.

Ed spotted Jack half way across the loading dock bay. Ed shook his head. "Man, are you a sight for sore eyes."

"I've just come to get a few things."

"Good thing you've come today. Tomorrow you wouldn't be able to get in."

"What? Why not?"

"The damned Institute's replacing us with machines. Look." Ed pointed to a tangle of wires around a mounting bracket above the door. "Can you believe that? Fifteen years with this piss-ass hell hole and they think they can replace us with a camera and a computer."

Jack slowly shook his head. "I'm sorry."

"And I guess you're owing me an 'Ed-you-were-right.'"

"Huh?" Jack looked up.

"Who do you think reported you to Garrette? That fuckin' bitch Leslie. You must have left something on your desk. She turned you in for the reward."

"Reward?" Jack asked.

"She's the new 'lab director.' Those three bitches have been struttin' around ever since you were dumped."

"There's no way they can let her run the show. That'll be a disaster."

"Do you care?" Ed asked.

Jack thought a minute. "Part of me does. I put fifteen years into building that lab. I hate seeing it go down the tube."

"Get used to it, Jack boy. This fuckin' institute is circling the drain. I know I don't give a shit. Man, I got almost fifteen years myself, Carl's got almost twenty, and they dump us like yesterday's garbage. You want your stuff? Go right ahead. I'm not going to stop you. Take anything you want. I don't give a shit." Ed held the door open for Jack.

Ed's grumbling curses faded quickly as Jack made his way to the elevator and pressed the button for the eighth floor. He got out and walked quickly to the office and looked down at the complex lock. He was somewhat surprised that he remembered the combination for the despicable security lock.

Jack pushed the door open.

"What are you doing here? Who let you in?"

Jack jumped, and looked up to see Leslie sitting in his chair, his former chair. "I just came to get my stuff. I didn't expect you here. I won't be long."

"You are not allowed here. You need to leave right now."

Jack repeated, "I've just come to get my stuff. I'll get it and leave. I didn't expect you. I don't even want to talk to you. I just want what belongs to me. I'll get it and leave."

Leslie's face was a mix of anger and fear. "Get out now. I'm calling security. You don't belong here."

"Save it. I'll have what I need and be gone before security gets here. I just want …" Jack looked at his desk. The pictures were gone, replaced by Leslie's family. "Where are my pictures?"

"I'm calling security."

Jack looked around quickly. The bookcase was changed. The books were gone. His eyes fell on the trashcan. Jennifer's picture, the one beside the trail, the one of his beloved beautiful Jennifer painted in sunset shades, was sitting at a forty-five degree angle in the trashcan.

He shouted, "What have you done?" He tilted his head to match the tilt of Jennifer's picture. There were other pictures in the trash along with his awards. "This is wrong! This is so wrong!"

Leslie had picked up the phone and punched in a series of numbers. The phone began ringing on the other end.

Jack turned to Leslie. "This is completely unacceptable. Take those out of the trash right now!" he demanded.

Leslie held the phone while it continued to ring unanswered.

"I said, take my pictures out of the trash. Are you listening to me?"

"Jack, you need to leave now." Leslie watched him as the phone rang twelve, thirteen, fourteen times.

"Damn it! Put down the phone. You had no right to trash my things. It's bad enough you've taken my lab, my job, my future — everything I was to anyone. I'm not going to let you take my memories, too. Put down the phone. If you're calling security, it's seven-thirty. The office isn't manned anymore until eight. It was in a memo last week. Look, this isn't hard; take my stuff out of the trash. Now!"

"I told you to get out. I'm calling the police." She punched in nine-one-one.

Jack shook his head. "I don't believe this. Are you so determined to destroy me that you can't even do something this simple so that I'll leave? You're very sick, you know?"

The telephone sounded an angry beep-beep-beep. Leslie held the receiver away from her ear and stared at the device.

"The call center workers are on strike. I heard it on the radio on the way in. Seems a lot of us are getting screwed this morning. The city's giving their jobs to robots, but the robot installation isn't complete. So let's just stop playing around. I'm getting really tired of this shit." He opened his carrying bag. "Pick up my pictures and my awards and put them in this bag. That's all I want."

Leslie placed the receiver in its cradle and folded her arms. "Pick them up yourself. This isn't your lab anymore, and I don't have to do what you say. It's my lab now."

Jack's face flushed red. He shouted, his voice cracking, "Pick 'em up!"

"No. Get out."

Jack's heart pounded. He looked into the open bag and spied his pistol at the bottom. He reached in, removed the pistol, and tossed the empty bag to Leslie's feet. His hands shook as he gripped the handle while trying to control his voice. "Enough. You've stolen everything from me. I've got nothing to lose. I won't take your humiliation. Now pick up the bag, take my pictures out of the trash, and put them into the bag."

Leslie continued her icy stare with the pistol pointed at her forehead.

Jack shouted, "Pick 'em up!"

"No."

A strange calm fell over him. Jack's hands grew steady. He focused on Leslie. His eyes narrowed. He squeezed the trigger. The forty-grain match-grade bullet left the muzzle of the pistol at a bit over fifteen hundred feet per second. Though her eyes would have recorded the flight of the bullet, it impacted her forehead before any nerve impulses could have traveled the optic nerve.

Had the .22 caliber projectile been a surgical instrument moving slowly in the hands of a gifted surgeon, it could have passed easily between the hemispheres of her brain. Instead, the hundred-forty foot-pounds of energy transferred to bone and tissue, and they traveled together in a shock wave through her skull, dismembering axons and synapses until the bullet exited behind her, taking with it all traces of humanity. She would not have perceived the sight of the bullet.

A round spatter of blood flashed onto the wall behind her as Leslie's head flopped backward.

"Oh, shit!" Jack looked down at the pistol in his hand. Hurried steps sounded in the hall. Jack turned around to see first Patricia and then Elsa appear at the door.

Patricia looked at Leslie. "Oh, my God!"

As she began turning to flee, Jack raised his pistol. How many times had Ed related aiming for the central body mass to stop an attacker? How many times at the range had Jack fired at his paper target, grouping all his shots in the center circle of the bull's eye over the heart of the target?

Jack squeezed the trigger. This bullet tore a path of destruction through Patricia's chest cavity, bisecting her heart. She fell to the floor, grasping her chest.

Elsa ran from the office door into the laboratory, closing the door, setting the lock.

Jack approached the lab door in a bright haze of confusion, blood pounding in his head. He held the pistol in his left hand as he entered the lock code with his right. The first attempt was unsuccessful. He reset the lock and tried again. The door opened.

Elsa held her phone as it chattered its angry beep-beep-beep. As Jack approached, she dropped the phone and ran along the central instrument table toward the ventilated solvent hood at the back of the lab.

He turned the corner and watched as she approached a series of solvent cases stacked high.

"Three days. Unreal." The technicians had long argued for buying solvent in bulk to save money and cut down on the frequency of orders. He had always objected on safety grounds. He raised the pistol, squeezed, and fired, hitting Elsa in the center of her back. She dropped immobile to the ground. The bullet struck her spine just below the fifth thoracic vertebra, sparing the nerves controlling her heart.

Anyone else coming in at this early hour would soon begin arriving, and life as he knew it would be over. He walked back to the office, stepping over Patricia's body so as to avoid the spreading red pool. He stopped at Leslie's feet, but did not look at her. He picked up his bag, put the pistol back in, and turned to the trashcan. He carefully recovered seven pictures of Jennifer, two certificates of appreciation, three first place debating trophies, his Duke diploma, and the ABRF lab certification. He turned and left the room, dousing the lights on his way. He would have closed the door, but Patricia's body blocked it.

By the time he arrived at the basement, he was shaking and feeling as though he might vomit.

He walked toward the loading dock exit.

"How'd it go?"

Jack turned to Ed. "Not so good."

Ed frowned. "Aw, man, you look like shit. Were they there?"

Jack nodded. He lowered his head.

"Yeah, they come in early so they can leave before four. Bet they were harassin' your ass."

"Uh huh," Jack agreed, his face ashen.

"Still, you don't look so good. You OK to drive?"

"Drive?" Jack was having difficulty envisioning his car, much less the route home.

"Hey, man, I'm drivin' you. You're in no condition to be behind the wheel," Ed insisted.

"You'll get in trouble."

"I don't give a shit. They want ol' TV eyes to watch this place? Let 'em. I'm taking early retirement."

"You don't understand. I'm hot. I'm marked. You don't want to be seen with me."

"Jack, boy, I didn't see you and you didn't see me. You came to get your stuff, you got it, and you're gone. It's that simple. If those bitches want to make a stink, they'll have to prove you were here. Ol' TV eyes isn't plugged in yet."

"It's not that simple."

"C'mon." Ed led Jack to an old car parked on the street. Ed wasn't willing to pay the monthly parking fee and arrived early enough each day that he invariably found a spot close by. "Let's go to my place for now. It's just half a mile from here. Let's get you some rest, and then I'll take you back to your car."

Jack followed in silence until they reached Ed's car. "Thanks."

"Don't mention it."

They drove to Ed's apartment, a four-room flat furnished with only essential furniture. Jack placed his bag on the floor by the couch and sprawled out, quickly falling asleep.

* * *

Elsa was conscious, completely aware of the cold tiles beneath her face. She could feel the intense hot pain of the bullet above the shattered vertebra, but nothing below. She waited until she heard Jack's footsteps receding in the hallway before attempting to move. Her efforts to reach forward with her arms were met by blinding pain. She would have to wait until coworkers from the other labs arrived.

In the quiet of the corner, she pondered the changes ahead. At the very least, she would be wheelchair-bound for a long time. Her husband, Jim, was not going to like that. They had fought frequently of late over his unwillingness to assume his share of responsibilities around the house. Then there was the matter of that woman at the bar. Elsa's immobility was going to be a problem.

Her thoughts were interrupted by a "pifff, pifff" sound somewhere above her. The sound went away momentarily and then returned louder. She felt a few droplets falling on her face and could smell the harsh organic fragrance of acetonitrile. Before running to investigate the sound of the gunshot, she had turned on the heating stir plate with two liters of solvent. The liquid had reached boiling temperature and continued to stir as the beaker became superheated.

She forced her arm to the side and tried to push away from the base of the hood. The dead weight of her lower torso made the effort extremely difficult, and the position of the bullet made every move excruciating. Still, she could hear the sound of the boiling growing lower. The fumes from the spilled solvent rolled down like a sheet to where she lay. So this is what Jack had been so afraid of. Damn him.

Elsa prayed for the lab sprinklers to turn on, but the ventilation carried the hottest portion of the fumes out of the room. She could feel the spattering liquid coming down like pungent rain. Her eyes stung, and she found breathing unpleasant. Acetonitrile was frothing over the edge of the beaker and running under the vessel with a popping sound. She grimaced and closed her eyes momentarily from time to time as she began to claw her way across the floor. "Damn Jack."

* * *

Thick vapors infiltrated the housing of the stir plate until a spark from the motor ignited that corner of the lab, with flames traveling along the streaming liquid into the neatly stacked paper boxes packed with more bottles of high-grade acetonitrile and propanol. By the time the triggers in the sprinkling system fused from the heat, the flames had moved into the solvent cabinet, whose doors were being held open by two towers of solvent boxes stacked nearly to the ceiling. They had saved seven dollars a bottle buying in bulk, over a thousand dollars overall.

A one-liter bottle of ethyl ether was the first to detonate, shattering adjoining bottles of flammable and caustic liquids, sending glass and fluids flying throughout the room. Gallons of hydrocarbons were aflame beneath the lab tables, protected from the sprinklers while the fume hood drew fresh air in from the hall to feed the flames. In the hellish inferno of the lab, the steel legs of the tables holding their instruments began to buckle as they softened.

The drywall separating the lab from the office blew apart with the explosion of bottles of nitro methane.

* * *

"Jack, Jack, get up man. You gotta' see this." Ed shook Jack awake and directed his groggy attention to the television.

Ed went over to the set and turned up the volume.

"What the hell?" Jack watched the coverage of the fire at the lab. Apparently it had raged for half an hour before fire units were called to the scene. "What time is it?"

"'bout noon." Ed stared at the television. "You didn't set the place on fire before you left, did you?"

Jack shook his head. He listened to the reporter as the video rolled.

"There were few people in the building at the time of the early morning blaze. Researchers have now accounted for every worker believed to have occupied the laboratories except for three research assistants and a laboratory supervisor who actually worked in these spaces and are believed to have perished in the explosion and fire. It may be days or weeks before fire investigators will be able to sift through the glowing embers to assess the source of the blast, but Fire Chief Tom Morgan has already speculated that, given the size and ferocity of the blaze, the laboratory was in massive violation of city codes regarding the storage of flammable substances. In addition, given the steel-melting temperatures sustained over more than an hour, it is likely that there will be no recognizable human remains to be found."

The commentator paused while the footage showed the exterior wall of the eighth floor explode outward ahead of a fireball that extended above the building.

Ed watched mesmerized. "They think you're dead. They probably found your car in the garage." He turned to Jack. "You think the bitches got out, too?"

Jack shook his head.

"Well, they probably brought it on themselves. I remember Cliff grousin' about having to haul all that shit up to the lab. It took half an S & P truck to bring that load to the dock."

Jack leaned back on the couch and closed his eyes while he listened to the rest of the report. The damage was extensive. The reporter even questioned whether the building could be salvaged.

Ed brought out a bottle of Jack Daniel's. He took a large draft and offered the bottle to Jack. Jack initially declined the offer, but needed something to take the edge off a growing headache. After a while, he took the bottle and downed his share.

Ed chuckled. "You hold your liquor pretty good for a ghost."

The fire occupied almost half of the news at noon. Jack began to feel the numbing effect of the whiskey when coverage switched to local economic news. The finance reporter was interviewing Dr. James Garrette. Jack strained to hear the questions. "Listen."

The story had been gathered the previous evening at a gala. The reporter pressed Garrette for details of a new drug called MetaStop being released by Plantagenet Pharmaceuticals. Garrette explained enthusiastically that MetaStop had proven in clinical trials to be over eighty-three percent effective in halting the growth of a wide variety of cancers even in advanced metastasis. He enumerated a long list of cancers it had beaten. Jennifer's was number seven on the list.

Garrette announced that the drug was in full production and would be available in quantity immediately. He estimated that sales of the cancer-fighting therapeutic would net company shareholders in excess of seventy billion dollars in the first year alone. The television report concluded noting that Plantagenet shares on the NASDAQ were up over sixty-five percent in the hour since the announcement.

Jack's cheeks grew red. "He let her die. They told me there were only milligrams of MetaStop; that every bit was needed for clinical trials. They have it in commercial quantities ready to ship. They told me I couldn't get near it. It had to have gone into production six, eight months ago. They let her fade away while they got their marketing campaign in gear." Jack reached for the wastebasket beside Ed's couch and threw up into it.

Ed turned back and forth between Jack and the television. "Aw, that just sucks."

Jack heaved several more times, and then sat leaning over the wastebasket with his eyes closed. "He has no idea the suffering that delay caused. And she wasn't the only one. There must be thousands and thousands. He has no idea."

"Actually, I doubt he cares. He's makin' another bundle off that stuff, and he's just marketing it. He doesn't give a shit if it's important to anyone as long as he's makin' the bucks." Ed sat in his chair and leaned back. "Yeah, the fat cat gets a little fatter and the little mice just keep on dyin'."

Jack breathed slowly, eyes still shut tight. "Someone needs to face up to him, to confront him. Someone needs to make him understand the suffering he's causing."

"Doubt that's going to happen anytime soon, Jack boy. When you've got that kinda' loot to spread around, you're not going to have many people in your face."

"Then I'll do it myself. Someone has to."

Ed laughed. "Yeah, right. You're a dead man pukin' your guts out in a dismissed employee's humble hovel — you're going to clean that up, I presume — a dead man who was lately fired after being turned in by three presumed-dead bitches. I'm no marketing genius, Jack boy, but I think you're definitely operating from a position of weakness."

"I'm going down to face him. Take me to my car."

"No way, good buddy. You can bet your wheels are impounded and being investigated."

Jack set the wastebasket aside, but continued to hang his head.

Ed watched him for a while. "Just what did you have in mind?"

"Not sure." He pointed to his carrying bag. "I'd show him her pictures, tell him how she died. I want him to apologize. Is that so much to ask? Isn't anyone willing to just say they're sorry?"

"Hmmm. Not a very elaborate plan. I guess I could take you down if you've got gas money. I'm about broke, but seein' as I haven't got much else to do, I might as well help you. Let's go." Ed took a final long swig of the bottle.

Jack stared at the bottle. Ed had finished most of it. "How 'bout if I drive?"

Ed grinned. "I've driven farther with more booze in my belly, but I'd hate to get pulled over with everyone all upset these days." He handed Jack his keys.

Ed's fuel gauge registered a hair above empty. Jack stopped on Patrick Street and filled the tank. He called to Ed, "Guess they'll start watching my card purchases soon, huh?"

Ed agreed.

Jack drove south on interstate ninety-five just at the speed limit.

"C'mon, Jack, let's get the lead out," Ed urged.

"And get caught? I can only imagine what they do with ghost riders."

Ed peered out the window. "Yeah, maybe. Good point. Poke along."

Ed dozed for about twenty minutes until he was awakened by the pull of the exit turning toward Mount Airy. He looked around. "I thought we were goin' down to headquarters."

"No. Too much security. I'll meet him at his home so we can have more quality time."

"How do you know where Garrette lives?"

"I was at his house for a reception last year after we won the Biopolymer Labs award."

"Well isn't that ironic? Now I don't suppose you think the cops are going to just let you park along his street, lying in ambush?"

"They're too busy. You slept through the news. Frederick's not the only place where the nine-one-one people are on strike. Apparently this is a nationwide strike now. That company made deals from Maine to Hawaii."

"What deals? What company?" Ed asked.

"Same one with the cameras that replaced your loyal butt … or were going to replace it. Once word got out big time, everyone's coming together and fighting it. So the nine-one-one system is essentially shot, and the police are having to go back to patrols to find trouble rather than the trouble coming to them."

"'Bout time, I say. I'm surprised the mayors and county execs haven't turned the cops on the nine-one-one guys."

"Actually, that was part of the story on the radio, came on about the time we were driving past Olney. Some of the executives tried to crack down, but they've gotten fierce resistance. It's a close community between law enforcement and the call centers. A lot of them share military bonds, either through service or family. It's like a revolt. You remember that thing over in P. G. County? College Park?"

Ed thought for a moment. "Sort of. The Exec fired the Sheriff."

"Yeah. The Sheriff didn't accept being fired. He and his deputies arrested the County Executive and some of his staff. The charges are real, but the chain of command is all out of whack."

Ed watched the passing scenery until they reached an obviously upscale neighborhood with tree-lined streets. The Garrette home sat on one and a third acres of trim lawn and controlled shrubbery. The house itself was a three story stone structure dating to the colonial era, but very twenty-first century cameras watched from posts along the perimeter.

Jack looked at the iron gate by the driveway. "Seems that ought to be closed during the day. And I see three cars at the end of the drive, including his 'Beemer.' I do believe Dr. Garrette is home." He drove in through the open gate and parked behind the BMW.

As they got out of the car, Ed looked at the back yard with its tennis court and swimming pool. "Remind me what we're doing here."

"We are getting an apology and engaging Dr. Garrette on his responsibilities to humankind," Jack replied.

"Oh. Why?"

Jack turned to his old friend. "Because it's the right thing to do, Ed. I don't know how much longer I've got, but I don't think I've got much to lose and not much time in which to lose it." He continued his course to the side door of the house.

Ed frowned. "I think you're experiencing some kinda trauma or something."

"If you have any qualms, feel free to go. Honestly, this only involves you peripherally. I won't be upset."

"No. No. It's just I'm not used to confronting the rich and powerful." Ed shrugged. "I don't guess I have all that much to lose, either." Ed looked around again. "What time is it, anyway?"

"About four-thirty."

* * *

"Nothing has changed since last night. And stop calling it 'my future.' You're not getting any guilt points for your blood money. Your so-called 'future' is built on inside trading — massive inside trading. I haven't had all that much law, but I can smell the stink already. And it's got my name all over it … and I didn't even know a thing about this until a few days ago. Plantagenet, Brisbane, who knows what else?"

Father and daughter had been engaged in their shouting match for nearly two solid hours. Both were showing signs of exhaustion. James Garrette sat at the end of the dining room table, silent.

Laura continued to pace along the far side of the room. "What are you going to do? This cannot stand. You have got to make changes. You have got to come clean. You're facing jail time, Father dearest. Jail time. Call Dick. He's been our family lawyer as long as I can remember. He'll find you

— us — a way out of this."

Garrette closed his eyes. His voice was drained of emotion. "I keep telling you. It's not that simple. There are forces behind these deals. Those forces are ruthless. They will kill you and me to protect their stake."

"What?" she asked, shaken by the last statement.

"They're cold. They're relentless. They will kill for what they want."

"Who?"

"The group behind Windham. The Trust is just their public face. Behind that façade is an iron network that enforces the cooperation of the Trust's beneficiaries."

Laura folded her arms, watching her father. "I think you're being a bit melodramatic, and I'm not buying it."

He opened his eyes wide and fixed them on her. "You'd better take it seriously. Do you remember Clyde Summerfield?"

"Of course. He owned some optics firm. He died in a ski accident about a month after he was here at the house. A ski accident, Father."

"He had come to talk to me about going public. He was tired of the whole mess. I tried to talk him out of it. Carlton sent each of us a copy of the autopsy showing he died of a broken neck at the bottom of one of the trails."

Laura waited, her arms still crossed.

"We — all of the Windham members — got the report the day before the authorities found his body. The report was dated two days later at a hospital owned by Windham. It's not that simple."

Laura sat down heavily in the chair at the far end of the table.

"You've already come closer to disaster than you could possibly know. Twice. First at the call center at College Park and then over in Laurel. Those men were enforcers. Bob Henderson is the leader of that group."

She had her head in her hands, covering her eyes. "Henderson? I remember him, though he didn't even recognize me at Laurel. They acted tough, but weren't very effective."

"No. You were just incredibly lucky. Henderson has serious short-term memory loss. Some kind of brain injury he suffered in Iraq in '08. But he was loyal to Windham before that and is specifically in service to Dr. Carlton. Whatever Max orders, Henderson executes. At College Park, Dr. Carlton intervened on your behalf. At Laurel, you got away before he got your name and he had to retreat before the cameras."

"This is a nightmare. How can …," she began.

The doorbell interrupted their conversation. Father and daughter exchanged grim expressions.

Garrette looked toward the kitchen. Whoever it was had come to the side door of the house. He turned back to Laura. "Have you done anything else I don't know about?"

She shook her head.

"Make yourself scarce. Let me see who it is."

"You look worried. Should I call the police?"

"No. We don't know who it is. Besides, I don't think that'll do much good today from the sounds of things."

Laura got up from the table and made her way upstairs, as fast as silence would permit.

Garrette went to the kitchen door and peered out cautiously. He opened the door and shouted incredulously, "Jack!"

"Dr. Garrette, we need to talk. You've …"

"We thought you were dead … in the fire!" Garrette exclaimed.

"No. I'm here to talk about Plantagenet. You and your people let my wife die." Jack's jaw clenched. "She died while you sat on a cure. You held off to maximize your marketing campaign while she suffered and died."

Garrette stood in the doorway two steps above Jack. "Look, we can talk about this in an appropriate setting. I'm not sure what you're talking about in particular. I'm sure there's a reasonable explanation. Let's meet somewhere and discuss this rationally."

Jack shook his head. "No, I'm tired of being rational. I haven't had enough sleep in the past week to be rational. Fuck rational! I want you to understand what you've done and that what you've done has human consequences. I want an apology."

"Excuse me?"

Jack threw up his hands. "Now what part of that was unclear? Understand. Apologize."

Garrette grew angry. "You do not come to someone's home and make demands like this. We will discuss this at an appropriate time."

As Garrette began to close the door, Ed rushed by Jack and put his foot against the doorsill. "I think you oughta' listen to what Jack has to say, Dr. Garrette."

Garrette tried unsuccessfully to move the door farther. He stared at Ed. "Who are you?"

"Friend of Jack's. Doesn't matter. I used to work for you 'til you tried to replace me with a damned robot." Ed was considerably stronger than Garrette, and the door slid open. "So let's just hear Jack out, and we'll be on our way."

Garrette had retreated into the kitchen. "This is home invasion. You're breaking the law."

Jack, shaking his head, followed Ed. "Why is it so hard for people to just say they're sorry? It's so easy to fix. I don't want anything that's not right and proper. Why is this so difficult?"

Garrette replied sternly, "You're going about this wrong, Jack. There is process. You don't barge into someone's home to get what you want."

Jack and Ed moved slowly, steadily toward Garrette as he backed into the dining room. "With all due respect, Dr. Garrette, the process isn't working. I tried to get MetaStop to save my Jennifer. I was told that there were only milligrams of MetaStop, that it was all being used for clinical trials. You and your people lied to us. People died. People died horrible, gasping deaths."

"I'm calling the police."

Ed chuckled and turned to Jack. "Guess he hasn't been listening to the news, either."

"Or he's bluffing." Jack pointed toward one of the dining room chairs. "Let's sit down and talk, Dr. Garrette. Now."

Jack's and Ed's backs were toward the living room. Laura crept silently down the stairs.

Garrette saw her and began talking to Jack. "OK, talk. I'm not agreeing to anything, though I will hear you out. And I'm warning you that there are going to be consequences for the way you've gone about this."

Laura had just reached the bottom of the stairs when she stepped on a plank of flooring that let out a loud creaking noise. She glanced toward the dining room as Jack and Ed spun in unison toward the sound.

Laura began a sprint toward the back of the house. Ed leapt from the dining room and bounded after her. She was fumbling desperately with the back door lock when he closed the distance and grabbed her with a bear hug. She struggled, flailing with her feet, kicking his shins.

"Ow! Chill, bitch. You're not going anywhere." He swung her around and marched awkwardly back to the dining room as she struggled in his grip.

Garrette's face was in his hands as they returned to the room.

Jack leaned on the table, his knuckles against the polished wood. He spoke to Laura without taking his eyes from Garrette. "We're not here to hurt Dr. Garrette or to take anything. It's just that events have gone too far, and there're things he needs to understand and fix. I'd be happy if he'd just apologize, damn it."

"Daddy?" Laura called.

"They're not from Windham. They're here for something else, although they've gone about it all wrong." He turned to Ed. "Let her go, please."

Ed shook his head. "I don't think so. She'll go get people, get guns, whatever. We didn't ask for much, sir. And now the stakes have gotten a lot higher. If I let her go, we've got nothing for the risk we've taken."

Garrette looked at Laura. "If he releases you, will you sit down?"

She looked back angrily. "Who are these people?" She had stopped struggling, but Ed maintained his sure grip.

Garrette opened his hand in Jack's direction. "This is Jack. Jack, my daughter, Laura."

Laura frowned, perplexed. "Jack Pullman?" She turned back to her father. "Jack Pullman who you fired?"

Garrette nodded.

She looked at Jack. "I thought they said you burned up in the fire in Frederick this morning."

Jack hung his head. "Obviously, I didn't. Look, I'm getting a headache. Why do we keep talking about the fire? I came here to make you understand the consequences of your actions with MetaStop. I came here for an apology. I know I haven't gone about this right, but you people have left me no choice. What does it take to get a little respect?"

"I want to hear this, too." Laura twisted her head toward Ed. "I won't run. Let me go."

Jack turned to Laura for the first time. "He can easily outrun you."

"I'm not running," she repeated.

Jack looked at Ed. "Let her go. Perhaps she'll sit and listen."

Ed was frowning as he relaxed his hold. Laura slipped loose, flexing her shoulders and rubbing her arms. She sat in the same chair she had left only a few minutes earlier.

Garrette nodded. "OK, Jack, you have my attention. Proceed."

Jack reached into his bag and pulled out the picture of Jennifer.

"Were you in the lab this morning, Jack?" Garrette asked.

"Yes, sir. I went back to get my things. Jennifer's office is holding a memorial service, and I went back to get my pictures and my wall stuff."

"Did you set the fire, Jack?"

Jack made weary reply, "Dr. Garrette, you are not focusing. We are here to talk about your role in MetaStop and the tragic consequences of delaying its release. For the record, sir, I had nothing to do with that fire. While I was at the lab this morning, I did see that in the very short time since you fired me, they had gone and done all the things I had forbidden when I was in charge of the lab. They had hundreds and hundreds of gallons of flammables and explosive solvents stacked to the ceiling, sir."

"How did you get into the labs?" Garrette continued.

"Pay attention, sir. Maybe we can discuss the lab at — how did you phrase it — an appropriate time and place? For now, I want you to look at Jennifer's picture. I want you to know that a wonderful human being died from your deliberate inaction."

Laura was gazing at Jennifer's picture with the sunset colors and chestnut hair.

Garrette would not look.

18 ENEMY WITHIN

Tuesday, May 20, 2014

Despite Garrette's apparent indifference, Jack began to tell Jennifer's story. He told about how they met, about her work with non-profits, about the terrible day Dr. Nielsen gave her the news of her cancer.

Tears streamed down Laura's and Ed's faces as Jack described her gradual losing battle, his desperate attempts to get treatments and insurance payments. James Garrette seemed to withdraw into a cocoon of silence.

Jack fidgeted as he finished his narrative. "I have a splitting headache. It's been a very long, very bad day. Do you have anything for a headache?" He turned to Dr. Garrette, who shook his head. Jack turned to Laura.

"As awful as your experience was, this is crazy. Why would I help you?" she demanded.

"Because it's the right thing to do."

Laura's face twisted in disbelief. "Excuse me. You invade our home and hold us hostage and you think it's 'the right thing to do' to help you?"

Jack put his hands to his face. "I'm sorry for my crude approach. It was never my intention to create this disaster. In the last few days, everything that's ever meant anything to me has been taken away. I just wanted some measure of justice. And it's proven far more difficult than I ever imagined. I just want someone to listen to me."

Laura stared, frowning, at Jack. Finally she spoke. "Upstairs, just to the right. In the guest room bathroom medicine cabinet, you'll find several headache things."

Garrette turn to Laura with a sullen look.

"Thank you." Jack climbed the stairs, wincing in pain with each step. He walked through the guest room, found the bathroom and medicine cabinet, and shook two large tablets into his hand. He looked around for a glass, but found none. Placing the tablets on his tongue, he rinsed his hands and then cupped them. He gathered water and drank it with the tablets.

Jack held his hands to his head, squeezing his eyes tightly. He sat down on the edge of the bed in the guest room outside the bathroom and exercised his shoulders back and forth. He leaned back gently until his head rested on the bed. "Just a few seconds. That's all it should take." Jack fell asleep immediately.

* * *

A fine rain fell on Washington, cooling the Rose Garden and muffling city sounds as purple dusk gathered on the South Lawn of the White House.

In the Oval Office, President Miller refereed a shouting match between the Vice President with his advisors and David Kincaid with his staff.

Vice President Bailey jabbed with his forefinger toward Kincaid. "We had them in our grasp two weeks ago, but we had to let them go. Now we're paying the price for our weakness. Now these monsters are tearing the country apart."

"That's crap and you know it! One more time, sir, do you have one teeny tiny shred of evidence that there is any conspiracy, foreign or domestic, involved in this?" Kincaid's face glowed red, extremely rare for him.

"Evidence? Evidence? From one coast to another, thousands of our first responders have gone on strike simultaneously. They've abandoned their posts, switched off their systems, and disrupted emergency services. In a matter of hours, these lowly, minimum wage workers have dissolved the basic national security network. You want evidence? Open your damned eyes." The Vice President turned from Kincaid to the President.

The President looked at Kincaid. "David, does it really seem plausible that such an organized shutdown could occur in the absence of a central organizing force?"

"Yes, sir, absolutely. We've seen spontaneous reactions like this throughout our history in response to all kinds of natural and man-made disasters."

The Vice President hung his head and put his hands on his hips. "Disasters? These strikes are the disaster."

Kincaid folded his arms. "Tens of thousands of highly skilled workers learned — not from their employers, but from news reports — that they would be losing their jobs in a matter of hours or days, that they would be losing their livelihoods just as state unemployment funds are being exhausted, that they were being replaced by machines with no history of reliability. These competent people know how to connect and marshal resources. That's what they're trained to do, Mr. Vice President. Faced with near-certain mass financial ruin and confronting callous official and corporate powers, they took the only logical step of fighting back." He turned to Miller. "Mr. President, the disaster is man-made. We should have known about this. We should have been deeply involved in a transition of this magnitude with so many lives at stake."

The office was finally quiet as the President looked back and forth between the two combatants. "Jim, I have to agree with David. Unless you can come up with something real, I see no reason to call these strikes conspiracies. The more we're finding out about this Brisbane Technologies and the company's relationship to the mayors and governors involved, the worse it gets. We've got economics driving unprecedented prosperity while at the same time financial crisis seems right under the surface, and it's scaring the hell out of our citizens. Those people on the lines know something is wrong, and they're dealing with it the only way they have left. The only question I have is how are we going to fix this mess. One thing I do agree with you is that the strikes are going to affect national security. Mr. Vice President?"

"Sir, the strikes have to be brought to an end immediately. Where we're not getting cooperation from local law enforcement, we may need to federalize some operations."

The President seemed shocked. "What? There's no way I'm authorizing anything that even looks like a federal takeover of civil services! First, I don't have the military manpower to even begin such an action. We've immobilized most of our fighting forces in Iraq and Saudi Arabia. Second, and far more importantly, I don't think we'd be in the right to force people back into jobs you're telling me are about to disappear. And just out of curiosity, why is it that you think we wouldn't get cooperation from local law enforcement? It seems they are most at risk from these job actions."

Kathy watched from her spot behind Kincaid as the Vice President's jaw clenched.

Peter spoke after a nod at him from Kincaid. "Mr. President, several factors join to make a strong bond between law enforcement and the emergency communications workers. I might add that these factors apply at all levels from city to federal. Many of the communications people are relatives of law enforcement or military. It's a natural family fit. They speak the same language and have similar perspectives. The call center workers are in more or less constant communication with law enforcement. They are the first responders' first notifiers. With all due respect to the Vice President, even if we had sufficient troop strength, I have considerable doubts that the military would move against those they see as 'their' people."

The Vice President struggled with his angry words. "Are you suggesting that our armed forces would put the interests of damned labor above our national security? That would be nothing short of a coup."

Peter remained calm. "Again, with due respect, sir, I don't believe there has been a precedent for pitting two elements of society against each other like that since the early days of the labor movement and then later in the civil rights era. And those interventions by the government are universally judged as having been wrong and destructive. History nearly always sides with strikers, not strike-breakers. Labor and national security are one and the same."

"You people in your ivory towers make me sick."

The President focused his gaze on the plasterwork of the ceiling as he pondered. "Jim, with all these call centers being replaced by machines, why are we not seeing the machines taking up the slack now?"

"Sir?" Bailey replied.

"The machines. The Brisbane machines. According to what I'm hearing on the news, these things are supposed to do the work of dozens of humans. But I'm also hearing on the news that the strike is having a huge and devastating impact on the communities affected. Why haven't the machines stepped in?"

"The installations aren't complete, Mr. President."

The President waved his finger. "No, that's not what the installers are saying on the news."

Kincaid turned his head quickly as Matthew raised his hand.

The President smiled. "Oh, good. Now we'll get some answers, even though I'm not sure I'll understand them."

Matt smiled in return. "Sir, I've been researching the telephone answering systems since this controversy began. I've spoken to the top researchers in A.I. — artificial intelligence — at the best university labs in the country, and not once did I encounter anyone who thought that computers were up to mimicking the human operators. They —"

The Vice President interrupted. "They don't have access to the research that Brisbane's been doing. Most of the best research for national security is conducted quietly outside the academic realm."

"Point well taken, sir." Matt nodded in Bailey's direction. "But many of my contacts have clearances higher than mine and work in commercial laboratories. They attend plenty of security conferences on these very topics. It's statistically inconceivable that even a company the size of Brisbane could foster the kind of advances and innovations needed to achieve a machine interface that could supplant even a lightly trained individual."

Bailey sneered, "It might be conceivable if you knew the innovative power of private enterprise rather than the 'we can't do it' philosophy of the college campus."

The President turned swiftly to the Vice President. "That's quite enough, sir! Matthew has never led me astray, and I'm definitely inclined to listen to him now. But we're not making anymore progress here at this point." He placed his hands on the desk, raising them up on fingertips. "Here's what we're going to do. Mr. Vice President, you will gather all the intelligence you have on any groups who might be involved. I want everything, but I want it documented. If what you have is speculation, you'd better damned well say so. And I want to see what you have on Brisbane Technologies. These people seem to be at the center of most of this, and I hadn't even heard of them until last week." He turned to Kincaid. "David, likewise, I want to know about Brisbane. What's their relationship with these local officials? I want you to find out whom to talk to in the hierarchy of these emergency centers — if there is a hierarchy. Do they have a spokesman? What are we able to do to facilitate a return to service? Get Cameron up to speed on everything you and the Vice President have. We'll meet back here at eight tomorrow morning, and you'll brief the press at ten. Understood?"

After a chorus of "Yes, sir," the Oval Office cleared, leaving the President alone.

"I really need a drink."

* * *

The Vice President and his entourage traveled downstairs and waited for the armored bus that would take them to his residence at the Naval Observatory. Aides held umbrellas above them as they climbed aboard the darkened vehicles and sped away into the night.

The drizzle of early evening had given way to a steady, warm rain. David Kincaid waited beneath the portico at the north entrance of the West Wing. Once all four staff members had assembled, they made a dash across the drive to the Executive Office Building, Kathy and Matt easily outrunning Peter and David. They were laughing as they stamped water off their shoes on the coconut fiber mats at the entrance.

Kincaid felt oddly at peace. "Well done, people. Your diligent research and thoroughness have served us well. Matt, not often will you have the President of the United States of America taking your side against the Vice President. Let's not get cocky, though. What Mr. Bailey said about this strike's organizing so fast is cause for concern. We have no idea what its trajectory is. So much is going to depend on just how far along Brisbane really is in its push to automate these centers. Matt, you've worked with Major Reed, right?"

Matthew nodded.

"Good. You and he need to get inside Brisbane and find out just how advanced their stuff is. The President and I obviously have confidence in your assessment, but we desperately need to have some hard evaluation."

He turned to Kathy. "We need numbers on the impact of job loss for different scenarios of readiness of these machines. Since there seems to be pretty tight linkage with military families, there will be federal financial involvement as a natural consequence. And that's on top of the impact of the state budget setbacks. Have you and Sarah gotten the unemployment briefing ready?"

She shrugged. "She and I were going to be rehearsing tomorrow morning to present to you and the President at ten. But …"

Kincaid sighed a tired sigh. "… that's when we'll be doing the public briefing on the strike. Right. Depending on how the briefing goes, can we meet — just the four of us — around one-thirty?" He extended his hand to include Peter.

She appeared glum. "We'll have to. I was hoping to catch a couple of lectures at the National Economic Summit over at the Smithsonian tomorrow, but this is decidedly more important."

Kincaid rubbed the back of his neck. "I'll get you a driver to take you over as soon as we're through."

Kathy smiled. "It's just across the Mall. It would be quicker to walk, and I usually jog — I keep running shoes under my desk."

He turned to Peter, about to speak, but was interrupted by his secure phone. "Yes, sir. Oh, no. Is that confirmed? No, sir. I hadn't seen anything on the boards. OK. We're on our way. Have some towels and coffee ready." He flipped the phone closed. "Sorry, team. Time to get wet again. To the situation room. The riots in Riyadh got out of hand — Saudi Army moved in and started massacring the rioters. Everyone piled on; and as best we can tell, the Saudi government has fallen, and the King and his family have been slaughtered."

They made their way back across the drive. The President had taken Kincaid's request seriously. There were towels and an assortment of coffees and teas awaiting them outside the situation room.

Kincaid walked in and looked up at the wide-screen map on the west wall showing symbolic flames from Riyadh to the Gulf port docks at Ras Tanura. Individual monitors were replaying clips of pitched battles, and the room was filled with the recorded sounds of gunfire and explosions.

"What happened?" Kincaid asked.

General Thomas turned to Kincaid. "The crowds in the streets are still upset over our people out in the desert by the Al Wadi pipeline. They've been marching for a couple of weeks. We urged the Saudi royals to show restraint, but something must have snapped this morning. The riots turned violent, and the army came down hard. But the army was outnumbered twenty or thirty-to-one, and they were completely overwhelmed. The rioters seized the army weapons, and after that, it was a bloodbath."

Kincaid continued to scan the monitors. "The President said the royal family is dead. Do we actually know that?"

"Yes, Mr. Kincaid. One of our sources in the household got word to CENTCOM before the line went dead. The crowd was beginning to torch the palace at that time. We've got a feed from one of the satellites coming up in a few seconds."

They watched a small monitor in one corner as a picture appeared. It showed thick, billowing smoke punctuated with bright flames. The streets around the palace were packed with people. Overturned vehicles, many engulfed in fire, littered the streets and alleys.

The President walked into the room. "Update, please, General."

"Sir, we can't confirm much more from the ground, but it's absolutely clear that the House of Saud has fallen and the country is in chaos."

"Anything we can do immediately, General?"

"We've closed our base and put it on a full war footing. We had beefed up security and the weapons cache as the situation got more and more unstable. General Johnson called for reinforcements yesterday morning, and we got another five hundred Marines to the base before the airspace became unflyable. The garrison has about forty days' worth of supplies, but they're pinned down and cut off by land and air. It would take an unthinkable military operation to extract them at least during the day."

The President closed his eyes. "Need I ask about the oil fields and ports?"

"No direct intelligence from the fields, Mr. President. We're not seeing any fires, so we would guess they haven't destroyed the oilrigs yet, but we don't know. The last word is that Ras Tanura is shut down. Tanker captains began refusing to go there last week, and the last one left the quay two days ago. Our aerials show the port deserted. We don't see any hostile action, but the Saudi army withdrew to Riyadh, so there's no protection, either. The port is basically at the mercy of the crowds. Bahrain has closed its border, and their border is well defended, but there's no oil coming in, either. Right now, the only oil from the region accessible to us is from Kuwait."

Kincaid turned around looking for Kathy. He found her in a far corner watching a screen filled with numbers. He approached. "What've you got?"

She pointed to the flickering figures. "Word of the overthrow hit the markets about twenty minutes ago. Oil's already spiked up twenty-seven dollars a barrel, and the price is rocketing upward. Sir, there was a shortage already. Everyone's basically been drawing down reserves. Worldwide flow stands at about ninety-five percent of core demand. If the Saudi flow has stopped, we just lost an additional thirteen percent. If the last tanker left port two days ago, the actual cutoff at the refinery gates is about three months away. Sir, I don't know if we even have models to predict what the prices will be at that point."

One of the White House staff members called out, "BBC just reported the death of the Saudi Royal Family … NPR just picked it up … now CNN."

The myriad phones in the situation room began to ring, more phones than people.

"Mr. President, Secretary Deatherage on line seven, Secretary Zink on line nine."

The President took the call from Treasury Secretary Deatherage and motioned for Kincaid to talk to Secretary Zink at State.

"Yeah, Chris." Kincaid listened to the phone as he watched his people moving about the room gathering information. With the President and Chief of Staff tied to their respective phones, the call from Defense was given to Peter, who listened for a while and then handed the phone to Matt. More members of departmental staffs began to appear. Phones were answered, and the distinct voices of the early hours merged into an indistinct cacophony.

The President's face was drawn. He motioned to Kincaid to join him in the hall. Kincaid nodded to his three assistants, who followed them up the half flight of stairs back into the Oval Office, where the evening had begun.

Kathy looked cautiously around the room.

The President smiled weakly. "Sit, please. Try to relax. Stretch out — take a nap if you can."

"Thank you, sir. I'll be fine."

A member of the evening kitchen crew wheeled a cart into the Oval Office with coffee, teas, fruit, and cheese. He prepared a cup of coffee with cream and two spoonfuls of sugar for the President, paused a moment after the President accepted the offering, and then departed.

The President drummed his fingers on his desk a moment while collecting his thoughts. "OK, team, tomorrow is going to be Hell on Earth. I seem to recall we had a press briefing scheduled tomorrow morning sometime. My brain's a little fried, so I don't remember exactly what it was about."

Kincaid offered a gentle reminder. "Ten, sir. Call center strike."

The President gazed once more at the intricate sculptured ceiling. "Wow. Was that really just yesterday we were talking about that? Seems like forever ago."

"Actually today, sir. Six hours ago," Kincaid confirmed.

The President closed his eyes and brought his chin to rest on his fist. He gazed into the distance. "Right. … Obviously our briefing will be much earlier. The European news cycle is in full swing. Our early news will need feed by seven at the latest. I'm guessing this is already impacting the European markets." He turned to Kathy.

"Paris CAC down twenty percent at the opening; DAX down thirty-two. Basically a third of perceived wealth vanished in under an hour."

The President nodded. "I asked Secretary Deatherage if we should consider closing the markets. He's pretty confident the automatic trading brakes will hold. He's more of the opinion that we should emphasize the safeguards and measures we will need to take as a country. Someone was talking to Energy."

He looked around the room. They all shook their heads.

"OK. I'll have someone find out who. Bill suggested that we have a skeleton of an emergency plan to present as the third item after the financial reassurance and the military response. I think Defense was talking to you, Peter."

Peter redirected the President's attention to Matt.

"Yes, sir. Secretary Banks laid out the situation in the Gulf. Basically, all our resources are already tied down in one way or the other. He's assuming that this will be going on for a long time and has ordered San Diego and Norfolk to prepare what ships remain for duty as soon as possible. He'll be here at four tomorrow morning with a more detailed script. CIA is essentially certain, based on really hard intelligence, that the crowds in Riyadh will be storming our embassy in the next twenty-four to forty-eight hours. He's initiating 'Operation Eastern Lights.'"

The President rubbed his eyes. "It's been a while. Refresh my memory."

"We'll use some of the large drones to create a diversion on the bluffs to the east of the capital — lots of light, noise — around midnight. That should draw most of the crowds. After about ninety minutes, we'll have the fast rescue helicopters come in, lights off, from the north. We set up the walled area to the north of the buildings for this very purpose three years ago. There are well-spaced landing pads for three birds, more than enough for the staff and Marine contingent. They've rehearsed this to the point that it should take less than five minutes. Major Reed says the embassy guard detachment is ready and waiting."

The President shook his head. "So what are we going to tell the American people, David? And when?"

"Sir, I've already sent for Cameron. I want to talk to her first, but I think we should be at the podium no later than six forty-five. Until she gets here, we can tell the pool to expect an early morning briefing."

"Right." The President closed his eyes and leaned back in his chair. "How is this going to end?" He opened his eyes to look at Kincaid.

"I don't know, sir. There are plenty of factors completely out of our hands. History will judge us by how we handle what we do control. I know it's hard to imagine it now, but we've got to get proactive and not reactive. We do know an energy shock is on its way, but we have a little time to be ready for it. We don't know what kind of government, if any, is going to emerge in Saudi Arabia, but I think we can count on its being hostile, at least for the near term. And we still have the serious problems of the state economies and emergency network strike. We need to find a solution to the strike immediately to get it off the table. We'll be calling in more horsepower on the state economies because we still can't figure out what's happening there. For the energy shock, we're going to have to let people know that they've got to prepare starting tomorrow. There's nothing new or magical in the preparations. They're all steps we should have been taking two decades ago."

The President looked around the room for more input. Seeing none offered, he spoke. "Well, we've got a long day tomorrow, and everything will be shifting under our feet. Go get some rest, all of you. You may want to stay close in. David, do we have some local arrangements?"

"The crisis quarters are ready across the way, sir."

"Thank you, David. Thank you all. I'll see you in the pre-dawn darkness."

They got up, left the White House, and made their third sprint of the night through the rain. The mood was somber compared to their first run.

"Where's the Vice President? I figured he'd be in the thick of this." Kathy removed the White House towel she used as a rain bonnet. She offered the towel to Kincaid.

"Thanks. He's got a smaller version of the situation room at the Observatory. I talked to him just before he arrived up there. He had suggested readying the fleet. I'm guessing he'll be over at the West Wing about four or so. Meanwhile, any questions about what we're going to need tomorrow?"

They all shook their heads.

"Everyone know where the crisis quarters are?"

They all nodded.

"OK. Try to get some rest, and I'll see you tomorrow morning. Shall we meet in my office and go over together, or do you want to head over to the back of the briefing room on your own?"

"Together," Kathy suggested. They all nodded.

"OK. Four-thirty. My office."

* * *

Each headed to her or his office to pick up material for the morning. As Kathy approached her office, she saw the light on. She peeked in cautiously to see Sarah at the computer, surrounded by her usual sea of papers.

Kathy spoke softly to avoid a start. "Hey, you should be home."

"I was just packing stuff up when red numbers started coming up on my screen. Looks like the Gulf is really bad. Guess that's where you guys have been."

Kathy nodded. "Saudi Arabia's gone. Tomorrow we start figuring out how to do with twenty percent less fuel in a few weeks."

Sarah appeared grim. "It's going to be much, much worse than that. Russia and Venezuela have been two competing suppliers among many. With that big a chunk of oil gone, they can make demands now. Big demands."

"Right. We hadn't gotten that far. Look, we could use you tomorrow morning. Do you have to go home tonight?"

Sarah wrinkled her chin in thought. "Not really. I was probably going to water my plants, but I think they're mostly dead anyway. Where could I stay?"

"There are rooms in the basement we call crisis quarters. Pretty Spartan, but quiet. They even have little travel shampoos and spare toothbrushes."

"Sorta like camping or a sleepover?" Sarah asked.

Kathy smiled, almost laughing. "Sorta."

"I'm in."

* * *

The President made his way toward his bedroom. He stopped by one of the anterooms where visiting bigwigs were normally parked while waiting to see him. He checked that the room was empty and crept to the cabinet on the far side. He removed a bottle of fine Kentucky bourbon and began pouring half a glass.

His Secret Service agent entered the room. "Sir?"

"Don't worry. It's been a stressful evening and I need something to take the edge off so I can get some quality sleep."

The agent nodded, grim-faced.

* * *

Wednesday, May 21, 2014, 1:15 a.m.

Jack started at a sudden loud noise. He peered up into the darkness. "What the …" He raised himself up on his elbows. "Ow. Better but not normal yet." Shouts echoed from the first floor.

He got up quickly, wincing. Making his way to the stairs, he moved quickly toward the light from the living room. Laura and Ed were shouting. Jack descended the stairs quickly through the dim light.

Rounding the corner, Jack looked over to see Garrette lying near the wall, a bad bruise on his cheek as well as some blood. Garrette didn't move. Jack turned to see Laura on the couch or, more exactly, partially on the couch. She seemed tied by one arm to a post of the furniture. Her legs were drawn up, ready to kick. Above her stood Ed.

Ed looked at Jack. In his hand he held his large knife, and his face had a crazed look. Ed had undressed from the waist down.

The commotion in the room halted for a moment.

Jack spoke slowly and deliberately, "Ed, what the Hell is going on?"

Ed swayed slowly over Laura. "Now, Jack." His eyes narrowed. He struggled to speak, slurring his words. "You just go on back upstairs. I'm gettin' a little payment in kind. This doesn't concern you. I'm going to enjoy myself, and then I'm leavin'. You just go on back if you don't want to watch."

"Get away from her, Ed." Jack could see a small plastic bag dusted with white powder near Ed's feet.

"No, Jack, I'm not to be denied a little fun. No. No."

Jack paused for a moment, then reached for his duffle bag he had left in the room. He dug deeply and pulled out his pistol. Turning to face Ed, Jack raised the gun, holding it calmly with both hands in well-practiced stance. "Get away from her, Ed. Come on. It's not too late. We'll leave and disappear, Ed. Just step back before it's too late."

Ed laughed harshly. "Too late? Jack, it's too late now. We're dead men. This piece of chicken is my last meal."

"Damn it! Why won't anyone listen to me? Stop now, Ed. Step back now!"

Ed's face flushed deep red. He turned the knife in his hand and gripped it firmly. Jack saw Ed's arm muscles tighten.

"Stop, Ed!"

Ed raised his knife and looked down at Laura. "Fuckin' bitch!" He swung the knife toward her throat.

Jack fired, and then fired again, striking the center of Ed's chest as Ed wheeled around.

Ed dropped the knife and clutched his chest. He looked up at Jack, his face twisted in pain. "Nice shots." He leaned back against the wall and shook his head. Ed closed his eyes and fell over.

Jack dropped the pistol and raced to Ed's side. "Oh, man, why didn't you stop? Why, why, why?"

Laura twisted her hands violently until she freed herself from the bindings and then scrambled for the pistol. Picking it up with one hand, she stepped back and pointed it at Jack. "Stay right where you are! Don't even think about moving." She crept sideways toward her father.

Jack placed his fingers on Ed's neck. No pulse. "He's dead." He hung his head. "After Jennifer, he was my best friend."

Garrette was breathing slowly as Laura placed her free hand on his side. She kept her eyes on Jack. "Your best friend downed some kind of powder and went nuts. You'd better hope to God that my father doesn't die."

She continued to move sideways until she reached the scattered contents of her purse. Switching her attention rapidly between the debris field and Jack, she picked up her phone and punched in a phone number.

"It won't work. All the call centers in the area are shut down," Jack said.

Laura watched Jack, who remained still. "I knew that." She cancelled the call, punched in Charlie's number with shaking hand, and waited for his voice. "Charlie, Laura. Our house has been attacked. There are two men. One of them just shot the other dead. I'm holding a gun on the live one. Dad was attacked first. He's alive but unconscious. I need to get him to the hospital."

* * *

Charlie had been walking the College Park picket lines with Anita since early morning. They had been joined from time to time by news crews, local police, streams of curious onlookers, and, finally, in the late night, two deputies from the Sheriff's office.

"Shit, I was wondering what had happened to you. Let me see what I can do. Nine-one-one's not working, but I'm guessing you already found that out, boss lady. Hold on." Charlie cupped his hand over the microphone and walked to the deputies' car. "Officer O'Connor, a friend of ours's been attacked in her house over in Silver Spring. Her dad's injured. Can you get her an ambulance?"

"Sure. But it'd be faster if she called the main number."

"She's holding a gun on one of the attackers now. It'd be a bit difficult for her to go and look up the number."

"Ah." Deputy O'Connor held out his hand for Charlie's phone as he reached for his note pad and pen. "Yes, ma'am. What's your address?" He jotted her information on his pad and handed the phone back to Charlie. After making the call to send help to Laura, he motioned for his fellow officer to head for the car and turned to Charlie. "Want to go with us?"

Charlie jumped into the back seat, and the patrol car wound through snarled traffic toward the beltway.

* * *

"Too much killing." Jack slowly shook his head as he knelt over Ed's body. He turned to look for a blanket.

Laura shouted, the pistol shaking in her hand, "I said, don't move!"

"I was just going to cover him up."

"You said he's dead. He doesn't need covering. So help me, if you move, I'll shoot you dead."

Jack continued to kneel by Ed's side. He turned his head slowly in Laura's direction. "You're holding it wrong."

"What?"

"You're holding the pistol wrong. The way you're shaking, there's no telling where the bullet will go. And the recoil's likely to knock it out of your hand," he said.

Laura moved her other hand to grasp the pistol. "Why are you telling me this?"

"If you're going to kill me, I want you to make it quick. I've seen too much suffering today. And your aim is bouncing all around, too high, too low. If you fired now, you'd hit me in the neck or shoulder. If you're going to kill me, aim for the heart or brain. You saw how quickly Ed died. He taught me how to aim. Ironic, huh?"

"You're nuts," she stammered.

Jack looked Laura in the face.

Her brown eyes were wide with fear as she licked her dry lips.

"I think you're right. I'm nuts," Jack said. "I'm moving slowly to sit down. My knees hurt."

Despite her two-handed grip, the pistol still shook. She lowered her aim as Jack instructed. Beads of sweat festooned her brow, and her voice wavered. "Why are you telling me this? Am I in the middle of some weird suicide pact?"

"I told you: I've seen too much suffering. If you're going to kill me, do it right. I've been pretty straight with you this whole time. I think I deserve that final little bit of respect." Jack crossed his legs and sat quietly beside Ed's body.

Laura glanced toward the window. "Jeez, I wish they'd hurry up."

Jack had closed his eyes. "Where are your people coming from?"

"Why do you want to know? And didn't I tell you to keep quiet?"

"No. You told me not to move. I'm not moving."

Laura shook her head and stammered, "Damn it. For someone in as dire straits as you are, you don't seem to be taking your situation very seriously."

"Sorry. I thought a little conversation might help you relax. You're gripping the stock so tightly; you're going to cramp up. Even if you don't plan to shoot me, you might pull the trigger unintentionally," he offered.

"I'm not planning to shoot you unless you make me. I'm holding you until the Sheriff arrives. After that, you're not my problem."

Jack shrugged and turned slowly in Ed's direction. Ed's body lay, face serene, against the wall.

After five minutes or so of silence, Laura released the pistol with one hand and flexed her fingers. She frowned. "OK, how do I grip it so that my hand doesn't hurt?"

"Not easy. They really weren't meant to be held for long periods. A pistol's designed for quick use. It's not a sniper weapon like a rifle. If you thought I were a real threat, you should have shot me by now and moved on. But you still don't trust me, right?"

"Not a chance."

"Fair enough. Then you should secure me. I'm hazarding a guess, but I sense that you have neither the background nor the strength to safely tie me up."

Laura cocked her head. "I don't even pretend to understand you, …"

"Jack."

"OK, Jack, I'll agree that I'm not interested in getting close to you. As far as I'm concerned, you're very dangerous. So where does that leave me?"

Jack thought for a few moments. "Ed provided security at the Institute. He usually carried a set of handcuffs in his back pocket. Where are his pants?"

Laura had relaxed while talking with Jack. The pistol no longer shook.

She found the pants and rooted through the pockets while keeping an eye on Jack. She extracted a set of steel handcuffs. "How do I open them?"

"When there's no hand in them, you just push and they ratchet through. But check his keychain. There should be a small key on that."

She continued her wary search until she pulled out a heavy set of keys. "Good grief. What did he do that he needed so many keys?"

"Like I said, Ed was part of the security service at the Institute up in Frederick."

"Nice. A drug-snorting rapist on the security detail."

"He was a complicated man. Over the years he apprehended more than a dozen thieves and kept a good watch. Like I said, he was my friend. Jennifer didn't think much of him. She was right in the end, obviously." Jack slowly shook his head.

"How do I know which key is the right one?"

Jack surveyed the collection from his distance. "Try the small golden one … there, that one. With the cuff closed, try opening it with your fingers while using the key."

Laura followed his directions, and the cuff sprang open. "If you can put the handcuffs on without the key, why do I need it?"

"At some point your people are going to be here, and you'll be turning me over to them."

"I see. And in the meantime?" she asked.

"In the meantime you need to anchor me to something heavy and unbreakable." They looked around. "Like the iron railing of the stairs, for instance. I'm going to slowly scoot over in that direction. When I get there, you slide the cuffs to me, and I'll put them on."

Laura's breathing had returned to normal, but she continued to point the pistol at Jack. "This is still weird, but it makes sense at one level."

"Thank you."

Laura moved parallel to Jack at a distance. "You still haven't explained why you're doing this, why you're telling me these things."

Jack stopped and hung his head, shaking it slowly. "Nobody is listening. Nobody. Since the wee hours of this morning …" He looked around. "… or yesterday morning. Can you imagine? I was so down, I was going to commit suicide with that pistol — the very one you're holding — but I realized how disappointed Jennifer would have been. I went to the lab to retrieve my pictures of Jennifer, but Leslie wouldn't give them to me. She'd thrown them away. She wouldn't listen; she only needed to hand them over. That's all." Jack looked up at Laura, his face twisted in pain. He shook his head and bowed it again. "That's all."

"I don't pretend to understand what you're going through, Jack."

"I thought you did. I thought you were listening yesterday in the other room. You and your father — and Ed. I just wanted Dr. Garrette to understand the horrible pain he caused when he withheld the medicine that would have saved Jennifer and so many others. I just wanted him to listen and understand. That's all. I didn't want anyone to get hurt. Now there's death everywhere." He continued inching toward the stairs. "And I'm the one who brought death. I just wanted people to listen and understand, and now there's death everywhere."

Jack stopped at the base of the stairs by the iron railing. "If you'll slide me the cuffs …"

Laura sent the steel manacles sliding noisily across the marble floor. Jack picked them up and secured himself to the iron rail.

"You're safe now, Ms. Garrette, unless I develop superhuman strength or Ed comes back from the dead. But do the both of us a favor. Take a look on the pistol just above the trigger. There's a little button. What color is it?"

"Red."

Jack took in a deep breath and let it out. "Without getting your finger near the trigger, push the button until it shows white."

Laura followed his directions. "What was that all about?"

"It's the safety. The pistol can't accidentally discharge now. If you need to shoot me, press the white button, and it's armed again."

Laura grinned for the first time. "I'm not planning to shoot you."

"Good. Now you'd better go attend to your father. I'm kinda hoping he doesn't come around before they haul me off. What did Ed do to him?"

"He hit him really hard on the side of his face. Daddy hit the wall and just collapsed." Laura was beside her father. She laid the pistol down a few feet away.

"You might want to get a blanket to keep him warm. I'm not that kind of doctor, but sometimes head injuries can cause heat control problems. And don't try to move him. He could have a concussion or spinal cord injury. Let the EMT people take care of that whenever they get here."

Laura looked out the window.

Jack continued, "You're right, though. Seems like a long time for them to get here. Things must be pretty messed up with the nine-one-one out of commission."

Laura stood up and circled her shoulders to loosen them. They made gentle popping noises. "You said you're 'not that kind of doctor.' What kind of doctor are you?"

"PhD. Chemistry. I was pretty good at it at one time — a few weeks ago. I ran a genetic synthesis lab in Frederick."

"Not the one that burned up?"

"Yeah, that one," he said. "I loved that lab. It was the best work I've done in my life. The DNA we synthesized helped unravel over a dozen serious genetic diseases."

Laura opened a door beneath the bookshelves and pulled out a wool comforter. She continued watching Jack but spoke calmly as she tucked the edges of the blanket around her father. "And Daddy fired you, right?"

"Yeah. But it had nothing to do with the lab."

"I know. Joanna Denton was here arguing about it with him yesterday … or the day before. I've lost track of the days, too. She quit, you know."

"I'm sorry. Seems like everything I touch turns to shit lately."

Laura sat down cross-legged next to her father. She tilted her head as she eyed Jack. "Her quitting was a matter of principle. She was yelling at him. So was I. Was the only thing you did …"

Jack completed her question, "I made love to Jennifer on a beach in San Diego."

"I was trying to be sensitive."

"It's OK. It was wrong and we got caught. I paid the fine. It should have been over at that point." Jack shifted uncomfortably at the base of the stairs. He leaned back, resting his head on the third step, arching his back against the first two. "But the incident took on a life of its own. That ticket I paid got copied and found its way to Dr. Garrette. He thought it serious enough that he fired me."

Laura watched Jack for a minute. She got up, went to the couch, picked up two pillows, and slid them in his direction.

"Thanks."

"You were making me uncomfortable." She returned to her post beside her father.

Jack smiled and placed one pillow beneath his back and one under his head.

She looked at her father. "That was the reason he gave you. But he was firing plenty of high-priced talent that week."

Jack closed his eyes. "I'm sorta comforted, I guess. Do you really think you should be telling me this?"

"No, probably not. But you're in enough trouble that it doesn't much matter. I don't know why I told you. You got me talking, just like you wanted."

Jack sighed.

Laura turned toward the window as a flicker of red illuminated the curtains. She continued to sit as the sound of the opening door came from the kitchen.

"Laura?" It was Charlie's voice.

"In the living room!"

Charlie entered, followed by the two deputies and two EMTs with a medical lift. The medics and deputy moved swiftly to Garrette. Charlie glanced around, first at Ed's body, and then to Jack as Laura pointed toward the stairs.

Charlie walked over to Jack. "She cuffed you?"

"He cuffed himself." Laura got up and picked up the gun. "He was afraid I was going to shoot him because I didn't know how to handle this." She gave the pistol to Charlie.

He examined it. "You couldn't have shot him. The safety's on."

"He told me how to set the safety. Trust me. It was ready to shoot." She looked in Ed's direction.

Charlie handed the pistol to O'Connor, who called in the serial number on his radio.

The senior medic called out. "Ma'am, we've got your father immobilized. It looks like he may have a slight concussion. That's serious, but he should recover. We're taking him to the hospital."

She approached her father as they strapped him to the lift. "Can I go with him?"

O'Connor turned to her. "Ms. Garrette, they'll take good care of him, I promise. We need you here to find out what the hell happened. When we're done, we'll take you to the hospital. OK?"

She nodded, and the EMT wheeled Garrette to the ambulance.

Laura turned to Jack. "Good call."

Charlie looked back and forth between Laura and Jack. He extended his hand. "Charlie Jones."

Jack reached out to shake hands but was stopped short by the handcuffs. Charlie began laughing, and he reached farther and grasped Jack's hand. "Sorry, man. That wasn't intentional." He looked over at Ed. "Hold on a minute while I have a word with boss lady."

Charlie got up and went over to Ed, motioning for Laura to follow. Deputy O'Connor joined them. The three stood surveying the scene.

"Tell us what happened — slowly." The deputy took out his note pad and began writing.

She crossed her arms. "They came to the back door and demanded to talk to Dad. Dad wouldn't talk to them, so he forced his way in. His name's Ed." She nodded in the direction of the body. "Jack calmed Ed down and got Dad to agree to listen to his case."

"Ed's case?"

"Jack's."

Charlie grimaced. "Don't use pronouns. This is pretty tangled."

Laura continued, "Dad agreed to listen to Jack's story. Jack worked for Dad. Jack's wife died, but Jack thinks she could have been saved by a medicine that one of the companies Dad consults for made, but held up releasing for marketing reasons."

She looked at Charlie's confusion-covered face.

Laura took a deep breath. "Jack told us his story. About the time he was finishing, he said he had a headache. I told him where the medicine cabinet was, and he went upstairs. But he didn't come back. Apparently, he fell asleep."

The deputy looked up from his notes. "Let me get this straight. These two forced their way in — with guns — but you felt comfortable telling him where to go in your house?"

"They didn't have guns displayed at first. I didn't know there were any guns."

Charlie and O'Connor looked at each other.

"After Jack didn't return, Ed got restless. He'd been pretty rough with Dad, so we didn't do anything. At some point he downed whatever was in that bag and started getting crazy. When he began coming on to me, Dad tried to stop him, but Ed attacked him and hit him so hard that Dad literally bounced off the wall. Ed was getting ready to rape me. I fought him off as best I could, but he was strong enough to tie me to the sofa. When I still struggled, he got out that knife." She pointed to the knife beside Ed's body.

The deputy looked around. "And the gun?"

"I don't think Ed had a gun. That was Jack's"

The deputy stopped writing. "I thought …"

Laura held up her hand. "Shortly after Ed took off his pants, Jack showed up and tried to make Ed stop, tried to reason with him. Ed wasn't listening. He started arguing with Jack. Finally, Jack got into his bag, the one that had Jennifer's pictures in it, and pulled out his — Jack's — pistol. Ed was still arguing and was about to stab me. He was aiming at my throat. But Jack shot Ed. Twice. Shot him dead." She grew quiet. Charlie and O'Connor gave her a moment.

O'Connor walked over to Jack. "I'll be talking to you later." He turned to Laura. "So Jack shot Ed. How did we get from there to Jack handcuffed to your stairs?"

"Jack dropped the gun after he shot Ed. I got loose, grabbed the gun, and kept it trained on Jack. I had no idea what to expect."

Charlie nodded. "And the cuffs?"

"Jack said I didn't know how to handle the pistol, and was afraid I'd shoot him accidentally, so he told me about Ed's handcuffs and anchored himself to the railing so that I wouldn't keep pointing the gun at him."

Charlie knelt beside Jack who had been listening to the narrative. "That was a smart thing to do. She can be dangerous. I should know." Charlie turned again to Laura. "Pillows?"

"Jack was uncomfortable."

Charlie shrugged.

O'Connor's radio chirped. He held it to his ear and looked down as he listened. "Right. Uh huh. I see. Really?" He looked up suddenly in Jack's direction. "I'm looking at him right now, I think. OK. I'll get back to you."

The deputy knelt down alongside Charlie and spoke to Jack. "Seems you've had a rough forty-eight hours."

"Yes, sir."

"The serial number checks out, apparently registered to you. High-grade target pistol. Jack's got no priors. That's the good news."

Jack closed his eyes.

"But according to the database, you died about thirty-six hours ago."

"He visited the Frederick lab before the fire." Laura answered for Jack. "He went there to get the pictures of his wife. When he came out, he drove down with Ed to confront my dad. He left his car in the Frederick garage so they think he was lost in the fire, too."

O'Connor eyed Jack. "Is that what happened?"

Jack spoke softly. "Basically."

"Did you have anything to do with the fire?"

"He wasn't —" Laura began to answer again, but O'Connor threw up his hand to cut her off.

"Jack, did you have anything to do with the fire?"

"I don't think so. When I ran the lab, we maintained a prescribed safe volume of solvents. My technicians were always irritated at having to order so often. In the brief time I was in the lab that morning, I saw boxes and boxes of solvents stacked to the ceiling."

"And they just happened to go up after your visit?"

"There were dangerous shortcuts I forbade that they wanted to do. I have no idea what happened after I left."

O'Connor's radio sounded again. He picked it up and listened. "Right. I'm on it." He turned to Laura. "Ma'am, I've got an urgent call. We'll take Jack with us if you're prepared to press charges."

Laura froze, watching Jack slumped morosely at the stair landing. He raised his cuffed hand, the cuffs making a metallic dragging sound against the iron.

"Ma'am, I have to go now. Will you press charges?"

Laura, still watching Jack, shook her head. "No."

Jack and Charlie jerked their heads up in unison.

"He saved my life. He did everything he promised. He acted inappropriately and will have to deal with that — with my father, no less — but he didn't harm me."

"Home invasion?"

"We let him in."

"Intimidation?"

"That was Ed. Jack saved me from Ed."

O'Connor turned to Charlie.

Charlie buried his face in his hands. "Somehow I knew I was going to get in the middle of this. Jeez. Get on your way, O'Connor. I'll stay here with the crazy lady and her captive."

O'Connor scowled. "I can't say I have a good feeling about this, but I don't have a choice if you won't press charges." He called to deputy Reese who had been taking notes on the scene. "Alex, you stay with them. Things are getting out of hand over in College Park." He turned to Jack. "You'll want to stay close, sir. We'll have plenty of questions, as will other people when this mess outside is over. You got that?"

"Yes, sir," Jack replied.

O'Connor folded his notepad and left. Bright red lights flashed through the window as he sped away, siren wailing.

After silence returned to the house, Charlie shifted from kneeling to sitting. He extended his hand again, this time far enough for Jack to reach. "Charlie Jones."

"Jack Pullman."

Charlie tilted his head, knitting his brow. "Jack Pullman? Debate champion for 2014?"

Jack chuckled. "Yeah. Can you believe it?"

Laura threw out her hands in exasperation. "Charlie Jones, how the hell could you know that?"

Charlie grinned. "Some of us read the news as well as make it. Ol' Jack here argued both sides of federal funding for job transition training."

Jack nodded.

"Which side do you believe?" Charlie asked.

"I argued both sides. Both sides have merit."

"Which side do you believe?"

Jack was mildly irritated, but was in no position to be angry. "I suppose my rational side would be against, but Jennifer was strongly in favor."

Charlie folded his arms. "You're a wuss."

"Charlie!" Laura shouted.

"Charlie's right. I've worn my righteous rational armor all my adult life. And what do I have to show for it? My true love is dead without my ever having shown her the passion she deserved. My best friend is dead because I wouldn't confront his monstrous side. My life's work is literally in ashes. I'm chained to the stairs of the man I came to convince by rational argument of his inhumanity. And the only reason I'm not on my way to jail right now is that someone I just met irrationally chose, despite her terror, to keep me out of jail."

Charlie stroked his two-day stubble as he stared at Jack. "Which side do you believe?"

Jack shouted, "Funding! Yes! You have to have compassion! Jenn was totally right!"

Charlie stretched out his arm, palm open, toward Laura. "Key."

Deputy Reese looked up from his notes. "What? He still could be dangerous."

Charlie frowned. "He had his chance. Give me the key, Laura. Have I ever been wrong?"

Laura shook her head. "I'm sure you have, but not this time." She closed her eyes and handed Charlie the key to the handcuffs.

Charlie unlocked the cuffs. "We're going to need someone who knows how to speak in public. Today's actions are just a hint of what's coming, and soon."

Reese turned from his note taking beside Ed's body. "Great. We barely had enough officers to deal with a relatively low crime rate a few months ago. We can't cope with what we're seeing now. How are we going to deal with more?"

"You're not." Charlie offered absent-mindedly as he watched Jack massaging his wrists. "There's a good chance we've reached a tipping point in society. I could see the American social system crashing down over the next few weeks. In fact, I'd bet on it if I were a betting man."

Laura sighed. "Charlie tends toward the dramatic. Don't pay any attention to him when he gets this way."

"I do not. Again, boss lady, have I ever been wrong?"

She frowned. "I don't keep track. But I sure hope you're totally wrong on this."

* * *

By five in the morning, the West Wing corridors were crowded. In the situation room Vice President Bailey and his staff occupied the north end of the room, Kincaid and his staff the south. Both groups were subdued as generals, admirals, and high-ranking State Department people surrounding President Miller and answering questions and offering options.

About five-thirty the President glanced at his watch. "Mr. Kincaid, I think it's time we alert the press pool."

"Yes, sir. The gate opened about fifteen minutes ago. I expect everyone to be in their seats by six, if that works for you."

The President nodded. "Who's on makeup this morning?"

"Tony, sir."

"Good. He makes me look better than the others do. I really don't want to look like I feel."

Kincaid nodded. "How much of the briefing do you want to take, Mr. President?"

Miller frowned, pausing for a moment. "I think about fifteen minutes is all I can stomach." He turned to Cameron. "How much opening have you got for me?"

"About three minutes, sir. We can start with our sadness over the loss of life, including the royal family. But don't dwell on them, since we will be dealing from now on with those who led the coup. Then we repeat our pledge to support neighboring countries in the event that violence spreads.

Finally, you should probably give a strong warning for the U.S. to brace for challenges resulting from the coming disruption of oil flow."

The Vice President turned from conversation with his staff. "Mr. President, I would strongly recommend toning down any conversation about possible disruption. Our markets are skittish enough. I'd recommend, instead, emphasizing our commitment to defending shipping lanes and our support for those oil-producing countries who ally themselves with us."

The President watched Kincaid's staff and smiled as Kathy and Matt instinctively and simultaneously crossed their arms. "No, Mr. Bailey, I think I'm fine with the concept as is. Otherwise we'll look pretty stupid in a few weeks when our refineries start running low. It'll seem like we had no idea what was about to happen. I suspect we're going to be answering questions about what we're going to do when gas prices start soaring the way Ms. Whiting is predicting."

Bailey looked in Kathy's direction. "If."

"Whatever. I'm going to tell them that we will be putting contingency plans in place over the next few weeks. We're just lucky that this is happening at the beginning of summer rather than the beginning of winter."

The President turned to Secretary Banks. "How can I help the military side?"

"Mr. President, Operation Eastern Lights is ready and will commence at midnight in the Gulf."

"Six in the evening, our time?" Miller asked.

"Seven, sir. We're making a big show off the coast of Qatar." Secretary Banks stretched his arms across a swath of a map of the Gulf region, outlining eastern boundaries of Saudi Arabia and Qatar. "Lots of noisy air ops and ship movements. Secretary Zink is advising local governments to avoid this area. That diversion should draw out most of the forces from Riyadh. By the time we light up the bluffs to the east, our transport helos should be able to move in with minimal risk."

Secretary Zink joined in. "Mr. President, it would be helpful if you could give a clumsy denial about any plans for invading from the sea."

Miller smiled. "Being clumsy should be easy this morning."

Cameron looked up from her notebook. "Twenty-five minutes, Mr. President. We need to get you down to Tony."

Miller nodded. "Right. David, Cameron, come with me. The rest of you go somewhere to watch. I'm sure we'll have plenty of clarifications to issue when this briefing is over. The situation is changing by the minute, so keep on your toes for any significant development. I'd rather be the one to announce them than find out from a question."

Sunrise painted the eastern horizon as Peter, Matt, Kathy, Sarah, and Anna crossed to the Executive Office Building. Glancing to the right, they saw the brilliant white glare of television lights illuminating various reporters giving their pre-briefing reports against the backdrop of the White House.

Peter shook his head. "This is not going to go well."

The others climbed the steps in silent agreement.

Kathy spoke up as Matt held the door open. "It was probably a mistake to concentrate solely on the military operations. He could easily get questions about the strikes or even the state budgets. I don't think he's really up to speed on those topics."

Peter nodded. "You may be right. But if he stays on for only fifteen minutes, we'll be OK. Mr. Kincaid's up to date and can defer any question if he needs to. The Riyadh story will be the hot topic of the hour and the President's ready for just about anything they're likely to throw at him." He looked at his watch. "We'll know in about six minutes. Let's watch in the TV room."

The TV room in the second basement was about as big as a typical living room and had a wall of television monitors tuned to a wide range of local and foreign news feeds and a collection of sofas and chairs arranged for viewing. Peter chose Ben Jacobs's report for sound and turned up the volume.

They sat down as the President entered the press room. Kincaid and Cameron followed him, taking their accustomed positions along the side of the room.

The President spoke, "Good morning. During the past twelve hours, a series of events have unfolded in the Middle East, particularly in Saudi Arabia, that have dramatically and irreversibly altered the lives of the people there. The continued upheaval we are witnessing will have profound implications for the world community.

"We must report with great sadness that most of the royal family of Saudi Arabia have been murdered at the hands of those who now control the streets of their capital. We may have had substantial disagreements with some of the policies of the royal family in regard to their dealings with their own people, but we join with governments around the world in condemning the violence perpetrated in their overthrow. History demonstrates that murder and assassination are never foundations for a just and viable society.

"Nevertheless, we are left with the reality of the present. The government of Saudi Arabia is essentially non-existent. The streets of Riyadh are awash in violence and destruction. The ports are closed, with the implications for world energy flow obvious. Led by our Secretaries of State and Defense, we have taken all prudent steps to protect our staff in the country and some time ago encouraged our citizens to depart from this area. To the best of our knowledge, no U.S. citizens have been killed or harmed in the violence. We are attempting through every channel available to us to establish contact with anyone in the country in a position of leadership. This is challenging, as we have not identified at this time any emerging leadership organization.

"Beyond the obvious tragedies of death and destruction that we have witnessed, we must acknowledge that the convulsions on the Arabian Peninsula will have far-reaching impact on the health of the global economy. The world has long depended on a reliable flow of crude oil from the Saudi fields. The near-certain loss of this supply is going to require major changes in our industrial practices and personal behavior in a very short time. I have assembled a high-level task force to produce a plan for dealing with the inevitable disruption resulting from this upheaval. In the coming days we will publish details of this plan. While our hope is that compliance will be voluntary and in the best spirit of our citizens working together, we will also be proposing a number of legislative measures to facilitate cooperation and to guard against any attempts to take unfair advantage of potential shortages and stresses that may result.

"I have time for only a few questions. My answers will of necessity be brief, as I must continue the intense consultations with all branches of our government and with leaders around the world. I will not pretend that this situation is anything but serious. But we will be facing hardships of the kind and magnitude that we have faced many times before. I have complete faith that we will rise to the occasion and that we will emerge stronger on the other side."

The President paused, then pointed to the senior White House correspondent for the first question.

Watching the monitors, Peter seemed relieved as the first questions focused on the timing of the coup and the fate of the royal family. "That was pretty good. The Vice President must have been shut out of the final preps. Sounds like it came straight from Cameron." Peter frowned as the President pointed to Ben Jacobs. "Uh oh."

"Mr. President, would it be too much to speculate that the administration did not see these events coming because of the overwhelming distraction of the financial crisis engulfing the country and was consequently caught off-guard?"

The President folded his arms, leaning forward in thought. He was silent for some time, and then looked up. "Ben, this is no time for 'gotcha' questions. What you witness is what is on the television at the moment … what you and your associates put on that television screen. I resent your implication that we were not paying attention. Like any living organism, the White House is engaged in a vast array of activities all the time. No, we did not directly anticipate the tragic outcome of the last few days any more than you did. We did not expect the Saudi army's brutal crackdown on dissent two days ago, in part because we had been assured by the Saudis of their commitment to restraint. While not excusable, the ensuing violence was certainly predictable. This whole area has long been a tinderbox, and the match was struck. Tell me someone beside the Lord who can predict now when the fires will subside."

Jacobs raised one eyebrow. "A remarkably fatalistic view, Mr. President."

Miller ran his fingers along the edge of the podium. "I think, Mr. Jacobs, what you are seeing is calm confidence that we have concentrated the best skills in this land to work on our many problems. What would you expect from me? Hysteria? Bellicose posturing? No. We have at home a problem of confidence as best we can tell. The problem is economic, and the solution will be economic. The causes, which we do not fully understand at present, will be sorted out and we will fix them. The problems we face abroad have diplomatic and military solutions. We sensed potential unrest some time ago and took the necessary precautions to safeguard our people, and we are even now seeking channels of communication, so that we may be a force for good in the region. If you have some information or suggestions as to how we may be more effective, Mr. Jacobs, you are free to offer them."

After an uncomfortable silence, Jacobs said, "No, sir," and sat down.

The President glanced briefly at Kincaid. "My chief of staff and our press secretary will handle the remainder of your questions. As you can imagine, my day will be filled with many intense meetings." He turned and began to leave, but stopped for a moment at the door and turned to the assembly. "But be assured, we have not been and will not be caught off-guard."

Sarah leaned onto the back of the couch in the TV room. "That was pretty good, I'd say."

Peter nodded. "Yeah. And they're not likely to try to trap the boss. Maybe Cameron 'cause they think she's new; but based on my few days working directly with her, I can't imagine they'll get anywhere."

Kincaid and Cameron took turns answering questions and exchanging contacts. The briefing ended at 7:16. After his off-the-record session, Kincaid returned to the office complex around 8:30. He arrived first at Kathy and Sarah's office.

"We still on for 1:30?" Kincaid asked.

Kathy looked up. "Sure. I guess I assumed a meeting about state unemployment numbers would be shoved aside, given what's going on in the Gulf."

"The President wants to maintain the appearance of normal function. He needs domestic news that can be fed into the press cycle at about the time we mount Operation Eastern Lights. Plus I think he's still chafing from Jacobs's dig. And, for my part, I hope you'll have some surprisingly good numbers for me." He smiled.

Kathy returned the smile, but shook her head.

Kincaid turned back to the hallway, searching for Matthew.

* * *

Peter, Kathy, Sarah, and Kincaid had assembled in a third floor conference room at twenty minutes after one. Anna joined them to screen interrupting calls. Onto the table, Sarah plopped a pile of folders heavy enough for the sound to echo in the room.

Kincaid convened the meeting. "OK, folks, let me know what you've got."

Kathy began. "Essentially every state is now reporting unemployment numbers well above what had been expected. Most of them are also reporting drops in tax revenue from manufacturing and, now, services. On the other hand, the national report shows manufacturing is level or slightly rising."

Kincaid tilted his head. "And we still have no explanation for the disconnect?"

"Not yet," Kathy continued. "At least nothing certain. Sarah has a few reports that favor the states' picture, though."

Kincaid turned to Sarah, who rooted through her pile.

She looked up in frustration. "Shit. I left that one downstairs."

"Go ahead and get it. Looks like it's the first report that's making sense, though I'd rather it had been a positive state report."

Sarah walked swiftly toward the stairs as Anna answered the buzzing phone. She handed it to Kincaid. "It's Tracey. Seems urgent."

"Put it on speaker." Anna pushed the speakerphone button. "Kincaid."

"Mr. Kincaid, I didn't want to interrupt, but you have a very persistent caller — Professor Brian Doctrow."

"Ah, Brian. He was my roommate at Yale. Probably here for the economic conference. Wish I had time to meet him, but not now."

"Yes, sir. I've told him how busy you are but he keeps calling back. He finally said to tell you two words, and if you wouldn't meet with him, he'll drop it."

Kincaid grinned. "And they are …?"

"Code tangerine."

The smile vanished from Kincaid's face. "Code tangerine? I'd hoped I'd never hear that again. Is he still on the line? If so, patch him through."

"Actually, sir, he's at the west gate."

"Have someone bring him up."

Tracey hung up, and Kincaid settled back into his seat, scowling.

"Sir?" Anna watched Kincaid as she set down the receiver.

He took a deep breath. "Brian and I were best friends at school as well as roommates. We got into a lot of things together. One night, we were … well, the details aren't important. Brian was the lookout, and he was to text me 'code tangerine' if our professor found out what was going on. He did, and I spent four hours crouched behind an antique table while Professor Jarnigan sat at his computer checking his logs. You can imagine I never wanted to hear that again."

Sarah reappeared at the doorway with additional folders.

Kincaid turned to her. "Oh, good. You're back. We're going to have a visitor. An old friend of mine, Professor Brian Doctrow."

Sarah approached the table. "The Brian Doctrow? The pipeline-theory Brian Doctrow?"

Kincaid nodded, amused.

"How do you know him?" Sarah asked.

"He was my roommate. You've obviously heard of him."

Corporal Tull walked quietly into the room, accompanied by a man dressed in a conservative jacket. His wire-rimmed glasses and graying hair all contributed to the look of a serious scholar.

Sarah continued, unaware of their entrance. "Heard of him? Brian Doctrow is an economics god. He's probably advanced the field of pipeline theory more than anyone … ever. He's got to be on the short list for the Nobel in economics."

Doctrow and Tull eyed each other. Tull grinned. Doctrow placed his hands on his chest and grimaced.

"So when's he coming?" she demanded.

Kincaid lifted his hand and pointed behind her. Sarah turned around, saw Doctrow, and dropped her head into her hands. The others did their best to stifle their laughter.

"Brian Doctrow, I'd like you to meet Sarah Tyler, our economic assistant. Sarah, this is, well, you know, the economics god."

Doctrow stretched out his hand to Sarah.

Kincaid stood up and began to move around the table. "We rely on Sarah for her quick grasp of the economic situation. She is invariably correct."

Doctrow nodded. "Good person to have on your team."

"I have to tell you, Brian, I think I finally impressed her when I told her you were my roommate. Maybe we can get a New Jersey rest stop named after you."

Sarah protested immediately, "Can't. He's not native to New Jersey." She immediately realized what she had said and stamped her foot. "I've got to stop doing that."

Everyone laughed, including Doctrow. "No problem. I would hope your other predictions come true though."

Kincaid introduced the professor to others in the room, thanked Tull, and sent him on to his other duties. He motioned for all to sit. "So I guess you're here for the conference. Sorry we've been a little too busy to get over there. I promised Kathy some time this afternoon, but now it looks like part of the conference has come to us."

Doctrow nodded again. He sat at the table uncomfortably.

"Well, Brian, you've got my attention. As I told my staff, I'd hoped never to hear those words again. What's up?"

Doctrow looked around the room. "Perhaps we should talk in private. With all due respect to your fine staff, some of my concerns may impinge on issues of national security."

"I appreciate your consideration, but we have a pretty close working group here. Seriously, I trust them more than I trust myself most of the time. Besides, unless you've changed in twenty years, I'm going to need Kathy and Sarah to translate."

"Fair enough." The professor seemed satisfied. "I'm here this week to report on my group's work. We've been doing some interesting work with parallel non-interactive leading indicators."

Kincaid turned to Sarah.

She stepped in without hesitation. "Statistics that mirror the behavior of the economy at large, but are usually ignored as boring. They tend to be very accurate trackers of the flashy processes and can usually be fed into our data systems continuously. When done well, they lead the other indicators by a few days to a few weeks."

Kincaid turned back to Doctrow, who was watching Sarah.

"You're right. She's very good." Doctrow shook his head. "Anyway, about two years ago, we were refining our models and making great progress. But then our numbers began to diverge from the national reports — unemployment, manufacturing, GDP, and so forth. At first we thought we'd added some bad assumptions into the new model. But when we ran the old model, which has worked for nearly a decade, we saw the same variance. I've got a presentation tomorrow opposite Sandy Bates. She and I have been competing for nearly fifteen years. I figured that I was going to look pretty bad, but she came over to me last night at the banquet and asked if my numbers had been flakey lately. Seems hers have been, too. We compared notes, and as best we can tell, we can extrapolate the split back to a point about thirteen months ago."

Kincaid sensed Kathy's and Sarah's growing interest. "OK. We're all seeing something of that nature. We're looking for answers, too. What's your point?"

Doctrow placed his hands on the table. "I need to know if you changed the fundamental economic computations starting about thirteen months ago without telling anyone."

Kincaid shook his head. "No." Then he paused. "I don't think so." He turned to Kathy.

"Sir, I don't know, either. Since they classified the raw data, I haven't been able to link the national numbers with any of our models."

Kincaid frowned. "I took care of that months ago. You should have full access."

"No, sir. We're still blocked. I know you ordered access, but we haven't gotten it. Who'd you send it to?"

"The request went directly to …" Kincaid stopped abruptly as the color drained from his face.

Peter leaned forward, alarmed. "Boss, are you all right?"

Kincaid gave a quick shake of his head. "Kathy, who over in treasury is in charge of those data?"

"Scott Thomas."

"Do you have his number?"

She opened her phone, searched, and wrote down a telephone number.

"OK. Everyone keep quiet. It's all in how you ask the question, as you know." He entered the number, putting on speakerphone.

"Resources. Scott Thomas. May I help you?"

"Scott, this is David Kincaid in the President's office. We've got a problem. Seems some academic types have found a problem with our numbers. They're going to be reporting on it tomorrow."

"Oh, God, No." Thomas's tone was a mixture of panic and dismay.

Everyone in the room stiffened.

Kincaid rubbed his face. "Now, don't panic. We're going to handle it. But we need to get the real numbers over here. I need you to lift the restrictions for Kathy Whiting and Sarah Tyler right now."

After a very long silence, Thomas resumed, his voice heavy with stress. "Mr. Kincaid, there's nothing I'd rather do. But I can't. The security directive will not allow it. You have to realize the position I'm in. Believe me, sir; this has been eating at me for a long time. I told them this wouldn't work."

Kincaid raised a clenched fist to his lips for a moment and then spoke again. "Scott, I'm in the President's direct staff. I represent the President. I fail to see how a directive can stop me from ordering this."

"Mr. Kincaid, please. I was given the directive straight from the Vice President that your group is specifically blocked. It's not right. I've felt awful about it, but it's the law, sir."

Kincaid looked around at his staff, who sat in stunned silence. "I understand. You've done the right thing, Scott. You've been most helpful. I'll be sure that the president is aware of your positive contribution, and we will protect you. I think President Miller can override this, right?"

"Yes, sir." Thomas's voice sounded more hopeful.

"Back with you in a bit. Don't go anywhere, and don't talk to anyone yet."

"Yes, sir. Thank you."

Kincaid pushed the button to terminate the call and stared at the console.

Sarah sat with blank expression. "Oh, shit."

Kincaid, still silent, looked up at her.

After a pensive moment, Doctrow spoke up. "Sarah's correct, invariably."

"OK." Kincaid reached for his jacket. "Everyone up. Let's go for a walk."

He led them down the stairs and across the drive to the West Wing, and up the steps to Abigail's desk.

"We need to see the President."

Abigail crossed her arms. "You didn't say 'good morning.' Even though it's not a good morning, you almost always say 'good morning.' When you don't, it usually means it's going to be a long, long day. Is this going to be a long, long day?"

Kincaid nodded.

She sighed. "He's wrapping up with some generals now. The British, French, and Kuwaiti ambassadors are next in line. I'm guessing you think you're going in ahead of them."

He nodded again.

She continued in a weary Virginia drawl, "OK. When the generals come out, you go in. If there's to be any hope of preserving his schedule, be brief."

Four military officers emerged from the Oval Office, and Kincaid led his group in behind them.

The President looked up from signing some papers. "You don't look British, French, or Algerian."

"Kuwaiti, sir."

"That either. And I don't see any smiles."

"Mr. President, may I introduce Professor Brian Doctrow. He's a leading economist attending the conference at the Smithsonian."

The President rose and extended his hand, glancing quickly to Kincaid. "Professor. Welcome to Washington and to the White House."

"Sir, Professor Doctrow and some of his colleagues have apparently found a core reason for the economic turmoil. We need access to the raw data used in computing the national statistics."

The President frowned. "David, we're obviously under a great deal of stress here. I've got a pretty full plate myself, obviously. Take care of it."

Kincaid spread his hands. "That's the problem, sir. Vice President Bailey specifically blocked access for me and for my staff right about the time the downturn started. I can't override that."

The President slowly sat down. "Oh, David, I've got a really bad feeling about this."

"Sir, you're the only one who can authorize us."

"What do I need to do?" he asked.

Kincaid handed Kathy's slip of paper to the President. "His name is Scott Thomas. He's the one responsible for system security. Scott's been playing by the book, but it's clear he wants to cooperate. I suspect he's going to need protection. We need to get access to those numbers."

President Miller punched in the number. "Scott, this is the President. … Yes, I bet you have been expecting my call. … Yes, unblock them. … All of them. The whole staff. Look, I'm going to be sending over someone from the federal marshal service. … No, for your protection. You've suddenly become a very valuable witness. … So do we have any questions? How long will it take? … Right now? Good. Thank you, Scott. We'll be talking later, I'm sure."

The President hung up the phone and turned to Kincaid. "You've got your numbers. I'll be over as soon as I'm done with the Brit, the French, and the —"

"Kuwaiti," Kincaid finished.

"Right. In a better time, that would sound like the beginning of a joke, wouldn't it? Go!"

They quickly crossed the drive into the office building.

Kathy and Sarah ran down the stairs to their office. By the time Kincaid and Doctrow caught up, Kathy's computer screen was awash in digits.

"Oh my, Professor!" Kathy called.

Sarah and Doctrow joined Kathy at the screen while Kincaid lingered in the doorway.

Doctrow's eyes darted around the screen for a while. He turned to Kincaid. "It's a classic inversion. We've seen them before, but only in a few third world countries where many of the banking systems had become basically shams after a coup."

Kathy faced Kincaid. "The public numbers look completely made up. They don't look derived from underlying data. So since civilian banks rely on the public numbers, the civilian banks are making flawed decisions based on the assumptions these numbers support. Because the numbers are so out of whack, the banking decisions are feeding a downward spiral. It's getting worse, and it's accelerating."

"Got it. What do we do now?"

The professor put his hands on his hips as he continued to watch the screen. "I have no idea. As I said, we've seen this in a very few developing countries. What typically happens is that the local banks simply collapse, usually accompanied by bloodshed. Eventually the IMF and World Bank come in, pick up the pieces, and patch things back together. But we don't have models for something on this scale. The financial swings could theoretically be larger than the banking system itself — the world banking system. The closest thing that comes to mind is the hyperinflation period in prewar Germany. And we know how that turned out."

"The President will be here in a while. Get whatever you can for him. He's not an economist, either, so make the presentation clear and succinct. We need a plan of action. I'll step back for now. Do your economic stuff." Kincaid remained at the door as Sarah, Kathy, and Doctrow submerged into the jargon of their field. He heard "inversion" and "out of control" often.

19 COLLAPSE

By the time footsteps of the President's party filled the passageway, all three economists had positioned several charts around the room with annotated currency flows, dates, major banks, and arrows pointing to choke points in the world financial system.

With his Secret Service escort, President Miller stopped in the doorway beside Kincaid. "How bad is it?"

Kincaid shook his head slowly. "Worse than anything I could have imagined. Every new number they look at points to bigger trouble. Brian estimates that economic imbalance is growing at a rate of over a billion dollars a day. The loss of wealth matches very closely what we've seen in the states. It appears state numbers were spot on. The data we released in our regular updates appear to be fabrications, systematic fabrications."

"How could this happen? Economic data are public. How can they not have been challenged?"

Kathy turned from her screen to Kincaid. He nodded for her to proceed. "Mr. President, finished numbers — GDP, employment, public debt, those sorts of things — are definitely public. But underlying data, all those thousands and thousands of little numbers collected by a small army of Treasury and Labor workers, have been classified for the past two years."

"Classified? Why?" The President's face wrinkled in incredulity.

Kathy opened her hands. "The reason given was that raw data were being used by foreign governments for corporate espionage and currency manipulation."

"And I'm sensing you don't buy that," Miller observed.

"No, sir. In over a half century that these data have been gathered, everyone in the world got those numbers at the same time," she replied.

"How could I not have been aware of the change to classify them? Seems that's a pretty fundamental action."

Kathy folded her arms in resignation. "We hashed out these decisions in working groups over a number of departments and agencies. Policy evolved over time, not without a lot of shouting, but I would imagine that intricate details of those deliberations were filtered out long before they reached you."

The President turned to Kincaid. "Vice President Bailey?"

Kincaid shrugged. "He was a primary advocate — probably *the* primary advocate — of those restrictions. In the end, with his chosen positions within different agencies, those philosophies prevailed."

"Do you think the fabrications were deliberate? I mean, is there any other explanation?"

Kincaid closed his eyes. "Sir, we have known about the gap in detail for only an hour. I'm not going to speculate." He opened his eyes and turned to Doctrow. "But I could always count on Doctor Brian to offer speculation, and he's been watching the spread from another set of data for some time."

Doctrow grinned. "This can't be an accident. For instance, it's as if a linear increase were systematically laid on top of GDP while a linear decrease, with different coefficients, were subtracted from unemployment. Look here." He moved to one of Kathy's screens. "We've taken those key economic reports as they would have been calculated from raw data and subtracted them from reported values for the past five years. Here …" He pointed to spots on the graphs where lines diverged. "… about thirteen months ago, data began to drift apart. And it's not a random drift. Each month, it's just a few fractions of a point — just a little, but the drift is constant. Believe me, in economics, nothing is constant."

Kincaid nodded. "Thirteen months. Right about when you thought your models were flakey."

Doctrow wagged his finger. "And Sandy Bates's models as well. The superimposed drifts match almost perfectly what we thought were errors in our models."

The President walked toward the computers. "OK. Let's assume that the difference is real and that it's deliberate. Now tell me why."

Sarah raised her hand. The President nodded in her direction.

"Sir, when all economic data are pointing up, it inspires confidence. People invest, spend money on manufacturing and goods. The economy does move up."

The President frowned. "I'm no economist, but it seems that sooner or later, people would — did — find out."

Kincaid said, "Perhaps the manipulator figured once the economy was on a roll, he could set the numbers back. I don't believe it myself, but I know people who think that way."

The President turned to Doctrow. "Would that work?"

Doctrow answered with one word. "No."

Kincaid raised his eyebrows. "Wow. I've never heard you give a one word answer."

"Maybe, once upon a time before computers, you could pull that off. Back then, economic reports were more a political tool than a financial necessity. Today, technicians at tens of thousands of terminals around the world are waiting for those numbers to plug into their predictive programs. Those reports move money within minutes, sometimes seconds, of their release. That's why we're seeing this hellish spiral. The algorithms behind programmed trading are highly optimized. I know; I've spent most of my life making sure they're the best. If you feed in bad data, then it is a near certainty that results will be suboptimal. That is exactly what we have now; only the deterioration is not linear after a while. It accelerates. In a few weeks or months, it will be impossible to jig the numbers enough to mask reality."

The Secret Service agent handed the President a phone. "Senator Kreis, sir."

The President looked at Kincaid. "He wants to reschedule our meeting on the tax cut. We were going to talk about it this morning."

"Yes, sir, I remember. Seems like a long time ago."

Doctrow walked over to President Miller. "Mr. President," he said soberly, "there isn't going to be any tax cut."

The President cocked his head. "None?"

Kincaid joined the conversation. "Brian has always been a tax cut addict. If he says no, he has good reason."

The President spoke into his phone. "David, there's been a development. We're going to be putting off this legislation for …" He looked at Doctrow.

Doctrow frowned and shook his head.

"… for the foreseeable future. … No, it's not just the Gulf. We've got more troubles brewing. Hold on." The President cupped his hand over the receiver. "How long until we have something definitive, something we can discuss with the Senator in private?"

Doctrow turned to Kathy and Sarah. "Two hours?"

They nodded.

Sarah added, "And half an hour to write it up."

The President returned to his phone. "Senator, let's have dinner this evening. Just you, me, and some of my economist folks. There's not going to be a tax cut. … I seem worried? No, try 'terrified.' I'll see you tonight."

He closed his phone and turned to Kincaid. "OK, it's general quarters. Get that fellow we talked to earlier." The President snapped his fingers trying to remember the name.

"Scott Thomas," Kathy offered.

"Yes, him. He seems to be one person we know who understands what happened from the inside."

"Yes, sir. I've got Federal Marshal protection for him. He should be on his way over now. We'll meet in my office." Kincaid turned to the others. "Are we good to go?"

"I'll get printouts of these screens, particularly graphs. It'll take me about fifteen minutes." Kathy turned to her consoles and began organizing her printouts.

Tracy rose as the group entered Kincaid's outer office. "Mr. President."

Miller nodded. "Ms. Atwood. Please let Abigail know where I am. Tell her to put everything on hold for at least half an hour."

"Yes, Mr. President." Tracey picked up her phone.

The Secret Service agent remained in the outer office. Once inside the office, Kincaid closed the door and took his seat. Sarah leaned against the wall next to the door. Doctrow had brought a small sheaf of papers that he spread out along Kincaid's desk. The President watched, detached.

"Doctor Doctrow. Hmm. That doesn't sound right, does it? Professor Doctrow, what do you think, tentatively, we should do?"

Doctrow frowned. Before replying, he scanned the papers he'd just laid out. "Well," he sighed, "you're going to have to release real numbers. But you surely must know that this release may be one of the largest market shocks … in history."

"Yes, that's got to be true," Miller agreed, glumly.

"The market's natural impulse will be to react to this news immediately. There will be mistakes. Big mistakes. Professionals need time to digest the implications. They need to take measured corrective steps. Plus, you're dealing simultaneously with the Gulf crisis with all of its direct and indirect market impacts. Not to mention a public service strike. Mr. President, I'd suggest a suspension of trading and perhaps banking restrictions at the same time you announce the revised data."

"True. But the Gulf crisis had been anticipated by a lot of good people deep inside the Pentagon and CIA. For that situation we have a pretty well defined plan. Just pray that things go well this evening over there." The President turned to Doctrow. "We're going to get you an emergency top clearance. Obviously everything you hear may be considered extremely sensitive. Understood?"

Doctrow nodded.

"He's cleared for ridiculous, sir. I've known him most of my life. With what we've got on each other, it would be mutually assured destruction."

Doctrow nodded again, grinning.

Sarah jumped as Kincaid's intercom emitted an angry series of buzzes.

Tracey's voice sounded with urgency. "Mr. Kincaid, the front gate advised that Mr. Bailey is inbound at high velocity, and he doesn't look happy."

Everyone in the room looked at each other.

"How the hell …?" The President looked at Kincaid.

"I'd guess Senator Kreis called him to find out what he could about our change on the tax cut. It wouldn't take long to find out that his blackout of my office had been lifted."

Sarah began chewing on her thumbnail.

The President put his hands on his hips. "He's up to his eyeballs in this, isn't he?"

Kincaid placed his hands on his desk. "We'll know in less than two minutes."

"I shouldn't be here for this." The President looked around for a way out.

"Sorry, sir. That's your only exit. He's probably heading down the steps now."

"Damn!"

"You can try my closet, sir. Not very dignified, but that's all I can think of at the moment."

The President shook his head as he opened the door on Kincaid's walk-in closet and shut himself inside. He could hear Vice President Bailey arguing with Tracey and the Secret Service agent as the closet door closed. Doctrow stepped back from Kincaid's desk.

"You can't go in there right now, sir. There's a private meeting …"

Kincaid turned to Sarah and pointed to her right. "Step back now."

As Sarah jumped to her right, the door exploded open, doorknob smashing into the wall where Sarah had been standing, breaking loose a chunk of plaster.

The Vice President focused on Kincaid. His face was red, his upper lip curled. He shouted at Kincaid, "You're going down, you god-damned fucker! You have broken so many laws, you're going to be put away forever!"

Kincaid calmly leaned back in his chair and folded his arms. "How long have you been faking the economic data?"

"You don't ask me questions, mister. You have breached security at the highest level. You have put this country in jeopardy."

"How long have you been faking the economic data? There's a whole conference of economists across the mall who know about it now. Your game is over."

"You have no idea what you're talking about, any more than those geeks do."

"What are you getting out of it? Was President Miller in on this?"

Bailey laughed as he sneered. "Ha! He has neither the imagination nor the balls to develop a program of this brilliance."

"How long have you been faking the economic data?"

"Are you retarded?" Bailey screamed.

The President quietly opened the closet door behind the Vice President. Kincaid looked Vice President Bailey in the eye. "Why did you do it?"

"The economy operates on faith. I gave them news they wanted and they've responded appropriately and well."

"That is a lie, sir!" Doctrow interrupted. "The economy operates on trust, not faith, but only so long as the information works."

"Who the hell are you?"

"Brian Doctrow, sir."

"Well, Bri, you can keep your prissy nit picking to yourself. You're probably up to your eyeballs in this breach, too."

"You monster. You hideous monster." President Miller's voice seethed, barely under control. His cheeks twitched in anger.

The Vice President spun around, stunned, to face the voice at his back. "Mr. President."

"Did you think … did you really think you could get away with this?"

"Sir, our program is working. Look at the markets. We've enjoyed one of the longest and largest periods of growth in the republic's history."

The President slashed the air with his arm. "Cut the crap, Mr. Bailey. This isn't one of your Chamber of Commerce booster crowds. The reason these people are here …" He motioned towards Sarah and Doctrow. "… is that our economy is collapsing around us."

"Sir, markets are not collapsing. They are at an all time high."

The President clasped his face with both hands and spoke slowly, deliberately. "But … it's … not … real. It's an illusion. It's an illusion built on reports that are fiction, reports issued under our authority, in my name. Millions of people are losing their jobs, their homes, their retirements."

Bailey answered quickly. "The right people are doing fine."

The room became deathly quiet.

The President finally spoke, "The 'right people'?"

The Vice President looked around. "Those who actually make this country work — who pay wages, take risks, create the capital on which we depend."

Silence returned.

The President walked around Kincaid's desk as his Chief of Staff moved his chair back. The President opened the drawer and drew out a piece of paper and a pen.

Sarah moved toward the open door to get a view of the proceedings.

The President placed the paper on the desk and the pen on the paper. He put his forefinger on the paper and faced the Vice President. "You will resign the Vice-Presidency effective immediately. Write the letter. We have witnesses."

"Sir?"

"It's over. You have abused your office as no one else in this country's history has ever done. You have trampled the sacred trust to which you pledged yourself. You will resign."

"No, sir." The Vice President seemed incredulous.

"Jim, this isn't a suggestion or request. This is an order."

Bailey put his hands out in front of him, "No, sir. You can't order me to do that. I will not resign."

"Then you will be impeached. I assure you that won't take long."

"I will fight it. And it will be ugly. And you will all go down in the process."

"Don't you threaten me. I'm making this easy for you. Write the damned letter."

"No. Now, if you'll excuse me, I have a schedule to keep." The Vice President turned around to leave.

Sarah still stood in the doorway, blocking his quick exit. He approached, expecting her to step aside. She didn't move, seeming frozen. He glared at her. She frowned in return and folded her arms. He seemed at last to recognize her. Scowling, he walked around her, moving out into the passageway.

The President turned to Kincaid, his voice unsteady. "David, tell me this isn't as bad as it seems."

"Let me get back to you on that, sir."

The President asked, "Should we have him arrested?"

"Sorry, sir. That's not my area. We're going to be calling Justice and a whole lot of other people in a few minutes. Probably we should leave proceedings to them. It's not like he has anywhere to go. Right now we've got three major crises each of which would challenge any administration. We need a lot more horsepower."

"Right. Senator Kreis isn't going to have much appetite once I hit him with all this." The President spoke to Doctrow and Sarah. "Please join us for dinner. I won't have time for you to brief me enough to talk intelligently to the Senator."

"Yes, sir."

Again the President spoke to Doctrow. "Professor, you seem to have a handle on this. Would you please stay with us a while? I'll set up an office for you with access to whatever you need."

"Yes, of course, sir." Brian bowed.

"Mr. Kincaid, I'm going over to the situation room to monitor that show. When you have a rough draft, bring it over. Call in whomever you need for our meeting with Kreis."

Kincaid nodded as the President prepared to leave.

The President turned around in the doorway. "We need to revoke Mr.

Bailey's access to just about everything. That's not going to be easy, since he's still Vice President."

"I'll do whatever I can, sir. Tracey and Abigail will work up some authorization for you to sign."

The President left.

Kincaid turned to Doctrow. "Well, roomie, you really walked into a hornets' nest. I hope you still have that gift for solving problems in clever ways."

Doctrow looked grim. "This is going to be rough, David. Everything I've learned over all these years tells me this is going to be a really bad ride." He began gathering his papers from Kincaid's desk as Kathy entered.

"What happened?" She asked, looking around the room.

Doctrow joined her and they turned around, making their way out. "I'll explain back in your office."

Kincaid and Sarah were alone. Her arms were still folded, but seemed more tightly wrapped, as if she were cold.

"Are you OK?" Kincaid asked.

"I'm not sure, sir. That was pretty intense."

Kincaid nodded as he motioned for her to walk along. "That it was. But you've got a great story to tell your grandchildren about that day you held your ground and faced down the Vice President of the United States."

They walked quietly for a time.

As the two reached Sarah's desk, she spoke. "I'm still shaking."

Kincaid put his hand on her shoulder. "Me, too."

* * *

Wednesday, May 21, 2014, 7:15 p.m.

Senator Kreis stared at the collection of charts before him on the table. His half eaten supper had drifted steadily farther away from him on the table until he nodded to a server to remove it. "Still, how can it have gone on this long? How could Vice President Bailey have scammed the entire United States economic system for over a year?"

"He didn't scam the entire system, Senator," The President repeated his answer to the Senator's questions. "He manipulated a very small number of figures in ways that were very difficult to track."

"But Mr. President, evidence was all around us in abundance. Emergency programs, state unemployment reports. Didn't your people track these things?" Kreis waved his hand toward the end of the table where the economists sat.

Kathy spoke, her voice on edge. "Senator, we have indeed been tracking those programs and reports for almost six months. The biggest problem was that those numbers we were getting from states were at complete odds with both federal reports and Wall Street. Your Congressional Budget Office had the same big numbers we had."

"But surely you had access to the real numbers." His face seemed almost pained.

"No, sir, we did not. And that is at the core of this crisis. Raw data were classified such that we were denied access until a few hours ago. Classified by Mr. Bailey, sir," Kathy replied.

"Who allowed him to accumulate so much power that he was able to override the President's own staff?"

Kathy grasped the table's edge. "With all due respect, sir, you did, in part. The Economic Security Protection Act of 2012 directed that the Vice President be responsible for preventing economic sabotage by keeping sensitive information from falling into the hands of those who would do us economic harm. The Act *specified* that the Vice President define which data were deemed worthy of protection. You were one of sixty-four co-sponsors, Senator."

Senator Kreis paused, frowning. "Right. Sorry. I didn't mean to belittle your work. We'd still be wondering what the hell was going on if you hadn't unraveled this. I apologize."

Kathy released the table and folded her hands in front of her. "Professor Doctrow and his colleagues deserve a lot of the credit. His research is what pinpointed exactly where we needed to look, and he's given us critical guidance in the last few hours by constructing a more lucid picture of where we are."

Senator Kreis turned and addressed Speaker Pelosi and the President. "What's done is done. Where do we go first from here?"

A military officer entered the dining room and handed the President a single sheet of paper. Everyone remained silent as he read.

The President nodded and handed the paper back to the officer. "Have Ms. Conklin prepare a press release. Have her run it by Secretary Zink and Secretary Banks."

"Yes, sir," the officer replied and left the dining room.

The President returned to the discussion. "Operation Eastern Lights has concluded. All embassy personnel and nationals who had taken refuge in the embassy were safely extracted. As planned, our pyrotechnics drew most armed fighters to the East. Unfortunately, a number of fighters didn't take our bait. They fired on our aircraft and on our troops, who returned fire. Three American soldiers were killed, seven wounded. An indeterminate number of opposing fighters in Riyadh were killed, at least forty. Within an hour, the embassy was overrun and attackers attempted to set it ablaze. Embassy staff had already destroyed all embassy documents over the last three days, so there was no compromise of intelligence."

After a moment of contemplation, the President returned to matters at hand. "Now, Senator and Madame Speaker, we need the following from you quickly. We've revoked as many authorizations as we are able to from

Vice President Bailey. We have a list of remaining powers that we can't override, so we need emergency legislation." He handed Kreis and Pelosi stapled two-page lists. "How quickly might you be able to get it?"

Kreis looked at Pelosi for a moment. "Probably noon tomorrow at the earliest." He turned to the President. "How many people know about this right now? We're going to try to do the deauthorization behind closed doors, but we're talking about over six hundred people who love to go before cameras. By noon tomorrow this town's going to be a three-ring circus. And by the look on your face, bad news is still coming."

President Miller nodded. "I ordered Vice President Bailey to resign. He refused. Attorney General Jakubowski has compiled a list of charges from what we already know, and that list is growing as we discover more. We anticipate arresting Bailey tomorrow morning. That should contribute enormously to the circus atmosphere. You'll want to brush up on Article One. I've already told him that his impeachment would be swift if he refused to resign, but he's determined to make that as ugly as possible."

Kreis looked at Kincaid. "David, this is the time for us to know about any skeletons in your closet. The people aren't in a charitable mood to begin with. Once all this hits the media, your maneuvering room will be extremely limited."

Miller nodded, "I know, Senator. The only way out of this is to keep it open, keep it truthful. I'm very sure we don't have any skeletons, but that will hardly matter if Mr. Bailey is committed to a path of destruction. We're planning an open-ended press briefing as soon as he's arrested. We hope that he can be taken someplace on the west side of town for formal charges. That will reduce somewhat the mob scene at the Capitol."

Pelosi looked down the list of charges and then turned to the Attorney General. "Ruth, I presume you have someone to flesh out this list."

Jakubowski replied, "Absolutely, Madame Speaker. Our senior staff are working around the clock. Expect our initial report to weigh in at several thousand pages. Our primary witness is in protective custody and has provided an enormous number of tie-ins. The most straightforward and best documented offenses would include falsifications of official reports."

"Protective custody?" Kreis inquired.

Kincaid answered, "As soon as we had the first firm data, we began finding associations with a number of high-powered shadow organizations. Not organized crime, but security companies with high capacities for violence. We thought it best to protect our source. By the time that our marshals arrived at Mr. Thomas's home, security from Brisbane Technologies was trying to 'talk' to him."

"Brisbane? The defense contractor?" Pelosi asked.

Jakubowski nodded. "They appear to have ties to the College Park shooting and Windham Trust as well. Dr. Tyler's research has begun to reveal a web tying these together."

The Speaker turned to Sarah. "What do we know about this?"

Sarah quickly swallowed her bite of steak and wiped her mouth. "Madam Speaker, we've had good data and stronger research programs for only a little while, but we find Windham Trust consistently near the center of these incidents. Brisbane Technologies is one company favored by the Trust and is the company behind the scenes in those call center automations."

The Speaker squinted, looking at Sarah. "And they were a party to a privacy invasion involving you, if I recall."

Sarah looked at Kincaid, who smiled and nodded. "Yes, Ma'am, so it would appear. They passed surveillance video to Reverend Richards. We've since discovered a number of links between Windham Trust and his Crusade for Moral Clarity organization as well."

"And the Vice President's connections to Windham?"

"Uncertain, Ma'am. A recently acquired member list did not have his name on it, and we have no documentation linking the Vice President directly to the Trust."

"But I can tell you think there's intense involvement."

Sarah sighed. "My gut tells me yes, but there are no data at present to confirm that."

"Good enough. Thank you." Pelosi returned to Jakubowski. "I'll have my staff get together with yours. I think we can strip him of his authorizations by noon tomorrow — maybe temporarily if there's any pushback, but we should have them removed by noon. I need to talk to minority and majority leaders on a bill of impeachment, but we'll send it to Senator Kreis for trial as soon as possible. It'll help if you have a really clean, prioritized list to give to my people so they can start. As soon as the press gets wind of this, though, we've got to be ready to move, and move in a really crowded environment."

"Understood." The Attorney General finished taking notes.

"President Miller," Senator Kreis said, recovering a little from his shocked gaze, "when you told me to put the tax cut on hold, I expected some sort of bargaining on another bill. In my wildest nightmares, I couldn't have envisioned this. You're caught in a real riptide here. But I'm pledging to you all the support you need."

"Thanks, David. That means a lot to all of us."

"And from the House as well, Mr. President. We'll be ready to move faster than we've done in two centuries."

"Thank you, Nancy, I appreciate it. OK, everyone here has an overwhelming number of priority-one missions to accomplish. Let's move out and try to make it through tomorrow."

The dining room filled with murmurs of plans and schedules. Players slowly dispersed to their respective offices.

David Kincaid turned to Peter. "Let's put some coffee on. It's going to be a long night. You have any of that high-test Kona coffee left?"

Peter grinned. "Yes, sir, I'm pretty sure I do. You're the only one who drinks it.

* * *

Jack sat on the couch and continued massaging his wrist. "Probably shouldn't have closed it so tight."

Deputy Reese had called for transport of Ed's body to the morgue. He looked out of the window at approaching dawn, and then turned to Laura. "Things are really backed up. There'll be someone out later this morning for his body. And someone from Victim's Assistance will contact you about cleaning services and counseling."

Laura watched Jack. "I'm not a victim."

Deputy Reese dropped his head. "That's what we call our unit. We don't have an 'Almost Victim's Assistance.'"

Charlie was eating a breakfast sandwich he had made. "She's like that. Just pretend you're agreeing with her and do what you have to do. I find that works pretty well." He looked at Laura, returning her glare. "In fairness, she's usually right. She's much better organized. And did I mention fearless?"

Jack nodded.

The Garrettes' home phone rang. Charlie looked at his watch. "Six-thirty. Do people usually call that early around here?"

Laura tilted her head back. "No, of course not. And I don't want to talk to anyone right now. Answer it, please."

"OK." Charlie picked up the phone and spoke, "Hello. Garrette."

Laura brought her head forward, clasping it with both hands. "He's like that. I don't even know if I'll ever figure him out. I'm not sure I want to. I'm afraid of what I might find."

Charlie continued his banter. "Say again? … Why? … No, I think I should know … Dr. James Garrette. … I don't think that would be a good idea. … Hello? Hello?" He put down the phone and turned to Laura and Jack. "We've got to go. Grab daddy's paperwork. Now."

Laura shook her head vigorously. "What? What are you talking about? I'm not going anywhere. Who was that?"

"Our early morning caller said, 'WT says sell it all.' When I challenged him, I'm guessing my Daddy impersonation fell short. He said, 'Stay right there. We're coming over.' I figure this would be one of those times when it's good to be disobedient."

Laura raised both hands. "Just hold on, Charlie. Who was it?"

Charlie leaned over, speaking slowly. "Our good friend Henderson. I've come to know and love that voice."

Laura dropped her hands. "Oh, shit, you're right. I'll get my keys. We definitely don't want to be here alone with him and his buds."

"No, Jack's driving. Henderson and his posse would certainly recognize your little sports car."

"It's not a sports car. Where are we going?"

Charlie shrugged. "Somewhere nearby. Tibet, maybe." He turned to Reese. "Deputy, I think it would be good for you to not be here as well."

"I'm armed. I think I'll be OK. It sounds like a crime is about to be committed."

"Very brave, Deputy Reese," Charlie replied. "I'll be sure to let your widow know. Henderson said *we*. If *we* includes Hercules, they're way more armed and, with all due respect, better and quicker at using their weapons than you are. If you'll recall, it was our brief encounter with them way back before everything turned to crap that left not one but two deputies with broken collar bones and set off the current spiral into devastation."

"Got it. I'll pull back and call in lots of reinforcements — if there are any."

Charlie turned to Jack. "OK, debate master, time to go. Fly casual."

As Charlie, Laura, and Jack headed toward the kitchen door, Charlie stopped at the table where Reese had been writing his report and picked up Jack's pistol.

"Hey!" Reese called.

"Sorry, Alex, we may really need this. It's not very powerful, but I'm told Jack is very accurate. You can charge me when this is all over. You'd better get moving."

They got into Jack's car, Charlie in front, Laura in back.

Charlie rubbed his chin. "Head into downtown Silver Spring, Jack."

"What's there?"

"A Denny's. I didn't finish my breakfast."

"Charlie," Laura groaned from the back seat as they turned the corner onto the main road.

"Laura, down. It's Henderson's van. And it looks like three or four more. Jack, just drive normally. He doesn't know you."

Charlie and Laura kept down for several blocks.

Charlie mused aloud. "I suppose he was telling your daddy to sell all Windham Trust stock. Wonder what that's about."

20 FOX HUNT

Thursday, May 22, 2014

Kincaid pinched the bridge of his nose, stretched his arms, and looked at his clock. Nine-fifty-one. He' been working with a single brief break for breakfast since 4 a.m. reviewing legal opinions and the torrent of data Kathy, Sarah, and Brian had generated between last night's meeting and early morning. Agents would move in on Vice President Bailey presently.

Early word from Capitol Hill was not encouraging, far more rancorous than expected. To everyone's amazement, word of the impending political earthquakes had not yet leaked. As far as Kincaid could tell, that alone remained on script. Though Speaker Pelosi may have achieved an agreement for temporary suspension of Vice President Bailey's authorities half an hour ago, he had not received word of a vote.

Kincaid had set up a working space in their television-lined conference room. He muted the sound so that he could work. Early morning news' main story detailed the embassy's fall in Riyadh. Congressional representatives interviewed going behind closed doors pronounced expected harsh judgments. Network news featured excerpts of Cameron's Saudi release, bland by intention. What little clamor generated thus far centered on the identities of casualties. Only NPR gave any significant airtime to the impending supply chain disruptions.

Senator Kreis postponed hearings on the tax cut bill "out of respect for our brave men and women risking their lives in the Gulf." He would await Bailey's arrest before tabling that bill. Two floors above, the economics team members had begun meeting on a coordinated response about an hour and a half before. Analysts and deputy assistant secretaries of Treasury and Justice had been trickling into the Executive Office Building, and word was that it had become crowded.

Peter returned from the team meeting with a sheaf of papers and a fresh carafe of coffee that he placed beside Kincaid's work.

"Thanks, Peter. I hope that new pile is going to tell me that things are going to be all right and that we overestimated the impact."

"Sorry, Mr. Kincaid."

Kincaid managed a trace of a grin. "C'mon, you promised."

"No, sir, not a chance." Peter shook his head.

Kincaid looked at his new stack of papers. "I don't suppose you could give me an executive summary of what's in there?"

"Upstairs, they say we need to 'fess up as soon as possible, no later than early afternoon. Their big debate is over whether to close the stock markets and banks simultaneously with our announcement and, if so, for how long. They're still developing models predicting what will happen after all is revealed. Best guesses are this crash will range from really bad to devastating. The only thing they had agreed on when I left is that there is going to be a crash and that every delay will make it worse."

Kincaid pulled papers in front of him. He leaned back in his chair and stared ahead.

Peter answered when the phone rang. "Yes, sir, he's here. Certainly, Mr. President."

Peter brought the phone over to Kincaid. "It's big boss, and he sounds particularly upset."

"Yes, sir?" Kincaid answered.

President Miller sputtered, "We've got a situation. Damn! I just got off the phone with Bob Matthews at Treasury. It's unbelievably bad. Get your … damn — I can't think … your money people … your economics people. Get over to the situation room. No, that's too crowded, and we need more connections. Head to the war room. I'll be down as soon as I get my waiting room cleared here." He hung up.

Kincaid looked at the receiver for a moment. "OK, Peter, let's go get some of our troops. We've got a situation."

"What?"

"I have no idea. He was short on specifics. He said to gather, I presume, our core economics team in the war room."

"Uh oh."

They bypassed the elevator and trotted up four floors. Kincaid breathed heavily. "I need to get more exercise."

Sounds of arguments guided them to their destination. They opened the door. "Please forgive our intrusion. Kathy, Brian, Sarah …" He looked around for others. "… Anna. With me, please. Everyone else, keep up your great work — quickly."

All four joined him in the hallway.

"Make sure you have your badge and an additional photo ID. I'll wait here."

Anna and Sarah ran to their desks to retrieve their driver's licenses.

Kathy turned to Peter. "Anything we need to know?"

"Not sure. Something really bad has come up, and we're heading way downstairs."

Anna and Sarah returned, and their party of six headed to an indistinct elevator in an obscure corridor. This elevator bore no up or down buttons, only a keypad.

Sarah whispered to Kathy, "Where are we going?"

Kathy held up a finger for Sarah to wait as Kincaid punched in a series of numbers. In a few seconds they boarded what looked like a freight elevator.

"We're heading to the war room."

Sarah's eyes grew wide. "War? Have we declared war on someone?"

Kathy glanced around. "I don't think so. If we were going to war, Matt would be here."

Sarah nodded, apparently relieved.

Four or five floors below where most business was conducted, the doors opened to a short corridor illuminated by shielded lights. Two Marines were posted at the far end. They were not those friendly, helpful guardians from above. These Marines were dressed in camouflage fatigues. One carried a rifle. They examined each ID and badge, comparing pictures with each bearer and judging signatures on cards with signatures on the sign-in sheet. Once they were satisfied with all six visitors, the armed sergeant entered code into a shielded box, and the door ahead of them opened with a loud clank.

Kincaid led into the room. Its walls were solid banks of monitors. Large world maps shone with cryptic notations, lines, and symbols. Serious-looking individuals, half of them uniformed military, manned forty or so consoles.

A Naval officer approached Kincaid. "Mr. Kincaid, Commander Lowe, Officer of the Deck. Have you been briefed, sir?"

Kincaid shook his head. "No, Commander, the President didn't communicate anything other than a sense of urgency."

Commander Lowe turned to a nearby petty officer. "Get Mr. Matthews on the line."

Kincaid turned to Commander Lowe. "Can you put him on speaker phone? We all need to get up to speed as fast as possible."

Commander Lowe nodded to the petty officer, and they could hear a phone ringing.

"Bob Matthews."

"Bob, David Kincaid here. I understand we have a situation. President Miller was sketchy on details."

"Yes, sir, about three hours ago, our DOTS network picked up a strong pattern of potential criminal activity."

Kincaid turned to Kathy.

"Data Observation and Telecommunications Synthesis. It's a series of programs we developed to detect patterns of financial transactions consistent with major fraud or sabotage. It can spot patterns within billions of transactions and flag them."

Doctrow turned to Kathy. "You've actually implemented that? I've only known it as a theoretical construct."

Kathy nodded.

Kincaid returned to Matthews. "So who or what's involved?"

"A series of large wire transfers to various Chinese banks from a cluster of U.S. accounts, initially belonging to Windham Trust, tripped our program. Once alerted, DOTS narrowed in on these accounts. About two hours ago we started seeing huge transfer attempts from Treasury funds to the same Chinese banks through Windham accounts."

"Attempts?"

"We have circuit breakers in our transfer programs to tell suspect sending accounts that transfers were processing, while in fact they're on hold until each transfer is manually verified as legitimate. Suspect receiving accounts get a message that their transfer is pending. That keeps connections open and often stops them from shutting down. It's how we've crunched a lot of drug money flow."

"How much money are we talking about, Bob?"

"It's billions with a 'b.'"

Kincaid let out a whistle. "I can't imagine, but any chance these are legitimate transfers?"

"No way, sir. I've seen a few accounts. National Parks maintenance budget, Agriculture food stamp funding, VA, that sort of thing. Big ticket items and nothing that has any business going into private Chinese bank accounts."

Kincaid turned to his staff. Doctrow's face registered nothing short of shock. "Bob, could this be hackers? Organized sabotage?"

"We checked that first, sir. There's no evidence of probing on these accounts prior to transfer initiation. Transaction security codes were entered systematically and correctly from time zero."

Kincaid bowed his head. "And who would have access to that broad a range of budget codes?"

After a short pause, Bob Matthews spoke, fatigue in his voice. "The only place where all that information exists in one place is in the White House Budget Office controlled by Vice President Bailey, sir."

The clank of heavy door announced the President's arrival flanked by senior officers from Treasury and Justice.

"What have we got, David?"

"There's a massive theft attempt underway, Mr. President. Billions of dollars from all over the federal government are being requested for transfer into a bunch of private accounts bound for China."

"Bailey?"

"That hasn't been confirmed, sir, but all evidence is pointing in his direction."

"I think we can drop polite pretense, David. As I left my office, I ordered his residence stormed. They should have him …"

The Officer of the Deck interrupted. "Mr. President, you have an urgent call from the FBI Director."

The President took the phone. "Yeah?" His face grew ashen. "What do you mean 'not there'? Where …? What?" He stood, listening. "No, I'll take it from here. Be ready at Andrews when he's back." President Miller handed the phone back to Commander Lowe and looked at Kincaid. "He's in Portland, Oregon, for a campaign visit. Portland. Oregon."

The President called to Commander Lowe, "Get me Vice President Bailey. Put it on speaker."

"Yes, Mr. President."

After several rings, a voice answered. "Vice President's detail, agent Stewart."

The President looked surprised. "Agent Stewart, this is President Miller. I need to talk to Vice President Bailey."

"I'm sorry, sir. He's returned to Air Force Two. He went with his private security and left us stranded here in Portland. He said he had to return to Washington urgently."

"Why private security?"

"I don't know, sir. He wouldn't say. We reported it up the chain of command. It's strange, Mr. President. He used a private helicopter rather than the armored limo."

"Did he say what was so urgent?"

"No, sir, but he seemed in an awful hurry. That's why I'm talking to you on his phone. He grabbed my jacket. I've got his phone, and he's got mine."

"Right. Hang on in Portland, Agent Stewart. We'll get you and your people back as soon as we're able."

"Yes, sir, Mr. President."

President Miller took a deep breath. "Officer of the Deck, contact Air Force Two and instruct them to hold at the end of the runway at Andrews when they return and await further instructions."

"Yes, Mr. President." Lowe snapped his fingers, and an Air Force major began the call to the Vice President's plane.

The President motioned for the others to gather around him. "All right, let's review where we are. We've caught most transfers and have them in limbo. We've got the Vice President localized on Air Force Two and are prepared to take him into custody when he arrives. Right?"

The two civilians accompanying the President nodded.

He turned to Kincaid. "Speaker Pelosi called me to let me know they've approved the suspension of his authorities, and I've already begun the implementation. She hasn't started the impeachment process yet and she doesn't know about this latest. The press are having a field day over the closed door session, but haven't gotten the story so far."

The Major shouted, bypassing the Officer of the Deck. "Sir, Air Force Two says the Vice President has not turned up, nor had he informed the pilot that they were returning. When they try to raise him, they just get the security detachment."

The President surveyed the wall of maps. "Where the hell is he? Can they find his helicopter?"

A civilian technician approached the President. "There are hundreds of craft in the air, Mr. President. We don't know the type, or configuration, or flight path. We don't have anything to go on."

"What about his phone? Can we track that?"

The civilian shook his head. "No, sir, he has the same kind as yours. It's designed to be cloaked so that it can't be used as a targeting device."

"Damn."

Anna spoke up, instinctively raising her hand. "Mr. President, the Vice President's phone is with Agent Stewart. The Vice President has Stewart's phone. Can we track that?"

Miller's face brightened. "Thank you. Of course. It might be easiest to just call him on that phone and order him to surrender."

Peter looked to Kincaid, who nodded and addressed the President. "Sir, at this point, he probably doesn't realize he's trackable. If you call him, he'll shut it down and might evade our search."

The Officer of the Deck had followed their conversation, obtained Stewart's phone address, and passed the information on.

"Bingo, sir." An army master sergeant called from a console several rows over. "We have a light on a cell tower in the Bay area."

The President scowled. "San Francisco Bay?"

"Yes, sir, I'm localizing it and putting it up on screen G-87."

Commander Lowe pointed to a particular screen that displayed a flashing circle that encompassed much of the southern end of San Francisco Bay. Another two circles appeared in a moment, and the flashing circle shrank.

"North of San Mateo, sir."

The process repeated twice more, and the master sergeant adjusted the scale of the map.

"Got it, sir. That's as good as it gets for now. SFO, International

Terminal, midway out concourse G."

The President folded his arms. "He's making a run for it. Stop him."

Lowe replied, "Yes, sir, we're on it. Agent Stewart called in again. He says he got some kind of coded message for the Vice President: 'WT is dead.' When the caller realized it wasn't Vice President Bailey, he hung up."

Sarah talked to herself. "WT. WT. WT. Oh, shit, Mr. President. Walter Thomas Bailey founded Windham Trust — WT. Vice President Bailey isn't just an investor. He himself *is* Windham Trust."

The President shook his head. "Well, that explains their trying to funnel the money through the Trust. Why China?"

Anna answered, "Mr. President, the Vice President had been our main negotiator in discussions on liberalized trade with China. He's made over a dozen trips to Beijing in the last three years. The talks were reported as not going well, and we still have no open inspections of banks, nor do we have any extradition treaty — for financial or any other kinds of crimes."

Kincaid turned to Lowe. "Is Bob Matthews still on the line?"

Matthews answered through the speakers, "I'm here, David. You guys better not discuss anything I'm not cleared for. This is an open feed."

"Right. We'll try. Listen, do you have any information on the target accounts in China?"

"Just coming in, David. So far, most of them seem to be controlled by higher-ups in the Party. While in name they're public accounts, in fact they're treated like the party officials' private funds. There is one particular account, though, that seems to be getting most of the targeting instructions. We don't know whose that one is. Haven't seen it before."

"Thank you, Bob. I think we've got a pretty good idea who that belongs to."

"Mr. President," the Officer of the Deck interrupted, "we've got SFO tower, Chief Reynolds, on the line." He handed the President a handset. "This line's not on speaker."

"Yes, Chief Reynolds, this is the President. The Vice President of the United States has boarded a plane about half-way out Concourse …" The President swung in Kincaid's direction.

"G," Kincaid answered.

"Concourse G. It's probably a flight bound for Beijing." The President paused. "Shanghai? OK. That still fits. Under no circumstances is that flight to leave, Chief Reynolds."

President Miller paused again, listening as alarm spread across his face.

"Find a way to stop it, Chief. That plane must not get airborne. That's an order."

He turned to the group. "The flight's already pulled away from the gate and is powering up."

* * *

In the control tower of San Francisco International Airport, Tower Chief Reynolds ordered Flight 781 to halt take-off preparations.

The aircraft did not respond. Instead, it increased power to the plane's starboard engine, turning toward the taxiway.

"Damn it, Flight 781, cut your engines and stand down immediately. That's an order."

The plane continued its slow arc as baggage trucks scurried out of its way.

The Chief picked up a handset. "Runway Security, we have a rogue flight, Concourse G, China Airlines Flight 781. Intercept and shut it down." His jaw dropped. "Say again."

He turned to his assistant. "Damn. I don't believe this. Runway Security is on the far side. A major drug bust got underway forty minutes ago. They've got every vehicle over there. There's no time." He watched as the jet lumbered away from the concourse. "But I'll be damned if they think they're slipping away on my watch. Get me ground support."

* * *

"I don't know what happened to the tower. It's tough developing a plan when we're here blind." The President turned to the Officer of the Deck. "Can we get a video feed of what's going on? Satellite image?"

Lowe shook his head. "No, sir, there's no reason we'd be monitoring that area. Satellites with useful imaging capability pass over maybe a couple of times a day. We'll check for the next one, though I don't expect it to be any time soon. We're still trying to get our connection back to the tower. Seems something is blocking our communication."

Sarah's cell phone buzzed in her pocket. She looked down at it. "How does the signal make it all the way down here?" She reached for it, puzzled.

"Repeaters," Kathy replied. "You probably get a better signal down here than topside."

She looked at the name on her Caller ID as the phone continued to buzz.

Kincaid turned to Sarah, frowning. He indicated with a movement of his finger across his throat to terminate the call.

"It's Ben Jacobs, sir."

The discussions stopped. The President turned first in Sarah's direction, then to Kincaid. "He's good, but not *that* good."

Kincaid addressed Sarah, "Answer the call. Don't answer any questions related to this. Be calm — creative ignorance."

She put the phone to her ear and spoke. "Ben Jacobs. How are you? How's our story coming?" She listened for a moment before looking up. "SFO? The airport? I don't know. Why?" She listened again. "Let me ask around the office, Ben."

Sarah cupped her hand over her phone. "Ben's here in Washington, but he had a crew at San Francisco International doing a story on the treaty impasse with Chinese aviation. When airport security shut down Concourse G a little while ago, they trapped his crew on that very concourse. When the crew asked security what was going on, they were told the concourse was being sealed on orders from the President."

Peter spoke up. "Maybe they can patch in their cameras so we can see what's going on."

The President turned to Lowe.

"That would take some time, Mr. President. We don't have any established links. We'd have to do a lot of connecting and transfers."

The President scowled. "Would the network have any auxiliary channels they could broadcast on? Something we could pick up here?"

Sarah turned her attention back to the phone. "I'm checking, Ben. Be patient. … Hey, look, I'm well aware of how busy you are."

Lowe broke in. "Mr. President. We have a call transferred from your office. It's Premier Yuan. He wants to know why we're endangering a Chinese aircraft."

Kincaid shook his head. "Sounds like the Tower Chief came up with something. Better keep the Premier on hold 'til we learn what he did. I've got an idea." He turned to Sarah. "Ask Ben if he can broadcast from Concourse G?"

"What?" The President turned to Kincaid. "Everything will be in the open if he does that."

"Sir, with all due respect, it's all going to come out in the open in the next hour or so anyway."

The President wilted. "Shit!"

Kincaid turned to Sarah and nodded.

Sarah took a deep breath. "Ben, we'd like to see what's going on ourselves. Can you broadcast what your crew sees from the window there? Maybe a Chinese jet?" She ducked her head. "'We' is 'we.' Don't ask. … Uh huh. … Yes, I understand. … Yes, I know. … This may be important — really important. Just a minute." She looked up, cupping the phone again. "He says there's no way the network would let him override their current broadcasts without a damn good reason — his words."

The President flung his arms. "They're in the middle of soaps — stupid mindless soaps."

Kincaid smiled. "Economics, sir. In fairness, he has to have a spectacular reason to break in. Talk to him."

As the President approached Sarah, she said, "Look, Ben, we'd really like that picture. Someone wants to talk to you." She handed her phone to the President.

"Mr. Jacobs, this is President Miller. You seem to have found yourself in the middle of an international crisis — again. There's a jet getting ready for an unauthorized exit from SFO, specifically China Airlines Flight 781. We've lost contact with the tower, and we're getting ready to talk to our Chinese counterparts, and it would be so helpful if we could see what's going on."

Lowe motioned for the President's attention and pointed to a screen to the right of the San Francisco map. The screen received feed from channel 8 and featured a gaudy "Breaking News — Special Report."

"Wow! That was fast! Thank you, Mr. Jacobs." The President handed the phone back to Sarah. He turned to Lowe. "Can we get some sound?"

* * *

"This is Ben Jacobs. You're watching live coverage of a major developing story. You can see in this picture an aircraft, tentatively identified as an Airbus A380 jetliner, China Airlines Flight 781, halted on the taxiway of San Francisco International Airport. Details are vague at this time, though sources indicate that the effort to stop this flight comes from the highest levels of the U.S. government.

"Our film crew with reporter Terry Ross were on the international concourse of the airport as the flight began an unexpected departure. Terry reports that the concourse had been sealed and that the plane tried to make a hasty exit, with jet blast rattling the concourse windows and the jet almost running over a number of service vehicles.

"As you can see, it appears that the jetliner has stopped and that the plane seems to be surrounded by a phalanx of fuel trucks. One can only imagine the consequences of this massive aircraft colliding with thousands of gallons of aviation fuel.

"What you see and what I have just told you are all we know for certain at this time. Many, many questions remain, including:

"Why in this time of rising tensions between the United States and China the United States would be willing to use this level of force at grave risk against what would seem to be a routine commercial flight with hundreds of passengers.

"Why did China Airlines Flight 871 attempt to make an unauthorized exit from San Francisco at enormous risk? What cargo or passengers could be worth triggering a confrontation between the two largest military forces on earth?

"How long have matters been festering till they reached a boiling point this morning?

"Why is there an absence of law enforcement vehicles on the scene?

"We are trying to get answers to these and a host of other questions. Our task has been made all the more difficult by a partial blackout of communications in the vicinity of the airport. We do not have audio from our on-site reporter. The live shots you see are being transmitted by line-of-sight to a receiver well outside the airport.

"We have also begun to receive reports here in Washington of extraordinary developments closer to home. For the past several hours, the Senate and House have been meeting behind locked doors, and access to the Capitol has been severely restricted. The extraordinary timing of these events combined with what appears to be all out civil war erupting in Saudi Arabia suggests the world may be in for some powerful convulsions in the hours and days ahead.

"We have an interview conducted just a few hours ago with Senator David Kreis as he made his way to the Capitol. At the time his answers seemed vague and ambiguous. In light of current developments, we now have context to his answers. The interview is unedited and not of our accustomed quality. We are playing it for you as we have it."

* * *

"Fuel trucks. Clever. Dangerous, but clever. Where the hell are his security people?" the President said as he watched the jetliner surrounded by aviation fuel trucks. The airport feed switched to a shaky, handheld traveling shot on-the-walk questioning of Senator Kreis. The President asked Lowe, "Have we got any communications back with the tower?"

"No, sir. We can't be sure, but we're beginning to suspect some kind of jamming. We got through to FBI and Homeland Security in South Bay, and they're converging on the airport."

As the audio of Senator Kreis's interview continued to play, the video switched back to the long camera shot of the idled jetliner. A long distance camera shot captured shimmering refractions of light behind the plane's engines. Vehicles with red and blue flashing lights joined the fuel trucks. The long focus exaggerated vibrations of the camera as Jacobs's crew panned across the length of the jetliner. The only objects visible were the dark windows of the plane.

"If it weren't for the jamming, I'd say it's time to give the Vice President a call," the President said softly.

"Mr. President," Lowe turned from a handset, "Navy ECWs have located the jamming source and are neutralizing it."

"ECWs?"

"Sorry, sir. Electronic Counter Warfare specialists. They're the ones responsible for survival during an electronic attack. I've got the tower chief back."

"Chief Reynolds? Masterful job stopping that flight."

"Mr. President, I don't know what happened to our comms. Thankfully, someone must have gotten the word to give us a hand. What do you want us to do?"

"Give us a second, Chief." The President turned to Kincaid.

Kincaid folded his arms as he watched the image of the jetliner on screen. "We need to take the Vice President and anyone with him into custody. Mercifully, they stopped the plane on the ground, so we don't have any territorial issues. So long as it's not airborne, we have complete jurisdiction. I'm hoping that he'll leave on his own. We don't want to be seen storming the plane on world-wide television."

"Do you think he'll leave on his own?" the President asked.

"No, not really, unless you're going to offer him some deal — which I don't recommend. Perhaps our best option is to have the Chinese invite his entourage to deplane."

Miller agreed, "Right. Sounds like I should take the call from Premier Yuan. You get the airport people ready to receive the Vice President." The President followed Lowe to a desk with a secure phone and interpreter.

"Chief, this is David Kincaid, Chief of Staff to the President. If you could assist us for a little while longer, we'll try to let you get back to running your airport."

"Thank you, Mr. Kincaid. While it's been an interesting change of pace, normal will be welcome."

"We need to arrest the Vice President. I'm guessing that it would be best to take him into custody there on the taxiway. Do you have a mobile stairway that you can bring up to that plane?"

"Yes, sir, we do. Did I hear right? Did you say to arrest the Vice President? *Our* Vice President?"

"I'm afraid so, Chief. It's a sad, complicated story. We think there may be some other people with him, personal staff or bodyguards. We'll need to take them into custody as well. Any police unit can arrest them. However, the Vice President, because of some of his special duties and privileges needs to be arrested by a federal marshal."

"Problem there, sir. Our security is over on the far side of the airport in a huge drug bust."

Kincaid shook his head. "Why am I not surprised? Is there no federal law enforcement officer in the building?"

The war room fell silent awaiting word from Chief Reynolds.

"I may have, Mr. Kincaid. It's a long shot. Give me a minute."

* * *

Dr. Rob Griesbach shook his head as he surveyed the just-opened package of ornamental ginger plants on the table. A few cents worth of insecticide — even a non-toxic growth regulator — applied a season before could have saved the plants a trip into fumigation. So far, he'd seen seven soft brown scale insects. No telling what else might lurk in the folds of the leaves. A few minutes in the methyl bromide vapors and the insects would be quite dead. So would sixty to eighty percent of the plants. The recipient would not be happy.

Nevertheless, Dr. Griesbach was happy to have caught the invader here at the point of entry. As the chief inspector for the Animal and Plant

Health Inspection Service of the Department of Agriculture, he stood as an unseen warrior protecting the nation's agricultural health from all threats foreign, at least as they passed through San Francisco International Airport. He smiled as he looked above his desk at his then-five-year-old's now-ten-year-old drawing of his father arresting two bulbous aphids. 'You're under arrest,' the balloon read. Today the fifteen-year-old had little regard for his father's occupation.

The phone's ring intruded on his thoughts. "APHIS. Griesbach. How may I help you?"

He listened. "Uh huh. Yes, I passed the certification. Sure. Badge and pistol are in the safe. Why?" He listened further, raising his eyebrows. "Say again?"

* * *

The President returned from his phone call. "I didn't make any progress. He clearly knew the Vice President was aboard, and claims that is his prerogative."

"Did he have anything to say about the money transfers? Is he aware yet that they're frozen?"

"He's a good poker player, David. He denied our request. I explained our position and reiterated our rights. That's where we left things. I think he's probably calling in our ambassador for a dressing down. What's the status out west?"

"You can see, Mr. President, that they've got a mobile stairway up against the door of the Airbus. The Tower Chief found a qualified federal agent — I'll explain that later — and we're ready for capture with backup from about forty state and local officers if the flight crew will just open the door. We'll have federal officers on site as soon as we can get good comms with them."

The President rubbed his jaw. "Unbelievable that it's come to this. History is not going to look kindly on today."

"I think we'll let history take care of itself. Let's see if we can get one person to leave one plane." Kincaid turned to Commander Lowe. "Do we still have Agent Stewart's cell phone signal?"

"Yes, sir. In fact, with continued sampling, we've located the phone about two-thirds of the way back in the plane."

The President nodded. "Put it on speaker and make the call."

The room listened as the distant phone rang once, twice, and a third time before going silent.

The President's face became the picture of disappointment.

"The signal is gone, Mr. President," said Lowe.

"Mr. Kincaid, Ben Jacobs wants to know what's going on," Sarah said.

Kincaid and the President both wore the same grim expressions.

Kincaid said to Sarah, "Take your time. Be sure to tell him exactly what

I say. We have delayed the departure of China Airlines Flight 871 because we believe that the passengers include witnesses to a serious crime. The administration has requested that the flight crew hand over these persons of interest; then the plane will be free to proceed on its scheduled flight. The administration is waiting for the response from the Peoples' Republic of China. No effort has been made nor is any expected to use force to extract the persons of interest, but the flight will remain on the ground until these legal requests are fulfilled." He turned to the President. "Will that do?"

The President smiled at last. "Wow. Did you kiss the Blarney Stone?"

"Speech class, University of North Carolina, a very long time ago." Kincaid nodded to Sarah.

"OK, Ben, do you have something to copy this? … Yeah, great. Would I know that? We don't have that kind of technology here at the office. Here goes. We have delayed the departure of China Airlines Flight 871 because we believe that the passengers include witnesses to a serious crime. … The administration has requested that the flight crew hand over these persons of interest, then the plane will be free to proceed on its scheduled flight. … The administration is waiting for a response from the Peoples' Republic of China. … No effort has been made nor is any expected to use force to extract the persons of interest, but the flight will remain on the ground until these legal requests are fulfilled." She waited. "No, I'm not telling you who the persons of interest are — yet. … Let me check." She looked up from the phone. "He wants to know if that's official and how long we're prepared to hold the craft on the ground."

The President's answer was quick and firm. "As long as it takes. Until the fuel runs out and beyond. Tell him."

"Ben, as long as it takes. Until the fuel runs out and beyond. … Yes, those exact words." She shook her head and addressed the President. "He wants to know who said that, sir."

After an exchange of glances, Kincaid answered. "A very high administration source. And yes, the earlier statement is official." He turned to the representatives from the State Department who had remained in the background. "I presume you're keeping Secretary Zink in the loop and will let me know if there's a problem."

One of the representatives nodded, "Yes, sir."

Sarah smiled. "A very high administration source, Ben. … Yeah, higher than me. Yes, those exact words."

The television coverage on the large screen returned from a commercial break. A red crawl continued across the bottom of the screen: "Special Report. Breaking News. Chinese Airliner grounded in San Francisco in escalating standoff."

The President put his hands on his hips. "Escalating?"

"If you're just joining us, the picture you're seeing is China Airline Flight

871 idling on the taxiway of San Francisco International Airport. Terry Ross and our own crew, who were on the international concourse covering a story when the jetliner made an abrupt and apparently unauthorized departure attempt, are providing the video. As you can see, the plane has been stopped; its progress halted by a collection of fuel trucks and security vehicles from an assortment of federal and local agencies. A set of stairs has been pulled up to the door of the plane, but the door appears to be sealed.

"We have just learned from very high administration sources that the flight will be blocked — and I quote — 'As long as it takes. Until the fuel runs out and beyond.'

"Early reports from Beijing suggest that this standoff on the west coast of the United States is not being well received in China. A statement appearing in the online edition of the Peoples Daily protests what it calls unprecedented interference in Chinese trade and is demanding the immediate and unconditional release of the aircraft. Our inquiries at the State Department have so far been met with 'no comment.' However, the level of activity at the Department suggests this crisis is kicking into high gear.

"How the San Francisco standoff relates to the overthrow of the Saudi royal family and the extraordinary secret proceedings on Capitol Hill remains to be seen. Indications are that there may be a link. A knowledgeable Congressional source has told us that the session is addressing grave issues at the urging of the White House."

The President asked Kincaid, "Are Kreis and Pelosi aware of what's going on here?"

Kincaid turned to Peter.

"I'll get right on it, sir."

As Peter left in search of a secure phone, the President said to Kincaid, "We have to close this up fast. By rights we can hold the plane in position forever." He looked at his watch. "It's already been an hour and a half, on the ground and powered down. That plane could stay sealed up for days. Meanwhile, there are a host of players staking their positions, and we have two or more major crises that individually deserve our full attention. What do we have that Premier Yuan wants enough for us to give it to him without creating a bigger mess?"

Kincaid talked into the air. "Bob Matthews, are you still with us?"

"Still here, David. They've brought in a TV. We're trying to hold meetings, but it's getting pretty distracting. How can we help?"

"At the opening, you said most of the funds were from inappropriate federal accounts. Do you have any more on where they were going?"

"A little bit. Cross-checking some intelligence files, we've identified about half of the accounts including those belonging to most senior party members. The main account, which constitutes about ninety percent of the transfer, is still unidentified. On the outbound side, we've also identified some private funds traveling the same path from some California accounts labeled 'CMC.' They're heading to another unidentified account."

Sarah volunteered, "Crusade for Moral Clarity?"

"Let's try that…" Matthews was quiet for a moment. "Bingo. That saved us some time. It looks like those were separate. Though they're big, normally we wouldn't hold them without more cause."

"Bob, before you unfreeze those, give me a minute; I've got an idea. Tell me this — can you redirect any of these transfers once they're frozen?"

"Sure. It's just a matter of re-labeling the origin or destination accounts. There are negative legal ramifications, to say the least."

"Right." Kincaid turned to the President. "Sir, I think we could make a deal here that would keep things very quiet."

Sarah grinned. "I know what you're thinking."

"Will it work?" Kincaid asked.

Sarah nodded, "Probably."

"Mr. President, if we can get the Premier on the line, I think we should talk. Bob, can you get a list of names and account numbers to Kathy right now?"

"Yes, she'll have it in a minute."

The President stepped back. "David, are we about to do anything illegal?"

"I don't think so. Clumsy, yes, but fixable."

Commander Lowe handed Kincaid a red phone. "The Premier asked for you."

"Mr. Premier. We appreciate your patience in this most grievous matter. You may be unaware that one of our party officials, the Vice President of the United States, has been discovered committing a number of crimes. It would appear that he has tried to flee to your country in an effort to profit from his crimes."

Kincaid stopped and listened to a prolonged response, moving his head side to side. After a while he transferred the phone from one hand to the other.

"Yes, Mr. Premier, we appreciate your proper concerns, and we wish to resolve this unfortunate event as quickly as possible. You may be unaware, sir, that our Vice President attempted to move a great deal of financial resources from our country and laws to what he perceived as a less regulated environment. He has been unsuccessful, Mr. Premier. If you check, you will find that less than ten million dollars has been transmitted. … Yes, I'll wait."

Kincaid relaxed, put his hand over the receiver, and turned to Sarah, grinning. "He's checking. The tone changed very rapidly."

Sarah grinned back. "Well, Chinese *is* a tonal language."

Kincaid shook his head. He straightened up again. "Yes, Mr. Premier. I understand. Apparently the Vice President's plans were not well conceived. He is unable to deliver anything to your country at this point. Well, that's true as long as we are not too busy. With the Vice President on the plane, we can devote our full attention to stopping those transfers. If we shift our attention to arresting the Vice President, I don't think we have the resources to stop the pending transfers destined for an account ending …" — Kincaid looked down at Kathy's most recent notes — "… 2619. Sir?"

Kincaid lowered the phone. "He's consulting his 'diplomatic staff.'" He turned to the air again. "Bob, are there any substantial amounts among the CMC transfers?"

"There's one for forty-three million. That's the biggest of those."

"Then get ready to move those funds to the account ending 2619."

"David, that's —," Matthews began.

President Miller closed his eyes, shaking his head, but said nothing.

"Temporary, Bob. We'll get it replaced before anyone knows what's missing. I'm sure the consequences could be severe, so I'm taking full responsibility. This is my decision. It has to be done. Just hold until I say so."

"Yes, sir, I'm standing by."

"Thank you, Bob."

* * *

Sitting in the black security van amid the whine of jet engines and the pungent smell of aviation exhaust, Rob Griesbach looked ill. "This is bizarre. My total law enforcement training was a two-day course that dealt with drug trafficking issues for the most part."

His companion, a deputy sheriff from San Mateo County, chuckled. "Don't worry. All you need to do is say your lines and step back. There are twenty of us to take it from there. That is, if they ever get this show on the road. Sometimes these things get really drawn out. Couple of months back we had a hostage situation. Guy holed himself up in his girlfriend's apartment for four days. In the end he shot himself. Waste of time. At least he didn't kill her. Listen, if these guys start shooting, just drop to the ground. We'll take them out."

Griesbach looked out his window. "Thanks."

The deputy chuckled, reclined his seat, and pulled his black ball cap over his eyes. "Not a problem."

The crackle of his radio cut short his rest. "All intercept units, take your positions. They're opening the doors."

"Roger," the deputy responded.

Griesbach patted the pistol at his side and took the leather badge case from his pocket. "First time I've used it."

"You'll be fine."

"Currency Act of 1978."

"He won't be able to hear you over the engines. You could just as well tell a dirty joke. What he will notice is the guns and cuffs. Let's go. It's show time."

* * *

The main screen showed the capture party positioning themselves on the stairs. The President turned to Sarah, extending his hand.

"Ben, he wants to talk to you." Sarah handed her phone to the President.

"Mr. Jacobs, I have ordered the arrest of the Vice President of the United States for a variety of crimes that we will detail in the hours ahead. Vice President James Thomas Bailey attempted, without success, to flee our country." He handed the phone back to Sarah and watched the screen with David Kincaid.

* * *

Outside their vehicle, the noise was deafening and the acrid smell of jet fuel overpowering. Griesbach clutched his badge as he ascended the stairs, a strong wind buffeting him all the way. He glanced behind at the two black-clad officers accompanying him and at the first ring of officers at the bottom backed by armed police in a second ring.

Griesbach stopped at the wide platform at the top and waited as the cabin door lurched open. The Vice President emerged from the doorway escorted by stone-faced Chinese handlers and squinted in the brilliant sunlight.

Griesbach held open his badge case. "James Thomas Bailey, you're under arrest for violation of the Currency Act of 1976. You have the right to remain silent. Anything you say can and will be used against you in a court of law. You have the right to have an attorney present during questioning. If you cannot afford an attorney, one will be appointed for you. Do you understand these rights?"

Griesbach looked into the sour face and over the engine noise could just hear the words fuck you. He stepped back as the assembly of law enforcement officers took custody of the men — seven in all — as they emerged. When the last officer had left the platform, Griesbach returned his badge to his pocket, descended the stairs, and climbed into the deputy's van.

* * *

The President turned to Kincaid. "I want him in leg irons."

Kincaid chuckled. "I think we'll leave that to the professionals."

"I'm serious. He should be made an example."

Kincaid watched as Anna shook her head. "Sir, that would be ill advised in the extreme. We're going to have to demonstrate total calm and control as we've never done before. Leg irons would not help that perception."

The screen showed the Vice President's arrest.

Ben Jacobs began his grave announcement. "We have breaking news of historic proportions. President Miller has just announced — and you are witnessing live — the arrest of the Vice President of the United States, James T. Bailey. You're watching the scene at San Francisco International Airport as federal agents are taking the Vice President into custody from China Airlines Flight 871, on which he attempted to flee the country. A number of unidentified fellow passengers appear to be included in the arrests. Beyond these few facts, we are very much in the dark about this shocking turn of events.

"We have been told by the White House that details will be forthcoming in the hours ahead just as a slew of new reports reinforce the magnitude of the upheaval we may be in for —. And this just in: Secretary of the Treasury Deatherage has ordered the closing of the stock exchanges effective immediately. No period of closure has been announced. Treasury has also announced that cross-border monetary exchanges will experience substantial delays in the days ahead. No reason is given.

"And this report just crossed my desk. I almost said, 'and finally,' but events are moving faster than we can report them, so there will certainly be more. The closed session of Congress has adjourned, and senators and representatives are streaming from the chambers. We have confirmed that the Vice President has been stripped of all his government duties earlier this morning. There's no word about impeachment from the Senate, though that will be coming for certain. Stay tuned as we assemble this, the century's biggest story."

The President shook his head. "David, I'm going back to the office. We'll assemble the cabinet. Have Cameron work up a release and schedule my torture session from the press as soon as possible. Treasury's already set things in motion on the markets. I can't hold all this in my head. Have your people close by."

"Yes, Mr. President." Kincaid turned around. "Peter?"

"Yes, Mr. Kincaid?"

"Work with State to see what we're going to have to do to patch up things with Premier Yuan. When you're finished, have IT get up as many circuits as possible in the conference room. The rest of us will meet you there. It's big enough to be our control room for a few days."

"Yes, sir."

The heavy door opened for the President as Kincaid and his party joined him. The President looked down as they walked back through the corridor. "Ironic, isn't it? Jacobs gave me all that grief back in March, and he's in position when it all comes true."

"He's pretty old school, sir. Part luck I supposed, but luck favors the prepared. He did his homework."

The President nodded as they entered the elevator.

Doctrow turned to Kincaid. "David, there are billions and billions of dollars out of place. That means a big chunk of our economy is frozen until we can get funds back into the accounts where they belong."

"That makes sense. I'm sure that's what they're doing over at Treasury."

"I talked to Bob Matthews while you were on the phone. They're doing what they can. Ironically, until security codes get fixed, we have much better access to Treasury's accounts than they do. I'd like to help them if possible."

Kincaid nodded. "Right. Kathy, Sarah, want to give Professor Doctrow a hand?"

Both agreed and exited the elevator with Brian Doctrow at their floor.

Entering their office, Kathy and Sarah sat down at their computers and logged onto the transfer pages. Doctrow spoke with Bob Matthews and relayed instructions for reversing the flow of money.

He put his hand over the receiver. "Mr. Matthews suggests that you copy and paste numbers rather than type them in. It'll be faster, and you're less prone to make a mistake."

As he relayed instructions, they began changing items on their screens.

After twenty minutes Sarah looked over to Kathy. "How many of these are there, anyway?"

Doctrow had continued talking with Matthews, discussing problems that loomed before them. "He says about twenty-two hundred."

"Wow." Sarah returned to her entries for about an hour and then began laughing.

"What?" Kathy leaned back in her chair, rubbing her eyes.

"Last month I applied for a Macy's card, and they told me I didn't have enough credit history. Just now — that last move — on the strength of my typing alone, I transferred more money than Macy's is worth."

Kathy smiled. "Yeah, it is getting a bit surreal. Let's get this finished up. We're about three-quarters through, and we have to start prepping our bosses for their news conference. That's going to be difficult."

21 THE NEW ORDER

Thursday, May 22, 2014

"Wow! That was unexpected." Charlie stared at Jack's car radio. They were parked in shade at the edge of a small park just north of the Washington Beltway.

Laura had been dozing in the back seat between news updates but joined in the discussion. "What are you talking about, Charlie? You've been talking about what a crook Bailey is since before he took office. Don't try to tell me you didn't see this coming."

"Yeah, I suppose, but not this quickly. I mean, really, forty-eight hours ago he was at the top of his game. Now he's in custody." Charlie turned to Jack. "Well, what do you think of that, my fellow ruffian?"

Jack was leaning forward, head resting on the steering wheel. "I'm just the driver."

Charlie chuckled and looked out the passenger window. "Ah, yeah. You go ahead and think that. You just enjoy your view from the edge of the storm surge for now. But don't think you're not going to catch some rain. Henderson and his thugs are employees of Brisbane, which is totally entwined with our beloved soon-to-be-former Veep and his Windham Trust. I'd like to hope the Trust hubbub draws them away from us. But I have a bad feeling about this."

Jack spoke softly into the wheel. "Their employer will be taking heavy fire from half the agencies of the U.S. government. They operate at or beyond the edge of the law. The past three years of lax enforcement have allowed them to build a web of cover and transit routes. Though the markets are shut down, they can move huge sums out of the U.S. as long as the telecommunications infrastructure remains intact. And they have a lot of incentive to destroy a great deal of paperwork. Everything is set up for a long period of white collar gang warfare."

"How do you know all this, Jack?" Laura asked.

Jack shrugged. "I read a lot, listen a lot. Most of these concepts come up in debates. It's not that hard if you keep up."

Laura sat up scowling. "You two are so depressing. I just want to go home, get something to eat, and decide what we're going to do."

"That's what Jack's saying, Boss Lady. No can go home. Likely they've set up headquarters in your living room. By now they've ransacked your place and realize we've got *that*." Charlie pointed at the tall stack of documents piled on the floor and seat beside Laura.

"Great. So where are we going? After sundown, there may be wolves."

"Got a point, Boss Lady. Good thing for you I deal well with ambiguity and uncertainty. At the moment, I have no more of an idea than you or Jack. Can't stay at Jack's place, though."

"Why not?"

Jack lifted his head off the wheel. "A lot of people think that I'm dead, that I died in the lab fire … whenever it was. If I show up suddenly, it's going to make a big splash. You'd be exposed in the spotlight."

"So we go to Charlie's?" Laura asked.

Charlie smiled. "Uh, not a good idea. First, the cleaning lady hasn't been around for a while. Second, Henderson's boys definitely know where I live and would very much anticipate our joint arrival."

"Well, I don't want to spend the night in a car, as 'sixties as that might be."

"Hey, Boss Lady, I knew the 'sixties. The 'sixties were a friend of mine. Boss Lady, these are no 'sixties."

"Aargh," she groaned.

"The 'sixties were fun. There wasn't so much money involved."

"People died in the sixties, Charlie," she reminded.

Jack spoke, his eyes closed. "The deaths — like Kent State — were tragic, but few in number. With the proliferation of high-powered weapons, the shrinkage of law enforcement, and the injection of billions of dollars into the mix, the stage is set for a bloodbath."

"OK. Enough. Will they be looking for Anita?"

Charlie thought for a moment. "No, probably not. She never had any monetary link to them. They were looking for a scapegoat. And as I recall, they thought she was dead as well. We're building our own little army of the dead. Kinda creepy."

"OK, I'm calling Anita." Laura drew her phone from her pocket. "Now what?"

Charlie turned around.

"Something's wrong with the signal," she said

"Was it charged?"

"Yes, Charlie. I grabbed it from the charger on our way out," she grumbled.

"Let me see."

Laura handed Charlie her phone.

"Hmmm. Yeah, shows a full charge. What's that little symbol there?"

Jack leaned over to see the phone. "Roving. Means it's not finding a signal. Usually means you're in a dead zone."

"In Silver Spring?" Charlie asked.

Jack took a deep breath. "Or it could be the first rain band of the storm. About two news breaks ago, they were reporting that the telecommunications workers were talking about joining the call center job actions. Phone service could suffer pretty quickly. We're used to an extreme level of reliability, but the service infrastructure is actually incredibly fragile. You almost never notice outages because you have people working twenty-four-seven swapping out components at the first sign of a flutter. If that work force pauses, the network would suffer almost immediately and could collapse in a matter of days. And that's assuming no sabotage or direct action."

"Do you know where she lives, Charlie? Or any of the others?"

Charlie shook his head. "But I'm guessing that the party's still going on over in College Park. We can hook up with someone there."

"I need to get gas. We're almost empty," Jack said.

"Right. Better fill up as soon as possible. If the phones go, so does the ability to pay the usual way. It's all networked. We better stock up on cash too. Telephones go, so does credit."

Jack started the car. He tilted his head to the radio. "Oh, boy, here comes the news conference. This will be interesting.

Laura leaned forward. "Turn it up … please."

* * *

Sarah, Kathy, and Anna entered the press briefing room early but it was already filled, every seat occupied, and reporters lining the sides. A larger than normal contingent of secret service agents was stationed around the room; and, for the first time in memory, a Marine stood guard outside the press room.

The White House scheduled the briefing for six in the evening Washington time, but President Miller still had not arrived at twenty minutes after the hour. Sarah craned her neck to watch as Matt and Peter entered. "OK, won't be long."

The room erupted in camera clicks as the crowd rose. Kincaid, Brian Doctrow, and Cameron walked in just ahead of the President.

President Miller strode directly to the podium. "Please be seated." He waited for quiet. "In the last twenty-four hours we have experienced upheavals of unimaginable scope on the national and international stages. If I had hours to relate to you the details of what has happened, the story would still be a mere synopsis. So, I will not be going into any depth at this time. Instead, I will give you an outline of the facts as we understand them and our plan for immediate action. Our staff will flesh out a few more details, and we will return frequently in the days and weeks ahead to give you progress reports.

"The order in which I relate these events has nothing to do with the relative importance of the facts, but is dictated by what is well known and what is not." He spread out the notes that Cameron had placed on the podium.

"First, at 3:37 P.M. Eastern Time, I ordered the arrest of Vice President James T. Bailey. The Vice President is charged with a wide array of serious crimes including violations of currency laws, fraudulent use of government funds, and flight to avoid prosecution. He attempted to flee the country this morning, but was intercepted, literally in the last possible minutes. You have no doubt seen the dramatic coverage provided by Ben Jacobs's dedicated crew.

"It gave me no pleasure to order his arrest. James Bailey — Jim — has been a colleague of mine for nearly three decades, from our days as junior congressmen. What his motivations were and why he believed his crimes could succeed are beyond my grasp. The criminal acts we have uncovered so far point to an array of weaknesses in our checks and balances.

"That's all I'm saying about the Vice President personally for now. The frauds committed involved the systematic manipulation of the economic data underlying our perceptions of the U.S. economy. Unemployment numbers were arbitrarily revised downward; GDP numbers were arbitrarily revised upward, and so on. In more open times, these manipulations would have been spotted long ago. But as a result of new powers to classify the data, the changes were uncovered only a few hours ago. I have ordered the complete declassification of all these numbers. Effective immediately, the raw economic data are available as freely as they were prior to 2012. With the correct numbers now in hand, we will be publishing corrected economic reports for the entire period of the manipulation. Now, I need to give grateful credit to our economics team and to Professor Brian Doctrow. Together they finished the puzzle that allowed us to understand what was going on.

"Regrettably, the corrected data tell us that the dire numbers coming from our state treasurers were broadly correct and that the economic recovery task ahead is daunting. Your federal government was already coming to the aid of the states even before we understood the magnitudes of the problems. We will be fully engaged in fixing those problems.

"Our economics team has had access to the complete corrected numbers for about a day, and we are only just now beginning to see the more accurate picture of our financial condition. We are taking those steps that are most clearly dictated by the new data. Many changes will require a more complete picture before we can proceed. For that reason, I have ordered the closure of the stock exchanges and banks for the next three business days. Our country's condition is serious, but overreaction and overcorrection could easily make matters much worse. We will be issuing specific targeted guidance in the days ahead so that investors can operate with confidence in the numbers they are using."

Two Treasury officials arrived at the White House door of the press room. As the President continued, Kincaid slipped quietly into the passageway to talk with them. After a short time Kincaid motioned for Sarah, Anna, Matt, and Kathy to join him.

"There've been some more developments. We're going to need the President as soon as he's through with his core briefing. Anna, we'll need you on the line to Europe. I'm going to introduce the rest of you and have Sarah and Kathy answer any financial questions. Matt will take questions on the diplomatic and defense fronts."

"You're kidding." Sarah folded her arms. "A month and a half ago, they were ready to destroy me. Why would they take me seriously now?"

Kincaid smiled. "Washington has a very short memory. They need answers. You have answers. It's pretty much that simple. Kathy will guide you on the limits of what you can reveal but just lay out the facts in the same understandable way you've done for the President and for me."

Sarah looked down. "I don't know."

Kincaid turned and began walking back to the press room. "I need you to do this. It's really not a choice."

Kathy, Matt, and Sarah followed Kincaid into the press room.

The President was finishing the final briefing page. Kincaid approached the podium and the President leaned over to receive whispered advice.

"Ladies and gentlemen, there is so much more to discuss. And we will do it. But even now events are moving that require our immediate attention. My Chief of Staff will brief you on the plan as it stands for keeping communication lines open."

The President departed the platform abruptly to a chorus of "Mr. President ..., Mr. President..."

Kincaid ascended to the podium while all other heads followed the departing President. Kincaid waited for attention to return to the front. "Seats, please." He folded his arms and leaned on the podium, waiting until the room became quiet. "I won't be with you very long in this session. I will be introducing our point people. Listen to them and direct your questions their way. They know more than I do, and they speak for the President. Please keep in mind constantly that we are still just learning what has transpired and that our analyses are, of necessity, raw. You already have copies of the President's official statements. I'll stop by here at ten tonight with additional updates. Who's the chief liaison for the press corps?"

A hand went up in the middle of the room.

"Good. Let's get together about a quarter to ten to go over scheduling some mini briefings for the next few days." Kincaid gathered up the papers remaining on the podium.

"I'd like to introduce some of the key members of what I guess you'd call our crisis team." He motioned for Matt, Kathy, and Sarah.

"Matthew Luskin is our technology and military liaison. He can bring you up to date on the situation in Saudi Arabia and on how we interrupted Vice President Bailey's unannounced departure from San Francisco."

He opened his hand in Kathy's direction. "Kathy Whiting is our chief economics advisor. She can fill you in on how the fraud was traced and on some of the numbers involved.

"And Dr. Sarah Tyler has provided much of the investigative background that finally allowed us to put the puzzle together. So, I leave you in their capable hands and will see you later this evening."

Sarah watched as Kincaid left the room. She warily approached the podium.

The room buzzed as reporters stood up and gathered their belongings. No questions came as the three stood at the ready. Some reporters made their way toward the north door and the outside.

Sarah's anxiety changed rapidly to annoyance. Finally she stepped up to the podium and pounded her fist. She shouted, "Hey, hey, hey! Where do you think you're going? This isn't over. There's a lot you need to know, a lot you need to tell your readers and viewers."

Several of the reporters turned quickly toward her at the sound of her angry voice, but then returned to their packing. Kathy looked at Matt, amused.

Sarah's face flushed. "Just because the big boys have left doesn't mean you've got your story."

One reporter raised the shoulder strap of his computer case over his head and looked at Sarah. "I've got my story and I need to file it. Fraud, escape, capture."

Sarah's hands were waving in the air. "But you're missing important details, details that matter to your people. We just stopped the biggest theft in history. Your people's money."

The reporter smiled dismissively. "OK, I'll bite. How much?"

Sarah put her hands on her hips. "We don't have the total yet, but I myself transferred back over twenty-five billion dollars."

The casual din that had started up after Kincaid's departure halted as abruptly as it had begun.

The reporter began opening his computer case. "'B' billion?"

Sarah kept her hands on her hips. "'B' billion. Twenty-five billion dollars. A hundred dollars for every man, woman, and child in American. And I was just one of several people transferring it back into our treasury."

The reporter sat down quickly as others reversed their departures, scrambling for abandoned seats.

He pulled out a writing stylus. "Where exactly did all this money come from, and why did it take you so long to uncover the theft?"

Sarah turned to Kathy. Kathy smiled and held out her hands for Sarah to proceed.

Sarah leaned forward on the White House podium and, resting her elbows on the top, shook her head. "How did Ron Kowalski put up with this day after day? There're about a hundred people in this room whose profession is to dig up stuff on the White House. You've got staff whose sole reason for earning a paycheck is to find embarrassing stuff here. Several of you have budgets bigger than our whole White House economics office. You couldn't penetrate the shields any more than we could for over a year. You want to know why it took so long? It was because the misdirection was conducted incrementally — just a little — under the cover of 'national security.' It wasn't until the economic data no longer matched any reasonable financial model that a few academics could say with confidence that the numbers were lies.

"We owe a lot to just plain luck that the economics convention was in Washington this week rather than next or in some other city. Had that been the case, we might be begging a foreign government to please send back our money … oh, and our Vice President. It took so long to uncover the theft … wait. Actually, your question is all wrong. It didn't take us so long to uncover the theft. These transfers had clearly been planned for months. But the thefts hadn't actually occurred. Within minutes of their mass initiation, they were detected, diverted, and stopped." Sarah straightened up, hands back on her hips, frowning. "So, you see, the premise of your question was entirely wrong."

She stared at the reporter, who stared back, unsure what response was expected.

"Do you see that your premise was wrong?" She put her hands on the lectern, drumming her fingers.

"Sorry." The reporter looked around at his silent colleagues.

Sarah continued. "OK. We almost all missed the clues because they were deeply embedded in protected data. As to where the money came from, it was from hundreds and hundreds of important but mundane government accounts — a few I remember were several hundred million from USDA school lunch program, seventy-five million from road upgrades for Grand Canyon National Park, three hundred million from Department of Veterans Affairs hospital construction and renovation. Things like that. Programs that matter to a lot of Americans."

Sarah pointed to the raised hand of a woman reporter.

"You said..." — she looked at her notes — "... 'Within minutes of their mass initiation, they were detected, diverted, and stopped.' How exactly were these transfers detected, diverted, and stopped?"

Sarah turned to Kathy and Matt and whispered, "What can I say?"

Kathy stepped up to the microphone and paused a moment for composure. "Our national banking system is designed for a relatively steady flow of currency. When there is a sudden surge or drop in that flow, it could indicate some component failure in the banks' accounting. Hundreds of computer programs send out notices when these anomalies occur. The system can execute a partial shutdown to avoid damage caused by extraordinary and potentially improper transactions or system failures, a lot like a circuit breaker in your home." She shrugged. "That's basically what happened. Those routine banking fluctuations happen many times a day, but normally on a much smaller scale and are the result of accidents, not deliberate manipulation. In this case, the anomalous behavior was judged destructive and the switches remained 'off.'"

Kathy pointed to a reporter in the back of the room.

"In all the confusion generated by Vice President Bailey, has the White House lost focus on the collapse of the House of Saud and the resulting loss of all that oil?"

Kathy yielded her spot to Matt.

"The tragedy of Saudi Arabia will be with us for a very long time. The violence of the last few days is the result of a long, tangled history of bad policies with deep roots and many actors. We had hoped that cooler heads would have prevailed. For now, the situation is completely fluid. We don't even know the names of any leaders of the coup — if, indeed, there are any leaders. Anything I would say today along those lines is pure speculation. As far as your question about focus is concerned, we do not lose focus. The public discussion may have shifted to the spectacular theater closer to home, but professionals in the Departments of State, Defense, Treasury, and on and on do not shift their attention away from their areas of responsibility.

"In regard to the 'loss of all that oil,' as you put it, while that is secondary to the human tragedy, we know that the coming disruptions will be profound. Our economy still runs on oil despite decades of warnings for us to move to more diverse and renewable energy sources. I am part of the group that will be coordinating our national efforts to deal with the immediate shortfall. Rest assured that we will be pushing for an immediate diversification of energy resources. You'll be hearing a lot from us very shortly about the actions, including serious sacrifices that we will have to make.

"Obviously the whole picture is vastly complicated by the newly-revealed weaknesses in our economic situation."

Matt rubbed his chin as he surveyed the attentive crowd. "I've got to be honest. I think we're in for some very hard times. So much of what we've come to depend on is missing now. If we fall back on the infighting and bickering that has characterized our national discourse for all of my lifetime, then day-to-day life is going to get really, really bad for most of us. I've heard my great-grandparents talk about a spirit of cooperation they remember from the Second World War and from the days of the space race. I've often wondered how much of that memory is real and how much is nostalgia. To the extent it is real, we need to recapture that cooperation right now. We can survive the coming troubles if we choose, but it will definitely be a choice. Did that answer your question?"

The reporter looked up from his note taking. "Unfortunately, yes."

Matt, Kathy, and Sarah continued to take questions round robin for another forty minutes. When the questions began to drift toward trivia, Kathy called a halt to the briefing. "Ladies and gentlemen, it's supper time. Go get your stories filed. We'll be back this evening with more unexpected news."

Ben Jacobs grinned and began clapping his hands. The rest of the reporters joined him. Matt departed with two defense analysts. A gaggle of reporters gathered around Kathy and Sarah, who deflected questions of substance while providing background about the emotional tenor of the day. Jacobs remained in his seat until the pressroom was nearly empty.

When only the three remained, Jacobs finally packed his bag. "Masterful job, Ms. Whiting and Dr. Tyler. I think that was the first true news conference I've been to here. I hope it continues for a while, but you know it's going to get nasty."

Kathy leaned on the White House podium looking down at her scribbled notes and reminders. "Doesn't have to."

Jacobs gave a weak smile. "In a perfect world, no, but it will. I guarantee it."

"Great." Kathy shook her head slowly.

He walked slowly toward the exit.

Sarah called after him. "Aren't you missing your broadcast?"

He glanced at the clock. "Yeah. The evening news is over. There'll be bulletins and updates for the rest of the night. I'll probably anchor a few of those. Hey. I was serious about you doing a good job." He swept his hand across the room. "Most of these hairdos don't have much of an understanding of what you do or what's at stake. You might want to bring some visuals. I don't know — a whiteboard or something. Events will be moving too fast for anything fancy, but your role in the coming hours will mostly be teacher."

Sarah nodded. "Thanks."

Sarah and Kathy left the press room, walking slowly toward the situation room.

"Wow! This day certainly turned out different than we expected," Sarah spoke.

Kathy nodded. "Yep. You really let them have it there at first."

"Sorry, I lost it. I got carried away when they weren't even curious enough to ask such obvious questions," Sarah winced.

"No, you were right. I have no idea what Mr. Kincaid will have to say about it, but you got their attention and got them asking the right questions. And you delivered some pretty good sound bites during the give and take."

"What do you mean?"

"You know. Short snippets for their broadcasts. Quotable stuff."

Sarah turned to Kathy eagerly. "So I might actually be on the news."

"Definitely. What are you doing?"

Sarah punched a speed dial number on her phone. "Calling Mom. She needs to get Aunt Ruth to watch. Aunt Ruth's got one of those instant recorders." She held the phone close to her ear. "Mom, Sarah. Listen; get Aunt Ruth to turn her recorder on to some of the news spots tonight. You might see me … really?"

Sarah turned to Kathy. "They've been watching it live. Even our stuff."

Kathy shrugged.

"So, Mom, what did you think … Mom, slow down! Yes. What?" Sarah looked down. "No, of course not, Mom. No. I wasn't expecting to be on TV today. It's not that bad. Of course it matters, but that's not the point." Sarah listened, frustration etching her forehead. "Yes, Mom, I will. Look, I've got to go. Yes, really. I have meetings with a lot of people. Love you. I'll call later."

Sarah closed her phone, returned it to her pocket, and walked on quietly.

"What was that about?"

"She said I looked like a disgrace, that I should have been wearing a suit for an important occasion like this."

Kathy grinned.

"She said it looked like I got it from Bloomingdale's basement."

Kathy surveyed Sarah's attire. "It's not that bad. Working garb. Where did you get it?"

Sarah looked down and began laughing. "Bloomingdale's. Some of it from the basement. Oh, man, leave it to your Mom to put things in perspective."

"I'm sure she's very proud of you," Kathy offered.

"I don't know. She wanted me to be a doctor and marry Lenny Cohen."

"But you are a doctor," Kathy reminded.

"Yeah, nice try. I brought that up, and she countered that she meant a 'real' doctor, like a pediatrician. Not a PhD."

"But you work in the White House on national policy."

Sarah shook her head. "The way she describes it to her friends is that I do meetings all day. Very disappointed."

The brightly lit commotion of the situation room loomed ahead. A familiar figure appeared in the doorway.

"Sarah, I need you to explain to Secretary Zink how you got the structure of Windham Trust with those computer models."

"Yes, sir."

He turned away momentarily, and then back to her. "And could you please get the data on cash flow for the Emirates? Defense and Treasury need to get some idea of the magnitude of the problem there."

"Yes, Mr. President."

She turned to Kathy. "I'll be right back. Save me a seat." Sarah ran toward the crosswalk to their offices, stopping only for her security check.

Kathy smiled, sighed, and shook her head. She continued her walk toward the chaos ahead.

* * *

"I can't imagine they're going to give us gas." Jack leaned back in the driver's seat with his head turned toward Laura.

She, in turn, leaned forward. "Don't underestimate ol' Charlie. He can be as irritating as anyone you've ever met, but he can be a charmer too. He's probably spinning some story about how secure this transaction actually is. Here he comes now."

Jack rolled down the window.

"He said to get eight gallons. That's all the pump will give without a signal from higher up." Charlie said to Laura, "When … if … the electrons start flowing again, you'll be charged for twelve gallons. He wasn't going to let us have any, but it turns out I've been through his hometown, and we talked about it for a bit, and I guess he judged us trustworthy. Or at least a reasonable gamble."

Charlie walked around the car as Jack got out to pump the gas. To Laura, Jack said, "I see what you mean."

"It makes up for all the aggravation the rest of the time," she replied.

Once they had their eight gallons of gas, Jack drove toward the call center in College Park. The crowd now numbered several hundred in the gathering dusk. Charlie, Laura, and Jack found Anita seated near those holding signs.

Charlie approached, arms folded. "Hey, Nita, not like you to slack off."

Anita smiled. "Hey, Charlie. Hey, Laura. The doctors say I have to take it easy for a week. They'd likely have a fit if they knew I was here."

"They probably won't be finding out. I think the phone lines are pretty much dead. We barely got gas to get over here because there's no communication."

Anita nodded. "Well, that's what they said. The regular Brotherhood has joined the strike. But here's the twist. We're only letting emergency calls through. Regular commercial stuff is blocked."

Charlie laughed. "Well, that is ironic, isn't it? But I like it. By the way, have you had any more scary visitors?"

"Naw, I think there're too many of us now. There are news cameras everywhere, and the sheriff's got cars at both ends of the road."

Charlie looked around before continuing. "I don't suppose you or one of the others has room for three guests for a few days. The scary guys with black suits and guns were after us this morning and are probably watching Laura's and my places."

"Sure, Charlie. Anything for you and Laura and …"

"Right. Sorry. Anita, this is Jack. Jack, Anita. We met Jack through a series of bizarre events. Right now he's our driver and logician."

"Your what?" Anita grinned, trying to decide whether Charlie was serious or not.

"He's helping us figure out what's real and what's not. Jack's won some serious debating contests."

Anita nodded. "We could use someone who's a good public speaker. The TV crews have been out here a couple of times to interview people, and we don't come across very well."

Charlie nodded. "We'll need to get Jack up to speed on the cast of characters. What time do you get off your shift here? We'll follow you home if that's OK."

"I don't have a specific time. Until I get back on my feet, I'm kind of a mascot. Just let Michael know. He brought me over. You can take me home if you've got room and save him a trip."

After Charlie consulted with Michael, Jack brought the car around, and he and Laura assisted Anita, one on each side, into the car. Charlie waved to the deputy on watch at the end of the block as they headed to Berwyn Heights.

* * *

May 22, 2014, 8:45 p.m.

"Ben said he wants all their names, not just most of them." WWDC senior news editor Tom Meacham looked at his clock. He had been in full operational mode through two complete shifts and was beginning to feel the fatigue. "Let's go over it again. How many people were with the Vice President on the plane?"

"Seven."

"Eight."

Tom folded his arms and bowed his head. "OK, Jim, seven based on …?"

"You can count every one of them descending the stairs from the plane, and we know them by name. We've got great images and positive IDs."

"Right. Steve, eight based on ...?"

"The clip of Bailey and his people moving down the concourse behind the SFO onsite. The quality's not great, but I definitely count eight. Seven of them match the seven on the exit stairs but there's definitely an eighth."

"OK, let's roll the clip again frame by frame. But make it quick. Jacobs is in make-up now."

Steve commented as the frames appeared on the high-definition monitor. "First frame, you see the big guy enter to the left. Hercules. He's the real bad ass. Next, next, next. These three guys we've accounted for."

"Can you blow it up some?"

"Yeah, a little, but it gets pretty grainy. There. Now in this frame Bailey enters stage left. But look. Too many arms. There's someone on his other side. Next. See? A little bit of another head. Next. You see the rest of the seven walking behind Bailey. Next, next, next. He passes behind the reporter's head and out on the other side. Next. There. That's the best shot of number eight. He's real, and he's obviously with the group."

Tom squinted and tilted his head. "Can you sharpen that up any? Put some noise filter on it?"

"Maybe a little. There. That's the best I can do."

"That guy looks familiar."

Steve's eyes grew wide. "Holy crap! You know who that is."

"Oh, yeah!" Tom turned immediately to his phone. "I need to talk to Ben. I don't care. He needs to hear this right now."

* * *

In mid-Pacific, at thirty-five thousand feet, a fierce sun reflected off layered clouds below. The first class lounge of Flight 781 dimmed to allow passengers some rest during the long flight.

The senior first class steward approached seat 7C where the passenger reviewed data on his laptop with papers spread out over two seats emptied by the Vice President and his followers. "Sir, the captain is pleased to inform you that we have departed the North American defense zone and will encounter no problems between here and Shanghai."

The passenger nodded. He lifted an empty wine glass for the steward. "I want a good California Cabernet."

"Sir, we have the finest wines produced in China for your pleasure."

The passenger raised his head, lips tightly drawn. "If I wanted your Chinese pond scum, I would have asked for it. I'm sure the captain has some California reserve in his personal stock."

"Yes, sir." The steward took the glass and stepped back. "Will there be anything else, Dr. Richards?"

* * *

Griesbach arrived home at six-fifty.

"You look beat," she said. "Rough day at the office?" She dried her hands on a dishtowel and returned his kiss.

"It was … eventful. Where are John and Lisa?"

"In the living room, in front of the TV. John's moaning and groaning because his teacher's making them write up a detailed summary of the news."

Griesbach made his way into the living room and sat on the sofa to watch.

As Lisa entered a text message, John turned to his father. "Did you see any of the action at the airport today? Vice President Bailey got busted."

"Uh huh. I heard something about that."

The splash screen for the evening news appeared briefly on the television and then switched to footage of the arrest. Griesbach could tell the cameras had been filming from some distance. Despite image stabilization, the picture vibrated and most of the edges of the plane image wavered from thermal irregularities in the air. Besides, he couldn't remember any cameras up close.

Ben Jacobs started the voice-over. "This was the scene only hours ago as federal agent Robert Griesbach mounted the steps to China Airlines Flight 781, and arrested the Vice President of the United States James T. Bailey, thus thwarting perhaps the grandest theft in all history. The Vice President is in custody, the money has been restored, the plot grows more tangled by the hour, and the nation is in shock. Our coverage begins in Washington, from where this saga began, and to where it has now returned."

Griesbach's attention drifted from the screen to his son. John's eyes were wide, his mouth open in admiration not seen since the arrest of the aphids.

* * *

Anita unlocked the door to her apartment and promptly oriented Charlie, Laura, and Jack. "It's small but quite comfortable. We have two bedrooms. Sheets and extra pillows are in the linen closet by the bathroom. The tub faucet leaks if you don't turn it off just so. Please don't turn it. The shower works fine. Someone can take the couch, too. It's pretty comfortable. Benny has buddies over sometimes for video games, and they wind up playing past midnight. We picked the sofa partly with that in mind. It'll pull out to make a bed if your legs are too long.

"There are a few beers and some sandwich fixings in the fridge. I'm running a little low after all the confusion of the last few days."

"How 'bout we restock you?" Laura asked. "We stopped at nearly every ATM on the way over to College Park. Only about a third were working, but we've got pretty good cash reserves right now."

Anita waved her hands as she shook her head. "No, I couldn't have you do that. It's my pleasure."

Charlie chuckled. "Not to worry, Nita. She's rich."

"Charlie!" Laura and Anita shouted their common irritation.

Charlie raised his hands as he shrugged. "Hey, it's true. Why do you think I put up with you when you're in your foul moods? Which is most of the time these days, by the way."

Anita laughed. "Charlie, if you weren't so lovable..." She turned to Laura. "A little help with the pantry would be very kind. There're not a lot of prospects for pay anytime soon. Especially now that the regular telephone workers are joining up."

"That probably explains our roaming signal on your phone." Jack had leaned back in the recliner next to Laura sitting on the floor; his eyes closed.

"Yeah, sorry about that." Anita turned to Laura. "Get me your phone numbers, and I'll put them in the database."

"What database?" Laura asked.

"The phone system's badly degraded, but not dead. When the telecomm workers joined the strike, we all agreed there'd be no sabotage, but it didn't take long at all for the little breakdowns to snowball. The system as a whole protects itself and prioritizes calls. For instance, if you pressed nine-one-one right now, it would go through even with the roaming sign. Half of us are on the picket lines, and the other half man the emergency call centers. We rotate. It has to be a real emergency, though. The CCs get dumped right away. We just hang up."

"CCs?" Jack asked.

"'Crap Calls.' Under normal circumstances, we deal with them if the load's not too heavy and the caller is sincere."

Laura smiled. She reached up and shook Jack's leg. "You were right about the maintenance."

"Hmmm," Jack murmured.

"Looks like he's found his spot for the night. I wouldn't mind shutting down myself. Aside from a little dozing in the car, I haven't gotten any sleep for … I've lost track. Two days I think."

"But about the phone numbers," Anita continued, "the system as a whole can recognize priority numbers and let them through. Most of us call center people, the maintenance workers, and some higher-ups in the government have priority." Anita handed Laura a piece of paper and pen.

"Charlie doesn't have a cell phone," Laura said. "He says he doesn't believe in them, so he always uses mine." She turned to look at Jack. "And I'm not sure Jack wants his in the system. Right, Jack?"

Jack stirred. "Huh?"

"Do you want me to give Anita your phone number to put in the priority phone database?"

Jack raised his head. "Probably not. I think I left my phone back at Ed's place in Frederick. Besides, most of the authorities — other than our friends who cleaned up at Laura's — probably still think I'm dead, and that might be best for now. If my number pops up in a database, it would raise questions we don't want to answer."

Laura handed the paper to Anita. "OK, then, one number."

"I'll put it in tomorrow and it should be active in a few days. You want the guest room? That's where the TV is if you want to catch up on the news."

"Let Charlie have it," Laura replied. "I just want some rest. The couch looks fine."

Charlie scanned Anita's bookcase. "For a fiery radical, your taste in books is pretty mainstream."

"Then you'll like the guest room better. Benny's dad's always sending us good books we haven't had time to read."

Charlie checked the guest room and pronounced the library adequate. Everyone prepared for sleep, pulling out pillows and light blankets.

Anita turned on the nightlight in the bathroom. "Good night, folks. Let's hope the next few days are better than Charlie is expecting." She left for her room.

"Are you comfortable, Jack?" Laura asked.

"Yes, quite. Thanks for asking. You?"

"Yes."

"By the way, Laura, I never properly thanked you for not handing me over to the authorities. You have no idea how messed up things have been in the past few days. A lot of terrible things have happened and I haven't had time to process it all. There's going to be a reckoning at some point."

"I'm not completely sure why I didn't, Jack. I hope I was right in the long run. But, after all, you did stop Ed. I'm sorry you had to shoot your friend."

Jack lay in the recliner staring at the ceiling in the faint reflected glow of the nightlight. "So much has happened. This time last year, my life was boringly routine. I was married to the most amazing creature who ever walked this planet, and I didn't realize how good I had it. Good job. Meaningful work. Then, slowly but surely, I lost it all."

"My dad was part of that," Laura offered.

Jack thought for a while. "I'm not about to blame him for my situation. He acted without having all the facts, and I probably could have straightened that out, though it might have required some lawyers. But other things have happened. I'm not sure that straightening out is an option anymore."

"Like what?"

Jack hesitated for a long time. "I need to process it." He was quiet another few minutes. "I'm sorry about your father. I didn't hear exactly what happened."

"Well, not so much to process there. Ed hit him really hard and almost killed him. I need to find out how he's doing without running afoul of Henderson and his storm troopers."

"I've no right to intrude, but I sense you and your dad had a falling out."

"It's OK. He got deep into the Windham Trust thing. He was making some warped decisions and we're living some of the consequences now," she said.

"Back when we were looking for gas, Charlie said we were on the edge of the storm surge. He's right. We're going to be tested. I'm probably not thinking too clearly at the moment, but I'm at your disposal for whatever I can do. I'm 'dead,' but I can still be useful."

Laura giggled. "Great. Unfortunately, Charlie has a ghastly knack for being right. I'm still hoping that things will blow over and we can just start correcting everything. Otherwise, I'm Joan of Arc, throwing my lot in with the army of the dead. Guess I wouldn't have seen that coming forty-eight hours ago … except that Charlie predicted it."

"I'll warn you: Jenn always said that I snored."

"Not to worry. My dad said I sound like an eighteen-wheeler in my sleep."

"Good night, Laura."

"Good night, Jack."

* * *

Monday, May 26, 2014, Memorial Day

"All right, people, let's get everyone synched up. I have a few items from the last couple of hours." David Kincaid opened his staff meeting notes. "First, the Vice President was successfully transferred to the federal prison in Danbury, Connecticut, as of three-thirty a.m. His questioning over the weekend in California was not particularly revealing. Two of the four companions who escaped custody at SFO have been recaptured. The media ruckus resulting from their escape subsided once pictures of our agents' injuries became public. Our primary concern is for one of the remaining escapees, a particularly violent individual who goes by the handle of 'Hercules.' He seems to be a central figure in running the dirty operations.

"OK. Synopsis time. James, the Gulf."

James finished handing out his briefing pages. "U.S. and Britain are beefing up the southern and eastern borders of Kuwait. Saudi Arabia is basically a wasteland. Once our embassy was burned, that which did not burn was demolished with explosives. The most recent flyover shows nothing but rubble. And Riyadh is clearing out. The major roads are impassible, and there's no food is coming in. Not only has no leader emerged, but also it appears that there was no dominant group in the overthrow. Most of our contacts have gone quiet, but our best intelligence suggests over twenty competing groups. The oil terminals are deserted, and the pipelines to those terminals are being destroyed by the hour."

James paused.

"Is there any non-catastrophic news?" Kincaid followed some of James's narrative on the sheets.

James looked up briefly, unsmiling. "No, sir. Those are the highlights for Saudi Arabia. On to Iran. The Supreme Council is still pushing their claims about the incursion back in April. They have, for want of a better term, ordered us to leave Kuwait and Iraq. The last report I saw confirmed troops massed on the border at Abadan and a big buildup of anti-ship missiles in the arc around the Strait of Hormuz. Those missiles are quite capable of reaching all the way over into Oman."

"And our reinforcements?"

"We've been ferrying troops in around the clock. We've matched the Iranian concentrations with a buildup in Basra and north of Baghdad. It looks like we moved early enough and made a big dusty show of it. The Iranians stopped their buildup as soon as we were truly visible. We've made a more limited buildup on the southern border. The fighting in Saudi Arabia seems to be internal strife. We don't see any hostile moves toward the north, but have beefed up surveillance."

Matt raised his hand. "How are we communicating our intentions to both the Arabs and the Iranians? The last thing we want is a misunderstanding."

"Right," James nodded and then turned to Kincaid. "I guess this would count for non-catastrophic. For the Iranians, we have transmitted our intentions through every open channel. We've even invited Iranian observers under U.N. escort to tour our defensive perimeter. They haven't taken us up on that yet, but the effort seems to have lowered the temperature. In part, they don't have much more to spare in military assets, since they're still facing a lot of internal strife. If we keep playing it cool, I think we've seen the peak of the conflict on that border. And we might just possibly get some contacts with Tehran out of it.

"To the south, it's anybody's guess. We've kept up a noisy, flashy patrol parallel to the border but we don't really see anyone watching."

"Who's doing liaison with NATO?" Anna asked.

"Admiral Bill Brown is our point man," James replied. "He's set up in the Roosevelt Room with phones and is bunking over in the executive office building."

"Good." Anna nodded. "He's a master at smoothing things out."

Kincaid looked around, as the room grew quiet. "Anyone else have any questions for James?" In the absence of questions, he nodded to Anna. "Diplomacy, please."

"We're got extremely grim realities on three fronts." She moved to a large map on the wall and waved her hand over the Gulf region. "The fall of the House of Saud splits the region into five distinct regions; the Emirates to the south, then Saudi Arabia, then Iraq-Kuwait, then Iran, and finally Afghanistan. There has been no cooperation between any two adjacent regions, so the whole area is basically gridlocked.

"On the periphery, Egypt, Israel, Jordan, and Syria are bracing for fallout. Within the first hours, we picked up indications that the Israelis might be looking to use this turmoil for operational cover. Ambassador Ginsburg met face-to-face with them and advised in unequivocal terms to stay out of the fray. He delivered the President's threat that we would give their neighbors our reconnaissance frequencies and would immediately suspend all aid if they did anything to further escalate the conflict.

"To the east, Pakistan seems an island of calm for a change. We've made limited use of their airfields, and we have kept them informed of all our movements. I think they're pretty uncomfortable watching how quickly Riyadh unraveled.

"In the rest of the Islamic world, the focus appears to be on the House of Saud, not the U.S. or our allies. So far we've gotten mostly good marks for our extraction. The world's attention is focused mainly on the loss of oil. I expect that to drive most of the diplomatic fallout as regards the Gulf for the near future."

Anna looked up from her notes for questions. Seeing none, she continued, "However, on the quasi-diplomatic front, we are going to experience a lot of turbulence from the continuing revelations about the Vice President's chicanery. Europe, Japan, and China are extremely concerned about how much damage he did shrouded in secrecy." She turned to Kincaid. "The President should be expecting a lot of harsh questions about how so much could happen outside the normal review process. Politically, this disaster has strengthened the position of those who were advocating delinking the dollar from the world banking systems. Kathy and Sarah probably have more on that than I do."

"Right," Kincaid weighed in, "the President is weighing whether we should hold some kind of emergency economic summit to clear the air and offer reassurances. We'll be meeting later this afternoon on that. Some of you will be attending, but the roster isn't finalized."

"Yes, sir. Whatever is decided should be announced as quickly as possible. The rumor mills are working overtime, and it's going to be difficult to sort fact from fiction pretty soon."

"I appreciate that. Part of the problem is sorting out fact and fiction here. Kathy, where do we stand exactly?"

"Mr. Kincaid, the bank holiday started on Friday and will continue tomorrow and Wednesday. We finished confirming the correct data sets late Saturday night. We posted the individual sets as they were verified and instructed banks to put the corrected sets in place before starting any transactions or analyses. But that's proving more and more difficult."

Kincaid looked up from the reports. "How so?"

Matt spoke, "The national telecommunications grid is failing. Rapidly. What started as a local protest over the automation of a call center in College Park went national after the underlying scheme to replace most of the workers was revealed. When some local jurisdictions began to push back, the regular telecommunications workers joined in. Whether by design or temporary neglect, the infrastructure is not being repaired at the same rate it naturally breaks down, and the national grid is how the banks communicate with one another, how they get their data, how they put money into the hands of their customers. Right now you'd be hard pressed to find a working ATM in most of the country. Automated payments, including most salaries, are getting through only sporadically."

Kincaid raised his hand. "Whoa. The local jurisdictions can't be pushing back, can they? When we were in with the President a few days ago, I thought you said that these systems can't work up to the commercial claims, that the technology wasn't ready."

"Correct, sir," Matt agreed.

Kincaid spread his hands. "Then …"

Matt rubbed his face. "It's complicated. A lot of the cities and counties had reduced their budgets in anticipation of the automation and to avoid taking back their tax cuts. Now their taxes are insufficient to fund their current workforce. On top of this, a substantial portion of the administrators is still convinced that the automated systems will work. Brisbane Technologies is still assuring them that their systems either will work or can be fixed."

"In spite of all the evidence that's come to light?" Kincaid asked.

"Yes, sir. They're listening to other voices. The talk radio shows are playing this as a labor issue. They're vilifying the workers, and some are even portraying the Vice President's arrest as a diversion."

Kincaid leaned back in his chair. "This isn't going to be easy, is it?"

"No, sir. And it's getting more difficult by the minute. Most of the traditional news is distributed via television. Most television is transmitted over cable and telephone lines, which are degrading. Talk radio is, as advertised, radio, which is still transmitting. In theory, you have reliable voices like NPR, but the percentages favor the talk shows. Ironically, the actions the telecomm workers have taken make a resolution much more difficult."

"Can we invoke any back-to-work orders until we can cool the situation?"

Peter spoke. "Sir, because of Mr. Bailey's links to Brisbane, and the speeches he's given, we don't have any more clout with the workers than we do with the industries. Whatever limited labor laws could be used would have to have the cooperation of both sides. Right now, we have neither. Have you seen the most recent polls?"

Kincaid shook his head.

"In five days we've dropped from sixty-plus approval to under ten percent."

"What about public safety?" Kincaid asked.

"The national grid is multi-tiered. For the present, emergency calls go through. That includes your phone, by the way, as long as you're using the White House-issued phone." Peter folded his arms. "Even if we did have any clout remaining with the workers, there is no unified structure to the strike. The national union never authorized it. They're claiming hands off, that all of the actions are spontaneous and local."

"What are we going to do, Peter?"

Peter looked up at the clock. "In three hours, you'll be meeting with Cameron, Senator Kreis, Tiffany Miller, and about ten other advisors. Then we will pray that the President listens and acts."

Kincaid looked down to the end of the table where Sarah was busy typing on her laptop. "Sarah, have you been catching any of this?"

"Sir?"

"You seem distracted."

Sarah smiled. "No, sir. James: dismal news on the military front. Tenuous bases, almost no wiggle room, and little margin for error in the Gulf. Anna: gridlock diplomatically. Everyone hates one another in a zebra stripe around the region. All our friends are frustrated with us, and the by standing nations are not expecting much from us. Kathy: numbers are in the toilet, but at least we flushed. We need all the banks and markets to use the new — actually old — numbers that we have, but we can't give them out effectively. Matt: we're losing the grid we've all come to love and depend on and are rapidly going back in time to pre-dialup days. Matt didn't say it, but he's going into search engine withdrawal, and he's scared shitless of losing all of his super powers to reach out and harvest information. Peter: everybody hates us, nobody loves us, and you have a meeting in three hours."

The room fell silent save for the faint sigh of air vents and the clacking of Sarah's keyboard. Peter and Anna were both grinning.

Finally, Kincaid spoke, "Right. If I could remember your exact phrasing, that's what I'd tell the President. What are you typing anyway?"

"While I still have that tier of access that Matt was talking about, I've got a flood of data coming in, particularly in regard to Windham Trust. Our way out probably depends on reversing what they've done. They're the organizing force behind a frightening percentage of the security companies. As far as I can tell, all the major investors in Brisbane are members, or whatever they should be called, of Windham Trust. They're the titans of industry, and they're the ones funding the talk radio. Someone's gotta tell me if I'm being paranoid, but the picture I'm getting is one of a giant parasite designed to suck the economic life out of the country. It makes perfect sense that Mr. Bailey was trying to shut us down."

She turned her laptop so that Kincaid and the others could see the image.

"Bailey is the big red sphere in the middle now that we know that he is WT. The blue lines are the feeder systems, companies feeding off federal, state, and local security contracts."

Kincaid stared expressionless at the picture. "And the yellow speckled shell?"

"I've labeled those 'defensive.' Those are legal firms, PR agencies, radio stations, and that sort of thing owned by Trust members. They function like a protective armor around the Trust. We're going to have to pick off the weaker ones to penetrate into the core. But the Trust seems to have deliberately structured their system so that it's self-healing. If I displayed the names, you'd see how awesomely redundant their defenses are. They had a lot of really smart people structure this beast. The armor plates are firms with strong positive ratings with the public and are cemented to the Trust by massive financial bonds."

Kincaid drummed his fingers on the desk. "You don't sound so much paranoid as admiring."

"Sorry, sir, but from an objective academic perspective, Windham Trust is a beautifully constructed entity. Matt could give you some bad guy parallels from science fiction." Sarah turned to Matt.

Matt rose to the challenge. "Death Star, mother ship from Independence day, Borg cube. Let's hope our ending is the same, but without all the nastiness in between."

Kincaid smiled briefly. "I remember the Death Star, but don't recall the others. Sounds like the plot has been explored before. OK, I think that everyone has an idea of what we need to do here. Sorry to spoil your Memorial Day, but we should probably meet again before the day is done. Peter, let's go up to see the President in about fifteen minutes. Sarah, I'd like you to show him your findings. If the Trust is our path out of this, he's going to need to mobilize our forces."

"Yes, sir. Saving now," she acknowledged.

The room slowly cleared as each staff member gathered piles of papers and briefings.

Sarah closed her laptop. "I'll be right back, sir. I need to pick up a couple of printouts he'll want to see."

Kincaid nodded. At last, only Anna remained. "Cheer up, Anna," he said, "we'll get through this."

She nodded. "Yes, sir, I know. Sarah's diplomacy recap was a bit grimmer than the reality. I'm just a little worried about something else. One of my friends from chorus, Laura, the one you met while we were looking for Charlie Jones, went missing at about the time the telecomm crisis started. I don't remember whether I told you, but her father is a senior official with an institute that has a lot of ties to Windham Trust. I've been trying her cell phone, but nothing goes through. It's my personal phone, so I guess Matt's explanation of the system told me why I couldn't get through. But I heard from one of the other chorus members that my missing friend's father was attacked in their home and that she may have been kidnapped."

They walked together toward Kincaid's office.

"I can have someone check and find out what's known if you'd like," he said.

Anna shook her head. "You've got a lot of really serious issues that are going to require your full attention. I'll drive by her place on my way home." She paused, a trace of a smile on her face. "I'll be glad when this is over. Seems like we got thrown into deep water right from the start."

Kincaid was quiet for most of the remaining walk. When they arrived at his office door, he turned to Anna. "I, too, hope this is over soon, but my instinct tells me we're in for some difficult times on the way. Like you said, you and Sarah and the others have been thrown into very deep water. But you were chosen because you're the best. You'll all perform heroically, and you'll all be proud of your contributions when it's all resolved." He took her hand and squeezed it. "Let me know if you need help finding …"

"Laura Garrette. Yes, sir. Thank you." She smiled at last.

Kincaid released her hand. Anna turned and headed to her office. He watched her until she rounded the corner. Sighing, he entered his office. Sarah and Peter were waiting for him.

"OK, Sarah, got your numbers?"

"Yes, sir," she replied.

Kincaid turned to Tracy. "Please let Abigail know we're inbound with an update for the boss."

Tracy nodded as they left the office.

* * *

Traffic in the Oval Office was heavy and noisy. Two additional tables had been brought in, as many as the confined space would allow. Several teams crowded into the office. Each team worked over the papers spread on their table while the team leaders shuttled between the table and the President's desk.

President Miller looked up. "Ah, David. Good to see you. Seems like it's been ages."

"Yes, sir, it does feel that way. We have updates for you on several fronts. Let me know when you're ready."

The President waved to a spot on his right. "Pull alongside. Whenever there's any slack, jump right in. Just so you know, Senator Kreis assures me that the impeachment is moving as fast as the Constitution will allow. You know, of course, that you'll be heading the search for a stand-in Vice President."

Kincaid took a deep breath and let it out slowly. "I haven't had time to think about it, but, of course, that does make sense." He looked around the room. "Where is the Senator, anyway?"

"He's on his way. He had a lot of papers to sign and lawyers to organize." The President eyed Sarah's laptop. "What've you got, cyber-warrior?"

Sarah grinned as she opened the machine and proceeded to explain the constructs on its screen.

As she wrapped up her tutorial, the President stared at the screen, rubbing his chin. "You know, this explains a lot. From the moment we took him into custody, we've gotten essentially nowhere. Justice is being bombarded by demands from his legal team. Wolfe Network is twenty-four-seven with conspiracy theories that we're 'covering up the truth.' It's like some bizarre bad dream."

"Yes, sir. He's in a very secure cocoon," Sarah assured.

President Miller leaned back in his chair. "So, how do we pry him out? We've got impeachment proceedings in a matter of days."

Sarah turned to Peter.

He held out a small sheaf of paper. "Sir, we have a plan that should address a number of issues."

The President took the report and flipped through it. "Have you vetted this, David?"

Kincaid jumped in, "Yes, sir. The team, particularly Peter and Sarah, did the lion's share of the work, but I stand by it."

"Executive summary, Mr. Benson?"

"It appears that Vice President Bailey is still directing operations of Windham Trust through his lawyers and associates. Now that we're getting a clearer picture of its operational structure, including names and companies, we can apply pressure to the structural members who hold government contracts. We've identified almost half the members for whom their loyalty would be a serious conflict of interest. They'll either have to side with us and let go the Windham civilian business, or side with him and lose their government contracts. We would expect a fair number of defectors — assuming they believe he will be convicted in impeachment and presumed follow-on prosecutions."

Miller raised his eyebrows. "Assuming they believe?"

Peter paused a moment. "Mr. President, Vice President Bailey has demonstrated stunning skill in organizing the shenanigans we've seen in the last few days. He has legal fund resources that are likely legitimate and are as large as or larger than any prosecution budget we've used in over a decade. Brisbane Technologies alone appears to be spending nearly a hundred thousand dollars an hour to counter the reports about their failed call center security hardware and software. We have to get our message out through the legitimate news organizations before the Windham PR machinery drowns it. Once those corporations establish a beachhead, it will be extraordinarily difficult to get any real information out."

The President's face was drained, eyes and cheeks sagging. "And how do we do that?"

"You'll be doing a live interview in about two hours." Peter flipped open the plans to the middle of the stack. Peter grimaced as he realized his impertinence.

President Miller raised his eyebrows. "I will?" He turned to Kincaid. "David?"

Kincaid smiled. "Indelicately put, sir. Sorry. We strongly recommend that you avail yourself of this opportunity. We set up a tentative appointment. The airtime will be there if you're willing to do the interview. Cameron is working on talking points and sound bites right now. You'll look strong, and I don't think we can afford any delay."

"The last few interviews haven't gone very well, as you'll recall. Who's the inquisitor?"

Kincaid bit his lip. "Ben Jacobs."

The President slapped his hands on the desk. Everyone in the room turned toward him. "You've got to be shitting me!" he shouted.

"Sir, he is hands down the most respected member of the press corps right now. We stumbled because we were not prepared. We've been working with him almost every day for the past month, and he's shown the utmost respect and integrity when we are open and honest. We need to launch the counter offensive now; he would provide us with the strongest launch platform. It would go a long way toward reassuring those companies that Vice President Bailey will be indicted, convicted, and imprisoned."

Cameron Conklin strode into the Oval Office cradling an untidy pile of briefing papers. She flashed her customary confident smile. "Are we ready?"

The President buried his face in his hands. "No!"

Her smile faded. She turned to Kincaid, who silently mouthed, "Help."

She resumed her cheerful smile. "Well, then, let's *get* ready."

22 END OF THE BEGINNING

Tuesday, May 27, 2014

Laura continued her inventory of Anita's pantry. "We can definitely help here, I'm sure. I even recognize some of this stuff from the pantry. Presumably we can afford to fill her up."

Jack was sitting at Anita's kitchen table eating a slice of toast while he finished some notes. "How big a list have you got?"

She showed it to him.

"Oh, yeah, we can cover that in spades. We stopped at nearly every ATM in the county if you'll recall. How much did we gather, anyway?"

"About eight thousand," she replied.

Jack chuckled. "We'll do fine. I've done most of the shopping for the past year. Looks like one fifty, two hundred dollars tops for that list. I take it you're not big on grocery shopping."

"Don't you go being judgmental," she snapped. "I've already got a permanent judge in Charlie. Shopping's not something I do. I set up and run million dollar projects and buy an occasional dinner. Not much in between." Laura clutched the list to her chest, frowning.

Jack smiled softly. "I'm sorry. I really didn't mean to come off as judgmental. You do amazing work. I've heard about your pantry and have no doubt it's saved a lot of people. Now, its contents were donated, which means you couldn't see the prices. Charlie filled me in on some of those pharmaceutical plants on the border. I'm guessing you've got professional accountants for that. You don't need to know the cost of a market basket because you're concentrating, as you must, on what you do best. That's fitting and appropriate. The world would be a better place if more people lived that way. I did not mean any disrespect."

Laura sat down across the table from Jack. "Thanks. I didn't mean to be so bitchy." She looked down as she pushed the list across the table toward him. "I'm just tired of everyone giving me grief. Seems my whole life is spent in opposition to something or other."

Jack picked up her list. "I promise I'll try to stay positive. I really do admire what you do." He added a few items to the list. "She likely needs laundry and bath supplies." He laid down his pen. "We can go to the grocery together this afternoon if you'd like. Change of scenery."

Laura sounded tired. "I'd like that. You told us what you did at the Institute. I'll be honest; I didn't understand much of what you said you did. That's Dad's department."

"Basically, we made DNA and protein for the other scientists. DNA's the code of life, like the letters of words in a book. The better you understand the words, the better you understand the story. Part of what we did was to make variants on the code — words with different letters. The researchers would substitute the new codes into organisms to see what happened."

"Sounds a bit esoteric," she offered.

Jack leaned back. "In isolation, it would be. However, in nature those misspellings are responsible for a lot of nasty diseases. Cancer comes to mind first."

"I'm sorry," she murmured.

"Yeah. Well, a lot of what drove me was the hope that the work I was doing might defeat some of those vile diseases."

Laura nodded. "And it will someday. When this is over, maybe you can go back to another lab."

Jack rubbed his face slowly. "Maybe. A lot has happened. I'm just living for the moment now and that's a new experience for me. Jenn always said I wouldn't get out of bed without a plan."

"I can believe that," Laura giggled. "And what exactly have you been planning this morning?" She pointed to the notes he had been working on.

"Charlie laid out the main actors in this drama yesterday and earlier this morning. I've also been going over your dad's financial paperwork. It gives a good picture of the opposition. No wonder our favorite men in black want it back. As for the workers' organization, I must say it isn't very tight. It's basically a labor super-organization, so you've got a broad array of powerful, well trained, and well-heeled groups opposing you — corporations, local and state governments. Even the bulk of the citizenry."

"Well, that's pretty obvious." Laura took a piece of toast from the stack and ate slowly.

"You've seen only the first wave, though, the tip of the iceberg. If this standoff isn't resolved soon, the ugliness of the past few days will seem tame. The stakes got much higher when the national telecomm workers started joining in."

"How come you know so much about labor relations?" Laura asked.

Jack shook his head. "That's not how I'm approaching it. This — our whole society — is an organism. As an organism, it has finite resources available and endless demands on those resources. A properly functioning being reaches a good balance between resources and expenditures. The more sophisticated the organism, the more dependent it becomes on communications — command and control — within the body. The communication itself costs a lot of energy. Our brains, for instance, are by weight the highest energy consumers in the body. That's kinda what Brisbane was doing in this model. They were siphoning off some of that energy budget with the promise of more efficient communications."

"You think they were right to do that?" Laura frowned.

"It's complicated. I think that kind of substitution — very smart, efficient machines for high cost humans using only a fraction of their capabilities — is inevitable. Still, Brisbane's gone about it all wrong. They're more like nest parasites. Cuckoos."

Laura tilted her head. "Huh?"

"Cuckoos and cowbirds lay their eggs in the nests of other birds. Their young grow faster and bigger, eventually pushing out the other babies. The duped parents wind up raising cuckoos and cowbirds."

"I think I see. Go on."

Jack smiled. "Brisbane promises to be everything the workers are. It comes in, takes over, and pushes the workers out. Though I'm not really savvy in the voice recognition field, I'm pretty sure they're promising a lot more than they can deliver. By the time the customers — victims, if you will — find out, it'll be too late. Brisbane will have the money. The cuckoo will have flown."

"Don't you think we've stopped their flight now? Isn't it obvious to everyone what's happened?" she asked.

"I wish it were so. Humans can support a huge load of denial. You could tell President Miller was up against it last night."

"Yeah, no kidding. He let that jerk Bailey run loose for so long. He brought it on himself."

"Hmmm. James Bailey, King of the Cowbirds," Jack suggested.

Laura laughed.

"Seriously, though, too many citizens try to personify the government as some outside third person entity. In reality, we are the government. Government is the conceptual thread binding us together. When the government is damaged, as it certainly is now, we will all suffer, and soon."

"You've been talking a lot to Charlie, haven't you?" She eyed him.

"He's very smart. He hides his brilliance under that mask of goofiness."

"I know. Sometimes I wish he'd be serious, though he'd probably be dangerous." She looked Jack over for a while, and narrowed her eyes. "Are you dangerous?"

Jack looked away from her gaze. “I’d never thought about it, but yes, I guess I am. Or I would be if I had any power. Jenn always said I was cold, too logical, missing a passion for good. I’m dangerous, but not bad now. Am I making sense?”

Laura nodded. “And are we ...” — she spread her arms wide “... this mishmash of labor and other groups that you are now part of ... good?”

“In the old days, I’d be tempted to say I couldn’t judge whether we were good or bad. We just were what we were. I’m going to step out of character and say we’re good. Our coalition supports the hopes and aspirations of most people. We work for the common betterment. We work to promote a network benefiting humanity. That’s all to the good.”

“You think awfully deep awfully fast,” she said.

“Character flaw.”

“I can live with it,” she said. “What about President Miller?”

“I think he sincerely wants to fix things,” Jack offered.

Laura shook her head. “What if it’s just a big act?”

“I’ve been a debater most of my life. As a debater, you learn to read faces, watch for tics, and listen to nuances of phrasing. I can tell he never was a debater. Most of his political career was spent behind a teleprompter. So when he’s unscripted, like last night, you get a much clearer read on his real feelings.”

“He did seem on message,” she agreed.

“Yes. His handlers or backup staff did a much better job of prepping him than in the past. His previous encounter with Jacobs was a total disaster.”

Laura closed her eyes and smiled briefly. “I remember.”

“Well, last night, though he struggled for just the right words at times, he was speaking from his heart. You could see it in his eyes, too. Even a great actor, unscripted, can’t fake the eyes. What was perhaps most disturbing was his fear of some of those corporations.”

“Fear? I didn’t hear fear,” she said.

“Oh, it was there. He realizes some of the corporations that were party to Bailey’s theft scheme and attempted getaway may be as powerful as or more powerful than the government itself.”

“What? They’re just a fraction the size of the government,” she countered.

“By mass, maybe. They control the communications. Or almost do. Their technologies are fragile and primitive at this point, yet those technologies are in place. If they actually work ...”

* * *

Wednesday, June 18, 2014

“And I say we lead with the Brisbane story. It’s got drama, it’s an outrage, it ties into the impeachment mess, and it strikes at the heart of

Wolfe's image." Ben Jacobs folded his arms.

"And it's technical enough we'll tune out half our audience." John Sykes, the news manager remained defiant.

"You, sir, are afraid of three marginal sponsors who're muscling you."

"Bullshit, Ben. I've defended every stand you've taken the past two weeks. Dammit, have you seen the poll numbers? Unbelievable as it seems, the public thinks we're in cahoots with the administration. A third of them seem to think Bailey is an innocent scapegoat, maybe even a hero."

Jacobs narrowed his eyes. "What about you, John? What do you believe? Do you think Bailey's anything other than a manipulative thief? Do you think that Brisbane has any motive other than harvesting every billion it can before it's shut down? What do you believe, John, is our responsibility in light of the facts we have gathered?"

John Sykes dropped his head into his hand. "Ben, what we've got and what we report don't matter if no one is listening. The public thinks you're on a single-minded crusade and you're losing your objectivity."

"The public? Unless you've got numbers I haven't seen, about ten percent of 'the public' is our regular viewership. Hell, I can find you three percent who think Hitler wasn't such a bad guy. A year, five years, ten years from now, the world will talk of this as our finest hour, when we kept liberty's light lit. What were you going to lead with, by the way?" Jacobs asked.

John Sykes put his hands on the table, tight-lipped.

"No, John, no, not the Olympics drug tests. Please tell me you weren't going to echo Wolfe's coverage of the drug tests." Jacobs waited in silence. "You were."

Sykes looked away.

Jacobs stood up. "Tonight, we will lead with the undercover tests of the Brisbane call center software showing it can't tell the difference between 'my house is on fire' and 'my horse needs a shower,' even when spoken slowly with a Midwestern accent. We will follow with the administrations plans for gas rationing, and then the attempted coup in Iran. Somewhere in the mix, we'll report how several Senators at the heart of the impeachment are coping with the pressure from some of their mega million corporate donors. Maybe, if we're not out of time, we might possibly mention the Olympian drug-testing scandal, though we'll probably push it to the web site since it's mostly re-reporting anyway."

"Ben, you're going directly against the top office. They're not going to be happy. Your job isn't really so secure."

"Don't you dare threaten me, John Sykes. The chair I sit in is a sacred trust. I will not dishonor it."

The two faced each other in stern silence.

Jacobs spoke first. "We're done with our discussion. Let's get the broadcast formatted. We've got three hours before air."

* * *

"Good evening, this is Ben Jacobs. We open our broadcast tonight with results of our undercover testing of the call center hardware and software at the heart of the increasingly tense and occasionally violent national telecommunications strike. The scale of the test failures we observed calls into question the entire process behind the installations, and in particular the company producing the products, Brisbane Technologies. What we discovered is that those machines simply don't work."

The footage switched to an office identified simply as located in Columbus, Ohio. The narrator picked up the story.

"We have gained access to one of the Brisbane Technologies call center model 731A units, and we have been spending much of the day testing the unit with simulated phone calls. The results will at time seem humorous until you realize, in the event of an emergency, these would be the machines taking your call."

The camera focused on the words printing on a monitor screen as the television audio played the phone call.

[Woman's voice] "Help! My house is on fire!"

[Printout] Hell, my horse is a shower.

[Old man's voice] "There's an intruder in the bedroom."

[Printout] Hairs on strudel in the red room.

[Child's voice] My mommy's not breathing.

[Printout] I vomit hot teething.

"In not one single instance, out of over a hundred tests we performed, with normal voice tones, did the system come even remotely close to a correct transcription. Records we uncovered and confirmed with sources familiar with the transition prove these very units were to go into operation within the month as the call center staff was reduced. We have found the same situation at four other centers we visited in Ohio and West Virginia. Calls to the manufacturer have not been returned, despite numerous attempts."

The camera returned to Ben Jacobs. "We tried to question executives and workers of Brisbane Technologies, only to find the rural Pennsylvania corporate offices locked down, and we were greeted by heavily armed guards when we approached their facilities. We will report on our encounters tonight in a special edition at ten, nine Central Time.

"The man most closely identified with Brisbane and its shadow parent, Windham Trust, is of course, the Vice President, James T. Bailey. For the seventh day, the Vice President's legal team has managed to stall the impeachment process.

"Today's delay resulted from a call from Mr. Bailey's defense for documents they claim will show the fund transfers were part of a White

House directed plan to gain intelligence on the Chinese defense infrastructure. The White House immediately and vigorously denied those allegations and opened all files to the impeachment committee members to review any documents. Still the move will delay the proceedings another three to five days. Sources at the White House have expressed their increasing frustration at the delays and have set up a special office in the White House itself, with congressional staff present around the clock, to respond rapidly to the expected future calls for papers and information. In a noontime press conference, North Carolina Senator David Kreis said nothing offered by the Vice President's team has altered the course of the Congressional investigation and he expected an indictment within the week. Senator Kreis praised the White House for its cooperation while strongly denying he had any interest in the Vice-Presidency when, as expected, the position becomes available. In one of his very few light moments of the interview, he said he'd 'leave shipwrecks to divers.'"

* * *

Wednesday, July 2, 2014

The East Room of the White House resembled a dinner theatre. Several large screen televisions occupied one end of the room. White House staff alternately sat watching the proceedings or milling around on the periphery of the room, quietly conversing. David Kincaid sat with his group at the back of the room near a small cluster of phones.

Anna spoke on one line with Jacques Cartier. Kincaid caught more of her French vocabulary than in the past. Chiefly, he sensed the somber tone of her conversation.

Sarah continued her data entry, glancing from time to time at the big screens without reaction.

Senate microphones carried by C-Span provided the audio accompanying the broadcasts. Other channels broadcast similar video distinguished mostly by the crawls along the bottom of each screen.

Anna completed her call and turned to Kincaid. "Monsieur Cartier expresses his grave solicitude. He knows the President is taking this hard."

Kincaid nodded. "The President was asking me this morning if there was any reason to consider a pardon."

"A pardon? That sounds like a particularly bad idea," she said, alarmed.

"Apparently that's what the Founding Fathers thought, too. Article Two, Section Two actually denies him that ability."

"Smart guys," she agreed.

"And he's made it pretty clear that he doesn't much want to talk." Kincaid looked in the direction of the President. "Tiffany's the only one who's had more than a few minutes of conversation with him."

Anna surveyed the room. "Any idea how much longer until they begin voting?"

Sarah spoke without looking up from her screen. "Three more Senators still need to testify, then the Chief Justice gives his legal instructions, then they vote. I'm guessing conviction at six-fifteen, give or take twenty minutes."

Anna folded her arms. "Tyler, you can't be tracking proceedings that closely and typing that fast."

Sarah looked up briefly. "Can too. They're moving at glacial speed. I can devote five percent of my attention to the trial without really missing anything. Six-fifteen, plus or minus twenty, final answer."

Kincaid grinned and shook his head. "Anna, I'm going to get some coffee. Can I get you something?"

"I'll go with you, sir. It's a little too gloomy in here."

As the two of them reached the door on their way to the kitchen, Sarah glanced up from her laptop and watched them depart. She grinned and returned to her programs.

* * *

By the time of the judgment vote, everyone in the East Room was seated and silent. The clerk systematically called the roll, pausing only after the sixty-sixth consecutive "guilty." Most cameras focused on the Chief Justice, seated at the podium, hands folded before him, head bowed slightly. When the clerk paused, he looked up slowly, sadly. He nodded and the clerk resumed the roll call. In the end the Senate delivered its guilty verdict with one hundred votes.

The President closed his eyes. "Time of death?"

Kincaid looked at his watch. "Six twenty-one p.m. Eastern Daylight Time."

The President stood up. "Is our official pronouncement ready to roll?"

"Yes, sir. I think it'll probably run at seven. Do you want to watch it here?" Kincaid asked.

"No. I know what it says," Miller whispered.

"Yes, sir."

The President left the East Room, which was silent save for the background noise of the Senate broadcasting to screens no one was watching.

* * *

3:21 p.m., Thursday, July 11, 2014

"Are you sure?" Jack leaned forward clasping his chin.

Nearly thirty members of the emergency committee, representing twelve states, had gathered in a nondescript Rockville office building.

Charlie repeated the question into his phone and waited for an answer. Grimly, he looked up. "At least. She's behind a barrier. She can see the front of the building, and there are at least five people on the ground bleeding and motionless. She heard a dozen or more shots and can see four security people with rifles. They've got masks over their faces."

"Is it private security or local law enforcement?"

Charlie listened further. "Not sure. The uniforms are dark, and she can't get a clear look at the armed men. It seems far more weaponry than any security force should have."

Jack turned to the others. "OK. Now you've got some big decisions to make. It's clear that the federal government can't protect you. In several of the communities, the local governments are actually still aligned with Brisbane, though that's shrinking. If you take up arms, as Martin is suggesting, there is no telling where it will end. You're rushing to the brink of a civil war, a civil war for more dangerous than our first one. Unlike that first Civil War, this one would have no lines of North and South. This war would divide the nation street-by-street, house-by-house. The quantity and quality of weapons available right now on both sides guarantee a bloodbath the size of Antietam repeated over and over across the country. Don't go there."

Laura spoke from four seats away on Jack's left. "People are dying already. Innocent people, defenseless workers attacked by thugs armed with the most advanced weapons available. As of now, we've got twenty dead at half a dozen centers. What are we going to do?"

"You're first going to decide on a national leadership," Jack insisted. "We agreed on that a week ago. You're splintered. You have no cohesive voice to demand the protection you need. Who are our defenders going to listen to?" Jack spread his hands and began pointing to various representatives. "Chicago? Dallas? San Francisco?"

Martin VanDorn conferred with several colleagues in his corner. He turned finally to Jack. "We want you to be our spokesman."

"I'm not a member of any of the unions; I'm only here to advise. I have no history in this work, and I would be singularly inappropriate to represent you."

Martin folded his arms. "Then who? Who has a better track record predicting what's going to happen since the beginning of this mess? You're fast on your feet, and you say the right thing first time around."

Jack looked around the room. "Have you got representatives from all the regions here?"

"We're missing Michigan, I think."

"Pick someone who's worked in the call centers," Jack said.

As the representatives of each of the regional offices gathered at the far end of the room, Charlie walked over to Jack, Laura close behind. Charlie sat on the table and watched the meeting as he spoke to Jack. "You know they're going to ask you again."

"Then I'll say 'no' again."

"Not that easy, Jack Boy. None of them have kissed the Blarney Stone like you. The opposition has plenty of hired golden tongues who're filling the airwaves with their side." Charlie watched Jack for a while. "There are other things on your mind, I'm guessing."

"Charlie, I meant what I said. I've got no currency. From a logical standpoint, that's sufficient. The upcoming battle is going to be a media event. My back-story is all wrong. Do we remember that a few weeks ago, I shot and killed … my best friend? How long before that's the story?"

"Got some points there, Jack Boy. Still, you're way ahead on communications skills. You've trained all those years for the championships. We need you. They need you," Charlie insisted. "Maybe you can be the trainer behind the scenes."

"I'll do whatever is needed as long as it's effective. It's time we started looking at ground rules. Things like 'no weapons.' You don't want to do anything to give your foe an excuse."

Charlie's face wrinkled in apprehension. "You're totally right, Jack Boy. I've been a pretty much uncompromising pacifist my whole life, yet even I want to strike out with each new murder. We don't know how far the Brisbanians are willing to go to preserve their turf. We don't know how many of them there are, and we don't even know how they communicate."

The gathering across the room broke up, and several members moved in Jack's direction.

VanDorn spoke first. "For now, I'll take the lead. We still need you to be the voice."

Jack began drawing diagrams on his pad of paper. "We were just talking about that. I can't be the speaker. I have issues you don't know about that would distract too much from your message. While you and I disagree on some tactics, you've got a good stage presence. After all the years I've prepped for the podium, I should know. I'll help get you ready, teach you to polish. Laura's got media connections we can start working this evening."

VanDorn pondered the offer. "That might work. I still say we need our own security. It looks like we can trust the locals here. Half the others aren't so sure. This is life or death. We need our own security. That's really not optional."

"Do you understand what I'm saying about a civil war? Do you disagree that this could spiral out of control?" Jack repeated.

VanDorn remained quiet for a moment. "It could. Let's make sure it doesn't. We still need to be prepared to defend ourselves."

"And how do you propose to do that?"

"The locals still have to go through the wires to talk to each other. We need to monitor their talk." VanDorn said.

Jack put up his hand. "Whoa. First, that's illegal. Second, you don't have nearly the manpower needed to monitor communications even if it were legal."

VanDorn stood with his arms folded. "Legal? Jack, they're killing us. I think 'legal' is getting a little fuzzy these days."

Jack leaned on the table. "The first element of battle is organization. Foundation requirement is rules, iron clad rules, rules to follow even under siege. Maybe especially under siege. In the end, organization beats force. Though it may not seem like it during the hard times, principle and organization beat force in the end. 'Legal' is only as fuzzy as you make it, Martin. Right now, Brisbane and their allies seem to have the upper hand. They have their own organization built for their own short-term interests. However, they are operating outside the law, and are doomed to fail in the end. If you go down that path, I'm out."

"I can't believe you're engaging in this theoretical exercise at a time like this," Martin continued, exasperated.

Jack shook his head slowly as he sketched flow charts on the paper. "Not theoretical, Martin. This is the reality. You call it an exercise. I know that it's truth. You asked me just minutes ago to be spokesman. I'll stand behind you on one condition, Martin."

"What's that?"

Jack set down his pencil. "Put me in charge of security."

* * *

Monday, July 28, 2014

Kincaid noticed that White House meetings were increasingly held in the situation room. Monday's gathering with the Secretaries of Energy, Defense, Transportation, and Homeland Security had just concluded.

Kincaid reviewed his notes for Peter. "The last tanker from the Middle East arrived in Galveston this morning. From now on, it looks like we can rely only on Nigeria and Mexico as major foreign sources."

"No progress with Venezuela?" Peter asked.

"No."

Peter sighed. "We're already seeing lines all along the East Coast."

"Transportation is set to roll with their recommendations and Energy will start rationing discussions this afternoon."

"That's going to get ugly really fast. Regular's already over five-twenty a gallon," Peter warned.

"Right. And it doesn't help that it's getting really difficult to get the word out. There is increasing urgency to get something out in print before the whole system shuts down. After the last incident in Denver, the telecomm workers are pretty galvanized."

Peter nodded. "VanDorn has threatened rolling communication blackouts if the strikers don't get federal or effective state protection. I don't blame them for wanting it, but I don't see where anyone can come up with that much coverage."

Kincaid added, "And we're getting a lot of push-back from the Hill and Wolfe Networks. We really have to move fast. One surprise was just how few homes have a regular radio any more. Matt pulled up some statistics. Fewer than thirty percent of American homes have a working radio. What radios there are, live in the cars. Over eighty percent have been getting all their information from cable or fiber."

"Sir, was there any good news?" Peter asked.

Kincaid grinned, but his grin soon faded. He wrinkled his brow. "No, there actually wasn't any good news."

Tracey entered the room. "Mr. Kincaid, Senator Kreis called to say he's running about half an hour behind."

"Not a problem. By the way, how's Janet working out?"

"Splendidly, sir. That was a smart move." Tracey left the room.

"Janet? Janet Black, the Vice President's secretary?"

"Yep." Kincaid smiled. "She was always a reliable ally over there. She's serving as liaison with the Speaker's office for us now. Janet has the institutional knowledge and gets along well with some very difficult people."

"Obviously," Peter agreed.

"When we dismantled the Vice President's office, she was one of the few people we wanted to keep."

Peter chuckled. "Probably one of the few who aren't going to jail."

"Yeah, well, she's going to be the real head of the search team for a replacement. As bad as things were under Mr. Bailey, he still performed a useful function running interference for the President. Technically, I'm the head of the committee, yet she's doing all the heavy lifting. She's really well networked."

"So does she have a list of candidates?"

Kincaid shook his head. "Sadly, yes. But to most of the obvious talent, we're poison by association. What was it Senator Kreis said yesterday? He does great with the sound bites."

"I think it was 'rats seldom swim toward a sinking ship.' Maybe he said 'never.' He likes the nautical references."

"He was a Navy man. I think he made commander before he got out and ran for office. Anyway, he'll be here in a bit to go over some names. We'll see if there are any patriots left who'll give their political lives for their country." Kincaid stood up to stretch. He went over to the coffee carafe, only to find it empty. He stared out the window. "You know, when I was little, I dreamed of being President. After twenty-three years in this city, and especially after the last two years, I can't imagine wanting the job."

"You need to get some rest, sir."

"I know. I know." He looked up to see Corporal Tull enter with the message traffic clipboard.

As Kincaid reviewed and initialed the messages, Tull looked down to Peter, who shook his head slowly. Tull frowned. Peter pointed to the empty mug. Tull smiled and nodded.

After finishing the traffic, Kincaid returned the board. "I put the message from Treasury on top. Could you please get that to the President right away?"

"Yes, sir." Tull turned smartly and departed.

"Where was I?"

Peter smiled. "You were whining about how the job isn't what you dreamed it would be."

Kincaid laughed. "Was I whining?"

"That's one interpretation. You're definitely not your usual optimistic self. That's what really tells me you need sleep," Peter said.

Tracey stepped to the door. "Senator Kreis is on his way. And the Marines are mounting a rescue mission."

"Huh?"

She stepped back as Tull entered with a fresh carafe and a small plate of fruit and cheese.

Kincaid brightened. "I'm saved. If there's a medal for this, I'll see that you get it."

Tull grinned. "The coffee's fresh. The plate is leftovers from the meeting down the passageway."

"Thank you." Kincaid lifted his hand in a wave.

As Tull left, David Kreis arrived. "Well, Chief, you ready for more bad news?"

* * *

Monday, August 4, 2014

Kincaid was finding it difficult to concentrate during the staff meeting. Not that he was particularly tired, relative to what now passed as normal. He had finally gotten a full night's sleep Sunday night. Earlier in the meeting, he had presented the latest list of people who had declined to be considered for the Vice-Presidency. Matt's report, though grim, had been presented as a Star Wars narrative, which left everyone informed while still sane. Kincaid's difficulty had nothing to do with Anna's presentation. She even had maps to project and some positive updates about new alliances. Kincaid found it difficult to concentrate because he was watching her. The strand of hair that always seemed to rebel, which she periodically cajoled back into its place with a tiny shake of her head. Her summer blouse with the ruffles at the edges of its fabric. Her carefully carved words so much the product of a careful interpreter. He was fixated on the little beauty mark on her left cheek when she began to turn from the presentation board in his direction. He quickly faced forward to find Sarah eyeing him from across the table.

She had obviously been watching him for some time, her Cheshire grin vintage Sarah mischief. She turned her head slowly toward Anna, then back to Kincaid with an inquisitive tilt.

Kincaid scowled.

Sarah continued her smile, slowly raising her finger across her lips.

Kincaid did his best to concentrate for the rest of the meeting. He had had his good moments for the day.

23 DARKNESS DESCENDS

Akron, Ohio, Tuesday, August 26, 2014

The Old Union Hall in Akron smelled of well-worn tile, old wood, old books, and millions upon millions of walking shoes. Jack smiled, remembering fondly the times as a pre-teen he accompanied his father to their own courthouse to file real estate papers. That old courthouse and this union hall were vintage 1930s construction — solid, completely manual labor. He could have followed his father into real estate, but chose chemistry instead. That technical bent and his love of debate laid a path to his current location and secretive meetings developing the security for a movement barely days old, only different from a national rebellion in the details.

"OK," said Jack, "we have tracking devices and they're working. Martin, are you pretty sure it's only about two thousand for the Brisbane people opposing us … real boots-on-the-ground dangerous people?"

"Yes. We've gotten the rosters, located each Brisbane guy at least once, and alerted our locals to watch for them," Martin confirmed.

"Well done. That really helps. And do we know who's paying them?" Jack removed his new glasses. He had not needed glasses for several years, but the stress of the past few months had expressed itself by a return to blurry vision.

"Not really," Martin replied. "Only a few are on Brisbane's official payroll. In some cases, it's obvious, like those locales where the county execs are publicly campaigning against us. But Brisbane has troops in places where the locals are friendly, too."

Laura broke in. "It would help if we just listened in. We essentially own the transmissions."

Jack leaned forward, elbows on the table, head resting in his hands. "I'm pretty sure we already had this conversation. We've talked about that possibility and we all understand that it would be illegal and detrimental in the end. And while the matter of legality may seem at times absurd given the forces arrayed against us, the point is that we have the moral high ground, that we have remained within the law, and that in the end we will be better served for staying there. Because of our comm links to each other, we have stayed out of harm's way from those thugs, and we've been able to leverage our good position with both local and federal law enforcement."

He watched Laura fold her arms and bite her lip as she looked back at him. After a moment he smiled. "Did I exaggerate anything?"

Laura shook her head.

Jack turned again to Martin. "How are the talks with President Miller's people going?"

"Slow. They're tied up with a lot of problems, so we seem to be seeing different people nearly every time. The oil shortage has them tied in knots. Our best meetings have been with a Matt Luskin. He's one of the President's trusted tech advisors and seems to move a lot in the inner circle and has gotten us some protection — out in Denver, for instance. He's interested in our organizational structure. We didn't help him out on that yet, and he didn't seem too upset, but he said we appear to be a well-run organization." Martin grinned.

"Yes?" Jack queried.

Martin continued, "He wanted to know who the 'Jedi' in charge of our security was. I think they really don't know about Jack Pullman. Most of the world assumes he's dead."

Jack rubbed his chin. "Probably best to keep it that way, eh, Charlie?"

Charlie chuckled. "You can't fight the enemy you can't see."

"We're not the enemy," Jack replied sternly.

Charlie folded his arms behind his head and leaned back in his chair. "If I were the President of the United States trying to hold together a country running out of energy, an extremely skeptical population, a big war just a hair trigger away, an outraged Congress, and a deposed Vice President in prison with no one stepping forward to take his place, I'd be real likely to regard a group seeking justice by holding the nation's communication grid hostage as a potential threat. We're damned lucky that Mr. Luskin appears to believe in us."

Jack thought for a moment. "Martin, let's make absolutely certain that the President knows we're really on his side."

Martin nodded and turned to Laura while pointing to Charlie. "Does he always squeeze so much into a single sentence?"

She leaned forward. "You have no idea."

"All right." Jack shut his notebook. "When do we next contact the administration? I have visions of closing this up and everyone's going back home if possible."

Martin checked his schedule. "Friday morning."

"Excellent."

* * *

Thursday, August 28, 2014, The Eisenhower Executive Office Building

Kathy called for numbers as she finished her report. Sarah waited for each query and typed in the appropriate commands.

"April GDP gap?"

"Seventeen percent."

"May?

"Nineteen percent until Bailey was uncovered. From then on, zero," Sarah called.

"June, July, and August?"

Sarah sighed, "That's what 'from then on' means. Yes."

Kathy grinned. "Hey, don't get snippy with me. I have to be completely accurate. Now, for unemployment. April?"

"Seven …"

The lights went out, plunging the room in darkness except for Sarah's computer. Beneath her table, the alarm of her uninterruptible power supply chirped.

"Well, that was money well spent." She glanced under the table at the device, and then began saving and closing documents.

The lights came on again.

"Does that happen very often?"

Kathy frowned. "No. Never."

Racing footsteps sounded in the hall as Corporal Tull sped past their door, pistol drawn.

"What's going on?" Sarah stood up.

"Sit back down. You don't want to be wandering about during a security alert."

"Why not?" Sarah asked.

"You might get shot."

Sarah sat down quickly. "How long will it last?"

"I wouldn't know. Since we have no idea what caused the power failure, we have no idea how long it will take to resolve." Kathy began sniffing the air.

"What?" Sarah asked.

"Diesel fumes. We're on emergency power."

* * *

Programming Palace Software, Camden, New Jersey

The room erupted in cheers.

"And Josh Ruark beats the game. Eighteen levels and over five thousand aliens. And I still have my sword left."

Mike Johnson laughed. "Yeah, it only took you thirty-eight hours. And you're the one who programmed it."

Josh spread his hands and then held his controller aloft. "Thirty-eight hours straight against the best players on the East Coast." He motioned to Lindsey Two and Lindsey One.

Lindsey Two had been playing opposite Josh for the entire game. Lindsey One had fallen asleep after her defeat in level thirteen, but awoke at the sound of Mike's voice and discreetly unbuttoned the top three buttons of her blouse, revealing the pink lacy top of her bra. She stared at Mike.

Mike shook his head. "Congratulations. I'll be honest: I had my doubts last month. Glad I kept quiet."

Lindsey One spoke up. "You're a smart man to have your doubts, Mikey. Ole Josh here was hav'n a bitchin' time getting the blast shadows to work." She moved very close to Mike.

Mike turned to Josh.

"I'd never tried that before." Josh explained, "But it worked — eventually. You just saw that in the final play."

The lights in the room flickered and went out. Josh looked frantically around as the hum of the computer fans was joined by a cacophony of power supply alarms.

Josh shouted orders. "Emergency shut down — scramble." He and the two Lindseys darted around the room to each computer, saving files and shutting down machines.

After about three minutes, Lindsey One called from the far end of the room, "I win!"

Mike laughed. "That was as impressive as the game."

Josh was alight in the glow of his monitor. "In five weeks you won't laugh. The game's ready for the automated testing now, over a month ahead of schedule. You'll be a millionaire by Christmas just like I promised."

The Lindseys had returned from their shutdown tasks.

"The company will be sharing the profits with your assistants, too."

Josh smirked. "Of course, like always. But unlike you, they're already millionaires."

Mike turned to Lindsey One. He didn't have far to turn. "Really?"

She grinned and nodded vigorously.

He turned to Josh. "Well, you're an honorable man. I'll let the execs know as soon as I can get back on my machine and send e-mail. Shouldn't be too long."

Josh turned to his machine. "I can probably tell you exactly how long." He pulled up a program and entered a few numbers, then began to frown. "What the hell?"

Mike and the two Lindseys gathered around Josh.

"This isn't a dropout at the building or substation. The shutdown is system-wide and spreading. Look. Connecticut 4 and North Carolina 7 just went critical. Bang. Connecticut 4 just went offline. This is bad. This is really bad."

"Are we under attack? And how are you getting all this with the whole power grid shutting down?"

Josh entered more commands while shifting to a national view on his largest monitor. "The communications grid is mostly optical, so it has about twelve hours of battery backup. My machine will go for three days. Plus the comm grid's got priority, and it's getting power from the remaining stations. I'm pulling up the reporter software from the failing stations."

"How can you do that?"

Josh shrugged. "I wrote it." He continued to check his software plant by plant. With each check, his expression grew grimmer. Finally he turned around in his chair. "Mike, I think we need to make ourselves scarce for a while."

"What?"

Josh continued, "All the plants affected are suffering catastrophic failures. It's happening during emergency shutdowns at the point in the program I was working on the day we left Brisbane. Every plant that's failed is using the very version I was working on. If I were still programming for Brisbane, that version wouldn't be ready for release for another five months. I'll bet they turned the project over to that idiot Mattock, and she released it."

Lindsey Two rolled her eyes. One was shaking her head.

Mike stared at the screen. "Can you tell what the plants were doing at the time of the emergency?"

Josh shook his head. "Not in much detail." He pointed at some small charts on the screen. "But for every one, you see a sudden spike in turbine bearing temperatures followed by what looks like frantic efforts to shut the turbines down. After about ten minutes, the power suddenly drops to zero."

Mike continued to stare at the screen. "But they're not all red. There's still lots of green left."

"Yeah, about a third." Again he pointed to areas of the little dialogs on the screen. "And you see the greens are all using the last version of the software that I released, or they're the nukes who use ancient software that's DOE approved. Some nukes even use mechanical systems."

They stared at each other.

Finally, Josh turned and began shutting his system down. "Like I said, you'll be wanting to make yourself scarce. There will be some very unhappy people looking for us really soon."

"I'll call Janice."

"Take her with you. Remember, we're talking Brisbane. No telling what they'll do. And forget the phone. Just get driving. You'll recall your phone wasn't working even before this."

Mike closed his eyes tightly. "Then how did you … never mind. I can't leave. Janice dropped me off this morning."

Lindsey One volunteered. "I'll take him. He and Janice can stay at my place. I've got plenty of room, and no one's going to come looking for the Johnsons at my place."

Mike wilted.

Josh smiled as he shook his head. "Michael, my friend, I don't see a better solution. Looks like a little devil's going to be your guardian angel today."

Lindsey One skipped to her desk through the darkness to retrieve her keys.

* * *

The Eisenhower Executive Office Building, Saturday, August 30, 2014

In the large conference room of the Executive Office Building, Matt took the floor when it was his turn as Kincaid's staff briefed the President and cabinet secretaries. Matt did his best to make the presentation lively. With the help of a lot of strong coffee, he kept the sleep-deprived audience mostly awake.

"OK," he began, "we've traced the events of Thursday with near certainty to a wide-spread software bug. There is no evidence of any terrorist attack or deliberate takedown of the electric grid. The cause appears to be straightforward — flawed software installed too widely with too little testing. That said, the magnitude of the damage is almost unimaginable.

"Quick synopsis: Thursday afternoon, August 28th, a cold front moved through central New Jersey, triggering a line of severe thunderstorms. Lightning hit a large transmission tower near Cherry Hill, New Jersey, taking down the power lines. The substations on either side of the break are programmed to automatically request power from alternate generating stations, in this case the Water Gap plant. Water Gap responded appropriately, but the total demand was higher than their generators alone could provide. At that point Water Gap should have stopped powering up at one hundred percent capacity and requested supplemental power from three of its neighbors, but the software was missing the stop algorithm and instead allowed the rotors to continue spinning faster. They far exceeded their design capability, and the bearings of the generators began to overheat. The operators initiated an emergency shutdown, but the software was using the same flawed algorithm for those procedures. Simply put, the buttons on the operator's screen were reversed. Instead of commanding the generator to shut down, the emergency button on their screen sent a command to increase power. The bearings — incredibly tough Iridium steel — literally exploded, and the rotors destroyed their housings and brought the plant to a flaming stop.

"With power now gone, the power-request command was passed to the sister plants, and they followed the same devastating cycle. At last count, there were twenty-seven deaths in the various plants. There would have been more, but the software had been designed to reduce staffing, and the plants were nearly empty. Before this software implementation, there would have been experienced crews on hand who could have shut down the generators manually before they could reach a critical failure situation like this. The senior — expensive — staff had been let go."

President Miller spoke up. "How long before we get that capacity back on line?"

Matt took a deep breath. "That's part of the even worse news, Mr. President. Machines like these are not off-the-shelf items. It takes foundries months to make each one, and there exists a finite capacity to manufacture them — typically fewer than a hundred a year around the world. Several dozen generators were offline for routine maintenance and are being readied for service in the next few days using older, tested software, but, all told, we've lost between sixty-five and seventy percent of the total electrical generation across the country, and it will be significantly down for no less than six to ten months."

Secretary Deatherage let out a whistle. "Six to ten months? Can't we reroute power from the stations that are operational?"

Matt nodded. "Exactly. That's six to ten with rerouting. And that's happened and is happening as we speak. But it's not a straightforward process. The nation's power grid is a patchwork of generating stations and distribution centers with different systems — some networked together, some not. In point of fact, it is this very diversity that saved us from a complete shutdown. Had they all been running the same software ... I don't even want to contemplate the straits we'd be in."

Kincaid motioned to Peter, who replaced Matt at the white board.

"Mr. President, Matt has described the basic underlying cause. I'd like to go over the plan we're developing to deal with the consequences. I emphasize that this is a work in progress among Energy, Homeland Security, DOD, and a host of others." Peter pressed a button, and a map of the United States appeared on the screen beside the whiteboard. "The green areas, and there are not many of them, are zones where the power stations were unaffected — either because they had not installed the new software and/or laid off their workers, or because they used entirely different control technologies or generating capabilities. For instance, mountain California is largely wind-powered; Tennessee Valley uses a lot of hydroelectric, and the coal-fired plants there are using twentieth century controls. Alaska and Hawaii are largely unaffected because their small-scale generators didn't require these sophisticated controls. The yellow areas are zones operating on sixty to eighty percent power because of diverse energy sources or because they can bridge to more reliable sources. The yellow area looks big, but it's largely low-density population. The red areas are our critical concerns. Though small in area, they're densely populated. They're concentrated along the East and Gulf Coasts and the Mid-West around Chicago and the great rivers. That would include St. Louis, Cincinnati, Kansas City, and so on. Our biggest concerns are New York and Chicago."

The President interrupted. "How did L.A. and San Francisco escape this?"

"Very diverse sourcing, sir — wind, solar, nuclear, geothermal — combined with a shutdown mentality borne of their earthquake preparedness. They've lost about twenty percent of their capacity, but have adjusted consumption to compensate … for now."

The President nodded.

"Back to New York, though. That whole area is running on maybe ten percent; and the distribution is uneven, with some areas completely without power and unable to get power. The New York metro area has an aging infrastructure and minimal shared connections among competing power companies. Manhattan Island is probably our worst-case scenario. There were over twenty plants supplying power. Now there is one. Everything — and I mean everything — on the island is dependent on electricity. Elevators in their twenty- to hundred-plus story buildings. Pumps for the water above about five stories. Even at the lower levels, the water will last only as long as water towers have water, since they don't have the power to replenish. The subway, telephone, radio, TV — the very means we have to get information to the public — all need power.

"Even if there were generators, it wouldn't help for long because there's no way to get fuel for them. The gas stations have no electricity to pump. There is no mechanism for bringing in fuel packaged for retail distribution. There is no reasonable way to evacuate the population."

The President's face drained of color. "And all of this because of a God-damned piece of software?"

Matt answered from the side. "Yes, sir, basically it boils down to that. Brisbane Technology's power control division."

President Miller hung his head. "I am sick to death of hearing that name." He straightened up. "Obviously we are doing something. What's working?"

Sarah stepped to the board.

The President leaned back in his chair. "Last time we heard from you, you were an economist."

"We're wearing a lot of hats these days, Mr. President. And the survival channels are basically the same as the economic lines: all supply chain. The software for cash flow can accommodate most goods and services.

"As you know, FEMA, the National Guards, and Army are coordinating getting food and water into the most stricken cities. We don't have the manpower to go to every city, so we're pairing smaller cities with nearby larger cities to share resources. We're also making maps of all the fuel stations in those cities and deploying mobile generators to key filling stations. These mobile generators are mostly National Guard units. There aren't nearly enough because the whole system was scaled to a Katrina-sized disaster — which, I might add, we used to think of as big, but was only about five percent the size of the current emergency. Anyway, these strategically-located gas stations serve as boosters to get food trucks into the cities. The food and water are beginning to move, but we don't yet know what we're going to do for money. The banks are obviously shut down; the people have almost no money, since we are a ninety-five-plus percent electronic economy. No state or federal budget is ready for the demands that the food, water, and fuel alone are going to run, much less the huge cost of building electric network jumpers to get the power flowing again.

"We're somewhat fortunate that it's not winter, in which case people and pipes would be freezing. But, being it's August, these cities have become extremely dependent on ventilation and air-conditioning. It's not just a matter of comfort. Millions and millions of people live in buildings that are essentially uninhabitable without electricity."

The President turned to his Secretaries. "Can we really be brought to our knees this quickly?"

Sarah continued, "Actually, sir, it gets worse, yet. Until we can get power to the sanitation systems, we will be developing a sewage problem. CDC has given us about four days to get the sewers back on line before there may be catastrophic failures and the risk of cholera and other diseases we haven't seen here in two centuries. Part of our accompanying fears is that the city populations will become desperate and begin attacking the food and fuel trucks. If that fragile flow becomes disrupted, we could be looking at millions of deaths."

The President turned to Defense Secretary Banks. "Do we have the people to protect the supply chain?"

"Frankly, no, sir. What we are doing for now is blocking the main arteries into the city and allowing only essential materials and services in. We're developing procedures for rescuing and extracting civilian supply trucks if they break down or otherwise get stopped."

"Otherwise?" Miller asked.

"Sir, we're not ruling out mob actions. We're drafting an executive order authorizing deadly force in the event of a major breakdown of law and order."

The President turned to his Chief of Staff. "David?"

"That order would be the last resort and such a contingency will absolutely not be made public. What we are doing in the public arena is putting radio stations back on line starting with the Emergency Broadcast Network. Unfortunately, because of our rather lackluster emergency preparedness, very few people have portable radios to receive the broadcasts. FEMA has a limited supply of solar powered radios for distribution. We're developing a network of block captains or the equivalent to distribute to, so that we have some way of getting word out. Tiffany is riding through these areas on her motorcycle, getting public attention and getting people on board with the network."

"Tiffany? My Tiffany?"

"Yes, sir."

"No one told me about this."

"It was her idea, and it seems to be working. The people love her and they listen to her. I'm sorry for the lack of communications. You know what it's been like."

President Miller nodded slowly. "Right. It's a good idea, of course." He seemed dazed. "What are our greatest vulnerabilities, David? Don't we need to declare martial law in some of these areas?"

Kincaid shook his head. "Sir, I'd counsel against that. First, we don't really have a mechanism or solid legal foundation for any form of martial law. But, more importantly, we need to have faith in the citizenry, that they will respond appropriately as long as we are obviously doing our part. Not that it's going to be a smooth ride, but we've endured so many crises throughout our history and come out better on the other side. I really think this will be another such time."

The President narrowed his eyes. "For such a pragmatist as I know you to be, David, you're sounding like a starry-eyed optimist. You'd better be right."

"Yes, sir."

* * *

The Union Hall, Akron, Ohio, Thursday, September 18, 2014

Jack looked over his shoulder. "All right, Martin, you've got the watch in this zone. You feel safe enough?"

Martin nodded. "Yeah. That Jersey programmer's gotten us the software to track the Brisbane assets. We know where they are and where they're going. He's planted bots in their phones to tag 'em. How about you? Are you comfortable covering that distance?"

"Uh huh." Jack continued to pack boxes of food into the back of the SUV. "We've got current maps with enough detail that we can stick to back roads. Some of Charlie's people have spotted snipers along the interstates — mostly Brisbane, some sympathizers. With their corporate resources, there's no telling how much they know of our movements. When we call, it's going to be brief just before we move. You keep off the phone, too. Expect your calls to be intercepted."

"Of course." Martin handed Jack the last box of bottled water. "What bothers me most is that the other side seems to be functioning pretty well even with the grid shut down. According to our reports, they can move even in areas with little or no fuel."

Laura emerged with a large box of batteries. "They're commandeering vehicles and fuel supplies. I just got off the phone with Florence, South Carolina. A convoy of Brisbane guards shot an entire family when they tried to resist. They're on the move, and it looks like they're heading to DC and New York."

Jack sat down on the tailgate, catching his breath. "To what end? Even in this chaos, they're not going to take over the government."

"But they can collect one hell of a toll." Charlie emerged from the union hall carrying two rifles.

"Oh, no, no weapons, Charlie." Jack pointed back to the hall.

"Jack boy, I've been a pacifist all my life. But I've been a pacifist because it was practical. Right now there are several thousand people who will want you, and, coincidentally, me, dead as soon as they find out who you are and where you are. I've been looking at the path we've mapped out. Between here and Denver there are at least five points where we could encounter the forces of darkness. If we do, they will try to kill us for certain. No weapons, no Charlie on this trip."

Jack turned to Laura. "I've got to iron out some details with Martin and then we've got to get a move on before they arrive. Can you please deal with our own terrorist here?"

Laura scowled. "I'll talk to Charlie, but this time, regrettably, I'm agreeing with him."

Jack threw up his hands before heading back toward the hall with Martin. "It's time to sow some confusion for Brisbane to draw down their resources. Keep them on the move and spread them out. How are our meetings with the feds going?"

Martin replied, "We're talking, but they're suspicious. I don't think the administration knows whom they can trust anymore. We've got control of the civilian comm grid; Brisbane still has most of the heavy hardware. Brisbane has firepower; we've got maneuverability. The government has almost nothing they control independently."

"Now that's sad." Jack hung his head.

"You're telling me."

Laura and Charlie added two more rifles and several boxes of ammunition to their stash before closing the back of the SUV.

* * *

The White House, Sunday, October 5, 2014

Anna Colbert and David Kincaid shared a corner of the enormous table in the Roosevelt Room surrounded by clutter. A stream of staff members in casual work clothes had replaced the pristine order of the old normal tourist times. The White House and adjoining Treasury building were now isolated pupae in cocoons of security.

"We're not going to get much done, are we, sir?" Anna looked up after the sixth staff interruption.

"No. I wouldn't mind if these were things that actually required my attention, but I seem to be getting this stuff because I'm the only one available."

Anna glanced at the clock. "Peter will be here in about half an hour."

Kincaid nodded. "A lot of this the President should be handling." He looked up from the papers before him into Anna's face, his eyes revealing a blend of sadness and worry.

"It's gotten really bad, hasn't it, sir?"

Kincaid paused as Corporal Tull entered with a small bundle of messages. Kincaid checked each with quiet efficiency, initialing at the bottoms, and handing the stack back to Tull. "Thank you."

As soon as the two were alone again, Kincaid spoke in a whisper. "Yes. The President stays in the family quarters most of the day. I don't think he's been drinking much now that the staff is really vigilant, but he isn't giving us the face time we need right now. We're trying to get him to follow the medical officer's directions, but I don't think he's taking the medication, so the depression is worsening. Plus, he's really worried about Tiffany's safety, which makes sense."

"Sure. Can she check in more often?" Anna asked.

"She does pretty good. I don't think there's been more than twelve hours when they haven't talked by satellite phone. And there're tracking devices in her bike. I think he's feeling so out of control and overwhelmed that he's just withdrawing. I'm going to go up and see him as soon as Peter gets here. Want to come with me? I warn you: it could be a bit unsettling."

Anna nodded.

Kincaid's work was interrupted four more times before Peter and Matt arrived. The smell of hamburgers preceded their entry into the Roosevelt Room.

"Where on earth did you get those?" Kincaid asked. "I thought carryout was a thing of the past!"

"The Five Guys over on I Street is giving everything away. They're down to their last few gallons of fuel to run their generators. After that, everything spoils. We all promised to make sure they get restarted when the lights come on again. Want some?"

Kincaid smiled. "Thanks. I don't think my system can take hamburgers any more. You'd better chow down before Sarah gets here."

Peter spread out a cloth to protect the table. "Not to worry. She was right behind us."

Anna helped gather papers from the table. She and Kincaid reached the door just as Sarah entered, her hair tangled and face flushed, carrying three oil-soaked bags.

She looked to Kincaid. "You won't believe what's happening over on I Street."

* * *

Anna and Kincaid sat in chairs on either side of President Miller's desk. The President swiveled his chair around as he spoke with scant emotion.

"I guess it's just not our season to catch any good fortune. I used to repeat that old saying, 'you make your own luck' or something like that. I find that a little hard to believe these days. How could this happen? We're the most powerful nation in the history of the world. How could this happen? And so fast?"

"The situation has stabilized, Mr. President. The systems we developed together and put into action are working. We know that."

"Fires in New York?"

"There're still fires, but the numbers are down, and they're putting them out now."

"After losing ...?" He turned to Anna.

"About a third of the high-rises, sir. With the strengthened community organization, the loss of life has been remarkably low — fewer than a dozen."

The President slowly shook his head. "Power, David?"

"The first cables from the Niagara grid have been connected and are working. The cables from Calvert Cliffs should be operational in two days."

The President stood up and walked to a window overlooking the South Lawn. "And how much will that give the good citizens of New York?"

Kincaid rubbed the bridge of his nose. "Three percent more than they have now. It'll power hospitals and groceries, sir. I think we need to appreciate that this is going to take some time still, but everyone is doing their part. And the people are getting the message that we are doing our part." Kincaid's tone showed his growing irritation. "With all due respect, this is no time for defeatism. There is a path out of this mess, and we are on it." He looked at clippings on the President's desk. "Frankly, I think you should be out following your daughter's lead." He picked up a front-page photo-spread headed with 'Heroine Rides to Gotham's Rescue!' Tiffany sat astride her Harley, in her black riding suit, her helmet under her arm, her head held high. "I swear, Matt could Photoshop FDR's head on her, and it would fit. The people will rally behind us if we lead."

Kincaid handed the President the article. For the first time since they arrived, his face wore a trace of a smile. "She's a natural, isn't she?" He turned the picture so that Anna could see.

"Yes, sir, but we've always known that, haven't we?"

"You're right." He placed the paper back on his desk. "We start our comeback campaign tomorrow. Which is …?"

"Monday, sir. Might I suggest making an appearance at Connecticut 4? They're installing a replacement turbine tomorrow. It was part of a regularly scheduled maintenance swap, but it'll be the first destroyed turbine site to actually come back on line."

"I see. Like a photo-op throwing a switch?" the President asked.

Kincaid continued, "Well, they'll actually just be lowering a huge iron rotor into a casing with a giant crane, but at least you'll be wearing a hard hat and safety goggles. There will still be several weeks of construction and tests before any electrons can flow out of it. I'll have Matt brief you."

Anna smiled.

The President smiled back reflexively. "Good idea." He grew pensive. "And I'd like to make a very quiet trip over to Danbury."

"Um, sir, we've discussed that. I can't emphasize how bad an idea I think it would be to visit Mr. Bailey in prison. There's nothing to be gained and a portion of our cases against him to lose by your presence," Kincaid warned.

"David, he and I worked together for twenty plus years. I thought I knew him. I can't rest until I can wrap my head around what was going on in his heart all that time."

"Time for that after the trials, sir. It won't be that long."

The President returned to the window and sighed. "You're right, of course. Let's get me up to speed so we can watch them drop that big ol' turbine in place tomorrow and make everyone happy again."

"I'll make the arrangements, sir. *We'll watch them carefully place the critical rotor into the very important turbine.* Don't worry; Matt will have you talking like an electrical engineer by this time tomorrow. It's a lot easier than speaking French," Kincaid replied, grinning.

Anna tilted her head, clearly amused.

With the President gazing out over the landscape, they left the Oval Office and took the stairs to the first floor.

"I don't think it's easier than French, sir."

Kincaid smiled. "You saved him that time. It's Matt's turn. Let's go let Matt know what he has to do."

They walked on toward the West Wing.

Kincaid smiled. "Are you hungry? It's almost dinner time."

Anna turned to Kincaid, concern on her face. "For hamburgers?"

"No. Oh, no. I have something more delicate in mind."

She smiled. "OK, I'm game."

"Funny you would phrase it that way."

* * *

The Old Roadways Warehouse,
Edison, New Jersey, Monday October 27, 2014

Josh Ruark operated now from the warehouse. A dozen or so telecomm volunteers sat at other desks lined up along the expanse of the floor, entering information. Décor was vintage storage space, brown and dusty. The digital clock on the wall had just turned over to eight in the morning. Lindsey Two wore her wireless headset sitting in front of a large screen.

"Right. And that's next to Westchester? Got it. OK. Give me the frequency." She typed in numbers as they were spoken to her. "Was that final number a five or a nine? Got it. Hold on … bingo. They're squawking. Thanks a bunch. Keep your head down, babe." She turned to Josh. "Got another baddie just north of New York City. She says he's heavily armed. Got him entered and tracking. We've over five thousand bad guys."

Josh continued programming. "Excellent. I'm backing up the database now. I've added some tweaks to the display. You'll be seeing a little bleb around each one now, showing their likely track. I also added a color scale — green for the good guys through the spectrum to red for the most-armed bad guys."

Lindsey Two leaned back in her chair to see his screen.

"It'll come up automatically on yours as soon as I'm sure it works."

She giggled. "I was just thinking how much it looks like those little hurricane tracking thingies you did a few years ago."

He smiled. "Yeah, that was good stuff. They still use it. But there we were tracking three or four objects, not eight thousand."

They turned at the sound of the door. Mike walked in.

"Whoa. You look like hell, man." Josh greeted Johnson.

"I didn't get much sleep."

Lindsey Two snickered. "Sorry, Mikey. We told you One has a thing for older guys. I hope Janice isn't too upset. Lindsey One can be pretty flirty, but she's honorable."

Mike shook his head. "If only it were that simple."

"Huh?" Lindsey Two removed her headset.

"She and Janice are getting along fine. Really fine."

As Josh covered his face, Lindsey Two grimaced. "Ooooo. Did we mention that the door kinda swings both ways with Lindsey One?"

Johnson plopped down in a chair. "No, you did not. But apparently it does for Janice, too. I didn't know that, either. Somehow I'd imagined that by this point in my life everything would be pretty staid and routine. Guess I was wrong."

Lindsey Two bit her lip and looked over to Josh. He shrugged.

She took Mike's hand. "Come on. We need your kind of help. Go splash some cold water on your face and get some coffee. There's some industrial grade java in the pot now. We're getting a lot of call center people in here now and need a supervisor to get them scheduled efficiently. You're good at that. Want me to talk to One?"

Johnson stood up and turned toward the coffee. "No, it's really not bad, I don't think. Just unexpected. When I left, they were in the kitchen fixing a big lunch for us. That's good, right?"

"Uh huh. She's a hell of a cook," Lindsey Two assured.

Refreshed by coffee and cold water, Mike introduced himself to the growing staff. He repurposed a status board that had been used for shipping schedules and began drawing time slots, filling in names of the workforce. By lunchtime the tracking had reached nearly ten thousand, including over six thousand they now called the Empire. The others were the Rebels.

Lindsey Two's screen now featured the new tracking markers.

Josh called to Lindsey Two. "How's Commander X doing?"

She scrolled to the west. "He's left Akron heading west-southwest."

"Any reds tracking him?"

"Nope."

"Excellent. How about Martin?"

"Looks like he's headed toward Cleveland. Don't see anyone after him, either." She scrolled back to the east. "But unless your software's screwy, something's happening up north of New York. Look."

Josh got up and came over. The red and orange blebs were distending, seemingly drawn toward a point. "What're they all pointing to? Overlay the map."

She flicked a few menus, causing roads and cities to appear, along with labels. Josh pointed to one label. "That looks to be their target. Connecticut 4, the power plant. I'm sure that can't be good, but it's not a nuke. What would they want with a coal-fired power plant?"

Johnson bounded over to Lindsey Two's screen. "The President's visiting there this afternoon. Connecticut 4 is getting one of the turbines back on line, and the President will be there to watch. It was on NPR this morning."

"Oh, shit." Josh put his hand to the back of his neck. "I'm guessing they don't know that the Empire's closing in. And that's a lot of firepower. See, they're all full red."

Mike turned to Josh. "OK, let's get word to them before it's too late. I'm sure you know where the President is."

Josh shook his head. "No, believe it or not. We had no reason to track him."

"Don't tell me you don't have access to his circuits."

"No, they're too secure — even for me." Josh clasped his chin, thinking. "But I've got an idea. The Rebels in Ohio have been talking with the White

House." He turned to Lindsey Two. "Get Martin."

She tried for several minutes. "He's not picking up. Either a dead zone or he doesn't trust the incoming number."

"Can we reach Commander X?"

"I don't have his number. There's a number for one of his lieutenants, though."

* * *

Jack was noticing the first changing fall leaves as they drove through the gently rolling hills south of Columbus when Laura's phone in Charlie's pocket rang.

Jack looked at Charlie in the rearview mirror. "Who is it?"

Charlie held the phone at arm's length to read the number. "Not sure. It's the same exchange in Jersey as our programmer guy, but the number's not identified."

"Make it brief." He turned to Laura. "Plot us a new route with a pretty big departure from the present heading as soon as Charlie's off."

She pulled out her map and began checking signs to locate their current position.

Charlie opened her phone. "Listening." He held the phone to his ear, mostly in silence. "Holy shit. No, I don't have any D.C. numbers, but I'll try to reach the others. I'll let you know if we don't succeed. Got that? Only if we don't succeed." He immediately pushed the end call button and looked into Jack's eyes in the mirror. "Twenty-three seconds. But I've gotta reach Martin. Brisbane's closing in on the President with armed troops. He's flying into an ambush."

"Go. Make it fast."

Charley succeeded. "Martin. Rebel Jersey comm center just called to say the Brisbane boys are about to ambush the President at Connecticut 4. About seventy-five heavily armed troops are closing in on the plant. Can you get word to them? OK. Call me if you don't. Out." Charlie ended the call. "Seventeen seconds. You're free to maneuver."

Laura scanned the road ahead. "Turn left, south, on State Route 104 in about three miles."

* * *

The Executive Office Building

The long table in the second basement conference room was awash in papers, as was the case with most tables in both the Executive Office Building and White House. Anna Colbert occupied the chair at one end, as she helped Cameron and Sarah craft Monday evening's economic address for the President. Matt and Peter huddled with technicians from Departments of Energy and Treasury, reviewing the scant progress made on restoring the power grid.

Matt was sitting on the other end of the table. His phone chirped.

Looking at the number, he answered, "Yeah, Martin. What's up? … What? How do you know that? When? Do you know how many? Shit. I'm on it." He flipped his phone closed and looked up at Anna. "Slide me your secure phone."

"This table's a national treasure," she said, frowning, pointing to highly polished cherry wood. "Scratches."

"The President's party is about to be attacked by heavily armed units allied with Brisbane."

Anna slid her secure phone the length of the table.

"Mr. Kincaid, Matt here. You're about to be ambushed. I just got word from the Rebels that at least seventy-five Brisbane people are closing in on Connecticut 4, heavily armed and dangerous. Yes, sir, I believe him. They've been tracking 'em for their own protection. Seventy-five, minimum, probably more. That's the number of phones the Rebels are tracking. I'll call in secret service and military from here. What defenses do you have now?" Matt listened carefully. "Yes, sir. You've got it."

Peter had already reached Homeland Security by the time Matt ended his call to Kincaid. Matt opened a call to the Pentagon. After a short exchange he got up and carried the phone back to Anna. "Several Homeland Security units will be on the scene with armored cars within twenty to thirty minutes. Air Force will have some high speed aircraft buzzing the site within three or four minutes to let the bad guys know that we know they're there. Elements from the Marine detachment at New London should be lifting off in a few minutes. I'll notify the Speaker of the House."

Anna turned to Peter. "Where did all this come from? How did it blow up so fast? We've been handling the crisis. I thought everyone was cooperating. Power's coming back. They predicted millions of deaths. We've prevented that. The serious press acknowledges we've done pretty good."

"I have no idea where this is coming from." Peter shook his head. "There wasn't any general violence on the radar. Homeland Security hadn't picked up any activity or threat chatter." He turned to Matt. "Could your contacts be overreacting to something? Do you even know what they're seeing?"

Before Matt could answer, both Anna's and Peter's phones rang.

Anna picked up and listened. "Yes, sir." She set the phone down, her expression grim. "No mistake. They're under fire. The President's group is inside the power plant, and the plant is completely locked down. Fortunately, the plant was hardened against terrorist attacks about eight years ago. The plant security people and the three Marines on the flight are already on the roof of the plant, but they're pretty lightly armed and don't have enough ammunition for a siege. They're just going to hold off individual attackers until reinforcements arrive."

Sarah looked uncharacteristically somber.

Peter finished his phone call. "Secret Service says they've got a good position with a clear-fire zone around the plant. The President, Mr. Kincaid, and the plant people are deep in the building with protection. The Marines and plant security have already taken out about a dozen of the attackers. I think the bad guys were relying on surprise and don't have a complete plan of attack. Corporal Tull says the attackers retreated to the woods beyond the fence when the jets came close overhead."

Anna turned to Sarah. "They'll be all right. He knows what to do."

Sarah's head was bowed as she nodded slowly. "I know. Jeff's a sharpshooter. He showed me the badge. It's silver." She looked up at Anna. "I'm scared."

* * *

Connecticut 4 Power Plant near Farmington, Connecticut

Jeff Tull held the radio communicating with helicopters carrying Marines from the New London Submarine Base. "Roger, Rescue One, this is Marine One. We're on the roof, one Marine each on the south, north, and west. We've got seven civilians interspersed. Heaviest concentration of enemy forces seems to be to the west, in the trees about a hundred-fifty yards from the plant. Everything we've heard so far sounds like small arms and rifles. I haven't seen anything resembling an RPG, but I can't say they don't have 'em. A squad of about a dozen rushed the main entrance, and we shot several of them before they retreated. Four aren't moving, and the other three are probably badly wounded. When the rest of the squad retreated, they took the weapons of the others, so I don't think they have much backup.

"There's a big field to the east of the building. We'll lay down suppression fire when you're in range. Is your craft armored? No? Then come in fast and low. See if you can get the coordinator to have jets buzzing about the same time. ETA? Roger. Looking forward to seeing you. Out."

Deep in the bowels of the building the President and Chief of Staff had finished their broken phone conversations with Washington. Thick concrete walls and metal beams of the power plant absorbed most of their phones' signals.

The President sat glumly in an office chair while Kincaid perused a detailed wall map of the area.

"Well, David, I'm sure this will make riveting news tonight. Good thing most people can't receive it, eh?"

Kincaid chuckled. "Ironic, isn't it? We've restored broadcast communication to the point that most people probably will receive it. At least the cameras were off by the time the gunfire began. All the video will be of the rotor fitting in place."

"Oh, well, so much for the people supporting us. Personally, I'm not feeling very supported."

"Mr. President, this is so serious I can't minimize it, but I believe it's isolated."

The President raised his eyebrows. "Based on what? We don't even know who those people are out there."

"No. You're right. But we don't have any mass uprising reported anywhere. And the folks who warned us seem to be tracking those who would do us harm. Matt and Peter have been working with them and so far trust this relationship."

"David, what if this is all one big ruse? What if it's a trap to bring down the whole damn system? What about that possibility, huh? I wouldn't have entertained that notion six months ago, but it seems very real to me now."

Kincaid turned from the map. "No. I don't buy that. Since August we've taken a huge hit to the technological skeleton of the country. We have — for a while — lost three-fourths of the centralized power and most of our electronic communications. We've lost a big chunk of the petroleum used to fuel our transportation. We lost most of the 'things' we thought were essential for our society to function.

"And yet … and yet … we're still up and running. While so many of us up at the top feared millions of deaths, rioting in the streets, disease, pestilence, and famine, the people exercised their initiative to fix the problem. Did you watch Ben Jacobs's interview last week with the diesel mechanic in the Bronx? That guy just showed up one afternoon, figuring that with the hospital running on emergency power around the clock, they'd need more maintenance on the generators than their normal staff would be able to handle. He and his son had been at the hospital around the clock for almost a month swapping off generator watches. They'd gotten several of their friends to organize a supply chain for spare parts, and a local electrical contractor brought in his people to alter the electrical distribution to prioritize the operating rooms and infectious disease wards. And do you know what they were proudest of in that interview? They all got their picture with Tiffany."

"Ah, the power of individual initiative."

"No! Definitely not!" Kincaid responded, frustrated. "The power of *community*. They couldn't have done it on their own, separately. I remember that guy quoting his third grade teacher about responsibilities to others and about duties to community. He said — and I particularly remember this — that 'it's a We-the-people thing.'" Kincaid folded his arm and looked down before looking back to the President. "The fundamental force that will save us isn't the technological power grid, or communication grid, or individual initiative. The fundamental force that will save us is the self-assembling grid of millions of individuals steeped in community responsibility and the work ethic of the common good."

Kincaid paused at the sound of intense gunfire from above, followed by the wup-wup-wup of helicopters, and then silence.

The President looked up to the source of the sound of gunfire. "Well, David, either our liberators or our captors have arrived. Do you have two speeches ready?"

Kincaid unfolded his arms and looked sternly at the President. "No, sir. Only one."

* * *

The White House

Anna, Sarah, Peter, and Matt joined the small group of Marines and infirmary staff at the edge of the Rose Garden awaiting the President and his entourage.

Sarah looked at the medics. "Did the Major say who was injured?"

"No, ma'am. Just that it wasn't life-threatening."

She turned to Anna. "Is Mr. Kincaid OK?"

Anna smiled. "I'm sure he is. He had Corporal Tull with him." She took Sarah's hand. "And I'm sure Jeff is OK, too."

"I know. He had Mr. Kincaid with him."

They waited in the cool darkness below the Executive Mansion. Cameron came out to join them. "The doctor said to distract the President with details of the speech if he's not tired and ready for bed."

Sarah shifted her attention between Anna and Cameron. "That bad?"

Anna shook her head. "This trip was supposed to lighten his spirits, get him engaged."

"Oh, dear," Sarah replied.

They heard helicopter rotors in the distance. The landing pad border lights came up brightly as the sound grew louder and the massive aircraft appeared in the glare, its shiny exterior marred by dozens of pockmarks. Marine One touched down on the south lawn a few minutes before midnight, and the pad lights were immediately doused. The assembled welcoming party headed to the helicopter as soon as the rotors began to wind down. The door opened and Tull was the first down the stairs. He and Sergeant Smith helped Corporal Brycynski hobble to the waiting stretcher. Sarah came up behind the three, picked up Tull's travel bag, and followed as the other Marines gathered their rifles and small arms. Up close, even in the dim illumination of the south lawn, the armored glass of the windows appeared undamaged, but a number of indentations from bullets could be seen in the side of the helicopter. Anna overheard snippets of conversation about "minor grazing wound" and "a couple of days of R and R."

Once the medics cleared the area, the President walked down to be met by Peter and Cameron. His face was drawn and fatigued as they ushered him toward the south entrance.

"Good evening, sir." Anna quietly greeted David Kincaid, the last passenger to deplane.

He walked over to her, clearing the downdraft of the nearly stopped rotors, and took a deep breath. "Hi, there," He said, "I am *so* glad to see you."

He opened his arms, and Anna stepped into them, holding tightly as tears streamed down her face.

* * *

A farmhouse near Booneville, Arkansas, Thursday, November 6, 2014

"This is taking way longer than I expected." Jack reviewed the map marked with their travels.

Charlie had just complimented their host as he took a second helping of country ham and grits. "You young 'uns are so impatient. When you think about it, we're actually evading our predators by using time travel."

Laura turned to her host and smiled. "Don't pay too much attention to him, Mrs. Cayce. We think he was oxygen deprived at some point."

Caroline Cayce laughed. "But ol' Charlie's fun. And useful, too. He got the windmill linked up again. That contraption hadn't worked for twenty years or longer. Now we've got water flowing around the clock."

Laura turned to Charlie, her eyes wide.

"Hey, boss lady, just because you've never deigned to ask me to fix things doesn't mean I'm not handy. You rich people just assume your friends can't work, either."

Laura shook her head and continued to talk with Caroline. "And we appreciate what your husband's been able to do for us."

She dried her hands on her apron. "Oh, they just love special projects like that. They've got the relays set up so that it looks like you're in the middle of Fort Benning, Georgia."

Jack nodded. "And it's working. I just got a note from Martin that the Georgia folks have been watching a Brisbane team driving around looking for us. We could really make some progress shutting Brisbane down if the White House would just trust us a little more. We've shared a lot of good intelligence with them, but they really haven't reciprocated."

"I'm sure they have their reasons." Caroline sat down to her own breakfast. "At least they shut down several cells up in New England and Maryland after that attack on the President."

Laura caught up with the news on her laptop. "But you know, I'm getting a queasy feeling about the President. He's been basically out of the picture most of the time, and on the few occasions he has spoken, he hasn't looked or sounded very healthy. Their reputation is so low they still can't get anyone to take on the vice-presidency."

"They didn't ask me." Charlie leaned back, enjoying his coffee.

"Ah, right. That does make me feel a whole lot better about the current situation." Laura continued her reading. "At least the country seems to be handling the oil collapse."

Jack looked up from his maps. "That's one of the reasons we're so far behind. It takes three days to accumulate enough fuel to move."

Caroline smiled. "But it's sure obvious when someone tries to jump the system. That's how they nabbed those Brisbane fellas over in Tennessee. And I have to say as an Arkansan in a farming community that it makes sense they've given priority to the farm equipment. It's harvest time, you know, and if those combines don't run, everybody starves. People out here're pretty much taking it in stride. Ms. Garrette, you were telling me last night what the fuel's down to."

"Around sixty percent out here, Caroline. You get a better distribution from the Gulf here in Arkansas. East Coast is about forty percent. At least their electricity's coming back. They turned on an eighth transmission cable into New York City last night."

"So there you go, Jack." Caroline took a big helping of scrambled eggs. "You need to settle down in one place for several days along the way. You're traveling roads that were built back in the forties before the Eisenhower highway system. You're taking the back roads to keep from getting killed. And you need three days or so to fill up that tank of yours to get safely to your next hiding place. I'd say you're right on schedule."

Jack thought for a bit. "Huh. You're right. You're absolutely right." He looked up at her. "And have I told you enough how much we appreciate your hospitality and shelter?"

* * *

The White House, Monday, November 10, 2014

"Matt, I have to admit, I don't think I've ever seen you truly angry." Peter was trying to calm Matt.

Matt pounded a fist on the table. "The President just had to put that call in to Bailey. Damn it, he just couldn't let that go."

Sarah folded her arms. "Did he tell Bailey that we know about the Brisbane chain of command?"

"No," Matt replied.

"Why are you so sure?" Sarah spread her hands wide.

Matt placed both of his hands flat on the table as he began to settle. "For one thing, we haven't told the President what we know. More directly, he didn't realize the call was on the monitoring loop so the whole thing was recorded. Mr. Kincaid and Major Reid have been reviewing the call. I think they may be confronting him with the conversation right now."

Peter frowned. "Have you listened to it?"

"No." Matt shook his head. "They feel it's too sensitive right now. And I'll give them the benefit of the doubt. What I have heard, though, is that

Bailey was a real ass. Apparently, he kept calling the President 'weak.' Over and over. He seemed obsessed with that. And apparently he said several times that he has more firepower than the President. A real arrogant ass."

Sarah reviewed her reports of asset allocations. "Well, he was right about that up until early this month. We're still unraveling some of the links, but back then Bailey could literally move weapons and forces from his prison cell in Danbury. Speaking of which, are we back in good graces with the 'rebels,' Matt? Sounded like our confrontation with them could have really messed things up."

"Yes, I think so. I feel bad about that. It was a classic ruse on Brisbane's part. I fell for the fake communications that looked like they were between Brisbane and Commander X. It's like the Zimmerman Telegram all over again a century and a half later." Matt appeared much more relaxed.

"I saw that telegram once over at the Archives." Sarah sipped her coffee. "Maybe we should be making paper printouts of our own messages. Otherwise, I'm not sure how the Archives are going to display what's happened this year."

Peter closed his eyes. "Can you believe all this has happened inside one year? Remember what it was like back in January?"

Sarah set her coffee down. "Nope. I had just arrived here if you'll recall."

Matt grinned. "Hmmm. There does seem to be a correlation, doesn't there?"

Sarah stuck out her tongue at Matt.

* * *

"Any idea what he wants?" Anna put her executive summary in a folder for Kincaid to take to the President.

"Not a clue. At least he seemed calm and collected. More inviting than anxious."

"Does he know what you and the Major have heard?" she asked.

"I don't think so. We've kept it really quiet so we don't stir up too much sediment."

She nodded. "Well, good luck. At least I can't imagine him firing you."

"Oh, that's comforting."

She grinned.

Kincaid walked up the flight of marble stairs, across the drive to the West Wing, and up toward the President's office. He got out his ID for the guard, but Corporal Tull shook his head.

"No need, sir. The President said to send you straight in, sir. He told me personally."

Kincaid turned to Abigail, who sat at her desk as unexpressive as he had ever seen her. Kincaid moved toward the door, looking back momentarily at Tull.

Upon entering the office, Kincaid surveyed the occupants. A cup of coffee in hand, Senator Kreis sat on the sofa to Kincaid's left. Speaker Pelosi sat on the sofa to Kincaid's right, while Chief Justice Warren stood behind her. Admiral Lautermilch of the Joint Chiefs was stationed beside the President. The minority leaders of Congress, several department heads, and Cameron Conklin rounded out the mix.

Kincaid paused a moment. "Please tell me we haven't dissolved the government."

President Miller laughed and held out his hand. "Have a seat, David."

There was one empty chair in center of the circle opposite the President. Kincaid sat down.

"Despite your people's best efforts, we've been unable to get any upright citizen to step forward and assume the responsibilities of Vice President," the president began.

Kincaid nodded and looked around the room. "Correct, sir, including several upright citizens in this very room."

"True. That's why I called them all here. We've talked about it for the past couple of hours and realized that there's only one person loyal enough and foolhardy enough to take the job."

Kincaid leaned forward and quietly buried his face in his hands.

"David, I'm asking you on behalf of the American people and with the unequivocal support of all those present here, as well as the people they represent, to accept the office of Vice President."

Kincaid bit his lip before answering. "We need someone with national standing, sir."

Speaker Pelosi answered. "You've been the face of the administration more than the President himself for these many months. Your trust numbers are better than anyone else's. You've proven yourself under fire — literally."

Kincaid stared at the floor. "Can I think about it for a bit?"

"We'd rather you didn't," The Chief Justice chimed in. "There are a lot of good personal reasons for you to say no. We're appealing to your sense of duty above self."

* * *

Kincaid returned to his office.

Anna looked up from her conversation with Tracey. "You're looking pretty serious, sir. What happened?"

"We need to call everyone together. Cameron will be over in a few minutes. We're going to be shuffling some assignments."

* * *

The Evening News with Ben Jacobs

"Our top story tonight is, of course, the dramatic announcement from the White House."

The screen cut to the White House briefing room, where the President was seen taking the podium, flanked by Senator Kreis and Speaker Pelosi. "I have today asked former Senator and the nation's current Chief of Staff David Kincaid to accept the responsibilities of Vice President of the United States. This request was made in consultation with the leaders of both majority and minority parties of the House and Senate and with the wise counsel of the Judiciary branch. David Kincaid has graciously accepted this awesome burden, subject to congressional approval. ..."

The President paused as the room erupted in cheers. The entire press corps rose to their feet. He smiled and waited for calm. "... Gee. I haven't heard that in a long time. Obviously, David Kincaid has won the nation's admiration going back to his days as Senator, but more recently for his calm and guiding hand that has led us through the recent times of peril. His record is long and public. His life has been an open book.

"The leaders of the House and Senate have assured me that the necessary deliberations will be thorough but short and devoid of the rancor that has so crippled our common enterprise for so long."

The news coverage returned to Ben Jacobs.

"Following his introduction as Vice President designate, David Kincaid delivered brief remarks regarding his acceptance of the challenge. This was followed by nearly an hour of questions ranging from his philosophical differences from former Vice President Bailey to his outlook for resumption of oil deliveries. When discussing changes in the White House staffing if he is confirmed — a near certainty — Mr. Kincaid indicated that his current well-respected staff would remain in place, but have elevated responsibilities. Following confirmation, Peter Benson, the current Deputy Chief of Staff for the President, would assume the duties of Chief of Staff.

"News of Kincaid's nomination has been greeted with universal praise from across the country and around the globe. In abbreviated trading, the New York Stock exchange jumped the maximum number of points before automatic programmed breakers halted trading.

"We will return with more coverage of today's announcement following this message."

24 BUMPS

State route 260 west of
Heber, Arizona, Saturday, November 22, 2014

Charlie adjusted the tilt of his front passenger seat. "You OK back there?"

"Yeah, I'm fine." Laura reclined as much as her seat belt would allow.

Jack smiled as he watched her in the rear view mirror. She had bundled herself against the mile-high November chill with a Navajo blanket purchased in Heber and had wedged herself comfortably between two travel pillows. Jack saw that her face was serene, her eyes closed while the low late afternoon sun painted soft, warm hues across her face.

Charlie reclined his seat back a little, but kept an eye on the road ahead. "That was a fine meal back there. It's been a while since I've had some real Sonoran food. I had forgotten how good it is."

"It was good, wasn't it? I hope it'll hold us 'til Payson. The road's pretty good for now but we're in for some mountain driving and we don't know much about the locals." Jack looked again into the mirror. Laura appeared to be asleep.

As they drove steadily into the deepening dusk, Charlie began a lecture on the Arizona mountain economy, the native Piñon pines and their role in the Native American diet. He was just getting to the subject of sustainable harvest when he bolted upright. "What's that ahead?"

Jack strained his eyes. "Not sure. Looks like either a wreck or a roadblock — about a half-mile."

Charlie reached beneath the seat and pulled out his binoculars. "Shit! Oh, this is not good. I see two, three, at least four men in black with rifles. I'm not sure how this happened, Jack Boy, but it looks like Brisbane and Commander X are about to have a close encounter of the bad kind."

Jack slowed the car to a stop and then shifted into reverse and began to drive backward. "Laura, up! We've got trouble."

"What?" Laura sat up, shedding her blanket. "Why are we backing up?"

Jack drove as fast and straight as he could, peering over his right shoulder. "Looks like someone's waiting for us. But at the angle they see us, backing up'll give us a few more seconds. If I just turn around, they'll start after us right away. Where are the rifles?"

"Three back here."

"And two in the trunk," Charlie added.

"Have they started for us yet, Charlie?" Jack asked.

Charlie raised his binoculars again. "Almost. They're headed for their vans."

"How many vehicles?"

"Two."

"OK. As soon as I round this bend, I'm coming to a really fast stop. Charlie, you get the rifles from the trunk. Laura, you get the ammo box from the trunk. I'll get the backseat rifles. Run as fast as you can up the hill on the left. There's a pile of boulders at the edge of the woods. Get down behind the rocks. I've got a plan."

Laura was breathing hard. "Can't we just outrun them? We've got some distance between us."

"Not with us in this and them in those. Their vans are powered for assault," Jack replied.

The two black vans were heading up the road toward the turn.

Once over the rise, Jack slammed on the brakes. "Go, go, go!"

Charlie and Laura threw open their doors as Jack pulled the latch for the trunk.

"Keep the doors open," Jack called.

As Charlie and Laura gathered the trunk rifles and ammunition, Jack piled pillows on the front hood and threw the blanket on top. He propped one rifle on the pillows, grabbed the other two, and raced up the hill to join Laura and Charlie crouching behind the rocks just as the vans sped into view.

Jack spoke softly. "Are these all loaded?"

"Yes, fully," Charlie replied.

"How's your aim, Charlie?"

"It's OK."

"Laura?" Jack asked.

"I've never shot at anything except in video games."

"That'll have to do. Charlie, you counted at least four. Let's assume there are six of them. You take the two on the left. Laura, you take the two on the right, and I'll take two in the middle. If there's any overlap, that's OK. Let's spread out so they can't concentrate their fire. If they're getting out, they probably have body armor. Aim for their sides, where it's thinnest. Be ready. Pick your targets. But don't fire until I start. Fire single shots. We may not have time to reload."

Charlie and Laura moved slowly away from Jack along the rocks. The sun had set behind the hills to the West, and the surroundings were dark save for the glare of the approaching vans' headlights shining on their car and the car's headlights illuminating the vans.

The vans screeched to a halt, and black-suited men piled out, each carrying a black assault rifle at the ready, each with a glistening black helmet. The men opened fire, concentrating their aim on the pillows and blanket on the hood. Jack held the car keys in his hand. As the men moved closer to the car, he pressed the panic button on the key ring lock transmitter. The car horn sounded rhythmic blasts as the running lights flashed. The men in black halted and raised a volley of fire at the car.

Jack counted five men. As best he could tell from the lights that came on as they left their vehicles, none had stayed in the cabs. He aimed at the midribs of the third man and fired. To his left and right, Charlie and Laura opened fire.

The third man fell immediately, and Jack aimed for numbers two and four in succession. Two were still standing after about a dozen shots. They had finally turned their weapon fire on the rocks.

Jack ducked beneath his boulder for a moment and called alternately to Laura and Charlie. "Aim for high chest now. The body armor has to be flexible, so it's thinner there."

The two men made their way up the slope, firing in bursts into the rocks and forest. The man on the left fell, and number five began to run toward them. Just yards short of Laura's hiding place, he went down in combined fire.

Jack watched the figures on the ground in the sudden silence. "Don't get up. Don't go near them yet. We're not necessarily safe."

After a couple of minutes of silence, Jack spoke softly, just loud enough for Charlie and Laura to hear him. "Reload. Then cover me while I make sure they're out of commission." He refilled his magazine as he listened to the other two doing the same.

"OK. Are you ready to cover me?"

Charlie answered briskly, "Right." Laura responded with quavering voice, "Yeah."

"OK. Cover me. Charlie, watch the three on the road. Laura, the two on the slope."

In the deep dusk, Jack crept down the hill. He approached each man in turn. Though they all lay still, he put his rifle barrel to the base of their heads and fired a single shot into each.

Finally alone on the road, he called to the others. "Come on. Let's get out of here. No telling who or what might be farther on ahead."

He was surveying the front of their car as Laura and Charlie arrived. The front window was gone, leaving only a shattered frame around the opening. Radiator fluid drained from half a dozen holes, generating a cloud of steam in the icy night air.

Charlie approached the remains of the pillow and blanket. "Very clever, Jack boy. I'm impressed."

"Give your enemy what he expects. Then hit him with what he doesn't expect."

Laura gazed inside the car. Dozens of holes pierced the seats. Bullets had passed through the front seats and riddled the back as well. "What now?" she asked.

"Obviously we need to get out of here. And clearly not in the transportation we brought. Charlie, check for damage to those vans. We'll take the one with more gas. Put the dead guys in the other, and we'll get it off the road. But let's get a move on. We've been lucky so far."

"Lucky. Yeah. Just what I was thinking." Charlie approached the nearest van, limping as he walked.

Jack called to him. "Whoa, there. What's this?"

"It's nothing. Not bad."

Laura ran to his side. "Oh, no you don't. Let me see."

Charlie stopped as Laura examined his leg. She turned to Jack. "Get me some strips of the blanket. Charlie, sit!" Her voice was commanding, and Charlie complied without protest.

After tearing the strips, Jack checked the two vans. Neither had sustained any damage, and the second one had nearly a full tank of fuel. As Laura bandaged Charlie's leg, Jack transferred their supplies to the second van and salvaged the rifles from the fallen men in black. Once finished loading the rear van, he carried the dead and placed them in the back of the first.

Jack and Laura helped Charlie to stand up and supported him to the second vehicle, where they secured him in the back seat.

"I'll drive the first one on ahead. There's a turn off into the woods on the right about a quarter mile back toward Heber. Follow me. I'll get the first van out of sight, and then we'll figure out what to do."

Laura walked to their van. Jack made a final check of the car and turned off all the lights except the hazard blinkers. He drove the extra van to the turnoff and about a hundred yards along a weed-strewn path, pulled it to the side, and left it with all the lights on.

Laura had moved to the front passenger seat. Jack turned their van around and drove out of the woods.

"You left the lights on," she said.

"Right. If there's any locator device in it, it'll be powered by the battery. The lights'll drain the battery in a few hours. By morning, it'll be off the grid. Judging by the brush, I don't think anyone's visited that spot for a while. The hazard lights on the car are LED. They should be good all night so no one collides with it in the dark."

"Think there are any locator devices in this buggy?"

"I hope not. I checked briefly, but I really don't know what to look for. There's the GPS up by the mirror there. That could have been linked to something so I unplugged it. I guess we'll have to check in the morning when there's better light."

Jack looked into the mirror, but the back seat was dark. "Hey, Charlie, you OK back there?"

"Oh yeah. Never better. I've always said it's a blast hangin' around with you guys!"

Laura shook her head. "He's going to be fine." She turned around in her seat to face Charlie. "Hey, you. You lost some blood, and that wound could get infected, so we've got to get you some real medical attention." She looked to Jack. "Which we will get … how?"

"Do you have any signal strength?"

Laura pulled out her phone and turned it on. "Three bars."

"Call Martin quickly. Tell him we're about thirty miles west of Heber, Arizona, heading east-northeast on Arizona route 260. Find us the closest safe house with medical capability."

She called and later received directions in a return call to a location near the town. She turned to Jack. "Just before Heber, take a right on Buckskin Canyon Road, drive one and a quarter miles 'til you see two red barns on the left. There'll be someone checking his mail out front."

Jack smiled. "Checking his mail in the dark. I like it. Especially since they'd have to be really bright red barns at this hour."

They drove through the darkness without encountering any traffic. After a few minutes Charlie began to snore in the back seat.

Laura murmured, "Thank you, Jack."

"For … ?"

"For taking charge back there. I probably would have fallen apart. Were you in the army or something?"

"Nope. My brain just gets detached from my emotions at stressful times. Yours did, too, by the way. You did what you had to do. And you told me you've never fired a real rifle."

She leaned back in her seat, staring straight ahead. "I killed some people tonight, didn't I?"

"Probably. If you didn't, you incapacitated them, and I definitely killed them. You didn't have a choice, really, unless you were prepared to just give up and die yourself. There's no question they intended to kill us without hesitation. No prisoners, no hostages."

She tilted her head toward him. "You seemed to have it all figured out down to how to dispatch them. Have you done this before?"

Jack struggled for an answer, his face barely illuminated by the van's instrument panel.

Laura sighed. "Right. Ed."

"Ed, yes." Jack nodded. "And there are other things I haven't processed yet. I've saved my emotional energy for some future time I guess. Jennifer had me figured out pretty well. She said I had a way of putting a thick wall between my logic and my feelings. That trait served me well in debate. I'm not sure it's so healthy outside rhetorical combat."

"It saved us tonight. And it's kept the movement safe against Brisbane and its armed thugs and their allies."

Jack wagged his head back and forth. "Maybe, maybe not. I just know when I let myself think about it that there's been a lot of death and destruction that has to be accounted for some day."

"And you don't think you'd get justice when this is all over? Or do you think the good guys won't win?" she asked.

"I don't know what to think. I don't really try to think too deeply these days. Seems everything I associate with goes badly wrong."

"Maybe we can run away, assume new identities after this is over."

Jack glanced at her. "We?"

Laura was quiet for a while. When finally she spoke, her words came softly and slowly. "I did say 'we,' didn't I? Why did I do that? You came into my life so violently. And you're right: disaster seems to follow you. And now there's all this stuff from the past you don't want to talk about. You know, I almost shot you that night back in May." She turned to watch his face in the dashboard lights. His expression was one of concentration, perhaps tinged with dismay.

She continued, "And yet … and yet, you seem to have become part of my life. You and I depend on each other for our very lives in this crazy tide we've been swept into. And you know, I care about you. I really do. There was a time not so long ago I wasn't sure I'd ever feel that way about anyone, ever."

The ensuing silence hung heavy. Jack spoke slowly. "I know the question on your mind, and you'd like the answer, but I'm almost afraid to say it. The last thing I was doing before we came up on the roadblock was watching you in the mirror. It made me smile to see you so peaceful in the pillows with the sunset brushing your face."

"Wow." Laura adjusted the vent controls to bring in a little more outside air. "I wish this fight was over. I wish things were back to normal. There's so much good stuff we could do together."

"They will return to normal. Our institutions are self-correcting, healing."

"They seem awfully broken to me."

"Eh. Bent. Maybe distorted for now. But not broken. These times will pass, and we'll help build things anew."

"Well, aren't you suddenly the optimist."

"You know, while you were dozing, Charlie was telling me about the fires they had here back around 2002. The area's all new vegetation now. Healing."

They drove on a bit farther until he leaned forward in his seat. "Well, there's Buckskin Canyon Road. How far to our mail checker?" Jack slowed the van for the turn.

"One and a quarter miles."

A bit over a minute later, they spied an elderly man at a roadside mailbox. Jack brought the van to a stop. The man approached their open window. He was the picture of the rugged Westerner, complete with boots, plaid shirt, and tattered Stetson. Jack leaned out the window. "Howdy, neighbor. Don't suppose you'd have room for three weary travelers, would you?"

His face broke into a broad smile propagating deep wrinkles across its breadth. "You boys and girl have had quite a day." He extended his hand. "Bob Palance at your service. Put your van in the barn on the right. The door's open. Bring in what you need tonight, wash up, and get some shuteye. We'll sort things out in the morning. Doc Locke's on her way here now to check out that leg. The sheriff'll get your car secured in a bit. He'll likely have some questions for you in the morning. Don't worry. He's a good man. He's on our side."

"Thank you so much." Jack drove slowly up a dirt path and entered the barn.

Jack and Laura were discussing how to get Charlie to the house when Bob showed up at the barn entrance with a wheelchair.

Jack put his hands on his hips. "I'd heard about Western self-reliance but I had no idea."

Bob laughed. "My late wife needed it. I would have given it away, but seems I keep getting guests who can use it."

Jack and Laura helped Charlie into the chair and wheeled him to the house, arriving just as Dr. Locke pulled up the drive. While the doctor tended to Charlie, Jack and Laura brought in some bags and settled in the rooms Bob offered.

Laura conferred with Dr. Locke as she prepared to leave.

"He'll be fine," the doctor assured. "We get a lot of hunting accidents much worse than that. Just be sure he takes these." She handed Laura a small bottle of antibiotics. "I've gotta go. Sheriff called. One thing about a small town is you get to wear a lot of hats. I'm the coroner too."

"Sorry," Laura offered.

Doctor Locke shook her head. "Someone's gotta do it." She turned and headed to her pickup while talking to Bob.

He returned and bade them good night. "I'm retired, so I don't set an alarm. You'll likely be here a while so make yourselves comfortable. I usually fix breakfast around eight. There're extra quilts and blankets in the linen closet. Leave the door unlocked. That's the way around here. Good night."

Laura smiled. "Thank you, Mr. Palance."

"Heh. It's an honor. I know what you're doing for us. Mighty brave."

Laura and Jack surveyed the spacious accommodations.

She examined a series of photos on the wall. "Looks like the ranch is or was a meeting place, at least part time. Church groups. Businesses. Girl Scouts." Laura smiled.

Jack gazed out the window. "So quiet. I haven't been anywhere so quiet in … I don't know. I caught a bit of the sky outside. If I weren't so exhausted, I'd go out and look again. The Milky Way is beautiful."

Laura walked over and put her hand on his shoulders. "Man, you are all tension. You need to loosen up."

He put his arms around her, and they rested their heads on each other's shoulders for a long time in the quiet darkness. Afterward, they made their ways to their separate rooms. Deep sleep came quickly for both of them.

* * *

Vice President's Conference Room,
8 a.m. EST, Sunday, November 23, 2014,

"Excellent, Matt." Vice President Kincaid finished his second cup of coffee as Matt ended his presentation. "That's really encouraging. So, Upper Manhattan is our worst case at the moment, and they're at eighty-seven percent electricity."

"Yes, sir. Technically, it's eighty-seven percent of wattage handling capacity. But New York's been the most difficult case from the start, particularly Manhattan Island. They had no generating capacity to begin with. All the power has to be cabled in over ancient transmission lines. It's involved more digging than any other area. Earth, it appears, is inherently difficult to move."

Kincaid nodded. "And next after New York?"

"Charleston, South Carolina, at ninety-six percent. Charleston had reached a hundred percent two weeks ago, but the blasts at their two main substations set that back."

Kincaid turned Matt's report over, loosened his shoulders, and surveyed the nearly-empty conference room. "How's the investigation going on that?" Kincaid leaned forward.

"FBI has unequivocally linked the devices to Brisbane. As we dismantle more and more of the old Brisbane network, the remaining elites are getting desperate and willing to inflict real damage to slow our progress. The FBI Director believes that the Charleston target wasn't so much the federal

Homeland Security forces as it was the telecommunications rebels. Both substations powered key switching units for the east coast networks."

Kincaid waved off a third cup. "You know, we have to bring this 'rebel' thing to a close. I understand why there was no trust in the early days. But today I don't see the labor unions as an opposing third division. Are there any areas of substance where we're in disagreement?"

Matt shook his head. "No, sir. In fact, we seem to have very cordial relations with a number of the leaders of the movement. The only barriers are the lingering suspicions on their part and — probably most importantly — their fear of the Brisbane remnant. As damaging as Brisbane has been to the government infrastructure, they've been ruthless to the unions. You've seen the reports. The Brisbane people have burned homes and businesses and have made credible threats against associates of the movement. Even with Brisbane's reduced presence, we don't have the manpower to adequately protect all their targets. The unions' only salvation has been their superior tactics. They have an awesome ability to keep Brisbane off-balance between projecting their own phantom movements and monitoring the Brisbane troop locations."

"Matt, again, just between you and me, aren't we ready to drop the 'troop' and 'rebel' metaphors? Aren't we coming to a natural endpoint?"

"I don't know, Mr. Vice President."

Kincaid cringed. "And drop the 'Mr. Vice President.' I looked it up. It definitely is proper protocol to use my name."

Matt grinned. "I don't know, Mr. Kincaid. In the spring, we never would have imagined this. We had no idea how large and strong and out of control Brisbane was. We had no idea how quickly the telecommunications workers could coalesce into an organization. We soon found that we had two fiercely opposing camps, each with the capability to cripple society. Brisbane has shown no hesitation to do that. The unions have shown every inclination to safeguard our national infrastructure. We've been in touch fairly regularly with Martin, the head of the telecomm faction."

"Oh, so we know who he is?"

"Yes, sir, we know who he is. We just don't know where he is. Their security chief has a marvelous ability to keep the leadership's whereabouts cloaked. Some of Martin's conversations lead us to think he's located somewhere in the Midwest, maybe Indiana or Ohio."

"And FBI can't trace those conversations?" Kincaid tilted his head.

"Sure — over the telecommunications lines. If we run the trace five times, we get five different, essentially random, locations. On the other hand, when we trace Brisbane calls, we've uniformly pinpointed their locations. Brisbane had tried to develop location cloaking, but the telecomm people seem to have it neutralized. And the union is able to manipulate the Brisbane forces. Earlier this month they forged a bogus location for our phantom buddy Commander X near Fort Benning and drove the Brisbane people right into our hands."

Kincaid smiled. "Ah, yes. The mysterious Commander X. Surely you've identified him by now?"

Matt rubbed his neck. "That may be the most bizarre part. He really remains an enigma. We don't know who he is. All of the analysis points to someone from outside the original unions. Homeland Security reviewed all the photos and recordings of the times and places leading up to the unrest and continues to come up empty. We've got no pictures, no recordings of Commander X. We've accounted for all the others. HS thought they were close at one point when they linked an abandoned car to two activists who've been missing since the early days of the conflict, but the man associated with the car is known dead and was never associated with the unions. Whoever he — or she, possibly — is, when this is over, we want Commander X on our team."

Kincaid nodded, smiling. "Yes, we do. Looks like you're finally out of paper. Got anything else?"

"One small note I read on the way over. We've arrested Dr. Carlton, the Windham Trust mastermind. Given his age and frailty, we don't think we'll gain much from his prosecution. He seems more than willing to cooperate if it keeps him out of jail. We've also finished our interrogation of the Mattock woman, the programmer behind the power disaster. Looks like pure incompetence compounded by Carlton's inability to recognize it. Other than that, I've got nothing more." Matt relaxed.

"Thank you, Matt. I don't say that often enough. Your background information has made all the difference in keeping me sane here."

"I appreciate that, sir. It's been a team effort. Kathy and Sarah have been essential with their economic analysis, and they've kept the people well informed with their weekly economics show. It's one of the highest rated shows on television. Anna, of course, has helped to keep the diplomatic front quiet. Back in June I would have expected the oil cutoff to have flattened us by now. But it's been just the opposite."

Kincaid smiled. "If you recall, I told you this was one of those classic not-a-problem-but-an-opportunity moments. Where are we this week?"

"I don't have the numbers ready, but we seem to have adjusted in a matter of months to a fifteen-plus percent drop in petroleum availability. I don't think anyone would have believed possible that there was so much slack in the manufacturing infrastructure. The demand for new energy-efficient … stuff … has actually helped pull the economy along. People aren't going to be spending much for Christmas unless they count the new cars and refrigerators as gifts. It's still circulating money, though."

Kincaid chuckled. "Right. And, to be honest, I'll admit I've always been just a little uncomfortable with the semi-enforced waste of the holidays.

What did Sarah call it? Dead weight loss? Maybe we can establish some better traditions out of this. I almost forgot to ask. Do you have good Thanksgiving plans? Will you make it to your folks?"

"Not this year, sir." Matt smiled. "We don't think a trip out to Oregon under the circumstances would look right."

"We?"

Matt grinned. "Juliet's coming over for Thanksgiving dinner. We'll have a video linkup with her folks and mine in the afternoon."

"Sounds a bit more serious than I last remember."

Matt shrugged. "Maybe. Will you and Miss Colbert ...?"

"She's invited me to dinner with her family in Baltimore. Just a quiet traditional Thanksgiving dinner."

Matt gathered his papers, trying to suppress another grin. "Good. That's good."

* * *

Mountain ridge above Buckskin Canyon Road,
Heber, Arizona, 8 a.m. MST

Jack surveyed the rugged hills and distant mountains from his perch on a boulder. "I had forgotten how beautiful the western landscapes could be. My family came out this way twice while I was growing up — on family vacations."

Laura leaned against him. They wore matching black coats taken from the Brisbane van. "So we're not up here to watch for hostiles?"

"No," Jack smiled. "We're up here because it's a nice place to be. Take a big breath. You won't experience air that clean for a very long time. Now, be totally still and don't say anything."

They sat together still and quiet for nearly five minutes.

Jack finally broke the silence. "You did not hear a single human sound. In this age that's remarkable."

"You thinking of becoming a cowboy, Jack?"

"Nah." He tucked his head down. "I could probably adjust to almost anything, but I really don't have the temperament for rural life. I'm too much of a techno-weenie."

She laughed. "A techno-weenie?"

"Yeah, that's what Jenn called me. She said I was a techno-weenie, but that she loved me anyway."

Laura paused and grew serious. "You miss her, don't you?"

Jack looked in the distance at the dark band of clouds approaching from the west. "Yeah. I try not to think about her too much. We have a lot of responsibilities to a lot of people. I feel like I have to keep a clear head. But sometimes memories will just bubble up unexpectedly. I do the best I can."

"I'm sorry." She laid her head on his shoulder. "Did you get much support from your family during her illness? I feel bad that I've never asked about that."

"And I didn't say anything. My mom and dad died when I was eighteen. They were just driving through an intersection when a runaway truck broadsided their car. I was in high school at the time. They called me into the office. The principal and the school counselor were waiting there for me. I immediately became my younger brother's guardian. I had to grow up really fast. Jenn always thought that was the root of my coldness. Maybe it's a mask I put on back then and have had a hard time taking off."

He turned to Laura. "What about you? What about your family?"

She took a deep breath. "Well, you know my dad pretty well. You two are on such good terms — obviously." She turned to see his eyes rolling. "My dad and I have been fighting with words for a long, long time. I know that we love each other deeply, but we just get on each other's nerves. We've got such different perspectives."

"And your mom?"

Laura huddled more tightly against Jack. "Yeah. My mom. That's a different story. When I was about ten, she left us to live with this wealthy insurance executive. She was going to divorce Dad and marry the exec. That was back just before Dad came to the Institute. We didn't have a lot of money back then, and she wanted pretty things.

"But the exec got tired of her, and she came back for a while when I was thirteen." Laura sniffed, fighting back tears. "But she didn't stay long. They got divorced and she remarried someone else, then someone else, then someone else again. I tried to be a supportive daughter, but I drew the line at number four. I told her she wasn't getting a wedding present from me until she'd been married to that guy for five years. She didn't take that well; we had a big blow-up and haven't really talked since. Dad took good care of me, though. Maybe he saw me as his conscience. With all the resources that came with his position at the Institute and, as we now know, all sorts of shady business, I was able to attend Yale, graduate, and gain full time employment causing trouble. Who would have thought?"

Jack nodded slowly. "Wow. Sounds like we are two losers of the first order."

"Yep. Other than being some of the leaders of a national rebellion against the forces of darkness. Like Joan of Arc." She quickly sat upright. "Oh, God! Just like Joan of Arc. That's exactly what Charlie said."

"What?"

"Back in the spring, when all this was just starting, Charlie said I should lead the resistance, that I was the perfect Joan of Arc. I reminded him how badly that turned out for Joan. I don't remember what he said about that, but I'm sure that it wasn't very comforting. Damn. I wish he wasn't right so often."

Jack began laughing.

"Yeah, you laugh. Just remember that you've got a bigger price on your head than I have."

They both grew quiet at the sight of a station wagon moving down the road and turning into the ranch driveway. As two figures emerged from the car, Bob Palance came out to greet them, throwing his arms around the driver. They seemed to exchange pleasantries, and Bob waved his hands in the direction of his barn. The second figure reached into the station wagon, withdrew a large black bag, and headed for the barn while Bob and the driver walked to the house.

Laura spoke first. "I'm betting that's Bob's son he was talking about last night."

"Uh huh. And the other is a co-worker who's going to do a bug sweep of the van. I think it might be a good idea to go down and join them. I'm sure they've got questions for us. And I don't like the looks of those clouds heading our way. I wouldn't want to get caught in a snow storm up here."

Laura scanned the approaching clouds, closer and darker now. "Nah. We may get a dusting of snow, but that's it." She turned to Jack, who was eyeing her quizzically. "I know my weather. I'm a pilot."

"A pilot?" he asked, eyebrows raised.

"Yeah. You don't think I could be a pilot?"

"I absolutely do. I just wasn't expecting it. You're full of surprises."

She smiled and turned to the cloud, breathing the clean air. "You just keep that in mind."

They walked down the trail, arriving after twenty minutes. Entering the warm house, they were greeted by the aroma of chili and fresh baking.

Bob and the driver were talking in the kitchen. Bob brightened at their arrival. "Jack, Laura, meet my son, Bob Jr." He turned to his son. "Junior, this is Commander X and … what exactly are you, Laura?"

Jack chimed in confidently. "She's Vice President for network integration and fund-raising."

Laura smiled, turning to Jack. "Yeah. What he said."

Bob Jr. extended his hand to each of them. "It's an honor to have you here with us. You're an inspiration."

Jack shook his head. "I just hope we haven't put you in jeopardy. I seem to have attracted attention you don't need."

"On the contrary. I've been talking with the sheriff all morning. He doesn't think those guys were here for you. He found a lot of paperwork in the other van. There was a convoy of several fuel tankers heading down the same road about ten minutes behind you. From the timetables the sheriff found in the van, it looks like those thugs were planning to capture the trucks. Obviously they didn't plan to keep any hostages. You probably saved those six truckers last night. No, you were just in the wrong place at the wrong time … at least from Brisbane's perspective. From where we stand, you were in the right place at the right time."

Jack sat down at the kitchen table. "I guess I'm relieved."

"The sheriff will be by later this afternoon. He'll have a few questions, I'm sure. I, myself, would like to know how you snuffed out five men armed with top-of-the-line machine guns wearing body armor while you essentially had game rifles and no protection? And why did you leave the lights on in the other van?"

Laura answered. "The Brisbane soldiers are trained for combat. They assume a battle against a well-armed, valuable, point target. They would have been trained to concentrate all their efforts on that well defended target. Their command model assumes central control over well-protected communications lines. Look at the attack on the President last month. Big assault with lots of firepower on a single building with only a handful of defenders. And Brisbane would have succeeded had the defenders not had the high ground and had the ability to slow their advance while calling in reinforcements from not too far away.

"Last night when we were under attack, Jack gave them what appeared to be a centralized point of defense. The glare of the light from our … former … car masked our withdrawal onto the hillside. Though we had the high ground advantage, we were lightly armed. Jack waited until their focus was fully committed to the car before launching our attack against their vulnerabilities. Because Brisbane's training would emphasize frontal assault with overwhelming force and superior technologies, they weren't prepared for an attack from the flank." She turned to Jack.

He smiled.

Bob appeared in the doorway. "Lunch is ready. Let's move this gathering into the dining room."

Charlie was already seated at the big family table. Two pots of chili sat on the table along with cornbread and a pitcher of tea.

"I don't have guests so often this time of year. It's good to have someone to cook for," Bob beamed.

Laura took a seat at the table between Jack and Charlie. "Feeling better?"

"Oh, yeah, I'll be back to my jogging in no time."

She shook her head. "You never move faster than a walk."

Charlie looked hurt. "Well, maybe I'll change."

The side door opened, and a woman in her twenties entered carrying an electronic device of some sort.

"Samie," Bob Jr. called out. "Everyone, this is Samantha. She's the hardware guru at the switching station. Samie, have a seat. We're just starting lunch."

Samantha nodded. "I'd love to. If you could put something aside, I'll be back in about twenty. I want to get this transponder up the main highway.

The tankers are still stopped up there. We're outfitting them with this gear. Homeland Security is riding shotgun, and as far as we can tell, the baddies think that they pulled off the hijack. By the way, whoever unplugged the GPS, smooth move. The people monitoring this have been blind since the firefight."

Bob Jr. turned back to the table as Samantha left. "Like you said, central control over well-protected communication lines. Samie will get the devices turned back on somewhere that's safe for us, and Homeland Security can watch who shows up to ask about them. You're safe here for now, and we can set you up with good land line comms and masking right out of the house. As of this morning, you're just outside Saginaw, Michigan, electronically. The feds need to find out where Brisbane's cached the ammo for the Detroit area."

Charlie shook his head. "Way to go, Jack. The world's most powerful ghost."

Laura filled her plate and passed the chili to Jack. "I see they uncovered another warehouse of weapons down in Huntsville, Alabama, yesterday. What does that bring it up to? Twenty-five? Thirty?"

Bob Jr. scowled. "Try seventy-one. Between the New Jersey folks and Homeland Security, we're putting together a really scary picture. We keep uncovering more firms who were really shadow divisions of Brisbane. Before we began breaking them up, it looks like they had over four hundred thousand de facto soldiers under their control and more weapons than the Marine Corps and county governments combined. They owned enough prisons to hold most of the top levels of government. Even as late as last week, Bailey was calling the shots from Danbury."

Charlie perked up. "This is a great conspiracy. I love it. But I thought Danbury is a federal prison."

Bob Jr. shook his head. "The government may own the stones and bars, but the prison guard force had all been privatized under Bailey. You know: 'cost cutting, free enterprise, the American way.' Of course, it was none of that. Even our county jail here was APC staffed. We kept the staff, but cut the ties."

"We are so grateful for your hospitality. But we probably need to move on," Jack said. He was enjoying a second helping of beans. "Not that I want to."

Bob Palance raised his hand. "We have all the communications you need. California is calm, and the Brisbane threat is easing. I'm here by myself, Bob Jr.'s busy with his family, and I love the company. You could stockpile another few more days of fuel rations. Stay through Thanksgiving at least."

Jack looked to Laura and Charlie, both nodding. "Mr. Palance, it would be an honor."

* * *

Eisenhower Executive Office Building, Friday, November 28, 2014

Anna and Sarah worked across the paper-strewn table from each other. Anna gathered a set of documents together and secured them with a large clip. "The French have been given the names of the Brisbane agents in Paris and San Rafael. Do you have the intelligence on Brisbane funding?"

Sarah handed Anna a small bundle of papers. "Check."

"And I have the Japanese agents. Do we have financials for them?"

"Here's all I have. We're waiting on some more data from Korea and China. There seems to be a link with some of the Chinese factory cities." She handed Anna a single page.

Anna collated the sheets, holding them upright as she clipped them. She looked over to Sarah who seemed uncharacteristically quiet. "Have a good Thanksgiving?"

Sarah's face clouded. "It was OK."

"Sorry. I thought you and Corporal Tull …"

"Yeah. Like I said, it was OK. We had a nice turkey dinner at my place. We called our folks. It was OK."

Anna waited for more, but nothing was forthcoming. "But … ?"

Sarah scowled. "I guess I was expecting something more, some … sign … or token." Sarah flailed the air with her hands. "I was expecting some sort of … you know … indication of commitment."

Anna nodded respectfully. "I see. Well, Jeff's a pretty cautious guy. From everything I've seen, he seems to totally adore you. But he's not the kind to be rushed."

Sarah got up and began pacing the room. "I'm not talking about rushing anybody. I just think … I don't know what I think."

Anna tilted her head. "Well, that's a first."

"And what would you be doing, Miss Does-everything-right Colbert?" Sarah put her hands on her hips.

"I'd be patient. I'd enjoy the journey; be thankful for the time. *Tres romantique, non*?"

Sarah's scowl changed explosively to anger. "What a load of crap!"

"What?"

"Don't go off with this French romantic bullshit. You people don't have a monopoly on feelings. We geeks have love, too, ya know."

"But …"

"We fall in love, we marry, and we have kids. Tons of kids." Sarah spun around and faced Anna again. "Did you know that scientists have a much lower divorce rate than diplomats? Huh? Did you know that? Well, not economists. But that's another story."

Anna leaned back in her chair, her mouth open, as Sarah tramped around the room.

"I don't know why I'm asking you, anyway. Why am I asking you for advice? I should be helping plan your state wedding."

"Excuse me!"

"I should be preparing to be asked to sit for the little Kincaids while Vice President and Mrs. Perfect go out for some …" She twirled her hand in the air. "… big state whoop-de-doo."

"You're nuts."

"Oh yeah?" Sarah moved in close, fists resting on the table. "I sit across the table from him in our meetings. When you're up front talking, I watch him. It's painful, Colbert. The man is so in love with you, it hurts. You can see it in his eyes. My God, he smiles when you're talking about quadrinational debt exchange. How sad is that?"

Anna folded her hands in front of her on the table.

Sarah continued, "And don't think I haven't been watching you, too, girl. I can see those vision recordings playing in your head. Reading a book under the beach umbrella while your knight in shining armor watches the kiddies playing in the surf down at Cape May. So domestic, so comfortable. You know it's right." She seemed exhausted, almost to the point of tears. "It's just with all the hate and destruction and thievery and ruin of late, I just can't bear to think of something so perfect not happening. I'm sorry. I have no right to tear into you like that. I was just hoping for something better. That's all." Sarah stood behind her chair and lowered her head.

Anna watched her for some time. "How do you do that?"

"Do what?" Sarah murmured.

"How do you get inside peoples' heads like that? You construct all these wild scenarios that turn out to be invariably correct."

"Oh, I don't know. Gift. Curse. I … Wait. So I was right! Yes, I was right! Spill it, Colbert. I was right about everything, wasn't I?"

"Almost. I'm sure that Cape May is wonderful, but David and I prefer Myrtle Beach."

"David? David? What happened to 'Mr. Kincaid'?"

"This is my story. Am I going to regret telling you this?"

"No. Sorry." Sarah placed a finger across her lips.

"It's hard to know where to begin." Anna leaned forward on her elbows. "Working together so closely over the months through all these disasters, we've gotten to know each other. It's like you keep saying — we were made for each other. I've never known anyone as considerate and morally strong. We've had dinners together and talked about so much."

Sarah had returned to her seat, listening intently. "Really? Like when?"

Anna grinned. "The first time we had dinner, just the two of us, was that day back last month when the Five Guys suspended operations. He invited me over. He had some Cornish game hens in the freezer, and we used up just about everything in his fridge to make the meal. It was quite good, actually. He's a pretty decent cook. Who knew? After dinner, we finished the reports we brought."

"You're killing me, Colbert."

Anna raised her eyebrows. "My story."

"Right."

"Like I said, we finished the reports and then watched a movie. Afterwards, he drove me to my apartment. He was oh so gallant. He saw me to my door and kissed my hand." She beamed.

Sarah folded her arms on the table and buried her head in them. "You drive me crazy."

"And then I kissed him back properly. Long and deep and passionate."

Sarah sat up abruptly, raising her arms as if in victory. "There's hope for the world after all. So where are we going next, and when?"

Anna frowned. "That's where it gets complicated, and where you are held to confidence."

"You're kidding. This is wonderful. What's to not like?"

"Well, for one thing, we have to be absolutely sure there're no conflicts of interest. I don't think there are. And then there's the age thing."

"Age thing?" Sarah asked.

"It doesn't feel like it to me, but there is a difference of about twenty years. We have to be sensitive to that."

Sarah waved her hand in dismissal. "Not to worry. I did a paper on that once. You're safe."

"You've got to be joking."

"No. Really. It was a class in family economics. We had to do several research papers. I did one on marital age disparity. You wouldn't believe how much data is available on that topic."

Anna shook her head. "No, I guess I wouldn't."

"Anyway, it turns out that in addition to the island of stability around the point where the mates are the same age, there's another big island of stability when the older partner is about twice the age of the younger. The old half age plus seven rule."

"I thought that formula was debunked."

"No, no, no, my dear Josephine. A lot of data support it. It was pretty easy to correlate for my paper. The older partner — as long as they're not creepy older — brings stability, worldly experience, and resources. The younger partner — as long as they're not creepy younger — brings reasons to live — like fresh perspective and vigor. Pretty much a win-win."

"Unless you're an older woman."

"Nooooo. Works both ways. It's just that Mrs. Robinson wrecked it for the older woman set. There isn't nearly as much data for the older female model, but the math is the same."

Anna stared at Sarah across the table. After about a minute, Sarah grinned her mischievous grin.

"OK." Anna shook her head. "Let's get back to work. We will not discuss this again for a long time."

They returned to their papers. After a brief spate of work Sarah looked up. "Plus, when he does finally kick off, you'll still be quite marketable. Like Jackie Kennedy."

Anna slapped the table. "OK. Enough. No talking until … until … the economy's fixed."

Sarah, taken aback by the economics reference, pondered for a moment and then flipped through some of her papers, finally looking up and grinning. "OK."

* * *

The Old Roadways Warehouse,
Edison, New Jersey, Tuesday, December 23, 2014

"Hey Joshie, are you doing something with the software?" Lindsey Two called over to Josh, who was busily typing in code.

"No. I won't have anything new for several days. Why?"

"My little red baddies are disappearing from the screen."

"Huh?" Josh came over behind her. "Manually ping a couple of transponders." He watched as she tried several different phones. "Ah, hell. Looks like they figured out how to disable the locators. That is not good. Call Martin. See if he can cut the links between the specific cells. We need to buy some time while I figure a workaround."

Mike Johnson entered the warehouse with Lindsey One and Janice.

Josh looked up. "Mike, looks like the empire has found our trackers. We're trying to slow their turnoff, but I don't know how long it might take to find an alternative."

They gathered around Lindsey Two's console.

"What's the last movement status you had?" Mike queried Josh and Two.

"The Middle Atlantic agents were still moving in on Washington. The rest were still wandering around. Maybe some movement toward Arizona." Lindsey Two brought up a picture from a few hours earlier.

Lindsey One spoke. "I'll let Matt know. Looks like the DC guys are blinking out the fastest. What about the Western forces?"

"Yeah, we've lost a lot of them, too." Mike scanned the four-state region. "We'd better let the Commander know. I don't think Brisbane has his location, but they seem to be concentrating their efforts there. Probably searching. What about us? Are we still cloaked?"

Josh rubbed the back of his neck. "We were as of an hour ago. Hard to say now. Give me some time. I'll come up with something."

Lindsey One looked up from her desk and removed her headset. "Martin says our guys have started blocking the cell routers starting with the higher-ups. But he says it's all manual and will take some time."

"How many have we lost?"

She turned to the screen. "We had nineteen thousand red dots last time I remember. We're down to sixteen thou' now."

Mike looked relieved. "All right. That's not good, but it could be a lot worse."

"Unfortunately, the outages are concentrated around the capital and Arizona. It's not random."

* * *

The President's Office, the White House

"Mr. President, a speech like this does have an impact." Cameron Conklin laid the polished copy on the President's desk. "The reason we don't have any proof is probably that it's so self-evident that no one has ever done a real study. For my own part, I measure the success of past speeches by whether we remember them historically. Have you ever noticed that we remember several great speeches from near the ends of wars and crises? An upbeat Christmas greeting would be appropriately soothing."

"I know you're right. But when I think about where we were this time last year …"

"Don't think about that, sir. It wasn't real. You've said so yourself."

"But the economy's in a ditch."

"Halfway out and climbing fast, sir, thanks in no small part to what we've done," Cameron persisted.

"So many of our former allies are gone, replaced by hostile regimes."

"Who besides Saudi Arabia, sir?"

"Saudi Arabia was a very important ally."

"The mishmash that replaced them is weak, disorganized, and contained. And we picked up Iran as a non-enemy for the first time since before I was born."

The President at last seemed to enjoy the exchange. "But Iran is not supplying us any oil."

"On which we are no longer so dependent since the emergency measures we took to diversify our energy usage and sources, sir." She turned impatiently to Kincaid. "You can step in anytime, Mr. Vice President."

Kincaid raised a hand. "You're doing fine. I was just waiting for the part where the President bemoans the attacks by Brisbane and the strike by the telecommunications workers and where you come back with how the number of attacks has plummeted and most areas of the country are enjoying full service again."

Cameron turned to the President.

"He stole our lines." The President smiled. "OK, tell Tony to get me prepped and we'll have a few takes. What time were you shooting for?"

Cameron scribbled notes in the margins of her copy. "Eleven a.m. Eastern Time on Christmas day. I've already checked with the networks. They're all willing to air it, even Wolfe."

Kincaid looked up quickly from his own notes. "Even Wolfe? How did you manage that?"

"You don't want to know," she replied.

Kincaid nodded. "Right."

* * *

Palance Ranch, Heber, Arizona,
Wednesday, December 24, 2010, 9:30 p.m. MST

Jack picked up Charlie's suitcase as Bob and his son loaded their pickup. "I can't believe we've imposed on you this long. You're a real hero, Bob."

"Imposed?" His face crinkled with a broad grin as the glow of the porch light fell across his face, revealing an ancient, wise visage. "I typically barely get by over the course of the year. Everyone who's come to visit you and stayed has chipped in pretty generously. This will be my best year since '02. Plus, it's good to feel I have an active part in this. And you and the 'missus' have contributed more than your fair share." He grinned even more, glancing in Laura's direction.

She rolled her eyes. "Just make sure Charlie behaves himself."

Charlie laughed. "That'll be the day."

Bob Jr. turned the pickup around and headed down the drive. Bob and Charlie waved from the back seat.

"Where exactly are they going again?" Laura pulled her coat tighter against the frigid night air.

"Overgaard. It's just to the east, along the main highway. Bob Jr. lives there next to the airpark. The Mogollon Airpark, to be precise. They'll set up an early warning system in case we get visitors intent on doing us harm. They want to cover the approach roads all around and the airpark." He looked skyward. "I was hoping for a clear night. Maybe see the Milky Way. Not tonight, though. Feels like snow." He turned to Laura. "What does the pilot think?"

"The pilot thinks you're not paying attention. It *is* snowing. Look at the light on the barn across the road."

"So it is."

They re-entered the house, still warm and fragrant from the evening meal. Jack turned off the porch light and went through the house checking doors and turning off most lights. He returned to the darkened living room where Laura stood watching out the window. In silhouette, she looked cold. Jack put several more logs on the fire and the fireplace crackled momentarily with sparks.

"It's beautiful out there." She spoke in barely a whisper, but the house was completely silent otherwise.

Jack joined her at the window. The snow came down in large, clumpy flakes. In the darkness, it was difficult to tell where the road lay.

"They're going to try to kill us, aren't they?"

Jack searched for an answer, but gave up. "Probably."

She turned to him. "I was hoping for a more cheerful answer." She moved over closer to him. The heat of the fire warmed their backs.

"You only asked if they'll try. That they will — and have been for some time now. But they'll fail — just as they always have."

"I'm not so sure this time. Up until now, we've known where they were. I don't feel secure any more. What if they can track us now? What if the tables are really turned?"

"We're a tiny ship in a big ocean. We've got lookouts and plans. We'll do the best we can."

The fire crackled behind them and the snowscape outside shifted in the wind. They watched in silence for perhaps ten or twenty minutes.

"I'm cold. Hold me."

Jack turned to Laura and put his arms around her arms and rested his chin on her shoulder. Her arms were quite cold. "Wait right here." He trotted to his room, returning with a heavy quilted comforter. Jack opened the comforter and wrapped it around them. He positioned his arms around hers again and clasped the edges of the comforter. Her shivering subsided after a few minutes. "Better?"

"Ummmm." She sighed.

The snow grew heavier and the wind picked up. The light of the barn was no more than a bright blur of snow, and the road had disappeared.

"Make love to me, Jack."

A period of silence ensued. "I'm not sure that's a good idea."

"Jack, we're being hunted like animals. We've got this one precious time. I want you to make love to me."

He hugged her tightly. "I want to. Believe me, I want to. But we're not …"

"Jack, stop thinking. I know what I'm doing. You have to have trust. In me. In you. Whatever happens tonight is the least of your worries. Live, Jack. Live for once." She turned around in his arms and embraced him, kissing him passionately.

They stumbled back to the couch facing the fire and spread the comforter on the couch. Undressing each other, they piled their clothing, one piece after another, on the floor.

"You're very beautiful, you know. I've watched you in the rear view mirror across the whole continent."

"Thank you. You're a good man."

Jack lay on the couch and Laura climbed on top. Not a word was spoken as she lost herself in exertion until she was spent. Jack could taste salty tears as he kissed her face.

"How do you like…?" He asked.

"Don't think, Jack. Don't ask. Just do."

They swapped places and continued, Jack kissing her on the face and body. The flames of the fireplace painted her entirely in warm, glowing tones. His ankles and knees and shoulders crackled as months of tension released with his climax. He pulled the comforter over them, and they lay in warm, moist embrace, kissing for a very long time.

Laura finally turned in his arms and pushed her back tightly against his chest. She took his hand and placed it on her breast. "I love you, Jack."

"Yes, I know. I love you so much."

"I know."

In a distant part of the house Bob's Swiss cuckoo clock chirped twelve times.

"What is today, Jack?"

"I'm not sure. I've lost track." Jack replied.

"I think it's Christmas."

Jack chuckled. "I'm not sure. I've stopped thinking. But you may well be right."

"I am. Merry Christmas, Jack."

"Merry Christmas, Laura."

25 LAST STAND

Palance Ranch, Heber, Arizona,
Thursday, December 25, 2014, 9:30 a.m. MST

Sunrise unfolded in a long, slow process. Having shed nine inches of snow, the clouds hung thin, even, and gray, bathing the living room in drowsy softness. Laura and Jack lay in permeating warmth beneath the quilted comforter.

Laura cautiously opened one eye and whispered, "Jack, are you awake?"

"Barely."

"The fire's gone out."

"That makes sense."

"So, it's going to be cold in the room," she said.

"Good reason to stay under the cover."

She giggled and turned over, touching foreheads. "Shouldn't we get up or something?"

"Let me think about it."

He didn't have long to ponder the question. They both jumped at the sound of a vehicle door slamming.

Laura raced low to the front window. "Oh, shit! Charlie's back with Bob Jr. I thought they'd be gone for two days."

She turned toward the couch to see Jack quickly sorting their clothes. Each grabbed their individual pile and ran to their rooms.

Charlie and Bob Jr. came into the house talking about encryption routines and call-blocking technology. Charlie headed for the living room as Bob Jr. went to the kitchen to start coffee.

Laura returned to the living room at the same time Charlie entered it. "Well, good morning. I wasn't expecting you back so soon. I just got up. It's really quiet here."

"Yeah, we needed to get some frequency lists and contact numbers.

Didn't want to activate the cell phones 'til we had blocking in place." Charlie walked deliberately but comfortably with his cane. "I think Jack has the numbers." Charlie sat down on the couch. His brow wrinkled for a moment as he placed his hand on the warm comforter.

He looked down and his face broke into a grin as he used his cane to nudge an item missed in their frantic cleanup. He looked up at Laura, who looked away, her arms crossed. Charlie chuckled. "About time."

She growled and reached down, snatched the panties, and then stomped toward her room.

Charlie called after her, "Can you ask Jack to get me the contact list?" Hearing no reply, he smiled, hobbled over to the fireplace, and began laying wood for the fire. He mumbled a Christmas song, "Chestnuts roasting o'er an open fire …"

* * *

The Old Roadways Warehouse,
Edison, New Jersey, Monday, December 29, 2014

Mike Johnson long ago had learned to keep staff meetings short and as painless as possible. Presenting last, he savored the happy task of explaining their final role with the government. He approached the end of his announcements. "So, more or less the second week of January, we will move back to Programming Palace."

Everyone cheered.

"Josh. To answer your earlier question, we did all the documentation needed for patenting the techniques you developed during the war. Now the government can, and almost certainly will, take control of those patents, but Matt at the White House has assured me that we will be properly compensated, both financially from Homeland Security and commercially with intellectual property credit. The Brisbane troop numbers are down enough and the federal forces up to speed enough that we can begin an orderly turnover of responsibilities."

Josh shrugged. "I'm OK with that. Anyway, we've got a game to release."

Mike smiled. "Right. Finally I just want to say something. Everyone has been a hero here." He rose from his chair. "I remember when Josh brought me along from Brisbane. I was happy for the comfortable life the job brought and for the freedom from Brisbane, but I'd be dishonest if I said I thought at the time that what I was doing was worthwhile or noble. Now I've seen what this team could — and did — do in the service of the country, and I cannot imagine anything that could make me more proud. Thank you. Thank you all."

With another round of cheers, the meeting ended, and nearly every person headed back to his or her station.

With everyone else out of the room, Lindsey Two approached Mike.

"Nice job, Mikey. Hey, I heard what you and Janice did for One on Christmas. That was sweet."

He smiled sheepishly. "She deserves it."

Two nodded. "You're right." She sat up on the table a few chairs down. "She deserves decent people around her. I've never seen her so happy. One's a nice kid. When she was with Josh and me, we treated her OK, but it wasn't — you know — family. Josh is a good man, but not what you'd call nice. He and I get on great. I guess our styles mesh pretty well, but our styles are on the rough side. One's softer. And while I respect her way, I'm not into it myself. I think that was kind of a gap in her life when she was with us. She seems complete now. And, like I say, happy. Just thought you should know."

Mike nodded. "Thank you. I hope you know that I value and appreciate your perspective. I'm glad to know you think we're doing the right thing. It really matters to me." He paused. "Are you and Josh doing anything New Year's Eve?"

She rolled her eyes and clutched her chest. "Oh, yeah. But you don't want to be too close."

* * *

Vice President's Conference Room, Friday, January 6, 2015

Tiffany Miller rested her forehead in her hand, her elbow on the table. "I appreciate your concerns, but I still think that my place is here and that Washington is as safe as any other location."

Kincaid shook his head slowly. "You may be right. But, out of an abundance of caution, we'd rather have the two of you split up. There's no telling what these people have in mind. What we do know is that several agents have spotted the last, most violent remnant of Brisbane in this area. These are the very ones who boarded the plane with Vice President Bailey back in May — Henderson and Hercules in particular. They're smart, they're strong, and they don't hesitate to kill. For better and for worse, you are the symbol of resilience. Our best analysis is that this final SWAT team intends to capture or kill you and your father.

"And despite our best efforts, Mr. Bailey seems to have been communicating still from Danbury. We're moving him in secret to the prison in Lorton. That dungeon has been completely swept, and we should be able to finally cut the cord between Windham and Brisbane."

She took a deep breath. "OK. Let me talk to Dad. He's pretty fragile and not getting any better. When would I be moving out?"

Admiral Brown spoke from the end of the table. "We're looking at the early hours of Monday morning. We'll have a convoy large enough to protect you, but I hope small enough not to attract attention. That would be a few hours before we move Bailey through the same area. If this Brisbane team gets wind of Bailey's movements, they'll be drawn to that and not to your movements. We'd put you up in Indian Head for now. The base is a special weapons area and has our most trustworthy troops."

She bit her lower lip. "What about Dad?"

Kincaid spoke. "We're beefing up security here, too. The past couple of nights, we've quietly brought in some heavy artillery. That's what's in those tents on the east side of the White House."

She shook her head. "That's not what I meant. Who's keeping an eye on him? I'm worried. He's been really distant lately. Spends a lot of time just looking out the window. I know that all of you have been doing your best to keep him engaged, but he's not himself."

Admiral Brown looked over to Kincaid, who nodded. "We've noticed that same thing, Tiffany. We've placed several trained counselors among the staff and are keeping watch over him. They've already recommended a number of steps to restore his old optimism. Right now, he's still blaming himself for Bailey's ability to get as far as he did. I think that once the trials begin, the focus will be on Mr. Bailey, where it belongs."

"How much of this does Dad know?"

"Everything."

"Is he on board with it?"

"Yes, reluctantly."

She placed her hands on the table. "Well, then, Monday morning it is. I'll tidy up things here. How long do you think I need to pack for?"

Admiral Brown shook his head. "Can't say for sure. Probably a week. We're pulling troops in from the whole east coast. We've got the city ringed already, and we'll do a house-to-house search if we have to. The battle ends here. I wish it were some place more remote, but they've brought the battle to us."

"And the rebels?" she asked.

"That won't be much longer, either. We've got bridges of trust, and they're ready to end the standoff as well. We still haven't managed to have a face-to-face with their Commander X, but that shouldn't be much longer. Their technical support, it turns out, was just a couple of hours away in New Jersey. They've been instrumental in helping us neutralize all but the most hardcore of Brisbane, but New Jersey's still keeping their leaders' locations secret. We don't have reason to challenge that. I just wish they'd hurry up and release the remaining communication lines. It would help restore a sense of normalcy."

She looked at Admiral Brown. "With all due respect, Admiral, your need to spirit me away to a secure weapons station doesn't inspire a sense of normalcy in me, either."

"Yes, ma'am. Point taken."

She turned next to Kincaid. "Where do I need to be when?"

"Four a.m., Monday, Roosevelt Room."

She nodded.

* * *

The White House, Roosevelt Room,
Monday, January 9, 2015, 3:40 a.m. EST

Tiffany stood beside the long table wearing her riding jeans and flannel shirt. Her winter coat was draped over her suitcase. "I didn't know that I'd have company." She extended her hand.

"Scott Thomas, ma'am. And this is my son Jeremy."

"Ah. It's an honor to meet you, sir. I can appreciate that they want to keep you in a secure location, too." She turned to the boy. "How old are you, Jeremy?"

"Ten. Are you who I think you are?"

She smiled. "Who do you think I am?"

"You look like the President's daughter, the one who rides the motorcycle."

She laughed. "Bingo. You want a ride when we get back … if it's OK with your dad?"

Jeremy looked up at his father expectantly.

"Probably. When we get back."

"Cool."

She grew more serious, kneeling down to look Jeremy in the eye. "Do you know what we're doing at this ridiculous hour?"

"There are some bad guys after us because Dad wrecked their plot. We're going somewhere they can't get us, and the Marines and Army are going to find the bad guys and put them in jail."

Tiffany rubbed her chin and nodded. "I think you've got it down pretty good. I'm glad to be traveling with such a level-headed fellow kid."

Jeremy smiled.

Kincaid, Anna, Peter, Sarah, Kathy, and Brian Doctrow joined them with the President for final instructions and encouragement.

At a few minutes before four, the Marine Corps officer in charge of the convoy came and escorted them into one of four identical black armored vans.

Sarah looked up and down the drive separating the White House from the Executive Office Building. Marines in full battle gear with rifles at the ready were posted at both ends of the drive. "I don't like the looks of this."

The convoy started moving down the drive. The front gate opened just as the first van approached and shut again as the fourth moved slowly out onto the pavement toward New York Avenue.

* * *

Corporate Center parking lot at the
intersection of U.S. 50 and the Beltway, 4 a.m.

Hercules paced the sidewalk in agitation as his radio operator waited for calls. "Why didn't they get that tracker installed?" His men had taken over the building closest to the intersection as their outpost.

The operator repeated his earlier report, "Mr. Henderson says there were too many feds around to get close to the car. But like he said, we've got spotters all along the route. Mr. Bailey's just south of the Delaware Memorial Bridge now and traveling at normal speed."

"Shit," Hercules growled. "It'll be after sunup when they arrive here. We can't be moving around in the light. Let's get everyone positioned now. And tell them to keep their heads down until I give the signal. Curfew expires at sunrise. We don't want any patrols spoiling the party."

His men began moving down the slope from the office park and started traveling parallel to U.S. 50. Each man was dressed in black. Each man was equipped with night-vision goggles, and each carried a rifle, two pistols, an ammunition belt, and three hand grenades.

At twenty minutes after four, a lookout spotted a convoy of four vans approaching from the west. "Incoming from the city. We've got company."

Hercules ran to high ground overlooking the highway. "What the hell? We've been outed!" He grabbed his radio. "All units on the east-west highway, take out this patrol on my mark." He waited until the lead vehicle was parallel to the man farthest to the west. "Now."

Hercules's troops unleashed a hail of gunfire. A rocket-propelled grenade struck the cab of the lead van. The following vehicles screeched to a halt, and troops poured out of vans one, three, and four, firing into the darkness. Hercules watched as his men decimated the defenders with machine gun fire and hand grenades. After several minutes of silence, he turned to an aid. "Get me down there." He took to the radio again. "I'm coming. I want to know what's in van two. Keep an eye to the west. We may have more company on the way."

The van driver sped down the off ramp onto the deserted highway, turned a hundred and eighty degrees, and made his way around bodies until he arrived at the second van.

"What's in there?"

"Dunno. It's locked from the inside."

"Well, open it," he barked. "There's probably a key or release lever in the cab."

One of the men opened the cab door. The dead driver tumbled to the ground. The man began pulling levers in the cab until he heard the clunk of a release in the rear. Hercules squinted his eyes as two of his men pulled open the rear doors while others trained their rifles on the space inside the van.

"Well, well, well. Look what we have here. Boys, I think we've just stumbled onto the crown jewel herself, the keys to the kingdom. Take her up to the office. As for these other two … if they're with her, they're probably valuable." He pointed his finger at Jeremy. "But one false move from either of you and these gentlemen will blow your brains out." He swept his hand behind him. "Just like the others. Believe me, we will."

Tiffany struggled against the strong arms of four men dragging her toward Hercules's van. She kicked their legs and for a moment broke free with her right hand, promptly gouging the eyes of one of her assailants. Additional men joined the remaining three. Once Tiffany was immobilized, Hercules came up to her and leaned in close to her face.

"I'd relax if I were you, Ms. Miller. I'd hate to have to terminate you right here on the highway."

She spit in his face.

"Tie her up. Get her to the office. We've got to get her somewhere they can't find her. You can bet there'll be a lot of people coming for her real soon now. We can use her to draw troops away from our main mission."

They used several sets of handcuffs and rope, securing her tightly in the rear of the van before driving back to the office building.

Tiffany's face was red as she shouted at Hercules. "Your cause is lost, you know. Your organization has been taken apart piece by piece. You won't get away with this. You're an idiot if you think you can."

"Shut up, you stupid girl. Don't you think it a bit ridiculous to tell me our cause is lost, given that you're totally at my mercy and we just demonstrated our superiority over your defenses? Stupid, stupid girl."

Tiffany remained unfazed. "You're the last shred of this plot. Your people have been systematically neutralized. You can't win."

The van proceeded to the office building, and seven of Hercules's troops struggled to drag her into the building.

* * *

Eisenhower Executive Office Building, 4:50 a.m.

Anna had fallen asleep on a sofa in the main conference room.

Sarah burst in, shouting. "We think Tiffany and the Thomases have been captured."

Anna jumped up and followed Sarah toward the White House. The separating drive had filled with marines and combat vehicles preparing for battle. Sarah looked around quickly until she spotted Tull buckling his flak jacket. He glanced up momentarily and caught sight of her. She set her lips tightly to stop them trembling and clinched her fist for him to see. He returned the gesture and then donned his helmet. She turned and followed Anna into the West Wing.

Tears streamed down Sarah's face.

Anna took her aside. "Do you think you'll be able to handle this?"

Sarah whispered, "Jeff knows what he's doing. He was in Desert Storm."

Anna continued. "Sit down for a while if you need."

Sarah shook her head. "Let's go. Whatever we can do, let's do it."

They entered the crowded situation room. Matt met them at the door and pointed to a map on a high screen. "The convoy was ambushed near the intersection of New York Avenue and the Beltway. They obviously had huge firepower in place. We had only a few seconds of communication from the convoy during the attack. We had video from the Maryland traffic cams for a little while before they shot out the highway lights. We could see them dragging Tiffany away and we could recognize one of the attackers on the scene as Hercules.

Sarah scowled. "That's right by the route they would have been taking Bailey."

Matt nodded. "Yup."

"So those guys were probably waiting for him. We basically drove her right into their stakeout."

He nodded again. "That's what I'm guessing.

Sarah surveyed the room until her eyes fell on the President, his head bowed as conversations swirled about him. She walked over to his side. "We'll get her back, sir."

The President looked up. His face was ashen. She shuddered at his appearance, so changed in the months since the troubles had begun. His face was now gaunt and weary-looking. When he spoke, it was with the voice of an old man. "She's all I've got."

"We'll get her back, sir. Trust me. I haven't been wrong yet, have I, Mr. President?"

He managed a thin smile. "No, you haven't, Dr. Tyler. No, you haven't. Thank you." He turned his attention to an aide on his other side.

Sarah looked up at the map. A series of green circles moved toward the intersection. She gritted her teeth and crossed her arms grasping tightly. She mumbled to herself. "C'mon, Jeff. Do your Marine stuff and get back here."

Admiral Brown faced the President. "Unless you tell me otherwise, sir, I'm extending the curfew in the Metro area. We need to keep this as uncomplicated as we still can."

President Miller nodded.

* * *

5:17 a.m.

Corporal Tull occupied the third seat in the last of six armored personnel carriers. His rifle was fully loaded, safety off. He closed his eyes in concentration.

Sergeant Smith interrupted the meditation. "Kinda' quiet there, Tull. What'cha thinking?"

"Don't fire until you see the whites of their eyes, sir."

"Sounds familiar."

"Bunker Hill, Sergeant, 1775. In part, it was to save ammunition, in part a nod to the inaccuracy of their muskets."

"Well, Tull, at least we don't have to worry about the second part. The Bostonians would have loved to have these."

"They were firing in broad daylight, sir. June seventeenth, as I recall. We're firing in the dark, presumably against entrenched forces. We can assume they've got goggles, too. And you've got that damned visual lag with the night goggles. If they take advantage of it, it's going to be some tough targeting."

Smith mused for a moment. "You think too much. Get ready."

Tull heard for a moment an ear-splitting roar and then felt himself alternately pushed against the side of the van or tugged forward against his seat belt as the van tumbled down the road, the result of a rocket-propelled grenade's striking the cab.

* * *

Hercules circled Tiffany. With her mouth taped and her arms bound firmly to an executive chair, the conversation was one-sided. "You, woman, are my ticket to the great unraveling of everything. Don't you think I understand that your Daddy's as trapped as you as long as I own you?" The other men in the room stood against the walls.

She rocked violently back and forth in the chair.

"Won't work, you stupid girl. Hey, you and I might get to be friends while I have you. Could happen. I've never had a piece of the high-priced chicken." He stood in front of her, leaned in close, and put his hands on his crotch, all the while grinning.

Tiffany leaned forward for a split second and then threw her full weight against the chair so that it tilted back. She drew her bound legs up to her chest and kicked forward, her heels pushing straight into Hercules's groin with a loud crunching sound.

Hercules fell backward, shrieking as Tiffany's chair toppled over. He struggled to his feet in fits and starts. "I'll kill you! So help me, I'll kill you. The only thing they'll be negotiating for is body parts, one at a time."

A Brisbane soldier burst into the room. "Hercules, we've got lots more inbound. We took out one vehicle, but they started firing back right-off and they've got big guns this time."

Hercules stumbled up, wheeled and started for the door, but doubled over in pain. He looked down. Blood oozed through his pants. He turned back to Tiffany. "You'll pay for this, bitch. When I get back, you'll pay." He took a rifle from one of the men and hobbled out the door, followed by the other guards.

Tiffany heard gunfire in the distance. She spotted an unplugged space heater halfway across the room, and inched toward it, dragging her attached chair. With much effort, she knocked over the heater and began rubbing her bindings along the rough edge of the back of the its casing. She sliced the first rope in about ten minutes, the second in five more.

With one arm free, she ripped off the gag, took a deep breath, and reached into her riding pants, pulling out her pocketknife. "Guess the gentlemen didn't expect a lady to carry a knife," she muttered. "How old-fashioned." Once free of her bindings, she approached the front door, turned off the room lights, and cautiously peered through the door. Several men were positioned on the rise a hundred feet or so away, their backs to her. The building light, though, would make escape difficult. She headed to the rear of the office and surveyed the parking lot through the large back window. The lot was wide and open, empty and unlit. The ground floor window nearest to her wasn't designed to open. She placed a chair below the window and grabbed a second chair, which she hurled through the glass. Backing up, she took a running start, sprang up onto the chair, then the windowsill, through the shattered window, and onto the pavement outside. One edge of the glass caught her riding jeans, tearing them and drawing some blood. Tiffany sprinted across the parking lot and over the low fence beyond the asphalt and off into the suburbs as the sound of gunfire and explosions faded in the background.

* * *

Hercules radioed his men along the Beltway to fall back and join the fight. The battle lasted over an hour into the sunrise. In this second battle the Marines had the advantage of better armor and heavier weapons. Hercules's troops were killed one by one. Around seven a bullet pierced his right lung, and he fell to the ground. In the ensuing silence the Marines advanced behind an abandoned van. As two stood guard, Brycynski opened the back door of van number two to find Jeremy and his father huddled in the corner for warmth.

"You guys all right?"

Jeremy nodded.

Brycynski turned and called out, "Somebody get me some blankets or coats or something." He turned back to the Thomases. "You're safe. We're with you now."

Lieutenant Jones led a squad in flak jackets from body to body, searching for signs of life. He finally approached Hercules propped up against his van, breathing rapid, shallow breaths. Hercules clutched his side as blood pooled on the pavement. Lieutenant Jones kneeled beside him. "Where's the President's daughter?"

"Fuck you."

"Don't make this any more difficult than it is already. Where is she?"

Hercules grimaced as he coughed. "I fucked her. I cut off her damned head and threw it in the Potomac. Good luck finding it, assholes." He descended into a coughing fit, bringing up volumes of blood. Hercules fell silent and slumped to the ground.

The lieutenant stood up and barked orders. "Search the area. She's got to be around here somewhere. Find her." He turned toward the troops in the rear of the convoy. "Take two units back to where Sergeant Smith was hit and render assistance."

* * *

6:41 a.m.

James Bailey sat secured with handcuffs in the back seat of a speeding Federal Marshall Service sedan, noting exit signs as they travelled the Washington Beltway from the Interstate 95 intersection toward the Woodrow Wilson Bridge. He adjusted his seating as they passed the Kenilworth Avenue exit.

In the rearview mirror the driver watched the former Vice President.

As the car approached the exit for westbound U.S. 50, Bailey slowly, quietly lay down across the back seat, adjusting his position as best he could to avoid strain from the handcuffs on each hand.

The driver slowed to a stop on the empty beltway at the center of the bridge over U.S. 50. He nodded to his companion, Marshall Randolph, who turned around to face Bailey.

"You can straighten up, Mr. Bailey. Take a look at the highway below."

Bailey struggled to sit up, and peered out the window to his right. In the early light of dawn, he saw the wreckage of the first wave of vans. He saw bodies, many bodies clad mostly in black. Soldiers and Marines arranged them in a row, stacking rifles in a pile at one end. A Brisbane van lay on its side, windows blown out but for a ragged edge of broken glass. Bailey gazed, expressionless, at the panorama of destruction and then sat back in his seat.

"You were going to have us murdered," Randolph spoke calmly. "You were going to leave my wife and two children; his wife and baby widows and orphans. You son of a bitch." He reached into his pocket and withdrew a folded sheet of paper. He flung it at Bailey. "You've been read your rights about a dozen times already, but I'll remind you about that silence thing. You can just shut up for the rest of the trip. You are now charged with treason, Mr. Bailey, levying war against the United States. That's on top of everything else."

Randolph turned back in his seat and motioned to the driver. "Let's go dump this trash."

* * *

8:00 a.m.

The White House infirmary staff stood ready as the first vehicles returned with the wounded. The rest of the White House team lent their assistance as best they could and gathered details of the fight.

Sarah carried a doctor's medical bag as Brycynski helped lift the stretcher that carried Sergeant Smith. Brycynski caught sight of Sarah's strained look.

"Tull was in the van with Smith when they caught the RPG. We haven't found him yet, but I'm guessing he's OK. There were three of 'em in the vehicle. The driver's dead, but somebody attended to Smith's wounds before we reached them. The sergeant's unconscious, so I'm thinking it had to be Tull." He talked as they carried the litter toward the medical suite. "We've got people looking for Tull. Ms. Miller, too. We don't know where she is but we think she may have escaped during the battle." He turned as they approached the building. "Mr. Thomas and his boy are arriving. See if you can lend them a hand. They've got to be shaken up."

Sarah handed off the medical bag. "Right. I'm on it." She dashed to the armored personnel carrier and kneeled down to talk to Jeremy.

* * *

Outside The Vice President's Office,
Tuesday, January 10, 2015, 4:30 p.m. EST

President Miller walked slowly down the hall toward Vice President Kincaid's office. The officer of the day should be preparing his briefing, and Ms. Conklin would have something for the President to say to the press, something no doubt encouraging despite the obvious chaos and ruin. He could hear Cameron's voice finishing some question, followed by Kincaid's voice.

"We don't know that. We definitely don't. All evidence is to the contrary — that she escaped from the room she was held in. How's the tracking going?"

The other voice sounded like Major Reed. "We've had dogs on the scene since about noon, but there's not much of a trail. She was probably in a ground floor office in the Corporate Center and likely escaped the office through the smashed back window. There were a few drops of blood, but not enough of a trail for the bloodhounds to pick up after that. She could have gone across the lot or out toward the beltway. In theory, she could have grabbed a vehicle, but it would have been hard to get past the firing line. Worst case would be one of the Brisbane troops could have caught her in the lot and moved her someplace else."

Kincaid mused. "But we're not putting any credence in Hercules's last words?"

"Negative, sir. He claimed he decapitated her and threw her head in the Potomac. Between the time of her capture, which we've seen on video, and our assault, his forces were in motion at that intersection. He couldn't have made it to the river in that amount of time. Plus there was little sign of violence, only a few drops of blood on the ground outside the office."

"Still, it seems we would have heard from her by now. That's a fairly densely populated area."

"Telecomm's out in that whole quadrant. Brisbane blasted the towers and substations just as Bailey was approaching D.C."

The Vice President shook his head. "That may be the most delusional part of this whole bizarre episode. How could they not know that their power base is gone?"

Cameron joined in. "Whoever blew up the network must still be out there. Even if the cause is lost, they can still do a lot of damage. If they have explosives, they're probably armed with more than that. We need to be open to the possibility that she's been recaptured."

Kincaid turned to Major Reed. "You haven't briefed the President in the last hour or so, have you?"

"No, sir. I was hoping to have something firm by now. And I presume you or Peter would be the appropriate one for that, anyway," Reed confirmed.

"Right. He should be here any minute. We're going over the public response. Does he know what Hercules said?"

"No, sir," Reed confirmed.

"I'd hold off telling him. It's as far-fetched as it is hideous to imagine," Kincaid warned.

Just outside the office, the President turned back and walked silently toward his quarters in the White House.

Kincaid rubbed the back of his neck. "Keep up the good work. This day won't be over for a long time. Keep me posted no matter the hour. I'll be staying here in the emergency quarters until this is resolved." Sarah appeared in the doorway with briefing papers. Kincaid turned back to Reed. "What about Tull?"

The Major replied to Kincaid, but faced Sarah. "I think I briefed you on what we found. We've got as many men looking for him as we can spare from our search for the President's daughter. Tull's smart. He'll keep his head down, and get word to us as soon as he can get an open line, I'm sure."

Sarah nodded. "Thank you, Major." She looked at Cameron. "I've got the figures you wanted for the President."

Cameron scowled. "Yeah. Thanks. He should have been here by now."

Matt appeared in the doorway next. "Matt, did you see the President on your way over?" Kincaid asked.

Matt shook his head. "No. Didn't see him. Mr. Kincaid, we just got a radio call from Ft. Meade. They've gotten a video featuring Commander X wanting to finish restoring everything."

"Well, at least one piece of good news. I hope they said yes."

"Almost. The Commander's people want some personal assurances from the White House. It's not much, but they were insistent. They want just a little face time."

"Well, set it up immediately."

"We haven't had stable comms from inside the Beltway since this morning. We can't even get a good link to transmit the videos from Meade to here. The video was recorded, but they're on lockdown up there, and we don't have anyone to spare here to courier the session recording."

Kincaid put his head into his hands. "So close, so close." He leaned back in his chair and turned to check the clock. "Major, could you please go see what's keeping the President?"

"Yes, sir."

* * *

Executive Office Building, 7:30 p.m. EST

Sarah finished briefing Anna. "So the President told the Major to have Mr. Kincaid handle the press for now. The President feels too shaky and doesn't think it would help the mood of the country if he went on. Cameron went up with the Vice President right after that, and I think they agree. The President knows that we haven't found Tiffany yet."

Anna shook her head slowly. "This is not good. I can appreciate his despair, but we really need him now." She looked up at Sarah. "Just between the two of us, do you think Tiffany's alive?"

"Absolutely," Sarah answered with a confident tone.

"Good. And we're going to find Tull as well."

Sarah nodded. "They're both fast thinkers and strong. They'd be back here now if only there was a way to communicate. I could see Mr. Kincaid's pain at not being able to finally close the deal with Commander X's people."

Anna gave a small smile as she gathered her folder and prepared to leave for the West Wing. "Who knows? We might have actually found out who he is."

Sarah stood by her window, overlooking the dark drive between the Executive Office Building and the West Wing. She watched Anna cross over, illuminated by the porch light. The Marines guarding the entrance snapped a crisp salute, and Anna nodded in respectful reply.

Sarah reached for her large coffee mug. The coffee was cold by now, but strong enough to be useful. She had not turned on the overhead lights yet, so busy had she been telling Anna all that had happened. The only light in the room was her desk lamp with its small pool of illumination. She followed its dim glow up to the articles tacked to her corkboard: the hue and cry from the Crusade over her volleyball game and the remarkable defense coming from then Chief of Staff Kincaid. Other clippings chronicled the descent into chaos and the constant heroic efforts of so many to keep the country upright.

She re-read the headlines, thumb to her mouth, biting her thumbnail. Finally she put her hands on her hips. "OK, so what would Molly Pitcher do?" Sarah thought for a bit more, then reached into her purse for keys and badge, put on her coat, and headed to the garage. She drove up to the north gate and halted as Corporal Jackson came over to her window.

"No one comes or goes tonight, Dr. Tyler."

She held up a White House envelope. "Special orders from the Vice President. I have to retrieve some critical documents from Fort Meade."

Jackson appeared concerned. "We don't have anyone to escort you, ma'am."

"I've got a secure route through the back streets and a tracking device." She held up her cell phone.

"I think I need to check with the Vice President, ma'am."

"He's with the President now. There's going to be Hell to pay if these documents are delayed. It's almost over, you know."

Jackson looked around. "OK. I can't say I feel good about this. Just be careful out there. We've lost a lot of good people today."

"Thank you, Corporal Jackson."

The gate opened briefly, and the yellow Volkswagen leapt into the darkness. She concentrated on any movement along the streets. The White House envelope, holding her pay stub, and her dead cell phone sat in the seat beside her. Whenever she could, she drove with her lights off, snaking through Berwyn Heights, Beltsville, and Laurel, avoiding the main highways.

Sarah arrived at the south gate of Fort Meade about 9 p.m. The gate guards initially resisted, but her credentials cleared, and she had the number of the intercept office at NSA. An MP arrived presently to escort her to the outbuilding where the intercept officer was waiting.

"I was expecting a military courier."

"No one to spare. We've got way too much going on over there. You have some videos for us?"

The officer took her into the office. A small stack of cassettes, disks, and papers sat on his desk. "I wasn't expecting you." He looked around the office. "I'll have to go over and get you a box or courier bag."

"Not to worry. I've got something in my car." She dashed to her Bug and returned with a bag.

The officer stared. "You've got to be kidding."

"What?" she demanded.

"A Bloomingdale's bag? To carry classified documents?"

Sarah stomped her feet. "What is with you people? We have to get this material to the White House, now! We don't have military we can spare in the city. You're on lockdown. If I get stopped on my way, which would you rather have holding these, a stylish NSA courier bag or an old Bloomies bag with lacy lingerie sticking out in the back seat?"

The officer closed his eyes, shook his head, and began loading the bright pink and lime green nylon shopping bag with cassettes, disks, and papers. He handed it carefully to her. "It's heavy."

She smiled. "Trust me. It's held much more than this in its official capacity."

They walked to her car. Sarah placed the bag on her back seat, reaching under the passenger seat to retrieve several slips and a bra, which she packed on top of the bag.

The intercept officer raised his eyebrows. "Do you usually …? Never mind."

He escorted her back to the south gate and saw her off into the darkness.

Starting at half past midnight, Sarah retraced her route back through Laurel, Beltsville, and Berwyn Heights until she was stopped at an intersection half a mile north of New York Avenue by a rifle-wielding man in his twenties she had not seen with her lights off. She rolled down her window just an inch and spoke through the gap with as much irritation as she could muster. "Look, I don't have any money or food. The gas tank is almost empty, I'm in a hurry, and I haven't had much sleep. It would be better for both of us if you just let me get on my way."

Holding the rifle in his left hand, the young man leaned on the side of her car. "What the hell are you doing in this neighborhood at this hour? And how have you managed to miss the curfew cops?"

She frowned. "I'm stealthy."

He looked her car over bumper to bumper. "In a yellow Bug with lights off?"

She shook her head. "Did you actually stop me to discuss techniques of evasion? I've got places to go and not much time. I haven't exactly figured out how I'm going to cross New York or Mass. Ave."

The young man took a flashlight from his pocket and surveyed her back seat. He stopped the light for a moment on the Bloomingdale's bag, but moved on.

Sarah took a deep breath and let it out slowly. "What do you want? I told you I don't have any money or supplies."

"Just chill, please. I'm part of the neighborhood watch team."

"With a rifle?"

He chuckled. "Yeah. Who knew? I'm just a student at American University. This block was bad before the troubles, but we could afford the rent. Since the telephones went down, it's gotten a lot more dangerous. Right now, though, we need your car."

Sarah tensed, preparing to step on the gas before fellow neighborhood watchers came to join him.

"And actually, we don't need your car, just the transportation. We've got a soldier in the office who was in an ambush on his way to the beltway this morning and got separated from his unit. He was trying to get back to the White House, but he's in pretty bad shape to be walking that far. We just want to get him to a medical facility."

Sarah unlocked the doors and flung hers open, nearly knocking the student down. "You mean a Marine, right?"

"Yeah. You know about that?"

"I've heard there's one missing. Where is he? I'll get him back. Move it!"

Sarah followed him down the hall in a nearby brownstone, nearly treading on his heels. Entering the second room, she caught her breath as she spied Tull in an old recliner in one corner of the room. He appeared to be dozing, his hand over his left side, left leg in a bandage. In another corner two young people, a man and a woman, sat at a table with papers and textbooks spread around.

The young man turned to them. "Who's she, Andy?"

Sarah answered, "I was just driving by. I'm willing to take your Marine to the clinic."

At the sound of her voice, Tull lifted his head slowly. His eyes focused, and he grinned, shaking his head slowly.

"Fine. One less complication. What are you doing out at this hour, anyway?"

"Shopping," Sarah answered.

The man at the table frowned and turned to Andy, who simply shrugged. "She's got a full shopping bag in the back of her car."

Andy walked over to Tull. "Think you can take just a little more walking, sir?"

"Yeah. Absolutely. Just give me a hand." Tull turned to Sarah. "I think it's just some cracked ribs."

The young woman spoke up. "We were going to get him to the local clinic in the morning." She looked at their clock. "Later this morning, that is."

Tull winced as he rose to his feet and took in a slow, deep breath. His uniform was torn, his face and arm bruised, his leg bandaged, but otherwise he seemed in one piece. He walked on his own slowly toward the door.

Sarah turned to the others. "Thank you for taking care of him." She cocked her head. "Andy, I need your gun."

"What?" His eyes widened.

"I've got to get across New York Avenue. What if Brisbane is still on the loose?"

He turned to the two at the table.

She persisted. "C'mon, Andy. I'll get it back to you. Look, the Marine is my witness. I promise."

Sarah began walking toward him.

Andy called out. "Hassan?"

Hassan closed his book. "She's right to be afraid. This war is almost over, and we haven't had to use it, anyway. Let her borrow it. You'll get it back to us, say, tomorrow, Miss …?"

"Sarah."

Andy lifted the rifle forward. "Sarah? Sarah Tyler?"

She frowned. "Maybe. Why?"

"I recognize you."

"Oh, great. I thought my volleyball days were over."

"Huh?"

"Volleyball, Crusade for Moral Clarity, Ben Jacobs," she offered.

"I don't know. Your economics briefings are part of our class every week. We have to analyze all your presentations."

She glanced at the table and spied a familiar text. "What's your major?"

"Economics. Grad students, actually."

"Oh, wow. Are you sure you want to get into economics? It's dangerous, you know. Guns, smear campaigns, wars." She paused. "So do you like our briefings?"

Andy nodded as Sarah took the rifle. "Of course. You condense the points really well, and you're funny. Plus, I like the cute redhead — Ms. Whiting."

Sarah put on a full-face frown. "What? I'm not cute?"

Andy winced. He stared at Sarah. Her hair was disheveled, and lack of sleep gave her a crazed look. He looked at the rifle — his rifle — she was holding and put up his hands. "Absolutely cute. I just meant that she appealed to me particularly. That's all."

"Fair enough. I'll put in a good word for you. She really needs to get out and meet more people. Andy. American University. Economics. Last name?"

"Andy Merz, Ma'am."

"He called me Ma'am. Does that mean I'm an officer now?" She asked, turning to Tull with a mischievous grin.

Tull shook his head and moved again toward the front steps. "No."

Andy and Hassan followed behind. At the street, they helped Tull ease into the passenger seat once Sarah had cleared most of the cookie and chip bags and the drink bottles. Tull relaxed as they laid a blanket over his chest and carefully brought the seat belt around him.

Sarah thanked them again and started her car.

Tull turned to her. "Take it slow. It'll be a new experience for you, but I know you can do it."

She eased her foot on the accelerator and moved deliberately into the street. They drove slowly southward through the darkness.

"I know you didn't need that rifle. What possessed you to get it?" he asked.

"Seems all my life I've had people looking after me. My brother, my family, my teachers, Mr. Kincaid. You. Tonight I decided I was taking charge. I knew what needed to be done and I did it. I drove to NSA, got the stuff no one else could, and I'm taking it back to Mr. Kincaid." She turned to Tull. "I even rescued a fallen knight. I did all that because I decided to. I guess I wanted to see how far I could push it. So I told him to give me the gun. And he did. No telling how far I could go tonight. I could take over the world." Sarah grew increasingly excited as she spoke, bouncing in the seat as they drove along.

Tull sighed, "You're crazy, but I love you."

She slammed on the brakes, pressing Tull into his seat belt.

"Ow, ow, ow, ow!"

"What did you say?"

"I said you're crazy!"

"No, no. You said you loved me."

"I did?"

"Yes, you did." She put the car in neutral, unbuckled her seat belt, reached over, and wrapped her arms around his neck, kissing him repeatedly.

"Ow, ow, ow."

"Sorry." She returned to her seat, buckled up, and resumed their slow journey toward the White House."

She looked back at Tull. "So did I get a good gun?"

Tull examined the weapon. "Rifle. It's an automatic rifle, not a gun. Specifically, it's a Kalashnikov rifle, also known as an AK-47. I can't say for certain here in the dark, but it could easily be forty years old or more."

"Bummer."

"Oh, no, that's good. The Kalashnikov is a durable design. It may not have the accuracy or light weight of our modern rifles, but it's lasted. It's easy to take apart to clean with practice, though I didn't get the sense that those students were into that sort of thing. Still, it could keep on working in dirty, wet, and sandy areas where our sophisticated arms jammed. The Kalashnikov has been a favorite of oppressors and liberators alike."

"And I've got one. Cool."

"On loan. You promised on my honor to return it."

"Yeah, you're right. Maybe I can get my own when this is over."

"Why don't we just get your picture with it? I'll clean it for them after the docs get me taped up. I don't think we want to check it too closely. The AK-47 is also a favorite with drug runners for the same reasons."

"Oh."

Crossing New York Avenue proved a non-event. Ten minutes later, they pulled up to the fortified northwest gate of the White House.

Corporal Jackson was the first to recognize her car. He stood beside the car glaring angrily down at her. "You lied to me. If Ms. Colbert hadn't intervened, I'd be in the brig now. But you're going to have to answer to her, and she's not a bit happy. You'd better hope you've got a damned good excuse."

"I do." Sarah pointed to her right.

Jackson bent down and broke into a wide smile. "OK, he'll probably do." He waved to open the gate.

"I've got to get him to sick bay. He's been run over and banged up pretty good."

She drove through the open gate and parked on the drive. Corporal Jackson had already summoned two medics and they were waiting to help Tull. Sarah reached into the back seat and grabbed her bag and rifle. She walked ahead of Tull and the medics.

At the door the guard stopped her. "Hold on. You can't take that ..."

Sarah's face was washed by a fatigue-induced haziness. Behind her, Tull vigorously waved off the guard's directions.

"Uh, you can't bring that in without checking it. If you don't mind, I'll take the rifle and get it secured."

She nodded and turned back to Tull momentarily. "OK. It's not actually mine. I borrowed it and need to get it back to Andy later today."

The guard nodded incredulously.

As the party passed into the building, Tull leaned over to the guard and whispered, "Thanks."

Anna was waiting inside, arms crossed sternly until she caught sight of Tull.

Sarah stopped and stood before Anna as medics accompanied Tull to the infirmary. "He's broken, but not too bad." Sarah watched as Tull rounded the corner, and then she turned to Anna.

Anna continued, "I'm furious. What possessed you to go out there? That was a job for the Marines. You could have been captured or killed."

Sarah nodded. "He was a bonus. This is what I went for. I knew you needed it and didn't have anyone else to go." She handed Anna her bag.

"You went shopping?" Anna took the heavy green and pink canvas bag.

"No, not exactly. Well, sort of." She removed the slip and stockings. "These are the videos of Commander X. We may be able to get in touch with him now."

Anna raised her eyebrows as she rummaged through the bag.

"The guy over at NSA said disk KS-207 is the most interesting."

Anna looked at Sarah, nearly asleep on her feet.

Sarah mumbled, "I'm really tired. If you don't have anything else for me right now, I'm going over to the crisis bunk room and take a nap." She turned to go, but stopped in her tracks, almost whispering, "Have they found Tiffany yet?"

"No, not yet. Major Reed's expanded the search to include a stretch along the Potomac, but he's pretty sure she's been captured."

"She's alive. They'll find her. It's going to be OK. I can feel it."

Anna nodded. Sarah turned and left the White House for the Executive Office Building.

* * *

Situation Room, The White House,
Wednesday, January 11, 2015, 8:15 a.m. EST

Anna replayed a particular clip from disk KS-207 for the fifth or sixth time when the Vice President arrived.

"Good morning, sir. Seems Sarah's crazy adventure may have paid off big time. Look at this."

Kincaid took a seat. "Did she really drive across town last night to Ft. Meade?"

"Yep."

"In a bright yellow car with her lights off?"

"Yep. Except it wasn't bright in the dark."

"And she rescued Corporal Tull?"

"She says that wasn't her intention, but yes. Here, watch this, sir." Anna replayed the clip, video taken with a long lens through a window of a meeting. A woman seated at a table got up from her seat and put her hand on the shoulder of a man at the head of the table. After some time of discussion, she placed her hand on the man's head and smoothed his hair as she appeared to speak.

Kincaid shook his head. "What am I seeing?"

"A lot on many levels, sir. The man seated at the head table is presumed to be the great Commander X. Significantly, FBI has tentatively identified him as the same person they came up with months ago."

"I thought they didn't have a suspect."

"The man in this video matches the description of a Jack Pullman, whom they linked by several lines of evidence to the beginnings of the movement. But he was ruled out because they thought he perished in a major laboratory fire up in Frederick right about that time. They're still researching Jack Pullman's history, but so far they show him to be a chemist and a debating champion, very skilled at logic."

Kincaid leaned forward. "Any criminal record, other entanglements?"

"No, sir. Squeaky clean as far as records go."

"And the woman?"

"That for me is the exciting part. You remember my friend Laura Garrette?"

"Your friend who disappeared — singer, social activist. She didn't think much of our administration."

Anna giggled. "You have a good memory. The woman behind Jack

Pullman appears to be Laura Garrette. And it's obvious from this and a couple of other clips that they're much more than simple colleagues."

"Can we reach them now?"

"They've moved from this location since it was filmed, and the trail is cold. But I've got an idea. It's a long shot, but I had Laura's number in my cell. If she's with the communication workers, it just might be active."

Anna pressed the speed dial button for Laura and waited only a moment. "It's Anna. Don't hang up. Can we talk?"

* * *

Crisis Bunk Room, 2:25 p.m.

"Rise and shine, Sleeping Beauty." Anna opened the door to the room, but left the overhead light off.

Sarah stirred. "Go away. It's not a school day."

"Your shopping bag had some real bargains. We got through to Commander X. It's almost over. We have a meeting arranged in about two hours with some of their representatives to coordinate the end game."

"Great. Wonderful. Now go away and let me sleep."

Anna leaned on the door frame. "Mr. Kincaid's putting together a team to negotiate the reintegration. He wanted people who could think outside the box. Naturally, you were the first one who came to mind."

Sarah groaned. "Am I that bad?"

"No, you're that good." Anna waited, but Sarah lay motionless. "Jeff's all fixed up and will be part of the entourage."

Sarah sat up. "Ugh." She looked down at her clothes. "Jeez, I've been wearing this for … two days, I think. I probably smell like a pit toilet."

Anna turned to leave. "Get a shower. Put on something fresh and meet in the Roosevelt Room at four."

"I don't have a change of clothes. They're all back in Laurel."

Anna put her hands on her hips and scowled. "You were supposed to keep three changes of clothing in your locker here."

"I never got around to it."

"I may have something that I can lend you. What's your size?"

"Six," Sarah replied.

"Six? I've seen you eat. How can you be a six?"

"Nervous energy?"

"Right. I'll find something."

"Oo. Can I have that plum skirt with the pleated blouse?"

"I said lend."

Sarah nodded. "Did I say 'have'? I meant to say 'borrow'."

26 CHANGING THE EQUATION

Wednesday, January 11, 2015

Vice President Kincaid entered an old brownstone apartment on 13th Street, leaving four Marines posted outside. Three mid-level secretaries accompanied him, one from State and two from Homeland Security. He was still uncomfortable with what little authority he had been given. The President just said to "work something out." No plan, no pledge, just the President's order to work something out.

As best they Kincaid's team could tell, Jack Pullman remained secluded somewhere in the West, most likely Arizona or New Mexico. Jack's control seemed solid and his intentions benevolent — at least to Kincaid, the leader of a cause who wished it were all over. With a little luck and a lot of cooperation from his own side, Kincaid could make that happen.

"Ms. Denton, this is Don Jackson from State, Jerry Moon and Crystal Benge from Homeland Security, and Kathy Whiting and Sarah Tyler from my staff."

She smiled. "Joanna Denton, Mr. Vice President. Jack Pullman has given me full authority to speak on his behalf. I have every expectation that we can be well on our way to normal by tonight, sir. Do you have authority to speak for the President?"

"I wish I could say that with certainty. If what you say is true, tonight will be a real turning point. My authority comes from the President, who has the final say. I promise you that I will negotiate in good faith. Execution still rests with the President, and …" Kincaid had not meant to begin the last part of his sentence. From a negotiations standpoint, he had already revealed a weakness. Too much information. He probably shouldn't let her know he didn't fully trust the President to follow through on everything.

Joanna registered her disappointment. "I see. Well, I think we expected that. But we need to do something now. We trust you, Mr. Vice President.

We'll go as far as we're able."

So began five hours of precise, well-mannered give and take.

* * *

President Miller couldn't taste his fifth whiskey. He sat in The Chair. Around him, the Oval Office was as tidy as any tour book ever pictured it. Priceless antiques adorned perfect furniture. The presidential seal woven into the carpet glared at him in baleful mockery. The only item out of place was the camera pointing at him. In the good old days, it would have been present only a few times in a presidency, intended only for a matter of utmost political urgency. Now, in these bad times, the camera was a constant reminder of his failures, the scornful eye of history watching him stumble.

He stood up, a little wobbly, light-headed. He looked at the clock — an old clock, to be sure, but well maintained.

"Nine-thirty." He mouthed the time to no one. "Eastern Standard Time. Ten-thirty Central … or is it eight-thirty?" He paused. "Who cares? Doesn't matter." He paced the perimeter of his oval cage, stopping each round to look out the window at the darkened city. Not much traffic tonight. No fires that he could see. He resumed his walk, looking at the paintings, looking at the doors. He doubted Kincaid was accomplishing anything. The traitor! Negotiating with those thugs like it was an appropriations bill. He should have listened to Bailey, killing them when he had a chance. He was a weak President. Too late now. Too late for everything. Bailey was gone. Tiffany … He wept.

* * *

David Kincaid felt a great weight lifting from his shoulders. Joanna and her people proved adept traders and extremely well informed. About nine-thirty they reached Jack Pullman. The Vice President watched Joanna relay their results, her tone positive. Kincaid had made very few concessions, really nothing he wouldn't have wanted as good policy to begin with. Selling it to the President and getting him to honor the package might be a challenge, but he felt confident.

She put down the phone, smiling. "Mr. Vice President, we have an agreement. If President Miller will announce the details in public, Mr. Pullman will put the word out and our troubles will be over." She searched Kincaid's face for his reaction.

It sounded so simple, so right. Everyone got what they needed, even what they wanted. But he knew the President would be uncomfortable with several of the details.

He rose to shake her hand. "Thank you. The ball's in my court now. I hope I've set your expectations properly. A few items might be tough sells, but sell I will!"

She nodded.

"But for now, I think a celebration is in order. This agreement is, after all, a cause for great joy. Let's adjourn. I know a sweet little restaurant just two blocks from here."

Kincaid's invitation was well received, and the two teams mingled, walking out into the night, still under the watchful eyes of the Marine contingent. The restaurant was preparing to close for the night, but more than happy to carry on at the sight of this crowd. The television in the bar aired an old movie on one of the commercial channels.

* * *

The President lost track of how many laps he had walked. No word from Kincaid. It was probably a trap. "Serves him right." He looked at the seventh whiskey on The Desk across the office, but it no longer held his interest. His stomach ached, and his mind seemed to burn as he walked.

He examined the doors of his cell. In the good times, these doors had no locks. Now they could be barred from inside. A stupid addition, he thought. Any force that could get beyond the Marines outside those doors would certainly make fast work of those last barriers. Stupid, stupid, stupid. He looked at the bars. He turned and looked at the camera.

* * *

It was no wonder Joanna was so skillful at the negotiating table. A graduate of the University of Chicago School of Business and Georgetown Law, she had been a senior counsel for the ACLU for nearly seven years before her stint with the Institute. They left their serious talk behind and talked instead of schools and kids, hiking and gardening. The movie seemed to be some sort of love triangle set in Italy but they weren't paying attention.

* * *

The President moved from door to door, closing them and carefully, quietly, lowering the bars. Once this task was complete, he walked over to The Chair. He took a look out the window at the darkness, then at the clock. Ten thirty … Eastern Time. Film at eleven. He sat in The Chair and surveyed The Desk. Whiskey bottle, glass. He should probably put them away. It wouldn't look good. He chuckled. "Who cares?" He leaned over and removed his .45 automatic from its drawer. The final protective layer when everything else failed. How ironic was that? He reached up to see if he was wearing a tie. He was. He straightened it. Everything had failed.

He looked into the merciless eye of the camera. This part of the technical drill he knew all too well. After all the broadcasts in the last year, he could operate the controls blindfolded in his sleep. He took a deep breath and pushed "Broadcast."

* * *

Corporal Tull stood attentively at the edge of the Kincaid party. He had stolen a few glances at the movie and was the first to notice the switch to emergency broadcast.

At his shout, all conversations stopped. "Mr. Vice President!" He pointed at the television from which the President was addressing the country, haggard and leaning slightly to one side.

"... This past year we have witnessed the disintegration of a once-mighty nation ..."

"What the ..." Kincaid was as perplexed as the others. He jerked around to the Captain of the Guard. Captain Meacham, a step ahead, removed the secure phone from its case. "Captain, get me the Officer of the Day!"

"Done, sir." Captain Meacham handed the phone to Kincaid.

"... forces of anarchy, cruel terrorists bent on the elimination of our way of life have seized this republic by the throat ..." The president staggered on.

Joanna stared at the image on the screen for a while. She turned to the Vice President.

"Major Reed, what ... Right! ... Go! ... Break it down!" Kincaid would give the Marines permission to do anything they asked at this point.

Everyone heard thumping and banging from the television as the White House detachment assaulted the main door to the Oval Office. On screen, the President turned to his left, momentarily distracted. He returned to face the camera, continuing without script. "... unfortunately, the enemy has found a disloyal following in the population, even a following inside our once-sacred government..."

The Vice President saw a bottle on the desk, saw the glass, and saw what looked like a firearm. "Major Reed! Pull the plug on the transmission. NOW!"

"Yes, sir!" came the reply on the other end of the line.

Six Marines were at work on the door. They managed to crack the wood at midpoint, but the wide bar inside made progress difficult. Reed barked out to two in line waiting to take their turn. "Smith, Brycynski — get over to that thing and take it off the air. He pointed to the elaborate console ablaze with lights, dials, and switches. Corporal Smith had originally trained for vehicle maintenance, Brycynski for carpentry. The closest they had come to electronics was a walkie-talkie or cell phone. But they leaped at the box and began flipping switches to what they hoped was off. Still, the broadcast continued.

"... Not all the failures can be blamed on these forces of darkness. I bear responsibility for my weakness, for not maintaining the vigil it was my responsibility to keep ..."

He slurred some of his words.

Smith and Brycynski neared the end of the controls without effect. Major Reed shouted, "Just rip it out!" The pair lifted the console. It was heavy. No matter. They began moving it away from the wall, nearly at a run. Cables and cords, plugged and hard-wired, snapped and popped, and the console went dark. It came down from their hands with a crash and toppled over.

* * *

Kincaid still held the receiver to his ear but said nothing. He knew Major Reed was doing everything a Marine could do. The Vice President listened carefully to the banging from the television and banging and shouting from the phone. The television screen turned to static and the sounds came now only from his phone. Smith and Brycynski had accomplished their mission.

In the headset he could hear wood splintering violently and chaotic shouts, including "No, no, no..." A very sharp "crack" sounded. The voices stopped. Kincaid lowered his head, listening only because he must. He recognized the Major's voice in a slow, mournful, "Ah, shit!"

Sometime during the melee, Kincaid stood up. All eyes were on him; everyone and everything silent save the crackle of static from the television.

A minute passed and then two as Kincaid held on, head bowed, silent. Major Reed finally returned to the line, calm but clearly shaken. "I'm sorry, sir. We did our best. He shot himself in the head. He knew what he was doing. He's dead, sir."

"Understood, Major. I know you and your men performed valiantly. You got the transmission off the air before the end." He took a deep breath. "Secure the area; get every medical person you can find. Obviously don't touch anything or turn off any more of the equipment for now. Secure all the area around the White House. I'll talk to the Chiefs. You're still in military charge at the White House. I'm heading there now."

"Yes, sir."

"Major," Kincaid finished, "you did well. You did your duty. The record will show that."

"Yes, sir."

Kincaid cradled the phone. He looked at Denton, her face already tear-streaked. He couldn't sort out what had or had not been communicated as he hung onto the phone, but everyone knew the outcome.

"Ms. Denton, be assured that our agreement is intact. It's an honorable and workable way forward. You, too, have done your duty tonight."

She choked on her words. "Thank you, Mr. President." She stood, and with her all the room rose in silence.

Kincaid nodded, lips tight. "I'll make the speech we agreed on. It's going to take some time — maybe a matter of days — to get everything properly written and all the other messy details we have to work out now."

"We will begin tonight, Mr. President. We know you're a man of your word."

President Kincaid turned to Sarah. "Dr. Tyler, please stay behind and work out a communication plan with Ms. Denton. Keep it flexible; keep it personal. The next few days are going to be chaotic." He turned to Joanna. "Sarah speaks for me."

"Yes, sir." Sarah had already picked up her attaché case and moved alongside Joanna as soon as Kincaid looked in her direction.

He made his way toward the door amid a chorus of "Good luck, Mr. President. God speed, Mr. President." He walked out into the cold night air and the waiting car. Turning to Captain Meacham, he observed the Captain ready and waiting for his next command. "Call the office. I need to talk to the senior civilian there. Have Corporal Tull accompany Ms. Tyler and provide whatever security and support she needs."

The Captain followed orders immediately and handed the phone to the President. "Ms. Colbert, sir."

Senior civilian. That gave him comfort. He took the phone. "How much do you know?"

Her voice warbled a little. "Just about everything. I was down the hall. I'm working with the Major."

"Good. Call in all the staff."

"Done," she said.

"The Chiefs?"

"Major's doing it now, sir. Admiral Lautermilch is in Pearl, but we have a good secure link."

"Cabinet?"

"All but Interior. He's out of range."

"Good enough. Hold on a second while I get in the car." He handed the phone to Captain Meacham. Kincaid looked up at Frank holding the door for him. If Frank shared any of Kincaid's anguish, he didn't let it show. Their guard contingent had already been joined by another twenty-five or thirty more Marines, some in dress, others in camouflage with nasty looking weapons. The night air filled with sirens. The President ducked into the back. Frank followed while the Captain sat in the front passenger seat. Kincaid bowed his head, rubbing his eyes with the fingers of his left hand. "How're we going to do this, Frank?" There was a moment of silence.

"Look ahead, sir," Frank intoned.

Kincaid raised his head, puzzled. Frank had a trace of a smile and was pointing south down 13th Street. Kincaid turned to look. The street was empty all the way, but he could see blue and red and white flashing lights on both sides, blocking every cross street at least as far as the Mall. In the clear, cold night with no other city lights, it was a dazzling sight, like an arrow pointing the way home or the lights of a welcome landing strip waiting on a dark, stormy night. The abstract array was a beautiful sight; there was no time to linger though. A dozen or so motorcycles ringed his car fore and aft, watching for a signal.

"The people are with you, sir. You're not alone."

"'Look ahead.' Thanks, Frank. Let's go." Frank nodded to the Captain, who gave a hand signal to the escort. The forward motorcycles pulled away, siren blazing, and the driver floored the accelerator.

Kincaid didn't even want to know how fast they were going. Captain Meacham handed him the phone, and Kincaid continued his exchange with Anna. "We obviously need to get on the air. Have three of the press pool meet me. Tell the networks that President Miller is dead and that I will be available to the three pool reporters on a not-to-interfere basis within …" He looked out the window as the cavalcade roared down the emptied street. They were doing eighty at least in downtown D.C. "… three minutes."

"Yes, sir. Who do you want?"

"Your pick. Smart ones. No fluff."

"Done," she replied.

"I know I'm forgetting a lot. What am I forgetting?"

"The Chief Justice is on his way — full escort. We're setting up lights in the East Wing now. What Bible do you want?"

With Anna in charge, protocol would serve a good and noble purpose. Kincaid's own Bible was at the Vice Presidential residence miles away, and he doubted that Miller's could be located easily. "You have one in your office?"

"Yes, sir."

"May I borrow it?"

"Of course." He could tell she almost laughed.

"Thank you. Is everyone being notified — officially?"

"Yes, sir. We're well down the list by now. The Secretary of State just arrived, sir. Do you want to talk to her?"

He paused. "Not really. We're rounding the bend now. I'll be there in a few seconds. You're doing great. Just keep it up." He handed the phone back to Captain Meacham. "I think that's it for now. Stick with me."

"Yes, sir. Until we're inside. The Code Captain will be relieving me at the door."

"Code Captain?"

"Yes, sir. Launch codes, bomb codes. That's you now, sir."

"Yeah. I guess I knew that, but I forgot. We still have those, don't we? Let's try to change that, shall we?"

The entourage pulled to a halt under the portico. Marines and soldiers were everywhere. Lights blazed, and a throng waited on the steps. Kincaid turned first to Frank. "I want you just behind me when the cameras go on so Cathy can see that's you're OK." Then he turned to Meacham. "I'm grateful you were with me. I'll try to get you and your men transferred to the Presidential detachment if you don't mind."

"It would be an honor, sir. God speed, Mr. President."

* * *

In the glare of camera lights, President Kincaid emerged from the car. Anna was waiting, Bible in hand, flanked by the Code Captain, Secretary Zink, and Chief Justice Warren. Farther up the steps he recognized Susan from NPR, Thomas from ABC, and Ben Jacobs. Then there were Defense, Justice, Homeland Security, and several others. General Myers, and a host of people he didn't recognize filled out the remainder.

He looked to Anna. "Tell me what I'm doing."

"The press has been told we will give them ten minutes notice before anything official, but that anything other than the Oath of Office could be hours away. Tony will get you ready for the cameras. Tracey and Cameron have been writing a generic address, but would really like some input. Support cables are pouring in from everywhere. France was first, Russia and Canada tied for second. Mexico and Palestine sent especially warm wishes, and Israel is nervous. Your quarters are being prepared. They should be ready by midnight or one."

As they walked up the steps, the crowd fell in behind.

"That sounds awfully cold."

"It's business, sir. You're needed here."

He nodded.

"Treasury is recommending a three-day bank holiday and closure of the markets."

"Sounds like a wise idea," Kincaid agreed.

"Well, you have to say 'yes' or 'no.'" You are the governing authority now."

He turned to Anna, studying her face. "I see. Make it so."

Anna turned to Secretary Deatherage, who nodded, pulled out his phone, and set the machinery in motion. Kincaid knew that Anna would have said something if she hadn't thought it a good idea.

As quickly as possible the urgent governmental matters were disposed of. Seventeen minutes after arriving at the portico, President Kincaid turned to the three pool reporters. "Susan, Thomas, Ben, you know how I operate. We'll keep things open as long as you're respectful. You're my shadows tonight as long as you're not in the way." He turned to Anna for verification.

She nodded firmly.

"What's the condition of the Oval Office?"

"Crime scene, sir. Lots of blood and damage," she replied.

"OK. I'm not going up there. If any of you feel up to it, let Ms. Colbert know. She'll arrange an escort. I want everyone to know the truth, but it is my personal request that you respect the dignity of the late President. You are a free press. I have only my personal praise or indignation to enforce anything. Do we understand each other?"

All three nodded.

"Here are the facts as I know them." Susan and Thomas each pulled out voice recorders. Jacobs talked to Anna, who called over one of the Marines to take him to the Oval Office. "About half an hour or forty-five minutes ago, President Miller took his own life in the Oval Office. You probably saw the same partial broadcast I saw. That broadcast was terminated on my orders. I do not know the exact details as to how it was ended. The President had barricaded himself in the office and was clearly distraught. He apparently died of a self-inflicted gunshot to his head, and he died immediately. I don't know the exact nature of the weapon or anything specific regarding his emotional state. I believe I saw a handgun on the desk in the broadcast, but I do not know if that was the weapon used."

The President continued his conversation with the reporters, but began to walk slowly down the hall to the stairs leading to the offices below. He glanced over his shoulder to Anna. "I'm going down to Cameron and Tracey. I've got some ideas on the address. You want to join us?"

"I'll be there in a few minutes. We have to make sure the East Room is ready."

"Actually, that's part of my idea. Just a suggestion. How about inside the Lincoln Memorial or the Jefferson Memorial?"

Anna pondered a moment. "Those have merits. Let us do some checks. I'll be down in a few minutes. You still need the East Room for other matters first." She motioned to Frank, and the two disappeared into an office off the main corridor.

Kincaid and the two reporters made their way down the stairs, first to Tracey's office, which was empty, then over to Cameron's office, where she and Tracey were at work with pages strewn over the large table. Cameron was at her computer. "Oh, good. We've got you a fifteen-minute piece — durability of democracy, command structure intact, nation on normal alert, etc., etc."

"Do we have a theme, a centerpiece?" Kincaid asked.

Cameron answered, "Not yet."

"OK, I think I know what I want. Frank said it to me, not exactly in this context, but it resonates: 'Look ahead,' or 'Look ahead, America.' No, I like just 'Look ahead.' When the President shot himself, I was meeting with Jack Pullman's representatives. We had — and have — an agreement that should put things back together. Let's pay proper respect to President Miller, but let's focus on the sunrise. Let's be looking ahead. Does that feel right?"

"Oh, definitely. That's good. 'Look ahead.'" Cameron typed quickly into her computer. She ran on the adrenalin that so endeared her to everyone in the White House.

"Part of the agreement tonight included the President saying specific phrases. I don't have those with me. Sarah's with Pullman's party now. Do either of you have her number?"

Cameron pulled out her phone and pressed a few buttons. "Yep."

"This is your time to shine. Your words have to lift the country. Take as long as you need. When you get an idea of a comfortable time-frame, let someone know." He turned to leave as Anna and Frank appeared. "Ah."

Anna spoke. "Jefferson is too closed in, but Lincoln is good."

Kincaid turned to his writers. "Your address will be delivered from the Lincoln Memorial." He glanced at his watch. "Depending on when you're ready, we may be giving this speech at sunrise at the feet of Lincoln. I'm picturing a small crowd — twenty or so early risers, some kids, some members of congress, some military in full dress, some in camouflage. Broad spectrum, lapel mike." He looked around at Anna, Cameron, Tracey, and Frank. "Thoughts?" He turned to Susan and Thomas. "Thoughts?"

Frank said, "Sounds good to me. But you've got an oath waiting right now."

"Right. I haven't looked at that since high school. Anyone have a copy?"

Anna reached out and handed him a single sheet.

David couldn't suppress a small grin. He looked over the text. "No … hasn't changed since high school. If there's nothing else I need to do right now, I should be ready in twenty minutes. Is that good?"

Cameron and Tracey looked at each other. Tracey mused aloud. "We won't have anything of the quality you need in twenty minutes. Sunrise…" She looked at Cameron, who nodded. "Sunrise is good. I usually jog in the morning. Sunrise tomorrow should be about six forty-five." She grabbed her phone and looked up the sunrise tables. "Six fifty-seven."

"You're my heroes. I'm off to see Tony. Are we go?"

"Yes, Mr. President. We … are … ready." Cameron returned to her screen, fingers flying.

* * *

Tony Amadeo had served seven presidents. His deft hands elevated their faces into the iconic images that endured in the minds of the public, in the annals of the press for all time. He was accustomed to working on moving targets, many of them arrogant, abrasive, and rude. He liked David Kincaid, regarding him as a respectable gentleman. He appreciated that the new president made an effort to hold still while rehearsing.

* * *

David Kincaid swore the oath of office as President of the United States of America in the East Room of the White House at 12:07 a.m. Tuesday, February 17, 2015. Chief Justice John Warren administered the oath of office. Kincaid swore the oath on a Bible belonging to and held by White House advisor Anna Colbert. On camera he was joined by Chief of Staff

Peter Benson, Senator David Kreis, and Frank Brady, the President's Chief of Security. In a gesture of support, communication workers re-enabled transmission of the ceremony to broadcast sites, and the early morning swearing-in was transmitted live to the world. It is estimated that nearly half a billion people witnessed President Kincaid's oath of office live.

"I do solemnly swear that I will faithfully execute the Office of President of the United States, and will to the best of my ability, preserve, protect and defend the Constitution of the United States."

President Kincaid did not insert his name, as has often been the tradition; he insisted that inserting his name was not true to the text of the Constitution. Nor did he add the words "so help me God" for the same reason and out of respect for the separation of church and state. After receiving the good wishes of the Chief Justice, the President announced that he would address the nation at 6:45 a.m. Eastern Time.

* * *

The White House, Tuesday, February 17, 2015, 5:13 a.m. EST

"Mr. President, Mr. President." Major Reed spoke gently to President Kincaid, dozing in the situation room recliner since about two-thirty.

Kincaid began moving his hand toward his face to rub his eyes, but stopped. "Bad idea. Tony'd have to start all over again."

Tony laughed from behind him. "Do not worry, Mr. President. I need to touch you up a little. Sunrise is a very different light from the camera lights."

"Ah." Kincaid nodded as Tony resumed his magic. The President looked up. "You haven't been up all this time, have you?"

"I've been down with Cameron and your word team. They have a good speech for you, sir. It was an honor to see them in action."

Major Reed sat on a stool next to the phone bank. "I think Tony knows it by heart. They tried all their lines on him."

Tony grinned.

Anna and Cameron appeared in the doorway, showing no evidence of fatigue. Kincaid watched Anna's calm and elegant bearing in contrast to Cameron's excited flutter.

Cameron held up a thin sheaf of papers. "Are we ready to rehearse?" She looked at the clock. "T minus one hour, forty minutes."

"Can I remember it that quickly? Do we have a podium to take over there?"

"Not to worry, Mr. President." Anna took a seat on the other side of the President from Tony. "Interior is setting everything up now. You'll have a teleprompter. We've already transmitted the text."

"My, things move fast. Do we have an audience?"

Cameron nodded rapidly. "I activated my calling chain. Phone service is already pretty much back. Last we checked, seven of the local stations are back on the air. Whatever you guys agreed on seems to have worked."

Tony finished his touch-up. The President sat up and began pouring over the text. After a while he glanced up at Cameron. "This is awesome. Well done."

She smiled and looked around. "I had a lot of help."

After his first silent read, President Kincaid recited the speech, repeating particular lines to try different inflections.

Major Reed kept an eye on the clock. At six-twenty he shepherded them to a limousine parked outside the West Wing. It held the Major, Frank, Peter, Kathy, Cameron, Anna, and the President. Matt, the photographers, and additional staff climbed into a second car behind them. With watchful escort, they pulled out of the drive and headed toward the Lincoln Memorial.

Kincaid continued to try variations on key phrases, already committed to memory. The group debated the merits of different versions as they cruised along Constitution Avenue. Kincaid looked up when the car slowed near Henry Bacon Drive on approach to the Memorial. The Avenue was filled with people crossing southward.

Cameron grinned as she pressed her hands to the window. "Oh, good! It worked."

"What?" Kincaid kept looking around.

She replied with pride, "You said you wanted a crowd. I told everyone I called to call everyone they knew within ten miles. After they called their chains, they knocked on their neighbors' doors and had them call everyone they knew. They're here with their children, and their parents, and their dogs."

The driver called back, "Very slow going, Major. I'm not sure I can get there in time without lights or siren."

The Major spoke on his radio, and several soldiers appeared alongside. "Let's walk. It's only a block."

The President nodded. "Good idea." He got out, and they walked briskly to the base of the Memorial and looked toward the Capitol.

In the morning chill the reflecting pool glowed the deep pastel oranges and reds of early dawn. Thousands upon thousands of dark figures gathered from the base of the steps, around the pool, out to the periphery, and back toward the Washington Monument. The Park Service had set up mobile speakers at intervals down the length of the crowd.

Kincaid took a deep, cold breath. "Amazing." He climbed the stairs to wait between the columns and the statue of Lincoln.

Cameron paced at the edge of the space. "We should have done a sound check." She looked at her watch and scowled. "Six minutes to sunrise. Hey, Colbert, I've got an idea."

"Uh, oh."

"No. Follow me. You sang with Laura Garrette, right? I sing with my mom — opera."

Anna followed as Cameron stepped out into the dawn. Kincaid watched their animated gestures calm as they approached the microphones.

"Oh beautiful, for spacious skies …" Within seconds the crowd self-organized into an *a cappella* choir. With two minutes to go, Cameron pressed on with the fourth verse, which went surprisingly well. As "… from sea to shining sea" faded, she and Anna turned toward each other, bowed, and stepped apart.

David Kincaid walked up to the microphones. His waiting speech glowed in the reflection of his teleprompter, but he looked beyond the glass. The cameraman nodded and gave a thumbs-up. The President gazed over the crowd, silent in anticipation. In the near distance the dark obelisk of the Washington Monument pointed heavenward. He saw the first rays of the rising sun glinting off the Capitol rotunda.

"Our dark night of testing has ended. Ten score years have come and gone, and still our liberty endures. That for which patriots shed their blood and to which citizens gave their treasure is intact.

"Technology's false comforts deserted us. Our species's inherent greed laid siege to our very existence. Some to whom we entrusted our lives, our fortunes, and our sacred honors proved unfit for the task.

"And yet … and yet … we gather this cold morning to celebrate the integrity of our system of governance. Though our hearts are heavy laden with tragedy upon tragedy, some still unfolding, we look ahead.

"Throughout our history it seems our battle cries have always begun with 'Remember the …'. I had always attributed that to our consistent lack of preparedness. But I know now that such is not always the case. I know now that sometimes we are simply called upon to remember what we have left behind because we are already looking ahead.

"Behind us are the ruins of our old economy, the scavenged corpse of a system that glided along decade by decade on blind faith in the practitioners who reigned over it. Look ahead, America, to a new economy, open and transparent, subject to the scrutiny of every citizen without barrier or objection. Look ahead, our friends and neighbors around the globe, to an economy dedicated to sustainability and moderation.

"Behind us are the charred and twisted remains of an structure that could be destroyed by a single point of failure, devoid of the human capacity to react and innovate when the script was gone. Look ahead, America, to a new era of diversity and accountability, an era of renewed respect for the craftsmen among us. Look ahead, our friends around the globe, to a reliable and eager partner in the search for technological justice and empowering enterprise."

The disk of the sun had risen above the horizon. The windows in the rotunda were blindingly bright.

"Look ahead. Look ahead to a period of cooperation and mutual support unmatched in the best days of our history. From the first moments of this peculiar journey, I have had the blessings of working with the finest, most generous public servants. Few of them you have ever heard mentioned. I have enjoyed the privilege of roaming this great land during the depths of our troubles, meeting those who simply believed it was the right thing to do to keep the power on and the services working.

"You know who you are, though I suspect you might deny it. Yours is the trust I must now earn. Yours is the standard to which I must strive. Yours is the counsel on which I will rely.

"Our healing has already begun. The scars of our ordeal will linger, and they will continue to serve as lessons and warnings. But the dark night of our testing has ended, and our new day has begun. Look ahead, America, to a new day of wonders we will achieve together. Look ahead, people of the world, to a new day of hope and promise. Look ahead."

The President bowed his head as the concluding words echoed from the broad sides of the buildings lining the Mall, to be replaced by a swelling ovation from the crowd after his brief speech.

He walked over to his staff. Anna smiled and nodded. Frank grinned a broad grin. The President turned to Cameron. "Do you have a closing number?"

"Sure," she chirped.

He lifted his arm toward the microphones.

She motioned to one of the Marines in dress blues and then turned to the President. "Sergeant Baines is in the Cathedral Chorus." Cameron and the sergeant went forward together, her hands offering half the explanation.

As Conklin and Baines began *The Battle Hymn of the Republic*, the President turned to the others. "Let's head back to the office."

Major Reed saluted. "Yes, sir. I'll call the car."

Kincaid frowned and looked up momentarily at the rotunda. "Don't do it for me. It's a wonderful morning. I think I'll walk.

Frank shook his head, talking to no one in particular. "I knew he'd do that. I just knew he would." The others laughed.

The President strode to the edge of the porch and selected one of the flags from the row of flags serving as backdrop. He lifted it from its stand and began walking down the steps toward the north side of the Reflecting Pool as Cameron, Baines, and the crowd continued the hymn. Peter and Anna flanked him even as security and the others formed a loose bubble around him.

The crowd parted while they passed, but it was slow going: nearly forty-five minutes to complete the nine blocks, 1.1-mile walk. The President reached out to children perched on their parents' shoulders, to seniors, and to workers who had paused on their way to their morning tasks. Cameron caught up with the group on Constitution Avenue in the vicinity of the White House.

They entered the White House grounds just after eight-fifteen. The President handed the flag to Sergeant Brycynski. "Have someone get this back to the monument, please."

* * *

Tuesday morning filled with all the urgent tasks needed to restore a sense of routine in the White House. The President and his staff remained in the dining room as the flurry of activities swirled around them. FBI and Secret Service investigators finished their Oval Office examinations at eleven even as the Secretary of the Army began preparations for President Miller's state funeral in accordance with Army Pamphlet 1-1. French Ambassador Bonet, as senior representative of the diplomatic corps, dropped in around eleven-thirty to express condolences and meet with the Army personnel planning the funeral.

Shortly before noon, Sarah arrived with Tull. "Nice speech, Mr. President. It presented really well. Where's Cameron?"

"We sent her to get some sleep. Were you there on the Mall?"

Sarah shook her head. "No. It was on TV. Even Wolfe. Nice touch with the sunrise. One of the cameras was behind you and you're kinda' outlined in a glow with the Washington Monument off to the side. I stayed the night with Joanna Denton." She pointed to Tull and smiled. "Jeff guarded the place."

Kincaid grew excited. "Ah. So what did you find out?"

Sarah raised a finger in the air. "She's got awesome tropical fish. She's got this big ol' aquarium with black angelfish. Black angelfish! I had some of them when I was a teenager, but they all died."

Kincaid hung his head while the others, including the ambassador, stifled their laughter.

Sarah pursed her lips. "Right. You probably meant what did I find out about the other stuff. It's all good. The phones are back to about ninety-eight percent. Everyone's pretty much back to work. The call center workers have instructions on handling the Brisbane equipment as evidence. Joanna let Jack Pullman, a.k.a. Commander X, know about the amnesty for the good guys, and he's happy with that. She also passed on your offer to have him work with NSA. He says he needs a little reflection time. Joanna will be over here this afternoon. We can learn a lot from their exercise. You should see the secure communication gear she had in her apartment, in addition to the fish. We're pretty much amateurs by comparison."

Kincaid smiled. "Thank you, Sarah. Let me know when she gets here. I'll try to stop by."

Major Reed entered and walked quickly to the President's table.

"Major, you look like a Marine with good news."

"We've located Tiffany Miller, sir. She's OK. As we speculated, she had been recaptured by some of the Brisbane people. Not part of the main group. It's actually probably a good thing. They were sensible and she was suffering from exposure. Apparently she had only a heavy sweater when she initially escaped. In fact, her captors were the ones who contacted us, and she's urging leniency. We'll check it all out. She'll be here in a bit to help with arrangements."

"That is good news. She can stay here as long as she wants. It's got to be an awful time for her. Knowing her, she will likely be an important contributor to our transition. Whatever she wants."

"Yes, sir," the Major agreed.

Tull and Sarah turned to leave. Sarah stopped when she saw Kathy. Sarah pointed her finger as she spoke. "Kathy, I need you to deliver something."

"What?"

"I borrowed a rifle from Andy Merz. He's an economics grad from AMU and thinks you're cute. Anyway, I told him I'd try to introduce you two. I've got his address somewhere. OK?"

Kathy waved her hands. "Whoa, whoa. Let me get this straight. It sounds like you traded me for a rifle. Is that basically right?"

"No. Well, not exactly. Yeah, sort of. Hey, he's a real gentleman and helped take care of my Marine."

Kathy shook her head as Sarah departed.

The President stood up. "Peter, I'll work out of the Vice President's office for now. If the forensic people are finished, I believe the White House historian, Smithsonian, and Archives will need access to his office."

"Yes, sir. They're already on it. I'd suggest moving operations there after the funeral."

"Right. Well, I have some business to attend to. Mr. Ambassador, thank you as always for your most valuable support. We'll keep in close contact."

"Thank you, Mr. President. You can count on the diplomatic corps for our unwavering support."

The President walked toward the dining room door. "Anna, do you have a moment?"

She got up and followed.

Ambassador Bonet smiled.

27 AIRSTRIP

Thursday, February 19, 2015, Mogollon Airpark,
Heber-Overgaard, Arizona

President Kincaid was true to his word and formalized amnesty for all the workers involved in the events surrounding what had come to be called the Call Center War. At Jack's request, the President had arranged for time out of the spotlight while the country restored its routine. Jack drove the van to the seventh small plane in the flight line at Mogollon Airpark. He and Laura got out and approached a man sporting a crew cut who was completing his preflight inspection of the white twin-engine Cessna.

He looked up at Jack and Laura and asked, "Mr. Jones for Puerto Vallarta?" The man wore olive-drab flight garb with a patch reading "Weaver." He glanced down at his board. "My manifest shows only a single passenger."

"There will be two," Laura said, folding her arms.

Jack remained firm. "There is one."

"Two," she repeated, "You need me. I know people. I have connections.

Jack seemed tired, very tired. "I have no doubt, but we've discussed this. You of all people know that I'm still a marked man with whatever remains of Brisbane. I'm dangerous. I'm dangerous just to be around."

Laura closed her eyes. Tears streamed down her cheeks, falling onto her sweatshirt. Arms still crossed, she stood near the craft's tail as Jack hauled his travel bag to the starboard hatch and struggled to push it into the opening. Jack and Laura continued arguing back and forth.

The pilot, his list finished, narrowed his eyes and headed to the shed at the end of the flight line.

As Jack continue to push on his bag, Laura stepped quietly toward the shed. "There's something I don't like about this guy," she said. She stopped short of the building at the sound of a phone conversation.

"Henderson, it's Weaver. The target arrived. ... Yeah, I got the transmitter rigged. The C4's under the port wing. At five thousand feet that terrorist is gone. But there's a complication. He's got a girl with him. ... I don't know. Someone named Laura. ... OK. It'll be tight, but then I don't plan to be aboard very long."

Laura ran back to the plane, halting just as Weaver emerged from the shed.

Weaver walked to the hatch and helped Jack finally push the bag into the plane. Weaver turned away, walking toward the starboard wing. "OK, All aboard. I'll just put things away. Be right with you."

Laura bent down, silently lifted a wrench from the ground, raised it with both hands, and took two long steps forward. The wrench impacted Weaver's head with a loud thud just as Jack looked up.

"What the Hell are you doing?" he screamed. Weaver collapsed onto the tarmac, his clipboard and cap flying in different directions. Jack raced, ducking under the wing, to aid the fallen man.

"Shut up, damn it!" she shouted. Laura scooted under the wing just as Jack passed under. She surveyed the underbelly, quickly spying a bulky contraption secured to the plane with six screws. "You need me, damn it. Look in his wallet. Back pants pocket. This little box was about five thousand feet from blowing you to bits."

Jack's attention bounced from box to the man and back. He pulled the leather wallet from the pocket and opened it. "Shit! Brisbane."

"Get a screwdriver. We've got to get this off."

"What's the point? We don't have a pilot, and there are bound to be other agents surrounding us."

"Just get a screwdriver. You forget, I know how to fly. Look — if there is anyone else, as long as no one knows he's down, they'll hold off, right?" She crawled on hands and knees to starboard and opened the pilot's door. "Ah ha. He had a 'chute in here. He'd put the plane on autopilot and bail before five thousand. You got that screwdriver?"

She returned to find Jack unscrewing the fifth screw while holding the box up with his left hand. The package dangled awkwardly. She reached up and lifted it so that both of his hands were free.

Jack mused, "I don't know much about explosives, but I'm guessing this is a lot. See the 'C4' there? That's bad. Are you sure this is all?" He looked briefly into her uncertain eyes. He sighed. "Right. Let's hope."

With the final bolt removed, the box released into her grasp. Jack replaced the bolts into the skin of the plane while she carried the package away. Looking around for a place to put the deadly box, she caught sight of Weaver's sprawled figure and set it down gently behind his back.

She turned around. Jack had just finished the sixth bolt.

"Get in!" she said.

"Is this thing ready to go?"

"I don't know! He was waiting for you. He seemed ready to fly you. He said, 'All aboard.' It's probably ready. Get in! If it's not, there's nothing we can do about it."

Jack tossed the screwdriver in Weaver's direction and clambered in on the passenger side. Laura frantically surveyed myriad controls, muttering. Jack fastened his seat belt, pushed back on the seat, and took a settling breath. He turned back to Laura still studying the knobs and switches row by row. He stared at her in helpless silence.

"Mine was a single engine plane. I have a license, and I've made seven good landings, but it was single engine." She displayed a hint of something — fear, frustration, defeat?

"If you can figure out how to make it go and stop, I'll watch the little dials to make sure we're going up. I think we're going to have to just trust each other. Not much choice anyway."

She nodded quickly. "Good." She finished her survey. "OK, I think I've got it. Check to the right."

Jack looked out forward, then aft. The next plane was easily thirty feet away. Behind, Weaver lay unconscious or dead amidst the tools and explosive. "You've got thirty feet to the right."

She flipped a switch and the port engine came to life. "Good." She flipped a second and the starboard engine answered. Laura spent a few seconds practicing moving the engines faster and slower bit by bit. At the peak of each attempt, the craft leaned forward slightly.

Jack glanced back at Weaver. Still no movement.

With her fingernail, she pecked on a gauge. "Pay attention! Watch this dial. It's our airspeed. My single engine plane would lift off at 170 knots. This plane's heavier. I'm figuring it should be going faster. Tell me when it's 200."

"Right."

Laura pushed the throttle forward and let go a latch that clearly controlled the brakes. The plane careened forward. "Work the pedals, work the pedals," she repeated to herself.

The plane wobbled down a side taxiway to the end of the main runway. She worked furiously with her controls as the plane turned in a sickening semicircle. Jack sensed the starboard wheel leaving the ground for a moment, and over half of the turn was on grass. Still, they arrived on the main runway near the centerline.

Laura repeated, "You watch our speed."

"Thirty!" he called out.

She brought the engines to a full roar, and they began hurtling down the strip.

"Fifty!"

At first she worked her steering hard and fast, and the craft swerved back and forth across the line. After about ten twists, she seemed at peace with the controls, and Jack could sense only hard forward acceleration.

"Ninety!"

Laura stared forward in grim determination.

"One-thirty!"

She glanced for just a second to left and to right. "So far, so good," she murmured.

"One-eighty!"

The end of the runway approached very fast. Perhaps this plane needed less speed, not more. If she tried too soon, though, they'd end up in a heap of flaming debris. Faster, she thought.

"Two hundred!"

She pulled the wheel and the plane leapt skyward, squeezing them down into their seats.

"Probably didn't need the full two hundred," she said, chuckling.

Jack smiled, and checked the altimeter. "Passing five hundred feet."

The plane rose steeply, leaving the airfield, heading out over the mountains.

"Passing two thousand feet."

Laura banked the craft to starboard.

"I'm pretty sure Porto Vallarta is south of here." He looked to the right, watching the airport disappear; small planes already little more than toys.

"It is. With the surprise they had for us here, I can only imagine what might be waiting for us down there."

"Passing three thousand feet." Jack finally relaxed. "Your thought processes are fascinating." She turned to look at him. Most of the tension in her face had relaxed. She was pretty again. Laura flashed a smile in return for his respectful admiration. "... us ...," he thought.

Laura explained, "I know there are a lot of small airfields up around Eureka and Arcata. I've got friends up there — activists. I think we'll be safe while we sort out what's going on. Do you still trust the President's word?"

"Yes," Jack replied without hesitation.

"Why?"

He continued, "President Kincaid's kept his word on everything else. He took a lot of big risks. I was blindsided back at the airport, but I have a sense that guy wasn't playing on the same team. Passing four thousand."

"Why?"

"I have a sense," he said. They exchanged glances. "I don't know. I can't prove it. I may not be brilliant like you, but I've got a damn' good track record with people overall, don't I?"

"I'm not brilliant," she protested.

"You'd better be. I'm in the passenger seat with a pilot who's never flown one of these things."

She laughed.

"Of course, you're not that good a planner. You didn't pack anything."

She looked ahead quietly for a moment and then turned to him, a broad smile brightening her face. "That's the least of your problems."

* * *

On the tarmac Weaver regained painful consciousness. He could see that the plane had gone, but couldn't remember anything beyond his conversation with Henderson. There would be Hell to pay for their escape. But he was in no frame of mind to fashion an alibi. He tried to get up, but lay back with the blinding pain. Instead, he reached to the ground with his right hand and pushed to turn over. As he rolled, he felt something solid and heavy pushing on his waist. He bent slowly to see what it was and found the box with its ten pounds of C4.

"Oh, cra—"

* * *

"Passing five thousand feet."

"OK. I'm going to six thousand, and we'll stay along the Pacific coast. As soon as I recognize some of the towns north of the Bay Area, I'll bring us down a little. I don't think anyone's watching, but I'd just as soon not be tracked. Enjoy the ride. It's a beautiful trip."

28 LUNCH

Programming Palace, Camden,
New Jersey, Friday, October 16, 2015

Mike Johnson sat, alone and quiet, in the lunchroom. He munched calmly on his turkey submarine sandwich, sipping occasionally from a pint bottle of two percent milk, peering absent-mindedly through rain-spattered windows to the park behind Programming Palace, gray, cool, and wet.

Josh arrived a little after one o'clock carrying a large burger, a packet of Ramen, and a beer. "Yo, Mike, why all alone? It's a warning sign, you know, eating alone." He put a pot of water on the lunchroom stove for his noodles.

"That's drinking alone. Actually, I was just enjoying a bit of solitude while I could. Kinda' peaceful here. Rain makes me drowsy, though. I may even take a short nap before I get back to the stockholders' report."

Josh settled into a chair across from Mike and began on his hamburger. "Yeah, I'm sure glad you're writing that stuff. Legal never really liked my prose."

Mike grinned. "I remember. Who would have thought it would come to this?"

Quickly turning around in both directions, Josh frowned. "By the way, where is everybody?"

"At the shower."

"Shower?" Josh asked.

"You've got to read your e-mails."

"I've been meaning to do that. So who's getting married?"

"Baby shower," Mike replied.

"Anyone I know?"

"Probably."

Josh continued, "Obviously we — or at least you — weren't invited.

Not that I'm into those sorts of things. Babies kinda creep me out."

"It's a women-only do. Two and One and Janice organized it. It's over at our place."

"'Your' place? So you're staying put, the three of you?"

"Uh huh. Funny how these things work out. Janice and I contributed half-interest in the house at Christmas. One protested at first, but we all agree now it was a good idea. Thanks, by the way, for that last bonus. You're too generous, but we'll put it to good use. Financial security makes amazing things possible."

Josh gathered some crumbs and put them in his mouth. "You're worth it, Mikey. So who got knocked up?"

"Subtle to a fault, as always." Mike shook his head as he smiled. "It's a double shower actually. One is throwing part of the shower for Janice."

Josh looked dumbfounded. "Heh. So you're gonna be a daddy?"

Mike nodded.

"Congratulations, Mikey. Hey, that's really cool. You'll make a great dad. Suits you, I'd say. Little League, parent-teacher night. And the other?" He began crumpling the burger wrapper, preparing to shoot the hoop with the trashcan.

"You really should read your e-mail. Janice's throwing the other half for One. They're due just a couple of weeks apart."

Josh thought hard as he tossed the wrapper. It missed by a very wide margin. He tilted his head, examining Mike with a confused look. "Then … ?"

Mike nodded slowly.

"Wow!"

29 JERSEY GIRL

The White House, Monday, November 23, 2015, 4:30 p.m.

President Kincaid smiled as he relaxed in the office chair. "So, she really has no idea?"

"Not a clue, sir," Anna smiled. "And our special guests are settled in at Blair House resting up for the evening's events."

"Well done!" He rose from his chair, leaned over, and gave her a kiss before heading to Cameron's office for rehearsal.

* * *

Grand Ballroom, The White House,
Monday, November 23, 2015, 7:30 p.m.

"I still regret that I have not met Commander X and Laura Garrette in person. I still sometimes wonder if they're real." The room filled with laughter as President Kincaid lifted a large medal from the case that Sergeant Tull held. "But I can appreciate their need to attend to family matters and will, for now, send our nation's heartfelt gratitude for their role in saving our union. On the other hand, it is now my great honor to present to you, Joanna Susannah Denton and Martin James VanDorn, as representatives of the dedicated call center workers of this land, on behalf of a grateful nation, the Presidential Medal of Freedom."

The President placed the ribbon of the medals around each of their necks, shook their hands and embraced them as they enjoyed a standing ovation. While they beamed, the President looked over to what had been dubbed "the kids' table." Peter, his wife, and his two children sat there, along with Kathy and Andy, Cameron, Anita, and Tiffany. Sarah sat at the table, facing the platform, but appeared not to be paying attention. Her hands were in full motion in the midst of some story she was telling.

The President turned to Tull, each flashing a mischievous smile. He nodded to Peter who whispered instructions to his son and daughter. They scampered to the back of the ballroom and slowly escorted an older man and woman and a young man forward, followed by staff carrying three chairs.

"Do we have any other honorees, Sergeant Tull?" He watched as Sarah continued her animated conversation.

"We have one more, Mr. President," Tull announced.

Sarah stopped, glanced at her program and turned it over. She shook her head.

"Sarah Tyler Tull, please come forward."

She jumped at the sound of her name, and the program glided about fifteen feet across the ballroom floor. Peter and Kathy helped her to her feet, and she began her walk to the platform as every guest rose in rowdy applause. It was then that she spied the newly arrived guests — her mother, her father, and her brother. By the time she reached President Kincaid, she was in tears.

"Now, why are you crying?" he asked.

She bit her lip momentarily. "It seems like the right thing to do?"

He laughed and then hugged her. After a bit, he raised his hand for silence. He took the citation and read it: "'Sarah Tyler Tull, during the tumultuous events of 2014 and 2015, your cool competence and innovative insight promoted the rapid unraveling of the schemes afoot to pillage our nation. Your clear understanding of economics, and your fearless pursuit of truth brought the underlying frauds and corruption to light, and helped bring their perpetrators to justice. Your courage in securing contact with the leaders of the communications workers, particularly your crazy, insane, hare-brained trip to NSA at midnight on the 11th of January, 2015...'" He paused as she jerked her head around to look at him, her mouth open. "OK. It doesn't actually say that. They wouldn't let me tell the real story there. '... led to a rapid and successful closure to this chapter of our national story. For these and other services, on behalf of a grateful nation, I present you with the Presidential Medal of Freedom.'"

Tull removed the medal from its box and assisted the President connecting the ribbon at her back.

The President joined the clapping for a bit, but then held up his hand for silence again. "However, as those of us on the inside are well aware, the Presidential Medal of Freedom is a limited tribute, and one whose past is, to say the least, checkered. There is, however, one lasting gold standard of tribute. I now call on the Honorable Mary Cunningham, Governor of the Great State of New Jersey to complete our evening."

Sarah turned to the President, skeptical.

The Governor walked up to Sarah, shook her hand, and embraced her. She then turned to the guests as they took their seats. "Sarah, you well know the grand heritage of our state. Since you were a little girl, your parents immersed you in our history of courage and industry, a history stretching back to pre-colonial times. We are a proud state, one of the first thirteen, a staunch defender of the Union in our great Civil War. Our heroes, men and women alike, rose from the ranks of regular citizens to do great things. Leave it to a Jersey girl to win a war with a shopping bag." The Governor paused, smiling during more raucous applause.

Sarah pressed her lips together and nodded to the Governor.

"Sarah Tyler Tull, you have joined the ranks of New Jersey's amazing heroes — heroes like Vince Lombardi, Alexander Hamilton, Thomas Alva Edison, Grover Cleveland, Joyce Kilmer, Molly Pitcher, …"

Sarah doubled over laughing.

The Governor turned to her, smiling, and continued until she finished with Clara Barton and John Fenwick. "Sarah, as you know, we are just completing the expressway for visitors to enjoy our great state's southern seashore. We have a new rest stop and we have a new hero. Young girls and young boys will learn that their only limit is their personal courage when they memorize the name of the Sarah Tyler rest stop, so established by unanimous vote of the New Jersey legislature." An aide approached the Governor and handed her a small black bag with drawstring. "In token thereof, I present you with the official keys to the rest stop."

Sarah bowed and took the keys. She held them aloft like an Olympic medal as her brother and parents came forward.

Ceremonies at an end, musicians began playing softly. President Kincaid smiled and stepped away from the front of the room. All eyes were on Sarah and her family, save one pair. The President exchanged a victorious thumbs-up with Anna, his beloved First Lady.

The End

30 DEAR GRANDSON

May 21, 2051

Dear Timothy,

I got your invitation to talk about my adventures during the Rebellion of 2014. I'll be honored to talk to your class, and I'm writing this to you as an eyewitness account of part of those dark days.

On Monday, January 9th of 2015, I was with my dad, your Great-Grandfather Scott Thomas. We were being taken, along with Tiffany Miller, to a safe place with guards because your great-grandfather was a witness against Vice President Bailey and his people. The Brisbane forces attacked our convoy as we were leaving Washington. I was really sure they were going to kill us, but they decided to keep us as prisoners for trading later.

The Marines who fought the bad guys in what I remember as a really loud battle rescued us. I watched as Hercules, the bad guys' leader, died. He was spitting out blood, but wouldn't tell the Marines where Tiffany was. I've shown you the bullet I picked up that morning, and I'll be sure to bring it to class.

When we got back to the White House, I stayed for a while with Sarah Tyler. I have a news clipping of me with her and President Kincaid. You can see her bag, which is in the Smithsonian now.

You're right that it was a scary time, or it should have been. Things were moving so fast I didn't have much time to think about it, and the people all around me were such heroes.

I got to sing in the choir at the National Cathedral when President Kincaid and Anna were married and was on the reviewing stand for the inauguration parade with President Miller when she became President in 2042. It has been a real adventure, and I look forward to sharing with your class. In the end, it's a great story of the strength of our democracy and your fellow citizens. I'll see you the night before, and we can go to school together.

Your grandfather,
Jeremy Thomas

United States Penitentiary, Terre Haute
4200 Bureau Road N
Terre Haute, Indiana 47802-8128
(812) 238-1531

Consolidated Federal Prisoner Progress Report Date: *November 23, 2015*

Prisoner #: *14-472-94576*

Name (Last name, First name, MI): *Bailey, James P.*

Conviction: *Filing false report, failure to report income, acting as unregistered agent for foreign government, theft of government property by deception, aiding and abetting armed insurrection against the United States, lying under oath, etc.*

Normal expiration of sentence: *April 21, 2145*

First Eligible for parole: *May 21, 2051*

Daily Routine: *7 a.m. Reveille and shower*
8 a.m. breakfast
9 a.m. exercise, North Yard
11 a.m. reading and reflection
12 noon lunch
1 p.m. counselling and group therapy
3 p.m. occupational therapy/classroom
5 p.m. supper
6 p.m. leisure in cell
9 p.m. lights out

Observation of counselor: *Prisoner continues to exhibit negative attitude toward rehabilitation, maintaining that he is being held illegally. Prisoner continued to be uncooperative in counselling and therapy. Insists on access to legal services beyond what is permitted in his sentencing. Has on three occasions since the last report attempted to access unauthorized communications, resulting in loss of free roam privileges.*

Recommended for Parole: ☐ Yes ☒ No

Reasons for recommendation: *Prisoner has resisted efforts toward rehabilitation, has been a disruptive influence, and is a demonstrated flight risk.*

Counselor: *Yolanda C. Dorsey, LLC*

U.S. Bureau of Prisons form 27-415, revised April 17, 1998

ABOUT THE AUTHOR

Baltimore author Clark Thomas Riley has written and published non-fiction since the 1970s in support of careers in college at The University of North Carolina, Chapel Hill, the United States Navy, Graduate Studies at The University of Chicago, biomedical research, and information technology. He began writing fiction in 1994 and has five novels finished to the first draft level. *What If They Lied (just a little)?* is his first novel to be published. Following this work will be a pioneer romance, a medical mystery, a spy novel, a liberation adventure, and a commentary on building the twenty-first century hobby greenhouse.

Other interests include teaching Sunday School, growing and speaking about orchids, publishing services, teaching, and social activism. The author can be reached at ClarkTRiley@gmail.com. You can join a moderated discussion of *What If They Lied (just a little)?* at http://clarkriley.com/whatif/